M000114127

to June who shared many memories of childhood with me — warm regards much love Jeanette

Seagate House

June 2012

Seagate House

Jeanette H. Fusco

Library of Congress Control Number:		2008904347
ISBN:	Hardcover	978-1-4363-4290-2
	Softcover	978-1-4363-4289-6

This book was printed in the United States of America.

To order additional copies of this book, contact:
Xlibris Corporation
1-888-795-4274
www.Xlibris.com
Orders@Xlibris.com
41383

CONTENTS

From the Author 13

Acknowledgments 15

Chapter One: Elaina Rose Hamilton
                       1941 19

Chapter Two: Willem Skyler VanHameetman
                       1582-1616 68

Chapter Three: Sergio Cadiz Scarlatti
                       1580-1614 125

Chapter Four: New Landings
                       1614-1625 176

Chapter Five: Destined Meetings
                       1695-1775 227

Chapter Six: Sunny and Ben
                       1773-1774 291

Chapter Seven: A Matter of Independence
                       1774-1787 352

Chapter Eight: Mission Impossible
                       1777-1787 390

Chapter Nine: Peter Cadiz Hamilton the Young Man
                       1914-1942 444

Chapter Ten: Closing the Circle—the Reunion
                       October 1988 492

Further Reading 539

Websites of Interest 542

In Memory of

Adele   Ted   Jeanette

My sister, Adele Kamish Bowden, and my brother, Ted Kamish and our wonderful childhood adventures on Long Beach Island for so many summers. I can still hear their laughter—and I still miss them.

Dedication

For my parents, Jessie and Ted, and my maternal Grandfather, Poppy, who started it all—for their love of the island.

Author with her parents
1941 Ship Bottom, Long Beach Island
My Dad, the Jokester

Poppy, maternal grandfather, at the bay
Ship Bottom 1942

From three came eleven

BEACH BABIES
Haven Beach July 1970

Nieces, nephew and author's children—
a sweet mix of water lovers

FROM THE AUTHOR

Long Beach Island, New Jersey begins and ends the Seagate story. I have drawn from many personal memories of the Island, which has been in my life since 1935 when my family first vacationed there. The memories continue to gather as each new summer adds its own. The face of the land has changed over these many years, but the magical aura that surrounds the island and draws us in, remains unchanged.

Seagate House is historical fiction. I have placed my fictitious characters in accurate historical settings throughout, with few exceptions. Some liberties were taken with the famous people mentioned, researching and revealing more of their personalities in an attempt to bring them even further to life for my readers.

Jeanette Kamish Fusco
Newtown, Bucks County,
Pennsylvania

September 2010

To our ancestors, blessed with ingenuity, grit, and an endless faith in a dream they dared to dream. They braved the vast ocean and the unknown hardships of a New World, never faltering to realize their longed for destiny—freedom from oppression, however it was presented.

The VanHameeteman name is factual, on the maternal side of the Fusco ancestral lineage. They immigrated from Ouddorf, Holland.

Thoughts are but dreams till their effects be tried.

William Shakespeare

ACKNOWLEDGMENTS

Special thanks to my loving and generous daughters, Cynthia, Elizabeth, Holly and Gina—to Sarah, a grandmother's blessing, and to Cathy for her time, interest and suggestions. My sincere appreciation to the many reputable and learned persons who crossed my path, generously sharing their time, knowledge and advice, helping me to bring this book to life.

Erik Fleischer
President, Craven Hall Historical Society, Warminster, Bucks County, Pennsylvania, for generously sharing his diverse, extensive information of the Revolutionary War and the history of the local area.
Craven Hall Historical Society
http://www.Craven-Hall.org

Edward Greenawald
The Moland House, 1641 Old York Road, Hartsville, Warwick Township, Pennsylvania, for his generosity in sharing his impressive knowledge of the August 21, 1777 *Council of War* at the Cross Roads, Warwick Township, Bucks County, Pennsylvania.
The Moland House, Hartsville, PA
http://www.Moland.org/

Dr. David P. Stern
Lab for Particles and Fields at the Goddard Space Flight Center in Maryland, (who is now retired, continuing as emeritus) for his extended kindness and freely shared advice on *ancient navigation.*
Educational Web sites: a central linking page,
http://www.phy6.org

Arlene Balkansky
> Reference Specialist, the Library of Congress
> For her kindness and generous research help.
> *http://www.loc.gov.rr/askalib*

Richard Albert
> Restoration Director
> Delaware Riverkeeper Network
> For his time and wide ranging knowledge of Henry Hudson, the Cape May area and the history of the Delaware River.
> *www.delawareriverkeeper.org/*

Donald N. Moran
> Son of the American Revolution
> Author, noted Historian of George Washington's Life Guards (The Commander-in-Chief's Guards), Biographer of numerous battles of the American Revolution, biographies of officers and the rank and file who fought in that war, and for his encompassing familiarity of that era. Don, my sincerest appreciation for your time, advice and generosity of spirit.
> *http://sons-of-liberty-sar.org/*

Leonore
> My dear friend of many years, for her continued interest and support.
> *An honest answer is the sign of true friendship.*
> > Proverbs 24:26

Cindy R.
> A caring and steadfast friend, who bravely jumped into the fray:
> *It is sayd, that at the nede the frende is knowen.*
> > Caxton's *Sonnes of Aymon*, 1489

Ruth P. Thomas
> Professor of French, Temple University, Philadelphia Pennsylvania.
> Thank you Doctor Thomas for your generosity.

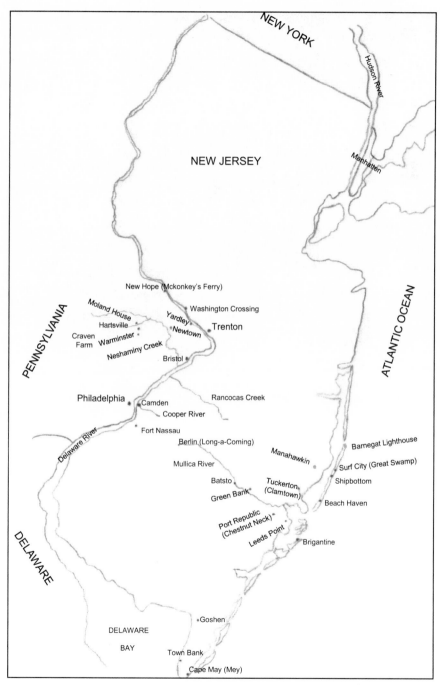

NEW YORK

Hudson River

NEW JERSEY

Manhatten

ATLANTIC OCEAN

PENNSYLVANIA

New Hope (Mckonkey's Ferry)

Moland House

Washington Crossing

Yardley

Hartsville

Newtown

Trenton

Craven
Farm

Warminster

Neshaminy Creek

Bristol

Philadelphia

Camden

Rancocas Creek

Cooper River

Delaware River

Fort Nassau

Berlin (Long-a-Coming)

Manahawkin

Barnegat Lighthouse

Mullica River

Surf City (Great Swamp)

Batsto

Tuckerton
(Clamtown)

Shipbottom

Green Bank

Beach Haven

DELAWARE

Port Republic
(Chestnut Neck)

Leeds Point

Brigantine

Goshen

DELAWARE

BAY

Town Bank

Cape May (Mey)

C.R. Fusco

CHAPTER ONE

Elaina Rose Hamilton

1941-1988

Elaina Rose was called Ella from her beginning. She was nine years old that October of 1941, but amazingly, more than forty years later, her recall remained startlingly lucid. The events surrounding that time were etched deeply into her memory with such searing clarity that she could never forget them—or how they had affected her ever since.

Ella left her townhouse and the heavy Philadelphia traffic behind her and headed east, over the Delaware River into New Jersey. If traffic ahead was light, she could make the island in less than an hour. She held the thoughts of this timeless strip of sand close to her. Memories made there were different. They were deep rooted and a major refuge in her life. The island brought happy memory offerings to her of hot, sun filled days, random, rainy afternoons and starry indigo nights. Ella willingly hugged all of this happiness to herself, feeling that she was blessed and that this narrow strip of land had an earth soul. She used to wonder why her beloved island was the setting for her terrifying childhood experience. Had synchronicity played a part and set the stage? She held no animosity toward the land. She had always felt the island would eventually give up the secrets surrounding the happening; she just had never known when.

The sudden appearance of the causeway's main span over Barnegat Bay always surprised her with its sharp contrast to the landscape. Its arched whiteness reflected the bright sunlight and it rose up, a stranger to the bordering flat marshlands. The long, rolling, cement carpet ushered in thousands of impatient drivers to the island during the hot summer months. After nightfall, strips of bright lights shining like holiday garlands, outlined the causeway bridge and welcomed weary travelers. Some had described the lights as a *string of pearls*, or a *pathway to heaven*. The bridge had been named for Dorland J. Henderson, an inventive, forward thinking engineer with the State of New Jersey's Department of Transportation. Mr. Henderson had designed the entire system, which contained hundreds of separate fluorescent lights and was the first system ever seen of its kind. However, the stretch was still called the *causeway* by the inhabitants and long time vacationers of the island. *Old habits die hard,* Ella thought.

She reached up to open the vent, letting the familiar briny smell of the saltwater marshlands greet her. Ella wrinkled her nose as pungent air assaulted her nostrils. She watched the crying gulls gracefully maneuvering the warm updrafts, easily pacing her car.

The modern causeway, built in 1958 was architecturally beautiful Ella considered, but she liked to bring back images of the narrow two lane macadam highway that had snaked across the marshlands and over the low sitting road bridges. She remembered how the old causeway had looked when she was a child. The highway ran by the old fishing shacks that squatted alongside the road and then continued across Cedar Bonnet Island. The rickety, planked drawbridge, the last link to the island, would finally appear. Sometimes it was a long delay, sitting in the heat, waiting for the drawbridge to open and allow boats through to the other side. The old drawbridge, no stranger to Ella, had echoed the thumpity—thump of the cars across the bay to the small town of Ship Bottom. The ricocheted noise was more noticeable in the summer evenings as it reverberated through the warm and quiet darkness. Ella recalled her mother remarking on Friday nights about the number of cars coming on to the island.

She hoped that the island would not sink. As a child, Ella had worried about that.

The first causeway had been built in 1914, when a toll was charged to cross. It had not taken the gulls long to learn to drop unopened clams onto the road to crack them open. Her father had told her that it had wrecked havoc on the old balloon tires.

Her destination was Seagate House, her uncle and aunt's beloved home on the ocean's edge. Uncle Peter was her father's elder brother.

Treasured childhood stories and photographs prompted her to look for the remains of the old railroad trestle, even though she knew it was long gone. Her mother, Kate had told her that a railroad used to run to Beach Haven; a violent storm had washed its tracks and trestle away and it had never been rebuilt. As a girl, her mother had ridden the train and she had shown Ella wonderful pictures from those days. Ella wished that she had been a passenger on that train, crossing over the bay to the island, seeing it from a different perspective. Remnants of the trestle had remained for years, sticking its wooden elbows up from the bay waters, but finally vanishing, defeated by time. When storms had battered the old causeway during nor'easters, the wind spit saltwater in great sheets of spray across the road and it had been frightening to ford.

Now the final portal to the island appeared—the traffic circle. It divided the towns of Ship Bottom to the south and Surf City to the north. From the circle, if you continued east by foot, you entered the shores of the great Atlantic Ocean which spread its grand, salty aroma over the entire island. Long Beach, a barrier island was only eighteen miles long and sat some six miles out into the sea.

Ella pressed down on the gas pedal. "We're almost there, Tucker." Her Border collie wagged his tail happily. Lost in memories, she had almost forgotten that he was in the back seat. *How easy the drive down is now,* she thought. When she was very young, they had lived in northern New Jersey, before her father's job had moved them to Philadelphia.

Bits of sweet memories emerged swiftly as she drifted back to a happy childhood, recalling those eventful trips to the shore. Images of the *beach* as the family always called the seashore, and the preparations for the drive down could never be forgotten. The summers she spent at Seagate with her family each season was to her, one of the most significant occurrences of the entire year. The long, hot drive through south Jersey was an event unto itself: there was no turnpike, no parkway, no air conditioning in cars and no going back for forgotten items.

Making ready was a major undertaking and required great ingenuity. Her mother, Kate wrote long lists and her father, Malcolm, became a tactical genius in car packing. The night before departure, Malcolm parked the big, green Dodge by the side door of their house. Her mother laid out their entire wardrobe for the summer. Augusta, her sister was too young to help much; but she could carry small items to the car. Ella carried her own clothes to the car, where her father squeezed great quantities of loose clothing into the car's large, oversized trunk. Suitcases were forbidden; the cases demanded too much space. When all the clothes and other odds and ends were finally pressed in, the *real* squeeze began. The inside of the car would be packed with sheets, pillowcases and blankets, carefully folded and stacked onto the big, back seat. Passengers had to sit on these; the trick was *not* to get the piles too high or they could slip forward, toppling a person off the seat if the car stopped short. Kate insisted on bringing her own linens to Seagate. She did not want to impose upon Hattie, Uncle Peter's long time housekeeper.

Finally, two small, wooden chairs for Gussie, as her sister was called and Ella were jammed in, onto the back seat floor. The big, green car was long and there was just enough floor space for the little chairs. Ella and her sister were the smallest passengers and this was their cross to bear. Their father carefully checked the house one more time before the big Dodge slowly backed into the street, its rear bumper banging the pavement as they exited the driveway and got under way.

Their first stop, about an hour later was the Weehawken, New Jersey Ferry terminal, where they collected Aunt Addie, Uncle Jim and their two daughters. They were Kate's brother's family. Living in Brooklyn and working in the city, they didn't need a car. Uncle Jim and his family had traveled from Brooklyn on the subway and then across the Hudson River on the Weehawken ferry. Ella laughed to herself now, remembering Uncle Jim's size—well over 300 pounds—she still wondered how they all had fit into the car. Her uncle was a mailman and his feet always hurt, so he would wear his slippers every day he was on vacation. Ella and Gussie thought this was just grand; walking around in your slippers every day! In the heat of travel, Uncle Jim's shirt was already stained with sweat.

However, there was a benefit to his weight; he was eligible for the desired front seat. Definite seating was always assigned: Kate sat in the middle of the front seat, Uncle Jim was next to her, his elbow crooked out the window, his head close to the inside roof of the car—Gussie and Ella sat on their little chairs; her aunt and cousins sat in the back seat. Aunt Addie had already sent their large black trunk via Railway Express to Beach Arlington, as Ship Bottom was sometimes called. The large trunk would arrive, *with a little luck*, shortly after they did.

The big car navigated through New Jersey on Route Nine to Route Seventy Two all the way to the island. Route Nine took them through Union City, across the soot covered Pulaski Skyway, through the heavy traffic of Elizabeth (where Malcolm filled up with gas for ten cents a gallon) and the smelly oil tanks of Linden, past the smokestacks and factories of Rahway. Then they would push on, crossing the Raritan River into South Amboy. If Aunt Addie didn't get car sick first and cause a sudden stop, Malcolm would let everyone out to relieve themselves. But that would have to wait until they were through the heat of the cities and into the cooler farmlands of southern New Jersey where there were plenty of woods. Freehold was the next large town, where vegetable, dairy and chicken farms occupied a fair share of the landscape.

Then it was on to Lakewood to pick up eggs at a chicken farm. Up next was Toms River, a sleepy little town where Ella then started asking, "Are we almost there? How much further?" Ella remembered the barrage her father had to endure the rest of the way. At Beachwood, just south of Toms River, she would watch for the tall pine trees bordering the highway and the sudden shine of white sand on the sides of the road. Seeing the sand drove all the children wild with anticipation and the barrage escalated, until they were threatened with punishment if they asked *how much further* one more time. Then Forked River suddenly appeared, then Barnegat, and finally Manahawken.

It was a ritual to stop at a gray, weather beaten shack on Bay Avenue, just before the causeway—its dilapidated tin roof extended out to shade a homemade wooden vegetable stand. They called him *the old man;* her father called him *Pop.* Ella was curious about this old man with the snow white hair and silver rimmed spectacles, who looked like Santa Claus. One time she peeked behind the curtain into a small back room when the old man wasn't looking. She thought he lived there all the time and she worried about him. The room held a neatly made bed and a wash stand beside the bed. Her mother told her later, that he didn't live there all year. It would be too cold. It was just his summer shack for selling his vegetables. Ella felt better.

They loaded the car with newly picked white corn, its silk strands hidden in the green husks still smelling of the earth. Wonderful, big, red, beefsteak tomatoes, bright green string beans, freshly harvested lettuce, juicy, sweet peaches, fat, round blueberries and other produce, fragrant with the black ground aroma. Kate would make her wonderful peach pie, that they all loved. Ella's mouth watered when she thought of the summertime treat. Everyone was given a big, brown, full paper bag to shove into any space available.

They had arrived! The excitement was evident. They would stop at a realtor for Uncle Jim to rent a place for his family. There were plenty of rentals to be had.

Ella thought that back then, one could not have possibly imagined what the island would be like nearly a half century later. It would be laughable now to think of coming to the island and stopping in a realtor's that late to secure a really decent place, although to present day, some still did. However, it was potluck and the penalty for renting late.

But this was the way it was then, and Uncle Jim rented a small cottage for $25.00 a week. His family would stay for two weeks. This would always be in the heart of Ship Bottom where one could survive without a car. If needed, the Dodge would pick them up for church or the movies on the weekends. All other travel was by foot.

Her father came down on weekends until his vacation in August through September.

Now there was unpacking to be done by Aunt Addie's family and the iceman would be scheduled right from the street. Most of the small cottages on the island had iceboxes. Ella and her family left the cottage and continued on to Seagate with its electric refrigerators. Seagate was about twelve blocks south of her cousins' cottage. Uncle Peter had a car, so if there was an emergency during the week, he was available.

When Ella visited her cousins during their two week vacation, she rode her bike on the back road. At times during her visits, the ice man, as the kids called him, was there. The young man was really a college student working delivery during his summer vacation. Ella loved to run after the ice truck with the other children and catch chips of ice from the big blocks that the iceman carved to fit different size iceboxes. They sucked on the ice and when it was hot, the ice tasted good.

What wonderful, happy, innocent days they were she recalled, as she neared her destination and focused on the present. She slept that night at Seagate House, deep in contented dreams, happy to be back on her island.

Early the next morning after visiting the kitchen for hot tea, Ella crossed into the library. She padded silently across the highly polished library floor, trailed by Tucker. His nails clicked a staccato rhythm on the gleaming wooden floors, interrupting the quiet in the room. The hem of her long, flannel nightgown edged the heavy, white socks she wore to keep her feet warm. Hattie had started a fire in the grate to ward off the distinct chill in the air and Ella silently blessed Uncle Peter's devoted housekeeper. Charles, Hattie's husband was caretaker of Seagate and he and Hattie took their stewardship very seriously.

October was beautiful at the shore, but it could be crisp in the opening and closing of the day. Carefully balancing hot tea, Ella lowered herself onto the cushion in the east window to gaze out at the vast Atlantic Ocean and the beach below. Tucker circled a few times, grunted, and then settled himself on the afghan that had spilled onto the floor.

The library was her favorite room in Seagate House and she sighed contentedly, sipping the steaming tea. Her eyes settled on the horizon, and she watched the warm, yellow sun slowly climbing out of the sea to turn on another day.

She altered her focus to the days ahead and the upcoming family reunion. Suddenly, she felt a rush of anxiety, fearing that the truth would elude her once more. She took a deep breath to calm her apprehension. She knew that the anticipation of approaching him with her long held questions caused her great upset. This time, she intended to force information from her cousin Ethan, who had held his silence too long. This time, she would confront him and hold him to the promise that he had made to her years ago. She was sure that something criminal and frightening had transpired at Seagate and the old fears still held her captive. She took another deep breath, attempting to still her anxiety and tried as always, to release the feeling that she could have done something then. What, she did not know. She had tried to intellectualize this guilt for so long that it was terribly difficult to release the emotional turmoil she still held; even though she had told herself numerous times through years of unrelenting regret, that in reality she had been a powerless child in the face of a bigger, stronger Ethan. Only recently, she had experienced a beginning shift of emotions and it was a welcome surprise. She savored the awareness, reveling in the start of herself pardon. She exhaled loudly, thanked God for the gift and hoped that she could now begin to move on from a more detached place. She did not expect an immediate wash of feelings, but at least she was able to grasp a beginning. How she would feel when she saw Ethan again, was another story.

The family was excited about this weekend's reunion at Seagate House. Preparations required a combined force of herself, Gussie, their mother and Aunt Mae, Uncle Peter's wife. Hattie and Charles were on the team. Invitations sent weeks ago had been returned with favorable acceptances. Seagate was a large house with seven bedrooms, huge parlors, porches, and enough room for everyone.

The reunion was wonderful to contemplate, but Ella knew that it also would be somewhat overwhelming. Her large family was an outgoing, somewhat raucous band, but always kind and caring and Ella loved them all. She was still consumed however, with thoughts of a confrontation with Ethan; yet, she knew that she must do it to move on. It had haunted her too long.

It was Friday, the day before the reunion. Kate and Gussie were already there. Ella expected her daughter, Sonya, with her two young children on Saturday. Her two sons, along with Gussie's daughters would also arrive sometime on Saturday. Malcolm had suffered a heart attack two years ago and was gone quickly. At times, Ella could hardly believe that her beloved father was no longer with them.

Ella shifted her startling, blue green eyes away from the window to observe the library around her. A smile crept across her lips as she watched a hanging crystal pick up the sun's first pale rays and dance them along the multitude of books that packed the floor to ceiling bookcases. A flash of light from the crystal caught her peripheral vision, and she eased herself out of the window seat and walked over to the row of cases. She reached up for one of the many photographs that stood on the shelves. The image of a young girl stared out at her from a silver frame. Ocean colored eyes fringed with sooty lashes, a cloud of curly, dark hair and a full mouth set with determination filled a face that glared back at her with a willful expression. Ella shook her head slightly, remembering how determined a child she had been and smiled at herself of long ago. Absent mindedly, she pushed back her abundant, dark hair, now beginning to streak with gray at her temples. Copious memories poured forth as she stared at the photograph.

When she was very young, she often had sensed prior knowledge of daily events and private things that other people held close. Her mother would smile, interested in understanding how Ella knew this and that. Ella did not know exactly what her mother had meant and she always hesitated in answering.

"Oh well," Kate had sighed on one occasion. "I think you have the gift. I am the seventh child of a seventh child, and I was born with a caul over my face and you are my daughter."

"What's a caul?" Her mother told her that it was a thin membrane covering over the newborn's face and head. Some believed that it was the sign of the psychic.

"Ugh," Ella had responded, although she did know what *psychic* meant; she knew that her mother was undeniably gifted with foresight.

"I saw great aunt so and so in a dream last night," Kate would casually mention, or something similar. "She may be leaving us soon." Ella knew that her mother had been right most of the time. Although the comments Kate made never frightened her, Ella always mulled over what she would disclose and what she would keep to herself. She learned in time not to be so forthcoming with her perceptions but to keep the knowledge alive within, unlike her mother who dispensed information so openly.

Ella disconnected from her reverie and placed the picture back on the shelf. She checked her watch and found that it was not yet 8:00 a.m. She had some time to sit and enjoy the quiet of the room and more memories.

"My three children," she sighed. Images of Adam, Sonya, and Polo elicited a smile. Polo was a nickname that Adam had given to his brother Michael years ago, because he loved to play the pool game, Marco Polo. At three years old, Michael had announced to Adam that he *was* Polo. It had stuck, and he was rarely called Michael after that. Ella wondered if she loved them too much. Did she worry too much? Although they were adults now and separated physically from her, emotionally they would always be tied to her heart.

Ella had studied art in college because of her interest in jewelry design and she hoped one day to own a small studio. She had put that aspiration on hold however, because she had wanted a family first. She had her children, but the marriage had not worked.

Now in her fifties, and years past the divorce, Ella was flying solo. She had many friends and there had been a few casual relationships. She felt the universe would send her the right man; that is, if it were meant to happen. Her art kept her busy. Initially she was a non serious jewelry designer who managed to work in her art as often as she could. She still aimed for higher education in her field; now to her surprise, her work had started to pay off. Her name was becoming known through client contacts as a custom designer and for the beauty of her own original pieces. Her close friends had networked well for her.

Thoughts of having her own studio had crept back into her mind and stayed there. *Forget the further education,* she finally decided. *This is probably why I have been stuck.* Uncle Peter had offered to back her, but she was uncertain which way she would finance her plans. She had invested and guarded her monies well from her share of the divorce settlement; there was enough to move ahead if she watched herself carefully. She had finally accepted Uncle Peter's offer as a cushion, and now she was successful and had paid back the monies owed.

There was never a lack of men in her life—that is, when she chose to have them there. She felt good about herself but still wondered if she was better off being on her own. Unless of course, her shining knight suddenly appeared. She wondered if he was still out there and thinking about it, laughed aloud. An expression her mother used came to mind: *There is a lid for every pot.* Ella wondered if she was the lid or the pot.

Still very attractive with her mass of glossy, dark hair and the surprise of her stunning, sea colored eyes, Ella put forth her exotic good looks and sexuality quite unconsciously. She had kept her body trim and healthy over the years, thanks to her love of riding and to Mr. Beau Jangles. She had lovingly raised Mr. Beau from a colt and tried to ride the gelding every day. Much to the envy of her friends, she was still wonderfully slim in her tight riding jodhpurs. Even with silver just starting in her hair, she appeared much younger than her age, probably due to her evident zest for life. Her friends were aware that she caught the eye of any male who was in close proximity, but Ella was rarely conscious of the interested looks that came her way.

Then Matt came into her life. He was the veterinarian for the stable where she boarded Mr. Beau. She had been seeing him regularly for nearly a year, but she was reluctant to acknowledge the fact that the relationship was becoming more intense. Time would tell she reasoned, although the more they were together; the more she wanted to be with him. She did admit that she missed him already. "Matt," she murmured, breathing in his name, seeing him in her mind's eye: tall, tan and trim from the outdoors, blonde hair, now half gray, dark blue eyes, sweet lips, and a loving disposition. She did not want to love him. She had never wanted to care deeply for a man again and so, it was dangerous to her. She needed to guard herself better.

Matt too, had known heartbreak and loss. A fatal automobile accident five years ago had killed his wife instantly. She had been younger than Matt, but there were no children. His wife had been unable to conceive and she would not adopt. Matt had taken his time coming back into the world around him. Nevertheless, he was a caretaker at heart and he loved all the animals, especially the horses. Ella felt that he was an old soul, wonderfully endowed with awareness and great empathy. Her caution had not worked; she could not stop herself from caring about him. She realized now, that it was becoming more than just caring.

Matt would be home soon from Spain. He had flown there to see the running of the bulls. She shook her head when he told her where he was going. She could not understand why he wanted to go and she felt that he would not be a watcher, but right there, into the fray. He only laughed and said, "Life is meant to be lived, Ella. We don't need a reason for everything. I have lived with restraints too long. Do we need to justify what we truly want to do if it's within reason?" She had felt that this was not within reason, but kept silent. His need to take such a step suggested to her, that his past relationship with his wife was not all that he had professed it to be. *I will not touch that subject with a fork,* she had decided. Nor had she asked him to join her for the family reunion. She did not want to be questioned by her family about her relationship with him. Not that she even knew exactly where their relationship stood. It was however, becoming quite evident to her that, in spite of her battle with herself, she loved him. "I have to put this on hold," she told herself, forcing her mind back to random thoughts of her island, retreating into her childhood happiness as she always had done when she wanted to distract herself. Tucker whined to go out, and she got up and went to the kitchen.

"I'll take him out," Charles offered from the back porch, adjoining the kitchen. "I have to run down to the store for Hattie, and Tucker can come with me if you like."

Ella handed him the leash. "Thanks. I appreciate it. I need to get dressed." While dressing, Ella remembered as a child how she was always ready and anxious to ride down to Long Beach Island.

"Don't open that door until we stop, Ella. For heaven's sake child, you'll fall out onto the driveway," her father had warned her more than once when they reached Seagate. Ella never listened and instead, fooled around with the door handle in her anxiousness to depart the car. Once out, she raced up the drive to the big house and flew through the back door, looking for Uncle Peter and Aunt Mae. Then it was on with her bathing suit and off to the beach, after pestering an adult to take her. She loved Seagate and just being there with people whom she cared for so deeply; especially Uncle Peter, who told her wonderful tales of her ancestors.

Willem Skyler VanHameetman was her Dutch predecessor. How many greats, she did not know. She heard this ancestor's story often when she was a little girl. No matter, she listened each time as though the telling was the first time. Willem had built sea gates in Holland to control the surrounding waters. He was born in Ouddorp, Holland; Uncle Peter told her that Ouddorp meant *ancient village* in Dutch. When he was older, the family moved to Rotterdam. Willem had sailed from Rotterdam to America in the early 1600s to escape the Spanish persecution in his country. His original destination was the port of New Amsterdam on Manhattan Island in what is now New York City. He was so disappointed and horrified at what he had found at the large port that he set sail and headed south to Long Beach Island. He had relied upon the word of an old sea captain he had met at the port, who spoke of this wonderful island. Willem would forever tell that it had been the best advice ever given to him. He and his family had settled on the island in the Great Swamp area near what would eventually become Surf City. Hundreds of years ago, great white Atlantic cedar trees, fed by a fresh spring aquifer, grew profusely in that area. The Great Swamp was washed away by a horrendous hurricane and the beautiful white cedar trees had been lost forever. No trace was left of the homes that her ancestors had built on the periphery of the Great Swamp, which was destroyed by the massive hurricane sometime around 1820-1821.

In the early 1800s, Cornelius Arent VanHameetman II, Willem's great grandson who was called Neil, had built the large brown cedar house overlooking the Atlantic Ocean. He had named it Seagate House in honor of his ancestors who had helped build and tend the dikes in Holland. Dikes were banks of earth constructed to control or confine waters. Holland was a land of water and needed dams to hold back the always flooding, encroaching sea. Irrigation management was necessary to preserve the little dry land that there was.

When Ella was a child, she had loved to gaze up at Seagate House from the bulk headed front yard. The house had been lovingly cared for by generations of VanHameetmans. Seagate had been dressed in cedar shingles, grown from the brown cedar trees in the area of the Great Swamp. The house was like a living thing, looming up over her. She had to tilt her head back to see the entire house. The white trimmed windows had looked out at the fathomless, endless sea for more than a hundred years. Ella was sure that the house remembered all that it had seen. A widow's walk protruded out from the front of the third story. The walk had been built in remembrance of the women in Holland who had waited and watched the sea for a husband or lover's return. It was now symbolic and reminiscent of the old seaside homes near the dikes in Holland. The entrance to the walk on the third floor was always securely locked. Ella knew that her cousins had tried to get out onto the walk, but they never had succeeded.

Twin red brick chimneys sat on opposite ends of the roof. Fireplaces are real heating systems, just not very efficient. The fireplaces were the only means of warmth until a central heating system had been installed. On cool nights, before the installation, the generations of family had great fun roasting marshmallows poked on long sticks held over the open hearths.

Highly polished wooden floors in the hallways, cut from lumber grown near Tuckerton, gleamed brightly. Varying shades of warm browns in the flooring complimented the lighter brown wall paneling in the big rooms. The large, black front door was crowned with a multicolored glass arc brought to America from Holland hundreds of years ago. The sun funneled light beams through the colored prisms, sending colored rays in dancing patterns of brightness onto the shiny, wooden floor in the grand foyer. The same semicircle of glass had been rescued long ago from a door in another house on Long Beach Island—a house, long gone, that had once stood in the Great Swamp area, the house of Ella's first Dutch ancestors in North America.

Aunt Mae loved Seagate and often told Ella the house was always full of family and friends, dogs and cats and children's laughter. Mae planted a variety of colored flowers that marched along the wooden, weathered gray front walk. In accord with the different seasons—pink and white in spring and summer, and deep gold and bright crimson in autumn. The walk ended in a T at the large bulkhead, which ran the length of the beachfront property, north to south. The bulkhead shored up the front yard like a fortress, buffering the sand and sea's constant encroachment. Yellow and white stones covered the front and back yards. Grass had grown there years before, but Aunt Mae had said that grass was a breeding ground for mosquitoes. Now the yellow stone blanket covered the yard, preventing the invasion of the little biting pests.

Sunbathers had a lovely view of the ocean from the large, open patio in the front of the house. The garage, which sat behind the house, was built years later and was dressed in the same brown cedar shakes. A small open patio was on the south side of the house, shielded from the blowing, north winds. Near the patio, protected by the house from the relentless winds, was a huge birdhouse, which replicated Seagate House and was home to many tiny wrens. Great grandfather Neil had built a carpenter's work of art, and Ella admired the workmanship of its gingerbread trim, tiny doors and little, white trimmed windows. No one could keep count of the many families of tiny, brown wrens that occupied the cedar birdhouse. It was a constant hub of activity. The family loved to sit and watch the constant motion of the little birds and their lively fly abouts. Ella filled the birdseed trays for the wrens when she was at Seagate.

In the late 1960s, the brown cedar shingles had become so discolored from time and the elements, that Uncle Peter had the house reshingled and painted white with a black roof and shutters. The house was stunning in its new coat, but Ella's childhood memory of Seagate's brown cedar shingles remained constant.

Sergio Cadiz Scarlatti was her Spanish ancestor. His bell stood in the backyard, between the house and the garage. Ella could never remember how many generations of greats Sergio was either. His ancient bell hung on a huge, wooden, elbow-like rack with a base fashioned from squared, dark, criss-crossed wooden pieces. Ella clearly recalled Uncle Peter sitting in the library, telling her stories of Sergio, who had come to America from Spain more than three hundred years ago.

"Sergio was shipwrecked, and chance landed him on the island, around 1614, if I remember correctly from the old journals. I often wondered if this was his destiny, or was he just thrown willy-nilly onto Long Beach Island's shore." Uncle Peter paused to think about that for a minute then continued. "Later the Dutch VanHameetmans arrived, I think around 1616—again, if I remember correctly. And without both our Dutch and Spanish families, there would never have been a you or me!" He winked at Ella and continued his story. "Sergio's ship had sunk in pieces on the shoals of the northern inlet, during a terrible storm. That's where the lighthouse is now, Ella. He managed to save himself and the ship's big brass bell. Some of his crew were lost, but most survived."

She recalled her mother remarking, "You'd think that he hardly had time to worry about saving himself, let alone

saving a bell in that stormy ocean!" Ella had guessed her
mother was tired of hearing about the bell.

Uncle Peter lifted his dark eyebrows in her mother's
direction and clucked his tongue. "I'll choose to ignore
that, Kate," he told his sister-in-law, while running his
hand through his thick, dark, hair, a gesture rising from
exasperation. "You have to remember what the brass bell
meant to Sergio and how he acquired it."

Ella thought now what a fine looking man Uncle Peter
was then, even if he had been an older man in her child's
eyes. He was tall and on the wiry side; he had told her that
he kept himself fit with exercise and a gentle heart.

Peter had graduated from a military academy in Western
Pennsylvania, and following in his father's footsteps, he
had enlisted in the army during the breakout of World
War I. *What a brave soldier he must have been*, Ella had
thought. She knew that he had been severely wounded
in something called the Second Battle of the Marne. A
fragment of metal had lodged in his leg. Even though
surgery had removed the metal, it would give him trouble
from the partial destruction of the bone for the rest of his
life. Ella watched him limp when he was tired or when the
weather was damp or rainy. It made her feel sad.

Peter's face lit up, and his dark eyes were wide as he
spoke further of Sergio's voyage. The historical bell held
great importance to the family because of the personal
history attached.

"How do you know so much about what happened
hundreds of years ago Uncle Peter?"

"There are family journals." Ella knew that he was
proud of that. The VanHameetman family kept their own
separate journals from the early times until now. Sergio's
family had also kept all their family records and they
were brought into the VanHameetman journals when
the families merged. "One person in each generation is
responsible for keeping the family history and the job was
taken very seriously, on both sides, I might add. The story
of Sergio and his involvement with the Spanish Armada
and the bell has been retold down through our family for

generations. Perhaps there has been some embellishment, but very little, I would think. We do have records."

"Where are all the journals now?" She had asked, wondering if he had saved all of them.

"I have them stored safely away." He smiled at her. "I am the keeper of the family records in this generation."

"Are you still writing in the journals?" She could not imagine him doing this.

"Yes. I update family news and family genealogy and I try to interweave the local and important world events of the times as well." Peter had retired early from the government and he worked part time now in Philadelphia and at home for his own consulting firm. He enjoyed Seagate and the visits from his extended family. He spent many hours organizing the family journals, which seemed to be an endless job—but he loved doing it.

"What happens when you die?"

"Ella!" Kate had scolded. "What a terrible thing to ask!"

"Don't chastise the child, Kate," Peter countered. "She's curious and that's good." He smiled at his niece. "Who knows who the next custodian will be?" Ella saw a tiny twitch of his mouth as he went on to tell her more about Sergio.

"Tell us about him when he was little," Ella had prompted.

"Our Scarlatti ancestors came from a beautiful area near the Gulf of Cadiz in Spain. My full name is Peter Willem Cadiz Hamilton. Hamilton used to be VanHameetman. But our family name was changed to Hamilton from VanHameetman years ago." He looked at Kate. "Malcolm must have discussed this with you?" he questioned, referring to her husband and the youngest of his four brothers.

"Of course Peter." Kate acknowledged.

"It's neat to be named after a town, like Cadiz," Ella piped in, grinning. "I think I will visit Spain when I grow up."

Peter smiled at her. Although he would teach her one day about the way the Spanish carried their names forward and how the Dutch newborns were named, he felt at that time, that she was too young to understand. It was enough, and it had nothing to do with the VanHameetman name change. He would tell her about that change sometime later.

"I wonder how Sergio and Willem met. Did they just bump into each other?" she giggled.

"Could be, Ella." He laughed. "I'm not sure if they actually had met on the island or elsewhere, or perhaps not at all. It could have been their children or grandchildren that encountered each other. I would have to go back in our genealogy and see the exact date of the marriage that merged the families." He paused to sip the coffee that Hattie had brought him. "It seems to me that it was a VanHameetman man and a Scarlatti woman who were first married."

"I would really like to read about that." Ella was interested.

"I'll tell you a little of the history of Spain at that time and why Sergio had to leave. In the late 1500s, King Philip II of Spain wanted England to change to his religion—Catholicism. Much of the matter had to do with the Queen of England who had refused Philip's hand in marriage. Sergio's Grandfather, Bernardo, did not agree with King Philip, even though Bernardo was Catholic, he protested loudly in public about the King's treatment of non Catholics. When he would not repent for his protesting, the soldiers arrested him.

Sergio's father, Alfonso, went to plead for his father, Bernardo, and then Alfonso was also thrown into prison. Sergio, being the only male in the family and still at home, was in danger from the King's soldiers. His family decided to hide Sergio as a ships boy. Later, the King attempted to invade England with his large Armada of ships—with the goal of trying to enforce his religion on others. This was the main thrust behind the Armada. Sergio's ship was caught in port in Lisbon, Portugal and his ship and crew were drafted into the Armada. That's how Sergio came to be involved. It was more complicated than that, Ella, but I want you to understand, so I've simplified it."

Ella agreed. "How old was he?"

"Probably eleven or twelve when he was first hidden, I would think. I believe he wasn't quite fifteen when he was conscripted into the navy. He had no choice. There was some humor about this, though. When Sergio and the crew were drafted into the King's navy, Sergio was hidden on one of the King's own ships. It was the safest place to be—right under King Philip's nose." Uncle Peter laughed.

"Their ship was so heavily damaged in the Armada battle that they were barely able to limp into a safe port. Thick fog caused additional navigational problems and that's where the bell came into play. Sergio rang that bell for an entire day, pinpointing his ship's location, preventing collisions. The King honored Sergio for his tireless bravery and perseverance. Sergio was given the great, brass bell to keep for himself. The King never realized who Sergio really was," Uncle Peter paused and smiled broadly at Ella. "Can you believe that?"

Ella drew in a deep breath and continued her reminiscing. She remembered her uncle again in her mind's eye, leaning his long, thin body forward in the chair. He loved to tell Sergio's story. "Many years later, our Sergio mounted the very same bell on the deck of his own ship and sailed across the ocean to America. I have a very old, oil painting of Sergio as a young man. I will get it out of storage and show it to you, Ella. Your cousin Ethan bears a remarkable resemblance to his ancestor."

"Is that what all that stuff is in that old trunk in the attic?"

"Some things are there. Most of our historical journals are safely kept in special storage along with the oil painting."

The family took great pride in the historical significance of the bell. People out on a stroll still rang Seagate's doorbell and asked to see this piece of history up close. Over the years, numerous articles about the bell had been written in the local newspapers.

Ella had tried to imagine the arduous trip her early ancestors had endured. She could not grasp how they accomplished the long ocean voyages in wooden ships fueled only by the wind. She had seen pictures of the sailing ships in books. She wondered if her ancestors were frightened, riding the rolling, ocean waves in fairy tale ships, on that vast body of salt water. She could not bear to think of the dangerous storms they probably had encountered out on the open seas.

Sometime later Ella remembered that her uncle had promised to tell her further about the VanHameetman name change to Hamilton. If this was her Dutch ancestor's name, why didn't she have it? Or why not Scarlatti, which was Sergio's last name?

Peter sighed and thought I should have realized that Ella would not let that drop. Oh, well, *I might as well try.* "You are related to both the Scarlatti name and the VanHameetman name. The VanHameetman name should really be yours. In Holland, the name was easy to pronounce, but in America, it was difficult. My Great Grandfather Neil, who built Seagate, wanted a more American name, so it was told. He was the one who legally changed the name VanHameetman to Hamilton. And when I was a young man, during World War I, when we were at war with Germany, anything that sounded German, even though it was not, was suspect. So I guess by that time, the family was happy that our name was Hamilton. I find that very sad, very sad. Your Aunt Mae's maiden name started with a Von. Her family changed their name during World War I. The name was a German derivative and although her entire family was American born, they had threats against them. They dropped the Von from their last name to make it sound less foreign. Uncle Peter did not wish to speak of it again. She knew that he had fought in that war against the Germans. Ella felt very sorry that he was so sad about this, but decided that she would rather have her name, Hamilton. It was easier to spell than VanHameetman.

Now Ella laughed softly, her memories were here and there and somewhat discombobulated. She thought of the time when she had felt her lot in life was unjust. Try as she might, it had been painfully difficult to accept her physical features. She saw her mother, Kate, young, pretty, with blonde hair, blue eyes and a soft round body that Ella liked to lean against. Malcolm, her tall, handsome father was blessed with a shock of dark blonde hair and bright hazel eyes. "Kate and Malcolm," she said aloud, gently shaking her head. Their names conjured up beautiful people in her mind. Even her sister Gussie was blonde and blue eyed. I could have been adopted, she would speculate, except for the proof of her birth certificate bearing her name and her tiny footprints stamped on the bottom. She would stare repeatedly at the important looking document, containing an official, round, silver stamp with jagged edges. Still, she questioned her heritage and her dark hair amidst the family blondness. Her mother had told her that she had inherited her exotic looks and dark hair from the Spanish side of the family, with a little American Indian and Irish thrown in; her blue green eyes were passed down to her from her Swedish Dutch ancestry. Kate had assured Ella that she would be a beauty one day. "Ella, my darling—this family of ours is a real melting pot!"

However, Ella did not care to be exotic, whatever that meant and it would be a long time before she could ever believe what her mother had said about her being a beauty. Ella did remember though, her mother saying, "Just you wait and see, Elaina Rose. You'll grow up to be a beautiful woman just like your Great Aunt Elaina." Ella recalled grimacing over that remark. "Please call me Ella," she begged. She felt Elaina Rose was too long a name.

"You're right, Ella. Elaina Rose is a mouthful." Aunt Mae had been listening from the other room.

Ella recalled that earlier in July of 1941, she was at Seagate with her mother and sister. Uncle Ramon, her father's brother, had dropped off Luke and Hope, her cousins, for a few weeks to visit with Ella. Uncle Ramon, her father Malcolm, and Uncle Peter were brothers. There was a fourth brother, Jerry, but Ella was not as familiar with him. He lived in California.

Cousin Luke was a daredevil and the girls worried about him. He always planted himself where the big waves crashed, refusing to budge. The waves thoroughly pounded his stubbornness and he would suffer numerous wipeouts before he admitted defeat. After lunch, the hot sun, the buzzing of the bugs, the sweet smell of the blooming flowers and the muted drifting sounds of the bathers in the surf caused the children to become drowsy. They were exhausted from jumping the waves in the warm, salt water and the trio retreated into the coolness of the enclosed, front, screened porch to take a nap. Listening to the soft surf noises, they dozed on the cool and comfortable, blue cushions that Hattie had scattered on the white, wicker chaises. Kate would rock Gussie to sleep in one of the old, cane rocking chairs, singing softly to all of them and then dozing off herself. Ella recalled how pleasant it had been in that safe haven.

The ocean was too rough for the children to venture out far and not conducive for learning to swim. Ella and her cousins first learned to paddle in the bay's calm, warmer, water. At the swimming beach on the bay, the big green float was anchored out a ways and after you had learned to swim and could make it out to the float by yourself, you were considered a swimmer; Ella had made it to the float unaided, in her eighth summer. Gussie would achieve success later at the same age.

On overcast days, they were back on the bay's shore to forage for crabs. Ella, Luke and Hope tied on their dirty, old sneakers, grabbed the crab nets and headed for the bay with Charles. They hunted the smelly, salt marshes for the hiding crabs, that were wearing their soft shells. Uncle Peter said that these crabs were his favorite seafood.

How well Ella remembered the dock on the bay, where they crabbed for the hard shells, with the new net that they bought each year from the Conrad Lumber Company. Conrad's was one of their favorite places; it was stocked with splendid fishing paraphernalia, where they could wander at their leisure.

A favorite past time was watching the small seaplane land right in front of the dock on the bay, near the swimming beach in Ship Bottom. She couldn't recall the owner's name now, but her memories of that small plane landing on the water had made an impression on her busy mind. She had been told that the man who owned it commuted from Philadelphia in the summertime.

Some Saturday nights, Uncle Peter would stop and pick up Ruthie and Virginia, cousins on Aunt Mae's side who often visited. He would drop off the children and accompanying adults a block before the Colony Theater in Brant Beach for the six o'clock movie. There was no parking in front of the Colony, so it was a quick drop on the previous block. The sidewalk before the theater passed through an area overgrown with holly bushes and other vegetation, harboring millions of mosquitoes. The tiny buggers swarmed out for an evening meal and anyone walking by broke into a trot. Walt Disney and Esther Williams movies were favorites of both the children and the adults. That year the girls decided to become professional swimmers.

There were two theaters on the island, the Colonial in Beach Haven and the Colony, nearer to Seagate in Brant Beach. The Colony Theater at that time was not air conditioned and could get very warm. The rear of the theater was not far from the ocean, so Mr. Coleman, a very tall, large man and the owner of both theaters, would open the rear doors to let in the cool, Atlantic Ocean breezes. However, in came the mosquitoes along with the breezes. Then he would walk up and down the aisles with his orange flit gun, spraying here and there to kill the tiny pests. The audience quickly learned to duck! No one back then knew how harmful the pesticides in the flit gun could be. Ella thought now, if one breathed in the fumes or the *fluid* got you in the mouth or face, how dangerous that could have been. But then, no one knew of those things.

Ella also remembered the *bug man*, as her kids called him, but that was years later when she had her own children. He rode in a small truck, and sometimes in a jeep, up and down the streets, blowing out clouds of pesticides to tame the mosquitoes; the children would run through the billowing clouds of pesticide, laughing and screaming. Ella was appalled now, recalling what they thought was fun. The parents had no knowledge of the harm these clouds full of pesticides could cause when let loose.

Returning to long ago Sunday morning memories brought Ella and her cousins back to the Colony to attend Mass—usually said by visiting Franciscan Friars. The small Catholic Church in Beach Haven could hardly accommodate the large summer crowds, so Uncle Peter chose to attend the lesser crowded Colony Theater for Mass. The altar was improvised on the stage, with two large fans placed on either side acting as air conditioning. However, this did little to cool the air on a hot, humid, Sunday morning.

The Franciscans wore sandals and dark brown frocks like Friar Tuck, much to the children's delight. They played guitars and sang, moving mass along quickly in the heat. The children wore bathing suits and went barefoot most of the summer, so wearing shoes caused them to hobble down the aisle. Sunday dresses and shirts, starched and ironed, scratched their sunburned backs ferociously and they barely tolerated the hour spent in church once a week. Uncle Peter shamed their complaining by telling them, "You kids have it too good. You can afford to give God one hour of your time on Sunday mornings for all that you have—even if you have to suffer a little." Ella thought they suffered a lot.

When Mass was over at last and the front doors were thrown open, the cousins attempted to race through the upper corridor to see who could exit first, but most times an adult would slow them down. The walk to church was not far, but Uncle Peter chose to drive so that he could stop at the bakery for the warm jelly donuts rolled in confectionary sugar, packed in big, white bags. Ella recalled him handing them the bag, warning them to eat just one donut each. By the time the car reached Seagate's driveway, the children had devoured at least two donuts each and acquired white powdered mustaches with jelly dripping down their chins.

Occasionally, after supper, while it was still light, Uncle Peter and Aunt Mae would take the children to the Boulevard in Ship Bottom for frozen custard. "You are such a pain, Luke. I cannot imagine anyone not liking frozen custard." Hope was appalled, and rolled her eyes at her brother. Nevertheless, Aunt Mae indulged him now and again, because this was his only dislike. Otherwise they walked to the big drugstore, where the college boys wore white uniforms and white hats and scooped gigantic servings of Dolly Madison ice cream. The trio spun around on red, leather stools in front of a long counter to order banana splits and sundaes. Seemingly infinite discussion ensued before they reached a decision as to what flavors of ice cream they would order.

"If you don't make up your minds quickly, they'll put you all out," Uncle Peter had threatened. Then they decided lickety split.

Atlantic City, thirty four miles south, was exciting and the visit each year was highly anticipated. They were awestruck as they watched the large, white horse with a young woman on his back, dive into the ocean from the Steel Pier. They noticed that the rider waited for the horse to decide when *he* wanted to dive. Then Kate and Malcolm liked to stop and watch the dancers in the large ballroom on the pier. The Steel Pier was famous; big name bands usually played there.

Before they left, they stopped to see the motorcycle driver roar around the inside of a gigantic, slatted barrel. They could not understand why he didn't fall down from the sides. Uncle Peter demonstrated the principle of centrifugal force to them the next day by swinging a bucket full of water around quickly, upside down, and the water stayed in.

Dinner at the Engleside Hotel was always a seasonal
treat for a number of years, until 1940, when the hotel had
its last summer. When she was small, Ella had thought
that the Engleside Hotel was a castle because of its many
turrets. The children were forced to behave when they sat
in the hushed and very sophisticated dining room, where
white uniformed servers hovered in attendance. Kate's face
was hidden behind the large menu, as she read from the
extensive offerings.

"I don't know what that is," Ella had whined. She
refused all suggestions except the desserts. Her mother
finally gave up and ignored her protests.

"The menu is very exotic," Aunt Mae had commented.
Ella realized later that exotic could mean anything not
local, like Green Turtle Soup Madeira, Sweetbread Patties,
Sauté of Squabs on Toast, Pineapple Charlotte, Montrose
Pudding in fruit sauce, Bent's crackers and other foreign
sounding names.

After the Engleside had closed, the family dinner out
was at the Baldwin Hotel, which was once known as the
Arlington Inn. "You should have seen the Baldwin in her
early days." Aunt Mae smiled dreamily, lost in reverie.
"When I was a girl, we stayed at the Baldwin a few times,
and it was wonderful," she sighed. "A horse drawn trolley
dropped the guests at the front door. The hotel was truly
something to see in those days. It had been the largest
and grandest hotel and restaurant for miles around."

"Horses? Real, live horses?" Luke had perked up. "How
long ago was that?"

"Before you were born," Mae drifted again into fond
memories.

After dinner, they had sat on the bench lined
promenade, as Kate called the small boardwalk to observe
the different people. "I see a lot of exotic looking people,"
Ella noted, now that she had a grasp of what exotic meant.
Her mother smiled.

Ella remembered a previous conversation Uncle Peter
had with her mother and Aunt Mae. He did not frequent
some of the larger restaurants, or hotels, he said, because

he knew that they were restricted. "What does that mean?" Ella had asked.

"Hotels or clubs who will not serve or house people because of their religious beliefs, are called restricted," he answered, shaking his head in disgust.

Mae had replied softly, "Is that legal? I just cannot believe that it would be allowed."

"For heaven's sake, Mae, are you not aware of what goes on around you if it doesn't affect you? Don't you believe what happened to that lovely young woman who was asked to leave? She is quite well known on the island. I'm sure you know who I mean," he insisted.

"I know. I know. It is so outrageous, that it is hard to believe. But what can we do about it?" She sighed.

"You should not frequent places that are restricted," Peter responded. "That's condoning the shameful behavior."

Ella could not understand what that was all about, but Uncle Peter never patronized certain places on the island; her mother then did the same. She remembered saying to the adults, "For heaven's sake, who cares what church you go to? That's silly."

Thank God that kind of behavior is against the law now, the adult Ella thought to herself, and returned to her reminiscing.

On a rainy afternoon, at least once in the summer, they had piled into the car and drove to the Barnegat Lighthouse at the northern end of the island. Old Barney stood proudly overlooking the Barnegat inlet, where it had once thrown its warning light over the entire island to steer ships away from the dangerous island shore and inlets. The lighthouse had been one of the most important points of light for coastal vessels bound up and back from New York. Strong currents and the always shifting sandbars, along with the rocky coasts, brought out the best skills in those pilots attempting to navigate the coastline. Uncle Peter had told the children that there had been smaller lighthouses overlooking the inlet before the present house was built. Congress ordered construction of a lighthouse in 1834. It had been lit in 1835, but the lighthouse was eventually ruled inadequate. Then in 1855, George G. Meade, who had earned historical recognition during the Civil War, designed a new lighthouse. The Barnegat tower light was 165 feet above sea level and a navigational lighthouse until 1927 when a Barnegat Lightship was anchored 8 miles off the coast to replace old Barney. Now holly, scrub bushes and low growing sea grass covered the entire area.

The lighthouse had been run down and deserted and remained unlit for many years. They wondered if all the talk about the lighthouse area becoming a park one day would ever come to fruition.

"I don't think we should go in," Uncle Peter cautioned as he watched Luke open the broken door of the lighthouse. He stood there for a minute, undecided. "I guess it wouldn't hurt to climb to the top, but you kids be careful." He was anxious about allowing the children to make the climb, but he had never been to the top himself. His desire to do so interfered with his judgment about being trespassers. He followed the children up the 217 winding metal steps, bad leg and all. Kate remained below with Mae.

The misty rain had lifted and the view of Barnegat Bay, the inlet, the island and the ocean from the top of the lighthouse astounded them. "I can see the mainland," Luke yelled excitedly. Ella never forgot her first climb and counting all of the 217 steps. Peter snapped a picture from their high point of sight and then they descended the narrow, spiral, metal steps to the ground. Before they left, Kate asked a man who had just come upon the scene to take their picture. The camera caught them at the base of Old Barney, smiling, laughing, arms around each other—captured forever on a piece of shiny, black and white paper. Uncle Peter later framed the photos and stood them on a library shelf, to recall his momentous, singular climb to the top of the Barnegat lighthouse. Ella never forgot it either, although there would be many visits in the future, that first climb would top them all.

Before they left for home, they visited the location where Captain Steelman, a privateer in the 1700s, had been murdered in the dunes by the infamous Captain John Bacon. Bacon, a self proclaimed Loyalist, pirate, then privateer, had attacked Steelman and his men and murdered them while they slept. Captain Steelman had previously confiscated a cargo of Hyson tea from a wrecked Belgian cutter and after unloading it on the beach, the men rested—probably the rum made the crew sleep more soundly. Bacon and his men then did their dirty deed, and after the murders, stole the booty. Afterwards, there was a metal plate laid in the ground, with the massacre's history on it. Ella always had wondered if this was Captain Steelman's real grave, or just a marker.

"Captain Steelman was buried in Manahawkin with the rest of the crew. That is just a marker," Uncle Peter had told her.

Later in the summer, Charles took the children on their annual visit to the fishery located on the traffic circle. "I only call you young'uns once to get up, or we don't go!" Charles would shout to route them out of bed. "It's six o'clock. Up and at 'em." They would grab the bag that Hattie had prepared for each of them, hiding a bun and a drink.

This was a pound fishery, where Charles as a very young man in high school had worked the fishnets during the summers, until he joined the Army. He was very knowledgeable about the workings of pound fisheries. "The nets are tied to those poles. The poles go out two miles into the water," he pointed to the tall North Carolina hickory poles 70 to 85 feet long, lying behind the fishery, ready to be set out in the water. "The poles are set about 75 feet apart, and you can see the tops of the poles eight to twelve feet out of the water. This is what holds the nets. You wouldn't think they were that far out, but they are. The width or the depth of the nets, relates to the depth of the water. The net rises from the ocean floor, whether it is 30 feet or 60 feet; it will vary. The square trap at the end efficiently captures any sea life that enters. The nets are changed every two weeks to clean them of seaweed."

The children had listened intently to Charles. They watched through binoculars as the large, open boats with small outboards came into shore, heavy with fish pulled from the nets. In earlier times, oars were used. The boat, which looked like a large, oversized rowboat, was hurled through the close breakers onto a horizontal row of logs that had been set down in the surf. The breaking waves slammed the boats down hard on the row of logs that acted as a moving plank, rolling the boat up onto the beach from there and a tractor, or in earlier years, horses hauled the boats up further on the beach. The fishermen then sorted the large catch into big, brown, wicker baskets, which were lined up on an old, open flatbed truck. What wonderful stuff came up and out of those nets!

"What is that?" Ella had asked one time, pointing to a large tropical sunfish that looked like a big car tire. The fishermen, busy as they were, stopped to answer the children's questions. There were hammerhead sharks, sand sharks, mantas, and all kinds of fish and crabs. After the sorting was finished, the flatbed drove the baskets further up to the fishery itself. The children were quiet on the ride home, mulling over the wonders they had just seen. "Next time we have to bring a camera," Charles commented.

Ella slept in a small, third floor bedroom at Seagate, which she considered *her* bedroom away from home. During World War II, there were strict blackout rules on the island. Aunt Mae told Ella that Long Beach Island was a barrier island, exposed to the ocean coastline to the east and the Inter coastal waterway to the west. Mae hung a black shade over the small window to keep the light in. Blackout shades were mandatory to avoid German submarines, called U-boats from being guided in by lights from the shore.

"There now, Ella, that ought to do the trick," Aunt Mae had said in her lilting remnant of an Irish brogue, as she pulled the dark shade down. Then she rearranged her yellow flowered dress, pulling it loose across her ample bosom. Ella knew that a war was happening, but she had never thought that the Germans might see her light and bomb the house. She did not understand that the danger was from the submarines.

"But you told me Germany was across the ocean," Ella had cried, imagining great explosions knocking the house down. "How can they drop a bomb over here?" Frightened now, she knew that she must warn Luke and Hope. They would need an escape plan if Seagate was attacked.

Mae continued making up Ella's bed and when she had finished, she stood back, pushing her heavy, dark red hair off her sweaty face. Noisily clucking her tongue, she shook her head at Ella, and addressed her niece's concerns about the bombs. "It's the submarines, child," Mae said. "They're called U-boats."

"I won't *ever* turn the light on, unless the shade is down, Aunt Mae. So, could you leave the window open just a crack so I can hear the ocean?" She certainly did not want any Germans to see her light.

"Very well," Aunt Mae answered. "But remember, if you do get up, first pull the shade down all the way before you turn the light on. We don't want a warden ringing our doorbell."

"I know, I know." Ella was upset.

The air raid wardens, as they were called, were neighborhood volunteers, who monitored every house after dark and reminded their neighbors of the blackout rules.

During that wartime summer, Ella and her cousins played in the warm tidal pools in the cool of the early evening. Sailors from the United States Coast Guard station patrolled the beach on their big prancing horses. Ella liked to watch the sailors dressed in their white sailor suits and hats, with tan spat leggings up to their knees. She especially admired their horses but she was never permitted to approach them.

The Guards watched the waters from the large tower standing on the upper beach and they patrolled the shoreline with Doberman pinscher dogs. Low flying blimps monitored the near coastal waters acting as submarine spotters, watching for any sub activity in the near waters. They also alerted any of the United States convoys traveling near in on the ocean.

The Coast Guard started to remove people from the beach at dusk, as the darker part of twilight set in. Ella and her cousins left the beach, which was closed after sundown.

One evening the family heard that U-boats had been spotted right off their beach, only a half mile or so out. Ella guessed it was a good place to land if you wanted to make war on America; she was glad that the Coast Guard was there to protect them. Ella had asked Uncle Peter why they called the submarines U-boats, instead of just submarines. He told her that U-boat is another name for U-boot, a shortened version of the German word, Unterseeboot, meaning undersea boat. U-boat was an English name, referring only to the German submarines in the World Wars.

Tar washed up on the beach from the sunken U-boats and occasionally, pieces of wooden crates marked with funny letters floated in. Charles had told them that the words were German. The empty crates probably had stored either fruit or other foodstuff. Once or twice, they had found oranges and apples in the surf. Luke had picked up a German sailor's hat from the beach and yelled as he put it on his head, "Look at me," pointing to the hat. Ella wondered about the German sailor who had worn the hat and what had happened to him.

Hattie had a tar station near the back door, loaded with old rags and turpentine to clean the tar from their feet. It was risky walking the beach because of the tar lumps that had drifted in to the beach from the sunken U-boats. Hattie's tar station worked twofold. Other than the tar on the beach, small, back streets would melt when the weather was very warm. The Boulevard was of a different material and never softened in the heat.

Uncle Peter announced one evening, that a group of German spies had been captured on the dunes about a mile south from their beach; they were thought to have been signaling a U-boat. The children wanted to walk down and look, but Kate said it would be foolish, that there was nothing to see at that point. That was so long ago Ella acknowledged, but how well she remembered the incident.

Gussie opened the library door noisily and interrupted Ella's mind wanderings. She peeked in and saw Ella somewhere in outer space.

"Oh, hi, Gus," Ella greeted her sister.

"Here's more hot tea," Gussie offered, as she set the pot down and looked at her sister. "Hattie sent it up. She was worried about you. How long have you been in here?" Gussie saw that it was useless trying to talk to her.

"Thanks, Gus. I'll be floating soon with all the tea, but thank Hattie for me anyway."

Gussie turned to leave but stopped to pet Tucker. "He's such a good boy. Does he have to go out?" She stood for a minute, looking at Ella, wishing she could help her. Other family members too, knew about Ella's frightened belief that something terrible had happened that October night at Seagate, so many years ago. She realized at times like this, when they were at Seagate, that the memories came back strongly to Ella. "Let's hope your awful mystery gets solved at the reunion. Uncle Peter told us that Ethan and Martine will definitely be here."

Ella stirred the fresh tea. "Are you sure Ethan is coming? I hope so, Gus. It's been too long, and I'm determined to finish it. And thanks, but Tucker was out earlier." She watched her sister close the door.

Tucker heard his name mentioned and laid his head on Ella's lap. "You're too smart, my lad," she whispered and softly stroked his lovely head.

She stopped for a minute to think why she had been at Seagate in October of 1941. She had always visited in July and August. She left the library, wandered up the stairs into her old room on the third floor and continued reminiscing.

In 1941, Ella's family had moved to Philadelphia and lived in a large, two story brick townhouse near Rittenhouse Square. Her father had been in a terrible car accident and had suffered serious injuries. Kate brought the girls to Seagate the morning after the accident. Their aunt and uncle would care for them, freeing their mother to visit the hospital. Hattie and Charles, sincerely concerned, had also offered to help care for the sisters during their father's recovery.

Ethan, Peter's son and only child, arrived at Seagate shortly after Ella, Gussie and Kate. "Who is that, Mother?" Ella had whispered, surprised at seeing the young man. She had not remembered Ethan.

"He's Uncle Peter's son, Ethan; he's your first cousin," Kate answered softly. "Uncle Peter is older than your father, so that accounts for the years of age difference between you and Ethan. I guess it has been too long for you to remember him; I think you were only about four years old when you last saw him."

She had been told that Ethan was in the army and that he was stationed overseas. When he returned to the states, Uncle Peter and Aunt Mae did visit Ethan and his wife, Martine in Washington, D.C., but not often. Ella recalled that after her childhood night of terror, no one had spoken of Ethan and when she had questioned Uncle Peter about his son, he was always vague. When Ella was older, she felt that Uncle Peter had become estranged from Ethan, but by then she had stopped asking about him because there was never anyone who would discuss Ethan. His name had become almost taboo.

Funny, Ella thought now, *there were pictures of him as a child on the library shelves, but none as an adult.* Still, she had never forgotten her involvement with Ethan on that dark October night, so long ago. Her childhood perception had captured Ethan in her mind's eye as tall and handsome, looking somewhat like Uncle Peter, with dark hair and fiery dark eyes.

She had written her memories in a little book and kept adding notes, so that she would never forget any of the details. Ella felt that she had been seriously marked as a child. Now as an adult, she desperately needed to know the truth to dispel the black memories she still carried. Returning to that dark night, she went back once more in her mind and carefully revisited the incident. She was still very sure, as she had been then, that she was not dreaming about the baby crying and the old bell clanging so loudly through the deep stillness of that night.

She picked up her tea, and walked over to the window. She stood there, quietly, looking down to the beach and leaned over to crack the window. Her deep concentration became trance like. Sharply etched pictures rose up and moved across the landscape of her mind, forming colorful, intensely emotional scenes, and the haunting began once again. Memories of that frightening Indian summer night of long ago drew her back. As the images became more vivid in her mind's eye, Ella shivered. She clearly recognized, that in her new awareness as an adult, she had never been able to completely outpace the demons that came forth from that intimidating night: the inky blackness in her room and outside her window, the strange noises, along with the untruths and the many unexplainable events had frightened her terribly.

The adult Ella shook her head slowly, somewhat in disbelief, as she recalled her inner capabilities as a child. She had known instinctively that Ethan had lied to her. Even now, she did not doubt her childhood impressions.

On that October morning, so long ago, her mother, Aunt Mae and Uncle Peter had left Seagate for Philadelphia to visit her father. They would see him that day, stay overnight in Uncle Peter's Philadelphia apartment, visit her father again the next morning, tend to a few errands and return to Seagate.

9:00 p.m. had been bedtime for Ella. That night, she quietly climbed the stairs to her snug little third floor abode. Gussie would sleep with Hattie so that she would not cry out in the night for her mother. Remembering what Aunt Mae had told her, Ella immediately pulled the black shade down before she turned the light on. When she was ready for bed, she turned the light off and then cracked the window a little bit so that she could hear the ocean. She pulled the dark shade up just enough to let the moon shine in to interrupt the awful absence of light. There was only a half moon that night, shedding partial light into her room and it was overcast, so the moon's glow was hardly constant. From high up in the gigantic old house, she watched the damp, swirling mist outside through the partly lifted shade. She hurried into bed and fell into a void of darkness, until little by little dim outlines appeared in the room, taking on sinister shapes. Other shrouded objects seemed to move with energy sucked in from the inky blackness. Her terrible fear of the dark always attacked her more acutely when she was not in her own home. Lying in terror, she was afraid to move one toe for fear that if she stuck it out from under her safe covers, the wolves would get her. There were rules in her terror though and she knew her blankets were a safe zone; the rules said that any part of her under the covers was out of bounds to all monsters. She used to wonder with whom she had made that agreement. When she was older, she realized that it was with herself, to help her cope with the dark.

She had thought that she had been wide awake, unable to sleep, when she suddenly heard the clanging of the old bell. It rang and rang, echoing loudly through the foggy night and across the dark beach. Who was ringing the bell? And why? Had a bomb been dropped? Were there foreign soldiers on the beach? She had desperately wanted to creep to the window and peek out, but she was so paralyzed with fear that she lay straight and stiff under the safety of her blankets. Time ran together, and she had no way of knowing the hour, not that it would have made any difference to her in her black abyss of terror. Logic instantly fled, and thoughts of horrific proportions continued to grab her. Her mind ran wild with another thought: *Could the ghost of Grandfather Sergio be ringing the bell? Has he come to take his bell?*

Then, as suddenly as the ringing had started, it stopped. She remembered how her intense fear caused her heart to thump up into her throat. Her scalp tingled in the sudden quiet. Her body was rigid and the frightening silence buzzed in her ears as she strained to hear any sounds at all. Then after a time that she could not measure, softly muted male voices drifted up from the beach, though not so soft that they did not carry up to her window. She thought she heard different voices and then water sounds, that she could not distinguish, followed by the extreme silence again. Suddenly, within the house came a muted fussing sound, that at first she could not understand, until awareness came abruptly. She realized that it was a baby crying—a baby far too young to be Gussie.

"Not really crying though. It was more of a whimpering, so soft and muffled it was," Ella murmured aloud then, thinking it would stick better in her memory and help her to validate her recollections later. She thought however, it was not so soft that she could not make out that it definitely was a baby. She could not understand anything she was hearing. Curiosity finally overcame her terror and she had managed suddenly to sit up, straining to listen more closely in the darkness. Her ears detected faint sounds of vague, shuffling footsteps and low murmurings coming from the first level of the old house. In the darkened silence, hushed whisperings floated up the spiraling, open stairwell and ricocheted down the hall to her room. Then all went silent again, so still that Ella once more heard the thumping of her own heart.

She had waited for a long time but heard no more. She decided to investigate in the morning when all of the bad things had left her room, when the bright sun would draw a path of light across her wooden floor and when everything would be as it should be in the first light.

The next morning at breakfast however, it was not all right. When Ella had asked Ethan about the bell, the baby crying and the voices on the beach, he told her that she had been dreaming and that she had a big imagination. No bell had been rung in the middle of the night, he had assured her and certainly, no baby had been crying. He would have heard it, he said. He sounded very unconcerned as she watched him butter his toast with his strong square hands. "Ella, my dear child, you have a very vivid imagination," Ethan repeated and laughed. "You had a bad dream, my little sweet."

Liar! She wanted to yell at him, but she turned away and said it softly to herself instead. Cousin Ethan, with his watchful dark eyes and his persuasive, smiling face, thought he could fool her. *He sure is used to getting his own way*, she thought, provoking her anger even further. She could not figure him out. She hoped that he was just secretive, not bad, just hiding his real self. Yet it was destructive to her. Ethan was young that summer, but Ella saw him as a man in her child's perception. He looked at her across the breakfast table with those intense see all eyes; then his expression suddenly changed. She felt he realized, that without a doubt she knew he had lied. She did not care what he said. He could not fool her. She knew what she had heard and she knew that he was lying to her, making her furious—furious that he had laughed at her in his lying.

"When is my mother coming for me? And where's Uncle Peter and Aunt Mae?" Swallowing a lump in her throat, she tried to hold back her tears. She thought of her father and the deep closeness they shared. *What if he died and left them?* She wondered why Ethan was here at Seagate. She had overheard her mother tell her father that Ethan's comings and goings from D.C. and other overseas places worried Uncle Peter. Ella had not known exactly how far D.C. was from New Jersey, but she had learned in school, that it was Washington, District of Columbia, capital of the United States and that the White House, where the President lived, was there. Everything now seemed awry; she felt isolated and needed her mother. She could not make sense of what was happening.

"Your mother must stay awhile with your father, Ella. He'll be as good as new, but he needs to be in the hospital right now," Ethan had told her, getting up from the breakfast table. "Your Uncle Peter had an appointment in the city first thing this morning. That's why they left yesterday and stayed overnight." He folded his napkin and laid it on the table as Ella watched.

"I think kidnappers were here with a stolen baby," she suddenly blurted out.

Ethan looked at her intently. "My god Ella. What kind of nonsense is that?" Shaking his head, he walked from the room.

She wondered how long he had known about Uncle Peter's appointment. Did he somehow arrange things so that the adults were gone overnight? How could he have managed that? *It would clear the coast for him,* she thought. She sat awhile longer, and then decided to go outside and look around. For what, she had no idea. There was something strange going on and she just knew instinctively that Ethan was involved. She didn't care what he had told her. Her little voice inside was very active, but of course she could not fully verbalize her suspicions as a child, nor was she any match for Ethan, then. She just knew what she felt. Ethan had trod on her feelings when he had laughed at her and treated her like a baby. She was determined to find out the truth of last night and confront him with his lies. Uncle Peter would be back soon and she could hardly wait to tell him. Mother did not need to know. It would upset her, Ella reasoned. Father was so sick; even though Ella wanted desperately to see him, she knew that she could not. Uncle Peter would have to fill her father's place.

"Are you finished here, Missy?" Ella jumped at Hattie's loud voice behind her. She pushed back in her chair as Hattie started to clear the table.

Nodding her head that she was finished with her breakfast, Ella stood up, then hesitated. "May I walk the dogs? I'll be very careful and watch them."

"Of course," Hattie answered, continuing to clean off the table. "Don't stay too long," she cautioned Ella. "I may need help with Gussie."

Each year when the season was over and the summer people left, Uncle Peter allowed her to run his three Scottie dogs—Winkin, Blinkin, and Nod—on the beach, providing she picked up after them. She loved all animals, but dogs and horses most of all. Quick, hot tears came now in Ella's adult reverie. She remembered with love the three darling dogs, now long departed. She fondly recalled the great joy they had given to all of the family and especially to her, on those golden days long ago.

She heard herself as a child calling to them once more and saw in her mind's eye the three little black imps racing toward her. *"Here, Winkin,"* she used to call, laughing, knowing that when the three dogs heard her, they would race down the wooden floors along the big hallway. They barked with excitement, sliding, and then skidding to an abrupt halt in front of her. They loved to run on the beach and they knew that it was Ella who ran them when she was at Seagate.

Suddenly it had occurred to her that she had not heard the dogs bark last night. Perhaps Ethan had locked them in a place where the dogs could not hear sounds; perhaps he had hushed them, or put them somewhere out of the house. She decided that was it. But where? Then she wondered why no one else had heard the bell. Ella thought about that and decided that Hattie and Charles *had* heard it since they were not deaf. Nevertheless, both Hattie and Charles had denied any knowledge of the strange noises and the bell ringing last night. She had to conclude that they were lying to her too. But why? She decided that she would never discuss it with them again, because of their lying.

Who else might have heard the bell? The street had been deserted. The summer people on their block were gone. Seagate property ran from the oceanfront, then west across the Boulevard to the bay front. Holly bushes and scrubby plants filled the open sandy lots between Seagate and the bayside. Probably no one had been around to hear the bell. No one had inquired at the house that morning about any unusual activity. Still, Ella realized that someone had taken an enormous chance of being discovered, since the police in the area certainly would have heard the loud bell ringing at that time of the night. Were the police involved too? She knew that lying came easily to Ethan. He had an excuse and a reason for everything she had heard. She was no match for him. What had he done? Now he frightened her.

Quickly, she edged over to the front door, not wanting Ethan to see her. She quietly let the Scotties out; then she darted rapidly across the front yard, as the dogs kept pace. She jumped off the bordering bulkhead, then scooted across the vanilla sands. The Scotties were too short legged to jump down from the bulkhead, so they scampered around to the ramp leading down to the beach.

She was still greatly concerned about the baby. Was the child stolen? Was it okay? Where was its mother? She stood on the beach, looking back at the house and her eyes traveled high up to her room. Her gabled window would have provided a good view if she had not been such a scary cat and had gotten herself out of bed to look out. She ran back up the ramp and made her way up to the bell and noticed that great handfuls of stones were flung up on the wooden base. Now she was very sure strangers had passed through because the previous evening, she had watched Hattie sweep the base clean. It looked like more than one person had rushed by. It was obvious that the stones had been kicked about. Then she saw the seaweed. At first, she thought it had blown up into the yard from the beach. Green, shiny pieces were scattered along the side of the house, back toward the garage and the rear door. That was a long way for seaweed to be blown. Perhaps it had caught on someone's shoe? Then she eyed the entire beach area and did not see any seaweed at all up on the sand. Someone had dragged the seaweed from the lower beach up to the house the night before. There was no other answer, she decided. *Here's the evidence* she thought, as she picked up pieces of seaweed and stuck them into her pocket. She needed to show Uncle Peter when he returned home. Sensing someone was watching her, she twisted around abruptly and saw Ethan standing at the window. He smiled and waved, but she turned her back quickly and walked away. She was determined to stay and play with the dogs and then sneak in later through the back door and up the rear stairs to her room.

"Ella! Ella! Mommy's home! Mommy's home!" Gussie shouted up the stairs sometime later. Ella heard Gussie's little voice ask their mother where she had been so long. It was early afternoon, and her mother's soft reply told Gussie, "I was visiting Daddy, and he is doing just fine." The dogs were carrying on; Ella knew that Uncle Peter and Aunt Mae had come in, too. She raced down the stairs to the front foyer to greet them all.

"How's Daddy?" Ella hugged her mother tightly.

"My goodness, what a nice hello." Kate smiled at her. "Daddy's doing much better. He will probably be coming home in a very short time. He sends his love to you and Sister."

Uncle Peter hugged her. "What's been going on since I left? Have you been behaving yourself?"

"I have something to tell you, Uncle Peter."

"What's that, Sweet Pea?"

Ella started to speak, but from the corner of her eye, she saw Ethan coming toward them.

"What's wrong, Ella?" Uncle Peter frowned when he realized she had stopped speaking because of Ethan's approach. Ella watched her mother and Aunt Mae drift into the parlor behind a chattering Gussie and bouncing dogs. She stood there with Ethan and Uncle Peter, wishing Ethan would leave.

"I have to go," and she had fled up the stairs, leaving Uncle Peter confused and Ethan not quite sure how to react. When she reached the second floor landing, she leaned back over the stair railing to look down and as she did, Ethan looked up at her and deliberately winked.

She ignored him, but she vowed to speak to Uncle Peter alone, just as soon as she could.

During dinner that night, Ella kept her head down, unable to look at Ethan, just wishing that he would leave. She sat sullen and withdrawn, refusing to speak to anyone. The phone rang suddenly with a startling shrillness and she jumped.

Hattie picked it up. "It's for you, Mr. Ethan."

"I'll take it in the library, Hattie."

"What's going on, Ella? Did something happen while I was away?" Uncle Peter peered sharply at her after Ethan had left the room.

She could only shake her head in reply. Tears were too close, her throat was closing and she could not speak. She sat for a minute, tracing the pattern on the Oriental rug with her toe. Her voice had deserted her.

"What's the matter, sweetheart?" Kate, who was sitting next to her, was quite concerned. She leaned over and put her arm around her daughter.

Suddenly Ella could not hold back her tears and she broke out into great, gulping sobs. They allowed her to sit and blubber for a minute.

"Come on, Ella, let's go to my office and have a little talk. We won't be disturbed in there." He took her hand, thanked Hattie for a box of tissues she had handed him and led Ella away from the table. He closed the door behind them and sat her opposite his desk in the big, red leather chair with the gold studs. He handed her the tissues. "I think you have something to tell me. Speak up, Sweet Pea. It can't be that bad."

"I don't know what happened," she whispered, "but I want to tell you about last night, when you and Mother and Aunt Mae were gone. *I think kidnappers stole a baby and they came into our house last night.* I heard the baby cry."

Peter looked closely at her. "What in the world?"

It was then that she blurted out the rest of last night's events. When she finished telling, she pulled a piece of seaweed from her pocket. "I found this by the bell," she handed him some seaweed. "That wasn't the only piece." She dug into her pocket, grabbed an entire handful of the green stuff and laid it on his desk. "And that's not all. The stones around the bell were scattered all over. I saw Hattie sweeping the bell platform clean the night before." He was quiet for a long time, staring intently at her. His face was very serious and suddenly, Ella was fearful again.

"You're sure you didn't imagine any of this?" Peter asked, and then paused for a moment. "You're a bright girl, Ella. You know the difference between lying and telling the truth. This is very serious. You know that, don't you?"

She nodded her head. "Yes, I know. But I think it's important that you know what happened, Uncle Peter." She felt it was vital that she tell him because she knew something dreadful had taken place and she had been unable to do anything about it. Then she thought *I hope the baby is still alive.*

"All right now," Peter said soothingly, seeing how upset she was becoming. "I don't want you to worry anymore. I will have a talk with Ethan. It's still light, so I'll take a walk around outside for myself." He rose slowly to his feet.

Ella knew the conversation was over for the moment. He was gone for awhile, but she waited for him and when he returned, she immediately questioned him. "Did you see any seaweed?"

"Yes, there was a little scattered about."

"I think the wind blew most of it away—*or someone had picked up the rest,*" she added softly, but meaningfully.

"I believe you, Ella. Don't get upset. It's all right. I do believe you." He walked her to the door and she went upstairs where Kate was reading a story to Gussie. Ella rested on the other bed; she immediately felt safe again being near her mother. Kate's words began to fade and Ella thought she must have drifted off because the next thing she saw was her mother covering her with a blanket and reaching over to turn the light out.

She sat up quickly. "I'm not ready for bed yet. I want to go downstairs." She took her mother's hand.

Mae had been upstairs when she heard the shouting from Peter's office and opened her door to see Ella and Kate heading for the stairs and she followed them. They were almost to the bottom of the stairs when the voices became louder. Pausing on the last landing, they listened quietly to the angry tones. Ella heard Uncle Peter—his voice was full of fury. She had never heard him raise his tone like that. He shouted at Ethan, and kept asking him how he was involved. Ethan kept telling him that he could not speak of it.

"You can't bring this kind of thing into my home," Peter raged at his son.

"You have forgotten about your own prior entanglements, Father," Ethan raised his voice and shot back. "Are you too old to remember why you did what you did?"

Peter did not answer, but thundered back at Ethan, "I'm questioning whether you know what you're entangling *us* in."

"I know who the enemy is, Father, whether you believe me or not. There are other forces at work that I cannot discuss. *It would put others at risk, and you should understand that,*" Ethan responded, his voice rising in anger to match his father's rage.

Ella moved to the bottom step to listen more intently.

"There's no need for you to be doing this," Peter stressed. "I want it finished *now*, Ethan!"

"You know that it's impossible to put down something started until it's finished, Father," Ethan stated. "This discussion is over."

Suddenly, the office door flew open and Ethan rushed down the hall toward Kate and Ella. Then he saw his mother with them and stopped.

"Little Ella," Ethan said softly, after looking up at Kate and Mae on the lower landing and then down at her. "One day, Ella, we will sit and discuss this fully, I promise you.

You're a very smart girl, but then you come from a long line of brave and intelligent men and women. I probably will not see you for a long time. Be good," he said and leaned down and gently kissed the top of her head, surprising Ella into silence.

She watched as Ethan turned to hug his mother, who had stepped down to stand by her. He picked up his suitcase that he had left by the front door, said goodbye to Kate, and walked out.

"Where is he going?" Ella felt guilty and that she was to blame for the terrible row. "I'm so sorry," she said and started to cry. "I didn't mean to make any trouble." Ella continued to question herself. *Why were they fighting? Why was Uncle Peter so angry? It seemed to be something more going on between them, rather than just what had happened last night.* She was frightened and upset by the shouting and thought if she hadn't said anything, this terrible argument would not have happened.

"*Will he come back?*" She was in tears.

Peter came out of his office and walked to the window where Aunt Mae was now standing. He put his arm around her as they watched their son's car drive down the road in the early dusk. "*It's not your fault, child,*" he said to Ella without turning from the window. "Ethan has his own agenda. I'll have to believe that my son is involved in something that is more important in the grand scheme of things."

"What do you mean?" Ella asked, tears still rolling down her cheeks. "I don't understand."

"This has nothing to do with you, child."

"But I want to know what scared me last night." She could not be consoled.

"We may never know, Ella." Uncle Peter lowered his head and sighed as though defeated. "I'm going upstairs. I will see you all in the morning." He turned and started up the stairs. Mae followed him.

Ella was devastated. She cried again in frustration, once more feeling in her child's mind, that she had caused the rift between Uncle Peter and his son. As angry as she was with Ethan, she wondered if she would ever see him again.

Her reverie stopped. She was back in the present and surprised once again, how clear her memories remained.

CHAPTER TWO

Willem Skyler VanHameetman

1582-1616

"And furthermore, Mother," Willem raised his voice from the entrance hall as he departed. *"I want you and Amalie to stop introducing your friends, daughters of friends, and god knows who else to me."*

A potpourri of wonderful aroma drifted across the old Rotterdam Market when Willem visited in the spring of 1588. He was a young boy that summer and for some elusive reason, that time seemed different to him—almost magical. He had traveled to market with his mother many times, but this time was like no other. Perhaps he was becoming aware of the beauty around him. Willem's mind was the artist that summer, observing and storing various images he saw. He chose to hoard waterscapes of small boats with bright, white sails on clear, blue waters, landscapes of lush emerald fields, beds of startling red and yellow tulips surrounding small white cottages, and the distinct fragrance of purple lilacs. He discovered that the wonderful scenes and scents persisted clearly in his memory, woven precisely in a skein of time, retrievable at will. Even the fragrance came forth as it was originally breathed in. The wonderful scents and colors which had been so intensely imprinted upon his memory, lingered strongly. When Willem was older, he could clearly call up those happy times at will from his vast collection of impressions and he used these images often when he was in need of an uplifting, or a calming of his emotions.

As much as he loved the great market, he was always happy to return home to his small village of Ouddorp, which lay on the seacoast in the low country of Holland. Ouddorp was a charming and very old village; the name meant *ancient village*. It lay on the small island of *Goedereede* in the Dutch province of South Holland on the North Sea. Ouddorp was usually a very quiet place, except for the continually patrolling Spanish soldiers.

When Willem and his mother had returned home from one of their trips to the Rotterdam Market, they found the streets of Ouddorp chaotic with rioting, ribald carryings on and the carousing of drunken townspeople of questionable morals as his mother, Marta, expressed it.

Willem was watching the goings on in the streets below from one of the second floor balconies of his home. He was not sure what all the yelling was about; he just liked watching the people.

"Willem," his older sister called for the second time. "Willem Skyler VanHameetman, you silly little boy, where are you?" This time he knew Amalie was angry because she called him by his full name. He sighed and decided to answer her.

"Here I am, Amalie." He inched out further on his belly to the end of the balcony; he did not want to miss anything. Reluctantly he looked away from the street to see Amalie hurrying toward him.

"What are you doing!" she shouted and pulled Willem by his ankles back from the railings and into the safety of the bedroom floor. "Mother sent me to look for you and well that I did, because in another minute you would have been over and into the street. You are so skinny; you could have slipped through the railings." She could not help herself—she laughed and relented. "Look at you, Willem. Just look at you." She frowned at him. "I think that you are old enough to at least comb your hair."

Marta heard Amalie's last remark from behind the balcony door. She watched her son reach up to pat down his thick, blonde hair. It was sticking up and out every which way. Marta had the same color hair. She smiled and told Willem that he would not mind so much when his hair turned white with age because there would only be a shade or two difference. Marta's eyes were a vivid blue, and Willem had also inherited her startling blue eyes. "Might as well take it all," Marta told him. "I promise you though, that I have not given you my stoutness. You are more a VanHameetman in your build." The children laughed.

She smiled now and hugged Willem to her. "No more hanging through the railing, Willie. Come in soon," she told them, and reminded Amalie to watch her younger brother. They were a family of six; Marta, Paul and children—Jacob the elder, Amalie, Hendrick and Willem, the younger, sometimes affectionately called Willie. Willem did not care to be called that, but when the family was excited and forgot, they would call him by his babyhood name.

"What are they doing, Amalie?" Willem asked and turned his attention toward the street again. "What is all the dancing and yelling about?"

Amalie knew about many things, or so Willem thought. She was a pretty, dark haired blonde with light, blue eyes, nearing her teens. Willem had noticed recently, that she and her friend Alison were growing outward everywhere and observed the older boys acting witless around them. The boys tumbled and punched one another while watching the girl's reactions out of the corners of their eyes. The two girls never looked at them, but later Willem heard his sister talking and giggling with Alison. He had eavesdropped on their conversation and was surprised that both girls had seen everything the boys had done. Willem mentioned this to his father, Paul, who told him that women were hard to understand. Willem nodded in agreement.

Hendrick, hearing this, just rolled his eyes. Hendrick was second born and very much taken with himself. He was as dark as Willem was light haired. Hendrick was tall and slim, with striking hazel eyes under thick, black lashes and blessed with a charismatic personality. Hendrick, the handsome one, Marta said of her second son. Willem noticed too, that girls blushed and stammered when he was around. Hendrick thought he knew the ways of girls and proceeded to instruct his younger brother. Their father laughed when he overheard Hendrick's grand statements and told his son, that he too, had a lot to learn.

Amalie had a way of making herself invisible when she was within listening range of private adult conversations; thus she accumulated information usually forbidden to children. Sometimes, if she was in a good mood and Willem was nice to her, she would share the information.

"Come in here, children, now. We do not know who is watching." Marta appeared once more in the doorway. She walked to the railing and leaned over to see who was out on the street. "Riffraff," she sniffed, peering down. "I know we are away from the unrest in the big cities, but I still do not like to take chances." The children could see that she was very unsettled over the street noises. "Twenty three years of Spanish occupation is a long time. I am tired of looking over my shoulder for the soldiers. I am tired of my Holland being ruled by the Spanish and called the Spanish Netherlands. It makes my blood run cold." She made a face. "I pray to God that I will live to see my homeland rightly called Holland and returned to us again. Come inside now."

Marta had tried to explain to the children the present political situation, but they were not interested until it touched *them* in some way. This was quite evident in the questions they had asked. Right now they had no idea why the people were celebrating.

"Are you taught in school why the Spanish occupy your country? Have you been told that the seventeen Dutch provinces are possessions of Spanish King Philip?" She was quite annoyed at their ignorance because she had explained this to them many times, but they did not listen.

"Why are we always at war, Mother?" Willem asked. He was young, but bright and he had heard so much talk but he was still confused. "Why is our Holland called the Spanish Netherlands? We are Dutch, right? How did King Philip get us?"

"King Philip has either acquired or inherited us, Willem—all seventeen provinces. Now let us speak of something other than the Spanish, unless you pay attention to what I tell you."

Willem knew what inherited meant, but he could not grasp how people could be inherited. He could not understand acquisition either. Making matters more difficult, Holland was a separate province. They were all Dutchmen, but his family called themselves Hollanders because they lived in the Holland provinces of the Netherlands.

"I will explain this to you one more time. I want you to know what is going on around you." She told them to sit down and listen. "King Philip of Spain was angry because Queen Elizabeth of England had refused his hand in marriage. He had asked her to marry him after his wife, Mary Tudor died. Elizabeth is Catholic, but she has fallen away from her religion and now practices Protestantism. She leans toward the Church of England. Philip had thought that if she married him, she would practice Catholicism again and England would follow. However, he was wrong. She hates the way he persecutes non Catholics. Then Elizabeth permitted her sea captains to rob his ships. Now Philip discriminates against any non Catholic. Elizabeth had enough of his cruel ways; she sent her soldiers to help protect the persecuted." Marta stopped to make sure they were listening. "There is a lot more, children, about Elizabeth's half sister, Queen Marie Stuart, called Mary, Queen of Scots and all that intrigue, but you would not understand it. Just remember that Queen Elizabeth of England hates King Philip and he hates her. Now Philip has sent his Armada of ships to invade and conquer England. The King came to the throne thirty three years ago. He rules part of Western Europe and Peru, Mexico, the Philippines and Flanders."

Marta shrugged. "Now he has decided to invade England and destroy Elizabeth. You would think he had enough countries under his rule—such a greedy man.

Such a foolish man. Yes, children," she said when they looked at her in surprise. "He is a very greedy man."

"Why does he need to rule more countries Mother, when he has all of this?" Willem asked, in his innocence.

"It is hard to understand, Mother," Amalie said. "We have already heard part of what you told us in school, from the teacher."

"Right now those ships in the King's Armada are fighting the English at Gravelines. The battle is right off Flanders in the North Sea. The townspeople are cheering the English and are *rioting against* King Philip and his Armada.*"

Willem still could not understand what was going on. He knew they all hated the fanatic Spanish King and certainly wanted his demise. The Dutch had no ships of their own; the Spanish occupied and ruled the provinces of Holland and the rest of the Netherlands. *How could all of this have happened,* he wondered.

"We attacked the Spanish Armada?" Amalie asked, mistakenly excited about the fighting. "Shout hurray! How many ships did we sink?"

"For heaven's sake, Amalie. I think you have it wrong, my daughter." Marta was exasperated with her. "You were not listening. Those are Spanish ships of the Armada, right off our coast, fighting the English. Did you forget that we are the Spanish Netherlands? Not the Dutch Netherlands," Marta sighed. "There is no Dutch fleet. I wish the King would just let everyone alone. We have endured so much strife and this unending vexation with the Spanish! You children have never known a peace time." She pursed her lips in disapproval.

The rioting continued for two days. "It would be difficult to find one villager who defended the King and his Armada," their father, Paul remarked, breathing out heavily in frustration. During dinner on that second evening of the town chaos, Paul remarked, that in all probability the Spanish troops in their area had been called into service in the larger cities. The small villages, such as Ouddorp, were free of soldiers now and no authorities were on hand to squash the rioting. The people were going wild. They had had enough of the Spanish occupation. Willem told his father that he heard the crowds chanting, *"Give us back our country!"*

"I do not know what this will mean to us, though." The children were concerned over the worried look on their father's face. "I hope the people do not get punished by the Spanish for rioting."

"How I would love to be on one of those English ships out there, banging away at the crazy King's fleet!" Hendrick had burst through the door into the dining room, clearly agitated. The excitement outside was contagious. "I think I would rather be with the English. I know they are not my countrymen, but they fight the Spanish. I do not know why Jacob stays at the university when he is old enough to join the English and have at the Armada. Why is there no Dutch fleet?"

"Let me straighten you out on a few things, son." Paul scowled at him. "Before I begin, why are you late for dinner?" Hendrick hung his head. "Why is there no Dutch fleet?" Paul repeated. "Where in the world would the Dutch obtain ships to fight the Armada? Just *think* a minute, Hendrick. We are the Spanish Netherlands, as I have repeatedly told you. I know that you are living in your own world, with nothing going on in there, but for god's sake, Hendrick! The Spanish have the ships, not the Dutch. The Spanish occupy us!" Paul raised his voice in annoyance and looked at Marta's face. "I think your mother has a few words for you, Hendrick."

Willem looked over at his mother's furious face and knew Hendrick was in for a lecture. No one criticized his brother Jacob, the elder son.

Hendrick hung his head, waiting for the onslaught.

"You have no idea what you are speaking of, young man. Only your age and lack of experience in life would permit you to make such a foolish statement. Your brother, Jacob is studying medicine; quite a noble ambition I would think. I thank the heavens every night for your Uncle's connections for your brother. It is not easy to get into university."

Hendrick realized that he had gone too far. He knew that his mother was referring to her brother Jacob, his brother's namesake, involved in government in Rotterdam. Hendrick quickly closed his mouth and remained quiet. He had said too much, especially about Jacob, who was the pride of the family.

"Enough, enough," Paul announced harshly from the head of the table. "Must I hear arguing at my own dinner table? And from my children? I am so tired of dealing with the Spanish, and I am tired of hearing about them. Maybe we should all leave here and start anew somewhere else!" He stood up, shoved his chair back and left the room.

Marta drew a noisy breath in and with tight lips and a stiff back, she left the table.

"Now see what you have done, Hendrick," Amalie scolded. "You have upset both of them."

"Did you hear what Father said? Leave here? Do you think he meant that?" Willem cried, not believing what he had just heard. Talk like that frightened him and he really did not want to think of leaving his home to go and live elsewhere. "I am not going. I would miss Grandpapa and my uncles and aunts and all my cousins," he whined. Willem could not understand the events exploding around him.

Willem's paternal Grandfather Adam, owned and ran the family shipyard in Rotterdam. As Adam's sons, Paul, Theo and Jan had matured, each had joined the family business. Presently, the three brothers worked in the shipyard in different capacities. Adam had refused to build warships for the Spanish. He had lied and told the local Spanish officials that he was cutting back because he would retire soon.

Adam presented a strong presence and possessed a fount of knowledge, that ran the gamut. He was a large man with snow white hair, piercing blue eyes, a booming voice and a good natured disposition. He was well liked. People often consulted him when they needed information about a variety of things. He was widowed, had a lady friend and was close to his sons and grandchildren.

On one occasion, Amalie had heard Grandfather Adam tell her father, that he refused to build ships for King Philip and would rather shut down than do so. "I just could not do that. The King and his Inquisitors are evil."

Later, Amalie told Willem that she had big news. "Guess what, Willie? Father is going to leave the family shipyard to be a banker. I heard them say that Uncle Theo is leaving the family business too."

"But I thought Father liked working with Grandpapa, building ships." Willem was upset to hear such news. "Why would he leave?" Willem could not keep it all straight, but he knew a little about shipbuilding. His father sometimes took him to Rotterdam to the family shipyard, where the shipbuilding was physically accomplished. Willem loved to watch a ship come alive from great stacks of wood under the carpenters' loving hands. He thought of a ship as a living thing.

Amalie tried to explain to Willem that there were too many of the family working in the business and not enough money to pay everyone. "Because Grandfather refuses to build war ships for Spain, he is losing business. Grandfather does not care what other Dutch companies have decided to do," she expressed with authority. "I heard Father tell Mother that right now there is not enough business to support three families and Grandfather. That is why Father will work in the Banking house. I heard the whole conversation," Amalie bragged.

"What does a banker do?" Willem wanted to know; he knew what a Banking House was, but did not really know what the bank did except save your money and sometimes give out money.

"Father has joined Mr. VanWagnor in his Banking House. Grandfather Adam gave Father some of our money for investment in the bank, and Father will be Mr. VanWagnor's partner. Father knows figures well and he can keep books. His bank will do all kinds of good things for people," she added.

Willem knew that she did not know either. He would ask Father later for his own satisfaction. "What will Uncle Theo do?" Willem continued questioning her.

"He wants to learn more about big buildings," Amalie replied. "Father said that Uncle Theo is rather old to apprentice to an architect, but Uncle Theo said he would not mind. You know he is the youngest of Father's brothers, so he does have time to change his work."

"You mean how to build big buildings? How to make bricks?"

"How should I know?" Amalie was tired of his relentless questions, especially since she did not have all the answers. "I just heard Father say that Uncle Theo was interested in city buildings."

"What will Uncle Jan do?" Willem asked.

"I do not know. You can go ask him."

Paul had traveled extensively for the family business throughout the Netherlands from his small office in Ouddorp. Now that the business had slowed, Paul went into banking, keeping books. He had kept the books for the family yard and bought certain woods for ship building; usually from Norway, where timber was plentiful, unlike Holland or the rest of the Netherlands. He would work part time still, buying timber and doing some limited traveling for the family yard. He would keep the books for the bank, and be more of an advertising, or community person for them. "I am so disgusted," Willem heard his father declare, "I hate being under the Spanish thumb, having to ask for a permit to travel in my own country!"

"How can Spain let you travel, Father, if we are at war with them?" Willem asked.

"Let us just say they are living here, occupying our country because we are a possession of Spain. They profit from my work, so we both have to make the best of it." Paul frowned. "It is difficult to explain, son. They call this politics."

It was Saturday again. The town had calmed down, although the Spanish soldiers continued their day to day patrol.

The family usually traveled to Rotterdam every third Saturday, but because of the battle off their coast, they had waited to travel to market. Willem loved to visit the great Rotterdam Market with his mother. Most times, Marta took their helper, Greta with them. Sometimes Amalie joined them. The family lived on the coast and the transportation to the Ouddorp docks was by horse and cart. Here they caught the boat to Rotterdam. Either Paul drove them to the dock, or Marta drove and left the horse and cart in the care of the stable. They bought the bulk of their fruit, vegetables, and dried meats, along with other necessities such as outer clothing and footwear from the Rotterdam Market. Marta and Greta armed themselves with huge shopping baskets and Willem and Amalie trailed close behind, carrying their small sacks.

The noises and the smells were singular to the great market. Willem loved the little goats that brayed gently. These lovely little soft furred creatures were raised for their milk, which was used mostly to make cheese. White geese and brightly colored chickens scrambled behind tents that were erected to protect the food from the sun. The tents covered big round chunks of an assortment of cheeses, made by the Dutchman who hauled the large pieces to market.

Marta told her children again, "Cheese and milk must be kept out of the sun and protected, or you could become sick if you eat spoiled food."

When Amalie traveled to market, she searched the peasant's baskets for lace and hair ribbons and other dainties that girls liked. Her mother loved the handmade, pure white collars with lace edging and the hand sewn nightgowns, scalloped and laced along the bottom.

Willem sought out Yanni, the old woodcarver at the market. He whittled dogs, cats, horses and the beautiful whales and dolphins he had seen on his former sea voyages. Besides the wonderful animals and the sea life, he carved little houses from different colored woods. Sometimes Paul would slip his son a silver dollar from the Baltic or a Levant silver lion dollar and Willem spent them collecting Yanni's carvings. A dollar could buy a lot, Willem had learned and he saved his money carefully for his next trip to see Yanni. The top of Willem's desk was a forest on one side, holding a myriad of animals. The top of his chest of drawers had been turned into a sea for all his beautifully carved fish. He set his houses on a small table near his bed.

Even though they lived in a small town, their house had a large backyard. Marta raised goats there for their own milk and cheese. She wanted a cow, but Paul told her, "There is not enough room for a cow in the goat's shed, woman. You have enough to do raising the goats. Be happy with Mrs. Kleetch's cows." Marta approved of Mrs. Kleetch because of her cleanliness, not only in her home, but also with her cows.

Marta and Greta baked their own breads and cakes and grew some seasonal vegetables, which they dried for the winter. Ouddorp had a smaller, local market and there Marta bought her fresh fish and other items to fill in the rest of their needs. However, they all enjoyed the commotion of any marketplace.

Marta and Paul felt that the small schoolhouse that Willem attended in Ouddorp was very adequate. They investigated the schoolmaster's curriculum quite thoroughly each year. The children were taught handwriting, reading, arithmetic and Latin. Amalie and Hendrick had moved on from the small school to the church academy. Hendrick would decide in a year or two where his interests lay, but Amalie would probably go no farther than the academy. Besides her regular subjects, she learned cooking, sewing, and needlework. Marta wanted Hendrick to attend the university at Leiden where Jacob was studying medicine, but Hendrick had no such aspirations at that time. Besides, he was seriously discovering girls, where he found himself most successful.

Willem was still young, but that did not stop Marta from telling him how bright he was and that he had a grand destiny. At that time of his life however, Willem did not have such goals; his greatest desire was to become a fisherman. His father smiled knowingly. "He is only a baby, Marta. He can be a fisherman now if he wants to be."

"I may even be a hunter when I grow up. I will sell furs and run a trading post in Norway," Willem declared. In school, his teacher had read them stories of Norway where great timber forests held a variety of large animals.

"You should see some of the animals; my teacher bought a book with the drawings in them. The animals are hunted and their skins are made into outer clothes for the hunters and they sell the rest for their meat. I could make lots of money, hunting and fishing," Willem imparted enthusiastically. "I would buy you and Papa nice things," he told his mother. It was exciting to speak of his plans. It was from that time on, that Marta would remember Willem being taken with his trading post idea.

After the failure of the Spanish Armada, explorations to all parts of the world had greatly increased the demands from other countries for the safer Dutch ships. This caused a sudden upsurge of business in their shipyard. Adam stood firm in refusing to build warships for the Spanish. However, building ships for exploration certainly was acceptable to the Spanish, who still received their taxes.

Paul ended his partnership in the bank and returned to the family business. "We are moving to Rotterdam," he announced unexpectedly at the dinner table shortly after he had made his decision. "I am tired of traveling between Ouddorp and Rotterdam. Now that I will be back at the yards, I want to eliminate the trip altogether." He knew that this would bring mixed reactions. He sat back and waited.

"But what about our friends?" Amalie and Hendrick cried.

"You can make new ones. This decision is very important to all of us. If someone else wants to go to work instead and help support the family, speak up!"

Amalie and Hendrick made faces and hung their heads.

Willem answered excitedly, "Will we be near the market? I will go with you, Father."

"Thank you, Willie." His father tousled his hair. "The rest of the family has decided to move, too. So you will have your cousins and aunts and uncles nearby." Paul decided that he had made the right decision; he would be back with the shipyard and living in Rotterdam and there were plenty of good schools in Rotterdam. Marta would enjoy deciding which were best for the children.

Uncle Theo had finished his two year architectural apprenticeship and now worked for the city of Rotterdam.

In time, Willem entered university in Leiden, as his parents had hoped he would do, to study agriculture and irrigation. He considered these two subjects worthy of his study. After graduation, he was led to heavy involvement with the sea gates, as the Dutch called the dikes, where he found the workings of the drainage systems challenging. New machinery and drainage ideas were being invented frequently. This was a land of water and the big windmills were used to drain off the polders or lowlands, which had to be managed if the country was to survive.

The occupation of Spain continued for eleven more years, until 1609, when a truce was called between Spain and the Netherlands. Not that it meant complete peace or the Netherlands' independence, but it did end the outright skirmishes between the Dutch and the Spanish.

1609 was a memorable year for the Netherlands too. Henry Hudson, the English explorer hired by the Dutch East India Company, sailed to the New World in the Dutch ship *Half Moon*. He searched for a new route to China but instead, discovered the vast territory of the Americas. Hudson returned with wonderful tales of a wilderness filled with bountiful wildlife, timber, and rich earth; although his description of both hostile and peaceful encounters with the natives was quite contradictory.

Willem had graduated and was doing well for himself working at a small sea management company where he had gained an excellent reputation. However, even with these achievements won, he constantly carried the feeling that something was missing in his life. It nagged him persistently, resulting in his somewhat arrogant, moody demeanor.

"My, you are the handsome one," Amalie remarked one day, looking up at her six foot two younger brother, with his flaxen hair and blue, blue eyes. "You ought to find yourself a wife." She smiled.

Willem ignored the remark from his sister, thinking that a change of scenery would better solve his moodiness. He was tired of his mother and sister telling him that he needed a wife. He was tired of living the quasi peace with Spain; he found the peace agreement with Spain a farce in most instances. Willem worked closely with the local government in water management and saw firsthand, how things really stood.

He complained to his father one day, "This close contact with the Spanish officials is wearing. They feel it necessary to constantly oversee my work. They involve themselves in the drainage projects without having any technical knowledge. Their presence and interference irritate me greatly."

"I realize how difficult it is," Paul commiserated. "Your generation has never known a peace time or your personal freedoms. Your mother and I have good memories from past years, before the Spanish were here."

Willem had known a few girls, although his mother reminded him constantly after she met each one, that they were not right for him or they were not exactly the marrying kind. *Perhaps I am too critical,* he wondered. He did not know exactly what the problem was, except that none of the women he met held his interest. *I will not be pushed into something that is not right.* There has to be more to marriage, he thought. Evidently, I have not met the right girl. He recalled a recent, rather harsh confrontation with his mother.

"What do you mean, Mother? Not the marrying kind. Are you saying that I am bringing girls from the street to meet you?" He was angry.

Marta was shocked. "I did not mean it that way, Willem. I just do not care for any of them that you have brought home so far."

"I truly do not think that you would care for *any girl* that I brought home to meet you! I think I will stop introducing anyone to you." He walked out of the room, greatly irritated. "And furthermore, Mother," Willem raised his voice from the entrance hall as he departed. "I want you and Amalie to stop introducing your friends, daughters of friends, and god knows who else to me. Thank you." He slammed the door, leaving his mother standing there with her mouth hanging open.

Afterwards, Willem was chagrined. He had never spoken to his mother like that, but he felt that the two of them playing matchmaker for him was insulting, embarrassing, and humiliating to any girl to whom they introduced him. If he allowed his mother or Amalie or his friends to introduce him to someone, he felt they expected something of him; he felt he disappointed them when nothing came of the introduction.

Willem wanted someone in his life, but he did not know how to find that someone. He tried not to think about it, but the more he saw Amalie and Hendrick and their respective spouses and children, the more he felt his aloneness. Willem was buried in his work, but he was not personally happy. The more he worked, the more depressed he became. He needed more of a challenge in his work and he left the smaller company for a position in the City of Rotterdam Land Preservation. As a hobby, he kept himself busy after work and traded any commodity that had value—which resulted in a nice nest egg for him. As time went on, he greatly enjoyed his new job and it became his salvation. There were not as many restrictions on the workers as there had been in his previous employment.

Amalie lived comfortably in a handsome manor house with her husband, James and their three children. James worked with her father, buying ship timber from Norway; James also dabbled in refined wool, one of the most highly exported products of Holland. He did very well.

Jewelry and silver smithing had caught Hendrick's eye, and he owned a large business. He and his wife, Gretchen, were raising four children.

Jacob, the elder brother and a family physician, had fulfilled his calling to medicine. Marta and Paul were very proud of their children and their spouses.

Even though the Dutch culture was advanced and they lived very comfortably, Hendrick and Jacob felt much as Willem did. They were tired of living under the daily oppression of the Spanish, most times subtle, but always present. The three continually discussed leaving Holland for the New World, even though it was all theory and talk. They spoke constantly of their grand dream of journeying to the virgin land of the Americas. They would sit for hours, repeatedly going over plans for their new life in this recently discovered, bountiful land. They read all the material available—however, they still did not move forward.

Eventually they had become frustrated, aware that their fragile dream could easily slip through their fingers. "I do not think that we will ever see our Holland and the Netherlands totally independent from the reigning Spanish." Willem was disgusted, and the sudden epiphany that they *had* to move finally prompted them to push ahead to bring their unending plans to fruition. They were tired of chasing a dream. In so many instances they were not entirely at liberty to make their own business or personal decisions. They were really not their own men under the oppressive Spanish, and this was the impetus that finally pushed them hard. They were not interested in claiming land for Holland—they wanted to claim land for themselves. However, it was undeniably a huge undertaking and total commitment did not come easily.

"We *have* to move forward. It seems as though it is becoming only a story we keep telling ourselves." Jacob kept nudging his brothers. He was frustrated with the delay. Jacob was much like his father in manner and resembled him physically, with light brown hair and hazel eyes.

"We need a large group to undertake the journey. You are aware of this, right?" Hendrick was impatient. "We need to approach our cousins. I would rather have family as crew." His brothers felt the same. We should pool our own resources of knowledge first, then share our ideas with our cousins."

They hinted to their sister of their visions, but Amalie did not take them seriously. She was completely disinterested, so they did not speak of it to her again. The brothers spoke to their cousins, who were close and all of the same generation, some married and some single. Their cousins' first reaction was that lunacy was afoot, but as time went on, some of the cousins found themselves seriously contemplating the exciting proposal. The idea grew in desirability and anticipation in their minds and was reinforced by the constant negative encounters with the Spanish.

Immediately, two cousins turned them down. The unknown consequences of a first voyage were too overwhelming for them. "Ships now sail to and return from the Americas to Europe. You always have the option of going back home after a year," Jacob reminded them. "We will encounter hardships, but that is to be expected. Joining a voyage like this is not to be decided lightly."

Willem understood their concerns, but the undertaking needed a crew and he agreed with his brothers; they would rather have kin.

Jacob thought about telling their parents of their plans. Willem and Hendrick were aghast. "Dear god! Do you realize what Mother's reaction would be?" Hendrick asked. Willem too, was shocked at the suggestion. They respected their mother, but they wanted to avoid confrontation with her for as long as possible.

"We will eventually tell the elders, but we have a great deal to accomplish first. We need to approach the family with a solid plan. We need all the help that we can get. But I think we should speak with Grandpapa."

They believed an untouched wilderness awaited, theirs for the taking, and they could not be dissuaded from their dream. For one reason or another, the brothers delayed the voyage, probably out of plain fear of the unknown. There was a vast territory in this America, open for exploration; the area stretched from the Connecticut River to the big bay.

In 1614, the Dutch East India Company announced its plans to increase its holdings in North America. "What about signing on with the East India Company? I hear they are looking for crews," Willem finally suggested. His brothers were surprised at his statement. "If this is the only way to get going, then we should seriously consider it." Willem decided that it was time to seek Grandfather Adam's opinion.

"Well, boys," Adam greeted his grandsons. "I knew something was afoot. Out with it." Immediately, he dismissed the East India Company idea. "You would be sailing for *their* glory and profit. I like your idea of your own voyage though," and without hesitation, he said, "I will give you a fluyt from the family yard." The yard built several types of ships, including the fluyt, and this magnanimous offer from grandfather was gratefully received and set the keystone in place.

"We have to figure out first what modifications will be needed to meet your needs. The fluyt is built to house a smaller crew. We can start with that advantage and progress accordingly as you make your decisions. First thing I need to know, how many will crew Willie?"

"I am aiming for ten to twelve."

"Good. We can modify the interior somewhat, but a ship too large would *not* be more advantageous." *Perhaps a bit larger*, Adam thought to himself. "I have some thinking to do. I will speak to Ignatius, my head builder, to see what he suggests. Give me the information you have now about the state of affairs in this exploration business. Gather the reading material that you have. I would like to read it all."

"There is more information that I am after," Willem replied, "but I will give you what we have." He handed Adam a copy of the *March 27, 1614, State General of Holland's Edict for the Encouragement and Promotion of the New World Lands.* "Technically, in 1498, John Cabot, Italian born, sailing for England, had been the first to sail the Atlantic Ocean coastline of America. He made three voyages, but not much is known about him," Willem added.

"Then in 1609, Henry Hudson sailed up the large river he named the *North River* and had referred to this area as the Hudson Valley. The edict had encouraged further exploration. Hudson then claimed all of the land for the East India Company, ranging from the port area, called New Amsterdam, to about one hundred and twenty five miles north into the Hudson Valley. The State General, from Hudson's description, felt that there were large, bountiful lands to be explored and acquired in the Americas. They encouraged all of those rich merchants to sail and claim new land for Holland. Many of the more wealthy Hollanders however, were interested in a large region, called New Netherlands, south of the Hudson River Valley area. It was reported that these merchants had already outfitted a fleet of five vessels to follow the Hudson trail."

Willem had spoken to a number of seamen who had sailed to and from the port of New Amsterdam which was situated on an island, that the Indians had named *Mannahatta*. Two tribes resided on the island, the *Shinnecock* and the *Canarsee*. Which tribe had named the island was uncertain. The island was near the mouth of the North River, with quick access to the ocean. "They report that the port has not been fully established to date. Only rough docks and some wooden houses used as shop fronts and offices have been built. It is an excellent location, although it will take some building up and getting some law and order in there to make it safe. It is no place to settle. They are hoping that the Dutch will take over and clean up the area and put in a decent wharf. I hope you all have noted that the *North River* is now called the Hudson River, as is the valley."

DUTCH FLUYTS

"We have read all of Hudson's logs, and he has described the Indians living in these regions quite thoroughly," Hendrick continued. "Jacob and I are looking into the newly forming communities in the port area and the Hudson River Valley. We discovered that a group of merchants from Amsterdam and Hoorn had received a three year monopoly for fur trading from the State General. They had formed the *New Netherlands Community,* within the New Netherlands region. However, the community was never colonized—it never did well, being quite isolated that far north. Most of the population had settled in the area of the Amsterdam Port. At the end of the three year monopoly, the agreement was not renewed and the land was opened to all Dutch traders. The settlement faced hostile Indians to the north, adding danger to the settlers; and the people were moved."

"We also spoke to sea captains, who had sailed in this region," Willem reported. "One of these captains told me that a few independent groups of Dutchmen had formed small villages near the port. I had thought about joining a community for obvious reasons of safety and companionship. Then in time, we could strike off on our own."

"There is still no governing law over the large, growing population in the port area. I have heard harsh talk of this port." Willem was steadfast in his feelings about the port, because of the lack of any law, but he still wanted to look into the further outlaying areas. And he wanted to check the small Dutch settlement about a mile from the port. His brothers suggested further exploration, into the countryside, within a hundred mile radius of the New Amsterdam port, to see everything, and then make further choices from there.

"That is a strange name for the island," Jacob commented, referring to *Mannahatta.*

"I heard that on Hudson's early voyage, his navigator, by name of Robert Juet, wrote that name in the Half Moon's log. It is from the Lenape Indian language meaning *island of many hills,*" Willem shared.

"Interesting," Hendrick commented. "Who told you about the name?"

"I was with Grandpapa the other day and I commented on the name. You know Grandpapa—if there is any information to be had, he has it!" Willem replied, and they all laughed. "And there's more from Grandpapa. With the different groups of people in and out of that region, *Mannahatta* evidently translates now as *Manhattan.* Grandfather said that this is the way Europeans refer to the island. He also hears this from the merchants who import goods into that area."

They looked at him and just shook their heads. Grandfather, who Willem usually called Grandpapa, was always coming up with something out of the ordinary, and most times, it was true. It seemed that Willem had followed in his Grandfather's footsteps with this tendency.

"I guess we will refer to the island then as Manhattan," Hendrick commented. "I think Willie is right. We need to see this place firsthand. It seems confusing with all those factions in the area. Hearing about the people around the port makes me a little anxious though. We will have the ship, and we really do not have to stay there."

Willem told them that he had read a large amount of information about Henry Hudson. "On former voyages Henry Hudson was looking for a northeast passage, from England to the Far East via the Arctic Ocean. "Here is one for you brothers—the word Arctic comes from the Greek arktos, meaning *Great Bear Constellation,* also called *Ursa Major,* familiar to any sailor. The constellation can be seen from most parts of the Northern Hemisphere. It was originally named by the North American Indians; the English called it *King David's Chariot,* the Irish called it *King David's Chariot* and the French called it *Great Chariot.*

"Willem, you are getting more like Grandpapa each day," Hendrick laughed after the astronomy lesson.

Hudson was also hoping to confirm that the Atlantic and Pacific Oceans were separated merely by a narrow piece of land. Hudson continued along the Atlantic coast in 1609, sailing south about ninety nautical miles from the island of Manhattan, when he discovered a great body of water and its capes. He was actually the first to record the capes leading into, and the big bay itself. *However, he did not name the capes.* The bay was recorded by his navigator, Juet. Hudson was unable to explore the entire bay, but he did manage to sail several miles of shore around the bay, when the *Half Moon* struck bottom. Juet recorded a tide running from the northwest, and suspected that a large river flowed into the bay. Hudson named it the *South River.* The *Half Moon's* hull and rudder repeatedly struck bottom and Hudson left the bay. The discovery of the bay and the suspected river was noted in Juet's journals, as I said. Hudson named this river, but evidently did not name the bay. Later, upon Hudson's continued explorations of the area to the north, the river, which Hudson had originally called the North River, was now being called the Hudson River, as I mentioned to you previously. And now the Hudson Valley will be called the Hudson River Valley. Upon the discovery of these rivers by Hudson, the Dutch laid claim to both rivers.

"I have also read Thomas West's logs. The Englishman, West, was also the twelfth Baron De La Warre," Willem reported. "I have heard that there is some controversy that he was the one who named the bay and the river after himself."

"What controversy?" Hendrick wanted to know.

Jacob jumped in. "Baron De La Warre, naming the large bay after himself, is what is controversial. The Baron was the new Governor of Jamestown in 1610 and had led the contingent who reinforced the Jamestown Settlement. Baron De La Warre saved the small colony from the abandonment of the remaining settlers there. It is reported by most, that De La Warre had never even seen the big bay on his voyage to Virginia in 1610, much less named it after himself. It is said that his deputy, Sir Samuel Argalls, of Lord Somers' squadron, hit a severe storm in that area and landed further up north on Cape Cod. On Argall's voyage back down to Virginia, he spotted the bay and assuming that it was the northern boundary of the Virginia Patent, he named the bay after the Baron De La Warre, which has translated to Delaware."

Hendrick joined in and told them what he had read. "The bay," as Willem reported, is about 100 miles south of the port of New Amsterdam. This results in a slightly milder temperature, probably about five to ten degrees. I have read a few accounts of the land along the coast to the south."

In 1611, Hendrick Christiansen, a West India trader and Adrien Block of Amsterdam, Holland had chartered a ship and had sailed to the Hudson River Valley. They returned to Holland with furs and two sons of Indian chiefs. The Dutch were flabbergasted with the boys and Christiansen named the young men, *Orson* and *Valentine*. In the following year Christiansen and Block received backing from leading merchants in Holland, and they returned to the Hudson River Valley in two ships, the *Fortuyn* and the *Tiger*.

"Interesting about Adrien Block," Willem now commented.

"Whooops. Here it comes. Another story that Willie has encountered," Jacob laughed.

"Do you want to hear this, or not?" Willem was annoyed. "I have to tell you though, that it is very interesting."

"Go ahead, Willem," Hendrick said, but he could not suppress a smile. "I do want to hear."

"Block was ready to return to Holland when his ship, the *Tiger* caught fire and burned. He decided to build a new ship and worked out of a hut on the shore of a small island, which he later named Block Island—of course after himself. He spent the following year building his new ship. He named her *Onrust*, meaning *Restless* in English. *Onrust* was of light draft, enabling Block to thoroughly explore some of the more shallow waterways."

Willem continued. "I know that Hendrick Christiansen returned to Holland and his ship, the *Fortuyn*, was then put into the hands of Captain Cornelius Jacobsen Mey by its owners, who resided in Hoorn, Holland."

Jacob followed up. "In the fall, all the ships of the trading squadron returned to Holland, all except the *Fortuyn,* which stayed on Manhattan Island for further exploration, under the command of Captain Mey. Mey landed the *Fortuyn* on the bottom of a cape, past the large bay, and gave the cape his name." Jacob hesitated. "I would like to see that area. And just in the past year, Mey sailed southward again and charted the coast from what the seamen call Sandy Hooke, located somewhat south of the port of Amsterdam. This time when Mey entered the huge body of water, he passed the capes of the bay. He initially gave his surname, *Mey,* to the Northern Cape, and his Christian name, *Cornelius,* to the Southern Cape opposite; to the *southern cape facing the ocean,* he gave the name *Hindlopen* or *Henlopen.* There was a very important business man in the Netherlands named *Hindlopen.* Mey probably knew him, but who can tell. I wouldn't be surprised if all of these names will change, as many initially named places do. The village of Lewes, right in that area of the capes, had been discovered by Henry Hudson in 1609."

"Mey and a crew of explorers in the *Fortuyn* explored the big Delaware Bay and sailed up the river, which flowed into the big bay. I hear there are some Swedish settlements starting up along the river, further up north." Jacob paused and then continued after he had something to drink. "The river that had been called the South River previously by Hudson, was now carrying the name of the *Delaware River.* From what I had heard, Argalls never even saw the bay, much less the river that flowed into the bay, which Hudson had named the South River. I would think that the South River picked up the name of the Delaware from the Bay. I heard that the Lenape Indians are also called the Delaware Indians."

"Here is what I think," Hendrick spoke up and summarized. "The Lenape first named the Delaware Bay, *Poutaxat,* and the river flowing into it, *Lenape Wihittuck,* which means the *rapid stream of the Lenape.* Hudson tried to navigate the bay in 1609, but struck bottom and he could not explore the entire bay, neither did he name it, but he took credit for naming the South river that flowed into the bay. In 1610, Argalls, was blown off course and sighting the big bay, named it after Thomas West, also known as Lord De La Warre. But Argalls never navigated the bay. That obviously makes the most sense, as far as the name goes. The bay translated very quickly into Delaware, and the South River very quickly into Delaware River. Then in 1611, Captain Cornelius Jacobsen Mey sailed along the coast, passed the capes of the bay and named them. I must look to Juet's log again to see if Hudson gave any name to those capes. I have never heard that he did and it was never written in his log."

"What does it really matter anyway?"

"I guess it would matter if someone stole your thunder," Jacob answered Willem rather sharply.

"I would think that Hudson could clear the entire story up. But much the shame," Hendrick replied, "he is no longer with us. Remember, also in 1611, Hudson's crew on his new ship *Discovery*, mutinied and put Hudson, his young son and seven others, who were reportedly sick, off the *Discovery* into a boat, out into the ice flows. The crew had had enough of the cold weather and icy conditions, I would suppose; but what a dastardly thing to do. The crew wanted to return home; Hudson wanted to continue exploring. I do not understand why they could not overcome him, rather than put him over the side. Hudson was never heard from again."

"I wonder if there is not another way to approach that upper Delaware River," Willem was off in thought.

"Not by vessel, evidently," Jacob said. "I have not heard of any exploring on the upper river—say, past those new settlements. It has been reported that the river there is quite shallow and loaded with large rocks and small rapids. Certainly a very small craft could possibly navigate past these obstacles, but no large ship could. Perhaps one could reach the upper Delaware River by land. I have read that the entire Delaware Bay area has been described as most pleasant; the natives in that immediate area were extremely hospitable to the white visitors, Captain Mey reported. The mouth of the bay is within a reasonable range of sailing distance from New Amsterdam on the ocean route. We know that he also told of the Indian settlements up the Delaware River."

"I think that this should be a future goal of ours, to explore further into that region," Jacob offered.

"Remember, we spoke of that, and considering the differences in the reports of Mey's experiences with the natives and Captain Hudson's experiences, we wondered if Captain Hudson was more aggressive toward the natives. I guess we will find that out for ourselves." Willem's main concern, after reading Hudson's logs, was that the area was so heavily populated with Indians. He hoped that Hudson's reports of hostile Indians had been overstated.

Grandfather Adam commented, "There is more than enough out there for everyone. You must be well prepared. This is your first duty to yourselves."

"I have checked a number of ships' voyages to see the weather reports in different months," Hendrick announced. "I have been to the docks and gathered information about weather encountered on a number of sailing dates. Of course, winter is not an option. The larger ship owners have perused the logs of the returning ships and have gleaned important information about the month weather, weather relationship. I told them why I needed the information and they let me inspect their weather records. The ocean crossings are averaging approximately thirty four days. I deduced from the reports that April and September were particularly stormy months on the seas." He looked around at his brothers and cousins. "I think we should set our sailing date to middle May. This would give us an arrival date around middle June, which would be beneficial to us from a point of weather."

"I agree, Hendrick." Willem was enthused. "Middle to late June, if, by the grace of God all goes well, would be an excellent time to land. I just heard of an English ship lost in a wintry storm in early April last year."

"That was an older model ship, *The Southern Cross*, if I remember correctly," Jacob stated. "Perhaps if the vessel was sturdier, like our new fluyt, they would have had a chance; but then, it was foolish for any ship to sail in April."

He was greeted by silence, and he knew that they all were thinking about the dangers they could encounter. He thanked God for Grandfather Adam's generosity and the help he had given them. He hoped that a May sailing would at least eliminate encountering wintry storms.

"I guess we all realize how fortunate we are to have one of Grandpapa's ships," Willem reminded them, knowing what serious dangers the voyage held.

Because sailings were becoming more frequent across the ocean to the Americas, from Rotterdam, London, Lisbon and other cities—letters, packages and supplies could be carried with some regularity. It no longer took a year to receive news of a tragedy, a happy landing, or of the quickly increasing population and the new settlements in different regions.

The brothers could now secure updated information from the new maps that were available from the multitude of crossings. They decided to sail across the Atlantic Ocean to the Hudson River and then make their way south to the Delaware Bay area.

Willem smiled to himself, thinking of his Grandpapa. Initially Adam had wanted to join them, but then decided that this was a young man's passage, so his participation in outfitting them gave him great pleasure.

"When you establish yourselves, I will visit. That is, if I live that long." Adam grinned at Willem, who assured him that he had a good chance.

"Grandpapa," Willem laughed. "You do not have one foot in the grave yet!"

Adam had laughed in response. "Well, maybe so, Willie."

"Have you decided how you will modify our fluyt?"

Adam hesitated a moment. "I have given this a lot of thought. You need a ship that is easy to handle, with large storage space and a shallow draft. She must be safer on the open seas and more efficient in the inland, low waterways," Adam announced, nodding his head to confirm the decision to himself. "Your fluyt already has all of those requirements."

Willem knew that the usual length of a fluyt was from four to six times its beam and its masts were as far apart as possible to allow room for a large main cargo hold. She carried light, mounted guns, and her rigging was relatively simple. Winches or tackles were used wherever possible, thus requiring a smaller crew.

"I am rethinking what I thought previously about not changing her structure," Grandfather Adam told them. "I have decided otherwise. I will enlarge the overall measurements of the ship, using the formula of length equals four to six times its beam. I intend to divide the cargo hold into three separate areas, and increase the aft cabin itself, within the ship's own measurements. Just this increase will make a big difference there. I am giving you one of my new fluyts that is being drawn up. I can add the outside restructuring. This will work well. I think I will increase her arms though, just in case. You will not be able to engage any large pirate ship, but you will be able to defend yourselves from smaller bands of thieves. At least you will not be sitting ducks. I will get more men working on her and make it a priority. She should be ready for your inspection in approximately two months and ready to sail in three months."

"Great News," Jacob grinned. "That should bring us up to the end of April, giving us time to load and finish our plans."

"What's the matter with the rest of you?" Adam looked at their worried faces. "Are you backing out?"

"No—Reality is just beginning to set in." Hendrick realized that their dream was actually coming to fruition and it was somewhat overwhelming; actually the reality was causing him some anxiety.

Timber was plentiful in the New World. Windows however, even the small, glass windowpanes that the Dutch had become so proficient in making, would not be available to buy. Glass was scarce. Willem had read that in 1608, a glass factory in Jamestown failed because of a famine in the colony.

They would carry a few of each window size, stored in the cabins, under the berths and hammocks. After they arrived, they would experiment; first with brick making from indigenous materials and eventually glass making. They would carry two small woodstoves, for cooking and heat which would be used in the community house, the first house they had planned to build. Hopefully, the building would be completed before the winter set in. The building would have fireplaces in most rooms, and one woodstove for cooking. If the community house was not finished, they had the two stoves that could heat the ship. They had read everything that was available about the local climate and they seriously took to heart the numerous comments about the frigid winters others had encountered. They figured it certainly could not be any colder than their own winters in Holland.

Willem reminded them of the report that the temperature was milder in the area of the Delaware Bay than on Manhattan Island and areas further north. "Every little bit of information helps. I find it difficult to understand how anyone would sail unprepared into the unknown."

Jacob was to gather information about the reported local herbs available for medicinal and cooking purposes. He had spoken to a few captains of ships returning from the Americas and he had found that not much information was available. "I will draw and label as I discover. I am hoping that we will become acquainted with some of the local Indians and learn of the medicinal herbs that they use. We will bring severe consequences down upon our heads if we do not plan to the very jot. I will pursue this diligently when we arrive. I certainly would like to know the Lenape people. They are farmers. They could be most helpful."

"If only I was a young man," Grandpapa kept saying. Willem felt sorry for him.

There would be no return to Holland across the wintry Atlantic Ocean after that first crossing. If necessary, the *Marta* would provide excellent shelter until the following spring. Although the ship would be crowded and sacrifices would have to be made, they could survive.

"I have heard that some arrivals lived in big, shoveled out holes in the ground, with a cover over the top. Good lord, never would I live in such a manner!" Willem was horrified. "I would rather live in a cave!"

"I am anxious to get under way," Hendrick declared. "I thank Grandfather for putting us on a schedule or we would never have gotten everything together. I think that now we need to finish up and start on a list of priorities to accomplish when we land."

"I would suggest that our first priority should be cutting timber for the community house and looking into brick making using indigenous materials. We will have the saw with us, and we will ask Uncle Theo to draw up simple plans for a few buildings. He is the architect," Jacob suggested. "I will speak with him immediately."

"You can use the ship to explore the area, as long as the weather holds, "Adam advised. "Send me a letter as soon as you arrive. There will be ships crossing through the rest of the summer. After that, you will have to wait for spring, if you wanted to return."

Willem agreed. He felt somewhat confident about who would be sailing with them. He and his two brothers, Jacob, Hendrick, two single cousins, along with Job and Arthur, were committed. *"Including myself, a crew of five so far,"* he thought to himself; and Job is familiar with *glass making*. He smiled to himself about that bit of good fortune. Grandfather had offered the services of Captain Hanson and Navigator Turbott, whom he would compensate. The group was happy to accept the generous offer. No one felt a first mate was necessary. The majority of his cousins, at one time or another, had worked and sailed on Grandfather's ships. They were well experienced in crewing and repair. Now the crew members totaled *seven*, including the captain and the navigator. Willem was still hoping that he would be able to round out the crew with family.

Gretchen, Hendrick's wife was excited about the plans even though the thought of losing Hendrick terrified her. After they had many conversations and pleadings, and because she knew how desperately he wanted to go, she acquiesced and told Hendrick, "You will return in a year and either stay here or take us all back with you. You must promise me this, Hendrick." He promised. This then, was the understanding between them.

Amalie's husband, James, asked questions constantly. Willem thought Amalie would beat James when he voiced his interest, so Willem spoke up. "You are terribly unfair, Amalie, to speak so harshly to James."

Amalie turned on him. She knew what was afoot, even if Willem was unaware that she did; Amalie did not want to discuss it. "You have no wife or children, Willem. Evidently, you are not leaving anyone or anything that holds any meaning for you. You are footloose and fancy free. You couldn't possibly understand anything but yourself and what you want to do!"

Willem's face turned red with embarrassment and he quickly left, ending further discussion with his sister. He felt both angry and embarrassed that Amalie should say such things to him. Amalie had no idea of the excitement and the dreams it held for her brothers. He had tried to talk to her about the voyage, but Amalie would not speak of it. Now he realized that there was too much at stake for her to let James join them. Her husband could be lost at sea, or killed or maimed by some dangerous hostile encounter and her children would be fatherless. Who knew what could happen to any of them once they landed on unfamiliar soil. He tried to dismiss her outburst as ignorance, but he knew that she had spoken the truth from her perspective, even though some of it was not his truth. Amalie had always followed a secure path; he realized that it would have been impossible for her to let

James go. He had to respect the legitimacy of her stormy response to him. He would apologize to her soon—after she had calmed down a bit.

Willem felt that there could be a surprise where his favorite, unmarried cousin, Elizabete was concerned. He hoped that she would become a crew member and without saying anything, he planned provisions for her privacy aboard the ship and brought the crew count to eight.

Cousin Domine was experienced in carpentry, bricklaying, and woodworking. Most of the architecture in Rotterdam was of stone or brick. There were few wooden buildings because of the scarcity of timber in Holland. However, Domine had worked on wooden appendages to the stone dwellings and with other wood that was incorporated into the outside décor of buildings. He was also a carver and knew the feel of different woods. It was common knowledge that brick and stone dwellings far outlasted wooden buildings, but bricks were too heavy to carry on board. The group would investigate what was available locally; they heard that slate existed in abundance. Willem considered cousin Domine's building experience most fortuitous and hoped that he would join them. Domine was single, but still undecided.

Willem's responsibilities, with the help of Hendrick, were the planning and gathering of supplies needed to survive the voyage and the coming winter. That would include weapons. They would attempt to foster a relationship with the local Indians, specifically the Lenni Lenape farming tribe. He needed them desperately, not only for their knowledge of the land and crop growing, they would be experienced in the hunting and dressing out of the larger animals along with the preservation of meat. Willem found these responsibilities overwhelming. Issues of life and death were hard to face. After much contemplation, he realized that each would contribute to the survival of the group in his own way. He decided this was the only way to think.

The foodstuff necessary to carry on their voyage was not Willem's field of expertise, so he consulted with one of Grandfather's friends, Mr. Green, a stores master. He proved to be of enormous help to Willem and after working with him, Willem felt that his lists were quite adequate. The lists provided for as many contingencies as was humanly possible.

"You cannot bring everything with you, Willem, or you will surely sink." Mr. Green laughed. "You are familiar with the sailor's basic hard biscuit or hard bread called hardtack? The usual way to make hardtack is with flour, water and some salt. When the hardtack contains cooked grains, vegetables and herbs, it is more appetizing as well as palatable. After it is cooked, it is cut up and dried. This is the basic food of seamen. You can pack other dry stuffs and use for a few weeks. If possible, take dried apples and cabbages. I would depend on fish rather than salted down meats. You might bring a very small amount of the meats, but I would not eat too much of that; besides it goes bad quickly. It would be better to stick to fresh fish." He paused to think. "You are bringing chickens and goats? Do not forget the feed for them. I hope that the chickens will lay and the goats will produce milk. This would be most fortunate. Not many sailors have that luxury."

Willem was writing everything down. "Why apples and cabbages? I have seen them occasionally at the market."

"I am sure you have heard of the disease called scurvy. It has been around for thousands of years. Hippocrates described it first. The thought now is that eating any dried or fresh fruit or vegetable will help to hold this disease at bay. They do not know why but fresh fruit, especially the citrus fruits and perhaps some vegetables, seems to repel this disease. The first symptoms are bleeding gums. You should be landed before that happens and you probably will not have any problems, but I would still bring these things with you. I will have to see how they preserve the cabbages. You should be able to use those for perhaps, the first two weeks. I have heard that the English naval ships are starting to carry lemons too, on their longer voyages. However, you have to preserve the lemons somehow. Perhaps in a water barrel? I will see if anyone knows anything of this. I think that you would have to import lemons from Spain."

It was middle February. Willem put the naming of the ship to a vote. "All in favor of naming the ship *Marta*, after Mother, say aye! All ayes it is then, me brothers! Mother should be pleased, if that is possible," Willem stated. They all laughed, but never with malice.

Jacob and Hendrick elected Willem to set up a family meeting and to make the initial announcement of their voyage. They would back him as best they could, they told him. "I protest," Willem cried. "Why do I always get stuck with the dirty work? One of you two can do it," he raised his voice to his brothers' backs as they walked from the room.

Hendrick later commented, "We have invited all of our cousins to join us, regardless of gender or occupation. I do not want anyone accusing us of omitting them."

Willem set about notifying his entire family of an important meeting concerning each of them. Willem told Adam, "Grandpapa, you must come and back us. We need you."

Adam reluctantly agreed. He knew what reactions to expect. "Pray for me, boys," Adam told his grandsons when the time came for the meeting. "This will be most unpleasant." He took a deep breath, winked at Willem and walked into the drawing room where the large family was gathered. Adam had been previously sworn to secrecy about the voyage. He too, knew what he was about to face when he revealed his involvement.

Evidently, Amalie had kept the news quiet, as Willem had requested her to do. He was surprised and silently thanked her.

The news of the intended voyage was not well received, which was no surprise. "But why do you want to leave your home?" Marta immediately asked, starting to fill up. "You boys have everything here that you need. Why are you risking your lives for a foolish dream?" Tears were already on her cheeks. "And you, Hendrick, leaving your wife and small children. Have you lost your mind? You were all raised better than that!"

"Mother, we are men, not boys. It is not a dream. My country has been at war or occupied since I can remember. I do not know if we will ever see true independence from Spain. They continue to harass us and dominate us in everything that we do, and I am tired of the oppression. I have no freedom to run my business without them sticking their nose into everything I do! The decision is between Gretchen and me and no one else. We want to be free, with our children free, to see the New World. There will never be another opportunity like this." Hendrick stated his feelings.

"I wish I were their age. I would be the first on board," Adam commented. "Marta, they are young and healthy and need to spread their wings. It is not as though you will never see them again. Ships are built better now and our own fluyt is well equipped and sturdier than ever. I have given them one of my best." He looked at Marta's face. In his anxiousness to help the young ones, he had forgotten that he had been sworn to secrecy. It was bound to come out sooner or later—oh well, *I guess it is sooner*, and he prepared himself for her berating.

"You have done *what*?" Marta bawled. "You were in on this from the very beginning, Adam?" she wailed. "My own father-in-law and like a father to me! You have betrayed me," she accused him, weeping into her handkerchief. It certainly would be traumatic for Marta, losing three sons, to what she perceived was an irrefutable fact—they would all be killed by some unknown encounter. There would be no surviving or returning home in her eyes for her sons. Willem did feel sorry for his mother, but did not hold to her ideas. Marta was hard set in her ways, even though they tried to reason with her, it was futile. But she was a mother and they were her sons and she was fearful that they would be lost.

"That is enough, Marta," Paul interrupted. "Get hold of yourself, wife! They have the right to do as they wish; they are all of age. I can understand their reluctance to discuss anything with you. They knew how you would act. Just look at you," he said, as Marta sat crying hysterically. At first, Paul had commiserated with her when they announced the voyage. But Marta was not going to stop her hysterics. "If I were just ten years younger, I would join them," Paul announced, shaking his head. "Go to it, men. If there is anything I can do to help, let me know."

The single cousins, Job and Arthur announced that they were committed to the crew, much to the delight of the group. Domine then joined them. This news brought unhappy resistance and cries from the mothers, which were to be expected.

Grandfather Adam could understand the mothers' dilemma. These were their children, and they were putting themselves in danger; perhaps they would never be seen again. However, he also understood the young ones.

Aunt Adele was terribly upset with her son, Domine's decision. She would wait until later to speak to him. She was private with her feelings; sometimes she wished she could weep and sob as spontaneously as her sister-in-law Marta, however unladylike.

Cousin Elizabete had not rendered her verdict. "What is your resolve, Bete?" Willem asked her, referring to her by her childhood name.

"I have decided to join you," Bete looked at Willem and then her mother.

"You have *what*?" Aunt Beth cried. "What kind of nonsense is this, Elizabete? I forbid it. Your brothers and now you? I absolutely forbid it!" She started to cry and dab her nose.

"Mother, I am well into my twenties, and I am entitled to make my own decisions." Bete put her dark, curly head down and in a barely audible voice continued. "You know I have not been happy since I put off my marriage to Nicholas. I want to set my course in another direction; I will go with you, Willie." She lifted her head now and looked at him with her big, brown eyes, and then turned to her mother. "I will be with my brothers, Mama. Job and Arthur will watch out for me." She turned to Willem.

"I would like to request a favor, Willem. I would like my best friend, Margaret Vanderbeck, to accompany me. You remember Maggie? We were in school together."

"I think we all know Margaret. You and she were always great chums. Have you discussed this with her?"

"Yes, I took the liberty to invite her. Maggie has secured permission from her guardian to join us. She has no immediate family. Maggie said that she wants to see the New World. She felt that this might be her only chance."

Amalie gasped. "Are you mad, Bete? You are going to a strange land filled with savages and dragging Maggie with you. Have you lost your senses completely?"

Bete only smiled at Amalie. "I know all the advantages we have here and how well we live. But it is not everything, Amalie. Maggie feels the same. Something is lacking in my life and since I had to break off my intended marriage," and she drifted into silence, twisting her handkerchief in her lap.

At that moment, Willem was sorry that he had been stopped from thrashing Nicholas, her intended. Nicholas had been unfaithful and when poor Bete found out, she had quickly called off their intended marriage. That was nearly three years ago; Bete no longer was the same happy person. "We would welcome Maggie on our journey," Willem said to her. "Unless anyone objects?" Willem thought perhaps that Bete too, was searching for that certain elusive something that was missing in her life. Willem suddenly felt a stronger kinship toward his cousin, understanding her feelings. "That brings our group to *eleven* with Margaret and Bete," Willem announced.

Amalie sat silent, her lips glued tightly together. Willem felt sorry for James. He was so anxious to join them, but it would be a risk to his marriage and James knew it.

"You will all be massacred at the hands of those red devils," Marta assured them, as she looked around the room at her sons.

"Mother," Willem replied, "That is just not so. We plan to return, and perhaps, after we are settled you will join us, or at least, visit us."

"Never, never, never will I leave my home to journey to an unknown wilderness with hostiles killing everyone," she replied fervently, sticking her chin out and up while patting at fresh tears. "Now if you will excuse me, I do not think there is a thing left to discuss. I would not set foot on that foreign land." That was her final comment as she swept through the door, weeping as she exited.

In the next few weeks, the crew formally christened their new ship, *Marta*. When Hendrick commented to his mother that her name would carry them safely across the sea, she relented a bit. However, she left them with the last word, "I will pray for all of you, that you come back with your heads on."

Jacob, Hendrick, Willem and their cousins Bete, Domine, Job and Arthur, along with Maggie, Turbott, the navigator and Captain Hanson made up the crew thus far.

Willem felt that he had taken care of everything that he possibly could, even the one problem that had been nagging him. Captain Hanson, Turbott and the two women were not part of the working crew—the working crew was four short. Willem was concerned that six men were not a sufficient number to work the Marta. He brought in Kruger and Jools, two of his friends. When they were younger, Kruger and Jools, a builder and farmer respectively, had often sailed with them. Willem had chosen them specifically for their knowledge. He was happy to welcome the two into the crew, bringing the new total to twelve, which seemed to be a splendid number in itself, like eggs in a basket. Usually the captain and navigator were not part of a working crew, unless an emergency arose. Grandfather had spoken with Hanson and Turbott and they already knew the circumstances and told Adam that they would join the working crew when needed. Adam felt that unless they hit bad weather, eight experienced crew could handle the *Marta*.

Among the travelers, thus far, was a metal smith who could adapt his knowledge to the forge, a physician, a navigator, an experienced sea captain, an agronomist, an irrigation specialist, a glassmaker, a farmer along with a carpenter, a builder and someone with extensive knowledge of ship's repair. With Bete and Maggie, they would have a seamstress, a cook, an animal tender, and whatever else the women desired to do. Six small goats and twelve chickens would sail with them to provide milk, cheese and eggs. Chickens reproduce quickly. Willem felt that they were far ahead of other voyagers. Their crew was diversified and well experienced.

Sometime in 1615, it was reported in the newspaper that the explorer Christiansen's adopted Indian son, Orson, had murdered him. The heinous deed had taken place near Fort Orange in the Hudson River Valley. Orson had been the son of a sachem, or King from a tribe in the Massachusetts region, specifically southward of Plymouth. There was no other information available.

"Dear god," Hendrick said. "Do not let mother see this."

The *Marta* would set sail for the New World from Rotterdam, May 15, 1616. Adam came on deck before she set sail, to wish them good luck and impart something to Willem. "Better that you do not think about the huge sea you have to cross. Take one day at a time, Willie and cross it off your calendar and before you know it, you will be at the doorstep of the New World. Godspeed to all of you," he wished. He hugged his grandchildren one by one and shook the hands of the rest of the crew. His face was awash in tears of happiness; but there was also apprehension in those tears, physically clouding his vision. Hendrick helped him from the ship.

The crew's excitement quickly became contagious as Willem turned to Hendrick and punched him softly on the arm. They both smiled at Jacob. "Can you believe what we have finally accomplished? We are almost away, big brothers," Willem shared his joy and Hendrick's wide grin mirrored his brother's elation. Willem's body tingled with sheer energy as he looked up at the deep blue sky and noted what a splendid day it was.

Relatives milled about on the dock, commenting on the beauty of the ship and cheering the crew onward, wishing them good luck. The *Marta* was a handsome ship, well constructed under Grandfather's loving hand and modified to fit his family's mission. Marta's name was clearly visible and stood out in bright green against the brown bow of the fluyt. It was time to get under way. Willem called for all moorings to be untied, and as a soft breeze picked up, he heard the sails pop gently full. He interpreted the sound as a good omen for the start of a voyage.

Willem turned to glance aft and saw Bete and her friend Maggie coming toward him. "God is surely smiling upon us," Bete said, beaming up at her cousin. "I pray that good fortune will stay with us the entire voyage."

Willem raised his hands over his head in jubilation as the *Marta* slowly headed out toward the ocean. He watched his family waving farewell, until the dock finally receded into small specks. He saw his mother's handkerchief, a tiny white dot and then it too, vanished as the *Marta* sailed toward the horizon.

Willem felt that the ship had been prepared properly and that she was extremely seaworthy, but he still prayed fervently that nothing had been overlooked—he knew that faith, determination and working together had gotten them this far.

Bete told him repeatedly to stop worrying. "There is nothing you can do about it now," she added. "We are on our way!" she shouted, and the men turned to join in her excitement.

Willem wondered where he would be in a year. *I cannot worry about a year from now. Today and the tomorrows will keep me well occupied.* He realized how fortunate they were that Grandfather had sent Captain Hanson and Turbott with them. Their sailing experience with fluyts in local waters, as well as in open seas, was well known.

Turbott felt quite confident embarking on this voyage. The ocean was big; winds could vary and usually blew against them, but he never felt lost. When the sun was shining, he used a cross staff to track its height above the horizon and estimate its noontime position, telling both south and latitude. On overcast days, there was the mysterious magnetic needle. On two passages to the Bermudas, he had hit the islands perfectly even though, once, the winds made his captain tack this way and that, motions a navigator had to take into account.

The trickiest part would be arriving at the New World. He knew its beaches were mostly sandy, but still, getting stuck in the sand and hoping for a decent high tide was not a good way to end a voyage. The time when the shore was expected to appear was tense for both navigator and captain. At night, some shippers then let out the smaller anchor, hoping that if the beach were reached, the ship would stop before hitting ground.

Just no storms, Lord, Turbott thought, *just no storms.* Sailing west from Rotterdam, they could estimate where they would land on the North American continent, but not the time of their arrival. If they wanted it more precise, he would use *dead reckoning*, which calculated their position by speed and time. That was more involved, but Turbott was well versed in it, should it be necessary. They knew the average time that recent crossings had taken, so they could estimate time. They would correct their landing point when they arrived. He knew that getting becalmed, or dead in the water and a storm near rocky inlets was their enemy. He would let the captain handle those situations.

Captain Hanson went over the planned route to the North American continent again with Turbott, Willem, Jacob, and Hendrick. The *Marta* would follow the modified course plotted by the Dutch skippers Block, Mey, and Christiansen. Turbott had already discussed the updated charts and had reread Hudson's navigator, Juet's log from his 1609 passage. Hudson had made his return trip in thirty four days. They hoped to eliminate a day or two, if the weather held.

Willem's excitement returned, and it was especially difficult for him to calm his exhilaration. Finally their vision was no longer the dream they had challenged themselves to fulfill; they had moved into reality. However, Willem still harbored anxiety; he felt responsible for everyone on the ship. Bete told him for the second time, "It is your choice, Willem. You cannot be accountable for everything and everyone. No one has asked you to do this." Then she gave up.

Willem moved over to the railing and turned to face the massive, dark blue waters that his eyes could not avoid. The great Atlantic Ocean would surround him for at least the next four weeks. When the *Marta* had sailed a short distance, Willem requested all hands on deck to join him in a prayer for a safe voyage.

A partial entry that first day from the ship's log read—*nineteen hours covered approximately one hundred nautical miles. All are elated.* However, Turbott was somewhat pessimistic by nature and told the crew that days like this were a gift from the heavens. "Considering that we left at 6:00 a.m so family could share bon voyage, rather than the midnight we had planned and losing six hours of sailing time, we have made fine time. Pray for swift winds aloft and calm seas. We have a long way to go me boys—over 3,000 nautical miles. We will have to sail approximately 100 nautical miles in a 24 hour period to arrive in 34 days."

"If we have good winds, perhaps we can do better than that." Jacob commented. Captain Hanson looked at him and shook his head.

"Come down and have a cup of tea with us, Willem," Maggie invited quietly toward the end of the next day.

Willem was at the wheel, and turned in surprise. His focus had been ahead and he had not heard her come up behind him. "Thank you, Margaret. I will come down in a few minutes."

"Call me Maggie. Everyone does." She smiled up at Willem, and her face lit up. He glanced down at her, and then turned back to really look at her. He could not understand, knowing her that long, how he had not recognized how very pretty she was.

Staring down upon her intently, he took in the full measure of her, noticing that she had pushed her bonnet back from her lovely face and she appeared almost ethereal in her persona. Her light brown hair, streaked with blonde from the sun, was tied back, but it sprang free in wisps and ringlets, framing her lovely, heart shaped face. He noticed her even, white teeth as she smiled up at him. For the first time, he really looked into her clear, hazel eyes, fringed with long, black lashes and he stayed there. He felt a tingling sensation throughout his body and an unconscious reflex caused him to pull his breath in sharply. After a few seconds of standing there and staring at her like a complete oaf, he repeated himself and told her he would be down to the cabin shortly. She turned her slim body to leave and as her lavender scent caught him, his senses were flooded with her. He thought himself to be going daft. He could not believe how her closeness had affected him so quickly.

Could it be that he had distanced himself from women that long? How could he have known her all these years and not really have seen her? He stood there, somewhat dazed for a minute, then apprehensively made his way down to the women's cabin, while Turbott relieved him at the wheel.

"It's me, Willem," he called through the louvered top of the door after knocking.

"Come in." Bete opened the door inwardly. "You look tired. Sit down and visit for a while and have a nice hot cup of tea."

"Thanks. I would enjoy that." He nodded to Maggie, tidying up in the corner. "You have made it nice in here," Willem observed as he glanced around. He noticed that they had hung a curtain over the small window for privacy. The feminine clothes, hairbrushes, and other paraphernalia lying about, made him somewhat uncomfortable.

Bete handed him his tea and sat down next to him at the small table. "I know we are only two days out, but it has gone so well. I will not be carried away, but it is better to think positive," she said. He nodded.

Because the women were not familiar with the ship's bells, Hendrick had posted a reference for them with the watches by the bells. He noticed that the list was tacked up on the wall. Time was kept with an hourglass and the ship's bells sounded the watches. The women wanted to learn the watches first, and then acquaint themselves with the bells striking every half hour of each watch.

"How are you doing with the watches?" Willem asked.

"It is confusing, but we are quizzing each other so that we will learn. I do have a pocket watch though, that I wind." Bete showed him the watch. "I like to know the precise time."

Middle Watch	Midnight to 4 AM
Morning Watch	4 AM to 8 AM
Forenoon Watch	8 AM to noon
Afternoon Watch	Noon to 4 PM
First Dog Watch	4 PM to 6 PM
Second Dog Watch	6 PM to 8 PM
First Watch	8 PM to Midnight

"You have brought lots of books," Willem commented as he continued his perusal of the small cabin. He noticed that one of the men had put up shelving for them and two cupboards were stored against the wall, making the cabin somewhat crowded. He thanked Grandpapa's foresight in enlarging the ship, along with the two aft cabins, allowing them to carry knocked down tables and chairs.

"You remember what an avid reader I am. I did not know if we would have access to books, so I wanted to have a supply on hand. Maggie brought more books in her trunk, too."

"I am sorry for the overcrowding, but I guess there was no other place to store those cupboards." He looked at Bete. "That small enlargement in the cabin's overall measurements certainly let you store things in here that otherwise would have been left behind." He paused.

"Have either of you had sea sickness yet? You are hardly seasoned sailors, and I was concerned."

"Do not be concerned about us, Willem," Bete replied. "All is well. We are thinking positive. Not to worry."

Maggie told him that she was growing mint and other herbs, both for consumption and medicinal purposes. "I am an avid gardener and like to be out in the sun. I have brought lots of seeds with me. I will plant them when we land. I think there will be enough growing time," she smiled at him.

The hot tea tasted good, and then he realized how bone tired he truly was. The second day had been good—long, but good—and now he needed sleep. He was not on watch that night and he was grateful. Willem thanked them for the tea and left. He willed his mind blank. Later, when he got to his berth in the men's community cabin, he immediately drifted off and slept the night without moving or dreaming or, at least, without remembering any of his dreams.

The ship's bells sounded the Forenoon Watch and rudely interrupted his sleep. Willem sat up abruptly, trying to orient himself. The warm morning sun cast yellow lines of light on the cabin floor. It was 8:00 a.m. Willem could not believe that he had slept so long. He took a quick look about and saw that the cabin was empty. He stood up, used the urinal, sighed with relief and then slipped his britches on over his under drawers. He adjusted the small reflecting glass above the washbasin to accommodate his six foot, two inch height and his broad shoulders. The water was cool on his face and head. He splashed his muscular chest down to his waist, dried himself and cleaned his teeth. He leaned into the looking glass, opened his clear blue eyes wider, and blinked at himself. His growing beard reflected in the glass and he smiled, remembering Amalie's horror when he told her that they were all going to let their beards grow during the voyage. Bete had volunteered to act as ship's barber and keep them trimmed. Rubbing a hand over his face, he noticed that the incoming growth was many shades darker than his thick, white-blonde hair. He had never grown a beard. He concluded that this new growth would match his dark brows. He drew a comb through his damp hair, grabbed a shirt, pulled on his boots and headed aft to the small community area.

"Well, good morning, sleepy head," Bete greeted him. "You certainly needed the rest. How are you?"

"Starved," he replied, scanning the area briefly for Maggie. "I could eat a cow," he told Bete and turned to see Maggie enter.

The two women had volunteered to cook in lieu of working on deck. They were very aware that this was not a pleasure ship and even though they were females, it was expected that they pull their own weight in other ways.

Marta had been appalled when she heard that Bete and Maggie would cook and care for the animals. She had begged Willem to take a cook and a cabin boy along, but he laughed and refused. Marta had not understood the necessity of portioning out the various duties and saving space for stores. Willem had reminded her, that she had always pulled her own weight at home, even though she did not realize it. Now she moaned that she was too old to change and that the new generations were not as genteel.

Bete and Maggie cooked on the large, contained hearth housed in a corner near the rear cargo compartment. Because the ship was packed with necessities, they used a common table in the stern cabin and ate in shifts. The crew took meals on deck when the weather was nice, because of the overcrowding. Captain Hansen was not ordinarily agreeable to eating on deck, but necessity at times, won.

"Good morning, Willem." Maggie said and smiled at him. "What would you like for breakfast? I am the cook this morning."

Willem just grinned back as he took in her freshly scrubbed face and clean, white apron over her blue and white dress. "Whatever the rest of the crew had." He watched her go to one of the small cupboards and take down a plate, eating utensils, and a cup. She poured fresh goat's milk from a nearby pitcher into the blue cup and brought it to him. She leaned over his shoulder from behind and once more, he caught her faint scent of lavender; it touched off in him a feeling of heady intoxication. Breathing deeply, he told himself that he would control his emotions, or he would get himself into trouble. He did not want to offend Maggie; he was seized with longing to grab hold of her. He knew they would be in close quarters for the voyage, so he quickly decided to avoid her whenever possible.

She came back from the small galley area with his breakfast plate full of eggs, sausages, buttered bread, hot, strong tea in another cup, and an apple. "Enjoy the eggs. The chickens have been rather excitable, but seem to have settled down. After two or three weeks, the butter will probably turn rancid. The smoked sausages have a longer life. Perhaps there is a place where we can store the butter and sausages in the cool ocean water?"

He held his breath quietly until she had turned away from him. "Let me see what we can do about that." Then he turned his focus to ship's matters for the day.

The weather held for the first seven days. Late in the week, they lowered one of the small dinghies over the side and rowed out a way to fish. They salted anything caught from the sea, keeping up with supplies. The journey went well into the second week; the course was maintained, much to the joy of Captain Hanson and Turbott. Sustained winds and mildly choppy waters held. Everyone pulled his own weight. Weather was always chancy and they prayed constantly that this wonderful weather would hold and it did through the second week.

Three weeks out, the great Atlantic Ocean turned rough in the afternoon. They dropped the large sails as the wind came around to the northeast in a stiff, cold gale that continued all night. The next morning appeared thick and foggy, with a moderate to brisk wind blowing the fog in and out in pockets. Light rain dampened the deck, and the temperature dropped. The wind held constant, allowing them to steer a true, fast course for a time. Then the wind and rain increased to a great force, and they sailed into a massive storm. Before they could lower the small sails, gale force winds ripped one sail down. Luck was with them; the sail landed on deck, but missed any of the crew.

"If you are not working the ship, go below!" Captain Hanson bellowed. "Those on deck, tie yourselves to a sturdy fixture." He thanked God that they had already lowered the large sails before the gale had hit full force.

Bete and Maggie hurried to their cabin, fighting the stiff wind on deck. High rolling waves pitched the sturdy *Marta* unrelentingly, crashing onto the deck and for the first time, Willem's stomach rebelled. He reminded the men once more, "All you men on deck, tether yourself to the solid parts of the ship. Watch the high ones as they come in!" he roared over the wind.

Turbott hollered to Willem, "I do not think we can hold a true course!"

Willem yelled back, "Does not matter! We will adjust later." Willem would not allow anyone to know how terrified he was. Then he remembered what Grandpapa had cautioned him: *Better you do not think about the huge sea around you,* and with this thought, Willem somehow managed to calm himself.

After three stormy days, the rain gradually ceased and the wind suddenly dropped off. They raised the small sails as the *Marta* coursed out of a dark rain forest, into a beautiful, deep blue pasture. The water continued to be mildly choppy, but the terribly rough waters and strong winds had fallen off. Twilight came and the moon sailed low on the horizon, lighting a wide path of glowing light on the black ocean. Willem and the assigned crew of Hendrick, Job, Arthur, and Domine continued the watch. They were soggy and tired, but relieved that they had weathered the gale. Willem went to his hammock after the storm broke, wet and dragging with exhaustion. He was unable to sleep at first because in his mind, he heard his mother nagging him about wet clothes. He managed to slip them off before he fell into a dead sleep.

Surprisingly, when the sun rose early the next morning, Turbott happily reported that they were not far off their path. "I am adjusting our course."

The weather was fair; it was windy, but to their favor. The stiff breeze pushed the *Marta* briskly along. The sea was still mildly choppy, and at times, a lone, large wave rolled the ship so that walking became hazardous. Willem was looking for the women when he spotted Jacob on deck. "Have you seen Bete or Maggie? I think I should check on them."

"I just spoke with Bete a short time ago. She told me that she and Maggie had fared well enough during the night. Bete was going on deck for some air."

"Oh lord, I did not want that. The footing is too dangerous." He knew Bete was cautious, but he still wanted to check on them. "I am going to their cabin to make sure they are both all right."

He had tried to avoid Maggie, but she was in his thoughts constantly; unconsciously he watched for her slim profile wherever he was. They had spoken a few times, but he still found it extremely difficult to be near her. The extent of his difficulties amazed him. Willem was not sure what was wrong with him. He had never felt this way or had been so bewildered by a woman. He would be relieved when they landed. He could get on with his life. But the thought of not seeing her was terribly depressing. He was confused with himself; he felt almost possessed, captured by his own emotions. Thoughts of her were becoming almost obsessive.

"Hello, in there," he called through the door, knocking softly. "Are you all right? It is I, Willem."

The ship suddenly rolled steeply, tilting the deck floor up at a precarious angle under his feet. At that moment, Maggie opened the door inwardly and Willem immediately slid through the open door. Unable to avoid her, he lifted her to him and they continued sliding. They came to rest, pressed together, standing against the far cabin wall. The roll of the ship had happened so abruptly that it had frightened her and she twisted in his arms, trying to gain a footing. Willem felt the length of her supple body move against him and a searing jolt of intense passion surged through his throat and raced down to his knees. It left him weak; he was dizzy with the fragrance of her and her warm, sweet breath on his mouth and cheek. Looking down into her startled, pale face, Willem tightened his hold. "It is all right, Maggie," he whispered. "I have hold of you. Do not be frightened," he managed to say. He felt her relax against his chest and they continued to stand, intermingled for a long moment. He did not see Bete.

"Oh, Willem," she murmured, urging herself even closer, breathing her sweetness upon him. "I have waited so long." She sighed, turning her face up to him as she slipped her warm arms around his neck. His senses were on fire and his desire was so fierce that it was drowning him. He lifted her up to him and his mouth found her warm lips; he felt as though her spirit had slipped into his. Maggie had touched something deep in him—even more than the physical—she had met his very soul. *She is what I have been seeking,* he knew, with absoluteness. His mind reeled. *Had he and Maggie been destined to meet?* At that moment, *he had no doubt that this was so.* Those thoughts raced swiftly through his mind as he held her tightly to him.

"Willem," they heard Bete calling. "Willem, where are you?" she called again, and he knew that she was on her way to the cabin.

Willem's head was swimming. He was trembling as he reluctantly released her. She was shaken and stumbled slightly as he loosened her from his tight grip.

"Do not say a word," she cautioned Willem. He could read the passion behind her clear eyes and he knew that he needed to gain control. "Bete is coming." Maggie stepped back from him.

Willem turned away from her as Bete came bursting through the door, completely oblivious to the situation

at hand. "Where have you been, Willem? I could not find
you, and I want you to take a look at Magda. I think she is
pregnant." Magda was one of the female goats. "All right.
All right, I will take a look." He glanced over at Maggie,
smiled slightly to her in frustration and left the room with
Bete.

Dear God, he thought to himself, as he followed Bete
quickly back to the animal pens. He raised his eyes to
heaven; *give me back that one moment, that is all I ask—an
incredible moment interrupted by a pregnant goat! Only
this mistiming could happen to me.*

After concluding that the goat was indeed pregnant,
which was good fortune, he came back on deck. He stood
on the aft deck alone, gazing absentmindedly at the *Marta*'s
wake. He was consumed now in the passionate heat of his
encounter with Maggie. He turned to the churning dark
waters to refocus himself so that he would be able to carry
out his duties. He was unable to speak; his body was out
of control, and his senses had betrayed him. This caused
him a great deal of concern. He already knew that he must
have her, not just now but forever. He could not believe the
swiftness of the thoughts that had run through his head
when he had held her. He tried again to clear his mind so
that he could think rationally. He was always in charge
of his physical self and what had happened, rattled him.
Certainly, the physical passion was intense with Maggie,
but there was something else he had experienced with her
that had never happened to him before. When they came
together, he felt whole.

He wondered what Maggie had meant when she had
said to him that she had waited so long. *Where in the
world,* he thought, *was I all those years to be so completely
unaware of her?* He decided to speak with Bete. She had
been Maggie's close friend since childhood and must
be privy to some information, he reasoned. Willem was
not ready to sleep that night, so he volunteered for an
extra watch rather than lie down in his cabin in physical
and mental torment, thinking of Maggie. However, after

thinking about the interruption of the pregnant goat, he laughed aloud to himself. *It was so preposterous* he could not think of another word to describe it.

To everyone's delight and surprise, the last week of their journey moved ahead rapidly and uneventfully. "Methinks that we are through the worst of the weather. Perhaps we will be able to gain a day or two if the winds hold and we remain free of storms." Captain Hanson was intuitively feeling the weather in his bones and then was able to forecast most of the time, quite accurately. Willem was happy to hear the news.

Maggie and Willem spoke cautiously in passing, but one day she put her head down and did not look at him. That morning Willem sought out Bete. Not knowing how to start such a conversation, Willem just fell right into the matter. "Have I missed something with Maggie all these years?"

"Why are you asking?" Bete raised her eyebrows in surprise.

"Because I love her," he answered simply and directly in a voice broken with emotion.

Bete looked at him searchingly. "Bully for you, Willie!" she said enthusiastically. "You have finally come to your senses and can see what is right under your very nose." She moved over to hug him. "I cannot believe this. Maggie has loved you since we were children, but of course you never saw her. She said that was not the reason she came on this voyage, but I think it was. What has happened Willem, to make you tell me that you love her?"

"What are you saying, Bete?" He hit his palm to his forehead in surprise. "Maggie has had feelings for me all these years? How could I have been so stupid? Why was I not told? Good god, Bete, I have always thought of Maggie and you together, as cousins, as family—I never saw her for herself. Could this have caused me to be completely in the dark to her feelings? And why has she been turning away from me the last few days?"

"She is concerned that she was too forward, that in my opinion, is nonsense. I do not know what happened to make you aware of her. She would not tell me, but I am sure she did not instigate it."

"Of course it was not her doing. There is something that I feel for her that I cannot explain. It is like finding something that you know, but do not know what it is until you find it again. I need to speak privately with her, Bete. Could you leave your cabin for an hour?"

"Certainly I will, and I think it is all delightful. I told Maggie that one day I had hoped she would truly be my cousin," she paused, lost in her happiness for them. "Can you visit tomorrow morning after breakfast?"

"Fine, I will see her then." He did not know how he would manage to wait that long, but he did. The next morning, he walked down to her cabin and rapped lightly on the door.

Maggie opened the door and smiled up at him with her beautiful face and his heart nearly stopped. "I was hoping that the ship would roll again," she murmured, casting her eyes downward.

"Do not say that, Maggie. I cannot stand it. I cannot even think of what happened, or I will lose my mind. We have to talk. The crossing is almost completed; we will be landing. I want to marry you as soon as we are settled. Time is passing—and I have lost enough time already," and then he was quiet.

Willem could not believe that he was speaking! *Me, Willem, who was always so cautious.* "That is," he continued nervously, "if you will have me."

Maggie sat down, and put her hand over her heart. "I have loved you, Willem, since the first time I saw you. I will always love you and yes, yes, I will marry you," and she got up, put her arms around him, lifting her face to his in an acceptance of his proposal.

"When will we make the announcement?"

"Can we wait until the last night? It should only be a few more days. We will be scandalized by not having a long engagement," she laughed.

"Of course, my love. Come here." He pulled her to him. "How I love you, Maggie. I will never let you go. I could never wait another year."

She laughed at his rambling, and then he asked her, "Why did you not tell me how you felt?"

"And what if you refused me, love? Suppose you were not ready for me before this?"

Was there some truth in the old wisdom that everything is as it should be and there is a time for everything? Willem guessed he would never know, but he was thankful that he had found her. There would be a lifetime ahead for the both of them. He would have a partner in the New World; if there was no priest to be found, Captain Hanson could marry them.

Five days later, just before twilight, on June 15, Willem heard his brother yelling loudly, "Land Ho!" There was a tiny line on the horizon that Jacob had spotted with his glass. Turbott's excellent navigating landed them almost directly on point. Captain Hanson confirmed the sighting and stated that they would not be into port until the following dawn. They were still far out; Turbott would now make sight adjustments.

The excitement was contagious. Willem looked over at Maggie questioningly and mouthed, "May I?" and she nodded her head shyly. She watched Willem rush to the wheel deck, where he rang the ship's bell to get everyone's attention. The sighting of land, along with Willem's bell ringing brought everyone on deck.

"I—no, we—have an announcement to make!" he shouted down from the wheel deck to all the friendly inquiring faces. "Maggie and I will be married as soon as possible after we land." Willem jumped down to the deck and hugged Maggie, keeping her tightly in the circle of his arm. There was surprised silence for a moment and then cheers and congratulations burst forth as Willem's family of brothers, cousins and friends gathered around them, carrying on raucously. Captain Hanson came forward to shake Willem's hand, to hug Maggie and to wish them both good fortunes. "Tis a lucky ship that has a new bride.

I expect you two will want to be married before Turbott and I return home?"

Maggie shook her head yes. "I will be married in the Americas. Think of that!" She laughed up at Willem.

"I am the happiest man alive," Willem whispered to her as they stood at the rail, surrounded by the deep blue waters of the Atlantic. His personal search was over and the void, which he had carried for so long, was now filled with Maggie. A new life was ahead of them.

Willem raised his face toward heaven and silently thanked his God.

CHAPTER THREE

Sergio Cadiz Scarlatti

1580-1614

Powdered debris lay sprinkled like dust on his dark curly hair; his face was stained with dirt, gunpowder and blood. *Fifteen years is too young to die,* he thought.

The great battle was drawing to an end. The galleon, *Juanita* had been caught in the midst of King Philip's great Spanish Armada. She had taken a near death blow from the English. The dark haired, dark eyed boy with the red sash inched his way across the ship's deck on his belly, praying that he would not heave his guts. Carefully avoiding the blown up dead, he rolled quickly into a large, empty storage bin. He pressed himself against its wall, where it was dark. He did not want Captain Lorca to see him. He curled himself tightly into a ball, ducking his head under his arms. He wanted the captain to think him dead. He lay still for a time, then cautiously lifted his head and swiped a dirty hand across his runny nose. He heard Captain Lorca calling to him, but in his terror he could neither move nor answer. He reasoned that ships boys do not fight and die and that was what he was: just a ships boy.

"Help me, Sergio boy!" Captain Lorca screamed. "I am hurt!" Silence, and then again the captain thundered, "*Sergio, you skinny bastard*! Show yourself. Help me, boy!" Lorca bawled. "I am hurt." Then there was no more from the captain.

"He knows that I am not dead," Sergio moaned softly to himself. "I have to get to him." Powdered debris lay sprinkled like dust on his dark, curly hair; his face was stained with dirt, gunpowder, and blood. He shook himself like a dog, trying to fling off the gritty dust. Bombs burst ferociously above and around the ship, raining black debris. He knew roughly where his captain had fallen and he determined that if an exploding cannon ball did not hit him, he could crawl to him. His determination to help his friend suddenly gave him the strength to lift up. "Please, God," he prayed fervently aloud, "do not let me wet myself." With Herculean effort drawn from his very insides, he suddenly burst free from his hiding place and darted quickly across the galleon's deck. He wove in and out to avoid the flying black death. He rolled and scrambled and became tangled in the corpse of a fallen sea mate; he shrieked, fought free and finally reached his captain.

"Santa Maria," Sergio murmured softly. He blessed himself and tried to catch his breath. The captain was propped up against the side of the wall, just under the lip of the railing. Sergio recoiled, seeing his captain holding his massively bleeding arm tightly against his chest. "I cannot do this!" Sergio cried aloud, looking at the captain's large shoulders and huge belly. He knew that he was too small to move the big man. Lorca's gray black hair was matted red; his dark blue jacket was ripped open across his chest. His face was a pasty white and bloody drool ran from his mouth, settling in his beard.

"I have to help him," Sergio whispered. Strong feelings brought tears to his eyes. He remembered with gratitude and love how fatherly and protective the gruff captain had been. *I would be in the King's prison but for him.* Random thoughts flashed across his mind in that moment, recalling the good times with his captain and yes, he admitted, some of the crew. They were funny and rough and sometimes drunken, but never vicious or mean—at least, not to him.

With great bravado, Sergio told his Captain, "Do not worry. I will take care of you." He did not know if the half conscious man had heard him. *Remove your mind, remove what you see and attend to him,* he thought and fell back into the moment. He pulled the red sash from his waist and wrapped it tightly around the captain's arm. "Keep it tight," he demanded of his Captain. Sergio was becoming more aware of his surroundings, and observed in amazement the amount of blood covering the deck. He was immensely grateful that he had once observed the town doctor tie a rope around an injured man's leg to stop the bleeding. "There," he announced, after a few more minutes. "The bleeding is slackening off. I pray that it will work with an arm too."

"*Thank you.*" Lorca mumbled.

Sergio pulled back in surprise. He thought the captain was still unconscious. *"Please, please, merciful heaven, do not let him die,"* he again prayed softly. He watched the captain's pain ridden face and thought that he was surely a goner. Then, after a few more minutes, he was hopeful. "The bleeding is slowing down!"

Sergio knew that this was a serious wound and might require cauterization. He would need to use a hot metal poker to stop the bleeding and close the wound. There was a poker in the medical closet.

"Just rest yourself." He sat down next to his captain, leaned back and took a deep breath to give his thumping heart a chance to leave his throat. He should loosen the sash as the doctor had loosened the rope, but he did not know how often.

"Sergio boy," Captain Lorca murmured. He opened his eyes and looked up at Sergio. The boy was barely starting manhood; he was tall, thin; not yet filled out, but reliable and trustworthy. His dark curly hair was awash in dirt, and his aristocratic features were smeared with blood and grit. He would be a fine looking man when full grown, Captain Lorca thought.

Sergio closed his eyes and willed his mind elsewhere at that moment. No one could ever have conveyed to him that war was so vile and filled with agony. He had seen the terrible bloodshed himself. Bodies and body parts were strewn everywhere—helter skelter—and he thanked God that they were dead. The wounds inflicted by the cannons were too terrible and grievous to describe. The horrific stench of the body parts from the heat assaulted his nostrils. Suddenly he gagged and could not stop. Their own cannon balls had been cast so badly, that they exploded when they were fired. Many of the non military vessels confiscated for the Armada had not been built as warships. The vessels could not stand up to the terrific recoil of the heavy cannon firing and the pounding of their own guns, that caused damage to their own ships. The crew had to watch for guns shaking loose and leaping across the deck, still firing and killing men. Then there were the *English Hell burners*. No gathering of Spanish ships at anchor, either in harbor or out on the waters were safe from these English fire ships sent into their midst.

Sergio wanted to leave all of this devastation and madness. He wondered if he would ever go home again, back to Cadiz. The *Juanita* had suffered major damage, and the fighting was not over. He silently questioned what he was doing in this bloody hell of a place, sitting in the midst of death and destruction. Why did he have to run from a crazy King who had ordered his Inquisitors to murder his father and his grandfather, all in the name of God? It was insanity.

"Sergio, boy," the Captain whispered hoarsely, now completely conscious.

Sergio leaned over and loosened the sash around his arm. "The bleeding has almost stopped," he told the Captain. He cautiously fastened the sash as a sling and secured Lorca's arm tightly in place, against his chest. "Do you think we should sear the wound?"

"Sit for a minute, and we will see how she does." Lorca laid his big head back and shut his eyes.

Sergio closed his eyes too, and mused how his father could have reasoned that being at sea was a safer place for him. His mind raced back over the events that led him to this terrible place of death from flying shot and exploding firebombs.

He knew that the *Juanita* had been badly hit. He could hardly believe that she had held her own in battle and that they were still afloat. He looked up at her square riggings, high bow and strong hull. He gave thanks.

"She did hold her own though." Captain Lorca startled Sergio as he seemingly reflected the boy's thoughts. Lorca sighed as they sat quietly, observing the disaster around them. "We fought bravely boy, and the men manned the heavy artillery well," he commented sadly. "How many are dead?" Lorca raised himself further. "How many are wounded?"

Sergio did not answer. The many walking wounded were helping the severely injured; he would take a count for the captain later. There would be many burials at sea. Sergio's anger and sadness intensified as he recalled details of why he was here, on this ship. He spoke his thoughts. "My Grandfather Bernardo was the instigator. He had no right to place our entire family in jeopardy. The King's men were only questioning him about helping his Protestant friend. He could have lied. He put my cousin, Francisco in danger too. And Grandfather did this without a thought for anyone else." Sergio's tone echoed his anger.

"Things happen, boy. Circumstances push them."

"Do you know what my mother told me? Grandfather had yelled at the Inquisitors. He told them that he would not bend down to that Spanish, fanatic King Philip." Sergio's voice escalated. "And then he told them that he would not tell them anything about his Protestant friends. Mother told me that Cousin Francisco had tried to calm Grandfather after the soldiers had left; she knew that they would report him. Hours later, Grandfather was still on a roar."

"What right do those vindictive hypocrites have to question me!" Grandfather had thundered.

Francisco had responded just as hotly, "Because you are one of the privileged and a Catholic, Bernardo, do not think that you are protected. You will be thrown into prison and, no one, not even I, will be able to help you.

You do not have to tell them anything. You are clever enough. Just lie. Humble yourself and his Inquisitors will soon forget about you. Do what I tell you, Bernardo." Francisco had warned him.

Grandfather had ignored him. "What kind of Christian behavior is this?" he ranted. "Because you are non Catholic means that you should be tortured and killed in the name of religion? What nonsense! The King is loco! Imagine, trying to convert all of England to his liking. If that is not madness, I do not know what is."

"Be that as it may, Bernardo, your family will be snatched away and used to bring you to your knees!" Francisco had shouted, desperate to stop the old man.

Sergio had listened to his father, Alfonso, trying to reason with Grandfather. "Think, Father! Try to stop your ranting for a minute. Do not forget that our cousin, Francisco is the Marques Alvarado Cadiz, and a very distinguished admiral. You should be grateful and not put him in such a dangerous position. He has put his honor on the line for you. Even though he is a second cousin, and we are close family, he can only do so much for you."

Sergio sighed, remembering how Grandfather had persisted; then finally his defiance against the crown had put the entire family in jeopardy.

Bernardo was a widower; his wife had died two years past. Sergio knew that was probably why he truly did not care what happened to him. He was angry though, that Grandfather had thought only of himself.

Sergio saw his life now in terms of before being a ships boy and after being a ships boy. Before, he was Sergio Cadiz Scarlatti, carrying his mother's maiden name. He lived in the city of Cadiz in Spain. Both his paternal and maternal ancestors had lived in Cadiz for hundreds of years. His father, Alfonso Cadiz Cruz, and his mother, Theresa Scarlatti Reyes, were born, raised and later married in Cadiz. They had inherited many acres of orange groves that had allowed them to live comfortably. The family was thankful for their way of life; they recognized and acknowledged that they were privileged. They treated the workers who tended their orange groves with great respect, for they were the men who enabled them to live this life style.

Cadiz was an important seaport located on the southwestern coast of Spain, near the Strait of Gibraltar, on a peninsula surrounded by bright blue waters. A wall encircled the city and there was only one land exit. The brilliant, blue green Gulf of Cadiz shimmered in the sunshine most of the year and the warm climate made living there a delightful paradise. The farmers grew fruits and olives and exported fish. Salt obtained by evaporating seawater was also an important export. Sergio was descended from the aristocracy, the founders of Cadiz, on his father's side. He wanted to emulate the career of his cousin, Francisco, the admiral.

Sergio's reflections stopped abruptly when he saw that Captain Lorca had dozed off and then he too, closed his eyes; but his ruminating persisted—at least removing his physical self from the present bloody surroundings. He thought about Columbus and his discovery of America nearly one hundred years ago. Sergio's city of Cadiz had become the headquarters for the Spanish treasure fleet's activities. It was a busy port; King Philip was often there. The King held prejudices against non Catholics and harbored other fanatical, bigoted ideas. Philip thought that Catholicism was the only true religion, causing him to be greatly disliked. No one could tell the reason for the extent of his terrible hatred of the English. Probably Elizabeth, Queen of England had contributed immensely to his anger when she refused him in marriage. His great plans to unite Spain with England had failed.

The Englishman, Sir Francis Drake, had previously made his way into Cadiz harbor and set many of the King's ships afire. This further fueled the deranged King's hatred for the English Protestants. Since Sergio could remember, Spain had been at unrest. The *Inquisition*, as his father called it, had continued for years. Sergio only understood, that if you were not Catholic, one wrong move in protest, brought grave danger down on your head from the local rulers in the King's name. The result was usually torture and death.

Francisco had warned Grandfather Bernardo that he had crossed the danger line, when he showed his blatant disrespect for the soldiers. He had also put his family in severe peril. He reminded them that Sergio was the only male child in the family. He advised Alfonso to apprentice his son out as a ships boy and to move his wife, Theresa and daughter, Isabella to Lisbon, Portugal. Distant relatives would take them in. "They will be safer there, Alfonso. No one would think of looking for them under the King's nose. If Bernardo continues to challenge the King, the whole family is in real danger."

"To rebel against all odds is foolish, not brave," Alfonso reminded his father, repeatedly. There were family members who would suffer; there were more subtle and anonymous ways to protest, Alfonso had cautioned. "Of course we disagree with the King's actions. Nevertheless, you must remember that the King has thousands of supporters who are cowards and bullies like himself. Now the King wants the English to convert to his religion, which is *loco*. Remember that his aims are not strictly at the English, though. In his derangement, this ruler would like the entire world to convert!"

"Well, my son," Alfonso had finally said to Sergio. "You have few choices. You can go to sea or flee with your mother and sister into hiding. I must stay with your grandfather. God knows how long you will have to stay hidden. I know that you are very young Sergio, but I still feel that you will fare better at sea."

Sergio decided that he would sail on a ship as a ships boy and make the best of it. He did not want to be near his home when the Inquisitors came for his grandfather. He knew that being the only grandson, he would be taken and used against his grandfather.

Francisco had arranged for Sergio to apprentice on Captain Lorca's packet ship, the *Rosita,* to learn the basics of seamanship. The packet ships usually ran a definite route in and out of the same ports, supplying and transporting various goods. This sturdy ship would be Sergio's first introduction to sailing. The secret apprenticeship arrangement would be dangerous and undeniably a noble gesture from Francisco to a family member.

Sergio was sent to Captain Lorca, Francisco's old friend. Lorca and Francisco held similar political leanings. However, neither could express their beliefs outwardly. Francisco had remained anonymous, when Captain Lorca advertised throughout the harbor for a ships boy. Sergio was chosen from the many applicants. Not a soul knew that the admiral was involved.

Sergio quickly reported to Captain Lorca, who was a large man of Portuguese and Irish descent. His blue eyes were intense under heavy black brows and he kept his dark beard neatly trimmed. The captain exuded strength and masculinity in his size and mannerisms. He was direct with others and clear in his communicating.

When he assembled the entire crew on deck as the *Rosita* got under way, the captain presented quite an impressive figure in his navy blue jacket with gold buttons and a matching captain's hat. He reiterated the common Spanish sailing laws to refresh the crew's memory, added his own ship's law and then mentioned, that there was a new ships boy. All eyes turned toward Sergio; crew members smirked and inspected him from head to toe. Sergio looked down at his feet and turned bright red with embarrassment.

"Listen carefully, you uncivilized lot," Lorca announced loudly. Sergio is my personal servant and apprentice; he is out of bounds to all! If any one of you motley crew so much as touches him, you will answer to me; severe punishment will follow." Then he lied by threatening, "The boy is my nephew by my sister's first husband and is family." He thought the crew would never be able to decipher that statement. "He has been put in my care, and God help anyone who forgets that!"

Sergio was not sure what all of that meant, but somehow, he felt safer for the captain saying it to the rough crew. Later, Lorca was stern with him. "You will receive no personal favors from me, boy. The crew is a mean lot. You are a young boy, innocent in the ways of men's carnal nature and I wanted to warn you. I am sure you comprehend some of what I am telling you, don't you?" Sergio nodded and thanked him. Although he was not completely ignorant of what the captain was trying to convey to him, he was still naïve in the lustful habits of the crew.

The *Rosita* was a larger packet and the Lisbon Shipping Company who owned her, assigned her routes that were more distant. Sergio was baptized in the ways of the sea during that first year. He learned much about ship restoration while watching the crew repair the *Rosita* at sea. Each man used his own tools. Sergio's ship vocabulary expanded rapidly and he was expected to apply the proper name to every ship's part. The seamen tended not to answer him if he referred incorrectly to a part or area of the ship. Sergio saw members of the crew fashion a new rudder and sternpost right on the ship, using a cloth pattern as a guide to cut replacement parts. The blacksmith made iron bolts, pintles and gudgeons from his forge. The men dove into the ocean, depending upon the season, repairing the hull when necessary, or replacing a broken rudder while under the water. It was advantageous to do ship repair out on the ocean when possible, making it unnecessary to put into port constantly for maintenance.

"The first mate primarily assists me, so I am assigning you to Mister Piper, my navigator," Lorca told Sergio. "I want you to know the rudiments of navigation."

Lorca was pleased with Sergio's progress and acknowledged how rapidly he learned. Sergio was taught to read maritime charts and shown where the popular trade routes lay over the five oceans. He learned of Vasco Da Gama who established the trade route from Europe to India and Asia and the Portuguese navigator Bartholomeu Dias who had rounded the cape of Africa in stormy seas to discover new lands. *What brave men they were*, Sergio acknowledged.

He gained root knowledge of the cross staff and how the wind coursed in different oceans. Mister Piper was surprised that the captain occasionally allowed Sergio to use his personal cross staff. He had never permitted anyone to use the staff before.

Sergio learned that north of the equator a wind rotator revolved clockwise, while south of the equator another spun counter clockwise. This had to be taken into consideration when the ship was sailing in different oceans. He also learned of the *doldrums,* located near the equator on the African coast. *Doldrums* lacked any kind of winds; they could produce *dead calm,* which meant no wind at all. Most sailors believed that this was the most terrible event of all. If left too long on the sea in a dead calm, the crew could suffer thirst and starvation, then death. However, windless seas could occur anywhere, but it was more prevalent on the African coast.

Sergio listened eagerly. He was like a sponge, absorbing massive amounts of information with great relish—the captain encouraged him and praised him. He watched the captain and his first mate closely, observing how a ship was handled on the high seas. The first year, he saw a world that he had never known existed as the *Rosita* put into the exotic ports of the Orient and the cold, blustery harbors of Europe. He saw the beautiful colors of the *northern lights*—the *aurora borealis* from the ship's deck, above the Norwegian Sea off Norway and Sweden. He watched the heavenly colored fingers of light paint sweeping swirls and cascades of tints throughout the sky.

They encountered frightening storms whose gale force winds pitched the sturdy packet ship up and down the gigantic swells of dark waters. The storm rolled the Rosita mightily on the icy, unforgiving North Sea below the Arctic Circle, off the coast of the Scandinavian Peninsula. Sergio thought many times that he would expire with the seasickness; finally, his body stopped rebelling.

"You will be working with my third mate now. The *Rosita* runs heavy cargo most of the time; the owners insist I carry a member to track the cargo and make sure it is properly off loaded and delivered. So my lad, you will be learning about loading and unloading cargo and the bookkeeping, including trade and profits. Sergio was happy that he had excelled in math, so the subjects were not difficult for him. He found the work interesting.

Captain Lorca was a good and knowledgeable captain; Sergio placed great confidence in him. He found the captain to be fair with him and the crew. Cousin Francisco was correct in his assessment of the man.

Sergio lacked friends in the crew, although there were some members who were only fifteen years old. These rough young men were not of the same rearing as Sergio. He simply had nothing in common with them. His interaction was limited to card games or joking together. The captain became his friend, teacher, and mentor. Slowly, the friendship evolved into a quasi father son relationship. Captain Lorca and his wife were childless. She lived in Lisbon and was accustomed to his absences; she had family there.

The following spring, they sailed into the port of Tangier in northern Morocco. Tangier was situated on the North African coast, at the western entrance of the Strait of Gibraltar. Here the Mediterranean Sea met the Atlantic Ocean, off Cape Spartel. They would sail further down the African coast, crossing the equator into the Southern Hemisphere and then coursing to Rio de Janeiro, Brazil. Here Sergio beheld the magnificent *Southern Cross* constellation, blazing in the dark Brazilian sky.

A letter written months ago had finally caught up with Captain Lorca. He called Sergio to his cabin for privacy, then told him that he had bad news. "Your, cousin Francisco, died in February." He hesitated. "He died of natural causes; a heart ailment I am told."

Sergio was shocked and intensely grieved; he stood silent for a minute, after hearing the sad news. "I am sorry for your loss my boy." Lorca patted Sergio on the back. "You and your family could be highly vulnerable now to the King's wrath. Your secret benefactor is gone." Captain Lorca's eyes filled. "I shall miss my friend. God help us all."

Sergio left the captain and walked the deck in grief. He later returned to Lorca's cabin and knocked softly. "I haven't seen my parents or sister since I left Cadiz." He was amazed that the time on ship had passed so quickly. "Letters cannot replace seeing my family," he reminded the Captain. "The last communication I received was months ago. Isabella did not mention my father, or my grandfather. I am sure she did not know anything about their situation. The lack of information has been causing me great anxiety. I must know what happened to Grandfather." Sergio was extremely agitated. "I have no idea where Cousin Francisco has been buried, either. I do not know if they brought him back to Cadiz, nor do I think that my father went to Lisbon to see mother and Isabella. I received only one letter from Isabella; she wrote, that she and my mother arrived safely at my cousins' home outside of Lisbon. My parents would have been tremendously distressed if they had not been able to attend Francisco's funeral. And what of my father?" he said, holding back his emotions. "I must find out. We live in terribly evil times."

Captain Lorca agreed with the boy but remained silent to Sergio's questions. He was concerned about many issues. Had Sergio's grandfather been put to death? The boy's mother and sister had been sent to Lisbon some time ago. Had the King's men been ordered to Lisbon to abduct them? The King would stop at nothing to punish those who defied him. He thanked God that Alfonso had gotten the women out of Cadiz so quickly; even though Lorca was worried about them, he still felt Lisbon was the better place to hide.

The Admiral had told Lorca more than a year ago, that Sergio's father, Alfonso had stayed with his father, Bernardo, and then he too, had been arrested. Lorca had never shared this information with Sergio. He felt it would have been a terrible burden to the boy; nothing could have been done about it. *Had he been wrong?* He thought about that now. He was concerned, that Sergio's father and grandfather were probably no longer alive. Scuttlebutt aboard the ship reminded him that the King was still on his prejudicial rampage. W*hat advice shall I give the boy?* he pondered. The *Rosita* would put into Lisbon in another few weeks. He made his decision. *I will let the boy visit his mother and sister.*

After leaving Morocco, the crew whispered that King Philip planned to make his dream come true. The King called it *restoring,* but in truth, it really was trying to force the Roman Catholic faith on all of England. In his mind, Philip felt that the English piracies against Spanish trade caused him further provocations that he must avenge. Other real or imagined acts of the English only stoked the fires. The King was furious with Sir Francis Drake and his damaging assaults against Spanish commerce. This and other animosities that he held against the Queen of England convinced King Philip, that a direct invasion of England was necessary.

"When I was younger," Sergio told Captain Lorca, "my father took me down to the docks and showed me the destruction that the Englishman, Sir Francis Drake, had perpetrated on Cadiz harbor. I never forgot that. I consider him a very bold enemy, not to be reckoned with lightly. Drake is uncommonly brave for defying King Philip. I still cannot understand how the majority of the people accept the King's decrees. Why are there no uprisings?"

"What would you do, boy? The King's men would cut you down as soon as look at you. There are too many of them," Lorca grunted. "They slither in and out and about like the snakes that they are. But remember, there are other ways to protest, my boy." Sergio recalled hearing that same statement from his father.

The *Rosita* sailed into Lisbon Harbor for supplies on a bright, sunny morning in October in the year of Our Lord 1587. Six years before, King Philip of Spain had invaded Portugal and occupied Lisbon and other large cities in Portugal. Lisbon was an important port and the King often stayed there. He had claimed the throne of the former Sebastian, King of Portugal who was killed in battle in Morocco. Portugal still held its own independence, but King Philip governed. Spanish troops were stationed there, because Philip would not tolerate chaos in what he considered *his city.* It was doubtful that the Inquisitors from Cadiz would be looking in Lisbon for Sergio's family, although Sergio knew that he would need to remain cautious when and if he visited his mother and sister.

The harbor was a beehive of activity. The crew stood on deck, scanning the harbor and watching multitudes of ships at anchor. Sergio overheard Captain Lorca speaking to Mister Piper, his navigator. "I think that blasted lunatic is starting to prepare an army. Look at the troops camped up in the hills over there." Lorca pointed to the far side of the harbor. "Look! Over there! They are loading warships!" Lorca saw that his worst fears were being realized. King Philip was on the move; this time he was serious.

Lorca's blood ran cold. "Curses! We ran right into their trap! We will not get out of this damn harbor," he moaned. "They will not allow any ships to sail. Mark my words, men. Just watch and see. Their warships need to be outfitted with crews. We will not have a choice in the matter. They will blockade the entrance to the harbor. How stupid am I, that I did not see this coming?" He slapped himself on his head in frustration.

"I wondered about those two naval ships meandering around the harbor," Sergio observed. "How could you have known what they were up to? You could not have seen those ships from outside of the harbor."

"Any ship that sails into the harbor that can be outfitted for war will be held in port for the King. We are forewarned! Sorry, me lads. We sailed right into it, I am afraid," Lorca announced. "I am sure the King's men are ordered to commandeer any packet, fluyt, schooner, carrack, or galleon. I am afraid that we are done for!"

"Can I be forced to serve in the King's navy? I am only a ships boy."

Captain Lorca nodded, commenting, "The navy will assume that you are a Spanish citizen, Sergio, me lad; you will be conscripted. You have experience on a ship now; I am afraid that there is no way out for you. Besides, who would you say you were? You are still hiding your identity. You must continue to do that. We will give you a bogus name. You will probably be safest on a ship after all. I'm afraid it is a no win situation, lad."

The King's navy soon commandeered the *Rosita* as Lorca had expected. A Spanish pilot ship stopped the *Rosita* and guided her into a berth where the crew and the ship could be watched.

"I must visit my family. I may never have another chance," Sergio told Lorca. "I do not want to go there one day in the future and find that my mother and sister have disappeared."

"Take every bit of identification from your body, boy and dress in peasant clothes. Depart the ship at first light. Few will be awake at that hour, considering the rowdiness and drinking that goes on here at night."

Sergio listened well. He knew the danger.

"I want you to take this document with you." Lorca handed Sergio papers. "It states that you are on a mission for me to scout supplies for the *Rosita*. You are referred to as the *Rosita*'s ships boy, Sergio Romano. You show them this and you should be passed through." Sergio knew that most ships had to scout for their own supplies, which would be needed, no matter if their ship were commandeered by the Spanish navy or not. *This is a clever ruse*, he thought.

"I visited with my relatives often as a child, so I have the way committed to memory. I am greatly concerned about my family." Sergio was fearful and anxious of what he would find, or not find.

"Be extremely careful, lad. Do not speak to anyone until you glean information of your family's state of affairs. Remember, my wife lives in Lisbon. We have a little place near the harbor; she always knows the climate of the times there. Jose Sandinista, the innkeeper at the White Dove

Inn, just outside of town on the Lisbon road is a close friend of mine; my wife also knows him. He can be trusted to find me, so I may get to you or your family. He knows where I am, always. Please tell your family that."

Sergio was told of a stable outside of town and with his small saved wages, he rented a horse to ride to the home of his Lopez cousins. He arrived in less than an hour at a small, isolated house, off the Lisbon Road. The cottage was almost completely hidden by woods on his cousins' property; it had been the groundskeeper's cottage. It was comfortable and Theresa and Isabella had requested the cottage, rather than living in the large house. It afforded them their privacy.

His mother and sister were at the kitchen door, watching to see who was riding in. When they realized it was Sergio, they fell upon him, weeping and sobbing. "Please, Mother," Sergio cried, "I cannot sit until you tell me what has happened."

Theresa put her hand to her heart and immediately began to relate the terrible story. "Grandfather was taken in for questioning soon after you left, my son. The Inquisitors knew, that despite harsh warnings, he had continued to help others escape from Spain. They questioned him repeatedly about his relationship with these people." She had to stop. No more words would come forth in her grief; Sergio and Isabella tried to calm her.

Isabella continued with great effort. "Oh, Sergio, we heard that Grandfather was openly defiant. He was so angry that he spit on the King's soldiers and he sealed his own doom. Can you believe that—spitting on the soldiers? They put him in chains, threw him in prison, then tortured and maimed him." Now his sister could not continue.

"They cut off his hands as an example," his mother sobbed, "so that Grandfather could never help anyone again. Francisco could do nothing for him; he warned your father to stay away." Theresa bowed her head and breathed deeply. "Your father was Bernardo's son and his blood. He could not leave his father hurt and in prison, so he went to beg for his life. Your father pleaded for him, but to no avail and because your father was tenacious in his begging, nonsense charges were trumped up against him."

Again, she had to stop for a moment, "Your father was charged with conspiring with your grandfather and your father was so angry over Bernardo's mutilation that he attacked two Spanish guards. They threw him into prison and added treason and assault to the conspiracy charges," Theresa wailed. "They later hanged your father. Grandfather lasted until December and left the earth around the holy days. His guilt was so overwhelming that he lost his desire to live. He blamed himself for the death of your father." Tears ran down her face.

Isabella wept as she told him that no one could help Grandfather during his last days. "They allowed his old servant, Julio, to care for him because Grandfather had given the guards so much trouble. Even Francisco was ordered to stay away. We wondered if you had heard of Francisco's death. He died of natural causes, a heart ailment. The Spanish Government took him to Cadiz and buried him in our church cemetery. Thank the heavens for that."

"Do you know where they buried my father? And where was Grandfather buried? What a terrible way to end your life." Sergio thought how much he had once admired Grandfather for living his beliefs. He hated him now for being responsible for the death of his beloved father. "I will never forgive him for what has happened," Sergio told his mother.

Theresa knew that her son would need to mature in many ways before he would be able to understand that it was his father's choice to come to Grandfather Bernardo's aid. However, she knew that it did not erase the horror that had been perpetrated.

"We were too frightened to ask where they were buried, Sergio. They would come and get us." She leaned against him for support. "Such evil! How could this have happened to us?"

Francisco had cautioned Theresa and Isabella not to return to Spain or to question the officials where Bernardo and Alfonso were buried. Prisoners were denied funerals and were buried in a common grave akin to a Potter's Field. Theresa was terribly depressed and ready to join her husband. "I should have gone and begged the King to let my husband have a proper funeral," she moaned. "I hope that he was not so cruel as to forbid a priest to be present." Sergio told her that he wondered if this could be possible, considering that the King was catholic himself.

"Sergio," she sighed, "I am so afraid that anything is possible. We did have a memorial service for your father and grandfather in the church here and Isabella and I felt better. Even though you could not be here, we felt your presence." Theresa was heartbroken. "And later, we said a prayer for Cousin Francisco. You know we could not attend his funeral."

"I will find out Mother, where they are buried if it is the last thing I do on this earth. This I swear. I will take you there myself," Sergio promised, although there was serious doubt in his mind that his mother would ever last that long. "I will find them and put them to rest properly," he repeated.

"Mother dwells on these thoughts day and night; the strain is disastrous to her health. Her heart is broken." Isabella's hushed tone alerted Sergio when their mother went out of the room for a moment. "She has been suffering physically for months. We thought it was a cold, but now I fear that it is far more than just a cold." Isabella confided to him that she did not think their mother was long for this world.

After Sergio's father, Alfonso had been put to death, Francisco visited Theresa and Isabella to express his deep sorrow. He had asked Isabella to deliver a message to Sergio when they saw him again. Perhaps his words could help him in some way. That had been Francisco's last visit.

Sergio now reread the letter and then folded it and put it into his pocket. He ran his fingers through his thick, dark hair, and put his head down to hide his tears. "Remember, should you need me, Isabella," Sergio reminded her, "you may reach Captain Lorca through the White Dove Inn."

"I do remember," she breathed a sigh of relief, knowing that she had a way of contacting her brother.

My Dear Sergio,

In time, the King and his cohorts will forget about you. Follow the seas and in years to come, other matters will fill your mind. Although you will never forget the horrendous deeds done to your family, you must push ahead. The sailing life is a good one, affording you greater independence. It will give you the chance to discover freedom from the tyranny in your own country. Do not let your family name die with you. Keep free from Spain until King Philip is dead.

Yours faithfully,

Francisco

"I do not know if I will be conscripted into the King's navy," Sergio was angry. "I will send you a message before I leave Lisbon if I cannot get to you myself." Sergio kissed the women goodbye and started back to the harbor and his ship, not knowing if he would ever see them again. His throat had closed at the thought. He mounted his horse and rode away.

When Sergio arrived at the ship, Captain Lorca was on deck and greeted him. "What news from the family?" Lorca was visibly upset after Sergio related the story to him. "That bastard!" he muttered of the King.

Lorca had spoken to a representative of the Lisbon Shipping Company, owners of the *Rosita*. He discovered that the company had not contacted the Spanish navy regarding the *Rosita*'s destiny. It was obvious that the Company would like the *Rosita* to leave port, but did not want to take the responsibility of confronting the Spanish. They knew it would be futile.

Captain Lorca was so thoroughly frustrated, that he decided to run. He allowed no one to depart the ship. He could not chance the men drinking to excess, opening their mouths in the tavern and spilling his plans, should any of them have guessed what he soon intended to do. He would hide the *Rosita* among the anchored, confiscated ships and slip out of the harbor. Until then, he had told only Sergio of his intentions. "I will tell the crew later. We will try to slip out of the harbor tonight, on the evening tide. I know that not one of my crew or meself wishes to serve on a King's warship. The moon is passing through its final quarter and it should be dark tonight." It had been chaotic since they had entered the port and Lorca suddenly remembered that they were low on supplies. "The hell with it. We can pick up provisions later," he stated.

The night was dark—there was a gentle breeze, much to their favor. Lorca told the crew his plans—not a man disagreed. They hoisted the small sails in an attempt to slip quietly out into open waters. The two Spanish naval ships blocking the entrance to the harbor meandered about on watch. Lorca hoped that the *Rosita* could slip past them during their roaming. After much maneuvering in the harbor however, the *Rosita* was spotted and Navy scouts sounded the alarm. Lorca had been caught red handed.

The King's naval officers immediately stopped and boarded the ship. Captain Lorca reminded them that there was no proclamation issued demanding, that all ships remain in harbor. The scout ships forced the *Rosita* back into a slip; Captain Lorca and his crew were then officially ordered not to leave their ship. Two soldiers were left to stand guard on the *Rosita*. A fast messenger was sent to the King's naval attaché, the Duke of Medina Sidonia, asking for disposition of the crew and the ship. The *Rosita* waited two days for a reply.

On the third day, a naval officer with his subordinate, boarded the *Rosita* demanding that the crew assemble on deck. The officer was in full dress regalia; his metal helmet reflected the morning sun's rays, while the large red plume springing from his helmet fluttered gently in the breeze. The officer stood rigidly on deck and read the decision rendered in the name of the King. The navy had confiscated the *Rosita* from the Lisbon Shipping Company and directed that it be used as a packet, supply or scout ship in the newly forming Armada. If the *Rosita* came through the fray, she would be returned to her owners. "The owner of the *Rosita* should be proud to contribute to the noble cause of Spain," the officer read.

Sergio and the crew members could not miss Captain Lorca's tiny smirk as this nonsense was announced. "I just bet the company will be proud," he muttered.

"Furthermore," Plume head, as the crew had named the officer reading the decree, continued. "The captain and entire crew are assigned to a Spanish naval vessel, to be designated in the Armada of our King. All men, after official enlistment into the Spanish navy, will be trained in naval warfare during the remainder of this year. There will be a short leave from duty, when approved. The Armada will set sail in the spring, in the Year of Our Lord 1588."

"Well, men, there it is. We are being conscripted," Lorca whispered to those around him. "Bloody hell!"

Sergio decided to ask about ships boys being drafted, even though he knew he should not be questioning anything. At the first pause, he jumped in and with his heart pounding, hesitantly asked, "Excuse me, Sir. Do these plans include ships boy?"

Plume head looked down at him, annoyed at the interruption. "How old are you, boy?"

"I'm nearly fifteen, Sir," Sergio replied in a small voice.

"Fifteen is the magic number. Consider yourself fortunate to sail on a great naval warship in this invincible Armada, and consider yourself no longer a ships boy. You are old enough to crew. Work hard, and learn everything your instructor teaches you." He rolled up the document and handed it to his assistant.

"Captain," Plume head called, looking around for Captain Lorca and when he spotted him, he motioned him over. "Have you understood everything that was read to you? You and your crew will leave the *Rosita* in this berth. Here are your orders." He handed Lorca a sheaf of papers. "You and your men will report to the Lisbon headquarters of the Armada at 9:00 a.m. tomorrow morning, to be sworn into the King's navy. The building is straight down the road from the dock. You cannot miss it," he advised. "My aid will be watching for you and your men. I have all the names here and I will look for each and every one of you," he warned as he departed.

"Blast them to hell," Captain Lorca muttered under his breath.

The stunning news silenced the crew. Reality spoken was harsh. The speculation had ended. They were all to fight in a war that was not their own. The men grumbled, swore and threatened to jump ship. "Listen, men!" Captain Lorca yelled. "Listen to me, you louts!" he repeated louder. "None of us want anything to do with this lunacy, but there does not seem to be any choice. You can take the chance of running, but the command is vicious and will hunt you down and hang you. King Philip is a fanatic and will use any means to reach his deranged ends. I have experience in fighting, so I will take my chance sailing with you mates, rather than running. I think you are a good and well seasoned crew." He lowered his head, shaking it slowly in disgust. "Where would you go?" he questioned, realizing fully now that it had been futile to think that they could escape from the harbor. "We are in the midst of a large fleet. If you jump ship, you would have to cross all of Spain to get to France or Africa. And how would you get there? The land will be crawling with the King's troops," he reminded them. The crew was highly agitated, grumbling amongst themselves while listening to the captain. "Write letters to your families; Sergio will help you. Tell them, that you have been involuntarily drafted into the Spanish navy and will be sailing with the Armada in the spring. I will get them delivered for you. What say you?"

The men swore angrily again and then threw their hands up in defeat. They agreed to stick with their captain. They trusted him. He would take care of them to the best of his ability.

Early the next morning, Captain Lorca addressed his officers and crew and told them to make ready to report to the headquarters for their new assignments. "Why do we have to give them the *Rosita*?" Sergio asked, even though he knew that the *Rosita* was not a fighting ship.

"The crew will be trained to man a larger warship. I do not like any of this," Lorca commented. He signaled Sergio to follow him. When they were alone, he said, "I want you to stay in the background and be silent about your true name when we arrive."

The headquarters building was set back off a dirt road and was a hub of activity. The crew waited at the tavern a few doors down for the captain's return with their orders and more information. Lorca appeared at the tavern a short time later and announced, "We will be trained on a naval warship for a few months. I will be in command. They have given me my own galleon, which is much larger than the *Rosita*, so another crew will be joining ours. The navy will pay you all a seaman's wage—at least we will receive that, by Jupiter! That includes you, Sergio. The Armada has been preparing for more than a year and a half. It will be a few months before we sail. Time for training, I would assume. I cannot tell you anything more except that our destination, as I am sure you all have guessed, is England in the spring." Lorca waited for any comments from the men. There were none.

"We are to report to the *Juanita Cadiz* this afternoon after you all have signed the enlistment papers. I know you were hoping for a carrack, but the galleon is much larger, which is greatly to our advantage. She can be three or four masted and is square rigged with multiple decks. Most times, she will be armed with cannons," he said, looking at all the scowling faces around him. "I am sure that you all know," he continued, "that the galleon is the next step up from the carrack, with more stability and less wind resistance than the carrack. She is faster and can be maneuvered easier, thus better for us. She usually weighs around 500 tons." He paused here and took a great swig of rum. "I am looking forward to seeing her. Our *Rosita* is not large enough to be outfitted with cannons. They will use her for a supply and runner ship. She has been a good packet and served us well. Now we need a fighting ship. Some of you have already been trained on the cannons, but the rest of you need to do that as soon as possible. We can hope she is a lucky ship, men." Lorca called to the innkeeper, "Bring us more rum all around, my good man!" He emphasized this order by banging his metal cup on the table, which brought grins from the crew. They would drink to the best of a bad situation and to safe passages.

They left the tavern, still mumbling and complaining, making their way to the headquarters building. The navy would officially swear them in. Only a few could write their name. Most wrote an *X*.

Sergio was astonished when he heard the name of the ship. Was this a relative of his, for whom she was named? He would ask his mother, that is, if he ever saw her again.

After signing, Lorca's men, along with the crew that would be joining them from another ship, walked back to the docks for a glimpse of their new ship. The crew was directed to wait on the dock. A Spanish official would accompany the newly conscripted officers out to the ship for an inspection. Lorca spoke to the officer and requested, that Sergio join them. The Spanish officer looked at Lorca in disbelief for a moment at his request, until Lorca explained that Sergio wrote well, and that he would be making a list of necessary items needed for the ship.

They spotted the *Juanita Cadiz* anchored in the azure blue waters, with the sun reflecting off her sails; she was a beauty of a ship. Captain Lorca spoke to his officers in hushed, reverent tones. "The gods have smiled upon us, men. We have ourselves a beauty of a grand galleon. She is faster and hardier than the carrack and she can certainly hold her own in battle." He was excited, as he shared the good news. "If we have to be in this navy and fighting, we have been assigned an excellent ship. I see a few cannons, but I would assume they will add more."

"You can tell all that by just looking at her?" Sergio was surprised.

"I have not sailed this many a year my boy, without knowing my ships. Keep your eyes open and your mouth shut."

They rowed up to the side of the *Juanita* and boarded her. Sergio finally told the Captain quietly, "The ship is named after my place of birth and probably *Juanita* was a distant relative. I will ask my mother about the name."

Captain Lorca grinned broadly and told Sergio, "I too, will see if I can find someone who knows the origin of the ship's name. We will keep it to ourselves," he directed Sergio. "This is more good luck for us! Imagine being on a ship named after your birthplace and perhaps, a relative for more luck! Write down all that I say, boy. That officer is watching us."

Sergio's eyes roamed the deck, stopping abruptly upon a large brass bell. From its appearance, he determined that it had just been struck from its mold. The bell was polished to a high sheen and was anchored on the wheel deck, above the captain's cabin. Sergio made his way over to the bell and stood in silent reverence. The date of 1588 was engraved deeply into one curved portion of the bell's wide rim. Evidently, the engraver had been told in advance, that the Armada would sail in 1588. It was a beautiful bell, Sergio thought, *regardless that it was a Spanish bell.*

After the inspection of the *Juanita*, Lorca and his officers returned to the docks. Right then, before the crews went back to their respective ships, Captain Lorca reminded them, "Up until now, the great lot of talk about the Armada's plans has been pure scuttlebutt. Nevertheless, now I want whatever you hear reported to me. The King is keeping quiet and has not issued official plans. Perhaps someone will hear something that has truth to it."

A few days later, the captains of the ships received news regarding the Armada's composition. "We have received information about the structure of the Armada. How true it is, I have me doubts," Lorca shrugged his shoulders. He had not seen the King's seal on the document. He then read the supposedly official dictate to his crew. "The Spanish fleet consists of approximately 131 ships, carrying roughly 8,000 seamen. There are 20 large, three masted galleons, which will be the major ships of the Armada. The largest of the galleons mounts 50 heavy, ship killing guns and carries 500 men. This battle force is rounded out with 44 carracks—the galleons and carracks will all be given added armament and high superstructures above the main deck for close combat." Lorca was satisfied to be commanding the galleon, *Juanita*. They would at least have a chance; her armament had been incorporated when she was built.

Captain Lorca told them, that the Armada fleet would also include four massive, square rigged galleasses. Many of the seamen, including Lorca, felt the galleys were too frail to survive the northern winds and rough seas. The Armada would also include 23 urcas, adequate as a convoy. The urca was a clumsy ship with its three-sail rig and wide bellied hull. Completing the flotilla was the 70 ton patache, smaller, but surprisingly, very efficient. She was a scout ship and carried orders from ship to ship. Most sailors knew, that in battle the pataches gathered to screen the lightly armed supply ships from enemy assaults.

"Now men, comes the big surprise," Captain Lorca announced. "I was notified that approximately 17,000 Spanish soldiers, along with 180 Catholic priests, will be sailing with the Armada." When Sergio heard this, he drew in a deep breath and crossed himself. *Where would all these soldiers and priests be berthed?* Lorca remembered seeing a large number of infantry soldiers around the docks, but the number alleged was astounding and the men found it hard to believe. They knew that not all of these soldiers were in the area. What would these infantry soldiers be doing in naval battles? Soldiers were usually berthed below, not allowed on deck to interfere with the crew's work. The crew recognized that the conditions of living below deck were horrendous. The rotten food, green slime in the drinking water, overcrowding, lack of fresh air and unsanitary conditions usually finished off a large number of men. The plague and other sicknesses ran unchecked.

"I hoped that we would not be carrying any infantry," Lorca said. "When I looked below on the *Juanita*, I had not seen anything that would indicate that."

Another crew member had a cousin who lived in town on slightly higher ground, affording an excellent view of the harbor. He had reported that he could only see about 65 line of battle ships. He saw no large army.

"They must intend to include the carracks in the line of battle ships. The flotilla is lacking in galleons and they are hoping that the carracks can pull their weight in close in fighting," one of the crew had ventured to hushed agreements.

"I agree with you, but I am very concerned over the lack of galleons," Lorca stated. "Perhaps they have not let it be known that there will be more of the large ships with us. They will need at least three or four more galleons to carry that amount of men."

It was a well known fact, touted by seamen who had seen the English fleet—the English warships were faster than the Spanish warships, better armed and carried heavier guns.

Scuttlebutt no longer, the truth was now confirmed; the talk hopped from ship to ship with the speed of lightning. The Spanish Duke of Medina Sidonia, who had stepped in to aid the King, was given complete command of the operation, even though he had relatively little sea experience. He was a capable administrator, but not a seaman. His plan was to sail to Dunkirk, France carrying 17,000 armed soldiers in large galleons. When the Armada reached Dunkirk, they would bring on board another 16,000 Spanish soldiers, who were waiting in France under the command of the Duke of Parma. The Spanish Naval office apparently intended to rely upon the supremacy of the Spanish infantry soldiers as boarding parties while the English ships were being engaged in battle.

"They better have those extra galleons. The carracks cannot handle this large a burden," Lorca announced. "What nonsense!" he roared. "I think we will be very lonesome out there on the high seas, with our few galleons. The English can outmaneuver us all over the water. If they are thinking that those Spanish soldiers can board the English ships in close in engagements, they are crazier than I thought."

"We have all heard the rumor that the English admiral, Charles Howard, is no more experienced than Admiral Medina Sidonia," the first mate put forth. "How true is this?"

"Even if it is true, the English second in command is Sir Francis Drake," Sergio responded. "The King hates him and for good cause. Drake's reputation alone infuriates the King." Sergio reminded them how Drake had burned the shipping harbor in Cadiz. "Drake is a force to be reckoned with. He more than makes up for Howard's inexperience." Sir Francis Drake continued to be a thorn in the side of the King. Even though he was the enemy, the crew inwardly cheered his courageous acts.

There also were rumors that the King's spies had reported that the English fleet contained nearly 200 ships, though this was not confirmed to the King's satisfaction. He was said to be angry because accurate information was not forthcoming. The English had also placed great reliance on their naval artillery skills, thus requiring fewer soldiers for boarding skirmishes.

"Can you imagine?" Lorca thundered. "Inexperienced admirals, insufficient artillery, and infantry on the high seas—and we are expected to win this battle! It is over before we engage. Maybe this is what it will take for someone to assassinate that crazy King!" The crew of the

Juanita would fight for their survival, but never for the King's cause.

After months of rigorous training and the restructuring of the fleet's ships, the officers and crew had not yet heard the Armada's sailing date. They knew that it was the spring of 1588, but no more exact than that. The taverns in the harbor were doing a tremendous business during the lull.

Sergio sought out Captain Lorca. "I would like to ask your permission to visit my mother and sister once more before we sail." Captain Lorca gave his consent, but advised Sergio that he would have to receive final permission from the Naval headquarters, since the crew had been ordered to stay inside the harbor. None could pass the sentries guarding the harbor perimeter without a permit. The crew did not care; they could get to the tavern in the harbor for an afternoon and night of drinking. They finally had accepted that there would be severe consequences if they fled.

Sergio gained official permission to go into Lisbon after explaining that he had family and a sick mother living there. However, his pass was limited to a five mile perimeter of the harbor. *I am safe,* he thought, *the cottage is within those boundaries.* The countryside of Lisbon was swarming with the Spanish, and Sergio expected to be stopped.

"I have my pass," he told Lorca, who was surprised that he had received it so quickly. Evidently the superior officer felt Sergio held no threat of desertion. "I cannot hire the horse again. He has been sold; but I was able to find a ride in a merchant's wagon, which will help me going out. I will have to walk back, but at least I can ride halfway. Bad luck for me."

Sergio had estimated that it would take him approximately one hour out and two hours back to the ship before dark. He had planned a quick farewell. As expected, the King's men were everywhere and checked him twice. He presented his papers and told the guardsmen that he would return before dark. He also told them that he was proud to be part of the King's navy. He thought he would choke.

Sergio came upon his mother and sister sitting under the arbor in the front yard, taking tea and cake. Theresa looked up as he rushed in. "Sergio, my son," she greeted him. "We did not expect you. What a wonderful surprise. I thought you had just been here." A gentle smile transformed her face. "Perhaps I have been dreaming?"

"It has been some time, Mother but, no matter. Here I am," and he leaned over to kiss her cheek. He saw that the shining had gone out of her lovely, brown eyes, and the unnatural brightness in them spoke of fever. Her memory had also suffered. Her dark eyes and sweet mouth were sinking into her face from the ravages of the constant illness. He remembered how Grandmother had looked before she died of the lung disease.

"Sergio," Isabella cried, throwing her arms around him. "How happy I am to see you, brother. Happy birthday to you," she said. "I know it is a little early, but I want to say it to you now." She paused. "You look well. Really, are you all right?"

He looked closely at Isabella and saw that she had grown up quickly. It probably had happened right before his eyes and he had never realized it. She was a young woman now and very pretty, with light brown hair swept back and big, brown eyes that had seen too much sorrow, too soon. She was a woman now. He felt very protective of his fair sister. It upset him to know that he could not offer Isabella and his mother his protection.

Theresa pleaded, "Come and sit with us. Have a piece of cake and something to drink. I wish we knew you were coming. Happy birthday, my son," she wished. "Am I ahead of myself? I think I was, last time I saw you."

"Not to worry, Mama. Wishing birthday greetings before birthdays are good too. I cannot stay long," he told her, although he did not remember her saying anything about his birthday, when last he saw her. She was becoming confused. "I will sit down for awhile. I have little time and much to say." The women sat quietly near him and listened as he explained to them that he had been conscripted into the Spanish navy, with no choice in the matter and that he would soon face a large battle. "There is no place to run, Mama. I am staying with Captain Lorca. The officials have our names; I think I will fare better sailing with him."

"Do not worry about us, Sergio; I beg you. We are safe here with our cousins," Isabella offered. Sergio reminded Isabella of the White Dove Inn again. She nodded. Isabella shyly told him that she was seeing a young naval officer stationed in Lisbon. "He is from an old Cadiz family," she shared. "I consider this a fateful coincidence."

Sergio cautioned her. "Be careful, Isabella. Censor your conversations with him about our family. You could be betrayed if someone revealed that you and Mama were in hiding from the King. Wait until he tells you honestly his true feelings about the King's policies."

Isabella assured him, "Louis is a fine man; his family is not in sympathy with the King. He is in the same position as you are, Sergio. Louis was drafted."

"Nevertheless, please be careful," Sergio warned her again. She promised him that she would take every precaution.

"Mama, our new ship carries the name *Juanita Cadiz*. I felt that perhaps she carried the namesake of someone in our family. Do you remember a Juanita on Papa's or your side?"

"I think so, Sergio. I seem to remember a great grandmother on your father's side," she answered. Her mind began to wander. "I just do not know what is happening here lately. Sometimes I wonder why I am here, in this little house. So many things were left behind in our own house when we fled. The lineage book is there. I do not even know what has happened to our home."

"I will not be able to go there until this action is finished. We will be going to sea soon. One day Mama, I will return to our home to see what has happened and I will retrieve what is left." He leaned over to kiss her, and he felt surely, that it would be the last time. Isabella was right when she had mentioned consumption. "I have to leave now. It will take me time to walk back. I do not know when I will see you again," he told them, as he made ready to leave.

"We will pray for you, my son," Theresa hugged and kissed him goodbye. His mother's frailness in his arms confirmed his former thinking; the lump in his throat silenced his voice.

Isabella came over and put her arms around him. "Brother, I will take care of Mother," she promised. "We will be fine." As he looked into her brown eyes, he saw the tears start.

Sergio left the two women standing with their arms around each other in the front yard of the little, white cottage. He started at a trot because he knew that he would break down and cry. His pace accelerated; he needed to be out of sight. He slackened his stride after a time when he was a good ways down the road.

Suddenly, he was startled by the appearance of two, dirty, ragged men behind him, coming up fast. He increased his speed until he was again at a run. *What more can happen,* he thought. He knew he could not outfight two of them. "Lord above, help me now," he begged aloud, and as he finished his pleadings to the Almighty, he came upon a bend in the road. Just ahead and walking at a fast pace, he saw a small band of the King's soldiers. Sergio blessed himself and all but fell upon them. "Help me!" he yelled to the large, well built lieutenant riding in front of the group on a big chestnut gelding. "I am making my way back to my ship in the harbor. I am in the King's navy; I am being followed by those two who, I am sure, mean me harm." He was winded and could only point back at the two rag pickers who by now, were almost upon him.

"Ho, you two. Halt!" hollered the lieutenant. He spurred his massive horse back toward the two, who now immediately halted. The sight of the soldiers and the big man leading them sent the beggars on the run into the woods, where they disappeared from sight. "I have no time for this." The lieutenant was irritated at the interruption and he ordered his men to continue onward. "We are headed back to the harbor. If you can keep up with my men's pace, you may accompany us. If not, there are two reserve horses in the rear. If you can ride, leap up on one, fall in with us and hurry. I have lost enough time already." The lieutenant urged his large horse forward.

Sergio leaped up on the bare back of the nearest horse, then fell in with the men. He was grateful that he had ridden since childhood. When they finally reached the harbor, Sergio again thanked the lieutenant and made out for the *Rosita*. It was their last night on their own ship. Tomorrow they would board the *Juanita Cadiz*.

The Armada had finally sailed in May of 1588, from Lisbon, Portugal. The fleet was out on the seas only a month or so, destined for England, when heavy gales forced the entire Armada back to the port of La Coruña in northern Spain on Biscay Bay. The crew did refitting to repair the damage caused by the tumultuous storm and the Armada was underway again in July, off Lizard Point, the tip of Southern England on July 29. It had been nearly three months since the *Juanita* had left Lisbon—the crew had yet to see even a skirmish. Small, advance skiffs reported that the main division of the English fleet was seen near Plymouth, England. They were dead to leeward, facing or located away from the wind, giving the Armada a great advantage. The next report came with a barrage of gun fire. The English fleet had managed by great ingenuity, to maneuver to the upwind side of the Armada, acquiring tactical superiority.

As the first English barrage overshot the bow of the *Juanita Cadiz*, Captain Lorca bellowed, "By Jove, what seamanship! Gentlemen, we are all dead unless we make a run for it. We are no match for the English and their guns. We will try to out sail them."

The *Juanita* survived three more encounters with the English and was involved in two battles. The British easily harassed the Spanish ships, avoiding all attempts by the Spanish to bring them into boarding range. Yet, unbelievably, the English were unable to inflict serious

damage on the majority of the ships in the Armada at
that time. The *Juanita* finally reached the Strait of Dover,
the narrowest part of the English Channel on August 6,
and anchored off Calais, France. From Calais, the strait
was about twenty miles to South Foreland, County Kent,
England. Much to Lorca's disbelief, the Armada was again
totally exposed to the English fleet that was anchored to
their west. Once more, the English had the advantage of
the wind.

The Duke of Parma, the King's Spanish Regent in the
Netherlands, was waiting in Dunkirk, France to cross the
16,000 Spanish soldiers over the channel to come to the
aid of the Armada.

The Duke of Medina Sidonia had sent a message to
Parma: *"I am anchored here two leagues from Calais with
the enemy's fleet on my flank. They can cannonade me
whenever they like, and I shall be unable to do them much
harm in return."* The Duke de Parma regretfully did not
even have fifty ships to send. He had less than twenty
ships, mostly disabled.

"The Duke de Parma has to move his troops across
the Dover Strait," Captain Lorca stated. "The Armada
cannot get near the strait to escort the troops. It is truly a
suicide mission for those infantrymen. The English ships
will blow them all out of the water. The King will get his
own men killed!"

The English had sent eight fire ships sailing into the
midst of the Armada, forcing the Spanish to weigh anchor
and flee or catch fire. There was no chance for Spanish
ships to get to the strait to cross over their soldiers. The
next morning, the Armada was scattered in all directions.
The report came later that day that the English had sunk
a goodly number of Spanish transport ships carrying
the infantry troops. The *Juanita* was still off the coast of
France, near Gravelines, when once more she suddenly
came under heavy barrage from the English guns. It was
here at Gravelines, along the coast of Flanders, between
Gravelines and Dunkirk that the battle continued all day.
By late afternoon, most ships were out of gunpowder; what

was left of the Armada was forced north. The English did not follow, but tried to finish off those ships that were still within their range. Charles Howard of Effingham, Lord High Admiral, was convinced that the Spanish ships were so thoroughly damaged, that they would sink before they reached any port.

Lorca commanded the *Juanita* to course toward the North Sea, shouting, "We have to escape the heavy artillery! Head north for the safety of the open seas." The command came too late. The *Juanita* had sustained a number of direct hits from English cannon balls. More shells hit the bow. Several of the crew were up on the high deck when a shell burst directly on them; they were thrown overboard or onto the lower deck, in pieces. Many men were killed; countless more were severely wounded.

Sergio, now watching over his injured captain, thought of his mother, his sister and the many long days that had passed since he had seen them.

Once the cannonading had stopped, the able crew members worked together to repair the ship as best they could to keep her afloat. The men took care of each other's wounds. Sergio stayed close to his captain. His mind would carry horrific images of the bloody annihilation for the rest of his life—the carnage that had surrounded him: blood, death, fallen sea mates tossed about like rag dolls and his captain's near fatal wound. Sergio would never forget that terrible day. He knew that the angels had watched over both himself and his captain. He thanked his Maker for permitting the few wounded survivors to live.

The first mate was one of the walking wounded; nevertheless, he had been able to steer the crippled ship toward the open seas, but he had no recourse except to go north, around the Orkney Islands. The remaining crew managed to pile the bodies of the dead on the aft deck for a mass burial at sea that afternoon. In some instances, body parts of the dead had been thrown immediately into the sea. This had to be done, because of the odor that would quickly accumulate in the heat. They would have a memorial ceremony as soon as they reached a port. The *Juanita*, along with the other surviving Spanish ships, passed the Hebrides near Scotland and located off the west coast of Ireland. However, some of the surviving ships were then blown onto the shoals by the fierce gales of the North Atlantic.

Days passed before the *Juanita Cadiz* limped into the Bay of Biscay, off the western coast of France, for a respite and partial repair. Lorca, still healing himself, held memorial services for those who had already been buried at sea. The *Juanita* then headed toward the port of Santander on the northern coast of Spain. Two days out from the coast, the *Juanita Cadiz* hit thick, gray fog. Navigating was impossible. Before the fog rolled in, Lorca was surprised to count approximately 30 surviving Armada ships that had caught up with them and were headed toward Santander. They had hoped for this. Seeing the damaged ships appearing to join the small fleet, the crew had cheered them on.

"Sergio!" Captain Lorca yelled. "Get up that pole into the bird's nest. See if you can navigate us through this damnable fog." He had already posted the walking wounded as lookouts. Lorca thought it would be ironic if he was killed by a collision from another ship, after surviving the terrible arm wound.

When Sergio reached the nest, he could not see a thing and started to climb down. "Captain!" he yelled, "The bell! We have forgotten the bell! I will start ringing it and keep ringing it until the fog lifts. I hope the others will hear us and ring their bells so we can avoid colliding in the fog."

Sergio scrambled over to the bell, grabbed the thick, hemp rope, setting the big clapper swinging. It hit the sides of the brass bell with such force that the sound echoed sharply across the water, hurting ears that came too close. The ringing accomplished its purpose, and Sergio rang the bell for most of the day. Finally, he descended from the wheel deck. "I need to relieve myself and get something to eat," he told whoever was on deck to report this to the old man. "My arm is ready to fall off."

In no time, Sergio was back at his post to ring the bell. This time, however, he tied a long rope to the clapper so he could ring the bell from a distance, or he thought he would surely go deaf from the noise. The fog eventually lifted toward evening. "I do not think I will ever be able to use my arm again."

The other ships rang their bells and within the fleet, only two ships came extremely close to colliding. The *Juanita* was now approximately a half day out of Santander and the crew knew that they would make it. The fog was sporadic the following morning; the wind picked up and blew the murkiness into pockets. Sergio again resorted to ringing the big brass bell, though intermittently.

The *Juanita Cadiz* limped into Santander, leading the procession, with only her small sails catching the soft wind. She neared the port, announcing herself proudly with her ringing bell. It ricocheted across the calm waters and all remnants of the fog finally lifted. They navigated in close, cast the large anchor, and the *Juanita* settled herself into the soft blows. Captain Lorca stood bravely on deck, his arm tied to his chest. Men who could stand, did so.

Valencia Des Solas, one of the King's aides, was in residence at the port of Santander and heard the commotion. He watched the remaining ships glide in—Sergio stopped ringing the large bell. Des Solas was amazed at the number of townspeople who had come out to welcome the ships.

Des Solas sent a message to Captain Lorca that he would like to meet with him and the bell ringer. Sergio's loss of family members was too close; Lorca felt there was no reason to take a chance. Des Solas might have recognized Sergio's name. He told Sergio to stay on the ship.

Lorca had met with Des Solas later, after he had seen the naval physician. When Des Solas asked who had rung the bell, Captain Lorca casually replied, "Oh, just the ships boy, Sergio." The conversation had gone no further. The captain however, did make a request of Des Solas before he left. He would like Sergio to have the bell. Des Solas agreed, thinking it would be good public propaganda to give Sergio the bell in the King's name for services rendered to his country.

When Captain Lorca returned, he announced, "Sergio, boy, the bell is yours—a gift from the King—to our brave bell ringer!" They both laughed long and loud, but Sergio was pleased. The bell had sung out thunderously, saving many of Sergio's fellow men. The King had nothing to do with it in Sergio's mind.

"I will keep the bell safe for you until you are ready to collect it. I think my sailing days are over, Sergio. Remember my small place in Lisbon near the port, overlooking the harbor. My old woman waits for me. I plan to finish out my days there. I will have the bell mounted near my house and when you are ready, come and get it. Instructions will be left for my family that the bell is yours, should I expire before you return. I am getting too old and I have had my fill of sailing." The captain hugged him; tears clouded his blue eyes. "I shall miss you, Sergio. You are like my own son. I thank you."

It was reported that many other ships with surviving crew had made their way to the beautiful Port of Santander. Sergio knew too well that he was fortunate to be one of them. He vowed that he would never serve on another warship. The flotilla was damaged and broken; there were no plans to resurrect the fleet. Now they needed to make their way back to Lisbon. Sergio decided that he would ship out, from Lisbon to Brazil or to the Canary Islands to avoid being commandeered again by the King. Before he left, he wanted to see his family, although he was concerned with what he would find.

Isabella had wept bitterly when she told her brother that their dear mother had passed away just weeks after he had left. "She died of the consumption," Isabella told him, but Sergio believed his mother truly died of a broken heart. Later, Isabella informed Sergio that she and Louis were to be married.

"But you are still young," he cautioned her.

"We are waiting another year."

"I am happy to hear that, sister. I look forward to meeting your Louis."

"Come with me." She took his hand. They walked into the small cottage to retrieve a package left for him by their mother.

"She wanted you to have this." Isabella handed him a well wrapped, brown packet tied repeatedly with strong yarn. "There is a message with it. Wait until I retrieve it, brother. I hid it well." She went to recover the letter and handed it to Sergio. He sat down to read his mother's small, meticulous writing hand. She wrote in the letter that she and Alfonso had wanted their two children to have the remainder of the family fortune, although it was now pitifully smaller.

Isabella reminded him, "It is terribly sad to see what is left of our inheritance, Sergio. Most of it was used to appeal Grandfather's case. When that was gone and Grandfather's own resources were depleted, Mother refused to allow the Cruz jewelry and part of her own dowry of gold doubloons to be sold. She knew that it would do little good. Father finally agreed with her, that you and I should have the remains of the family inheritance, so they secreted away what they could for us. I have other jewelry and family heirlooms that I will keep should we need it sometime later." He reminded her that they still had the groves and the house in Cadiz.

"I would rather have Mother and Father here with us." Isabella broke down, weeping. "How I miss them both." Sergio kissed his sister's cheek.

"I will be shipping out as crew member within the next few days on a Brazilian exploratory ship. I want to leave the country until things calm down. Never again will I sail on a warship for a tyrannical King, or for anyone else."

Isabella embraced him. "Even though I will miss you, brother, I feel it is the safest thing for you to do. I will stay here in Lisbon with our cousins. Once we announce our engagement, Louis' family has asked me to stay with them. I would have you meet him, but he is presently out on maneuvers. Louis would like to leave here too, and journey to the New World in the future." Sergio nodded his head.

"Please take my inheritance and hide it in a safe place," he said and handed the packet back to her. "Promise me one thing, Isabella. You will not leave Lisbon until I see you again. I will do my best to put in and out of Lisbon. I do not want to find you gone without a trace. Please promise me that, sister," Sergio urged.

"I will be here, unless something unavoidable transpires and I have to flee. I will leave a message for you at the same place that we had arranged before." She handed him a slip of paper. "Here is Louis' last name and address. I have written down his family's address too."

Sergio would sail on trade ships first as crew, then working himself to second mate, then first mate. His friend, Tomas, who he had met when they crewed together both on the *Rosita* and the *Juanita*, sailed with him and the two became as brothers. Tomas was a very large, muscular man with dark hair and dark roving eyes that saw all. He was kind and gentle unless he noticed abuse around him, and then he reacted, sometimes violently against the abuser. Whenever Sergio was in Lisbon Port, he visited his sister, but never took his inheritance. He knew that he would need it in the future.

In time, Sergio had put into Lisbon to give his beautiful sister away. Isabella married her Louis; Sergio was thankful that his sister was happy and with an old, well to do family who loved her. How proud he was to lead her down the church aisle. He deeply regretted that neither of their parents was there to share in Isabella's happiness.

"Why are you smiling, Isabella?" Sergio asked her as they stood in the rear of the church before the music sent them down the aisle.

"My Sergio, my little brother—what a handsome man you are." She glanced at his tall, slender but muscular body. "It is hard to believe that skinny little boy who was all arms and legs and big brown eyes grew into you." She reached up and smoothed out his dark, unruly curls. "We must find you a wonderful woman to marry, so that you will know the joy that I have." She turned to listen to the music. "It is time to begin."

Two years after her marriage, Isabella delivered her first son, Fernandez, and Sergio became an uncle.

King Philip died a few years later, and a quasi peace reigned, but Spain declined. Now, with the new King in residence, Sergio longed for a chance to sail on the Spanish discovery and trade expeditions. Eventually his goal was to secure a ship of his own.

When Sergio was still free because of the unsettled life he led, he sent a letter to the naval attaché at the King's court. He had waited to do this for a number of years after the death of Philip II. He wanted an appointment as an officer in the Spanish navy, then onto a Spanish exploration ship.

Captain Lorca had kept meticulous records of Sergio's voyages. The records, along with Sergio's logs, opened the doors with a glowing report of his seamanship, detailing his experience over the past years. The captain had kept in touch with Sergio through letters for those years. Sadly, Captain Lorca had passed away a short time before. His wife sent the Captain's records on to Sergio.

Not long after, Sergio did receive his officer's commission.

What was erased from the records was Sergio's sympathies to the plight of falsely charged political prisoners whose fate was already sealed. Many of Sergio's previous voyages had been with the network of captains who identified with his beliefs. They had hidden escaped, falsely accused prisoners on board ship and dropped them in foreign cities.

During this time, through different avenues, Sergio was able to gain information of the location of his father and grandfather's final resting place in Cadiz. Sergio took his first leave from the navy, after his ship put into the port of Lisbon. The ship would be idle for two to three weeks.

Knowing this, a scheme had formed in Sergio's mind. He planned to accomplish a number of things, among the most important tasks: he would have his mother's body exhumed from her Lisbon grave to rebury her in Cadiz, he would travel to Cadiz to see what had happened to his father and grandfather, and he would attend to the old family home. He solved the matter of traveling to Cadiz by convincing his superior officer that they could run cargo from Lisbon to Cadiz, while their ship lay idle in the Lisbon harbor. He told his superior, "It will make money for the King's coffers, if we can run cargo to Cadiz and then return to Lisbon with a load."

He had worked on the ruse of the cargo plan for a month, before the navy was convinced. Then they too, thought it a good idea. He had already contacted a company in Cadiz and its affiliate in Lisbon who were interested in a shipping price below market.

If Isabella and he had to travel overland, it was 218 miles from Lisbon to Cadiz, along the Iberian Peninsula—it would be risky, at best. There was a trail, but it was reported to be full of highwaymen and pirates who put in from the Atlantic Ocean. He went to the home of Louis and Isabella to tell his sister of his plans. "I am satisfied that I was able to convince the navy to make this run, and I can use the ship and a light crew, too," he told her.

Isabella took him to the cemetery in Lisbon where their mother had been buried and they made plans to have her exhumed and laid in a new casket for travel. The administrator of the cemetery agreed to do this. He would bring the casket to the dock and load it on the ship in one week. All would be in order and ready to sail from Lisbon the following week.

When they docked in Cadiz, the ship would be anchored for a week with a skeleton crew, who did not mind at all spending time there. Sergio had rented a horse and a larger carriage to carry their mother's casket to Saint Michael's cemetery.

Sergio had written two months previously to Monsignor Loma of Saint Michael the Archangel Church—the church of Sergio's childhood in Cadiz. He had explained the family situation and had asked for the prelate's help in finding where his father and grandfather had been buried.

Monsignor Loma had looked into the matter and through a letter advised Sergio, that the King in his fury had done a cruel and despicable deed. He had buried the two Catholic men in a common plot of land, where the paupers, criminals, and murderers were interred. The land was not holy ground and their plot of earth had not been blessed by a priest. No other holy man had attended the burial.

When Sergio found out, he thanked God that his poor mother never knew while she was on the earth. He had been fortunate that his father and grandfather had been interred together and that the Government records had indicated the names and grave numbers. Identifying them would have been impossible otherwise. There were numerous, unmarked mass graves, showing the King's tyrannical depravity by his disrespect for the dead.

"What a cruel, heartless deed the King has done," Isabella could hardly speak.

"I know," Sergio said, putting his arm around his sister. "Now we can have them buried properly; we will have a priest this time," he assured her. "I am happy that they all will be together at last."

Monsignor Loma had also written in his letter to Sergio, that he would help in exhuming his father and grandfather from the ungodly place where they had been buried, outside of Cadiz.

The Monsignor would petition the Government in Louis' name for permission to exhume the bodies of his in laws and bring them to the church for burial. The prelate soon discovered that none of the Government workers really cared who was asking for exhumation. Sergio knew that this would take a number of weeks to accomplish. He was relieved that he had requested the Monsignor's help two months prior.

Finally, the second letter had arrived from the Monsignor that the exhumation had been completed and that the bodies would be in caskets at the cemetery. The caskets would be taken into the church on the date of Sergio's arrival. On that day, he and Louis carried Theresa's small coffin into the church and placed his mother beside her husband, Alfonso, and her father-in-law, Bernardo.

Sergio prayed for his parents and asked God to help him forgive what his Grandfather Bernardo had done. It was some comfort to him, knowing that they would rest together in the beautiful cemetery next to the church. They prayed for his Uncle Francisco, who was already buried there. Sergio and Isabella could visit the cemetery whenever they were in Cadiz.

Later, in their rented carriage, they drove past their old home near the church and found it still standing, although in desperate need of repair. The orange fields behind the house held trees dry and broken from lack of care. Isabella wondered if the trees would ever grow and produce fruit again. Sergio and Louis stepped out of the carriage and walked into the open house. Isabella stayed in the carriage, too saddened to look into their childhood home. The entire house had been vandalized, stripped clean; even some of the decorative ceilings had been ripped down. Sergio and Louis stood in the doorway, upset, but not surprised.

"Sergio! Isabella," someone was calling. A figure came running across the fields. Sergio recognized Antonio, the son of their father's business partner, Joseph, who had passed years ago.

"Good lord above," Sergio exclaimed hugging the man. "Antonio, how are you?"

"I saw your carriage and could not believe it was you and Isabella. I knew you would return one day, when you could. They have destroyed your beautiful home, Sergio." Antonio was upset. He turned to acknowledge Isabella, still in the carriage. "The soldiers came looking for the rest of your family after they killed your father. You were all gone. They ransacked the house and stole all that was left. My wife and a few of the other men still here, had fooled them. We had a feeling that they would come for you. We went into the house before they arrived and carried out anything important that we could. We have it stored in Guido's old shed, down the hill, behind the barn."

"Heavens," Isabella stepped down from the carriage and fell upon Antonio, weeping. "How kind you are to look out for us. How can we ever thank you?"

Sergio was stunned and at a loss for words. "Thank you, Antonio. Please know that we cannot begin to tell you how much we appreciate all of your help. I will have the contents that were rescued from the house sent to Isabella and I will arrange for the groves and the house to be sold. Thank you again for your kindness."

"Come and have something to eat," Antonio invited, and they sat together in the back yard of his home and ate together. Guido, who had managed their orchards, joined them.

It was difficult for Sergio to imagine that the Church had acknowledged the late King Philip as a good Catholic. He could not fathom why Rome had not excommunicated him for his heinous deeds. Then he realized the power of gold, along with the distortion and greed of men who hid their wickedness behind a religious facade. Moreover, it would seem men are men, be they priests, or the Church hierarchy itself. Thenceforth, he would remember that it is the human element that distorts the good in all religion, powerfully driven by man.

Sergio was becoming restless, and in time his yearning to explore the New World became almost obsessive. He read Henry Hudson's findings again and learned that the Dutch were making inroads into the New World, claiming new regions not only for themselves, but also for England. He requested a commission on a Spanish ship sailing to the New World. He had not forgotten his sister's words about leaving for the Americas, but he wanted to be there first, to welcome them. He knew neither of them would ever return to Spain to live.

Tomas gave him some advice. "Hold your tongue, Sergio, and your temper. Relay your sailing experience to the attaché and that you are from the town of Cadiz.

Mention to him the honorable award of the bell given to you by the King."

"Wouldn't King Philip be turning over in his grave if he knew to whom he had accorded the honor?" Sergio laughed, and Tomas howled with him.

"Use Des Solas' written recommendation," Tomas reminded him, "to lend an element of credibility." He laughed again.

Sergio would sail on a Spanish exploratory ship coursing the ocean routes, charting maps and becoming knowledgeable in many areas of the world, while waiting for his own ship to command. His goal was to sail to the shores of the New World of the Americas, explore the area and make ready for his sister to join him.

May 1614

> Having proven myself, the Spanish Government has finally given me command of my own ship. I have named her *Theresa*, in honor of my dear mother, who will surely look down upon me. I will follow the route of the Englishman, Henry Hudson. The English and the Dutch are still settling this area, and they desire further firsthand information on these new findings. The Spanish as well, seek further knowledge of this new land. My ship should be completely loaded and ready to sail within the next few weeks.
>
> *Sergio Cadiz Scarlatti*
> His personal diary

Within those prior weeks of sailing, Sergio had made his way to Captain Lorca's small house near the sea to collect his bell. He had rented two sturdy mules and a large cart to move the bell. He intended to install the big bell on the deck of the *Theresa*, putting his own mark on his ship.

When he reached Captain Lorca's house, an old man answered the door. Sergio introduced himself and told the old man, that he knew the captain had passed away and then offered his condolences.

"I am Alvaro, Fernao's brother."

Sergio looked at him, standing in the doorway, not understanding who Fernao was.

"Captain Fernao Artur Lorca—my brother," Alvaro repeated.

"I am so sorry. I never knew his first name. As a matter of fact, neither did I know his middle name. I do apologize, again." Sergio was amazed. "He and I became very close in the many letters that we had exchanged, but he had never mentioned his true name."

"Well you know the captain was Irish and Portuguese. Our Irish mother gave him Artur, and myself, Conan as middle names. My brother was the elder. My Portuguese father gave us our first names." Alvaro smiled, remembering past times. "The captain told me to look for you. He was a very old man when he died."

Sergio remembered telling the captain the last time he had seen him, that he would live as long as Methuselah. Even though it had been some time since the Captain had passed, Sergio found it difficult still, that his beloved friend had crossed to the other side. "I am so sorry that he is gone and that I will not see him, just one more time." Sergio's voice quivered. Good memories quickly flashed across his mind and hot tears assaulted his eyes. *Fernao Artur Lorca—how they would have laughed over that. No wonder he never told anyone.*

"And Captain Lorca's wife?"

"My sister-in-law, Anna died a few months after him."

"Again, my condolences." Sergio felt badly. "I wanted to thank her again for sending me all the documentation that Captain Lorca had kept. It was most helpful."

"You have come for your bell? I dug it up after my brother died and stored it in the old shed. He was so concerned when he hid it for you, that he buried it. He knew that the King and his soldiers would never find it."

"I cannot thank you enough for doing this," Sergio told him.

"He left you something else, Sergio. You know he spoke of you so often. You were like a son to him."

Alvaro came down from the upstairs of the small house with something wrapped in a large cloth and handed it to Sergio.

"What is this?" He opened the bundle to find Captain Lorca's cross staff. Sergio was beset and could not speak; the lump in his throat prevented any sound of his voice. "Dear god, this was most precious to him. I wish I could thank him." Sergio had to sit down for a few moments to compose himself.

"Oh, I think he knew how much you would appreciate this gift. He is probably looking down right now. We will go out to the shed for your bell. It has been taken apart, so it is easier to manage. I will help you load it." Sergio thanked him for his help and for keeping the bell.

"Before he died, we had quite a conversation about you," Alvaro mentioned. My brother said to ask you one question. *Do you intend to continue carrying any miscellaneous cargo?"*

Sergio smiled and nodded; he knew exactly what the captain had meant. Politics still ran the country, and although the present monarchy was nowhere as fanatical as King Philip had been, many were still being unjustly accused.

"*Good.* He said if you said yes, to tell you *good.*"

The last time Sergio had seen the captain, he had told him that he was planning to sail to the New World—Lorca had said, "How I envy you, son, taking your ship to the New World. Ahhhh, if only I were ten years younger, even five." They both had grinned. "If we never meet again, Sergio, take care of yourself." Sergio was not sure what Lorca's admonition meant at that time, but he decided he would be extra cautious in all things. He hoped the advice was not a bad omen.

Alvaro and he packed the bell and the cross staff in the wagon and Sergio departed.

In June of 1614, the *Theresa*, a Spanish exploratory ship, with Sergio as captain and Tomas as first mate, carrying a full crew, sailed out of Lisbon harbor with a cargo of various items for the savages in the New World.

"Promise me that you will bring me something unusual from the wilderness," Isabella had requested as she hugged her brother farewell.

Now he watched his sister and her husband waving goodbye from the dock. Louis held their elder son, Fernandez, and Isabella held their son, Francisco, named after their cousin, the admiral. Sergio knew that he would be back for the little family; when, he did not know.

As Sergio set sail, he whispered, "Holy Mother, thank you," and he looked at the deep, blue sea, which would show him her many moods in the month ahead. Finally, he was captain of his own ship; he smiled, quite pleased with himself.

Near the end of the voyage, Sergio was thankful that other than some sporadic squalls, this sailing had been uneventful, almost as though the gods had smiled upon the *Theresa*. They made landfall; Sergio stood on the upper deck searching the near horizon. He spotted an island and to the south, he spotted another, shorter island. Were these the two islands Hudson had seen that were noted in his log? It was then that the weather quickly changed; the sea became rough, the wind picked up and conditions worsened rapidly. Sergio gave the crew further commands, then hastily went to his cabin to retrieve the ship's log. He had only written a short paragraph and had intended to add more.

Sergio heard the men shouting. He grabbed the log, wrapped it in its oilskin, and hurried to the deck. He saw that the men had downed the sails quickly. "Tie yourselves in," Sergio yelled to the crew. "We do not want anyone washing overboard." The men immediately tied long ropes around themselves and fastened the ropes to sturdy parts of the ship.

July 17, 1614
Log of the Theresa

Landfall made this date in the same area Hudson had explored. We encountered some squalls, but otherwise the trip was uneventful. Closing in on land and we have encountered a heavy squall line—weather becoming more violent.

The wind howled like a banshee, and the rain came down in sheets. Tomas shouted over the wind to Sergio, "We have to get out of this open water. We need to maneuver into the inlet of the larger island. The wind and rain are too heavy; I do not know if we can avoid those rocky boundaries on either side."

The first mate could not hold the rudder steady—the *Theresa* was carried toward the rough, swirling inlet, out of control. Suddenly, a great sound emanated from her bowels. A low moaning came from her insides, likened to a death knell, and she became rooted on a bar. Someone yelled, "A bar! We have hit a sandbar!"

A giant wave mounted high and crashed mightily over the *Theresa*; churning waters mixed with sand tore through her hull. Another gigantic wave followed, washing over the ship and with a tremendous lurch, she broke free from the tip of the bar. The *Theresa* hit the shallows as she washed into the inlet and the rocky bottom ripped a large hole in her stern, flinging men around the deck and into the water. Sergio remembered yelling, "*Santa Maria, we have hit the shoals.*" The last thing he saw through the sheeted rain was a sandy beach, then all went dark.

CHAPTER FOUR

New Landings

1614-1625

The summer darkness does not descend until almost nine o'clock, so there is time before retiring for stories around the fire. The old Iroquois storyteller manages to sneak in a few tales for the delighted children.

Sergio regained consciousness two days later. The bright, morning sun shone warmly on his face and he thought that surely, he was dead and in the afterlife. Fear kept his eyelids glued shut.

"How are you, young fella? We thought you were a goner." A gruff voice was near his ear. Sergio was in a dark tunnel and so disoriented that he did not understand. Could this be God speaking to him?

He forced his eyes open, trying to focus on a large blur standing over him; the pain in his head was ferocious. It took him another minute before he was able to make some adjustment to his surroundings. He blinked hard. Someone was sitting in a chair by his cot. His eyes made out an aged face bent over him. The man spoke with a strange accent, and he was difficult to understand. *I am fortunate*, Sergio thought, *that I have some knowledge of the English language.*

"Where am I?" Sergio croaked.

"You are on Long Beach; tis a barrier island off the coast. We pulled you in from the sea during the storm two days ago. You caught the beginnings of a nasty nor'easter. You suffered a bad whack on the head and you were water logged. We were concerned that you had swallowed too much seawater, but I guess we did get it all up. Rolled you back and forth over that there barrel," the old man said, nodding towards a huge, empty drum. "This here is our whaling camp. We stay here on this island during the warmer months, but a few of us hardies live here all year. Captain John Stephen Weber is me name," he announced, pointing proudly to himself. "Call me Captain John, or Captain Weber, or just plain John. Whatever suits ye. You were lucky that the ocean had warmed up. The sun is out now; thank the Almighty. We have had rain and cold for the past days. That was a nasty one, that nor'easter; stuck here, that it did."

"What of my men? What of Tomas?" Sergio sat up too quickly. He fell back onto the blankets; the room spun, and his stomach churned. Looking around, he saw that he was in an old hut like cabin, lying on a cot. Warmth emanated from the squat, brick chimney with its long pipe sticking through the roof for ventilation. Amazingly, the sun had managed to penetrate the window cut by the side of his cot to add light and more warmth to the little hut.

"I will stay here forever until I wake up from this terrible dream," Sergio decided. He did not want to move.

"Thirteen of your men made the beach. They washed up on shore after your ship tore apart on the shoals in the inlet." Captain John gestured north. "Your friend Tomas is a tough one. He managed to make the beach without help. He told me that there was a crew of eighteen, plus you two. That makes twenty total. You have seven dead, and six of the dead have floated in." Sergio turned his head wanting to hear no more. He did remember though, that the weather had turned bad so quickly that within a very short time the *Theresa* was out of control.

"We saw your ship foundering out there and we went up the beach a piece to see what we could do. From what we could figure after seeing that tear in her hull, we were sure that she was hung up on the end of that close in bar. That storm must have extended the bar. The wind and wild water dragged her and rocked her off the sandbar, then washed her onto the shoals. She never had a chance and left a trail of timber and men in the water. By the time my friends and I got to you, pieces of her timber and some wrapped cargo were riding in. The wind was still blowing and sheets of rain made it hard to see. Your men swam hard and were tossed up on the beach like rag dolls by the waves; that they were. We dragged you out of the water and stayed near the wreck a spell, until we were sure you were all right and all your parts were working. Then we carried you here to get you to shelter. Not much left of your ship," he observed.

"Where are the bodies?" Sergio swallowed hard, trying to release the lump in his throat. He still could not understand how the storm had come up that quickly. Was there anything he could have done to prevent the deaths? He offered a prayer of thanks for all who were saved. Seven of his men were dead though; one was still missing. *They must all have a proper burial.*

As though reading his mind, Captain John told him, "Storms come up fast here. Nothing you could have done to avoid that nor'easter—big ones, those ocean storms." John shook his head. "The sea will give up the last body. I will send my friends to search the beach to see if they can find him, now that the rain has stopped. You can be sure we will give the dead a proper send off. I promise you that. God smiled on you, my boy. We pulled you in last." The captain got up and carefully examined the large wound on Sergio's head. "You took some crack on your head."

"How can I thank you?"

"Just get well. We were glad to help."

"Could you ask Tomas to come in, please?" Sergio needed to see his friend. He lay quietly, lost in grief, ruminating, wondering if he could have kept the *Theresa* away from the inlet's shoals. He was overwhelmed and just wanted to lie in the quiet warmth of the cabin and the morning sun. He did not want to think what lay ahead. He did not hear Captain John come back until he spoke again.

"A large piece of your mast washed up with a ship's bell tied to it. Know anything of that?"

Sergio shook his head, yes. He glanced past the captain and spotted Tomas's huge shoulders filling the doorway; his head was wrapped in a red bandana.

"Yo ho, Sergio my friend! Thanks to Jupiter, you made it. Your bell brought us good luck." Tomas grinned, flashing his white teeth and contagious smile. He leaned down and hugged his friend.

"Tomas my friend. You had a good swim I presume?" Sergio asked. "The water temperature suited your gentle nature?" Tomas rolled with laughter, long and loud, helping to give Sergio the impetus and courage to move forward.

Sergio had done everything correctly and not one of the crew blamed him. Every man that sails knows that he is placing his own life in jeopardy. He does not put blame on another, when an act of God occurs. This was the unwritten code.

After the burials, all but two of the surviving crew ventured further inland. They were firm in their decision to walk along Indian trails the one hundred miles or so north, to the newly settled Hudson River Valley area. The small band hoped to sign on to a ship at the New Amsterdam port and return to Europe.

"I think this a very foolish move, men," Sergio had told them. "You know nothing of the dangers, nor can you imagine the animal predators lurking in the woods, hostile Indians ready to scalp you, and who knows what. You are ignorant of what lies in wait to kill you before you cover a short distance. It is unfamiliar territory," he repeated. The men left anyhow. Sergio was concerned, but he could not stop them.

"Those loggerheads have made their minds up," Captain John reminded Sergio. "They are adult men. They ain't children. I agree that it is a bad decision, but they need to take that burden on themselves."

Basel and Big Red, two of the crew, stayed on the island with Sergio. He was thankful that they remained with him and that he and Tomas were not the only crew members left on Long Beach.

July 22 1614
Final Log of the ship *Theresa*

The ship's log was saved. I make this final entry to close the log of the *Theresa*, now in pieces, after she hit a bar and then foundered on the rocky bottoms of the northern inlet of this island, called Long Beach. The *Theresa* was a good ship and served us well. Seven of my crew drowned or were killed by falling timber. We have managed to save a small amount of cargo for trading. The shoals that surround this inlet spare no ship. From this time forth, I will write in my own journal.

Sergio Cadiz Scarlatti
Captain of the *Theresa*

Captain John Weber sat on his makeshift wooden chair, his pipe in his mouth, sucking on the empty stem. He told Sergio and Tomas of his explorations over the area, traveling on Indian trails well over one hundred miles. "Yes, Sir, me boys," he coughed and then grinned, exposing a gap in the side of his mouth, which once had housed a tooth. His weathered face was worn like fine leather; a once white, shabby captain's hat of sorts was perched on his head. Sergio saw Captain John's shaggy, gray dome as reminiscent of a wooly ram. His thick hair was somewhat unshorn and it curled over the back of his collar. Observing his pleasant features, Sergio thought that he must have been a fine looking young man years ago. His short, gray beard, neatly trimmed around his chin, matched his bushy gray eyebrows, sheltering his very blue eyes. Sergio looked into his wise, perhaps playful, bright eyes. *Probably inherited those from his Scandinavian father,* Sergio considered. The captain was a Swede by birth; he had previously informed Sergio. The Lenape had dubbed him *Blue Eyes Laughing.*

"However did they arrive at that name?" Sergio asked. They both laughed. Sergio noticed that John was extremely clean with his person, and this spoke well of him. He was medium tall, quite thin, but wiry, probably healthy, despite his lean appearance. He was actually a right hardy soul, worthy of note in conversation. He had told Sergio that he was getting on, what that meant as far as his age, was anyone's guess.

Captain John repeated that he had scouted for hundreds of miles, and no one knew the range better than he did. "Yes, indeed," he exclaimed and spat a wad of brown stuff into the nearby bushes. "I have traveled south too, past the entrance to a big bay, then down around a cape with my Iroquois friends. Mind you, traveling ain't easy."

Sergio thought that perhaps this was the large bay that some called the Delaware; explored first minimally by Hudson, then thoroughly by Cornelius Jacobsen Mey, aboard his ship the *Fortuyn.* He also had recently named the cape in that area *Cape Mey*, after himself. Sergio had heard this from his first mate.

Captain John seemed comfortably settled into the wonders and dangers of the New World. Indian friends had led him to the island years ago. "I have no family waiting for me in other places, no kith nor kin," as he told it. "Never was." Any kin were long gone now. He was truly a free spirit. "I have made a number of trips to *Mannahatta*, as the Indians call that island far to the north. Yes, sir, the port is on that island—still in its early years. They call the port area, New Amsterdam, and the New Netherlands area covers all of that range. The region is still more or less in its beginnings." Captain John told them he always came back to his island. "I hold no brook with the civilized world."

August 1614

Captain John Weber, an old whaler of the island, mercifully rescued us from a tempestuous storm that landed the *Theresa* on the inlet shoals. The last missing crew member washed up on the beach south of their camp. We are here nearly a month on this barrier island, mending our broken bodies and weary souls.

After fashioning coffins from wood salvaged from the *Theresa*, the men gave the dead decent burials. Captain John is of the mind that the salty sand helps protect the bodies. I feel that the body does not hold its meaning once the soul departs, the body being only the housing. Others have strong opinions different from mine. However, we all agree that the bodies should be buried and the graves marked properly.

Sergio Cadíz Scarlatti
His Journal

Sergio met Davey, Captain John's close friend. John called him Old Davey most of the time, even though they were both near in age, as far as Sergio could deduce.

"How do Capt'n Sergio," Davey said. He offered a firm hand; his spirited brown eyes looked straight at Sergio. *They make a good pair*, Sergio decided. Davey certainly had an energetic aura about him, and his dark, almost black eyes spoke of his Indian ancestry. His father had given Davey a Danish name, which no one seemed to remember. His Lenni Lenape mother found it too hard to speak, so he ended up with Davey—even his father called him Davey.

He talked continuously, but Davey was interesting and highly informative in his knowledge of the area. He wore a lightweight, tan buckskin shirt of soft, beaten leather; old pants were held up with a sash of sorts; a leather band wrapped around his full head of gray brown hair and a pigtail hung down the back of his neck. His skin, probably a light brown was now burned dark from the summer sun and wrinkled from too much exposure. Soft shoes called *moccasins* encased his feet and a necklace of shark teeth hung from his neck. Davey's bright, clean teeth were truly unusual, especially for an older man. Most men of that age had brown teeth worn down to their nubs. Suddenly Sergio pictured Davey walking down a busy street in Cadiz. He had to stifle his laughter.

Davey told Sergio and anyone else within earshot, "The New Netherlands region covers massive territory, and it would take a good long time to trek through and see the lot."

Davey was native born and he had lived in and around Long Beach Island and *Manahocking* most of his life, working with the whalers. "There are other whaling stations along the coast," Davey divulged. "I visit my friends during the summer. They are not social; but I have known them for many years. They avoid ships near the shore. Very clannish, these whalers. My mother was a Lenape," he repeated to Sergio. "Lenni Lenape means *real men* or *manly men,* or *original people.* They call this land *seheyichbi.* That means *land bordering the ocean* or *long land water,* as best as I can interpret into English."

He paused, collecting his thoughts. "My father was a sea captain from Bornholm, Denmark. Bornholm is an island in the Baltic Sea," he added. "I come from a long line of whalers, so I was told. My father shipwrecked off the southern tip of Long Beach, hunting whales. He and a few of his men made it over to the small, inland village of *Manahocking*, where he met my mother. I was raised among the Lenape and lived with them for many years; learned their language well."

He paused to light his pipe. It did not catch so he put it down. "When I was a young lad, my father left the island and took me with him on a whaling ship that put in a few miles out. We made port in London, where I stayed with him some." He had never been to a big city; he was amazed at what he had seen. "Never did get up to my father's home in Bornholm. Inherited the love of the sea and whaling from him, I would guess. I signed on early as ships boy on a whaler out of London—lost track of my father. Later, I captained an English whaling ship."

"Where's that damned corncob," he muttered, looking for his pipe, which he suddenly found under his chair. "When I was finished with the whaling life, I found one of my friends who sailed his whaler near Long Beach. I wanted to come back to my home in Manahocking. The island was not marked on any map that we knew, but my whaler friend was aware of the island's location. They put me off in a small dinghy with a sail near the northern inlet. My friend, the captain knew of the dangerous shoals and the strong tides in both inlets of the island. He would come no closer. It was a chance I was willing to take. I had to maneuver near half a mile or so into shore, but I was strong and in good health. My father never returned to Manahocking, and I never saw or heard from him again." He knocked the used tobacco from his pipe and refilled it. "Best thing I ever did was to marry Singing Woman; her name is translated from Lenape talk. We have a daughter. You will meet her soon." He grinned. "My wife comes from wonderful people."

Sergio listened keenly, not to miss a word. Davey told him, that he doubted that his mother had any other knowledge of his father and it was so long ago. He told it now almost as a story, a fable, and with little feeling about the entire tale. Sergio noted that Davey did speak English well; English seemed to be in the majority. At least most spoke enough to express their needs. *My English improves the more I speak it*, Sergio noted to himself.

Davey continued sharing his knowledge. "The New Netherlands area ranges south of, and slightly west of the big bay—then north, hundreds of miles. The range encompasses the Hudson River Valley expanse, including *Mannahatta* Island and the port city of New Amsterdam on that island. It is in the best of possible positions to shipping routes."

With this and other information, Sergio realized immediately that *Mannahatta* Island was bordered by the

Hudson River, where it emptied into the Atlantic Ocean. "I now understand how important the port is, being that close to the open sea," he told Tomas.

Captain John shared stories of his many journeys to *Mannahatta* via canoe with the river Indians, as he called them. As best as they could figure, these Indians, known as the Iroquois, were from the far north; they are a small group that has settled in this area. "The Indians know the shortest route to follow. I have charted the passage on rough maps, setting down a well marked course. The Indians laugh at my maps and me. They commit to memory very easily, marking the trails and water routes with natural signs; there were many trees and rocks and land formations along the way."

This barrier island, on which they sat, called Long Beach had a shorter barrier island beyond its southern tip, so Davey informed them. Not much was known of that shorter ribbon of land. Not many visited there. They referred to it as *Short Island*. Sergio had spotted the two islands in his glass before the *Theresa* sank.

"These islands were marked on very few maps if any, that I recollect." Captain John paused slightly as he attempted to remember the history of the area. "I am not quite sure. Indian friends tell their own stories about the beginning. I have little contact now with the outside world. I visit with my whaler friends who occasionally anchor in the vicinity, and I make yearly trips to the port at New Amsterdam. That is the extent now of my wanderings." He stood up to stretch himself and paced a little back and forth. "I explored the region in my early years, but now I find that I no longer enjoy such a rough regimen, traveling for unlimited periods." He sat down and was quiet.

Sergio tried to summarize what he knew of the discoveries in the area. "You know Henry Hudson, the Englishman, spotted your island first in 1609 from the *Half Moon* and writes of it in his log. He sailed past here, south, and saw the large bay, but he was not able to navigate the big bay waters. Hudson's ship was not light enough in her draft—the *Half Moon* repeatedly struck bottom. His navigator, Juet noticed a river flowing into the bay, which Hudson named the South River.

Hudson later sailed from *Mannahatta* Island north, on the North River that he had originally named. However, in a short time the North River was being called the Hudson River. I do not know if Hudson himself did this renaming. Those facts are a little murky. He explored that area further north into a large valley; evidently the valley came to be called the Hudson River Valley, which would be quite obvious. He returned to England and set out once more. His new ship the *Discovery* was funded by the Virginia Company and the British East India Company. His luck turned bad on this voyage. After months at sea, the crew wanted to return home, but Hudson wanted to explore further. The crew mutinied and set Hudson, his son and eight crew members adrift in a small boat, out among the ice flows. Some said that they sent supplies with them, others said not true. However, Hudson was never seen again. Only eight of the *Discovery*'s thirteen mutinous crew survived to return. They were arrested, but none were ever punished for the mutiny. Perhaps they held valuable information of the New World as yet unknown, and had bargained with that information. I guess we will never know what truly happened."

Sergio had studied Hudson in detail. He had read Hudson's navigator, Juet's entire logs of the Hudson voyages. "I guess our Captain Hudson did not fare so well in the end. It is a shame, because I consider him a most courageous explorer."

Sergio collected his thoughts. "Captain Cornelius Jacobsen Mey," he reported, pronouncing each syllable with pleasure, "from Holland, with his ship *Fortuyn* out of Hoorn, Holland, came after Hudson. Mey sailed south from the Hudson River Valley, past here, so I have heard. Mey thought *he* was the first to explore this area."

Captain John laughed, hearing that statement. "The Lenape Indians told me that they had seen a ship awhile ago, and they marked down the letters *Fortuyn* written on the bow of the ship. Must have been sailing pretty close to the shore for them to see the name. I was up to the port last June, so I missed Captain Mey. I heard about his exploration when he returned to New Amsterdam. I cannot understand how he missed the whalers on the island, unless he is not saying. Heard tell he named the inlet where you wrecked, Barendegat, in Dutch, and marked it on his map. Means *Inlet of Breakers* in English. Since I heard that, I have taken to calling the bay here *Barendegat,* too. Then it shortened to *Barnegat.* Down a little further south, there is a large area of bays. Mey evidently sent his men down there to explore. Named the whole area *Eyren Haven* in Dutch, which in English means *Harbor* or *Haven of Eggs*; broke it down on his map into Great and Little Egg Harbor. Good name that is, fitting to the area," he agreed, drifting off in thought. "The whole region is overrun with seabirds, large and small. The Indians harvest eggs down there all the time. I surely would like to get a copy of Mey's mapping of that area. Maybe this year down at the port," the captain hesitated, trying to recall other information he wanted to share."

Captain John then spoke of a place on Long Beach Island itself, called the Great Swamp, south of where they were camped. The Swamp was accessible by Indian trails or sailing on the bay or ocean. "It is an unusual area," he shared. "In the middle of the island, the Great Swamp covers almost two hundred acres. High dunes circle and shield the acreage, which are fed by a fresh water aquifer. Some figure the fresh water comes from a huge underground aquifer that lies under an extensive area southwest of here. The Indians call it the Pinelands; they say that this aquifer extends under the Great Swamp. Some call this huge area the Pine Barrens; it must contain at least one million acres, so it was thought. That is indeed hard to comprehend. The Pinelands or Pine Barrens is densely populated with pine trees, cedar and oak and other species. Over on the mainland, near our village of Manahocking, great red-brown cedar trees also grow profusely and our small lake is cedar colored."

Captain John freshened his pipe. "But back to the Great Swamp. Because of the fresh water, the ground is extremely fertile, allowing a forest of Atlantic white cedar trees to grow on that stretch of land. You can see the forest from the land and from far out on the sea. Wild birds and other animals live there because of the fresh water and it is just like a grand fairy tale realm, but it is real. I have seen it meself!" Captain John was quite emphatic and shifted in his chair. "Most will not believe me when I speak of it."

Sergio was astonished and anxious to visit the Great Swamp. He made the captain promise to take him to this extraordinary place when he was healed.

"To end my information about the Pineland expanse—a portion of the expanse lies just west of *Manahocking*, which in Indian gab means *good corn ground,* and would be the area that contains all those animals that the Indians hunt. I would not think that this is the only area of the Pinelands that contain these animals."

Unrelated to what they were speaking of, Sergio told Tomas, "I need to get to New Amsterdam and find a Lisbon bound ship."

How many times Sergio had said this to him, Tomas could not remember. "I know you need to contact Isabella, but you cannot go to the port until you can travel. Basel and Big Red are leaving for New Amsterdam with the Iroquois," Tomas said. "They plan to find a ship sailing to Lisbon, or as close as possible. I feel that Basel is trustworthy and could carry a letter to Isabella for you."

Sergio was quiet for a time. "You are right, my friend. Basel can be trusted. I will ask him to do me this favor."

Tomas and Sergio decided to stay put on this different, almost mysterious island of Long Beach for a spell, at least until Sergio was well healed. Captain John's shanty near the beach was fine for the summer when they fished with the Iroquois Indians for the smaller catches of fish and hunted the bay marshes of the island for crabs, mussels, clams and oysters. The Indians dried and preserved their copious catches with salt, evaporated from the bay's water, or from seaweed. Other methods of preserving were baking their catches in the sun.

Captain John warned them, "When October comes, you must start moving inland to my shack in *Manahocking*, or as some call it, Manahawkin. I sometimes forget. You are welcome to use this shelter to spend the coming winter. I come and go during that time, according to the weather."

Sometime later, Captain John felt that Sergio's head wound had healed satisfactorily. He took him to visit the large Lenape tribe, along with a smaller Iroquois group summering on the Barnegat bay side of the island to clam, crab and fish. Sergio noticed that both tribes practiced the same regimen in their fishing and clamming. After observing the Indians using their feet to dig for clams in the bay's thick, black mud, Sergio asked the captain if he had tried it.

"Best way to dig 'em up." Captain John winked. "Just has to be low tide, or you will be diving for 'em."

Captain John's whaling friends traveled both south and north from Long Beach, along the Atlantic coast in the bitter, cold months of February, March, and oft times, November. They hunted the migrating giants that swam down from the north, spouting and diving as they skirted the coast on their way to warmer southern waters. They harpooned the whales from open boats launched into the ocean. Captain John stayed in his winter housing in Manahawkin most of the time, but when the weather was pleasant, he would visit the island. He enjoyed the camaraderie of his friends, but felt he now had his fill of the actual hunting of the big ocean game. Now he helped with the processing of these huge mammals.

"Whale oil is an extremely valuable commodity, and that is the reason why these hardy men tolerate the bitter cold winter months camped in their old wooden huts on the beach. They are a tight bunch, and cautious. Too many pirates have stopped on the beaches here, so my friends are very suspicious of outsiders," John finished then added, "and rightly so. They have a crow's nest of sorts, built down the beach a ways to spot the whales and and unfamiliar hostiles who may wander onto the island from the ocean side."

Captain John shared what history had been told to him by his Indian friends, which was not much. "This island and its immediate surrounds have been inhabited by the Indians for hundreds of years. No one is sure exactly how long. Directly across from Long Beach, on the mainland, there is a site which contains a huge mound of clam and oyster shells. This tells us there was a large village there early on. The mound probably measures in size at least 24 X 100 X 200 feet, and maybe more. Some of the shells may have disappeared for various reasons."

Sergio commented to his friend, "I am sorry that there is not much history told, Tomas. There is so much to see, but I guess the Indians record their history verbally; perhaps much has been lost." He was quiet, lost in thought, wanting to see it all. His head wound was healing nicely and he pestered Captain John about the promised trip into the village of Manahawkin. A trip to the Great Swamp was postponed. "Good god, man, you need to heal first. That is the most important thing you have to do. You cannot be wandering all over, until you are well." Captain John tried to impress this upon Sergio.

The Lenni Lenape lived the rest of the year on the mainland in their village. "I am as accurate as I *can* be when I translate. It is difficult converting their talk into English because many things can be said in only a few Indian words." John told them it was Old Davey, who always held the last word when interpreting.

Toward the end of August, Captain John and Davey felt that Sergio was ready to travel further. "We are preparing for an overnight journey inland to the village of Manahawkin. The Lenape should be back home by now from their fishing and clamming. I know you want to see their village and the location of Captain John's winter shack. Do you think you are ready?" Sergio still tired easily, even though it was a relatively simple trek. He was not about to tell Davey that he could not travel. The trip was approximately six miles, usually done in less than two hours. However, they planned to take the entire morning should they need it, considering Sergio's lack of stamina.

"It is too bad that you have no horses," Sergio remarked.

Captain John grunted his agreement. "The Lenape have several horses that they traded from the Iroquois, but are loath to sell or trade any of them. Perhaps at a later date we can see if we can deal directly with the Iroquois."

Tomas, Captain John, Old Davey and two of Davey's trusted Lenape friends would leave the following morning. Tomas would mark the trails well on his own map. He and Sergio would have no guide when they returned to Captain John's wintering cabin near Manahawkin before November set in on Long Beach Island—that is, if they decided to stay the winter.

"You will have to be satisfied to visit the Great Swamp area later," Davey told Sergio. "There will be time to see all of it." Sergio had to acquiesce.

Early in the morning, the accompanying Lenape carried their light weight canoes to the bayside. They launched their craft into the bay, somewhat south of the northern inlet and again headed south on the bay, until they reached the Great Swamp area; then turned west, paddling across the open bay waters. They arrived at an extensive area of swampy lands, heavily laced with water ways. They paddled through the marshy area until they arrived at dry land. They easily lifted their light canoes and left them where the marshes stopped then trekked the rest of the way to Manahawkin following the old, well worn Indian foot trails. They used no maps. The Lenape Indians maintained the well marked trail year round, greatly accelerating the trip.

The travelers arrived at the village mid morning. Sergio was very interested in observing the natives' homes. He had never seen anything like these shelters. Bent saplings were fastened together to make a rounded roof. The sides and roof were then covered with some sort of bark and cornstalks. Dirt was packed around the long rounded sides and doors were positioned in either end. A roof hole let out the smoke from the inside fires. Mats created from cornstalks provided beds and seating. The rounded houses were clean and comfortable.

The bay's salt water yielded bountiful harvests of fish, crabs, oysters, mussels and other shellfish; the inland freshwater rivers and lakes in the Manahawkin area provided the natives with snapping turtles and diamond back terrapins found in the marshes, along with a few fresh water species of fish.

"It is a bounty out there," Davey told them: "Otter, beaver, deer, bear, mink, bay lynx, fox, muskrat, quail, grouse, prairie chicken and wild turkey are plentiful. No starving here," he said. "The fowls' breeding season is always abundant with the eggs of heron, black duck, mallard, railbird, gull and tern, and other birds that I have spotted—but I know only the name that the Lenape use for them."

The Indians told Davey that they had killed elk further inland in areas of thick pine trees. Davey had to explain to Sergio what elk was. "What do you think of that, lads? Elk in this area? I guess anything is possible." Davey raised his eyebrows.

The Lenape were just finishing their harvesting. "Look at those fields," Captain John said, waving his arm over lush green acreage. This is what the Indians call maize, or *mahiz*, which in native gab, means *that which sustains us.*"

Sergio knew about corn. It was also called maize, or in its ground form, *masa* or *masa harina* in Spanish. Christopher Columbus had brought samples back to Spain and it had been cultivated in Spain since then, he told Davey. *The Indians must have been growing maize here for some time,* he thought. Sergio looked out over the expanse of acres and acres of unending ears of yellow maize. "I have not seen anything like this in my travels," he commented.

"I do enjoy their maize soup and their cakes and puddings," Davey said. Sergio laughed.

"This is quite common in our country now," Tomas added, "but Sergio is right. I have not seen it grown to this extent."

"The Indians pound the maize bits or nibblets into meal in a stone mortar, then mix it with water to make a mush. It is a staple of their diet. Come, we can walk over to the other fields and see what they grow there." The captain pointed out different native vegetables to Sergio. "Here are sweet potatoes, tomatoes and two kinds of beans, peanuts, squash, peppers, pumpkins and more."

Sergio looked over the fields and then at Captain John. "I am not familiar with anything except the potatoes, tomatoes, maize and beans. You have to remember, that I was raised with citrus trees, bearing oranges and lemons. Their cultivation of vegetables and herbs is truly amazing," he commented. "I left Spain at a very early age, so I cannot remember much about our agriculture. I do remember different kinds of beans, though."

"The Lenape turn the soil and prepare it for crops, then keep the soil free of weeds through constant watching," Captain John explained. "They are ever vigilant using seaweed leached of its salt for fertilizer. They harvest great schools of herring and oft times King crabs which they break up and plow under, also as a fertilizer. That way the ground can be planted year after year continually yielding bountiful crops."

"I think we will accept your kind offer, Captain John. We would like to use your shelter for the winter," Sergio announced a little later. He and Tomas had inspected Captain John's winter shelter, and were pleasantly surprised. The shelter was more like a small house than the hut Sergio had anticipated. They would return in October to prepare the little cottage for the winter. He knew that he would not be able to make the trip to the port at New Amsterdam before the winter set in. Sergio prayed that Isabella had received his letter.

The group then made their way back to Long Beach to finish out the summer. They had much to prepare to tide them over the winter in Captain John's small dwelling. If they were to use his shelter, wood would have to be cut and stacked, food dried for the winter, and more. The Lenape had offered their help in supplying the men with their winter stock of food. Sergio was still mulling over his plans; however there did not seem to be any other choice.

May, 1615

I find it difficult to believe that we have been on Long Beach Island for nearly a year. The little quarters where we stayed were quite adequate and the Lenape group was very helpful to us over the winter. I am thankful that I am alive and healed.

Captain John speaks much of the group of sociable Iroquois Indians living on a large river about twenty five miles north on the inner waterway.

The large river that he speaks of must be north of here, flowing east to empty into the Atlantic Ocean. Captain John has traded with this tribe for a number of years and has great trust in them. The Iroquois are very different from the Lenni Lenape; John says. They originally lived further north, but he is not sure where. This particular group may have broken off from a large tribe. Captain John has accompanied their traveling group many times to the trading post and the port on Mannahatta Island. It is more feasible for us to go in the Iroquois convoy for protection and timely travel. They will take us next month, in their large dugout canoes, for a price. We will bring the salvaged and stored stuffs the *Theresa* was carrying. Much of the cargo was trading goods, wrapped in oilskins to avoid water damage. We will take what we are able for trading at the port. The Indians will lend us two canoes for that purpose and two paddlers—again, at a price. We still have a large number of stores remaining to trade with the local native groups. We will depart Long Beach in early May. Captain John expects to make the port, which is approximately eighty six nautical miles, within a long day, God willing.

Sergio Cadiz Scarlatti,
His Journal

Davey informed Sergio, Tomas and Captain John, that the Iroquois would collect the travelers on the bayside and canoe north up the inland waterway, exiting at the northern inlet, into the ocean and then paddling north to a small river. "Opposite this river," Davey continued, "there is an inlet, where the canoes will turn out into the ocean and steer north approximately twenty five nautical miles, hugging the coast until they round a small, sandy peninsular. Then they would head out into the open sea a short ways, crossing through the narrows that the Italian, Giovanni da Verrazzano noted and then into the mouth of the Hudson River and the port of New Amsterdam." Sergio could hardly wait to depart.

"The port is heavily populated because ships arriving from London, Lisbon, Amsterdam, and other world cities support it. It is still early summer and hopefully, you will hear from your sister. Let us hope that Big Red was able to get the letter off to her on a ship to Lisbon, or better still, he gave it to her in person," Tomas was hopeful.

"I hope that Big Red and Basel were able to catch a ship to Lisbon themselves," Captain John wondered. "Before Big Red left, I advised him to tell Isabella of a shipping office on the wharf, which holds messages and packages for a nominal fee, but it is well worth it. Big Red will tell her how to address her letter to me, which would be better because I am well known there. I plan to return to Long Beach toward the end of July. A few of the Indian group will stay at the port into August and can bring you back to the island, if you want to stay longer. Let me know what you and Tomas plan to do," Captain John requested.

Sergio glanced at Tomas. "I think we will reserve that decision until we see how things go. But now, we have to prepare for our trip to the port." Tomas nodded his head in agreement.

Sergio commented a little later to his friend. "I think it will give us a better sense of the area." He paused. "Bring anything that holds meaning for you." Tomas knew what Sergio had in mind and he gathered his important items together.

As they prepared to leave for the port, Sergio observed those around him. He recognized how truly beautiful the Iroquois people were—varied shades of black hair, skin somewhat tan colored, with red undertones. He admired their well formed features: large, brown to black eyes, thin, stern lips, prominent noses, and firm chins. The Iroquois men were tall, strong of physique, muscularly slender of build, with handsome and intelligent faces. Many of the women of this particular group were very beautiful. A few spoke some words and phrases in English, but none were truly proficient. Sergio laughed when he heard the few English expressions they had learned. Of course, most of it was cursing. It was humorous though, to hear these Indians speak English with a slight Captain John or Davy accent. Captain John did wonderfully well in their language and Sergio admired his grasp of such a difficult tongue. Davey was raised near this small group of Iroquois as well as his Lenape tribe and he had the last word when they struggled with a meaning, or an understanding of a communication of many words.

Most canoes sat two paddlers and passengers. The men paddled strongly and swiftly for extensive periods. The trip so far has been easy and enjoyable for us, Sergio noted, thankful that he did not have to paddle. As a passenger, he was able to observe and appreciate the countryside from their big swift canoes. They are skilled and experienced travelers. As I watched them, I noted how each is responsible for his own contribution to the larger group. The older children were called upon to act as lookouts for debris in the water even when riders were transported in front seats. The children just squeezed in.

They have brought their wives, children, dogs, and a great quantity of supplies for trading—furs, pipes, feather apparel, moccasins, and foodstuffs. The Iroquois were gregarious outwardly, Sergio noted, yet quite serious in their demeanor as hunters, protectors, and navigators. He realized what Davey had said was true, so he held back, always the observer, and hoped that in time, they would accept him further into their group. They were a tight clan.

Sergio did not want to ram in and risk resentment, or even shunning. He enjoyed watching the interaction between the adults and the children. The young received affection openly and are quite pampered by their mothers. Indian children are gently tolerated by the adult men and often bring patient smiles to their strong faces.

This Iroquois tribe was so different in appearance and behavior than the peaceful Lenni Lenape farming Indians, who were shorter in stature, darker skinned and overall heavier. He wondered where the Iroquois origin of migration had been. Davey had told Sergio that the Iroquois had mentioned landmarks of their roots, but those landmarks were not familiar to him and he could not interpret where any of these landmarks were. He told them that perhaps there were tribal stories referring to their beginnings—that is, if they could be understood. Davey had been told that there was a large tribe of Iroquois further north and in Canada.

The Iroquois scout was cautious as to where we would camp when we neared the port. His choice was a sheltered area of woods on the southern perimeter of the port—an area easy to defend. In his wariness, we camped in these woods for the night and I watched the children doing their chores—gathering wood for the fires and setting up the fishing nets. The women started the fires and began to cook as the men unloaded the canoes. The summer darkness did not descend until almost 9:00 p.m., so there was time before retiring for stories around the fire. The old Iroquois storyteller managed to sneak in a few tales for the delighted children. Davey interpreted as quickly as he could and I enjoyed the stories along with the children. They are a fun loving and jovial group, but efficient in all that they do.

Davey tells me that they can be ferocious in their fighting. Do not be fooled by their fun loving ways he says, which are reserved only for interactions within their own tribe. We feel privileged to be included.

The scout stayed behind with a few others as we went into the port. Now I know why they brought their dogs.

Even their canines have responsibilities and act as guards for their camp.

Davey brought me a letter from Isabella last night. It had been held at the shipping office at the port. She and her family are well and are anxious to see me. I have no idea what our future plans will be.

June 1615

How bitterly disappointed we are with this community. It abounds with thieves, cutthroats, and murderers. I have been told that the area has grown immensely in population in the last few years; yet so little has been accomplished in the way of true settlement. Few decent people live here in this growing region of human degradation. The proper gentility or religious live away from the seaport itself. The Dutch are the only civilized residents in this area.

You must be self sufficient; the Dutchmen know this. They come into port only to stock up on supplies needed in their own villages. They have managed to make bricks for a few of their small, well built homes. Their group includes various artisans; they have knowledge of the sicknesses and are clean. However, their so called benefactors are not supporting them.

I write this so I may never forget what I have seen here in this terrible place—a hell hole on earth, a God forgotten place. None here at the port live properly. Most live in filthy, crowded huts and there are few, if any dwellings truly fit for human habitation. I am told the death rate is atrocious, especially among the children. Certainly, these settlers are not the skilled artisans needed to make a village prosper. No order has been established; there is no law to maintain a decent way of life. The inhabitants of this port area are the dregs and outcasts of society from all over the world. All mercies, morals and manners have fled. People have starved; some have fed on the dead, which is cannibalism. Such horror! Outrageous drinking is prevalent, which only leads to more chaos. It is every man for himself. No one, it seems can enforce rules in this lawless society; the church holds no influence; births and deaths, so I am told, are not routinely recorded or any kind of records kept as a civilized society does. We have been told by one of the Dutch settlers, that most of the children are illegitimate, unsupervised, and roam unchecked by an adult. I doubt if most here wash in a year and they stink! At first sight of those people, one notices the bad or missing teeth, especially in the women. Whatever causes this malady, no one seems to know. Perhaps they are not aware that one has to clean their teeth to keep them healthy. Ignorance brings severe sicknesses. I have heard of humans drinking from the same dirty wells of the horses and cows and of course becoming sick. No human should drink foul water; the pox is rampant, along with the fever diseases and the bloody flux.

Captain John remarked that the Indians burn all manner of clothing, bedding, or any cloth stuff that meets any of those diseases. They have learned quickly because these sicknesses were unknown before the outsiders brought them here. The people in the port are so sickly because of their ignorance of basic health care that they succumb quickly to the widespread diseases.

There have been other settlements, but they too, have failed. I hear that many settlers have died during the first years of settlement alone. The hostile natives have killed over a thousand settlers, mostly in two massive raids in the area to our south. If you are not part of a group, says Captain John, life is brutal in an egocentric society, lacking any kind of communal bonds or the slightest human decency. Captain John assures me again, that there are villages where people work together, but after this, I would have to see it to believe it.

Sergio Cadiz Scarlatti
His Journal

Sergio knew that he had no monies or decent goods to use for bargaining at the port, only the salvaged cargo from the *Theresa*. Now, he understood fully why Captain John continued to return to his island. He knew however, that he could not live as the captain did, either.

"If I had a shipload of building materials and other necessities, I would consider staying on Long Beach, but I would never stay in this filthy port town," Sergio told Tomas. "I will return to Lisbon, and with my inheritance, I will outfit my own ship properly and return to the Americas when I have made ready."

Tomas shook his head in agreement. "I agree with you Sergio. I would return with you. I do realize, that we have a lot of work ahead of us. No decent man could live in this hell hole; we must be properly outfitted for surviving the return."

Sergio reminded Tomas of the inheritance that he had waiting for him in Lisbon and asked him to become his partner in preparing for their return to the New World. Tomas told him that he had saved his wages for years and intended to invest it in the ship they would have built. Sergio was pleased. If he could manage to find a ship returning to Lisbon, they knew that they would be on board. No matter that they had no monies, they would work for their keep, in any capacity.

June 16, 1615

I write this entry from the berth of a Spanish galleon in the New Amsterdam harbor. We have been in this miserable port town too long now and Tomas and I made a quick decision to ship out when we heard of this galleon sailing to Portugal this date—to Lisbon! What good fortune! God knows when another ship would be departing.

I will present myself in person to my sister, Isabella. There is no time to return to Long Beach Island with Captain John. It was difficult saying goodbye to him. He has done so much for us; I pray that I will see him again. I have asked him to keep my bell, and he promised to wrap it and bury it in a place among the dunes on the Island. Only he and I know the exact spot. The captain says to remember that he is a hearty old man still and perhaps, if we return within a few years, he will be here. He offered to loan us money for our passage to Lisbon, but we declined and would rather crew for our keep. We never did hear from my crew members who ventured out from the island soon after the wreck.

I realize with great clarity that one has to be well outfitted with, at a minimum, the bare necessities to subsist in this wilderness. We shipwrecked on the island on a whim of the Universe, though I am sure that there was a message in that. However, I am still trying to figure out what it is!

We have been able to see the conditions firsthand in this port. Now that I know what I must accomplish to endure in this wild New World, I would return, prepared and able to survive on my own, but not in New Amsterdam.

Sergio Cadiz Scarlatti
His Journal

Sergio put down his pen, sighed, stretched, and then walked over to the porthole of the large galleon as it glided out into the open ocean waters. He smiled to himself, for he knew with certainty that he would return to the area of Long Beach to retrieve his bell. Right now, all he could think of was seeing his beloved sister, Isabella and her family.

July, 1616

On the same dock a year later, during a July visit to the port, Captain John looked out over the New Amsterdam harbor. Lots going on, he considered as he observed the activity both in the harbor waters and in the town, abutting the wharf. At that moment, he was reminiscing about Sergio. How he loved that boy, almost like family he was. When he thought back, he was amazed at himself becoming that close to Sergio in such a short time. However, he had never been sorry for his fondness for the boy; he felt that Sergio was the nearest to a son that he would ever have.

He glanced out into the harbor, admiring a lovely Dutch fluyt as it came slipping in, its small sails filled with the gentle breeze. He watched the ship intently and commented aloud, "The Dutch certainly know how to build a ship." He repeated the remark to the general space around him. He got up and walked to the edge of the bulkhead and put his hand up shielding his rheumy old eyes from the sun. "Wonder where she's bound from," he continued speaking aloud. His watery eyes squinted to follow her course in. "The *Marta*," he whispered to himself and watched the ship as her anchor caught and she settled into the wind. Three young men lowered her dinghy and climbed down the rope ladder.

"Ho, there," Captain John called. "Ho there, the *Marta*!" he yelled vigorously in Dutch across the harbor's still waters.

"Ho there, old timer," a tall, blonde lad waved and shouted back in Dutch.

"Well, at least there is a welcoming party," another young man commented. The three laughed as they rowed into the wharf.

"Pull that oar, Hendrick," someone in the dinghy commanded. "We are going to hit the bulkhead too hard! Pull it!" The others in the dinghy were annoyed with the one called Hendrick. However, Hendrick was smiling at the old man standing on the wharf rather than paying attention to where he was rowing.

"Keep your drawers on, Jacob," Hendrick finally replied and stood up to throw the old man the fore rope. "I can see the bulkhead. I am not blind!"

"Real beauty of a ship there," the old man remarked in rough Dutch as he grabbed the young man's hand to help him up.

Willem hopped onto the wharf. "Thanks, old timer. What might your name be?"

"Captain John Stephen Weber, native to Sweden, occupation whaler, since retired, now of Long Beach, along the coast south of here." He offered his hand again. "I come to the port once a summer with my Indian friends to visit and trade and get drunk," he told them, slipping into broken English.

"Willem VanHameetman here," the large young man said, hardly able to contain himself from laughing at the old man's remarks. "You say you travel with your Indian friends?" He was surprised at what the old man had said. He was even more surprised that the old man spoke their language, though rather roughly. Willem noted his brothers' faces reflected the same startled reaction once they too, had stopped laughing.

"Sure. They be good friends and protectors. If not for them, I maybe would not have survived through many sick times on my island. What's your story?" he asked Willem, stunning him into silence with his directness.

Willem was taken aback. He looked down at this cocky old man because he was not sure why this odd fellow, by name of Captain John Stephan Weber, was so interested in them. Willem nodded his head slightly at his brothers, who were now on the wharf, indicating that they should keep their mouths shut until they found out why he was so curious.

"Sorry. I have overstepped meself." Captain John caught their caution. "It is not my business, but I guess when I see decent folks pulling in here, I want to warn them of the dangers."

"I'm Jacob, the elder and the best of us three brothers, and what dangers?"

"You watch yourselves here laddies. There are gangs of ruffians and thieves, runaways, pickpockets, and renegades, and they all come here looking for the easy life. They would rob you as soon as look at you; stick a knife in your gizzard in the blink of an eye. Just watch yourselves, laddies," he turned to leave.

"Wait a minute, Sir," Willem grabbed the Captain's coat sleeve. "We did not mean to offend you, but we do not know you. I thank you for the warning. We will take it to heart. We hope to see you again and talk more." He released the old man, but not before he added, "Where did you learn to speak our language?"

"Spent some time with my Dutchmen friends near the port and picked the lingo up. I will look for you later. You boys do pretty good with the English."

Willem told the Captain that they had planned to visit the small Dutch settlement to see how the group was progressing.

"There is not much you can do for your Dutch friends. They should return home. It is a sin how the company has deserted them." Captain John expressed his strong opinion.

Captain John left, but not before giving them a further warning about the port and the riff raff there. "What do you think of that?" Hendrick asked. "Think the old man is loony or what?"

"I think not. But we will soon find out." Willem headed to the street.

He immediately noticed the wandering groups of unkempt, tough, young men and the dilapidated shacks, storage sheds and outbuildings occupying most of the wharf. They investigated most of the town and returned to the ship.

Willem had spoken with the two women before they departed the ship. The men did not want Maggie and Bete leaving the *Marta*. Bete did not like Willem telling her that she and Maggie could not go to town. "We have come so far and we mean to see it all. It affects us too, Willem."

The brothers thought about what she had said, and they agreed it held merit. If they did not let them see the town, they would never hear the end of it.

That afternoon, seven large men and two women rowed into the public dock in two dinghies. Gangs of toughs and drunkards hung about the wharf now, and they took to leering at the women. Maggie and Bete ignored the toughs as best they could until the lewd comments spewed forth. Willem was angry. "We were fools not to bring our muskets."

"Perhaps we should wait until later and come back," Jacob suggested. Willem motioned to the rest of the men to stop rowing until they decided what to do.

Suddenly, they saw the wiry captain running full speed down the wharf and plow into the midst of the largest gang. He carried a good sized wooden plank and started swinging wildly.

"Move out of here, you louts!" he yelled as he swung his wooden weapon. "Make way for decent folk!" he roared. The group dispersed under his rage.

"We will get you, you old fool!" they threatened, shouting obscenities back at him as they scurried for cover from his ferociousness.

"Just try, you bunch of garbage," Captain John shrieked. "Just try!" he yelled at them again. "I will have me friends chop your heads off for their stew!" he bellowed.

Willem saw fear distort the faces of the marauders when they saw two of the captain's Iroquois friends running swiftly down the wharf toward them, brandishing their tomahawks. They scuttled off without hesitation.

"And never come near these fine folk or, by god, I will have the whole Iroquois tribe on your backs, you filthy scum!" Captain John roared in finality.

"Oh, Willem," Maggie whispered as she grabbed his arm. He saw her face, pallid with fear. He was furious that she was so frightened by this indecent bunch. He was more upset with himself for exposing her to such foulness. He had momentarily forgotten that there were persons of this mentality.

"This is not a good place," she whispered to him as they rowed into dockside where the captain and his Indian friends waited to give them a hand up.

"You must be Captain Weber. Thank you so much for your help." Maggie smiled and held out her hand. She had calmed down a bit. "I am Maggie, soon to be Willem's wife, and right now, I am very scared." She turned to Willem. "I am sorry that I did not listen to you, Willem. I cannot abide violence, and if this is what is here, I don't want to stay." She looked at Captain John. "I do admire your spunky swing, Sir." She held back her laugh and winked at him.

"Maggie!" Bete chastised her, but she was secretly glad that Maggie had regained her dry wit.

"Oh, for heaven's sake, Bete, I am only funning with him. And he did go at them with such great gusto!" She turned to acknowledge Captain John's Indian friends.

"It is not a good place to settle permanently, you betcha." Captain John grinned back, appreciating her attitude. "You would do better coming south a ways with me to my island. This port will be safer once they get some law in here to keep this scum at bay. Decent folks cannot be exposed to this. I do not know how that little Dutch group you intend to visit stay there. They spend all of their time defending themselves to the exclusion of working at settling."

"Thanks, John," Willem said. "I think we will see what we can do to help those people and then we will leave. There is nothing here for us. Perhaps we will visit your island. Will you sail with us and help me with navigating?"

"Oh, I would indeed!" John's lined face lit up. "It has been a long time since I have been aboard a beauty like your *Marta*. I will be ready whenever you want to cast off. I do indeed want my ride. I will send word to the Iroquois that I will not be traveling back to the island with them."

"We sail on the morning tide," Willem replied. "I calculate that to be around 6:00 a.m."

Willem was anxious to get under sail, and they left on the early morning tide. Captain John and his two Indian friends had slept on the Marta, so there was no delay in leaving. "I have set my course south," Willem told John and added, "I am certainly looking forward to this Long

Beach that you so love. I hope to find it as pleasant as you describe. We are certainly due for a turn of luck."

"No doubt at all. You will like it fine, laddie." He looked up at Willem and told him about his Spanish friend, Sergio Scarlatti. At first, Willem was not interested in a Spaniard for obvious reasons, but as Captain John's stories grew, he found himself taking a liking to the fellow as another human being, explorer, adventurer, and seaman. Willem could understand Sergio leaving the port if he had come unprepared through no fault of his own.

Leaning on the ship's rail, John remarked that he was stunned at the ship's speed. "I am enjoying meself immensely," he grinned.

July 1616

An old Swedish captain first greeted us and then warned us about the port being dangerous. Keeping his warning in mind, we explored the town. Even though we had been cautioned, we were still surprised to find the place so rough and full of unkempt seamen, renegades, drunkards, and other unsavory characters.

Outside of the immediate port is the small Dutch settlement. We ventured approximately a mile down a dirt road cut through the underbrush and shortly came upon a tiny building with a cross on its roof. We found a group of Dutch families, some still living in crude wooden huts. They had built a few small brick homes. However, it will take some time to replace the rough, wooden shacks still in use. The Dutch families were brought here by the United Netherlands Company in an attempt to settle Dutch Colonists on this large port island. The settlers have been here since 1614 and have been sadly neglected by the company. They were extremely happy to see us and hoped that we would settle near them. From first appearances of this place, I would find settling in this area, very unlikely. We did discuss brick making.

Bete and Maggie insisted upon seeing the port area and a nasty encounter occurred with some roughnecks on the wharf. Captain John, who we had just met, came to the rescue with his Iroquois friends before the encounter escalated and saved the day. He will sail south with us to his island of Long Beach, which we are anxious to see.

Willem VanHameetman
Personal Journal

Willem hugged the *Marta* to the coast, rounded an elbow of land and noted he had entered an inner waterway south of a sandy peninsular. Captain John drew a rough map and marked the route for him.

Willem quickly realized that he was facing tricky navigating through the northern inlet of Long Beach and turned the piloting over to Captain John. Willem watched intently as the Captain navigated the *Marta*, so he would be able to negotiate the inlet himself in the future.

They cast anchor on the bay side of the island, in a calm lagoon. They would start exploring the island at sunup.

1616
Maggie's Diary

Willem and I were married by Captain Hanson on the *Marta* before we sailed to the island. No two people could be more in love or happier than Willem and I.

Captain Hanson and Mister Turbott were fortunate to book passage back to Lisbon and we left them at the port.

We will forever treasure wonderful memories of our arrival on Long Beach and of those first days that we spent exploring this beautiful island and the surrounding waters. We sailed the *Marta* up and down the inland waterway, on the bay side from one end of the island to the other, casting anchor here and there.

We explored the Indian trails throughout the island on foot, leisurely and happily. We were amazed at the multitude of footpaths and how well the Indians had maintained them.

First summer 1616:

After thoroughly scouting the Great Swamp area in the middle of the island, we knew nothing could compare to this extraordinarily glorious area, and we settled near the southern border of the Great Swamp. Here, we had access to fresh water.

Bete and I planted a large garden and although we thought it would be too late to harvest any vegetables, we were pleasantly surprised at the good crop we had grown. Our method of brick making from the natural components in the soil basically worked well, although they turned out somewhat different than the bricks made in Holland. The Lenape Indians were quite curious about brick making.

Before the winter set in, we were able to build our first community house of brick and wood, along with a small barn to house the animals. Uncle Theo's building plans were simple and complete. Our first winter was very cold and damp, but we were all able to stay warm, in the newly built community house with its two fireplaces. How many times we thanked ourselves for bringing the small, wood burning grates which we used to supplement the fireplaces. The cedar from the area is wonderful and plentiful, although hard to cut. The Lenni Lenape Indians have taught us their method of splitting the cedar a little differently; we then used the wonderfully smelling, long lasting wood throughout our two buildings. The large tribe of Lenni Lenape, along with the smaller band of Iroquois, have been so helpful to all of us in every way. Although the Iroquois and Lenape are very different, we certainly appreciate all that each has to offer. The summer brings both groups to the shores of the bay for the sea bounty. They dry the various sea catches and prepare them for the next winter. They also supplied us with yams and dried fish that winter and will help us with our larger planting next spring.

Second summer: 1617

The second summer the men added to the community house, enlarged the barn and built a small house for Willem and me. Bete stays with us.

We made plans to build a dock for the *Marta* and our men asked the Indians for their help. We could not believe the number of men from the Lenape people that came to help us. They were interested in how we constructed a dock; we were interested in their building methods. If we had not had their help, the construction would have taken the men another summer.

Hendrick, along with cousins Arthur and Job, returned to Rotterdam the beginning of the summer. Hendrick kept his promise to Gretchen. He felt that the Great Swamp area should be their home and Hendrick returned with his family, along with Arthur and Job, the end of the summer. I dearly love Gretchen. We have always been close friends and I have missed her. The family would have to stay in the large community house until next year. A small house had been started for them, but it would be finished in the spring. For that winter, the larger community building would house the single men, Hendrick and family, and any visitors that might stop on the island. Captain John and Davey have given freely of their time where and when they were needed and we are very fortunate to have them.

Bete and I have planted an extensive area of maize, or corn and other vegetables familiar to the Lenape. They have shown us how to fertilize the ground and that second year we produced a bountiful crop. We had brought both seeds and grafts from apple trees and we planted them last year. They are doing nicely.

The Lenape are farming Indians and they helped us set out and plant a very large garden. There are vegetables here that we have not seen before; we are becoming able preservers. Lenape help again.

That year, after we visited the New Amsterdam port, we found that the survivors of the small Dutch settlement were hoping to ship back to Holland, for obvious reasons. However, Reuben and Isaac, two men from the settlement had decided to stay on. They moved to the island, into the community house.

Our Bete was taken with Reuben, and Reuben returned her affections. They were married in the spring. We have learned that out here, nothing is to be put off. Most times, second chances are not given. I am constantly on the lookout for young women for our single men.

Third summer: 1618

In 1618, the beginning of our third summer, Hendrick's house was finished, and another small home was built for Bete and Reuben. We are growing.

Bete and I are becoming quite proficient with the needle, fashioning the heavy animal skins into winter outerwear. The Lenape chief and his wife are helpful in showing us the method they use to sew their clothes. They prepare the hides for us. We do not know how to skin or cure hides, nor do we have any desire to learn. We are able to purchase blankets from the Lenape, thank heavens. Now we barter for spun wool at the port and over the winter we weave our own blankets and other heavy outer wear on the loom that we brought with us.

We will be the teachers of our children, and although Gretchen's children are quite small now, she has brought schoolbooks from Amsterdam. The natives are asking to be taught English. What a challenge!

We had six starter pigs shipped from Holland on the same boat that Hendrick and Gretchen had returned on. They join our healthy goats and chickens and we have bought domesticated white geese from our Lenape friends. The Iroquois traded us three beautiful horses this spring. It will be wonderful to ride them, unshod on the soft, sandy Indian trails here on the island. Before the horses, all travel was by foot and of course, water. I wondered how the horses arrived here on the island. The Iroquois told us that the horses were from a Spanish shipwreck many years ago. The horses had made their way to shore. Evidently the crew and passengers had drowned in a storm. Thank heavens that the men had enlarged the small barn for our growing animal family.

We had one minor skirmish that summer with hostile Indians. The Iroquois Chief and a group of his men heard of the foreign hostiles crossing this territory and came to protect us until they had passed through. The intruders had come armed and dangerous, but soon changed their minds when they encountered the Iroquois chief and his warriors. I was surprised to see how fierce the Iroquois could be with their painted faces. I thanked God for their protective presence.

Margaret (Maggie) VanHameetman
Her diary

Maggie leaned back in her chair, and closed her eyes. She brought to mind more of their lives from the past years. Both the Lenape and the Iroquois were founts of information regarding foodstuffs and medicinal herbs. Jacob was fascinated with their knowledge and learned to identify and use all of the plants and flowers, herbs, tree bark and roots in his healing. He has spent a great deal of time with Spring Moon and her father, Kachina, a Hopi Medicine man. Davey told us his name meant spirit, sacred dancer. Jacob has learned valuable healing techniques from them.

Shortly after Hendrick and Gretchen's return, their son Toby, cut his leg badly. The wound festered, and he came down with a high fever. Jacob was prepared to bleed him, which was the current accepted medical technique for an infection. Kachina was present. He was appalled once he understood Jacob's intentions. Old Davey interpreted for Kachina because the situation had become quite explosive and the language was more than Jacob could handle. Kachina told Jacob that there is a fixed amount of blood in each person's body, although the body can make more if it loses small quantities. However, the body is weakened and dies when it bleeds or is bled too much. He laughed at the stupidity of bleeding.

"I am so embarrassed," Gretchen confessed. "Thank God my son will not have to endure the bloodletting. I have always thought the treatment to be barbaric, and could not understand the reasoning behind it. Toby is too young to suffer that." Kachina asked if he could treat Toby in the Indian way; Gretchen gave him her permission. Spring Moon entered the room with green mold that she had harvested from the woods and applied the mold to the wound. When Jacob expressed concern, Spring Moon explained green mold grew naturally in the woods and was harvested in a certain cycle of its growth. When harvested in the right cycle, it could heal an infected wound. Kachina then prepared a drink from the bark of a tree and gave it to the child every few hours. His high fever broke and within a short time, the wound's redness had greatly dissipated.

Jacob was amazed at the medicinal potions being so readily available. *How long had the Indians known and used these cures,* he wondered. Jacob's curiosity with Kachina has led him into becoming quite a master in his use of local herbs. The following summer, Jacob stayed at the port and, armed with his new found knowledge, treated those in need. "When Jacob becomes too taken with himself, we call him shaman." Gretchen could not suppress a smile.

When childbirth came upon Maggie, she leaned heavily upon Spring Moon. Romy, their daughter—small, but feisty, was born in her parent's small house and was joyously received. She had come into their lives nearly four years after they were married. Maggie experienced a miscarriage after Romy and Spring Moon warned her then not to have another child too quickly. Maggie and Willem were so concerned about a pregnancy that they kept apart. Spring Moon saw Maggie crying and after learning what was wrong, gave Maggie a strong herb drink. "This will keep you from having babes. It will not make you barren, but it will keep you free until you desire to be pregnant. You should stop the drink a month before you try to become with child."

Maggie discussed this with Willem, who appeared rather hesitant; he was concerned that it might cause her health problems. "The Indian women use this regimen routinely to time their pregnancies with their traveling," Maggie told him. Then Willem agreed.

Jacob was amazed when Willem told him what Spring Moon had offered. He watched Maggie closely those months to see that there were no ill effects from the plant concoction.

Maggie had waited a time after her miscarriage and felt she was doing well, physically and emotionally after the loss. She felt it safe to stop the herb medicine. Subsequently, Hans, a beautiful light haired, blue eyed, good natured son was born. "I feel we have completed our family," she told Willem and Jacob. "Willem and I have a delightful daughter, and now a son. I thank God for Spring Moon." They did not keep to the Dutch tradition of naming the children, but instead, entered new names into the family. "I do not think I will try to have ten or more children. I know that many of the children die young, but I am convinced that with the help of the Lenape, our children will be strong and live a healthy, happy life."

Willem was preparing the ship for her yearly voyage to the port of New Amsterdam. The *Marta* was being stocked with supplies for trade and for their own consumption. The food sold at the port was still questionable, so they stayed to their own provisions.

Willem thought how fortunate they had been to have the *Marta* standing by these past years. It had been a wise decision to anchor her here on Long Beach Island, on the bay side in a sheltered cove. He raised his hand to shield his eyes from the bright sun and looked over at the small Indian compound in a straight line of sight from the ship. Captain John had suggested the spot to Willem. The *Marta* was anchored right under the watchful eye of a small family of Lenape camped on the bay's shore though most of the year.

Willem stood on the wheel deck and his eyes caught Maggie. He let go of his mental wanderings to look at his wife, thinking how beautiful she was with the sun shining on her bright hair—his Maggie, his never changing Maggie—how he loved her. The gods had smiled on him the day she stepped foot on the *Marta*.

"All right then!" Willem yelled. "Let's make ready to cast off. We have a busy time ahead of us." He leaned back over the railing to watch Hendrick pull up the gangplank.

"Yo ho!" Captain John yelled to Willem.

"Yo ho!" Willem shouted back, remembering the first time he had heard that greeting from the captain. He laughed at the now standing joke. "All aboard! We need to get under way. Hopefully we can make the port during daylight."

Later, Willem was silent, tired from a busy day. Captain John had taken the wheel. He realized that Captain John was staying with them more often now, in one of the rooms in the community house. Willem thought he might be lonely or just tired of living in solitude on the beach or in his Manahawkin cabin. John was like a grandfather to all of the children and loved to be with them. He and Maggie appreciated that.

"A nice sail today and a beautiful evening coming up," Captain John remarked after dinner to Willem. "Just look up at that beautiful sight," he said, bending back to observe the first faint sprinkling of stars visible in the heavens. "Cannot remember when I had a nicer day," he repeated, as the port came into sight. "Think the darkness will drop in before we get close enough?"

"I think we will stay out here, away from the crowd," Willem decided, after seeing how mobbed the harbor was. "It is nearly dark, and it will be too difficult to anchor near in. He ordered the crew to down the sails, and drop the dragger. When they were as close as Willem chose, they cast anchor. "We can come nearer in, tomorrow morning."

Willem truly enjoyed coming to the port now, because the area had been secured in the last few years. The riffraff stayed near the docks where the ships came in and the British, who were starting to build in the region, had taken an interest in the port area. They were now on patrol. It was safe for the women, who loved to visit the small mercantile shops, looking for imported goods from the trade ships which arrived daily.

Jacob came onto the wheel deck for the last watch. The *Marta* was at anchor for the night; Willem was dead tired and went below.

Captain John was on deck early the next morning and greeted Willem. "Ready to move in closer?" he asked.

"Morning to you, John," Willem was somewhat annoyed at John's persistence and he did not speak further to him. Willem turned his face from the blinding rays of the early morning sun and after he had assessed the crowded harbor, he announced, "It is like a damned obstacle course in the harbor. I do not like threading through those anchored ships. We are not the size of a dinghy, you know. The wind has picked up some. I have to think about this."

Willem again surveyed the situation and realized that they were really quite far out; further than he had thought. "Take a depth reading, Jacob, if you please," Willem asked a few minutes later.

"Sixteen feet," Jacob reported, as he pulled up the weighted hemp rope.

"What's your take on the wind, Captain?" Willem looked up at the flag flying above him. He wanted to make sure that it was safe enough before satisfying Captain John's request.

"A bit gusty, me boy."

"We can try to get in a little closer. Weigh anchors," he ordered the crew.

"Hendrick, hoist the small sails," Willem hollered. The winds were picking up and it was tricky, but they needed some movement. The harbor was full and that presented an even larger problem. "I still want to stay out a ways; give ourselves plenty of room. Too many ships at mooring and we are gaining speed." He looked up at the small sails and saw how they were billowing. The *Marta* was coming in close now, but still too fast Willem felt, and he called for another depth reading and shouted, "Down sails—depth reading please."

"Fifteen feet," Jacob reported.

"Drop the dragger—we are still coming in too fast!" Willem hollered, and over the small anchor went, dragging and bumping along the bottom helping to slow the ship. The men were alert, waiting for Willem's orders—they were coming up on a large group of ships—*Thank God we were out a ways*, Willem thought.

After a few minutes, the order came as the *Marta* had slowed down considerably, to where Willem finally yelled, "Cast anchor!" The *Marta* jerked as the huge anchor grabbed and she turned herself into the wind.

"You will have to row the rest of the way in," Willem said to anyone who did not like where they were anchored. "There are too many ships in the harbor to maneuver any further." He breathed a sigh of relief. The wind had had its way with the *Marta*, and now Willem took command. "Weigh dragger," Willem ordered.

Suddenly they heard the old captain yell.

"What in the hell is the matter!" Jacob shouted from the aft deck. "Damn—what is that old man up to now?"

"Willem!" Captain John shouted. "It is him! Sergio has come back to us! It is really him!"

"Calm down, Captain!" Willem roared back and yelled to Jacob, "Watch the old man so he does not fall overboard." Then he shouted to Captain John, "Are you sure it is your friend?"

"Over there. Two ships to the right! See the sloop marked *Theresa II*? That is Sergio's ship. He lost the *Theresa I* on the northern shoals, and now by heaven, he has the *Theresa II*. I will take the small dinghy and row over there!" Captain John shouted, barely able to contain himself. "He kept his promise, he did! Can you get us in closer?" he hollered to Willem.

"No, by Jove. The anchor is stayed. No closer! It is too dangerous to chance colliding with another ship, or running over another ship's anchor rope. You can row over!" Willem thundered, annoyed with this commotion. "Just wait a minute to make sure she settles."

The wind gusted and once more, the *Marta* jerked, twisting in the changing small blows, repeatedly settling herself. Jacob yelled over to Captain John, "Wait until the ship grabs steady again. We have to stop completely before you lower the dinghy, you old fool!"

Yet, before the *Marta* came to an absolute stop, they heard the dinghy slap the water. *That crazy old bugger*, Jacob thought. He could not wait. *We could have hit him!*

"Where the hell is he?" Willem yelled. "Has he fallen in?"

Then they heard Captain John yell, "Ho! The ship. Ho the *Theresa*."

Willem watched as Captain John rowed the dinghy alongside an enlarged, modified sloop. A tall, dark haired man leaned over the side and shouted something down to the Captain, then dropped the rope ladder over the side for him.

"Sergio! Sergio! Is it you, me lad?" Captain John cried, as he slowly climbed the ladder onto the deck and then hugged the dark haired, well built man in front of him.

"Of course it is me, you old goat." Sergio laughed. "I told you I would be back! Later is better than not coming back at all!"

"Come, my boy," Captain John demanded. "Sit for a short spell and tell me of your last years. I can hardly wait to hear."

"Put that off until later, my friend. I have my sister, Isabella, her husband, Louis and my two nephews with me. And Isabella's friend, Evita, and I might add, soon to be my wife—and her brothers, Renaldo and Delgado, and sister, Marbella," Sergio announced with a grin. "Quite a crowd." He laughed. "Remember Tomas?"

"Most certainly," Captain John replied. "But first, congratulations on your upcoming marriage. It took you long enough," he grinned and then abruptly got up and started across the deck to grab a second large, solidly built, dark haired man.

"Tomas, my boy, how are you?"

"By Jove! Captain John! You are a welcome sight. How have you been?" Tomas grinned, affectionately hugging and then sweeping the old man off his feet.

"Fine. Just fine. But just look at you two! Sure a sight for me old eyes you are. The two dark ones, but big and strong and handsome lads ye be," he cried. "I do remember how you looked when we fished you two out of the drink. Both half dead you were. But tell me, what plans are afoot?"

"Hold on, whoa!" Tomas interrupted loudly. "I do believe I was the only one who came ashore on his own two legs!"

With that explosion from Tomas, Captain John laughed and admitted that it was so.

"I came back to Long Beach to collect something that I left with you," Sergio said, in response to the captain's question, before Tomas had interrupted. "Surely you know what I mean?"

Captain John shook his head and smiled. "I pledged to you that I would take care of it and I did! But what is your final destination? Things have changed some in the port, although I do not think you would want to settle there just yet."

"We intend to sail around Cape Mey, into the Delaware Bay and up the Delaware River to the new Fort Nassau settlement that the West India Company has just established. It was led by Cornelius Mey," Sergio told him. "The settlers arrived last year. It is new, and I have not heard much about it. I plan to build a trading post there. Too bad, that we have to sail around the Cape to get there."

Tomas spoke up. "We did come prepared this time. Building tools, a few windows and doors and other materials for a house—two houses in fact. Wood can be harvested on the spot; we can subsist independently on the *Theresa* if circumstances dictate."

"Enough talk, now," Sergio butted in. "I want you to meet my fiancé and sister and her family and the rest of the group. "Evita," Sergio held his arm around her waist and urged her gently forward. "This is my friend, Captain John Weber, who saved our necks the first time we landed on his island."

Captain John looked at Evita and admired the young woman's beauty. Sergio certainly had done well. She was slimly built, with an abundance of dark hair piled high on her head. Curly strands peeped here and there and her flashing dark eyes looked directly into Captain John's, as she held out her hand to him in greeting. "I am so pleased to meet you. I have heard a great many wonderful tales about you and your grand reputation precedes you," she smiled at him. "Sergio has described this island beautifully. I am so fortunate to finally be here."

Before Captain John could answer this lovely woman, he heard Tomas yell, "Whoa, Francisco! Hold on to that pup," and he reached out to grab Francisco, Isabella's younger son who was racing down the deck after a young dog.

"Give me that dog!" shouted Fernandez, his older brother, who was in hot pursuit. "That is my dog, and I never told you to catch him!"

Tomas grabbed the boys, one under each arm, and introduced Captain John to Isabella, her husband Louis, their two rowdy sons, Evita's sister, Marbella, their two brothers and finally he stopped.

"The big one, I know well," John said, quite serious, and then he grinned and went to hug Tomas, who swung him about once more. He noticed that Tomas was with Marbella, another pretty woman. Captain John grinned, happy for Tomas.

"I have a load of cargo to drop at the port. Foodstuff from Lisbon and Amsterdam—should fetch a handsome price. Then I plan to sail south," Sergio paused. "I would like to stop and pick up my bell. Would you like to accompany us on the *Theresa*, Captain?"

"I certainly will sail back with you. I can row into the docks from here and catch up with Willem in town to let him know my change of plans."

Sergio watched the old man climb down the rope ladder and get himself into the dinghy, then turned his thoughts to his own affairs. He was happy to see Captain John and pleased to be back in the New World, but this time, on his own terms. He and Isabella had sold most of their inheritance to build their new sloop. Along with Tomas' generous input of money and Sergio's sale of the family land and house, they had paid for the building and the stocking of the *Theresa* with monies to spare.

Sergio and Isabella had sold the family home in Cadiz, and had received a fair price, even though it was in disrepair. It was the land that had brought the larger monies. Sergio and his sister had managed to keep their mother's two necklaces and some other pieces of fine antique jewelry.

The *Theresa* was outfitted to meet any necessity, and she was large and very comfortable. She carried foodstuffs for a year and Sergio knew that they would be able to fish and hunt to add fresh meat to their diet; hopefully they would be able to buy or barter for vegetables and perhaps some fruit. He still wanted to be independent for a time. Right now Sergio had cargo to unload and told Captain John, that he would see him later.

"Blast, blast! Where has that Dutchman gotten to?" Captain John ranted as he walked through the small port town in search of Willem. Now louder, "I will not walk around town again." He suddenly spotted Willem down the street in front of the blacksmith and hurried toward him. "I have turned around this town three times. Where did you go?"

"We have been in and out of some of the shops. How did you fare?"

"By the heavens, it is Sergio," Captain John announced happily. "He is back, with his sister and her entourage on their way up the Delaware River to a new settlement, that the West India Company is planning to build. I believed they call it Fort Nassau. Sergio and his sister's husband, Louis, are planning to open a trading post there."

"My goodness," Maggie smiled. "That is wonderful that you met up with him again, Captain. He must have been happy to see you."

"Sergio is unloading the *Theresa* right now. Then he plans to sail south, stopping at Long Beach Island some time later. He will drop me and collect something he left there, and then continue south, around Cape Mey. At least this will give us some time to catch up on the past years."

"Good luck and a safe trip to him," Willem wished Sergio well. *This Sergio must be a good friend*, Willem thought and felt a little sorry that he would miss meeting him, but he was busy picking up supplies himself. He told the Captain that he would see him back on the island and then went to find Maggie.

Hendrick and his elder son, Toby, had become visibly ill on the *Marta* when they had sailed back to the island from the port. Gretchen reported that both had been feeling sick for the last few days. After being home nearly a week, there had been no improvement. Gretchen rushed over to Willem and Maggie's early one morning soon after, terribly distraught and announced that both her husband and son were losing ground rapidly. Their fevers had soared, and they had broken out with a rash. Maggie called her niece Caitlin, Gretchen's daughter and told her to run and find Spring Moon and her father. "Tell them to hurry, Caitlin. Tell them Hendrick and Toby are very sick. We will meet them at your house." She took off running, with her brother Mitchell in hot pursuit.

Spring Moon and Kachina arrived quickly and entered the house. Suddenly, the two Indians stopped at the door of the bedroom where Hendrick and Toby were bedded and would go no further. They were visibly agitated.

"What is it?" Willem asked, but they were unable to convey the manner of the illness to him in English.

"Tell us please. What is wrong?" Gretchen was frightened by their behavior.

Willem then sent his nephew Ryan, Caitlin's brother, racing to look for Old Davey to interpret. Willem knew that Old Davey was on the island and he whispered thank you, turning his eyes upward. He remembered that Captain John had not yet arrived with Sergio.

"What is going on?" Old Davey asked, arriving out of breath from running after Ryan. The boy was almost hysterical over the bad turn his father and brother had taken.

"Hendrick and Toby are very ill. Spring Moon and Kachina will not go past the doorway. They are scaring us," Gretchen replied. Tears welled up, and she could barely speak.

Davey asked a question of Kachina, and he replied quickly, motioning with his hands and speaking rapidly and then, greatly upset, the Indians left the house.

Willem turned to Davey. "Bloody hell, Davey. What is going on?"

"It is the pox. It is the smallpox! They probably picked it up at the port. I heard something about this two weeks ago. We must isolate them immediately," Davey said, still puffing from the run. "Twelve to fourteen days is the harboring time, before the disease shows itself. The Indians have no defense against it, and it scares them half to death. They will not touch or tend anyone with the pox. They suggested a few things, but told me that they cannot stay near the poison."

"That is ridiculous," Jacob stated, his tone showing his disbelief. "I saw only a mild rash and low fever. How could he know it is the pox?"

Gretchen ignored Jacob and turned to Maggie. "We need to make the small room in the barn ready. The weather is mild, and they will be fine out there. We have to get them isolated. Dear Lord, the pox!" she whispered. Her face turned pale.

"What are you doing?" Jacob appeared in the doorway, openly irritated. "There is no way, that they can tell it is the pox, it is too early to diagnose."

"I swear to God," Davey shook his head. "The Indians can smell it."

Gretchen suddenly spoke up. "Both Kachina and Spring Moon have been right about every medical problem that has befallen us, have they not? I am sorry, Jacob. I trust Spring Moon and her father's advice. Compared to them, our medical knowledge is primitive." She turned to Maggie. "Come. Help me make up the beds."

Maggie nodded. "I am afraid I will have to listen to Spring Moon and her father, too. Sorry, Jacob, but that is what Gretchen wants."

"I will examine them again, right now," Jacob announced, still openly aggravated. "The pox starts off with a tiny round rash on the trunk." He asked Hendrick, "Do your muscles ache? Do you have a headache or backache?"

"All of that and I think I have a fever and I am sweating."

Now Jacob was concerned and his attitude quickly changed as he took Maggie aside. "Well, if it is the pox, the fever will recede along with that mild rash. Then it comes back with an eruptive rash, mostly on the hands, face, and feet first, and then it spreads. Back pain, headache again, and nosebleeds are part of the accompanying symptoms. If they get through a week of this, they have a chance. I have heard of taking a small bit of the pox fluid and cutting it into a healthy person's skin. This is supposed to give the person some immunity from the disease. I don't know about that," Jacob frowned. "But I hear that the exchange must be done when the person is healthy. It is too late for them. I need to examine Toby. I have not seen him in the last few hours."

After examining the boy, Jacob told Gretchen and Willem, "He has the rash and his skin is eruptive. He has been vomiting and has diarrhea. I am really sorry to say that I do believe it is the pox." He agreed both father and son should be isolated.

"Kind of strange, it was," Davey said, remembering what Spring Moon and Kachina advised. "They said not to catch their breath or touch the poisons as they explode. Poisons in the breath will go into you and yellow poisons from the body sores or yellow mucous from the nose or from any part of a body opening will go into you. There is no cure except the strength of the body for ten days. Does that make any sense?" he questioned. "I'm interpreting it word for word rather than change anything. They also said to keep the sick ones entirely to themselves. Do not let any of the family, especially the children, visit them or touch them right now."

"I understand. They are saying not to breathe in their breath or touch the open eruptions or anything with mucous or blood on it. Who knows how they come by their information." Jacob sighed. "I know; I need to have more faith in the Almighty. He surely must be leading Kachina."

On the sixth day, Jacob came and told Willem, "Our brother Hendrick is not going to make it. Toby is holding his own." Jacob broke down and wept. Willem put his arm around him.

Two days later, Hendrick died. After Bete had cried all day for her much loved cousin, she reminded everyone that they had done all that they could for Hendrick and now they had to get Toby through this terrible illness.

"We must remain vigilant and protect ourselves. Toby has not yet fully recovered. I do not think he is still contagious, but who knows? Take no chances, please," Jacob directed.

"Heaven above," Maggie moaned, and reminded all of them to pray for Toby.

Willem approached Gretchen, who was stunned and silent in her bedroom. He had to explain to her that burial should be immediate and that all linens should be burned. She agreed. "He really does not need his body now. Hendrick's spirit has flown, and he is with God. I am the sorrowful one, left behind to grieve. He is in a place of joy. I have to care for my four children now. What has to be done must be done." She started to get up and Willem caught her as she collapsed in grief.

Just after this sadness, Sergio stopped on the island, to retrieve his bell. He and Captain John heard what had happened. Before Sergio left, he gave Captain John two beautiful, hunting spaniel pups as a gift. The pups' mother was related to the same litter as the two dogs his nephews had. Sergio told Captain John, that one pup was for him and the other for Hendrick's son, Toby. Sergio's hope was that the young dog might help in Toby's recovery. Sergio departed shortly after.

"What a thoughtful thing to do," Willem said and saw that Toby had fallen in love with the beautiful hunting spaniel. He named him Tracks. "Be thankful that Toby has survived; we will keep our brother, Hendrick always in our hearts." Willem was devastated over his brother's death.

Willem, along with his family and Jacob, accompanied Gretchen and her children home to Rotterdam the following May.

Marta and Paul finally met their grandchildren. There was a large family reunion and Willem and Maggie spent a week with them, before returning to Long Beach Island. It was not long after that they heard of Marta's passing. "I am so thankful that we did get to visit mother," Willem bowed his head.

Paul in time, settled on Long Beach Island with his son and Maggie, as he had said he would do.

Gretchen never returned to the island.

CHAPTER FIVE

Destined Meetings

1695-1775

"Get my long glass, quickly!" Christian shouted to Florence, who flew to the cabin and raced back to hand him the glass. To Christian's horror, he saw the giant, pirate sloop. It was not flying a flag; rather she announced herself with her black color. Christian could hardly believe the outright, bold maneuver.

Romy, daughter of Maggie and Willem put her pen down, closed her journal, and was thankful that her parents had not lived to see the Duke of York's negligent actions. They would have been horrified at the treatment given to Richard Nicolls, the brilliant, no nonsense Governor of the middle colonies, admired by most of the Colonists. He did not deserve the attitude of the Duke of York, the King's brother, who had given land freely to his own undeserving friends.

August 1700

My mother, Maggie, wanted continuity in our family and made me promise that I would continue the family journal. After she crossed over, years ago, my father, Willem, did not stay on this earth but a few months. This was no surprise to any of us. He could not live without her. I thought that no one could take my father's place in my life, but realized much later that I probably should have gone on to look further for a husband. But then, perhaps my life was already determined. I am an old woman now, but I have had a wonderful life as a teacher, close to children who have touched my heart. I have my brother, Hans and his wife Sanne and my wonderful nephews, Christian and Kurt, with their beloved children. There are cousins, too, who keep in touch. My health is good and my life is happy and full.

I am adding the history and growth of the area as notes. Mother did not write of Peter Minuet, the Duke of York, who had tried to set up a patroon system around 1658. The Dutch West India Company initiated this system by granting titles and land to its invested members. They hoped these grants would encourage immigration to America. It became rather complicated, requiring the selected patroons to recruit settlers to stay on this land for a certain amount of time before the land would belong to the patroon. My father feared the system had overtones of slavery. It was somewhat successful further up north along the Hudson River. It never did well in this area.

Romy VanHameetman,
Daughter of Maggie and Willem VanHameetman
Her Journal

Notes: *On the history and growth of the area:*

In 1664, the Duke of York, the brother of King Charles, granted his two supposedly trusted friends, Lord John Berkeley and Sir George Carteret, a substantial portion of his holdings here in the New World. Jersey was named for Sir George Carteret's birthplace, the Isle of Jersey in the Channel Islands. The Jersey lands encompassed all of the territory east of the Delaware River and south of a line on the Delaware River to north on the Hudson River. Our newly formed province is relatively small, consisting of four and a half million acres, more or less.

Richard Nicolls, then a good Governor of the middle colonies, was appalled at the grant given by the Duke of York. Nicolls had been encouraging settlers from New England to come to the wonderfully fertile lands that now embodied the new province. When Nicolls heard what the duke had given away, he was disgusted. The fiasco of the duke granting this perfect region to Berkeley and Carteret, who had no idea of its real worth, not only in monies, but also in excellence of quality, was more than Nicolls could bear. He had requested to be relieved.

Just recently, Jersey was arranged into counties. Settlements are being established as towns all over this area. There is Mount Holly, Burlington, Bordentown, and just recently, Haddonfield. Of course, Shrewsbury was settled years ago. Who knows what the next fifty years will bring.

Romy VanHameetman
Her Journal

Seeing an old letter tucked into her mother's journal, Romy picked it up and saw the name, Scarlatti. She remembered the name because it had such a different, melodic sound to it. Romy opened the letter carefully. She did not want to tear the delicate, old paper. Her mother had kept the correspondence for many years. Romy felt that she was traveling back in time; Sergio would have been long gone.

Reading the letter, Romy thought of the many things that had transpired over the years when she was a child. Captain John Weber had spoken of Sergio with great fondness. Romy would always remember Sergio's kind gift of the beautiful spaniel he had given to her young cousin, Toby after his battle with smallpox, that had taken his father.

Sergio was long dead. Maggie was elderly when she received this letter from him, Romy realized. Evidently, her mother had written to Sergio upon the death of dear Captain John, although the letter had taken some time to find him.

December 24, 1650
Town Bank, Jersey

My Dear Maggie:
   Thank you for your letter dear lady, advising me of Captain Weber's passing some years ago. This response is long overdue. Your Indian friends finally tracked me down in Town Bank. I am an old man now, but my mind is clear, and how well I remember Captain John and his kindness. Evita, my dear wife, passed away a few years ago and I miss her more each day.
   After a troubled start, we left Fort Nassau and came to the southern cape, where we have done extremely well with our shipbuilding business. I have a son, Mario Cadiz and a grandson, Nicholas.
   Sometimes we cross into each other's lives, contribute significantly and then resume on our own path to complete our life journey. I feel that Captain John Weber was one who crossed into my life, helped me to heal my body and my spirit, directed me mentally and then moved on. Through Captain John Weber, you and your family then intersected my path, however minor. Perhaps it will happen again between our future generations, dear lady. I hope that you and I will meet in a sweeter place. My kindest regards to your wonderful family and Indian friends. My prayers are with all of you.

                              Your faithful servant
                              Sergio Cadiz Scarlatti

   Strange that Sergio spoke of the shipbuilding industry, Romy thought. While her brother, Hans had supplied lumber to the many new shipyards springing up in the area these last years, he had never spoken of meeting any of the Scarlattis. Hans had never gotten into the actual shipbuilding end because of the lucrative cedar business. Romy knew from old journals, that her father, Willem had known of Sergio but never had met him in person as far as she knew. Captain John Weber was the link between Sergio and Willem.

Coming back to the present in her ruminating, brought her brother, Hans to mind. Hans and his wife Sanne had two sons, Christian and Kurt, who had carried on the lumber business. Romy was very close to her sister-in-law, Sanne and thanked heaven that she had Sanne in her life. Christian, her nephew had married Florence. Kurt his brother, was yet unmarried, but Romy was always on the lookout for suitable girls for Kurt.

Christian asked his Aunt Romy if he could look at the old journals kept in the attic. He told her that he was very interested in the family history. Romy was delighted by his curiosity and gave Christian and Florence the keys. Shortly afterwards, the two sat in the attic, rummaging through old journals from the early 1600s.

"I cannot believe all of these old journals, Florence. It gives us a complete family history, including the trip over here on the *Marta*." He looked up at his wife. "Someone really should do some organizing."

"Perhaps they were too busy during their settling years to keep up the journals properly." Florence hesitated. "Just think about it, Christian. Coming here to a strange place, no home but the *Marta*, and you wonder how they managed to accomplish all that they did."

Christian agreed. "I heard Father mention these journals. In fact, more than once, saying that he should do something about organizing the ledgers. I *will* do it. I will start with the chronology and then sort in increments, but I will do it."

"I can help you," Florence offered. "I am really interested."

"Good. I think I will update the history of this area on a separate sheet of paper as Aunt Romy has done and keep it in the journal. It is much too lengthy as an entry, but it is important history. I can see where Maggie wanted to put events into perspective by adding some history of the times. I like her idea. I will have to catch up on our local area and family history, too. This has not been worked on in some time." He thought a minute, "The log of the *Marta* should be separate." Florence agreed.

Notes on the local history of the Philadelphia area

In March of 1681, William Penn, a Quaker from England, received a charter for a large expanse of land, which he named Pennsylvania, meaning Penn's Woods. The charter was in payment of a loan made to the English King, Charles II, by Penn's father. We all agree that Penn has made the most of it, not as some others have done. He is laying out a large area on the Delaware River as the central city of this expanse. Penn named the city, *Philadelphia*, meaning *City of Brotherly Love*. In October of 1682, he expanded the city by purchase, west to the Dutch named Schuylkill River, making the city a 1,200 acre rectangle from river to river.

The land surrounding the city is rich and fertile; our extended family investment group, formed years ago, voted to purchase the standard package offered by the city leaders. The package included a tract of five thousand acres, a building lot in the planned city, and a dividend of eighty acres in the Liberty lands north and west of the immediate city limits. It was too much for one family to handle, so we divided the responsibilities among our extended family.

The lot that we purchased within the city is speculative. We will decide later how we will use it.

The five thousand acre tract has many possibilities; We will address this at a family council meeting.

The rich eighty acres in the Liberty lands, west of the city, has already been planted in wheat by our cousins. We expect a profit this year. The wheat will be ground, bagged and brought into town for local citizens' purchase. We have also started a planned distribution to some outlying areas.

A *Free Society of Traders* was instigated, but it only lasted until 1686 because the individual merchants protested the bindings of the society. Regardless, the city continues to grow rapidly. Dissolving the restrictions placed on the merchants by the society has helped this growth. The demand for artisans in all fields—coopers, weavers, tinkers, masons, tailors, millers, shoemakers, jewelers, silversmiths and all kind of experienced people—is still great.

Philadelphia City is flourishing nicely, yet, there is the proverbial fly in the ointment. We find it ludicrous that there is considerable dissention already among the churchmen. We Dutchmen came to the New World because of the religious persecution from the Spanish. Although we are Catholic and our church had many tribulations in Holland, we did not feel that any of our fellow citizens should be persecuted for practicing their own religion. Now those very same sons of immigrants, who came to the New World as we did, for independence in all areas, are starting up again in petty battles amongst themselves. Penn, as a Quaker, holds fast to his beliefs and makes sure that religious freedom is accorded even to Catholics. In 1708, celebration of the mass started regularly in Philadelphia. This pleased us immensely. However, there is still a continuing intolerance toward Catholicism. We praise Penn's stand on freedom of religion. We had been without a priest for many years, except when we were able to attend mass at Shane's Castle in the Pinelands or by traveling into Philadelphia. Shane's Castle was really a log cabin where a traveling priest stopped when he could. However, besides the distance, there was never any regularity in scheduling. The cabin was located near the junction of Indian trails from the Delaware to the Great Egg Harbor Rivers. We have baptized our own children and said mass together in our compound for many years. Sea captains have performed the legal civil marriages. When a priest came through, he had many ceremonies to perform again. Catholicism is only one of many religions practiced and in this great diversity I believe, is Philadelphia's strength, although there will always be prejudice by some.

Meanwhile, during the late 1600s, the Carolina Colony, Maryland and Delaware were established and northern Jersey has become more populated. Elizabethtown named in honor of Lady Elizabeth Carteret, was settled in 1665. Already people are dropping the word *town*, from the name.

In the 1630s, the Dutch expanded their small settlement on the southern tip of Manhattan, to the wild and uncharted areas of Long Island. Carteret granted patents to sixty five settlers, mostly from the easterly Long Island villages and small towns, formerly in the New Haven Colony. They were land patents, held by Carteret, called proprietorships, or supreme titles to land, originally acquired within America by treaty.

The patent granted the rights to land under the treaty to the person named on the patent and to their heirs and their assigns forever. However, I hear that some patents, especially those granted in Virginia rendered the grantee just short of ownership of the land. Some patents required an annual *quit rent* be paid by the grantee as compensation to the proprietor.

A second tract of Jersey land was granted in April 1665, known as the Navesink or Monmouth patent, and this tract extended from Sandy Hooke to Barnegat Bay and up the Raritan River for twenty five miles, forming a large triangle. When Colonists first came to this area, oysters were so plentiful that oyster reefs covered more than thirty five square miles of the estuary, specifically the area from Sandy Hooke up the Hudson River as far north as Ossining, in western Raritan Bay; the Navesink and Shrewsbury River, the Arthur Kill and the newly named Newark Bay. Newark Township was founded soon after and the town and the bay I hear, were named after Newark-on-Trent in Lincoln County, England. Newark town in Jersey is very large; lots were laid out, as was a church, a marketplace, a wharf, and a mill. We will sail the *Marta* there and see this place, which I hear has grown immensely in a short time.

A 1664 designated proprietorship, now called New Jersey, ended its propriety in 1702. The proprietors, Berkeley and Carteret, felt that they also had the right of government under the Jersey patent of June 1664. The Duke of York had only the right to grant them soil and not the right of government. However, the Duke continued to assert that Berkeley and Carteret had the right of government. This assertion continues to cause trouble and most of the Colonists feel that proprietorship is outmoded and resent being asked to pledge an oath of fidelity to the proprietor. They want their rights, especially in levying their own taxes. We agree that the proprietorship is outmoded; I question how the taxes will be handled.

End of addendum notes.

Christian VanHameetman

1709

Over the years, we have been privileged to meet other Dutchmen from Manhattan, the Staten Island area and the Middle of the Shore on the mainland in Jersey. Staten Island has been heavily populated by the Dutch. The island was first inhabited by the Algonquin peoples, specifically the *Raritan* and other Indians related to the *Lenape*. European and British contact, as far as we know was first by da Verrazano and then Henry Hudson, an Englishman, who established Dutch trade in the area. Hudson named the island *Staaten Eylandt* after the Dutch parliament, *Staten Generaal*. For the last forty years there had been trouble with settling Staten Island because of the difficulties between the Dutch and the local Indian tribes. Ouddorp was the first permanent Dutch settlement. My uncles and cousins who settled on Staten Island were able to marry people from our native country. I was extremely fortunate to meet my wife, Florence, who was raised on the mainland near Middle of the Shore and was half Dutch.

Our immediate family clings to Long Beach Island in the Great Swamp area, where we are relatively cut off from the mainstream of thinking. We sail up to the port of New Amsterdam once a month with our cargo of cedar and this is when I am in touch with the local and English news. I bring the newspaper back for my friends and family, so that we may keep up with current affairs, both local and foreign.

We continue to add houses and outbuildings to our compound on the borders of the Great Swamp. We feel that a compound offers greater safety. Our complex is surrounded with a high cedar wall for added security. The wall structure was erected and completed years ago.

Cattle have been passed down through generations. We have bred and cared for them faithfully, therefore they thrive and flourish. They are marked and left to graze out in the Great Swamp. A huge, fresh water aquifer feeds this entire area, so raising cattle is possible.

It remains quite isolated on our island, although the population is slowly increasing. We are still off the main path, so to speak, and we are fortunate indeed that the local Lenni Lenape Indians are our close friends. To date, our surrounding wall has never been breached. The wall was built to protect us from animals, hostile Indians, pirates on the bay and any sort of danger from the mainland.

We derive our major income from lumber, so we must stay in close proximity to the enormous acreage of white and reddish brown cedar. Many years ago, we built a ramp and dock on the bay side, near the outer boundary of the cedar forest. Hired men from the area, along with my cousins, haul the cedar and load the *Marta* from our dock. We are fortunate that the ship draws only a few feet of water and we are able to navigate freely in the bay and the inland waterway. We can navigate the bay and cross over to the middle of the shore with the *Marta,* fully loaded at high tide. We attempt to constantly update charts of the local bay waters, although there is much shifting of the channels, which makes this extremely difficult and most times a waste of time.

The Great Swamp cedar is much coveted because of the hardness of the wood, which renders long term use. There is an unlimited amount of cedar; however for every tree down, we plant a seedling. The cedar brings us more monies than we ever dreamed of, not that any of the women complain of that! We do a great deal of bartering for goods in bulk portions at the port. Most times, this is more satisfactory than money because there is no common monetary exchange yet. However, the English pound does dominate. In large family investments, returns are equal, percentage wise, to the individual family investment. This makes buying in quantity possible. We have no trouble hiring experienced woodsmen because we have a fine reputation and pay well. Over the years, we have become more adept at raising our own crops and salting our own meat and fish.

We are very thankful that we are five to ten degrees milder in the winter months, than the port to our north.

Christian VanHameetman,
His journal

Christian always gave thanks for the accessibility and the great bounty of the wonderful cedar through the years. At times, they had found it difficult to keep up with the orders. He laughed to himself thinking, *most people would love to have such problems.* The magnificent cedar had been the major, consistent part of their livelihood, and it had given them the means to maintain the *Marta.* However, her age was showing; but because of their faithful maintenance of the ship, the family was still able to sail her to New Amsterdam nine months of the year, and every two weeks to the mainland, delivering the stripped cedar. The *Marta* was dependable and had made it possible for contracts to be met. However, ships too, had a life span. They knew a decision was eminent, but they kept putting it off.

Monies were so confusing that many refused to use it, turning to bartering instead. All Christian could remember was that twelve *pennies* (or *pence*) equaled one *shilling* and twenty *shillings* equaled one *pound*. This was the standard in England.

Many of the Colonists felt cheated when dealing with the English. The monetary system in place was too confusing. English money was referred to as *sterling;* Virginia monies were called *exchange rate.* The exchange rate in Virginia was probably about 85% of an English *pound sterling* out of England.

Then there was the *pistole,* a Spanish gold coin, called a *doubloon* which was worth approximately .83 of a *pound* English. The .83 represented slightly more than 18 *shillings.* The pistole was better known and used in Virginia. To confuse the Colonists even further, the *pistole* was often related to the French gold *Louis d'or,* which was worth from 18 *shillings* to just over a *pound* English. The French gold *Louis d'or,* also called a *French guinea,* was worth 21 *shillings* when used in dealing with *larger pounds.*

Another common coin, called the *Spanish peso,* or *piece of eight*, also called a *dollar,* was worth a little less than one quarter of an English *pound*, or four *shillings,* six *pence.* Most Colonists bartered, unless they were dealing in larger *pounds.*

Christian was lost in thoughts of travel one evening after a large dinner and he had started to doze in his favorite chair. Journeying from the island to Philadelphia was a long, tiring day. The easiest way to travel to Philadelphia was to sail the *Marta* south, around Cape Mey, into the Delaware Bay and up the Delaware River into Philadelphia; but that was too time consuming. If you sailed straight across Barnegat Bay, the channels to Tuckerton were better marked, and checked frequently; the *Marta* sailed at high tide. From Tuckerton, one could hire a horse, or a coach and horse from a local livery, to Coopers Creek Ferry, then continue on to the ferry crossing at the Delaware River. This ferry led to the center of Philadelphia.

When the weather was good, the family used their wherry to sail across the bay. The wherry was a long, open boat, similar to a rowboat, with a sail and used in local waters. They also kept two horses and a carriage in Manahawkin. It was the cheapest way to travel in that area and they could dictate their own schedule. They did this for years. And, one could then bypass the Coopers Creek Ferry and cross the Delaware River further north, but than one had to backtrack into the city.

The young men loaded their horses onto the *Marta*, sailed to Tuckerton and rode their horses to the Delaware Ferry, bypassing Camden, and then to Philadelphia.

The Delaware Ferry was cheap enough—six pennies a person, twelve for horse and rider. However, if the ferry was an open barge and the weather was unfavorable, the ferry did not sail.

For those that were not riding horses, you could rent a horse and buggy when one arrived in Philadelphia. Some Stage Coach runs were being established, but getting to the coaches was the problem. Christian hoped that the Stage Coach runs would be broadened.

"Christian, Christian! Wake up!" "Did you hear that the new meetinghouse over to the Middle of the Shore is nearly finished?"

"Good lord woman! Are you out of your mind? You scared me half to death with your yelling and just as I was comfortable and dreaming."

"But this is important, Chris."

"You mean over to Tuckerton." He rearranged himself more comfortably in the chair. Evidently, the tasty supper had dulled his senses, and he had drifted off in the big chair. He sighed and shook his left leg which had gone to sleep with him. He knew that Florence would not relent, so he decided to pay attention to what she was asking. Florence always grouped Tuckerton, or Clamtown and

Fishtown as the Middle of the Shore. They felt the Quakers were a spiritual group who practiced what they preached. So they attended the Quaker's religious services as often as they were able. However, Christian was not aware that the meetinghouse, which would also be more of a social hall, was nearly completed.

"Oh, yes," Florence revealed. "Mr. Edward Andrews deeded the land to the Friends last year. Cedar shingles cover the building, which is quite attractive. I hear tell there are four stained glass windows that people are making a fuss over."

Christian smiled, remembering that in the early sixties, his ancestors had brought stained and clear glass windows from Rotterdam and had installed them in their homes on Long Beach Island. "Do tell." He suppressed a grin. "And what do you call the glass over the front door in our Community Building?" He reminded her of the lovely crown shaped, multicolored glass that was set in place above the large, black, front door. "I bet the meetinghouse has nothing like that. Need I remind you that the glass topping that door was made in Holland."

"Hollanders have always been ahead in many things," she acknowledged. "But we are rather isolated out here, in case you had not noticed," she added, raising her eyebrows for emphasis.

Florence got up to retrieve her lacework. "Look at your shirt." She chastised him on her return trip to her chair. "A button is off again, neat and tidy, Christian—neat and tidy. Such a handsome man you are, but so unkempt."

"Where is that damnable pipe?" He had gotten up from his chair and was hunting in drawers, opening and slamming them shut, greatly annoyed. "Oops, there you are." He took the pipe down from a small wall shelf. The large looking glass that hung on the wall above the shelf reflected his shaggy, sandy colored hair. His shirt was not tucked in and really did not fit his broad shoulders. He leaned closer into the glass to capture more of his height and his deep blue eyes. He sighed. It was never important to him, being neat. He was always very clean with his person, but that was as far as it went. It was bothersome, but Florence had asked him numerous times to be more aware of his appearance. He decided that he would really make more of an effort.

Florence was a pretty, young woman with dark hair and light blue eyes. She wore her hair back, tied with a long ribbon, and was always neat in her person. Her exotic looks leaned towards her Spanish grandmother, whose family had settled on the mainland years before.

"Perhaps your brother will be able to meet someone at the new meetinghouse to his satisfaction," Florence nodded over at her brother-in-law, Kurt, who was sitting with them reading the newspaper. Then she turned to wink at her husband.

Kurt pretended not to hear her and Christian added, "Who would have him?"

Kurt grinned and pushed back his dark blonde hair. He usually tied it behind his neck, but it always tended to pop out. He was a good looking young man, although he was not aware that he was. Kurt was smaller in statue than his brother, but solidly built and his dark eyes never missed a thing. Christian and Florence liked to poke fun at him, but never in a mean spirited way.

Florence changed the subject back to the meetinghouse. "I would like to know if the new meetinghouse is finished, or when it will be finished. Are they building it near the Andrews Gristmill? I heard from a neighbor that the mill was near the mouth of the creek. I am trying to place it." She was relentless.

"The new meetinghouse is along one of the side streets," Christian told her. "You cannot see it that well from the main street." Christian knew that his wife, like the rest of the women, could hardly contain themselves thinking of attending a social at the meetinghouse. It was not important to him whether they built it near the mill or whether they even built it. He did not care about a social being held or anything about a meetinghouse. Suddenly, he felt guilty, knowing that his pretty, blue eyed Florence never had the opportunity to attend parties or socials.

"I have not been over that way in awhile, so I really have no news when the meetinghouse will be finished," Christian told her. "I just remember someone told me that it was under construction." He picked up his newspaper, indicating that the conversation was over. Florence gave up on that particular discussion. She had fought the good fight for now and would resume later.

Kurt chimed in, "Tuckerton, Middle of the shore or whatever as you said, is really expanding. I agree with you Chris. It is time that they gave the town a legitimate name—and just one." He shook his head in confusion. "What they really need in that area is a good boarding house where people can stay in comfort, especially now that there will be a meetinghouse. God knows what many of those taverns hold in their beds."

"I plan to take a run over there, probably in a month or so," Christian replied.

"Can you ask someone if the meetinghouse is finished and when the first social is planned?" Florence was back at her quest for information.

"That I can find out for you. I feel Tuckerton is probably safer now that both the town and the small harbor have grown. There are some decent people settling there." Christian had never left the *Marta* tied down in Tuckerton unguarded, because of the riffraff that frequented the area near the harbor. However, law and order had been established recently. "Please, no more about the meetinghouse if I do this for you?" He tried to set a bargain.

"I heard that there is a constable walking around now, at the least," Florence had the last word.

Changing the subject and before he forgot, Christian told her "I think I will put a Tuckerton trip on hold. I will be sailing to Goshen in a few days. I heard that a new shipyard is being built on the upper cape. We can sail the *Marta* on the ocean route, which is easier, so I can investigate. If it is true, I want to get in first to supply the lumber. They will need large quantities of good oak and cedar, plus other local woods for ship construction. Do you and the girls want to come along?"

The girls chirped in a chorus. "Papa, Papa, take us with you. We want to go on the *Marta* with you! Please, Papa," his three young daughters cried in unison. Two were light haired like their father, and one dark, as their mother. They had been taking in the conversation without Christian's noticing and now they jumped about and clapped their hands with excitement.

"Well, Florence, what do you think? There is an inn located in Romney Marsh. It came with the highest recommendations. The small village is supposed to be quite lovely. I thought we could cast anchor off Town Bank and take a carriage from there to Romney Marsh, which is inland. It would be a treat for you, my dear," he said to Florence. "We could stay off ship."

He watched his wife look over to his mother, Sanne, who lived with them. She had just entered the sitting room with her friend, Litonya and heard the last of the conversation.

"Go ahead, dear, I can hold things down here."

"We will be gone at least five days, Mother."

"Georgia is here with me," Sanne nodded, indicating her sister, who was on an extended visit. Georgia had traveled from Philadelphia to visit and now that she was getting older, an extended visit was always in order—the traveling tired her out.

"And I can ask Litonya to stay and help me," Sanne reminded them, looking over at Litonya. "And Billy will be around," she was referring to one of her many nephews.

Christian glanced over at his mother's Lenape friend, and thought her Indian name, Litonya, meaning *Darting Hummingbird,* suited her well. She was tiny, moved quickly and was always busy. She loved his mother dearly.

"Are you sure, Mother, that you would rather remain here?" He was uneasy about leaving her. Christian knew that his father and brother would want to sail to Goshen. Even though his father, Hans, was getting on, he was still spry. Other family homes and the outer wall

JEANETTE H. FUSCO

surrounded the compound. And then there were the dogs. The house backed the big cedar woods, but the island was relatively safe because it was not easily accessible from the mainland. Christian knew that cousin Billy would be overseeing the lumber business and would be around, but probably off in the woods somewhere with the other men. He then decided, that he would inform the Lenape chief, Kitchi, that he would be gone for a number of days, perhaps even a week. Christian depended upon the Lenape people, as his ancestors had done. His instincts were on high alert, but he was not able to decipher them, so he doubled his efforts to keep his mother safe. He would find Cheyvo, headman of the Iroquois, who was on the island for the summer with his group. He needed Cheyvo to be aware that he would be away. He would ask both men to be more vigilant of pirates and marauding bands of outlaw Indians on the bay, during his absence. He thought about the two men and their Indian names. It was amazing how the Indians used names with such remarkable appropriateness—Kitchi, meaning *Brave*—Cheyvo, meaning *Spirit Warrior*.

Those thoughts were running through Christian's head when his mother's words broke into his strategies. "Thank you, but I will stay home," she declared. "Then it is all settled."

"All right," he told her, but the uneasy feeling did not go away. "I will need Papa and Kurt to help sail."

"We have to drop a load of cedar in Tuckerton," Kurt reminded Christian the next day.

After many years, the family still had complete access to the Great Swamp cedar—no one had challenged them. Years ago, they had written to the original Dutch East India Company and had informed them then, that the VanHameetman family had settled on the island. They also had applied to the proper authorities in England, namely Dr. Daniel Cox, for the rights to the area; not that they felt the British really owned anything, but they desired some sort of so called legality for themselves. "Did the family ever hear from Daniel Cox when they wrote to him back some years? I just read something very interesting about Dr. Cox. It was written by a Mister Scull, a noted biographer." Christian looked to his mother.

"Not that I ever heard," Sanne replied.

Christian excused himself and came back with papers in his hand. "In 1684, Dr. Daniel Cox, of London, had acquired an extensive interest in West Jersey, and in 1686 an interest in East Jersey. The former Governor Byllinge died and in January, 1687, Cox purchased from Byllinge's family their landed property in West Jersey, together with the right of government in the Province, under the grant of the Duke of York to Byllinge. Dr. Cox, in consequence, then became Governor of West Jersey. Shortly after, on September 5, 1687, he addressed a letter to the Colony, detailing the circumstances connected with the transaction, and explaining his views as to the future. Mr. Scull advised that the above mentioned Daniel Cox, *being resolved to sell his interest in Land and Government of the Colonies of East and West Jersey, the land Amounting, by a moderate calculation unto one million of acres, whereof about 400,000 were surveyed and the Indian purchase was paid. Besides the purchase of ye land many thousand of pounds have been expended upon the establishing of a whale fishing, which will bring for ye future very great profit. There were also large forests of timber suitable for masts for vessels, immense vineyards for the curing of raisins and the manufacture of wines. Also, there were underlying lands which were rich in deposits of iron, brass, copper and lead. Besides these, there were oyster beds, fisheries and other industries in profitable operation.* Christian laid the papers down. "I have heard of this," Sanne said. Christian continued reading notes that someone had made in the margins.

"However, Dr. Cox *never* visited America. This fact is expressly stated by John Oldmixon, a well known English historian. Cox made John Tatham his agent in the Jerseys, the latter being a resident of Bucks county, Pa., in 1681, where Tatham owned extensive tracts of land. In the fall of 1687, the Assembly of West Jersey acknowledged Dr. Cox as Governor. Cox appointed Edward Hunloke his deputy, but soon after he commissioned his agent, John Tatham, to be his deputy Governor to govern in his name. Tatham was a Jacobite, and as such by principle, this disqualified him, and the Assembly rejected him. The cause assigned for his rejection, that he was a Jacobite, leaves no doubt as to his religious belief. James II, of the house of Stuart, was then upon the throne of England. His followers were known as Jacobites. To be a Jacobite and a Catholic were synonymous terms in those days. Notwithstanding the action of the Assembly, John Tatham continued to act as the agent of Governor Cox, and to take part in public affairs," Christian sat back in his chair. "What do you think of that mish mosh?"

Sanne added to the mix by telling Christian that she had remembered Governor Cox selling his pottery works in 1688. The sale was advertised in the local newspaper and listed the inventory along with some other information. "Just give me a minute and I will find the article. I saved it and tucked it into my journal. I was interested in some of the items that were for sale." She returned in no time with a yellowed clipping and read the following:

"Governor Cox advertised that he had erected a pottery at Burlington, *for white and Chiney ware, a great quantity of ye value £1,200 have been already made and vended in ye country, neighbor Colonies and ye Islands of Barbados and Jamaica, where they are in great request. I have two houses and kilns, with all necessary implements, divers workmen and other servts. Have expended thereon about £2,000."* The *'white'* ware corresponded with the *'white stoneware'* produced by William Miles, of Hanley, Staffordshire, England, and the "Chiney" ware was similar to the "crouch ware" made at Burslem. It had all the elements of porcelain, and had John Tatham given his kilns a harder fire his ware would have been semitransparent. The pottery was built at the suggestion of John Tatham, who had some knowledge of the advantages resulting from the combination of clays, and he thus established the first pottery built on this side of the Atlantic. The pottery was located near Mahlon Stacey's mill, on the Assanpink, in Trenton."

Sanne lay her papers down. "I am not sure who bought this pottery business. Assanpink Creek is a tributary of the Delaware River in western Jersey," Sanne reminded them. "If I remember correctly, the name is from the Lenape, meaning *stony, watery place.* I do believe the river rises in Monmouth, about a mile north of Clarksburg. It runs through a very rural area westward and empties into the Delaware River."

"No one had ever contacted our family. They thought they would receive some reply from their request, but over their years of settlement on the island, no communication was forthcoming. They wanted to know if it was necessary for them to petition to claim, or to buy the land, or to acquire by settling on it, so my father told me." Hans had joined the discussion.

Mainlanders would come over from time to time and chop cedar from the periphery of the Great Swamp and that was their right as much as the VanHameetmans. Acres and acres of cedar trees afforded plenty for all. However, cutters from the mainland had no way to transport any significant amount of lumber over to the Middle of the Shore. Therefore, they saw very few outside cutters; that was fine with them.

The family owned a rather primitive saw, set up in a rough shed in the woodland's borders. The saw was carried on the *Marta's* initial voyage, years ago. Cutting the trees was not the only requirement. The large cedar trees had to be stripped of their tough bark in order to cut the downed trunks into slabs. Barking, peeling or stripping was a seasonal job, when both men and women from the mainland were hired by Christian in early summer to do the stripping. The saw had served its purpose earlier, but now that they were receiving orders requesting more diversified slab sizes, they realized that they would have to look into purchasing a new saw.

"If we have an emergency order," Christian declared, "the Andrews Mill can do the slab cutting temporarily for us, although I know it would be inconvenient and add cost to the order." Christian remembered saying this some time ago and decided that buying a new saw was long overdue. He would make this a priority.

The *Marta* had dropped her cargo of cedar in Tuckerton. Christian then set sail from Tuckerton, east on Barnegat Bay and then south, through the southern inlet and out into open ocean waters. Kurt was up on deck, and they had been cruising south only a short time. He suddenly bellowed, "Christian! Chris! Look behind us! Do you see that black ship? Behind us! Behind us," he motioned, yelling loudly and repeatedly. At first, Christian did not understand him until he turned to see where he was pointing.

"Bloody hell, it *is* a pirate ship!" Kurt shouted, "She is picking up speed!"

"Get my long glass, quickly!" Christian shouted to Florence, who flew to the cabin and raced back to hand him the glass. To Christian's horror, he saw the giant, unmarked sloop. She was not flying a flag; rather, she announced herself with her black color. Christian could hardly believe their outright, bold maneuver.

"They were waiting for the next ship along. They spied us from the other side of the Brigantines to have come out in such fast pursuit." Florence was standing near Christian now, her hand shading her right eye from the bright sunlight; her left eye was glued to the pursuing sloop through a one eye, smaller, long glass. Kurt hurried over to her.

"How do you do that?" He often saw her using both eyes like that and was amazed. He probably just talked out of anxiety.

Florence was too busy to answer him. *"Bloody hell Kurt! There are at least twenty or thirty men on deck that I can see and probably more below,"* Florence drew her breath in sharply. In her excitement, she had sworn, but right then, she did not care. It was a pirate ship—monstrously sized, black and she was fast in the water. She handed Kurt the glass.

"Wha wha what kind of a draft do you th th think she draws?" Stuttering slightly and breathing very fast, Kurt watched the pursuing black ship through the glass.

"A lot more than we do," Christian answered from the wheel, knowing what a shallow draft their *Marta* drew—only the smallest amount of water necessary to submerge the rudder and cover the bottom of her hull. "We have to take a chance on the inner waterways, Kurt. No chance to outrun her." He watched the approaching black ship cutting swiftly through the water.

"She has to weigh a goodly amount of tons. Look how low she sits in the water." Kurt shared his brother's take on the sloop.

"Where is that map of Captain Mey's? I mean the rough, original chart of this part of the passage. All the channels around the Brigantines," Christian demanded. "Somebody! See if you can find it! Quickly!"

Christian continued coursing south and saw the larger Brigantine channel coming into view. "We are going in," he hollered to the crew and steered west. "We have no choice! Where is that damn map?" he yelled, frustrated. Kurt hurried to Christian at the wheel deck, map in hand. "Sebastian!" Christian shouted to one of Florence's cousins on the lower deck. "Come and relieve me at the wheel."

"Look here, Kurt. Someone has marked up the channels that weave through these small islands." They both studied the rough chart and noted Cornelius Mey's name on the bottom, but there was another name on top. Evidently, someone had copied Mey's map, marking some changes. "Oh well," Christian said. "We are into it now. I doubt that Mey would have put his name on the map if it had not been drawn for him. It looks like someone had tried to update it. Hopefully the better for us. Where is that damnable pirate now?"

"I think they are hesitating. They are not sure what to do." Florence was frightened.

"Keep your eye on them," Christian directed. "From the looks of this map, we will be hidden quickly. We will have to decide which channel to follow." He paused, studying the map. "There are more than a few paths marked here. I think we should course in west, then find a large channel headed southeasterly. What say you, Kurt?"

"Agreed."

After a few minutes, Florence shouted. "They are turning back! They probably have no information about these islands, not that we do either, but at least we have a map—of sorts that is, and a shallow draft." She let her breath out in a sigh, lowering the small glass from her eye.

"Smart move, me Captain," Kurt muttered to the pirate captain from behind the long glass.

Christian laid the map beside him and took the wheel from Sebastian. He would thread the *Marta* through small and large channels and hope for the best. They would say a prayer that they would find their way out. Evidently, Captain Mey had neighboring Indians or others familiar with the Brigantine Islands help him draw the map, because without it, Christian knew that they would have been lost. *Thank God for the compass* he thought. At least I know which direction I am going.

He remembered that their Indian friends had told them of tributaries and small creeks that would bring them across the top of the cape to Dennis Creek. This route would cut the sailing time enormously to Goshen and other towns on the western side of the cape. However, Christian would not think of taking the *Marta* on these small streams and creeks because of the constantly shifting bars and extremely low waters around that area. *If I had the time*, he thought, I would go with the Indians to chart the inland tributaries and streams with greater accuracy. What a godsend to navigation if there was such a map; but then, who could swear that even once charted, the depths and shifting bottoms would remain constant. *What would be the use.*

They had sailed a ways west, then turned southeast. Time passed and following the map, weaving carefully through multiple channels, they found themselves in a larger waterway, which opened to the ocean. The crew cheered, seeing the great Atlantic.

Christian breathed a sigh of relief. "I think we can continue around the cape, Oceanside, up to Town Bank. Just watch for pirate ships."

"There's another Man-of-war," one of the crew pointed out.

"Fall in behind that Man-of-war," Christian ordered. "Full sails!" he demanded. "With the British in view, I do not think the pirates will bother us."

Christian was already thinking about the return trip. He decided to replenish their food supply when they arrived in Town Bank, should they be hemmed in on their sail back home. "I have some ideas that may alleviate our worry about those bloody pirates," he said in hushed tones to Kurt. "I will tell you about it when I get more information. In the meantime, we have a British Man-of-war in view."

The Man-of-war was a very large three masted ship. She could be up to 200 feet long, carrying up to 124 guns. Four were at the front, eight at the back and 56 on each side. The guns altogether needed three cannon decks to hold them. Her maximum sailing speed was approximately eight or nine knots: one nautical knot equaled approximately 1.5 land miles. The Man-of-war was a category itself.

The sloops-of-war were small, but deadly warships. The British rated all vessels with 20 guns or more as a sloop-of-war. However, this included very small gun brigs and cutters. So a sloop-of-war could be anything that carried more than 20 guns.

The *Marta* trailed the Man-of-war to the bottom of the cape, Oceanside; as Christian started to break away and head north up the cape, the British turned in too. The crew cheered once more, knowing that they would be safe sailing up the cape. The Man-of-war continued on and the Marta cast anchor in the small Town Bank Harbor. They rowed the dinghy in to the small dock.

Christian had noted in a recent newspaper article that the cape, named after the explorer Mey, had been changed to May. He was curious how that had happened and he decided to put out some inquiries when he returned home.

The Hands Inn at Romney Marsh was inland, about fifteen miles or so north of Town Bank. Florence and the girls were anxious to set foot on land after their close encounter with the pirates. Christian had seen another larger, English sloop anchored in the harbor at Town Bank. This was what he had been looking for. *What luck*, he thought. He would explore his idea as soon as the opportunity arose. "If this trip does not turn my hair gray, nothing will," he remarked to Kurt.

Christian had remembered the name Scarlatti and the letter that Sergio had written years ago to his grandmother, Maggie. He knew that Sergio had been elderly when he wrote the letter, and was of course long gone.

"Florence, do you remember my mother telling us that Sergio Scarlatti had a son, Mario, and a grandson, Nicholas and that they had settled somewhere on the cape?" He was curious, and although it would probably come to naught, he intended to inquire in Romney Marsh and Town Bank to see whether either the Scarlatti or the Cadiz name was known in the area.

"I was informed that there is a livery hereabouts, where we can hire a coach. I hope that it is within walking distance. I do believe Romney Marsh is on or near Shamgar Hands old plantation land between Crooked Creek and Gravelly Run. I have heard much about it, and I am anxious to stay there for a good meal and a comfortable bed." Christian sent a crew member to find the livery; luck was with them. The livery was within walking distance of the Town Bank Harbor.

"Oh, Papa, what pretty black horses," the girls were excited, as they stood watching the livery owner harness two of his best horses for the family's ride to Romney Marsh. They piled in, and the coach jerked ahead.

Christian had already given orders to the *Marta's* crew and had asked his father whether he wanted to accompany them to Romney Marsh.

"I would rather stay here with the men on the ship than in some strange inn. We have plenty of provisions. Kurt should go with you." Christian expected that answer from his father. He knew how very set in his ways he had become.

"Settle down, now," Christian told his daughters as the coach pulled out. He realized that they were in a state of great excitement, savoring all of the newness. "We have a ways to go. The driver says it is about a twenty five minute ride from Town Bank to Hands Inn at Romney Marsh—if we go at a steady clip and if the road is in proper shape. The weather is fair, so we should make it in good time."

"I hope they have a room for us." Florence was worried.

"It's still early in the day, and I think we have a good chance." Christian tried to assure her.

"This coach is worse than the *Marta* with its rocking," Kurt complained, trying to settle back into his seat.

Exactly twenty minutes later, the coach pulled up in front of a large, attractive, well kept stone building, and the driver announced, "Here we are, folks. Enjoy your stay. Let me know if and when you want transportation back to your ship. I will wait a few minutes to see that you are settled."

Christian thanked the driver. "Wait, girls. Where are your manners?" Florence called, but they had been sitting far too long and could not contain themselves; they were off and running after their father, with Florence in pursuit.

"Oh my," Florence commented as she peeped into the large dining room on their way to find the innkeeper. "This is lovely. And what delicious smells are coming from the kitchen."

A rotund, but robust looking gentleman with a long, curled, white mustache, smoking a clay pipe approached them. He was certainly an eye catcher, in his green, velvet waistcoat, topping slim, black, stovepipe pants. He introduced himself as Daniel Hand, cousin of Shamgar Hand, the original proprietor of the inn. "May I help you?" he offered his hand.

"Yes, Sir, you may," Christian replied. "I would like a large room for my wife and family." Then he motioned to Kurt. "Would you have a smaller room for my brother? Or what arrangements can we make for him?"

"You are really in luck Sir. I have two large rooms left, both with a sitting area and two double beds. We also have bachelors' quarters, where we keep single beds for single gentlemen. Would that do?"

"Nicely, thank you," Kurt confirmed. "I will let the driver go," and he walked outside.

"We will all be coming down for dinner tonight," Christian stated, winking at the girls, who were staring wide eyed, at Mr. Hand's attire. This was the first time the young girls had stayed at an inn. Everything was new and exciting for them, and surely Mr. Hand was not ordinary. "May I hire a coach from here to return us to our ship in Town Bank, in a day or two?" Christian asked Mr. Hand.

"Yes, you can; I will arrange it for you." He called a boy to carry their bags upstairs."

Christian thanked him and the family settled into their room to clean up and rest a bit. "Thank heaven they had a room for us. I did not look forward to sleeping on the ship." Florence was happy.

Before dinner, the family took a turn around the lovely little town of Romney Marsh, founded and named by Shamgar Hand for a village on the Strait of Dover, off Kent, England.

Kurt had spoken with some of the local politicians he had met in the tavern. "There has been bitter dissention among the local citizens in naming Romney Marsh as the political center and county seat. Opposing views wanted either Dennis Creek or Goshen," Kurt informed them. "Dennis Creek has large shipbuilding activities, a big timber business and direct connection by water with Philadelphia. But Romney Marsh won out. Many wondered how that had happened."

Evening found the family comfortably seated around a large circular table. Their choice of food was wide and when it was served, proved to be just as delicious as the smells Florence had commented about earlier. Notably on the bill of fare were starters of fresh oysters and clams, mussels, or crabs, pulled right from the Delaware Bay. The main courses included wild turkey stuffed with cornbread dressing, served with a cranberry orange relish, roasted yams, and assorted fresh vegetables. Or, as Christian chose, the specialty of the house: the tavern's roast beef with Yorkshire pudding. The rest of the family chose the turkey. They topped off the sumptuous meal with a choice of blueberry pie, fresh peach pie, or chocolate cake, all still warm from the oven, sporting mounds of freshly whipped cream.

"I cannot move a fig," Florence commented. "I am absolutely stuffed with this wonderful dinner. Who would expect to find such a meal in this out of the way place? I am glad that we stuck with food that we know, although I would like to have tried some of the unknowns. Perhaps next time?" She smiled at Christian.

"And *they* cooked it all. How much better does that make it, my dear?" Christian laughed.

Darkness was closing in and Florence took the girls up to the room. The brothers strolled into the attached gentlemen's bar for a whiskey, hoping for some stimulating conversation regarding the state of the politics in the area.

"Have you come across the name Scarlatti or Cadiz in your years in this region?" Christian asked the bar keep. "I am not sure which name he would be using."

"I have only been in the area a year or two. Cannot say the name rings a bell. Sorry, mate."

During dinner, Christian had noted that there were a large number of English soldiers in the dining room and in the bar. *Their bright red coats are not to be missed*, he thought as he slowly sipped his whiskey. Once more, he approached the keep. "Is something going on, or is there a special mission afoot? I have noticed there are many British in here tonight. Is that usual?"

"One of the muckety mucks from England arrived yesterday. What you see here is his contingent of officers and mind you, they be all army. They leave for the port of Newark in a few days, escorting some nobleman from London, I do believe. He would be visiting the Governor there. Yes, that he is. You probably missed their sloop. They must have arrived in late afternoon."

Christian wanted to find out when the escort sloop was leaving for Newark, which was north of Long Beach Island. *By Jove*, Christian thought, *this may work!* His immediate intention was to ask British officers if the *Marta* could trail their sloop-of-war, south, around the cape and north to Long Beach Island. They would get escort protection two fold—both on the bay and on the ocean. No pirate ship would dare attack these heavily armed, smaller sloops-of-war patrolling the coasts, which were also referred to as escort ships. This sloop was carrying a contingent of English army officers, along with naval officers and crew. Christian laughed softly when he told Kurt what he had in mind. Kurt grinned. Christian immediately approached a lively group of British and struck up a conversation with the officers. He sympathized with them as they bemoaned the fact that they were army duty escorts on a navy ship.

Christian returned to their table to tell Kurt the news. "They are pulling out of Town Bank Friday morning. They told me that following their sloop would not be a problem. They would be delighted to help us. I spoke with Captain Harrison, and he said he would meet me on his ship, *H.M.S Victory*, Friday at noon, sharp." The brothers could not believe their good luck.

"Good timing, I would say." Kurt was quite satisfied, thinking that this would give them the time they needed for another day at Romney Marsh, a trip to Goshen and back to Town Bank to follow the British to Long Beach Island. He smiled to himself, relaxed, and finished off his whiskey.

"Ho there, matey." A deep voice interrupted from a table behind, startling the brothers. "I heard you questioning the keep about the Scarlattis. May I ask why you inquire of the name?" Christian turned around to see a dignified older man and noted his full head of thick, gray hair, his healthy complexion and the immaculate, white jabot he sported at his neck.

"Yes, Sir," Christian turned his chair fully around to face him, and held out his hand to the gentleman. "Christian VanHameetman here, and my brother, Kurt. The Scarlatti name comes up in our ancestral family journals. I am curious to see if there are any Scarlattis in the area. I know it was many years ago, but I thought I would ask anyway."

"Well, Sir, "he said, shaking Christian's hand, and nodding to Kurt, "Pleased to meet you—John Mulholland here, originally of County Antrim, Ireland at your service. Yes, I know of the Scarlattis. Still in this area, originally at Fort Nassau, then up to Town Bank, then further up the cape to Goshen, in the shipbuilding business. I believe they started one of the early trading posts over by Fort Nassau years ago. It was overrun by hostiles, and then the Scarlattis went to Town Bank with their post, where they were very successful. They entered into the ship trade in Goshen, and did very well for themselves, so I have heard. It would be Nick Scarlatti that you are looking for, elderly now, with a grandson of his own."

"That must be Sergio's grandson, Nicholas. He mentioned this in his letter to my grandmother of a son, Mario, and a grandson, Nicholas. Christian was surprised and pleased to hear that Mr. Mulholland was familiar with the Scarlatti family. He had not had much hope of locating them. "We are on our way to Goshen. I heard how the ship trade is growing up there and I wanted to see for myself."

"Ye be in the ship trade, laddies?"

"We are in the lumber business, Sir. Cedar wood to be exact. From up north along the Atlantic coast," Kurt responded.

Mulholland raised his bushy eyebrows. "That wonderful, hard, cedar wood from the barrier island? I know of the wood. Wonderful, indeed. Are you looking for business around Goshen?"

"We have to see the lay of the land first. Then we will contact the Scarlattis and tell them of our previous connection. I would not mind doing business with their yard." Kurt told him.

"You tell them that John Mulholland of County Antrim helped you track them down. I know you will like that Scarlatti bunch. Originally from Spain, you know. Cadiz, I think. On the coast."

"Thank you, Sir, that I will," Christian said. "Now if you will excuse us, Kurt and I will turn in. We have some busy days ahead of us, starting right on the morrow. Sailing down, we ran into pirates just south of Long Beach Island and were forced off our ocean route and into the Brigantines. We had no choice but to negotiate those small islands. We have made return plans with the British to trail their sloop north, up the coast." Christian paused. "I want to stay in open waters. Navigating is easier; we can make better time. Damned bloody pirates!"

"Good luck to ye, lads. Hope I run into you again." Mulholland got up to leave.

The sausages were round and fat the next morning, accompanying a flat fried cake mixed with apples, lighter than a fritter. This was the inn's specialty, aptly named apple pancakes. The delicacy was liberally covered with maple syrup and sweet butter. Both children and adults stuffed themselves, again.

Christian told Florence of the conversation regarding the Scarlattis. She was pleased and as anxious as he was to meet them. They looked forward to another day in Romney Marsh and their last night at Hands Inn. They would return to Town Bank tomorrow to pick up the *Marta* and continue on to Goshen. Florence remarked that it was worth the trip to see Romney Marsh and for the lovely stay and wonderful food at Hands. "I agree," Christian said. "By the way," he added, "Mr. Hand advised me to look for the Goshen Creek when we sail. There are few waterways into the bay as you sail north from Town Bank. The Scarlatti's have put up a small sign for buyers or visitors coming up the bay. Their business is not far from the entrance to the bay. He told me of an old man who watches for ships coming in. He earns a little money by giving visitors a ride in his wagon into town. Let us hope that he is there when we cast anchor. Mr. Hand said it is too far to walk into the village itself."

During their ride back to the *Marta*, Florence told Christian, "I know how much you enjoyed the pancakes Chris and I thought I would make them at home for you." She smiled. "I visited the cook early this morning." Christian reached over to hug her. She knew how much he loved his sweets.

The *Marta* arrived near Goshen and the sign appeared quickly. They cast anchor and dropped the dinghy. They were fortunate to see the old Indian man coming towards the dock. He offered to take them into town in his large wagon. "Do you know of the Scarlatti shipyards?" The old man nodded his head. "We would like you to stop there, if you please," Christian asked.

"You were fortunate that I saw your ship. I was on my way to town, which is the other way, when I happened to see your top sails," the old man offered. He took them to the shipyard, where they were immensely impressed at its size, including the ongoing additions. It was still early, and the gray mist was just lifting under the sun's warming rays. They asked the old man to stay, should they not be able to secure a ride back to the ship. As they approached the yard's office, they noticed an elderly gentleman sitting on a bench, most likely enjoying his first pipe of the day. He stood up and removed his cap to Florence and the girls and said, "Good morning to you, lovely ladies," executing a grand sweep of his chapeau to them, and turned to Christian and Kurt. "Looking for someone, lads? Maybe I can help you."

"Why, yes," Christian responded, "perhaps you can. We are looking for any of the Scarlatti family."

"You have business with them?" The gentleman inquired, smiling broadly. Christian noticed what fine white teeth he had for an older man; probably because he was deeply tanned, the whiteness was exaggerated. His dark hair was streaked with gray, and as the sun caught him fully in the face, his brown eyes flashed with mischief. He was indeed a very handsome fellow. *Methinks he knows it,* Christian thought.

"We might," Christian said, deciding to play a little cat and mouse in return. "Then again, it might be something more personal. Would you know what time they come down to the yard?"

The friendly fellow then tapped his pipe on the bench and grinned at them. "I am Nicholas Scarlatti. And who ye be?"

"Christian VanHameetman, Sir. Referred by one John Mulholland of County Antrim, Ireland, whom we met at Hands Inn. And this is Florence, my wife, and my three daughters, and Kurt, my brother." Christian paused to compose himself and to be at the ready to continue the conversation.

"Yes, I know Mr. Mulholland well. Fine fellow he is. And your business, my lad?" he asked, looking at Christian.

"You are referred to in my Grandmother Maggie's journal as Sergio's grandson, Nicholas. Is that correct?" Nicholas was caught off guard, *which I am sure did not happen often,* Christian noted.

"Your Grandmother Maggie's journal? How did I come to be mentioned in her journal?"

"Captain John Weber was a mutual friend of your Grandfather, Sergio, and my Grandfather, Willem VanHameetman. Captain John was a whaler for many years and camped near the Great Swamp on Long Beach. I have an old letter that Sergio wrote in response to a correspondence from my Grandmother, Maggie, telling him of the death of Captain Weber. My Grandfather, Willem, as a young man, knew the Captain well and often spoke of him as quite a character, but mostly he remembered him for his kindnesses. I wanted to meet the Scarlattis after reading of them in my grandmother's journal."

"By Jove boy! You have taken the wind right out of my sails, I can say that. Sergio was my grandfather. My father,

Mario, was Sergio's son. My father would tell me stories of Captain Weber and his visits to Fort Nassau, when my father was a boy. I only wish I had known Captain Weber. I do believe the news of Captain Weber's passing was delayed for a time, as my father told it. Evidently Sergio could not be found." Nicholas shook his head in wonderment, hearing this information. "Sit yourself a spell and tell me all of your family. My Grandson, Sergio, will be here soon. Yes, Sergio," he repeated when he saw Christian's reaction to the name. "We call him Serge for short; we wanted to keep the name in the family."

Christian had almost forgotten the waiting driver—he asked Nicholas if there was any transportation back to the dock where the *Marta* was at anchor.

"Of course, I will take you, or Serge will. Let this good man go."

Christian thanked the driver, handed him some money, and bade him farewell. Then they sat talking for a spell until the girls started getting restless. Just before they decided to depart, they saw a horse and wagon approaching. "Here he is now," Nicholas said, as he watched his grandson pull up in a horse and wagon.

"My goodness," Florence remarked. "What a comely fellow he is." She had taken in his deeply suntanned face, dark, wavy hair and green eyes. "Must run in the family."

"My son, Roberto was his father. We lost both Roberto and his wife Jenny in a typhoid fever epidemic when Serge was quite young," Nicholas told them. "Roberto was our only child."

Serge leaped down from the wagon and laughed at Florence, showing the same fine, white teeth as his grandfather, and bowing low to her, he said, "Why, thank you. Such nice compliments from a lovely lady." Florence blushed, knowing that he had overheard her flattering remark. He looked over to the three, giggling girls standing beside their mother and said, "And who are these beautiful little ladies in their finery?" This set the girls off into shrieks of laughter.

"Mixing the blood makes for handsome, strong offspring," Nicholas offered with a smile. "My mother was Iroquois and Swedish, named Brigitte, but we called her Orenda, her Iroquois name. It means *Magic Power*. My father always said that she had bewitched him. She was the most beautiful woman God ever put on this earth." He sighed. "My father, Mario, loved her like nothing I have ever seen the like of—God rest his and her soul." He thought of his parents whom he had loved deeply, who had died in a terrible flu epidemic, that had wiped out hundreds of people.

"You must have cousins here, too, Nicholas. I remember reading that your grandfather brought his sister and her family and friends from Spain on his return trip." Christian was trying to put all the names together that his parents and grandparents had discussed over the years.

"There's a whole parcel of descendent Spanish families living hereabouts. Thank goodness for Isabella's friends who sailed with our family. They brought new blood into the area. Some of our countrymen settled in New Amsterdam, although I heard there were not too many who stayed back in the '60s and early '70s. The lad here," Nicholas added, pointing to his grandson, Serge, "married Evangeline Rose, the prettiest girl you'll ever see. She is from the area around New Amsterdam, and is of Dutch, Swedish, and Spanish descent. They have two lovely children, Emilio and Rose. Married young, they did. We have not carried names forth as most Spanish do, because we have diverse cultural backgrounds involved."

"Congratulations, Serge," Christian offered, and Florence and Kurt joined in. "Your father told us that perhaps you and your new wife will be settling near here."

"Could be," Serge answered. "We are not sure yet."

"Let's talk of business," Nicholas said, and they stood for a further moment as Christian repeated the story of his cedar involvement to Serge.

"You mean you are the fellow who brings that Great Swamp cedar to New Amsterdam?"

"The very one. We are looking to supply the yards in this area. I would like to get another ship or contract to lease a ship to bring my cedar down here." Christian wanted to test the waters.

"What about your runs to New Amsterdam?" Serge asked. "That must be quite a money maker for you."

"I would keep that going, of course," Christian replied.

"I can use all the cedar wood that you can bring. You can see all the diverse species of wood in this area—but I am not interested in anything but the cedar. In fact, I would like you to bring all of your cedar up here and forget about New Amsterdam," Serge proposed. Christian raised a doubtful eyebrow, but Serge repeated what he just said to him. "I mean it, Christian. I am serious. We can use all of the cedar that you can haul, but before we even talk about that, my family is opening another yard in Dennis Creek. We are advertising for a number of different suppliers. Goshen Creek empties into the Delaware Bay, as Dennis Creek also empties into the bay and then right up the river to Philadelphia. Are you aware of the growth going on up there? Dennis Creek would be the ideal location to supply Philadelphia with ships and lumber and your cedar. We wanted our Goshen and Dennis Creek yards close. We would restock the new Dennis Creek yard differently and build our larger ships there. We have plans for the Goshen yard too. We can take everything you can bring us; we would give you one of our ships to use to sail the lumber over to us. The big problem for you is that there is no waterway across the top of the cape to Dennis Creek. You would have to sail around the cape and up the Delaware."

"This is quite a coincidence. I had seen an advertisement in the Philadelphia newspaper, but it was another name. That is why I decided to take a trip here. Did you advertise under Dennis Shipyards?"

"Yes, that is right." Serge nodded. "Some coincidence, that is. But we are glad that you found us."

"Any chance of the VanHameetmans investing in your new company?" Kurt asked, thinking he could only be refused.

Nicholas winked at him. "There is always room for a competent hard working investor. Right, Serge?"

So there would be room for us, Christian thought. *This is something that I have wanted to do for a while. All that money,* he thought, *rather, all that saved family gold.* Their hoard was in safekeeping, just waiting for a place to call home. The family felt banking houses were not satisfactory places to hold their gold and other shared assets. It would be easy pickings for the British, if they so intended.

"I have to catch my breath on this," Christian said, thinking how much a contract like this would bring into the family coffers. However, he was one who did not make rash decisions; he was well aware of the dangers lurking in the Delaware Bay. That entire bay area was a nesting place for bloodthirsty, thieving pirates who thought no more of cutting a man's throat than saying good morning. He was not about to risk his life or any of the others to ship lumber. *He kept those thoughts to himself for the moment.*

"How would you like a tour of our yard?" Serge asked. "We have an excellent reputation here in Goshen. We would like to carry that to Dennis Creek."

"You know there are a few small yards springing up near Tuckerton," Christian ventured. "How deep is the Goshen Creek?"

"Goshen Creek is usually deep enough, but we build only a few larger ships. Dennis Creek would allow us to build the larger exploratory ships. Right now we are building packets. We change specifications to fit the buyer's needs—mostly commercial fishing boats. What you see here is only a small portion of our Goshen yard. We have another yard next to this one, just up the creek kept for sorting, some assembly of small structure and storing lumber. We had already started stripping and cutting plank and assembling small structures for ships, but not actually building a ship. It was better that we kept that business separate. That is why there are no ships here. We were amazed that there was a tremendous call for ship parts all over this area. It turned out to be a great business." Serge looked toward Nicholas.

"We know about Tuckerton. Perhaps in the future, we can think about that area. Right now, Dennis Creek it is," Nicholas said and led the way out into the yard.

The Scarlatti family certainly knew something about building ships. Innovation and excellent artisanship carried over into beautiful ships. Even though the packets were their moneymakers, Christian saw two larger carracks in their other yard under construction. He felt that he and Kurt would like to discuss a future business venture with the Scarlatti family. From what he saw, it would definitely be a gold maker. However, the risks that would accompany such a partnership, were another matter. Kurt agreed with his brother.

Nicholas had suggested that they take the ship to Philadelphia and visit the city. Florence was in agreement. "I have never been to Philadelphia. What a treat it would be." He heard the excitement rising in Florence's voice.

Christian was growing concerned now, about the crew and leaving his mother that much longer on Long Beach. Work was waiting for them on the island. They had been gone for a time already. He was reluctant to extend the trip, but more important, they would be on their own on the return voyage, at the mercy of the pirates.

Christian worried about what he had heard in town—the pirates were extremely active up and down the coast. He needed to trail the English ship back to the island and they were departing Town Bank Friday at noon. "Florence, have you forgotten about those pirate ships? Why would we want to jeopardize our family and crew's safety on the return trip? What was I thinking, putting a visit to Philadelphia ahead of our safety concerns." Christian put his arm around Florence. "We can take a trip in the future, or sail over to Tuckerton and go overland to Philadelphia."

"There's no decision there," Nicholas was concerned. "I did not realize the real danger. Under those circumstances, I feel as you do. You have to follow the British and return home."

"Something has to be done about these damnable pirates," Kurt commented. "If we ever intend to ship lumber to Goshen, we would be sitting ducks on the open waters."

"I heard that the Jersey Government is very concerned about the thieving scoundrels, as is Pennsylvania. You know the Judge of the Admiralty in Pennsylvania to the Lords of Trade? I believe his name is Colonel Quary. He has captured some of the pirates, along with their ships. Can you believe that some of them are from as far away as Madagascar? Seems they are all over, from the north in New Amsterdam waters, to the south and the bottom of the cape and into the big bay. I would not be able to come around the cape into the bay safely, Serge," Christian admitted. "We can go pretty far up the protected inner waterway when we go to New Amsterdam, but the Delaware Bay and the open ocean is becoming more dangerous. I think we will have to schedule with the British from now on when we go out into the ocean or the Delaware Bay."

Nicholas nodded his head in agreement and told Christian that he understood that no profits were worth risking lives.

"Why don't you think more seriously about the Tuckerton area?" Christian asked Serge. "That Middle of the Shore area is growing rapidly and is an excellent location, especially for us. Transporting cedar directly across Barnegat Bay would be very easy. Tuckerton is easily accessible by water, yet sheltered from the ocean. This is probably where we will open a yard. I hear this area has become one of the larger ports on the Eastern seacoast, if not the largest. Opening a shipyard there would make us as much money as your Dennis Creek."

"I am sorry to interrupt, but it is 10:00 a.m. We have to get back to the *Marta* and make ready. You have to speak further with the officer in charge. We certainly cannot miss the British. The captain advised us strongly not to be late." Kurt was becoming anxious.

They bade the Scarlattis farewell, knowing that they would see them again. Christian realized, that in a short time they felt more like family than just mere names in his grandmother's diary. The Scarlattis were honest, industrious, and family oriented—wonderful qualities in a Dutchman's eyes.

They quickly piled into Serge's wagon and returned to the *Marta*.

Once on board and on their way, Christian remarked, "We need to have a serious discussion when we return home. A family meeting is in order." A plan was forming in his mind. He would open a shipyard in the Tuckerton vicinity. This had been suggested previously at a family finance meeting, but had gone no further. When they had toured the Scarlatti yard, he had carefully noted the layout of the yard. Of course, it was a quick perusal, but he did manage to get a halfway decent overview.

If they were to go ahead with that plan, he or Kurt could visit relatives in the Rotterdam area who were still in the shipbuilding business. He had been mulling that over in his mind for some time now. Occasionally, he was able to secure newspapers from Rotterdam on the incoming Dutch ships at New Amsterdam. More than once, he had seen articles about the VanHameetman Yard, or their advertising for men. Their yard was one of the largest in the Netherlands. His relatives had been involved in shipbuilding since the early 1500s. *They could learn much from their cousins*, he thought. He wondered why he had never thought of contacting them. Then he realized that he had only become familiar with the yard when he saw the recent advertisements in the papers. Certainly VanHameetman was not a common name. Christian decided that either he or Kurt should write to them; he wanted to know how they would be received. In the meantime, he would present his idea to the family about building a shipyard in the Tuckerton area. The family needed to invest its large hoard of gold, presently in safekeeping—safe, but stagnant.

The crew made quick work of weighing anchor, and in short time they were off, sailing back south to Town Bank. They cast anchor near the British sloop, the only ship moored in the small harbor. The crew released the dinghy for the brothers, and they rowed over to the *H.M.S. Victory.*

"Ahoy, the ship," Christian called.

A seaman leaned over the side and yelled down to them, "What is your business with the *H.M.S Victory?*"

"Permission to speak with the officer in charge on a matter of grave import; referred by Captain Harrison of the British Army," Christian shouted back, not knowing if Harrison was aboard yet.

The officer in charge called down to them, "Permission to come aboard." A seaman dropped the side ladder.

"Christian and Kurt VanHameetman of the *Marta* secured over yonder, Sir."

"And what can I do for you, laddies?" The officer replied and introduced himself as Captain William Smythe. "Captain Harrison is not aboard." Smythe stood before them, a very tall man with a long, gray, curled mustache and bright blue eyes. His broad chest, enclosed in the brilliant scarlet of an Englishman's jacket, clearly displaying his rank, told them he was not a seaman, but an English soldier and an officer.

Christian quickly summarized their previous conversation with Captain Harrison and Captain Smythe had no objection to them trailing close behind his ship. Smythe was definitely in charge, probably because of his escort duties, although there must have been a naval officer somewhere on board.

"Do not worry about those bloody pirates when an English sloop-of-war is in the waters, me boys," he bragged. "We will blow them to smithereens before they even see us, and they know it. Does not matter how large their ship is. They will not have a chance," he stated with authority. "Think the *Marta* can keep up with us?"

"Without effort, Sir," Kurt responded with a grin.

"Pretty confident of her, are ye, lad?" Smythe winked.

"With our sails full out, we can outrun pretty much anything except that giant pirate sloop we encountered coming down. She was manned by a crew of more than thirty," Christian added, shaking his head in almost disbelief, remembering the overall size of the pirate ship.

"But she does not have the guns, the trained men, or the maneuverability of a sloop-of-war," Captain Smythe gloated. "We had one encounter on the ocean side of the cape. Chased a large pirate ship for a ways, out into the ocean, but she did not want the clash, and she ran." He smiled and added that they were ready to weigh anchor. The brothers rowed back to the *Marta*.

The journey south around the cape and north to Long Beach Island was unremarkable. The *Marta* crew did spot a smaller, very suspicious looking, black galleon away to the west, but the galleon stayed far from them. They coursed north along the coast and slipped into the southern inlet. They waved farewell to the British crew and steered in, following the inner passage north, up the bay side to the southern boundary of the Great Swamp. It was the first time that they were thankful for British aid—strange indeed, they admitted.

As they approached their waterfront, they knew that something was afoot and dreadfully wrong. They spotted family members on the bay beach and on their dock, waiting. Evidently someone had seen the *Marta* sailing up bayside and had spread the word of their arrival.

"What has happened?" Florence was nervous when she saw people milling about when they came in close. Hans watched anxiously from the deck.

As they tied down, they quickly learned of the terrible news. The day after they had sailed, hostile Indians had come in a small group of ten or twelve, canoeing down the bay to the Great Swamp area. As soon as Christian and Kurt heard the news, they knew it had to be renegades, cast outs of their own tribe—only God knew what deeds they had committed. These Indians were the most dangerous. The hostiles had hugged tight to the shoreline, using the trees and brush for cover and were able to avoid the watchful Lenape group. The outlaws had entered the thick undergrowth of trees and with great stealth, had crept through the heavy brush and reeds toward the family compound. Sanne and Litonya had been *outside the wall*, gathering mushrooms and wild strawberries when the renegades surprised and murdered them so that they would not shout the alarm. Sanne's sister, Georgia had been in the house when this happened, which had saved her life.

Hans collapsed at the news of his wife, Sanne and they carried him into the house.

When Florence heard the horrible story, she cried hysterically, "Merciful Heaven! They were planning a grand feast for our return." She later learned that the Lenape Chief Kitchi's young daughters, Alsoomse and Nuttah, had been soft shell crabbing in the shore rushes, which had hidden them when they saw the hostiles' canoes slip silently past.

"We could not tell what tribe they were and my sister and I hid ourselves in the rushes until their canoes were out of sight. Then we ran to find our father. We could not find him and we did not know what to do!" Nuttah lay down on the grass and wept. Between sobs she told them, "Chief Cheyevo and his men were on the beach; the Lenape men were on the bay, too far to help us."

Alsoomse, younger daughter, spoke English well. Her name meant *Independent* and through tears, she told Florence, "My sister and I heard the screams but could do nothing. They would have killed us, too, if they had seen us. Sanne and Litonya never had a chance, and by the time my father and his men arrived, they were already dead."

When Nuttah, *My Heart*, elder daughter could get hold of herself, she told them, "I am thankful that our father arrived before the renegades desecrated the bodies. His men managed to kill three of the foreigners, wound two, and the rest ran off. My father is still not sure where these hostiles came from or to which tribe they had belonged." Nuttah was in a state of shock.

Christian was sick with grief over the killings. He could not understand how this could have happened. "Where are the two who were wounded?"

"Chief Cheyevo took them," Nuttah answered.

Christian did not comment. It was Indian punishment, and Cheyevo would take care of it. Christian did not care.

The Iroquois and Lenape, along with the family loved Litonya. Cheyevo of the Iroquois spoke with Lenape Chief Kitchi and they concluded that the group were cast outs, the unholy and unclean of all. They could have come from anywhere.

Florence was in shock; she dearly loved her mother-in-law, Sanne. The little girls could not understand why anyone would kill their beloved grandmother and Litonya. Nor could Christian understand such a senseless act. Hans was in shock.

"This is why there is a strict rule that women are not permitted alone outside of the compound, ever," Christian emphasized, "and the men, too, move only in groups. Our good fortune of isolated incidents and none encounters with hostiles is not by chance; there are rules to avoid any contact. The walled compound further enhances these rules. I do believe that this is the first instance where one of the family or friend has been murdered. Why Mother and Litonya chose to blatantly ignore the rule and go outside of the wall is difficult at best to fathom. The mushrooms and strawberries, which were of such great import at the time, cost them their lives." Christian put his head down and wept softly. It was a difficult and sad lesson learned by all; certainly a price too dear to pay for the rewards of berries and mushrooms. Aunt Georgia told Florence that she had been too tired to go with her sister and Litonya. Her nap had saved her life.

After months of grieving, Florence knew they had to move on. She had to set an example for her family. It had been hard for Christian. Hans did not speak for months after his wife's death. It was a terrible time or everyone.

Sometime later, Christian called a meeting of the Family Council. They decided unanimously to secure land and look into building a small shipyard in the Middle of the Shore area. "We need to put our savings to work," he explained. "Kurt and I will follow through and make a trip to Tuckerton to investigate and survey potential areas around the water for the new yard. If we find it satisfactory, we will purchase the land." After being reminded, Christian told the group, "I know that we need to put to work those eighty acres of land and the lot in Philadelphia. We should consider that soon."

Two weeks later, Christian announced, "I think we did well. It was our good fortune to find land and secure it at an excellent price so quickly." Nodding his head in agreement, Kurt was pleased with the purchase of 500 acres of ground fronting a long inlet near Little Egg Harbor.

"The price was right. I have certainly investigated land values. It is a large piece of land with direct access to water, and bargaining in gold gave us a substantial abatement." Christian smiled. "The family will be pleased."

The building of the new yard moved forward. They would start small, enlarging as they grew. Kurt posted an ad in the local paper and on the town bulletin board for men to clear the land. It rendered good response. It was a start.

"If I am in charge of the start up of the new shipyard, I need to get moving," Kurt said. "My plans are coming together for the trip to Rotterdam to visit the ancestral shipyards. You remember that I wrote a letter to the VanHameetman Yard in Rotterdam. I enclosed a copy of our genealogy, showing our place in the line; a Charles VanHameetman recently wrote back. He welcomed the idea of a trip from Cousin Bill and me and they kindly offered their home for our stay. Charles said that his family would be happy to help us in any way that they could. The letter was very welcoming. I am looking forward to meeting them. While I am there, I will look into enlisting a master shipbuilder to work with us for a year, here."

"That would certainly save a lot of time than if we had to search for a competent master builder." Christian was pleased. "I think it is a good idea too, bringing Cousin Bill with you. He can get into the business side and you can oversee the building of the yard." As an afterthought, he said to Kurt, "You two had better brush up on your Dutch, or better still, learn to speak Dutch properly."

Kurt and Bill sailed to Rotterdam and were greeted warmly by their extended family. They were most impressed with the large and profitable shipyard their cousins ran in Rotterdam. The journey paid off handsomely; Kurt was able to persuade a distant cousin, Olaf, a master shipbuilder, to spend a year with them in Jersey. Olaf, as a VanHameetman, made it abundantly clear that he would agree to teach *only* family members all he knew of the trade, from the design to the building of the ship. He would bring numerous plans with him, which could be modified to suit the local waters and buyers' requests. He would teach no outsiders the VanHameetman's century old, well guarded plans and certain other *secrets of the trade*, as he called it. This was strictly family related tutelage.

After Olaf arrived, and under his teaching, the men learned quickly and, as a result the business was off to a solid start. Because of the variety of the local lumber available, including the precious cedar from the Great Swamp, their ships were immediately in demand. Word had grown and spread quickly of Olaf. Christian laughed. "We certainly cannot complain about our profits." Both private citizens in the area and the English placed orders for packets, commercial fishing ships and merchant ships. The family avoided building warships for anyone.

The next large family event was joyful. Kurt and Cynthia were to be married in the spring. Cynthia was a lovely English Irish girl, with the beautiful English rose complexion, light strawberry colored hair, and dark blue eyes. In time, Kurt's life was very full when they had two sons, Andrew and Simon just a year apart.

"We need to retire the *Marta*," Christian announced once more to Kurt. "She has been repaired too many times. She is a very old ship and I do not want to see her rot to her demise. We should build the *Marta II*."

"I agree. It is time. I know we have been putting it off. Take some of the old lady's cedar, just a small amount and incorporate it into the new *Marta*. Good luck will come from that." Kurt was definite in his request.

"And, the problem exists on the open ocean waters or the Delaware Bay. With a shipload of cedar we need an armed escort. Thank God we can sail to the mainland and Tuckerton. Our neighbors and friends are fearful of losing their cargo and their lives to pirates," Christian acknowledged. "The big bay and the ocean routes are too dangerous to sail and there is no way out of the local waters."

"I would like to see the Scarlattis more often, but that is impossible unless they travel overland by coach, which is a long, tiresome trip." Kurt was angry and frustrated that the Delaware Bay waters were so infested with pirates. They could sail over to Tuckerton and meet the Scarlattis there, but it was a long ride overland, from Philadelphia to Tuckerton but a safe one. The British were patrolling in that area.

"We have been so fortunate having the Scarlattis as close friends. I think of them as family," Florence agreed, and added, "Yes, but it would be nice to see them more often."

May 1745

Years had passed too quickly Christian thought. He dwelled more in the past now. He recognized this, but he did not care. He enjoyed ruminating on pleasant memories. Florence had left the world a few years prior and he missed her terribly. Now he sat in the fading afternoon sun, trying to warm his old bones before the sun slipped low. Christian adored his three daughters, married for years to honest and hardworking men, whom he thought of as sons. Grandchildren had contributed greatly to their joy. He liked to think about the Scarlattis, remembering all the good times that they had had with the family. He instinctively knew that he would leave soon to join his beloved wife. Their lives together had been full and rich and he looked forward to the continuance of their relationship on the other side.

Christian asked his elder daughter to bring him the current family journal. He knew that the request would upset her, so he said, "I want to make sure the journal is ready to hand to Andrew in the future."

Christian had done an admirable job updating and sorting the immense amount of paperwork that had been left. He felt that his nephew, Andrew would do a good job, and he had intimated to his nephew that he wanted to leave the journals to him. He and Florence had discussed this and Florence had agreed that it should be Andrew, who had expressed his interest in these memory books. He was satisfied that Andrew could be held to his word. He would send for him within the next few days to extend his request personally. He sighed and turned his face to the fading sun to receive its last bit of warmth. He was content. He looked forward to meeting Florence in the gloaming.

Christian's decision was wise. He died soon after. His brother Kurt joined him within six months. No one was surprised. They had been very close as brothers and they ended together. They both would be sorely missed.

June 1746

My Uncle Christian had impressed upon me the importance of the family journals, as they have become our written VanHameetman legacy. Many family members have been on this island since my ancestors arrived on Long Beach in the early 1600s. I am the third generation to be born on the island, and a sixth generation VanHameetman from Adam. Important events are recorded in our journals and the Quaker Church, that tell the stories of our immediate family, from Maggie and Willem on down. It would be too much for us to record others' genealogies. We hope our relatives are as diligent.

Andrew VanHameetman
His journal

Andrew sat in silence, recalling former times. The journals and their memories had caused him to stop and reflect upon his life. Andrew definitely carried the VanHameetman genes. His hair was pale blonde, his eyes a deep blue, and he had the height in his genes. He was temperate in his demeanor, and consistent in his manner of conduct. He now wore glasses, which he had resisted for a long time, until his wife harassed him to the point of annoyance and he gave in. He had to admit that it was a joy being able to read and see clearly again. His wife, Marie was of Swedish descent. Rather than the blonde hair one would expect from a Swede, Marie was tall, with wonderfully, thick, chestnut colored hair and dark eyes. Something else had crept in there," Marie would laughingly say. She was raised on the mainland in Batsto, near the Pine Barrens expanse. Batsto meant *bathing place*, in Swedish.

Andrew had met Marie at the Quaker Meetinghouse in Tuckerton and they had courted for two years. He recalled, *much to the dismay of his parents* that many a courting trip had been made to the southern part of Long Beach and over to what was once called Short Beach. He had recently mentioned to Marie that it was bought by Reuben Tucker of New York. Mr. Tucker had bought the entire smaller island from old man Warrington who was the original white settler and owner. It will now be called

Tucker's Beach, and we hear that Mr. Tucker plans to open a hostel there. "We still call it Short Beach." Andrew remembered those courting trips and found it amusing that his parents had worried. Even after their marriage, Andrew continued to tell them that he had always been a gentleman, and that they should have had more faith in his character.

He and Marie had settled on Long Beach Island, in the family compound years ago. They had lost their first son to *summer complaint* at ten days old. Marie had finally asked the Lenape medicine man about this. She called in one of the translators to help. The shaman had tried to explain that an infant born in the beginning of summer was more prone to the ailment. The baby starts with diarrhea from milk or food commonly soured from the heat, which leads to vomiting and more diarrhea and the infant's body loses fluid, even if the baby is nursing. The fluid cannot be replaced rapidly enough. Better that the baby is born in the beginning of winter and when summer returns, the child is older and stronger.

In the next few years, Marie and Andrew were blessed with two healthy boys, Benjamin and Jack. Both boys were born in the beginning of winter. Andrew watched his sons with great interest. The noticeable differences in their demeanor, even at an early age had shown clearly. He was amazed that two brothers could be so dissimilar.

Andrew spent three days a week on the island supervising their lumber business and two days in Tuckerton, managing the family's small shipyard, with his brother, Simon. Ben and Jack were only young boys, but they often accompanied their father and his brother, Simon to the shipyard. "I hear there is a new industry springing up in the great Pine Barrens," Andrew mentioned to Simon. "I intend to take a trip over to the Barrens to investigate." Andrew was always on the lookout for sound, new business ventures for the family.

"Really? Are you referring to the bog ore extracted from the streams? I did hear a little bit about it. A company

has built furnaces to melt the ore down and they have
erected a number of sawmills to cut the lumber for the
furnaces. Immense amounts of wood will be necessary
to keep those furnaces hot enough to melt the ore. It is
an exciting concept and I can see great potential there,"
Simon agreed. "I would like to go with you, but I am so
tied up with that new packet, that I think I should pass
any involvement in anything new right now."

By early 1749, the Pine Barrens had been cut without
thought for the future. Numerous sawmills had been
erected to accommodate the early building needs. The
settlers were arriving in great numbers throughout the
area and they all needed wood to build cabins, barns,
outbuildings, and of course for cooking and heating.

"I would like to personally congratulate Mr. Benjamin
Franklin of Philadelphia," Andrew told Simon. "Mr. Franklin
saw the problem early on and objected to the wrongful
treatment of the environment in the Barrens. He suggested
ways to preserve this vast area and he urgently championed
conservation to moderate its reckless ruin."

"I hope Mr. Franklin's interests in the Barrens will
cast an influence on the problem and will slow down the
cutting until reform can be instigated," Simon offered. "Or
at least planting anew what has been cut. We have been
doing that in the Great Swamp area for years."

"Did you know that Charles Read of Burlington is
erecting an ironworks at Batsto? He just bought land
from John Munrow. Mr. Read is continuing negotiation
for purchase of more acreage in the area. He has already
secured permission to build a dam on the Batsto River to
provide waterpower," Andrew shared.

"Isn't that a tributary of the Mullica?" Simon
questioned.

Andrew nodded his head. "I would like to learn more
about the bog ore business and exactly what Mr. Read
is doing before I suggest that the family invest. I wonder
how the dam will affect the Mullica in time."

Simon changed the subject. "If England continues to tax us as she has done with the Sugar Act, sure as there is a sun in the sky, there will be a revolt. People can only take so much of others leeching from their hard work." Simon was angry and expressed himself loudly. "And then for the British to have the audacity to announce that they will soon introduce this new Stamp Act! One can hardly believe the boldness of it!"

Simon was quiet for a moment, and then looked at Andrew. "I wanted to tell you that I have asked Jennifer to marry me," he grinned. "She has accepted and we intend to be married soon. I would guess that would be in the next six months."

"Wonderful news, my brother. I know you will be happy. We are all fond of Jennifer. Did you tell Marie?"

"Not yet, but I will."

"Jennifer was raised near Tuckerton? Or Clamtown—I keep forgetting."

"Yes, really not that far from Batsto."

"Will you stay on the island?"

"I have been thinking about building a house at the end of our compound. If we end up doing business with Batsto, we will move over to Tuckerton. It's not that far from Batsto."

"If this Batsto business turns into something that we would be interested in, we have to think about who would supervise the lumber end of it. It will be a huge job supplying the furnaces."

Simon glanced at Andrew. "I prefer to stay with our shipyard, but I also realize that the cedar business is becoming too much for you. You need help there. See how you feel about Batsto after your visit. I am inclined to think that this will be young men's business; that is, if we become involved in a war with the British. Batsto will become a very important factor."

"Perhaps you are right." Andrew would have to think about that.

1765 Stamp Act
With notes on the Sugar Act of 1764

The Stamp Act was set into law by the British, titled, *Duties in American Colonies Act 1765: George III.* This was the first direct tax on the American colonies. Again, the Parliament claims that the act was to offset the high costs of the British military in America. For the first time, the Americans would be paying tax directly to England and not to their own local legislatures. It required all legal documents, permits, commercial contracts, newspapers, wills, pamphlets, playing cards and more, to carry a tax stamp.

1765 was a busy year. In July, the *Sons of Liberty*, a secret organization opposed to the Stamp act, formed a number of branches in colonial towns. It has been reported that the groups use intimidation and violent behavior in their opposition. Their intent basically, is to stop American merchants from ordering British trade goods, forcing the British stamp agents to close down. "I guess that someone needs to stand up against the Brits!" That was Marie's take.

Parliament recently passed the *Sugar Act.* The British claimed that this was to eliminate the war debt brought about by the French and Indian War. They also claimed that the act was to help pay for the expenses of running the newly acquired territories, and the Colonies. The act increases the duties on imported sugar and of course other items, such as textiles, wines, dye, and coffee. Duties will be doubled on foreign goods *reshipped* from England to the Colonies. Then the Parliament had the audacity to forbid the import of foreign rum and French wines to the American Colonies. That would cut into the double tax to us, with the reshipped goods.

Andrew VanHameetman
His journal

"Well, boys, Mr. Ben Franklin surely underestimated the people's reaction to the Stamp Act. Just watch him do an about face." Andrew had joined the conversation. His prediction was to come true. Franklin soon became an advocate of repeal. Although Andrew thought highly of Mr. Franklin, at times he wondered whose side Franklin was on: the common man—or the Congress that could further his ambitions.

"The intended tax on imported goods is disgraceful," Andrew commented. "This Stamp Act is bringing the Colonists together in such hot anger, that the British may not be able to squash it. The Colonists feel that the English Parliament has no right to impose taxes on us like this. The Philadelphia merchants have worked long and hard to establish their businesses and exports from England are at high enough prices already, without adding an extra tax. And guess what? I have heard that none of that tax is going to their national debt, as the British previously claimed and promised!"

"Any bets that this will lead to a boycott of English goods? It looks like the *Sons of Liberty* had it right." So said Simon.

Some of the English Parliament thought that the British army should be used to implement the Stamp Act of 1765; while many others applauded the Colonists for opposing a tax passed by a legislative body where they were not represented. The Colonists in turn, abandoned their prohibition of imported British goods.

"I cannot believe that this is happening. I do not see how England can assert that America is rightfully theirs. No one seems to know either, when I try to discuss this. How has this come about?" Marie could not understand.

Andrew tried to explain. "You have to remember that The British did establish the first settlement in America at Jamestown, Virginia in 1607. Of course it was settled by English Colonists. Tobacco seems to have started the slavery issue, as some believe. It was exported heavily and became extremely profitable. These early business men needed more hands to cultivate and harvest their product.

This is when Virginia imported Africans to cultivate the farmlands which resulted in the Virginia Colony soon becoming the wealthiest and most populated British Colony in North America. Perhaps the British did not expect the establishment of the additional Colonies to grow as they did, then prosper on their own as independent Colonies.

When the French and Spanish both withdrew from the regions, the British now felt that the remains were definitely theirs. It was easy for them because there was no competition. As the Colonies grew, they became more independent of England. The ever increasing influx of immigrants, the number of permanent Colonists and the establishment of large cities further confirmed to the Colonists that they no longer needed England. I think it must have been a huge blow to the aristocracy to be told that they were no longer considered the motherland. However, that is not saying that there are still many Loyalists who would never give up their allegiance to Great Britain. And that is my take on why Great Britain thinks the way they do."

The Scarlattis had become quite successful, due to their meticulous work, honesty and loyalty to their clients. Their yards in Philadelphia and Dennis Creek were the most prosperous. They had closed their Goshen yard to put their efforts into their Dennis and new Philadelphia yard.

Over the years, the families had seen one another when possible, usually during the summer and Christmas holidays. Serge's son, Emilio, and his wife Francesca with their two children, Sunny and Ricardo, had visited a few years past, over Christmas. This year, the Scarlatti's would journey to the island to spend the holidays with the VanHameetmans. Simon thought about Serge, who was an elderly man now. He had seen him recently when he was in Philadelphia. Regardless of his age, Serge had looked as superb and as dapper as ever.

"I can hardly wait for Christmas this year," Marie commented. "Having the Scarlattis with us will be wonderful for the holidays." The *Marta* would pick them up in Tuckerton.

Christmas 1765

This is my Christmas entry, which is notably family oriented and on this day, I leave all politics out of the journal.

We had set the date of December 22 for our annual Christmas party for our friends, local relatives and our Lenape and Iroquois friends. This year the Scarlattis will be with us.

The holiday turned out grand; as did the annual party. Marie, with the help of sister-in-law, Jennifer, decorated our large home beautifully with local pine and flora woven into large wreaths, which hung in the windows and on the doors. My brother, Simon and I cut down two lush, deep green, finely proportioned pine trees with the assistance of my sons, Ben and Jack, who are now old enough to help. Marie and Jennifer are planning the cooking, and all that goes with a grand holiday. We decorated the trees with the fine Dutch ornaments passed down from family. White beeswax and green holly berry scented wax candles burned in the windows, and the young people with their friends strung popcorn and cranberry garlands and hung them in tiers on the trees.

Our Indian friends brought us two large geese and two magnificent turkeys, hunted in the local woods. Marie made corn pudding and cornbread and resurrected a variety of local vegetables that were dried last summer.

Emilio would bring his special homemade wine, with a most delicate bouquet, just a tad dry; and Francesca would bring her homemade chocolate sweets and other tasty cakes from Philadelphia.

The Scarlattis finally arrived via the *Marta* on December 21. We reminisced over old times, ate a lot, laughed a lot, sang carols and enjoyed ourselves immensely. The Scarlattis have a grand sense of humor and we love being with them.

Emilio and Francesca's children, Ricardo, in his early teens and Regina, about twelve years, called Sunny, are well mannered and a joy. Our sons, Ben and Jack, a little older, got on well.

The women remarked that Sunny, even at this young age, is a beauty, with her beautiful, auburn hair. "She is a delightful young girl," Marie praised Francesca, for the way she had raised her daughter. We treasure making new memories and hate to see our friends leave for Philadelphia.

We look forward to visiting Philadelphia next year, joining the Scarlattis for the holidays. God knows what next year will bring.

Sadly, Serge passed away right after Christmas. We will miss him.

Andrew VanHameetman
His Journal

October 1768

In the last three years, the animosity between England and the Colonies had decidedly heated up. In addition to the *Stamp Act of 1765*, the British then imposed the *1767 Townshend Acts*, proposed initially by Charles Townshend. This new act levied import taxes on common products, such as lead, paper, paint, glass, and tea. The revenues were to be given to the British Governors and others that were usually paid by town assemblies. The tax was not a direct tax, but rather a tax on imports, which made them slightly different than the Stamp Act. There were hot incidents of protests here and there but nothing full blown, where a Colonist or a British soldier was harmed.

Andrew had just finished reading about the most recent British interaction with the Colonists. He called Marie and Simon into the sitting room. "I am not surprised to hear this news, although it spells conflict sooner than I would have thought. The British have sent in troops to safeguard

Loyalist interests in Boston. They were going to send in one regiment, but then decided to send in four! Can you imagine? Those are heavy troops."

"Was anyone hurt?" Marie asked.

"Not yet. But that aggressive behavior on their part is looking for a place and time for an outbreak of violence to happen. That is not all. I heard that it was General Gage who brought in the Yorkshire Fusiliers with other foot regiments. They landed the soldiers on October First. With all those British soldiers in Boston, there is bound to be a confrontation sooner than later." Andrew was very concerned.

"I wonder what the real story is." Simon asked. "Do you realize how many men that is? A usual British Regiment of Foot holds the staff officers, a grenadier company, a light infantry company and eight battalion companies," Simon shared. "That totals 478 men, more or less. Four times that number would be around 2,000 men. Their average ocean crossing time, with a load like that is about eight to ten weeks; however sometimes it can take longer. I have heard that the officers travel with their wives and servants, faring much better than the ordinary soldiers who live in abominable conditions in the lower part of the ship. There was a crossing that was spoken of that took 116 days, 100 men died of dysentery, and 800 men required treatment due to other diseases." They were both silent, mulling over the British plan.

"Mark my words," Marie offered. "Open conflict is around the corner. That Townshend Act just finished off any of the small businesses."

"To make things worse, Commodore Samuel Hood has sent in the 50 gun *H.M.S. Romney*. I think the ship arrived in May, escalating undercurrents. It is like a powder keg, ready to blow," Simon added.

February 1770

It had been relatively quiet once more, outwardly, at least. This surprised many of the Colonists. Then the conflict started up again with continuing clashes in Boston. Simon informed Andrew of the latest news out of Boston. "Good Lord, an eleven year old child was murdered in Boston."

"What in the world, now?" Andrew was surprised.

"A mob was demonstrating in front of the house of an Ebenezer Richardson, who was known by the Colonists as a Loyalist and an informant, so it was reported." Simon was upset as he told Andrew the story. "During the demonstration, someone in the crowd threw a stone and hit Richardson's wife who was standing in her doorway. Richardson came to her aid and then menaced the crowd with his musket." Simon stopped for a minute, collecting his thoughts to make an important point. "But the musket was not loaded. With this threat from Richardson, the crowd, who did not know that the musket was empty, proceeded to break down Richardson's door. I guess that was enough for Richardson and this time, he loaded his gun and fired into the crowd, seriously wounding a child, by name of Christopher Seider. The child died later."

"What was a child doing in the midst of an unruly mob?" Andrew asked.

"I have no idea, but mark my words Andrew; this will not be the last of it. I feel that the heavy presence of the British military is causing most of these incidents. And now, a child has been killed; how very sad."

March 5, 1770

Only a month later, Simon's prediction had come true. Andrew told Marie and his sons, that what had happened was no surprise to him. Andrew read and then summarized an account of what had happened.

"A serious incident had occurred outside of the Custom House in Boston. A young apprentice by name of Edward Gerrish, looking for a fight, had yelled loudly across the street to a British officer, named John Goldfinch, that Goldfinch had not paid his bill from a certain wigmaker. The wigmaker happened to be Gerrish's supervisor. It was later made known, that Captain Goldfinch had indeed paid the bill and that this was only a ruse on Gerrish's part, to instigate a fight. Captain Goldfinch did not answer, not wanting a scene and it was thought to be the end of it.

However, Gerrish came back to the Custom House later, continuing his complaints against Captain Goldfinch. Gerrish had brought companions with him and they started throwing snowballs at Captain Goldfinch.

Gerrish also exchanged insults with the sentry on duty, a Private White, who it seems, had enough of Gerrish's antagonizing and left his post. Private White confronted young Gerrish, and then hit him on the side of the head with his musket. Gerrish's companion, Bartholomew Broaders, continued to argue with Private White. The argument grew louder, and the crowd escalated into an angry mob.

The mob then grew larger and more unruly, and continued to harass Private White. White abandoned his sentry box and retreated to the Custom House stairs. The British Officer of the Day, Captain Thomas Preston watched and decided it was time to dispatch one non commissioned officer and several soldiers of the 29th Regiment of Foot. Fixing their bayonets, the soldiers went to relieve Private White.

When the soldiers moved forward, the crowd pressed around them. The Redcoats loaded their muskets and fell back to White at the stairs. The crowd soon numbered 300 to 400 angry Colonists who had formed a semi circle around the soldiers. In the chaos, a British Private, by name of Montgomery was hit and knocked to the ground. When he was able to get to his feet, he fired his gun and yelled to his comrade soldiers, *Damn you, fire!* or *Fire and be damned!* Both yells were reported. Montgomery's cry escalated as the mob began to taunt the soldiers, yelling, *Fire!* It was then, that the soldiers fired and hit eleven men—five died.

Three were Americans: Samuel Gray, a rope maker, James Caldwell, a mariner, and an African American sailor by the name of Crispus Attucks. *The three died instantly.*

Another young man, Samuel Maverick, only seventeen years old, was stuck by a ricocheting musket ball and died a few hours later. A thirty year old, Irish immigrant, Patrick Carr was injured and died two weeks later."

Royal authorities have removed all troops from the center of town and on March 27, the soldiers, along with Captain Preston and the four men who were in the Customs House and said to have fired shots, were indicted for murder." Andrew then passed the newspaper around.

"How terrible," Marie commented. "You just cannot have that many soldiers and crowds of angry Colonists in the same city, when you know that there is such animosity between them."

"What will happen now?" Ben and Jack asked. They had been sitting quietly, listening intently to their father. "What happened to Edward Gerrish and Broaders, who started it all?"

"There will be a trial, to be sure. We will have to wait and see. They are already calling this *The Boston Massacre*." He shook his head sadly. "I am sure this will not have a good ending. However, it has been a long time coming and both sides are pushing it. Heaven help us, boys."

Andrew knew there was grave danger ahead. No one had to be a genius to realize that. Ben picked up the newspaper to read about the incident, then he handed the paper to Jack.

1770
Notes on the Boston Massacre Trial

The trial had been set for October 24, 1770. However, it seems that no lawyer in Boston would take the case. The Colonial Government had been adamant about giving the British soldiers a fair trial, so that there could be no retaliation from the British.

British Captain Preston was desperate and had sent an appeal to John Adams to take his case. Adams, although contemplating running for public office and an ardent patriot, agreed to help. He, too, wanted a fair trial. John Adams, Josiah Quincy II, and Robert Auchmuty acted as the defense attorneys. Sampson Salter Blowers would investigate the jury pool.

No one really could say whether Paul Revere had been present at the actual Massacre. However, it was suspect. He had drawn a meticulous map of the positions of the wounded and dead bodies that would be used in the trial of the soldiers involved. There had been some conjecture, that Revere could not have drawn such a detailed map and later a metal engraving of the event, unless he had been present. However, no witnesses could, or would come forth to confirm his presence.

The town of Boston hired Massachusetts Solicitor General Samuel Quincy and Attorney Robert Treat Paine to handle the prosecution. The trial was delayed for months, because of the heat it had stirred up on both sides. This delay was quite unusual for the times. The juries were chosen from towns other than Boston. Captain Preston was acquitted. The jury did not believe that he had ordered the troops to fire. His trial was over on October 30.

The enlisted soldiers' trial opened November 27, 1770. Adams had put forth that if the soldiers were in real danger from the mob, they had the legal right to retaliate; therefore, they were innocent. At the most, they were guilty of manslaughter. The jury agreed with Adams; six of the soldiers were acquitted. Two of the soldiers were found guilty of murder; they had fired directly into the crowd. However, Adams used a loophole in British Common Law and their crime was reduced to manslaughter. Two additional privates were found guilty of manslaughter and had their thumbs branded. The jury evidently believed, that the soldiers did feel threatened by the crowd. Patrick Carr, the fifth Colonist victim agreed and sent a deathbed testimony, delivered to the court by his doctor.

Two years later, the mounting volatility continues. It must reach a peak of explosion. At times, we wish it would come to a head.

Andrew VanHameetman
His Journal

CHAPTER SIX

Sunny and Ben

1773-1774

Sunny tossed her auburn hair back and sprang up lightly into the saddle of the big palomino. Ben drew in a quick breath. *"By god! A stallion,"* he murmured, *"and what control she has of him."*

A ndrew sat at his desk sorting legal papers and paused to light his pipe. He had read one of the old journals the night before and was still thinking of what Maggie had written, now yellowed with age, but legible. His great grandparents, Willem and Maggie had settled on the island in 1616. He thought of the early primitiveness they had faced and how his family had depended upon the Lenape and Iroquois for their initial survival. He leaned back in his chair to continue reminiscing. He thought of his father, Kurt and was thankful for the many years he had with him. His mother had died young and Andrew saw his father's physical and spiritual strength through her sickness and passing. His father had never remarried. *So many memories.* Recently he had received a letter from his best friend and cousin, Zachary, who lived near Boston. How he would love to see him; it had been a long time.

He straightened up in his chair deciding that he would speak to his wife, Marie about his plan. He knew that she was not going to agree with his decision. He would wait until tomorrow.

The next day Andrew announced unexpectedly to Marie, "I am thinking of taking a trip to Boston in December. I may take the *Marta*. It would be the easiest way to travel," He was quiet for a moment. "I have not made up my mind yet."

"Where in the world did that come from?" Marie thought that perhaps he wanted to take the *Marta II* on a long voyage since she had been newly built. After they had christened the *Marta II*, the family unanimously decided to burn the *Marta I*. They did not want her rotting in her berth. They had taken a small piece of wood from the *Marta I*, as Simon had suggested and incorporated it into the new ship. They would sail the old girl, who had served them faithfully, out on one last run into the ocean; then set fire to her there. She belonged to the ocean—and they would let the ocean claim her.

"I guess I am just tired of hearing about events in Boston, without seeing things for myself. We have our own ship and I can take advantage of that. I need to experience Boston first hand. I have recently read in more than one Boston newspaper that the city has reached a state of quasi calm, whatever that means. It has been three years since the last big incident of the Boston Massacre." He looked up from the newspaper. "Aggression and hostility between the Colonists and the British is reported to have simmered down. I want to see for myself what the true state of intercourse is between them. Boston certainly is the best place to observe this." *If I am ever to get there*, he thought, *I should take advantage of the present tranquility.*

"From what I have read, the Philadelphia newspaper tells me that Boston is not the safest place to visit." Marie was worried.

He then leafed through a number of recent Boston newspapers, showing her that each one had reported the same, as to the present state of tranquility. The reporters evidently believed that everyone seemed to be going about their own business. "I would really like to go, Marie. I need to take advantage of this lull. It seems that the larger events have ceased for awhile. I can handle the continuing minor problems, but who knows? I would like to be ahead of that and I would like to see my old friend, Zach and the Scarlattis. I am going to go ahead with plans and write to Zach and Emilio."

The family acknowledged how fortunate they were, living on Long Beach Island, removed from much of the chaos caused by the British. "They are everywhere, Father," Ben, Andrew's elder son, told him. "They know this Island, but I guess it holds little interest for them. I cannot figure out if they know about the cedar, or the necessary stripping of the bark before it is cut. I am sure that they have no idea of the preparation of the trees before they are cut into usable slabs."

"What could they do with it? Ship it back to England? I doubt they would bother. British interests probably crossed off Long Beach Island from their list long ago. Evidently they *are* unaware of other natural riches that the island holds," Andrew told his son. "I am not sure that they have seen our salt farms."

Ben and Jack had attended school on the island, taught by Jonathon Newell. Jonathan was a second cousin to Marie and had received his education from Princeton in Jersey. They used the community house in the VanHameetman compound for their classrooms. Jonathan, a young widower had a calling for teaching and Andrew, along with the other parents considered themselves most fortunate to have him. Jonathan's younger sisters, Bettina and Susan taught the little ones. His elder sister, Lindsay, along with their mother, Stacey taught the middle grades. Jonathan taught the older students. The children were accepted at age six for half days, and graduated at age sixteen. They were taught reading, writing, arithmetic and manners or etiquette and the ability to read the bible. However they were more fortunate than most. They were being taught by an educated teacher. At sixteen, more curriculum was added to those subjects, if they wished to go further with their education. They would be schooled for college entrance exams; Queen's College and Princeton were located in Jersey. However, not many went on to higher learning.

Ben and Jack had completed their schooling at age 16, and felt that they wanted to join one of the family businesses. They knew that they were privileged, but they were taught that one had to work. Their parents often reminded them, that there were no free rides.

The small VanHameetman Shipyard on the mainland, just outside of Tuckerton did export some ships. They had been building wherries, fishing boats, transports, and some small packets. Foreign buyers paid dearly in high export taxes, which were collected by the British at every ship's sale. It was a no win situation for the Colonists and a win win for the British. Andrew had kept the number of ships they built secret. Recently they were building packet runners, disguised as fishing boats; perhaps the runners would be helpful for the Colonies, for what Andrew felt might be in the near future. The Colonist British situation, wrought with constant confrontations created ongoing unrest.

Andrew swore repeatedly, "I never want to see my ships being used by the British against us. I am sick to death of the nobility's arrogant attitude and their constant meddling into my business." He was angry. "I do not want them to know of our back orders. The ruse of fishing boats has worked so far, but cannot last forever. These British aristocrats have never known or completed an honest day's labor." Andrew was bitter. "I do not think any one of them has ever gotten his hands dirty. They have fed on others' industriousness, or they had been left a heritage. Our ancestors left Holland because of the persecution by the Spanish and now we have it here in our country, victimized by the British!"

"Andrew, you need to be careful. You must not speak your disgust with them so loud. You know it can be dangerous if you voice too much animosity outside of our home. Those hateful Loyalists are everywhere, always watching. It is enough to make your blood run cold."

"Who knows who they are? Sorry, Marie, I should call them Tories. Perhaps some of my own friends are still loyal to England; but they keep their persuasions hidden." He had seen more than a few businesses confiscated from the Colonists on trumped up charges. *Who was responsible for that? Who had set up those Colonists?* He wondered. *Was it the snooping, spying Loyalists?* Andrew would remind his employees and family to be cautious in speaking of the shipyard's business in public.

Ben overheard the conversation between his mother and father and chimed in. "We Colonists pay the outstretched British hands everywhere, but are forced to hold our tongues and of course, this only escalates our anger. I would never have believed that this could be happening in America!"

"And the damned pirates are everywhere. They attack ships, randomly and relentlessly. No one is safe from the viciousness of these bloody buccaneers. I cannot say where it will all end. They hold no mercy for their captives—not crew, passengers, or children. Those victims who have family that bargain for them and pay the ransom—the captives are eventually murdered anyway. All morals have fled. May they burn in hell." Andrew was disgusted.

The only ships that the pirates did not plunder were the large Men-of-war that patrolled the coast, diligently monitoring the thieves.

"Those English Men-of-war and their sloops-of-war patrol vessels have no trouble capturing any of the converted merchant vessels used by the pirates. The British shoot a warning at them; but it is just a tactic to run the pirates off. Those devils dare not come within British range. There are very few pirate ships large enough to challenge a Man-of-war."

"I recently read in the newspaper that the British were patrolling the Chestnut Neck region on a twenty four hour basis." Andrew was ecstatic. He found this news almost too good to believe. "I must write to the British Admiralty at Leeds Point and arrange to trail a Man-of-war north, up to Boston." He had planned to do this, and now decided to go ahead. "That should certainly assure us of a safe trip. Our only problem will be the weather. We need good sailing winds and fair weather so we can keep up with the British. December can be pretty chancy, and we could become sitting ducks." Andrew pursed his lips in contemplation, realizing what might be waiting out on the ocean, if they were not able to get British help. "If the weather turns, we could anchor close in and wait it out, but then he would lose the British protection. Where is the almanac, Marie. I want to consult it for those dates."

"I guess you have already made your mind up," Marie remarked. She still felt it was dangerous. He did not answer her.

"I would like to ask the Scarlattis to join us. It has been too long since we have been together. I have seen Emilio in Philadelphia, off and on, but the young ones have not been together in quite some time. I am going to ask them to sail with us to Boston and then return to the island as our guests for the holidays. It would be nice to share our Christmas with them again." Andrew remembered the past good times they had. "What think you of that?"

"How nice," Marie was enthused. "Has it been that long since we have seen them?"

Andrew doubted that Emilio's wife, Francesca would come along to Boston, but perhaps she could meet them on Long Beach Island for the holidays when they returned.

He realized that he would have to bite his tongue when he wrote to the small contingency of British stationed at Leeds Point. I know that the harbor is definitely under English control. "I have not heard that any decree has been rendered against entering Boston harbor," Andrew told Ben. The irony of taking the trip was that it would be with British help. He sat down that day and wrote his letter; he would wait for the reply and then contact Emilio, and if all went well, he would also write to his friend Zachary. Andrew planned to take Benjamin and Jack on the voyage to Boston. Both were able seamen. There were a few other experienced seamen on Marie's side who would want to join them and he would be able to round out an experienced crew with family.

"Simon can hold down the fort until I return from Boston; unless my brother wants to join us," Andrew told Marie. She had enough younger cousins in the vicinity to help Simon with the day to day work if needed.

"What say you boys?"

"Sounds good to me," Ben answered. He was hardly a boy anymore, as he often reminded his father. Brother, Jack was not far behind him in age, both were just into their twenties.

A week later, Marie announced, "This was delivered this morning from the British Admiralty." She gave the letter to Andrew. His request had been confirmed. He was to meet the British navy's Man-of-war, the H.M.S. *Queen of the Seas,* at noon on December 14 on her return to Boston. She would be in the ocean waters off the southern inlet of Long Beach Island, and would wait until 1:00 p.m. for the meet. "They will look for the *Marta* on that date." Andrew gave the letter to Ben and asked him to put it in the *Marta's* log book. The *Queen* would be in Leeds Point on December 13, loading stores and would continue north on December 14.

Andrew was happy with the news and sat down and wrote to Emilio. He would ask Emilio and his son Ricardo to crew with them.

Simon had decided to stay on the island. Being Andrew's brother, he was also a belt and suspenders man. Andrew knew that this habit annoyed his sons, but then they were young and in a hurry with everything. Andrew felt relieved. Simon would take charge.

Zach had written back quickly telling Andrew how very pleasantly surprised he had been to hear from him, and that he was looking forward to seeing him. He was familiar with the Green Dragon Inn where Andrew would be staying and he would be pleased to see him there around noon on December 15.

October 30, 1773
Rittenhouse Square
Philadelphia

Dear Friend Andrew,

    We received your letter with great enthusiasm. I have never visited Boston, strange as it seems, because Boston is not that far north on the ocean route. It is a place that I have longed to see and I think you remembered this. I would like to accept your most gracious invitation and ask your permission to bring along my daughter, Sunny, who has the wandering blood of her father. My son, Ricardo, and I would like to crew. We thank you for the invitation. Ricardo is a good sailor and would be quite helpful on the journey. Francesca will not be joining us on the trip to Boston, but she accepts your kind invitation to spend the Christmas holidays on the island. I will arrange for her travel before we leave.

    We will sail up the Mullica River and meet you in Green Bank on December 13, in the afternoon as you requested, spend overnight on the ship, and then make the meet with the British 'H.M.S. Queen of the Seas' at noon on December 14. I have ascertained from the British contingent in Philadelphia that they have heavy patrols in the area of Chestnut Neck and the big bay. Therefore, the Chestnut Neck area should be relatively safe to navigate.

    We will ride our own horses from Philadelphia, and make our way to Long-a-Coming Village and Green Bank, where the Mullica River rises.

    I can secure a flat bed barge; they make the trip routinely down the Mullica. I am not sure of the exact draft of the Marta, but I know she pulls very shallow and I think you can sail her up the Mullica to Green Bank. If you find this not to your liking, we can make other plans. I will go on the assumption that you can make it as aforementioned.

*I have arranged for our horses to be picked up in
Green Bank and brought back to Philadelphia.*
   *We accept your kind offer to sail us to Tuckerton
when we leave for home. We will make our plans
depending upon the pirate activity in the area.*

Your faithful friend,
Emilio

Emilio's response arrived within a week on the mail coach to Manahawkin. A Lenape friend carried the letter to the Island for Andrew. Emilio was excited about the invitation from Andrew and accepted his invitation for the voyage to Boston.

December was upon them too quickly, and they set about stocking the *Marta* with necessities for the trip. Although they planned to stay in one of the Boston inns, Andrew reminded his sons, "Our ship will be at the ready to handle any sort of emergency. We certainly do not want to be stranded in Boston." Andrew and the crew left Long Beach Island near noon, on an unusually mild day for December, allowing them ample time to meet the Scarlattis in Green Bank. Andrew went over the plans again: they would collect the Scarlattis from Green Bank, meet the English Man-of-war the next day at noon, trail the *H.M.S. Queen of the Seas* to Boston, and stop outside the harbor to present their papers. *I am satisfied*, he told himself. He would see his friend Zachary on December 15 in Boston.

Andrew watched Ben at the wheel and saw how much of a VanHameetman he was—in coloring, build, and temperament. He had a self confident but distant demeanor and scrutinized the world from his blue green eyes. Ben did not converse lightly or at length. His height, suntanned skin, and shock of wheat colored hair turned many a woman's head, but Ben was oblivious of his effect on women or of their longing glances. His shoulders were broad and his waist slim, above strong thighs and legs, well muscled from working long hours in the supervising and cutting of the cedars. Andrew had placed Ben in this position some years ago and Ben had more than fulfilled his expectations. He gently but firmly cared for the cattle and horses and although he had a stable boy to help him with the dirty work, he was always ready to pitch in.

Jack resembled his mother, Marie, in coloring: dark eyes and dark hair. He had a tall, slim build and a somewhat suave and at times, manipulative manner which sometimes dominated his personality. He was handsome, dapper, well groomed and well liked and underneath his outward charisma, he was usually quite caring. However, Jack was used to getting his own way, especially with his mother. He was engaged to Glenda, a lovely girl from Middle of the Shore, and Andrew and Marie were hoping he would marry and settle down. Time would tell.

The *Marta* cruised through the southern inlet of Long Beach and after a short sail, entered the mouth of the Great bay and then up the Mullica River. They passed Leeds Point where the *Queen* would be taking on cargo. They would meet the British the following morning when she sailed back out into the Atlantic from Leeds Point.

The sun had traveled into the west the following day, when they cast anchor at an agreed upon location set out in Andrew's second confirmation letter to Emilio. They soon spotted a large, open barge gliding downstream in the calm Mullica waters. Ben, Jack, and Andrew were on the *Marta*'s wheel deck. As the barge came closer, they could see Emilio standing in the front. He spotted them and waved enthusiastically. Andrew could not miss Sunny with her auburn hair, standing near her father. She was holding the reins of a beautiful, golden palomino. Ricardo was next to his sister, gripping the reins of a big, reddish brown hunter.

Sunny had been a little girl when Andrew had seen her last. He soon realized that this was no little girl whom he and his sons were watching. She was dressed in fitted, specially made, brown leather riding trousers, dark brown boots, and a cream colored, close fitting, silky blouse tucked into her pants. Her tan suede jacket was tossed over her shoulder because of the warmth of the day. A wide brimmed, tan suede hat was pushed back and lay on her shoulders. Her wonderful deep red hair reflected the bright sunlight.

Andrew rarely turned his head to admire a young woman, but Sunny clearly was an exception. As the large barge tied down and they got ready to exit, Sunny tossed her auburn curls back and sprang up lightly into the saddle of the big palomino, rode him off the barge and dismounted.

Ben drew in a quick breath. "By god! A stallion," he murmured, *and what control she has of him.*

"Did you ever see such a sight," Jack commented softly, making a statement rather than a question. "That is little Sunny? I cannot believe it. How old is she now?" Recalling when they had last seen her, Ben thought she was probably around nineteen or twenty, a few years younger than he was. Ricardo was probably about Ben's age.

Andrew confirmed his sons' guesswork. "Stop your staring," he told them. They were both leaning over the ship's rail, unable to take their eyes from her. "She was like a cousin to you boys."

"I would like to greet them. Come on boys, and stop your gawking! It is only little Sunny." He turned toward the crew. "Lower the gangplank please."

"Andrew," Emilio said, offering his hand. His wide brimmed black hat was now in his other hand. He was elegantly fitted in black riding trousers, a short, black, riding jacket, and a white, silk shirt. He was charming, of medium height, well built, and quite handsome with his dark eyes and dark hair. He exuded enthusiasm as he greeted Andrew with a firm handshake, then a bear hug and a back slap. "Really good to see you all," he said, looking first at Andrew and then at his sons. He extended his right hand to Ben and then to Jack while holding tight to his horse with the other. "We have to stable the horses first. We can catch a ride back to the ship in the wagon from the stable. You remember, Sunny?" he asked as he turned to put his arm around her, coaxing her forward.

Sunny smiled, moving forward toward Andrew and then into an embrace, saying, "Hello, Uncle Andrew. I hope you do not mind me calling you that." He did not, and looking at her smile, he recalled why Emilio called her Sunny, and then she was again, the little girl he remembered.

Her eyes were big and light brown, fringed with long, dark lashes; her full mouth covered straight, white teeth and freckles were scattered across her slightly upturned nose.

"My goodness, you have turned into a real beauty." Andrew smiled down at her. "Do you remember Ben and Jack?" he asked, turning her over to his sons.

"Charmed," Jack responded, putting on his most appealing airs, while moving forward to hug her. "You certainly have grown—in all ways." He smiled, not missing her full blouse and tight fitting pants, thinking he had never seen such a beauty. Then, he found himself at a loss for words, which rarely happened to Jack.

"Still as clever as ever, I see," she responded with a smile. She quickly pulled back from his hug, catching Jack off guard with her directness. Evidently, she perceived immediately that women were probably somewhat tongue tied around handsome Jack, who was master of the compliment.

"Ben?" She started toward him, then stopped abruptly, when she realized that he was not receptive to her intended hug. She backed off and said, "When I saw you last, you took me hunting for soft shells in the reeds by the bay's edge. We were kids. Do you remember? You were my hero."

"I remember, Sunny," he answered, looking down at her. He had never forgotten her. Now he wondered what was wrong with him. He knew that she was about to hug him and he had stood there like an unresponsive bungler, and was totally mortified! *Curses, I missed my chance.* He could not see beyond her, as the sun framed her wonderful, auburn curls with a brilliant halo. He knew he would have to look at her face, and when he did, he was not sure if he would be able to breathe, much less speak. He was close enough to catch her scent and then he froze. *My god, what is wrong with me? I feel like a twelve year old schoolboy.* He found himself instantly self conscious, so thoroughly taken with her that he wanted to remove himself from her presence so he could get a grip on himself. Nevertheless, his inner self had firmly rooted him there; he was unable to move his big feet. He knew that Jack was shaken too, and that he found extraordinary, because Brother Jack always knew what he was doing, especially with women.

"Have you raised him from a colt?" Ben asked, changing the subject and genuinely curious about the magnificent, large stallion. "May I touch him?"

"Yes," she answered. She pulled her horse's head down toward his hand and looked up at Ben's closeness. She was immediately lost.

"May I ask his name?" Ben asked, barely able to speak. He was too embarrassed to look at her.

"Tonio," she answered quickly, trying to recover from a flood of emotions.

"Jack, Ben, Uncle Andrew," Ricardo said. "Remember me?" He extended his hand and laughed. Ricardo was also dark haired, taller than his father, and immaculately groomed. He projected a very strong presence; his shocking, blue eyes caught one off guard. "That is all right. I am used to playing second to my little sister. I have to beat the boys off," his eyes flashed with mischief.

"That is a pretty big horse for a little girl," Jack commented. "He is beautiful."

"Tonio's gentle as a lamb, but he will not let anyone else on his back," she said and reached into her pocket for a sugar lump. "I suppose most are afraid to ride him, being a stallion and so large."

"I think we had better get going," Emilio interrupted. "We have to get the horses to stable. The wagon from the stable will take us back to the ship."

Jack and Ben hesitated. "Do you need any help with the horses?" Emilio shook his head no; Andrew and his sons started back to the *Marta* to wait for their return.

It was obvious to Andrew that both of his sons were thoroughly taken with Sunny. *Jack is used to having his way and, always, the pick of the girls,* Andrew thought. But, methinks, this time it will be different. We shall wait and see. Sunny is a delightful young woman, from a wonderful family, and either of my sons would be most fortunate if a relationship developed with this lovely Scarlatti.

They had a quick dinner on the *Marta* and then lots of catching up conversation. Andrew had designated the smaller cabin for Sunny and the other cabin for her brother and father. "We will stay in the common area," Andrew told his sons. He turned to Emilio and Ricardo. "I am very relieved that you two will help crew." They planned to set sail around 10:00 a.m. the next morning back down the Mullica River, through the Great bay and then out into the Atlantic to meet the English. "We have a busy day tomorrow and we have to meet the *Queen* on time, at noon. Better early than late," Andrew announced. "Where did you put that letter, Ben?" It contained their pass for the Boston Harbor.

"I stuck it in the log as you asked me to do. I guess we have to keep that Jack flying."

"That was part of the bargain and certainly a little enough price to pay." Andrew knew that Ben was unhappy about flying the Union Jack.

They sailed back down the Mullica next morning, passing Leeds Point. "There she is," Ben said, pointing to a large Man-of-war that was just hoisting her sails, preparing to depart. She had finished loading her cargo. Andrew turned the wheel and steered the *Marta* away from the *Queen,* giving the vessel room to maneuver, and they fell in behind her. They sailed out of the Mullica River, through the Great bay and into the Atlantic Ocean, following closely behind the *Queen.*

After seeing all the heavily armed Men-of-war about, Andrew stopped worrying, thinking, *not a pirate or a privateer would dare come near us.* "Great timing," Emilio said, "it will give us a head start leaving."

"Just good luck that we caught her here. I had expected to pick her up near the southern inlet of Long Beach Island." Andrew was happy.

"Great sailing, Andrew," Emilio complimented him.

"Thanks. That was just plain luck. We still had time for the meet, although I would rather be early." Andrew offered. "Now, I can relax."

"The *Queen* is signaling us," Ben yelled to his father. "They have hoisted another flag. Shall we answer her?"

"Jack, Emilio, Ricardo," Andrew shouted. "How well have you studied your semaphores?"

"Not as well as I would have liked," they answered, one by one.

"The *Queen* is acknowledging our appearance. We are the receiving ship and must respond."

Andrew pulled a flag from the wooden box on deck. "I thought you two were going to study your semaphores; you too, Ricardo. That is something I would like you all to learn." He handed the flag to Ben and waited for him to hoist it. "I can tell you a little of the history of the semaphore. Signaling at sea has been around from the time of the ancient Athenians, perhaps even older. De la Bourdonnais, a French officer conceived the first numeric flag code and everything going forward was based on his creation. Initially a different flag was assigned to each number 0 through 9. Then he devised three sets of flags with a dissimilar meaning on each. This could make 1,000 different combinations of three flag signals." Andrew paused, wanting to word this simply.

"De la Bourdonnais then created a dictionary, assigning a meaning to each single flag and combinations of several flags. The Bourdonnais system was a great leap forward in sophisticated naval communications. However, the system was never adopted by the French navy. About 25 years later, another Frenchman, Captain Sebastien François de Bigot Vicomte de Morogues, founder of the French Marine Academy at Brest, published his *Tactique Navale ou Traite des Evolutions et des Signaux* in 1763."

"That is quite a mouthful, just his name," Jack interrupted. Andrew did not respond to his comment but continued the history of the flags.

"While Bigot de Morogues' signal code followed most of the Bourdonnais meanings, he also included a provision in his code for ten numeric flags, which could be hoisted in 336 combinations of up to three flags each. Then he added both a preparatory flag to signal that a coded message would be transmitted and a flag requirement that the receiving ship acknowledge the signal. I would surmise that this also lets the transmitting ship know that the receiving ship is knowledgeable of the signaling system."

Sunny was listening too. "Good lord, Uncle Andrew. How can you remember all of that? By the way, I can translate that from the French."

"You speak French?" Ben asked her.

Sunny smiled and nodded her head. "It literally means, *Naval Tactics or Treatise on Developments and Signals*. This relates to placing the Navy, or armies of the sea in the appropriate order and regulating all of their movements."

"That's quite an achievement, Sunny." Andrew was impressed.

"Four years of it at the Academy, Uncle Andrew."

Andrew smiled at her. "I found this whole subject most interesting so it was easy for me. I do not have a problem remembering a subject if it interests me. The Royal navy was far behind the French, until Admiral Kempenfelt had the dictionary translated into English in 1767. And that is where we are now, in 1773. So remember, attend to that first chance you get, boys."

The temperature had fallen considerably, as befitted an early winter morning, when they approached Boston on

December 15. Ben remarked, "I am amazed at the size of this harbor and the activity afoot." Their overnight sail had been uneventful, except for the multitude of pirate ships seen in the distance during the daylight hours. Andrew figured that their voyage had been approximately three hundred nautical miles; the winds had been variable; they had made excellent time. They followed the *Queen* in slowly as day broke and cast anchor just inside the harbor. The British then boarded.

"Good morning, Sir," a smartly uniformed British Officer came aboard. Andrew saluted him and showed him their paperwork. The *Marta* was cleared and they were issued a pass into the harbor. Numerous ships, European and local, were at mooring.

"I did not realize how busy the port would be," Emilio remarked, looking around him.

They had rested a few hours and Andrew came onto the deck early and stood sipping his coffee and taking in the harbor view. The young men were still in their bunks.

"Good morning, Uncle Andrew." Sunny joined him. She too, had been up early. "I brought some baked goods with me when we left. Would you like a bun?"

"I think a little later, but thank you." He noticed that she had found the coffee. He looked around him and remarked, "I have never seen so many ships in one harbor." He turned to her. "I think we will have a nice day."

"Good morning father," she turned to greet Emilio.

He smiled at her. "And where is your brother? Not that I have to even ask."

"Their stomachs will soon get them up and going," Andrew commented.

The young men arrived on deck around 9:00 a.m., with food in hand and joined them. "Look at those ships," Ben remarked turning 360 degrees to catch it all.

"I think we can maneuver in a little closer. We really are far out," Ricardo commented.

Emilio looked at his son. "Are you serious? We are not sailing a row boat. I think we are fine here. We can easily row over to the wharf in the dinghy."

"I did notice Redcoats patrolling there. Usually, I would worry about the dinghy being stolen, but with the patrols, it seems to be fine." Andrew looked around. "Suppose we need to make a hasty retreat? I would rather be in good position to do so."

Ricardo, Ben, and Jack grumbled about the longer row in, but saw the safety in what was said and stopped their complaining. "You all are young and healthy. You can row over to the wharf. It looks as though the main street of town starts a short ways from there," Andrew pointed out. "Take one of the crew with you so he can bring the dinghy back. Some of the crew may want to go into town later. We can take the other dinghy."

Ben saw Sunny standing by the rail, watching the entire goings on in the harbor and he walked over to her. She looked up at him and smiled and he did not know what to say. He wanted to touch her. "I will see you in town, later," he finally said. She would have been surprised to know how her presence had affected him.

"I will look forward to it," she replied, thinking how much she wanted to spend time with him. She knew how impulsive she was, but realized immediately that Ben was very proper. He left to go ashore. She breathed deeply, watching him from the railing.

Andrew shouted down to them, "Boys, I want you to be careful and not stir up any commotion. Do you hear me?" He shouted again. They were young men, and knowing how curious they could be, Andrew was concerned. "No confrontations with the Redcoats!" he yelled again. "And do not forget to meet us around noon for lunch at the Green Dragon on Marshall Street, right in the center of town. The trio smiled and waved. Andrew felt certain they would ignore his warnings.

Sunny, Emilio and Andrew went inside and had a leisurely breakfast, then made ready to enjoy Boston. One of the crew pulled the dinghy over to the gangplank and they climbed into the little boat, and rowed to the wharf. There was a British regular standing guard over the tied down row of dinghies. "Wonderful," Emilio noted. "I would guess a number of dinghies have been stolen up until now."

Emilio hailed a carriage and told the driver, "The Green Dragon Tavern and Inn, my man, on Marshall Street." He turned to Andrew. "The inn was recommended highly by a friend," and as an afterthought he added, "I hear it is a Grand Lodge of the Freemasons."

They booked three rooms, refreshed themselves, and went back into the streets for a look about. "I told the boys that we would see them at the inn around noon for lunch. They have their clothes packs with them and should drop them off," Andrew told Emilio.

They had planned to spend a week in Boston, then return to Long Beach Island and celebrate Christmas. It was difficult to place a specific time of arrival at the island; they had to arrange their return trip with the British, hoping that the good December weather would hold. The British Admiralty had given Andrew a southern schedule for their armed packets and frigates. Seeing the large number of black ships in the distance on their trip north, it was clear that they would need an escort home.

"This damned Stamp Act, is downright reprehensible. It is shameful. The citizens are so bogged down now with these bloody taxes and they add more. Taxation without representation in the English Parliament is unjust," Emilio was angry. "Just a minute," he continued. "Look what I picked up last week in a tavern in Philadelphia." He pulled a folded notice from his pocket and handed it to Andrew.

Andrew read it and shook his head at the anger expressed in the handbill. "The pilots on the river will surely notify the authorities if they spot this fellow Ayres and his ship, Polly. It says here that he is trying to bring more tea in and they are not having it. If I were Ayres, I would run for the hills and stay away from Boston," Emilio commented.

To the DELAWARE PILOTS:

The Regard we have for your Characters, and our Desire to promote your future Peace and Safety, are the Occasion of this Third Address to you.

In our second Letter we acquainted you, that the Tea Ship was a Three Decker; we are now informed by good Authority, she is not a Three Decker, but an old black Ship, without a Head, or any Ornaments.

The Captain is a short fat Fellow, and a little obstinate withal.—. So much the worse for him . . . . For, so sure as he rides rusty, we shall heave him Keel out, and see that his Bottom be well fired, scrubb'd and paid.—His Upper Works too, will have an Overhawling.—and as it is said, he has a good deal of Quick Work about him. We will take particular Care that such Part of him undergoes a thorough Rummaging.

We have a still worse Account of his Owner;—for it is said, the Ship Polly was bought by him on Purpose, to make a Penny of us; and that he and Captain Ayres were well advised of the Risque they would run, in thus daring to insult and abuse us.

Captain Ayres was here in the Time of the Stamp Act, and ought to have known our People better, than to have expected we would be so mean as to suffer his rotten TEA to be funnel'd down our Throats, with the Parliament's Duty mixed with it.

We know him well, and have calculated to a Gill and a Feather, how much it will require to fit him for an American Exhibition. And we hope, not one of your Body will behave so ill, as to oblige us to clap him in the Cart along Side of the Captain. We must repeat, that the SHIP POLLY is an old black Ship, of about Two Hundred and Fifty Tons burthen, without a Head, and without Ornaments,—and, that CAPTAIN AYRES is a thick chunky Fellow.—As such, Take Care to avoid THEM.

Your Old Friends,
**The COMMITTEE for
TARRING and FEATHERING
Philadelphia, December 7, 1773**

Andrew thought further about the handbill and realized it was the third bill published. "We will have to find the other two. I would be interested in what else they have to say about this Polly ship and Captain Ayres." Emilio was curious and thought he would make it his business to find the first two handbills.

They walked to Griffins Wharf and a few ships moored out a short distance, caught Andrew's eye. "Over there, Emilio," Andrew said, pointing to three large ships at mooring. "Look how low they are in the water. Good lord, if they were any lower they would sink. Somewhat of an overload, I would say. Wonder what their cargo is? What names are those ships bearing?" He hesitated, shading his eyes trying to read the names. "Looks like *Dartmouth*, *Beaver*, and *Eleanor*. I would say they have been here for at least a month. Look at the green algae buildup. And look around toward the front. The hulls have old tide lines on them. Could be massive trouble if this is foodstuff and the British try to unload it. I can see riots starting, with this crowd milling about."

"If it is foodstuff, that would be pretty precious cargo, considering the shortages in food around here. That would sell for a pretty penny. I wonder to whom it is consigned. Then again, it could be something else. Perhaps guns and ammunition." Andrew ventured.

"It has to be something that keeps; if it were food, it would have turned rotten sitting there. If it were weapons, that would be real trouble. Those ships are loaded," Emilio repeated. "I am getting a very bad feeling. I do not like the atmosphere here already. I think we ought to change our plans. I smell trouble brewing, and playing out soon. I suggest we stay a day or two, keep to the safety of town, let Sunny do her Christmas shopping, then head back to Long Beach Island. We do not want to be caught in any mob violence," Emilio paused, and asked, "I wonder what kind of food the inn will be serving, with all the shortages."

"My friend, you are just like the boys!" Andrew laughed. "They would be concerned with food if they were before a firing squad!" He shook his head. "I would guess that we will be served rather plain food; perhaps meat and potatoes, something quite bland, or perhaps just potatoes." Andrew laughed again and Emilio joined him, not one bit offended. "Let us give the city a chance. We have just landed."

"Oh well, I am hungry. I guess we can live with whatever they serve us," and he stopped talking and frowned. Now Emilio was worried about Sunny. "Where has she gotten to?" Annoyed, he looked around, searching to see which store she had entered. "After those recent reports in the newspaper about the present tranquility, I certainly did not expect this amount of chaos. I guess one really cannot believe everything reported in the newspapers. *Calm in Boston?* I think not."

Andrew agreed. "I am concerned about the boys. Three young, spirited lads prowling about, defiant of the English soldiers is definitely a dangerous mix."

"I think we should get to the Admiralty's office and make our return plans as soon as possible." Emilio was becoming more worried. They did not want to be stayed in the harbor.

"My sons voice their anger each time they read of another tax levied by the British Parliament. When they speak to their merchant friends who are trying to make a go of their businesses, they listen to them complain of being taxed to death on their exports and imports. How can the Colonies grow with all these taxes being funneled back to England?"

"What is happening to our personal rights?" Andrew was disgusted, and now he was worried, and even more concerned about their return voyage. "We need to look into that schedule the Admiralty gave us. They have an office on the wharf to handle legalities. They told me at Leeds Point that I could make my arrangements there for the return trip. I do not want to be caught in anything like that Boston Massacre riot," Andrew repeated, pulling the sailing schedule from his pocket that he had previously secured.

Emilio suddenly spotted Sunny and called to her. He was thankful that she had taken his advice and stayed in the many upper class stores near the inn, which was a more tranquil area.

"I do love the shops father. I have already picked up some Christmas presents. I am sorry I took so long." She chattered on, all excited. "There they are," Sunny caught sight of her brother with Ben and Jack, walking toward them.

"I was becoming worried," Andrew was relieved.

"This city is steaming." Jack's excitement was apparent.

"Ready to blow." Ricardo was visibly agitated.

"We must leave earlier than we had planned," Emilio told Ricardo. "Andrew agrees with me. From the animosity brewing on the streets, we are liable to be caught in a pitched battle right here. The hostile talk is everywhere."

"Did you manage to get rooms for all of us?" Jack asked, changing the subject. "I would rather not sleep on the ship."

"Yes we did. The Green Dragon Tavern and Inn is just a few doors down on Marshall Street." Emilio pointed toward the direction of the tavern. He looked at the boys intently and cautioned, "I do not want Sunny anywhere on the streets by herself. Right in this area of the inn, she is safe enough. There are too many rough Redcoats and other riffraff milling about, especially down by the docks. Ricardo, need I say more?"

Andrew caught his sons' glances as Ben and Jack took in Sunny from stem to stern and could pretty well guess what they were thinking. It would not be a good idea for Sunny to encounter a bunch of ragtag scoundrels, strutting about on the streets looking for trouble, much less a group of rough, young Redcoats. Andrew repeated to his sons what Emilio had just said about not leaving Sunny alone for a minute.

"Today is December 15, which is almost over. I think another day here is sufficient. We will plan to leave the morning of the seventeenth. We are going over to the Admiralty office to make arrangements, *now*." Andrew turned to Emilio. "Look here." He pointed out a larger packet ship on the schedule. "The *Stella Maris* looks like a good bet. It is noted that she is a Royal Mail Ship, but has room for a few passengers."

"What armament does our Star of the Sea list?"

"The pamphlet only says that she is heavily armed and leaving at 9:00 a.m. December 17, running to Cape May. Perfect!" Andrew was satisfied.

"Come on, Ben," Sunny said, as she grabbed the opportunity to loop her arm through his. "Help me with my Christmas shopping." She smiled up at him. "We have little time, and I have a lot to buy."

"Shall I come along too?" Jack asked, quite surprised and somewhat annoyed that Sunny had chosen Ben. Then he felt silly and awkward that he had asked to join them.

"Thanks, old man. I think I can handle this just fine." Ben smiled down at Sunny, adorned in a bright yellow wool jacket with a dark brown, fur trimmed hood. Her jacket topped a long, brown suede skirt, and her hands molded matching gloves. She had tucked one hand into her dark fur muff for warmth and would have liked to have put her other hand into Ben's jacket pocket, but she did not dare. *He probably would run*, she thought. *He is so proper*. Little did she know of Ben's true feelings.

Ben was already intensely aware of her arm in his. He thought he would burst with pride that she had asked him to accompany her.

"What a fine couple they make." Much to Jack's dismay, he had overheard the remark Emilio had just made.

"Ricardo and I have something we need to do." Jack was irritated. "We will see you at the tavern around dinnertime."

"Give me your sack, Ben. Jack and I will check in and leave them at the inn. We will see you later." Ricardo had caught the annoyance in Jack's voice. "We will meet you later," Ricardo told Ben.

"If you have things to do," Andrew said to the young men, "Go ahead. But please be back for dinner at the inn before dark. I am meeting my friend Zach for lunch, as I told you." He turned to Emilio. "What say you join us for lunch right here. Perhaps Sunny and Ben will stop by. I would like Ben to say hello to Zach. He has not seen Ben in some time. It is just noon. We will have time to eat first and then head over to the Admiralty office to make arrangements to meet our *Stella Maris*. If it were up to me, I would like to leave Boston sooner, but Sunny has her heart set on buying up half of Boston."

"There he is," Andrew headed into the Green Dragon and spotted Zach at the bar having a drink. "How are you old friend," they shook hands, then hugged. "By god, you are aging well. You look the same as you did last time I saw you. How many years is that?" Andrew asked.

"Well I try," Zach answered. "Good timing. How have you been? I would say it has been five years at least!"

"This is my friend, Emilio. More like my brother." Andrew introduced Emilio to Zach. "And this is Sunny, his daughter."

"How do Emilio. Any friend of Andrew's is a friend of mine," and he turned to Sunny. "I would keep this pretty one under wraps!" He smiled at her then shook Ben's hand. "By Jove, Andrew, you raise the big ones," he said, looking up at Ben. "How have you been son?" Ben laughed and told him fine.

"Not to worry, Sunny. He is harmless. Has a daughter of his own about your age." Andrew smiled at her. "Flatters all the women; yes he does. Never changes. How is daughter Dolly by the way? And your wife and boys?" Andrew asked Zach.

"Everyone is just fine and sends their regards. Let us get a table and eat. I am hungry." Ben and Sunny took their leave and the men sat down.

An hour later, and the conversation was still going strong. Emilio pulled his watch from his waistcoat pocket and pointed to the time. "We have to get over to the Admiralty office."

"I understand how important this is after what you have told me," Zach took a last sip of coffee and started to gather his belongings.

"I am sorry that we have to leave but I am glad we had this time together and that you met Emilio. He will know who I am talking about now. Dangerous times call for diligence. Next time it is your visit to the island." Andrew shook hands and gave Zach his coat.

"It was a pleasure meeting you, Emilio. I hope we meet again." Zach shook his hand. "I have to get back to the store. We are taking inventory and I should be there. It was a pleasant ride here and it was nice being in the saddle again. I have not had this long a gallop for some time. Safe trip home to all," he said, and left.

Andrew and Emilio left the Admiralty office a short time later. The *Marta* had been cleared to follow the *Stella Maris,* heading south, leaving Boston on December 17, at 9:00 a.m. Now the men could relax.

There was to be a massive meeting at the *Old South Meeting House* near the wharf on December 16 regarding the status of the tea ships in the harbor. There had been a meeting previously on November 29, and a handbill had been posted in Boston for all to see.

"Have you read this handbill?" Emilio asked. "It has been posted from last month. Riot material! Could that be the cargo in those ships that we saw this afternoon?" He handed the bill to Andrew.

Friends! Brethren! Countrymen!—That worst of plagues, the detested tea, shipped for this port by the East India Company, is now arrived in the harbor; the hour of destruction, or manly opposition to the machinations of tyranny, stares you in the face. Every friend to his country, to himself and to posterity, is now called upon to meet at Faneuil Hall, at nine o'clock THIS DAY (at which time the bells will ring), to make united and successful resistance to this last, worst, and most destructive measure of administration."

Andrew was stunned. "Of course! If that is so, then there will definitely be trouble brewing at that meeting tonight. There has been a big stink about those ships, if indeed they are the ships in question. They were prevented from being unloaded when they came into port. The enormous taxes that have to be paid on this tea are being protested!"

"Blast! Where are they?" Emilio again expressed his concerns to Andrew about the young ones. They had been told to stay in the area of the inn, where it was safe. "I guess there is nothing we can do right now. I would like to stop and see a few merchants down on the wharf, myself. That area is relatively safe. I saw a ship's compass in a shop window and some other things I would like to look at more closely," Emilio confessed. "If we are to buy any gifts, we better do it now. We cannot leave, so we might as well do what we have to do." The two headed off to do some Christmas shopping of their own. Andrew remarked to Emilio that they only had another day in Boston.

Sunny and Ben had one encounter, which could have escalated. They ran into a dozen or so soldiers in the ranks, who started to make lewd remarks about Sunny. A British officer heard them from across the street and walked over to intervene, abruptly ending a potential confrontation. "Thank you, Sir," Ben was grateful for the intervention. There were too many in the group for him to take on, and they were armed and ready.

"Finish up, Sunny—back to the inn for us. It is too dangerous on the streets."

The following day, December 16 was tense, but uneventful. Andrew hired a carriage to take Emilio, Sunny, and himself on a tour of Boston City to see the lovely churches and other buildings. The young men were not interested—they had a few other places to visit. Boston had become quite populated in the last few years and there were many shops and lovely inns to see. "I wonder where the boys went in such a hurry." Sunny suddenly asked.

"Probably to do some shopping. I doubt if they finished yesterday," Andrew guessed. "I would think that Jack would be buying something for Glenda. She is his fiancée," he told Emilio and Sunny.

Around 4:00 p.m. Emilio pulled his watch from his waistcoat. "I truly have enjoyed the day, but we should get back to the inn."

That evening, after they had consumed a rather large meal on their last night, Andrew commented to Emilio, "Well, that food was very good—better than I had expected. Evidently, this inn serves everyone, the British included." Andrew sat quietly, contented and full. He continued to peruse the dining room.

"Perhaps that is why the food is so good." Emilio grinned.

"What about dessert?" Ricardo asked.

"I think I will have the bread pudding," Ben decided.

"I think we will all have it—and with hard sauce," Emilio added.

Sunny was lost in her shopping sacks, which she had brought to the table. She finally found what she wanted and showed them a few of the Christmas presents she had bought that day. "I really found some lovely gifts, but I cannot show them all to you," she smiled. "The Revere Silver Shop is extraordinary and I thought Mother would like a lovely silver bowl. You know, Mr. Paul Revere is a master silversmith. I am so glad that I did get to see Boston, but I am ready to go home now."

"We need to leave the harbor by 8:00 a.m. to rendezvous with the *Stella Maris* at 9:00 a.m. in the open waters. Everyone get a good night's sleep. It is late and time to retire."

"If you boys do stay up, please stay in. We do not want any trouble—get to bed at a decent time," Emilio told them. They had seen large gatherings starting over at the *Old South Meeting House* and Emilio was concerned. The young men were of age, however through inexperience, he felt that they might not realize just how dangerous a place the city was, especially at night. He wanted them off the streets, safe in their rooms.

Emilio's snoring kept Andrew awake for awhile, but he finally drifted off. Hours later, shouting and yelling from the streets woke them. They were too tired to see what was afoot and Emilio got up and closed the window to shut out the noise. Before he went back to bed, he rapped on the boys' door to make sure that the young men were in. Ben assured him that they were in bed, and Emilio went back to bed and fell into a deep sleep, until later, when he heard a banging on his door.

"Father! Father!" Sunny was pounding on his door. "Get up, please. Get up!" She yelled and Emilio jumped out of bed, rushed to the door and tripped over his boots, which were by the side of his bed.

"What is it? Are you all right? What is it?" He opened the door and stood there in his long underwear, confused with sleep, and a smarting toe.

"They have dumped the tea into the harbor," she was greatly excited. "They have dumped all of the tea! The town is in an uproar! I have been listening from my window to the town crier since sunup. Oh, Father, do get dressed so we can go out into the street!" She moved down the hall, and started to bang on the boys' door.

"Wait a minute! Just a minute!" Ben shouted, still half asleep. "For god's sake. Let us get decent, and we will meet you downstairs."

"What is she talking about?" Andrew was not fully awake. "What tea?"

"I have no idea, but we better get dressed. Now I hear her banging on the boys' door." Emilio hurried to the window to look out into the street. Full sunrise had yet to happen, although dawn had broken and there was just enough light to see.

Twenty minutes later, they met in the breakfast room, then went out into the street to join in the commotion. The crowd milled about and suddenly the mob started to sweep them down toward the docks. "Hold on to me, Sunny," Ben ordered and grabbed her arm. Their fathers and Ricardo and Jack were somewhere behind them.

When they reached Griffin's wharf, they were shocked to see hundreds of casks of tea floating in the seawater. Some casks holding large bricks of tea were broken open, others were still intact; all were drifting randomly throughout the inner harbor waters. They stood and listened to the loud, excited talk around them. Apparently, during the night, some 150 men led by Samuel Adams and the *Sons of Liberty* had painted their faces to disguise themselves as Mohawk and Narragansett Indians. They had boarded the three English ships and dumped 342 chests of tea into Boston Harbor in protest of the British Parliament's tax acts. Sunny heard that someone saw the ships' manifests, listing the number of chests.

What a magnificent act of rebellion, Andrew thought. Obviously, this was the cargo being held in the three heavily laden ships that he and Emilio had seen yesterday. "At last," Andrew said softly to Emilio. "A stand has been taken by us Colonists!"

"This will surely bring retribution from the British. No time to waste. Out to the Marta; hurry!" Emilio's voice was tight with apprehension. "We are setting sail immediately."

Andrew's face was a chalky color. "I cannot take a chance that the British may close the harbor and seize the *Marta*. With all this chaos, we can slip out. We have to get into proper position behind the packet. I do not care if we are too early. We can circle around the area outside of the harbor until we spot the *Stella Maris*." Andrew was uneasy and fearful, not only for himself, but for those with him.

Within the next minute, Ben and Sunny appeared. "All right, you two, get yourselves back to the inn and packed up. We need to go."

"Imagine, Father." Sunny said, as they worked their way through the mob. "Ninety thousand pounds of tea, worth over ten thousand sterling—dumped into the sea. I heard it said!"

Andrew found Ricardo and Jack in the chaos near the Green Dragon. "Get your belongings and be back in the front room quickly! It is a little after 7:30 a.m. We will leave at 8:00 a.m.," he told them.

"What about breakfast?" Jack asked, and Ricardo laughed.

"Are you serious?" Andrew was always amazed that their stomachs seemed to be their first priority. "We can eat on the ship," he added, as he rushed them into the inn. Then, looking at Ben, he noticed some sort of grease or soot on the back of his neck and asked him what it was.

"You do not want to know," Ben answered immediately, but quietly. Suddenly, Andrew did know and he looked at the three young men.

"You were all involved?" He was stunned.

"Not here—not now, father." Ben turned away from him.

"Clean yourselves up," Emilio commanded— *now.*" He was also aware of what the soot was. "The rest of Boston does not have to be privy."

"You were all part of it!" Sunny exclaimed excitedly.

"Be quiet. No more," Emilio said sternly. "Go and pack, all of you. We have to leave." He knew what the punishment could be if the boys were caught. "Hurry," he warned them. Emilio was frightened and with good reason.

They were quickly on the *Marta,* well ahead of the scheduled meeting time; Andrew and Emilio breathed easier. Because it was so early, the crew was onboard, as was the extra dinghy. They weighed anchor and sailed well out of the harbor, circling, but staying within sighting distance to watch for the *Stella Maris* as she departed.

It was not until they were well out of Boston Harbor, trailing the *Stella Maris,* that Andrew and Emilio would allow any talk of the incident. They called the trio together and asked them what had happened and how they had become involved in the escapade.

Ben started the conversation. "This is exactly what happened. I will tell you the timeline of the entire events leading up to the dumping of the tea. Yesterday afternoon, when you and Uncle Emilio and Sunny were out sightseeing, we wandered around the tavern, just to see what was there. We came across a group of men in a back room, having quite an agitated discussion. They drew us into their conversation but not before quizzing us first who we were, what we did, and so forth. We asked them just what was happening with the British. They told us that in May, the British Parliament had authorized the East India Tea Company to export half a million pounds of tea to the American Colonies. The East India Tea Company was to sell it without the English Parliament imposing the usual duties and tariffs. It was Parliament's attempt to try to save the corrupt Tea Company from bankruptcy! The company could undersell any other tea available in the Colonies, including smuggled tea. Their profit could save them from failure. Can you imagine that? The Colonists would help the East India Company avoid bankruptcy. The disruption to American commerce was unacceptable to many, including Samuel Adams of Boston."

Jack picked up the story. "The ship *Dartmouth* had already arrived November 28. The *Tea Act* required that the tax be collected within 20 days. Shortly thereafter the other two ships arrived and were moored in the harbor and all three were waiting to be unloaded. They were carrying tea from the East India Company. Then we were told about the meeting on November 29 in *Faneuil Hall*."

Ben took over. "*The Boston Committee of Correspondence* had invited surrounding towns to join in the meeting and they had all assembled in the room of the Selectmen. There were so many people there, that they had to move the meeting to the *Old South Meeting House*. At the House, a resolution was put forward and passed by the people, that the tea should not be unloaded, that no duty should be collected and that all of the ships should be sent back to where they came from. They also put forth that Francis Rotch, the *owner* of the vessel *Dartmouth*, should be told that it would be at his peril if his ship was unloaded and that the *Captain* of the Dartmouth be warned not to land the tea. This resolution was also passed. Orders were given to tie down the *Dartmouth* at Griffins Wharf and twenty citizens were to guard and prevent the *Dartmouth* from unloading."

Ricardo jumped in. "A letter arrived at the meeting from the owners of the ships, asking the meeting to wait until they could write to England for instructions how to proceed. They received a resounding refusal from the meeting and a statement: *Not a pound of it shall be landed.*"

"Were those the exact words?" Emilio asked.

"Correct," Ricardo confirmed. "The meeting also resolved that two other tea ships were expected within the hour and were directed to be docked alongside the *Dartmouth*—similarly under the volunteer guard. The meeting ended and riders would be dispensed to carry the news should there be an attempt to unload the tea by force. Then on December 14, another meeting was held in the *Old South Meeting House.* It was resolved that Mr. Rotch be ordered to immediately request a clearance for his ship and to leave the harbor. His cargo had been landed except for the chests of tea. However, the Governor had intended to prevent owner, Rotch's ship from sailing before all of the tea was landed.

The Governor had written to the English ministry, so we have heard and has asked them to prosecute some of the leaders of the *Sons of Liberty* for high crimes and misdemeanors. In addition, he further ordered Admiral Montagu to prevent the departure of vessels from the harbor. He has placed two armed ships at the entrance to follow these orders. Along with those instructions, he commanded Captain Leslie, who was the naval officer in command, not to let any ship pass out of the range of his big guns without a permit signed by the Governor, himself. They told us to try to attend the meeting that evening at *Faneuil Hall.*" Ricardo pushed back in his chair and looked at Ben to take up the conversation.

In the lull, Andrew commented, "I cannot understand why we were allowed to enter the harbor, unless we had arrived too early and orders were not yet in place. A lot

of the Governor's commands must have been ordered
during our time there. Perhaps his orders did not apply
to incoming ships. Thank God we are out of the harbor
now. I wonder if they will close it down."

"You have seen the chaos this had caused." Ben shook
his head. "Yesterday evening, the largest meeting was held
at the *Old South Meeting House,* which had filled quickly
and then spilled over into *Faneuil Hall.* We were there. Two
thousand men from neighboring towns attended and seven
thousand men were at the *Faneuil* and they overflowed
into the street. Then the report came that the Customs
House officers would not give Mr. Rotch a clearance for
the *Dartmouth,* before it was completely unloaded!"

"Can you believe that?" Jack was agitated. "This
command was thought to be ordered by the Governor,
who then rode back to Milton, thinking that he had won
a victory. Such arrogance!"

"*Not so,*" said the people adjoined there. "They were
not having any of it." Ben was in complete agreement with
the people after hearing the surrounding circumstances.
"After the crowd heard about the refusal at the Custom
House, they sent Mr. Rotch to the Governor's place in
Milton and told him to request the Governor, *in person* to
release his ship."

"When they reassembled a few hours later, Mr. Rotch
had not returned. The crowd of men at the meeting
was asked if they would still abide by the resolutions
passed if the Governor refused Mr. Rotch's request to
return to England without unloading the *Dartmouth.* The
enthusiastic crowd overwhelmingly shouted affirmation.
Josiah Quincy was most earnest. He is a rising attorney
and spoke eloquently," and Ricardo repeated what Mr.
Quincy had said.

*It is not the spirit that reposes within these walls that
must stand us in stead. The exertions of this day will
call forth events which will make a very different spirit
necessary for our salvation. Let us consider the issue. Let
us look to the end. Let us weigh and consider, before we*

advance to those measures which must bring on the most trying and terrible struggle this country ever saw.

"We have to confess that we did hear Attorney Quincy speak. We pushed our way into the Meeting House. We knew something important was happening. Everyone was so fired up we could not resist. It was then that we came back to the Green Dragon where we had initially found that meeting and we became involved," Ben admitted.

Jack disclosed more. "We had seen some of the men at the meeting whom we had previously met in the tavern and they told us that they would be back at the Green Dragon and that we should join them. We did, and again they questioned us at great length about ourselves. They asked us how we had helped the *cause*; I guess we gave them the right answers because after an intense examination, they invited us to join them for a drink. Then they told us that they were a group of the *Sons of Liberty*. Well, you can imagine how grand that was! We had heard about this group for so long and *now to meet some of them!* They had already brought us up to date on the state of affairs and what had happened in the previous meetings. They told us that they had a mission to complete for the *cause,* and they would be grateful if we would join them. We decided to go with them, even though we were not fully aware of what they intended to carry out, so we asked them. They told us that we had missed the *Indian war cry,* by some of the men at the Meeting House. They were resolved to dump the tea into the harbor waters and that *war cry* was an affirmation of that intent. They could not have those tea ships unloaded to the Colonists detriment! And we agreed."

Ben broke in. "Last night, we joined a large group of these patriots, down on Griffin's Wharf. We all disguised ourselves as Mohawk or Narragansett Indians. You cannot imagine the number of men out on the street then, disguised as Indians, most covered in blankets with soot on their necks and faces—hundreds of them! They divided us into three groups, to board the three ships. Our group was under the command of Leonard Pitt."

"Three groups rowed out to the three ships and boarded them all at the same time. After we were on board, one from our group went to the captain and confiscated the keys to the hatches and asked for candles. The captain asked us not to destroy his ship or rigging. We were ordered to open the hatches, grab the tea, cut or split the chests with our tomahawks and throw it overboard so all the tea would be ruined by the water. Eventually, we helped throw all of the tea into the harbor waters. Evidently the other two groups had one person who also directed the captains." Ricardo was pleased with what he had done.

"There were only a few crew members on board guarding the cargo, but you would be surprised how they helped us. Not one of the crew sounded the alarm. *We were surrounded by British ships, which were armed. They made no effort to stop us.* Then, we all left. No one spoke to another; we only knew one person's name, Leonard Pitt. We assumed that everyone would keep the secret." Jack could hardly believe that he had been part of something this enormous.

"You have taken our breaths away." Sunny sat quietly, agreeing with her father, unable to digest all of the information.

Andrew was flabbergasted. "I heard back in November that the *Dartmouth,* loaded with tea had been at mooring and was prevented from unloading. Evidently, the other two ships came in shortly after. That means they had been docked there for nearly a month. I had forgotten about that."

"We walked right past them." Emilio looked over at Andrew.

"Adams and the Boston Whigs feared that the tea would be confiscated for failure to pay customs duties, and eventually become available for sale. They really had made the decision, and that was to dump the tea overboard so the *English could not seize it.* I think it was a real blow to the British, in another way. The British love their tea and to know that all that tea was ruined, would really upset the English people. Perhaps it would let them know that the Colonists were serious about their *cause.*" Ben could not believe it either, that he had been part of this great event.

Jack turned to Sunny. "By the way, Sunny, I do believe I saw your master silversmith there, too."

"You mean, Paul Revere?" She was shocked.

"Is he not a member of the *Sons of Liberty*?" Jack paused, letting that thought sink in before he went on. "I cannot be one hundred percent sure, but I am about ninety five percent, that I saw him there. You know that many of the members of the *Sons of Liberty* are Freemasons too. We know that Benjamin Franklin and others belong to the Freemasons." Jack then went into almost a dissertation. "December 16, 1773, to be remembered in infamy, when the Colonists took a stand. We have been privileged to witness this historic moment—and actually be involved. A brave group of Colonists, disguised as Mohawk Indians, crept aboard the ships and dumped the chests of tea into the Boston Harbor. I think it was one of the best things I have ever done! Other well known persons were also involved and their identities would surprise you! *We want our liberties*, was the cry."

"What is the matter with you, Jack? If any of the Tories or British officers heard the last part of what you just said, you could be hanged. Are you not mature enough to realize that the people participating in this are all patriots and you could get them hanged too?" his father was angry. "Do you know how dangerous that escapade was? If the British navy ever got hold of you, that would be your end!"

"Bloody hell, Jack—speaking like that. Are you mad? You sound like you were interviewing for the newspaper. You had better keep your mouth shut when we are off the ship and I mean that. You are extremely lucky that you did not get caught and or shot!" Ben had a hard time keeping his voice down.

"I did not mean anything by that." Jack was contrite.

"Easy, Andrew," Emilio interrupted. "They are young men and fed up with the British control. You and I would have given our right arm to be involved in an event like this. Am I right, or am I right?"

Andrew admitted, however grudgingly, that Emilio was right. *I would have been right in the middle of the fray, given the opportunity.*

"Perhaps you should tell the boys about our passengers who accompanied us to Boston? What say you, Andrew?" Emilio questioned him, trying hard not to grin.

The three young men and Sunny showed surprise. "What are you saying, father?" she asked.

Ben could not believe what he was hearing.

"I had a few tense moments when the British Harbor Master inspected the ship before they issued us a final pass into the harbor—even though I knew that the runaways were well hidden," Andrew told them.

"It is dangerous, this slave business, Andrew. I am glad I did not know until later that they were aboard. I have to tell you at first I was angry that you would put us all at risk, but after learning the entire story of these slaves, I would have done the same thing," Emilio admitted.

"They needed to get to Canada, and the meet up had to be that first night, or I would have had to find shelter for them for another thirty days. As it was, they were taken off the *Marta* in the middle of the night and are safely on their way to Canada." Andrew was sorry, knowing that he had risked everyone's safety. It had been a difficult decision. He had never advertised to anyone what he had done and told Emilio so, but then thought to himself, *I will never do this again.* Then he reconsidered, *well, perhaps not until the next time.*

"Until the next time Andrew?" Emilio raised his eyebrows and smiled, knowingly. Andrew did not answer.

The young people sat wide eyed, and Ben told Jack to close his mouth before he drooled. "Father, are you saying that we were carrying runaway slaves to Boston?" Ben was surprised.

"They were headed for Canada. I was happy to get them to Boston. Let us not speak of this again."

They all knew that this Boston Tea Party, as it already was being called by the crowd, would trigger the end of one era and the beginning of another. War was on the horizon; the goal right now was to get the *Marta* back home into familiar territory. Trailing the British mail packet offered them a great measure of safety; the backup of the Union Jack enhanced that measure of safety, holding the pirate ships at bay. The pirates had kept a low profile, knowing that the English were outraged and dangerous.

The weather was clear, the winds brisk behind them, and the *Marta* broke off from the safety of the escort and turned into the northern inlet of Long Beach Island, happy to be out of the openness of the ocean.

"No pirates!" Ben shouted. "We have made it!"

They arrived on Long Beach Island a few days before Christmas. The family greeted them at the dock and it was good to be home.

A few days later, it was reported that they had rung the State House Bell in Philadelphia upon hearing of the Boston Tea Party. The Assembly had voted that Captain Ayres would neither be allowed to land his black ship Polly, or bring tea to the Custom House in Philadelphia. Ben read the newspaper to his father.

"Good for the Assembly!" was Andrew's take.

"But I wonder about the *State House Bell*. I had heard that the tower holding the bell was rotted and they were afraid to ring the bell." Sunny reminded them that she had mentioned this before. "You know, a few of the abolitionists have started to call this the *Liberty Bell*. That bell is quite old now, and with that crack in it, I would not like to be standing near that weakened, old rack!"

"I know a little of the history surrounding the bell," Andrew told them. "It was ordered by the Pennsylvania Assembly in 1751 to memorialize the 50 Year Anniversary of William Penn's 1701 *Charter of Privileges,* Pennsylvania's first constitution. It refers to the rights and freedoms valued by all. *Proclaim Liberty throughout all the land unto all the inhabitants thereof,"* is engraved into the bell, from the bible, I believe—*Leviticus.*"

"My goodness, Andrew," Marie interrupted. "You have an astounding memory!"

"You know my interest in history, Marie," and he continued. "The bell had been ordered from Whitechapel Foundry, out of London. The bell arrived in Philadelphia around 1752. I have to put my thinking cap on. I remember reading about this in the newspaper at that time. I don't think it was hung until the following year."

Ben walked in with a reference book. "You are correct, father. And here is a quote from Isaac Norris II, the day they hung the bell. He was a merchant and statesman and the son of Isaac Norris, Mayor of Philadelphia at one time, and then a member of the Supreme Court. *I had the mortification to hear that it was cracked by a stroke of the clapper without any other viollence as it was hung up to try the sound."*

Andrew finished telling them what he knew of the bell. "I know that the bell was recast a few times. The first time the job was given to two Philadelphia foundry workers, named Pass and Stow. They had added too much copper, and they tried again. Norris was still displeased and he requested Whitechapel cast another bell. However, the new bell was no better and so they left the second final casting by Pass and Stow to remain. Pass and Stow then put their name on the bell. It was rung quite often back in the fifties, to call the Assembly together, and to call the Colonists to discuss the Sugar Act and the Stamp Act—those I distinctly remember. I do not know if this was the State House Bell, as Sunny said, but bells were rung."

"I do not think the general public will ever know about the bells," so said Sunny.

"Who cares as long as there were some bells rung," was Jack's take.

The Christmas holidays were jubilant, and being with the Scarlattis was as ever, prized to all of the family. Earlier, on Christmas Eve day the family greeted friends from the island and the mainland, who had drifted in and out to wish all a Merry Christmas, Season's Greetings, and a prosperous and healthy New Year.

Sunny had gone out into the cold earlier with Ben and Jack to choose a tree. After much deliberation on her part, she cried, "There it is! That is the tree for us!" She rushed over to a large, beautifully shaped, pine tree. She watched Ben and Jack cut down not one, but two large trees. They set up one tree in the parlor for everyone to decorate and stood the second tree in the large foyer. The house smelled deliciously pungent with pine from the trees and garlands and the baking ginger cookies. Colorful, fresh greenery decorated the banisters. Pine garlands, tickling noses with their aroma, were draped above the doorways. It was a remarkable sight on that Christmas Eve.

The large table was covered with a beautiful, antique, handmade, ivory lace tablecloth, passed down to Marie from her Grandmamma, Sukie. Heavy silver, highly polished, was set out beside Marie's best dishes. Wonderful food covered the long, banquet table; splendid silver candelabras lit the huge room.

At dinner, Andrew held his glass high and gave a toast. "On this wonderful Christmas Eve, I give thanks to Him: for my wife and my sons, for close friends, for relatives, and my country. I pray that our new America will have peace, tranquility, and freedom, and that the British will return to England and their own celebrations. May we be together many more Christmas Eves in such warmth and love."

"*Hear, hear,*" echoed throughout, and they toasted each other with superb champagne served in thin, gold rimmed Swedish crystal.

The passing of the journal to a new generation was a solemn family occasion. *What better time to make my announcement than at the Christmas Eve table after a sumptuous dinner,* Andrew thought. He stood up and asked, "May I have everyone's attention, please?" Standing tall and proud at the head of the table, he tapped his wine glass gently to catch the attention of the diners. "I would like to make an announcement." He turned to Ben. "The one who keeps the family journal makes the decision when the time is right to pass the journal on to the next custodian. I have decided it is now time for me to do this, because now is a giving and sharing time." He paused and looked around at the many faces focused on him. "I inherited the duty as a young man and feel that it is a young person's task. I would like to pass the journal on to you, Ben, my elder son, if you will accept it. Remember, there is no disgrace or dishonor in refusing the legacy, if the inheritor feels that he cannot do justice to the keeping. We have emphasized this and found it to be a good rule," Andrew reminded everyone. "What say you, my son?"

"Thank you, Father," Ben stood up, with pride at being a VanHameetman and honored to be asked to continue this family tradition. "I accept with sincere thanks. It is an honor to be the custodian," Ben paused. "I tell you that I will do a good job." He smiled down the length of the long banquet table to the applause and praise of *Hear! Hear!* Then he sat down. "I will tell you about this later," he whispered to Sunny, who was sitting next to him, dressed in an emerald green velvet gown, with the Scarlatti antique emerald and diamond necklace adorning her neck.

After the evening feast, they gathered in the drawing room and handed one another gifts. Francesca played the harpsichord and the group gathered around her and sang Christmas carols. Sunny, with her bright and caring ways, received more pleasure from distributing her carefully chosen Christmas gifts bought in Boston, than she did in receiving. She and Ben sat on a small couch together. Ben handed her a small package with a bright red bow and whispered, "Merry Christmas. I hope you like it."

Sunny smiled, and her lovely face lit up, which touched him deeply. "I know I will, Ben. How kind of you." She opened the package to find a beautiful, gold locket on a chain. "Oh, Ben. How lovely! I will treasure it always." She leaned over and kissed him on the cheek, then she handed him her gift of a small silver compass, engraved with his initials, created by the Revere Silver Shop. Ben was ecstatic.

"I will keep it always." He reached out to put his hand on her arm, resisting the urge in front of others to draw her to him.

Sunny smiled at him and fantasized, *if he would have it, I would jump right into his lap, in front of God and the entire world and I would not care.* She smiled to herself, enjoying the shocking thought, and the response it would certainly have brought from the diners.

Andrew noticed Jack's angry expression as he watched the exchange between Ben and Sunny. He was concerned with his younger son's jealousy, knowing that he was engaged to Glenda. She was spending Christmas Eve with her family on the mainland and would see the VanHameetmans on Christmas day. Andrew decided to put his worries aside and not let it ruin his evening. He would speak with Jack later.

On Christmas Day, they gathered in the large common hall of the community building erected years ago, near the far end of the family compound. At the time the hall was built, it was necessary to house families there. In time, enough homes had been built to accommodate everyone. Now the hall was used for congregational purposes and the schoolrooms.

Andrew remembered as a young child, asking his mother where all the people would come from to fill the big hall and the multiple rooms within. She told him that the family was growing in leaps and bounds and that this large hall would be needed in the future. Andrew smiled to himself because, as a child he had looked for the people leaping and bounding about the room.

The extended family had come from Tuckerton and the Middle of the Shore area for the annual Christmas reunion—it was a time of joy and thankfulness. This year, they celebrated a special and rare pleasure. Father Michael deCosta, Emilio's friend, and a priest of the Jesuit Order in Philadelphia was spending Christmas with them. The priest had accompanied Francesca to the Island. Emilio had been surprised when he saw him. "Merry Christmas, Father, and I wish you health in the New Year. My wife certainly has amazing powers of persuasion. I am absolutely delighted that you could join us." He hugged the priest. His presence added another dimension to their holiday pleasure.

Father Michael deCosta, thin, gray haired, slightly stooped and rumpled, was getting on in years, ready to retire. He was looking forward to spending his days fulfilling his writing ambitions set aside so long ago. "I am greatly pleased to be here with all of you." He waved his hand over the large group, blessing them all. He had known the family for years and was pleased that he had chosen to spend the holidays with them.

"How wonderful to hear mass on Christmas day," Andrew smiled at Marie.

"Yes," she responded, smiling. "It is just wonderful. You will excuse me please. I need to help the women set up the altar in the common house hall, for a noon mass." Marie, as usual was taking care of others.

Andrew turned to see Jack and Glenda entering the room. Jack did not look happy. He was heading for Ben and Sunny who were on the other side of the room. He walked ahead of Glenda, in an ungentlemanly manner, ignoring her. Andrew could tell that Glenda was upset, being treated so disrespectfully by Jack, especially in front of everyone; then he lost track of them. Later, he found Marie and asked her if she had seen Jack with Glenda.

"Glenda just caught me in the foyer and told me that she was leaving. I was surprised because I know that she had planned to stay with us overnight. Jack was going to bring her home tomorrow and visit some friends in Tuckerton. She certainly could not make the trip to the mainland after dark tonight. She said she was leaving and going home with Josie Donahue. Josie is Ben's friend and Glenda knew her from school. After the fracas with Jack, Glenda approached Josie and asked her if she could stay overnight at her house. Josie's father is coming here to pick Josie up so Glenda will go home with them. I asked Glenda how she would get back to Tuckerton tomorrow; she said that would be arranged for her and for me not to worry. I asked her if Jack knew she was leaving and she told me that she really did not care whether he knew or not. She said to me that she had broken any relationship with Jack and she was sorry that she had to tell me, but that she wanted me to know. She asked me to tell you, too."

"Good lord Marie," Andrew shook his head. "I cannot believe that Jack has treated Glenda so abominably, but she is well out of it. I just do not know what to say to him. I am terribly disappointed at his behavior." Andrew frowned. "He needs a good thrashing. I know that he has been after Sunny. I just do not know what to do with him."

"What are you saying? Sunny only has eyes for Ben! I am appalled at Jack's behavior." Marie drew in a deep breath, took Andrew's arm, steering him in to the beginning of Mass.

After Mass, the huge buffet was set—its sumptuous array of food was definitely one of the highlights of the Christmas season. Each family contributed their own specialty; their loyal Lenape friends joined them, as they did each year, bringing their delicious delicacies to the festivities. It had been an extraordinary day.

Shortly afterward, Ben heard that on Christmas Day Captain Ayres' much hunted and detested tea ship, *Polly* had reached Chester. The *Polly* had followed closely behind another ship and had managed to slip into port. Evidently, Captain Ayres from the *Polly* tea ship was too frightened to sail into Philadelphia, which was his original destination. The Whigs in the Chester Port sent a messenger to Philadelphia, announcing that the *Polly* had been spotted coming into Chester. "To make a long story shorter," Ben said, "Captain Ayres did go into Philadelphia where 8,000 Colonists had been assembled in the State House Yard to protest the tea ship unloading. They demanded that

Ayres return to England. Captain Ayres was allowed time to replenish his supplies for the trip back to England and being a wise enough man, left soon after." Ben ended his story with "*Good riddance!*"

Lord Earl Dartmouth wrote to Governor John Penn, so it was reported, that the people of Philadelphia had insulted the Kingdom. This was very serious and would lead to important consequences. His Lordship wanted a full explanation.

Methinks his Lordship will have a very long wait, Ben thought.

"I doubt if *my lord* will ever get a full explanation. The arrogance of them!" That was Andrew's thought on the matter.

Andrew had spoken to Ben about Jack's unbelievably pompous, irresponsible behavior. "Jack had left Glenda on her own to get herself back to Tuckerton. I am assuming that Josie's father will take care of Glenda. I know the man, and he will do the right thing. If you see Josie or her father, please say something to them and make sure Glenda got home. I will definitely get to them and to Glenda's parents as soon as possible."

Marie piped up. "How disgraceful is this? I cannot believe my son's behavior!"

"It is hard to believe that Jack just left Glenda alone to find her way home. If Jack approaches Sunny in any disrespectful way, I will knock the stuffing out of him. I mean that, father. He is a spoiled brat!" Ben was furious.

"I will speak with your brother about this attitude of his, although I do not expect it will do any good. I am also going to speak with Glenda's parents at some time. I need to apologize for Jack stranding her and not seeing her home. Good lord! He has not been raised that way!" Andrew was beset.

"Andrew," Marie was looking for him the next morning.

"Yes, my dear, what can I do for you?"

"I would like you to ride over to the Donahue's this morning. Do you remember where they live? Just south of Harvey Cedars. You need to speak with Josie's father. I want to make sure that Glenda is all right. If not, then I think we should help out. I am totally embarrassed about the situation."

"I was thinking of doing that. I will leave immediately. And you are right, it is terribly embarrassing." Andrew dressed and went out to saddle his horse.

Ben called after him. "Do you want me to come with you, father?"

"Thanks Ben. I need to handle this one," Andrew answered and rode off.

January 1774

I am pleased to make my first entry into the family journal. After a wonderful New Year's celebration, the Scarlattis and Father deCosta left January 5, for home. They sailed on the *Marta* to Tuckerton, where they hired a carriage to Philadelphia.

The pirate activity in the Delaware Bay prevented the *Marta* from sailing to Philadelphia.

The only bad note of the holiday, was Jack's unbelievably arrogant and nasty attitude in stranding Glenda. We are shocked at his behavior. My father picked up Glenda and Mr. Donahue and brought her safely home on the *Marta*. Mr. Donahue saw Glenda home and returned on the *Marta* with us. To say the least it was embarrassing for our family to have to cover for my brother's wrong doing.

The weather is unseasonably mild this year, and we are back to work, stripping and cutting the cedar. After our encounter with the Boston Patriots, I am a changed man. We saw and experienced Boston. We are forced to acknowledge the full extent of the oppressive treatment of the British and we are tired of their ongoing pompous attitude. We know our enemy. However, I do admit that we did use the British to our advantage. Father does not feel that we will be sailing anywhere for a while except to Tuckerton to deliver our cedar. We will wait and see what upheaval this Tea Party has wrought in the grand scheme of things.

Benjamin VanHameetman
His Journal

Ben's mind was constantly filled with thoughts of Sunny. He could not understand what was happening to him. He found that he could not stop himself from compulsively replaying in his mind in great detail, the events of the last two weeks that he had spent near her when she and her family had visited for Christmas. He kept remembering, the smallest minutiae and would draw forth wonderful images of their rides together on the island before she left for home. He saw her in his mind's eye upon his beautiful, dark horse, Roscoe and each time he thought of her, he felt the blood leaving his head and going straight to his knees. He dreamed of Sunny and himself in ways that set his mind reeling. *How can one little person affect me like this?* He was baffled, well aware that these feelings, now becoming almost an obsession in their intensity, started on the day that they had met again as adults. When he was with her at times, his desire had been so strong to embrace her that the fierceness of it had startled him.

He had acted the gentleman and in that way, he was proud of himself. Jack was a complication that had made him angry and the extent of his anger surprised him. As for Jack, Ben knew that he too, wanted Sunny and the thought of Jack being with her was unbearable to Ben—even though he knew that those thoughts were only daydreams in Jack's mind.

Knowing how Jack's thoughts were running in regard to Sunny, Ben felt like killing his own brother when he had seen him near her. The strength of his feelings for Sunny held a passion that was new and startling to him. *Good lord*, he addressed himself, *you are acting like a woman.*

He had always thought himself a somewhat calm and confident person, but now he was confused. His rambling was interrupted by his mother's call.

"Ben? Ben, are you here? Where are you son?" she called.

"Sorry, Mother. I was lost in my thoughts."

"I just wanted to chat for a minute. I see you moping around, somewhere in a far off place. What in the world is bothering you? Can you speak of it?" She knew already that Ben loved Sunny deeply. She thought it would help him to speak about how Jack was involved in the relationship, but Ben was a man now and she realized that she should not interfere. She loved her son and hated to see him so miserable.

"Thanks, Mother, but I cannot." He dropped his eyes, disheartened.

Oh well, she thought. *I might as well have at it.* "Ben, if you want her, then go after her. Let nothing stop you." She sat down next to him and looked him in the eye.

He was surprised. "How did you know? Have I been as obvious as Jack? I could wring his neck. Jack's behavior has been abominable."

"Listen to me, son. I know that you are no longer a boy, but sometimes young men are confused with matters of the heart. You have always been a kind person and aware of others' feelings. Sometimes though, you are inclined to stand aside and let others take the prize. This time, I want you to reach out for what you truly want; if it is meant to be, it will happen. This time, do not stand aside, or you might regret it forever." She leaned over and smoothed back his shock of thick, light hair as she had done when he was a boy. "I hope you have not resented me for intruding into your privacy."

"No, Mother you have not. What you just said means a lot to me. And I will follow your advice." He bowed his head again. "I know I will have to take it slow and easy with Sunny, but I will win her because I love her with all my heart. How she feels about me, I truly cannot say, and it is driving me crazy."

"You need to find out then." She knew that her son was caught between his essential duties and Sunny.

It was critical that he get back to work. The demand for cedar by the local shipyards had increased—a demand that was kept secret from the British. Ben was overwhelmed with work. Wealthy merchants from Philadelphia to Tuckerton were contributing funds to the Colonists' cause. Shot and cannon balls from the Pine Barrens' furnaces were being stockpiled for the militia, for what many of the Colonists knew was on the horizon.

"I know that the Batsto furnaces will be important to the cause, when the fighting breaks out," Ben had told his father.

"The militia will need shot for their muskets and in great quantity; and packet ships, disguised as fishing boats will be an asset." Andrew agreed. He did note that Ben had said *will need*.

That night Ben decided he must write to Sunny to say he wished to visit her in Philadelphia. In the meantime, however, he would let day to day hard work take his mind from her until he saw her. He needed to calculate the weight in raw cedar he would need for their shipyard and the yards over on the mainland. His head was spinning. He would avoid Jack and wait for Sunny's reply. He also knew that his greatest fear was that Sunny did not feel as he did.

He needed to speak with Ricardo about the exact amount of indigenous timber near Batsto that would be needed to keep those furnaces hot enough to melt the ore. He thought that Ricardo had underestimated the number of men that would be needed to cut the timber. However, that would be easy to rectify. Ricardo would have to tack up another Help Wanted Bulletin on the local Town Crier's posts.

February 1774

The weather is fair, and mild for February, making it possible to deliver great amounts of cedar to our yard in Tuckerton to be used for packet ships. Tuckerton is just across the bay, and we do not need to go out into open waters. We have received orders for ships from as far away as the Connecticut Colony. Father had to tell them that we cannot build war ships, or the British will confiscate them. British Men-of-war and sloops are off our coast daily, heading north to Boston and New York.

No shots have been fired, but our First Continental Congress has assembled, debated, resolved and finally, adjourned. Friends returning from Boston report that the city is bursting at its seams with the hostilities afoot.

The Massachusetts Bay Colony is trying to raise an army which they will call the New England Army. A fresh act came out of the British Parliament that all the Colonies have been forbidden to trade anywhere except in England or the British West Indies.

The entire New England fishing fleet has been barred from the North Atlantic fisheries. The days of so called peace are fast ending.

Benjamin VanHameetman
His Journal

In spite of the upheaval he believed was coming, Ben noted that at the present, it had been quiet on both sides. *Perhaps the calm before the storm?* He knew that he must go now to visit Sunny. He had not heard from her. Why am I procrastinating, he asked himself. Deep down he knew though. He still did not know if there was reciprocity in her feelings for him. Their letters remained friendly, except for a slip up here or there, as he interpreted it. *What did she mean by writing that?* He would wonder. *Did she have a secret meaning for me?* The next moment, he would feel that it was his imagination. New orders had been exploding in their lumber business and shipyard, and he had truly given himself over to them. The orders had been pouring in. However, he did not want to take a chance of losing Sunny. He was caught up in inertia.

Then Jack told him that he planned to be in Philadelphia the middle of the week and he intended to stop and see the Scarlattis. The thought of Jack being with Sunny drove Ben wild. The brothers nearly came to blows when Ben brought up Jack's fiancée, Glenda.

"You have treated Glenda abominably," Ben raised his voice to Jack. "Father told me at Christmas what you had done. I did not speak of it because it was your own business. But I did not approve of how you did it. I am happy that Glenda is well shed of you, because you are nothing but a rotten rogue. And furthermore, do not presume to think of Sunny in any other way, but as a family friend." Ben was outraged at his brother's behavior.

Jack too, was furious; his face turned red; he yelled back at Ben, "How dare you try to take Sunny from me! I intend to visit her soon."

"What kind of nonsensical remark is that, Jack? How could someone be taken from you, who you never had? It is all in your mind, Jack, which I think you are losing." Ben finished the argument by telling him that their father had told Emilio that you were engaged to Glenda. How could you think that he did not tell Sunny? She will not have anything to do with you, Jack," Ben was furious. "I am sure Sunny knows how you ended the relationship with Glenda."

Jack stormed out yelling over his shoulder, "We will just see about that! And mind your own damn business!"

Jack had intended to visit Sunny the following month, without his family's knowledge. However, he had not set a date. After the row with Ben, he left for Philadelphia immediately, on a Tuesday and had lied about his destination. Jack returned home two days later, and Marie asked him where he had been. "I had business in Tuckerton for two days and stayed over at the tavern. I wanted to get away from here." He was annoyed that his mother had *interrogated* him.

The day Jack returned, Ben received a letter from Sunny, telling him that Jack had been to see her. He noted the date and was surprised at the speed that he had received the letter. He called to his mother to ask her when the letter had arrived and how. "It came special courier this morning." Marie had been surprised. "Is everything all right?"

"Sunny has asked me if it is possible for me to come to Philadelphia to see her." Ben recognized urgency in her letter, and told his father, "I will be leaving for Philadelphia on the morrow." He realized now, how torn he had been between his duties and his need to see Sunny. "I will be gone for a few days. I must see Sunny. She is upset. Jack lied to us about going to Tuckerton last week. He visited her the first day, and then went to Tuckerton; I would imagine for an alibi."

His father shook his head, dismayed. "I am at a complete loss as to why Jack was there. Has he spoken to you about Sunny?"

"He does not know that I know he had gone to see her. He has not spoken to me about his visit since his return. We had only discussed the business he supposedly conducted in Tuckerton, which I now know was a ruse to get to Philadelphia. The only way I know he visited Sunny was the letter I have just received from her. She wants me to come and see her, and it sounded urgent. She posted it special courier because it was dropped off at the house this morning. After I read it, I sought Jack out and pointedly asked him how Sunny was. He was surprised that I knew. I did not mention Sunny's letter. He told me the visit went very well and now that he was unencumbered, he was going to ask Sunny to marry him!"

"*He said what?*" His father was dumbfounded.

"I cannot even repeat it. I was stunned and could only stare at his smug face for a minute. Then I left the room, because if I had stayed another minute, I would have smashed his face. Jack has evidently gone after Sunny with a vengeance. You know what Jack does when he wants something. He is not satisfied that he had Glenda, who had loved him dearly and who he previously had claimed he wanted to marry but he tossed her away." Ben felt sick. "I am at a loss as to what I will do," he whispered. "Suppose Sunny agrees to marry him?" He was frantic. "You know father, that this is a very serious relationship for me. I want to marry her."

"I know Ben. This is ridiculous, son." Andrew was now furious. "What is the matter with Jack? He constantly runs roughshod over everyone. No one, not even his family, is safe from his wanton ways." Andrew did not know what to say to his miserable, elder son. "Ben, I am about to say something that truly disagrees with me. Jack is my son too, but he has definitely gone too far and has run amuck. I am sure Sunny feels nothing like love for Jack. I saw you two together; she definitely has deep feelings developing toward you. I want you to get on your horse, go to Philadelphia, and set things straight. This cannot go on. It has to stop, *now*."

"I am going to Philadelphia," Ben told his mother. "I am not waiting any longer. I am so angry with myself for not going to see her."

"You should have gone sooner, Ben. Right after I spoke to you," she said. "You must take care of yourself and your personal life. I know how busy you have been, but where do you come in?"

"I am so outraged at Jack that I will put everything aside and leave. I have some urgent business at Batsto," he said, "and I will go to Philadelphia from there."

"Good. Go, and good luck," Marie said.

The *Marta* was scheduled to make a run to Tuckerton the next day, with a load of cedar. *The hell with Batsto*, Ben thought, as he led his black hunter, Roscoe, aboard the *Marta*. I will stop there *after* I see Sunny. From Tuckerton, he departed the *Marta* and rode overland to the Delaware River crossing directly to Philadelphia, bypassing Cooper's Creek. He did not want to be held up by ferries. Sunny had previously sent him directions to her home, near Pine Street and Rittenhouse Square. Ben quickly found the big, three story, brick house in an upscale section of the city. A maid answered the door and told him that Miss Sunny was behind the house in the stables. Ben hurried around to the back; his heart was pounding at the thought of seeing her again. He did not know what he would do when he saw her, so he just let what would happen, happen.

"Ben!" She cried out as he rounded the corner and came into her view. She was in one of the open stalls, grooming Tonio when she spotted him. "Oh, Ben," she cried again. She flew from the stall and physically threw herself at him.

He grabbed her close to him and held her tightly while she sobbed into his chest. Ben did not know what had happened and he swore that if Jack had done anything wrong, he would kill him; but then he knew that he would not. It was his anger speaking. Sunny stopped crying and looked up at him.

"I could not care less about being forward. I do not care about anything at all except that I love you, Ben," she told him, pressing herself closer still. "If you say you will not have me, Ben, I will just die." She put her head down into his chest again, unable to look up at him, and repeated, "I will just die."

They stood entwined for a long moment. Ben wanted to stand there forever, never moving, with the feel of her body against him, her warm, soft hair under his chin and her sweet smell enveloping him. But then she peeked up, clearly waiting for his answer.

"I love you, Sunny; I want you more than anything I have ever wanted in my entire life. I was so afraid that you did not feel the way I did; I would have died a slow death if you did not love me," Ben whispered to her. "Come, be my love and marry me, Sunny. No one will ever love you the way I do."

"Oh, my dear sweetheart," she sobbed, then threw her arms around his neck and hoisted herself up higher. He lifted her rest of the way so that he could cover her warm mouth with his; when he felt and tasted her lips, the intensity of his feelings dazed and overwhelmed him.

She clung tighter, and Ben knew that he had to separate from her or in just a matter of moments, he might lose control completely.

"Sunny, my dearest Sunny," he whispered. "We cannot do this. We have to stop." But she pulled his head down, covering his mouth with her warm sweetness again, burrowing into him, and it took all of his willpower to part from her. "Wait, Wait a minute." He lifted her away from him. "Just stand there with some space between us, or I will lose myself. We have to talk."

She smiled at him through her tears. "Oh, I am so happy. I just cannot believe that you love me, too." She started for him again, saying, "It must be that I have waited so long and now I want to kiss and hug you forever." He had to hold her at arm's length.

"Sunny, Sunny," Ben murmured. "What has happened to make you so upset, dearest? When I received your letter, I could not wait to get here and then Jack told me that he intended to ask you to marry him. I could not believe it. What is going on? Did Jack do or act improperly to you? I will thrash him if he did," Ben said with such anger, that she pulled back, startled.

More tears rolled down her cheeks as she stood looking up at him. "What is the matter with Jack? He told me that he loved me. Is he mad? I have never given him any kind of encouragement, but he acted as though I had. I did not invite him here. He invited himself. I told him that I loved you and he acted surprised, then angry like a little boy not getting his own way. I had to see you. I was not sure if you felt anything between us as I did." She sobbed and gulped all over again. "I did not want to say anything to my parents about it, because I was not sure how you felt, and I do love you so Ben."

"What in the world is going on out there?" Francesca interrupted, suddenly coming out of the back door with her little dog Fritzie tucked under her arm. "Are you all right?" she asked her daughter. "I heard all the commotion. I thought I heard you crying." She frowned up at Ben. He stood there, silent and bewildered, with his big horse Roscoe in tow, and Sunny with tears running down her face. He was captive to the two women and could not move.

"Oh, Mother, I am exceedingly fine. Ben has just asked me to marry him. I know we have not seen much of each other since we have grown up, but we have known each other for such a long time and I do love him so. I think I have loved him since I first saw him!" Sunny answered passionately.

"My goodness Sunny, do try to calm down. Why all the tears then? Are they tears of happiness?"

"Everything is fine now, Mother. Everything is just fine." She tucked her hand into Ben's and repeated, "Everything is just fine." At her touch, his feet became unglued.

"We need to go inside and have a nice cup of hot tea," Francesca advised. Like most mothers, she thought a cup of tea calmed every stormy sea. "I think we can all use a settling down. Ricardo should be home soon and I know he would like to see you, Ben. And I am so happy for the two of you," she said with a big smile. "Just wait until your father hears the good news. I know he will be as pleased as I am."

Emilio and Ricardo walked in later and Francesca could not wait to tell them the news. After dinner, Ben and the family sat around the fireplace in the drawing room to discuss marriage plans. Ben was comfortable with them.

"I cannot tell you how happy and pleased I am that you two have found each other. I have always hoped this would happen since you were both young. Where do we go from here?" Emilio asked.

"It would be nice to be engaged for a time," Sunny offered. "What do you want to do, Ben?"

"That would be the proper thing to do, I suppose." He actually thought that he would have preferred marriage immediately, but he knew he would sound very forward in front of her parents. "I have to tell my parents the good news first and as far as the marriage plans—whatever you want Sunny. It is really fine with me." He was beset and could not believe what had just happened. This was such a monumental turn of events he thought; *perhaps*, he was dreaming and would wake up any second.

"I am engaged!" Sunny proclaimed, excitedly. "May we announce it formally in the newspaper? That is if there are still any papers left that take announcements."

Ben and Emilio laughed. "This is now woman's territory." Emilio smiled; Sunny and her mother got up and went into the library.

"Excuse me for a minute," Emilio said. "I need to get myself another cup of tea. I will see if Mrs. McKenzie has more in the kitchen." He hesitated. "I have changed my mind. This calls for something stronger than tea. This is a celebration! We need some libation! Will it be whiskey or wine, Ben?"

"I will have the whiskey, Sir." He thought it might bring him out of shock.

As soon as Emilio left the room, Ricardo, who had been quiet while all the animated conversations were going on, asked Ben, "What is going on with Jack? Sunny was quite upset; I was not sure what the state of affairs was between you two, or how Jack fit in."

"Jack does not fit in, in any way. Jack presumes where and when he should not presume." Ben was angry. "I will take care of it when I get home."

Ricardo waited for him to say more, but he saw that Ben was finished. "I will trust you to do that. I know it will be difficult because he is your brother, but I know you will straighten it out. Good luck, Ben. I am truly happy for you and Sunny. You know how special she is, and I am glad that she chose you."

Ben told Ricardo that he could not yet believe that Sunny had accepted his marriage proposal. He assured Ricardo that he would always take care of his sister.

Ben took his leave from Philadelphia the following morning. He stopped in Batsto, then started back to the island, not looking forward to confronting his brother about his lies. Jack always assumed, that if he wanted something badly enough, it would become reality. In the past, it had worked for him because he wore people down; but this time Jack had gone too far. Ben knew that he did love his brother, but Jack was difficult at best and, at times like this, just rotten.

Ben preferred not to speak to Jack immediately when he returned home. He chose to wait for an opportune moment to make his announcement; he did not know if Jack knew that he had seen Sunny. At dinner that night Jack was present, but Ben continued to avoid him. He was still angry, and suddenly he decided to hell with it; I will announce my marriage plans, right here and now and then demand an explanation from Jack about his uninvited visit to Sunny.

"Mother, Father," Ben stood up from the table. "You know I was in Philadelphia the last two days visiting Sunny. I had received an urgent request from her to come to her home." He looked at Jack and paused. "I was extremely concerned with the message and rushed to see her. It seems that Jack upset Sunny terribly when he was at the Scarlatti home recently. Not only was he insufferably overbearing, he came home to tell us that he was about to ask Sunny to marry him. This marriage idea may have some bizarre foundation in Jack's mind, but certainly holds no meaning for Sunny. *I think you are living in a fantasy land Jack, and completely out of your mind!*" Ben addressed him directly; his voice got louder. "Whatever made you think that Sunny regards you in that way? Has she ever given you any indication that she would even consider becoming your wife?"

Marie started to interrupt.

"Mother, please; I must finish this. Could you wait for just one more moment?" Marie sat back in her chair and remained silent.

"However Jack, I do want to thank you." Jack glanced up at him, surprised. "Sunny and I have had feelings for each other since we were children. The trip to Boston brought these emotions out, but I was too uncertain of myself to act on them." Jack looked up at him and sneered, shaking his head.

"Sneer all you want, Jack, but guess what? I will come right to the point, because if I hesitate *I will knock you right off that chair.*" Ben started to move toward him; his rising voice had startled Jack, who quickly pushed his chair back to put a little distance between himself and his brother.

"Ben," his father sent a warning voice and he started to get up from his chair. "For heaven's sake, stop; I know that you are angry, but control yourself!"

"I am finding that difficult indeed, father. This selfish, inconsiderate boor has compromised Sunny. He has acted in an ungentlemanly, rude, arrogant manner and I would like to beat or horsewhip him soundly! Do not push me, Jack, or I guarantee you will be sorry." Jack started to get up, and Ben shouted, "I am not finished!" He moved in and pushed Jack down hard into the chair. "I have asked Sunny to marry me, and she has accepted. As of two days ago, we are officially engaged. We intend to set a marriage date as soon as possible."

"Oh, Ben," Marie could hardly contain herself. "I am so happy for the two of you. Are Emilio and Francesca overjoyed? I would imagine so, getting a fine son like you." Tears came quickly as she got up and hugged her elder son.

"Congratulations, Ben," Andrew said and came around the table to shake his hand. "Such a lovely girl." He smiled. "I cannot wait to welcome her into our family as a daughter. Good work, son!"

Jack was stunned by the announcement and sat very still, his face a chalky white. "But *I* love Sunny. This is not fair! She was meant for me. What is the matter with all of you?"

"All is fair in love and war, Jack," Ben answered him. "How many times have I heard that from you? Fair? Fair? You tell me how fairly you have treated Glenda in the last three months, you spoiled brat. Disgraceful, that is how! You and your behavior have embarrassed our family and hers. I am not one fig sorry for you Jack, because you have been using and abusing the people around you for years, but this time, it will not work for you. Sunny and I will be married soon. Who needs a long engagement?"

"I wish I could help you, Jack," his father interrupted. "But what Ben says is true. It is a terrible way to learn a lesson. Evidently, you really did not love Glenda; she is well shed of you. You have treated her abominably and you have disgraced us with your outrageous behavior, as your brother says. You were not raised that way. Maybe you ought to think about that for awhile." Andrew was disappointed with Jack and he had to say his piece.

"How is that, Jack?" Ben asked. "What say you, brother?" Ben repeated. "You seemed to have plenty to say recently. Why so quiet now?"

"You have said it all. What would you have me say? You can go to hell!" he responded, not looking at Ben directly. He shoved his chair back, threw his napkin to the floor and stormed out of the room.

"He needs to grow up and realize people's feelings are not to be trampled upon," Ben stated.

"You know, he really is a good person underneath all that bravado," his mother did not know what to say. "I cannot believe Jack said that to you, his own brother."

"He needs to grow up," Ben repeated and left the room.

Jack rushed from the house the next day; they heard later that he had joined the militia. Ben was still too angry to have any sympathy for him. *Perhaps the militia can knock some of that arrogance and superiority out of him,* Ben thought.

Marie was in tears at the terrible row her sons had had and at Jack's leaving. Andrew walked around for days without speaking, ruminating over the dreadful argument, questioning whether he should have stopped it. He had finally decided that they were men now. They had to settle it themselves.

Ben knew it would take months, if ever, for him to forgive Jack. His parents hoped that in time, the terrible rift would heal. Ben felt it might be a long time before they would see Jack again.

CHAPTER SEVEN

A Matter of Independence

1774-1777

"Curses," Ricardo whispered to Ben. *"We almost made it. If Huro had not spoken to Cox, we would have been signed up with the New Jersey militia and long gone."*

Sunny and I could not wait; we were married the following June of 1774 by Father deCosta in Sunny's Philadelphia parish.

April 19 1775

Notes on Lexington and Concord Massachusetts

What we have been expecting for some time is over the horizon and upon us. The King's men have been engaged at Lexington and Concord, in the Massachusetts Bay Colony—the war is upon us.

What set this in motion were a number of major events: there was no representation in the British Parliament for the Colonists, the increasing, excessive taxes imposed upon the Colonists were the final straw that broke their backs, the Boston Tea Party and the Boston Massacre had never stopped simmering. These were but a few of the inflammatory events. We colonists have had enough!

The British thought they could strike a huge blow and prevent the coming rebellion of the Colonists by ordering General Gage, British Military Governor of Massachusetts, to destroy the Colonists' reported military stores in Concord, Massachusetts. The command came out of London. Gage ordered the Light Infantry and Grenadiers from the Boston Garrison to make ready for the secret raid to destroy the Colonists' stores.

The British Lieutenant Colonel Francis Smith and Marine Major John Pitcairn led the initial advance, marching north via Lexington to Concord. After leaving General Gage's headquarters, Lord Percy overheard talk from the street that the British regulars were preparing to march on Concord. He immediately advised General Gage, who then ordered Lord Percy to prepare his brigade to reinforce Colonel Smith, if necessary. Lord Hugh Percy marched with a back up column from Boston six hours after the first column. It was approximately ten miles from Boston to Lexington and seven miles from Lexington to Concord. Gage did not tell his officers their destination; he hoped to keep it secret until the last minute. He was determined to keep his plans quiet.

However, Boston's patriot eyes watched every British move. Paul Revere had become suspicious when he saw British landing boats being pulled from the water, supposedly for repairs. He felt that something was clearly afoot, but he needed confirmation on what he had seen. On April 16, Revere rode to Concord, knowing that this was the location of a storehouse of militia arms and the temporary location of the Provincial Congress. He warned the community that it was most likely that the British would raid their military storehouse. The townspeople immediately hid the munitions in wells, barns, behind walls of their homes and even in the swamp. What Revere and the other patriot intelligence did not know, was the route that the British would take to Concord. What the British did not know was that the American militia had received word *that a British raid was to be expected*

*and that the Colonists had moved most of their stores
to safe locations.*

On April 18, Revere was notified by a stable boy
that the British were readying boats for crossing the
Charles River; two other sources acknowledged that
initial report. Now they were almost sure that the
British were coming by water; however, they could
not take a chance of being wrong.

On the evening of April 18, 1775, Dr. Joseph
Warren of Boston received the news that the British
Regulars were active and on the move. He sent for
Paul Revere and asked him to ride north to Lexington,
to inform Samuel Adams and John Hancock that the
British were on the march to Concord. It was still
not known definitely if the British troops, numbering
somewhere around 700 men would arrive over land
or by sea.

Paul Revere was then serving as a courier for the
Boston Committee of Correspondence. Revere accepted
the task from Dr. Warren and set out to alert the
Colonists of a large British troop movement.

Charlestown, located on a peninsular just north
of the city, was the capital of the Massachusetts Bay
Colony. Bostonians usually considered Charlestown
to be part of Boston city.

Before Revere left for Charlestown on his way to
Lexington, he arranged with Robert Newman, the
sextant of the Christ, or the Old North Church in
Boston, for a signal to alert the countryside about
the manner in which the British would arrive. Christ
church was built in 1723, and was the oldest church
in Boston then. It had already acquired the title *old*,
even though it was only 52 years.

Newman was to hang one lantern in the church
spire if the British came by land, or two lanterns if
they came by sea, via the Charles River. The signal
would come from the tallest building in Boston and
could be seen not only in Charlestown, but also for
miles in the surrounding area. This would absolutely

confirm the route of the mounted British officers who were serving as cavalry.

They were initially correct—the British troops marched from Boston, crossed the Charles River in the waiting boats and advanced toward Concord to demolish the Colonists' Military stores. Newman had hung two lanterns in the Old North Church spire. Paul Revere left Boston on foot and rowed across the Charles River, close behind the marching British.

He arrived in Charlestown and headed to Colonel Conant and other *Sons of Liberty* members. Revere needed to verify that they had seen the two lanterns in the church spire.

He then went to Deacon John Larkin, a patriot supporter, to borrow a horse to ride the countryside and alert his fellow Colonists of the approaching British regulars. Revere was reportedly given a small chestnut mare, a Narragansett Pacer named Brown Beauty. He was warned that there were a number of British troops in the surrounds and he narrowly avoided being captured just outside of Charlestown. He rode out of Charlestown, along the Mystic River to Medford and then on to Lexington. It was said that Revere shouted, *"The regulars are out,"* to the surrounding countryside as he rode. He arrived in Lexington around midnight.

The British arrived in Lexington the next morning, just as the sun came up and the loud ringing of the local bells sounded the alert of the Redcoats' arrival.

Captain John Parker of the Lexington Militia had collected his men on Lexington Town Green to face the British column. The British Major, John Pitcairn, arrived at Lexington Green with his regulars, only to see this formidable group of Captain John Parker's 77 armed Minutemen in formation across the green. Others, who had been forewarned of the raid, accompanied them.

The British Major Pitcairn ordered his men to surround the group and disarm the Minutemen;

Captain Parker ordered his militia to disperse. Three shots rang out—two struck Pitcairn's horse and one struck a Private named Johnson; no one knew who fired the shots. The British then fired at the Minutemen and the others, killing eight and wounding ten. The Minutemen and their supporters retreated into the woods to avoid the British fire. They were severely outnumbered and fell back.

The British continued their march onward to Concord to search for the Colonists' supplies. They found none. It was reported that no citizen of Concord had any information for the British as to what had happened to their stores.

A note on the Minutemen:

The first Massachusetts Provincial Congress, in October, 1774 directed the establishment of the Minutemen from the existing militia—*to enlist one quarter of ye least of the number of the respective companies, and form them into companies of fifty privates at the least who shall equip and hold themselves in readiness on the shortest notice.*

Revere, along with William Dawes, had continued on to Concord, where Dr. Samuel Prescott subsequently joined them. The three then continued alerting their countrymen that the British were heading their way. The group was stopped by the British; Dawes and Prescott escaped. Revere was interrogated and released. His horse was taken. However, he had made it to Concord.

The North Bridge in Concord saw several hundred militiamen fight and defeat three companies of the King's regulars. The British then fell back to open fields, unable to hold off the militia who now fought from behind walls and fences, or from any cover. They had established a new strategy in warfare. No longer did they stand in lines and face the enemy, which in fact, was foolhardy. This 18th century strategy was dictated by their weapons, which were extremely inaccurate, short ranged, and with a slow rate of fire (3 rounds a minute). Heavy smoke would obscure the enemy. The Americans preferred to fight frontier style, from behind cover. More Minutemen came into the fray soon after, inflicting heavy casualties upon the British, harassing them as they marched back to Boston. The accrued militia blockaded the narrow land accesses to Charlestown and Boston and continued the battle.

The fighting took place in Middlesex County, Province of Massachusetts Bay, within the towns of Lexington, Concord, Lincoln, Menotomy and Cambridge, near Boston. This marks the start of open conflict between England and the Colonies. God save us all!

June 1775

As the war breaks out, I am in contact with Mr. John Cox, Philadelphia merchant, trader and ardent patriot. After a lengthy conversation, we wonder if he is related to Daniel Cox, the absentee owner of land on the island. Mr. John Cox has requested an agreement with Ricardo and me to supply him with lumber for the Batsto furnaces in the Pine Barrens, located in West Jersey—not to supply our cedar, but other indigenous varieties of wood in the area. The Batsto furnaces will supply shot and other munitions for our fighting men.

The Continental Congress has been discussing the formation of a Continental Army. It would be a daunting task for Congress to create an army to defend the 13 colonies.

A little more than a year ago, my brother Jack left our home after I announced my engagement to Sunny. To date, the family has received one letter, scant in content, telling us only that he was in Newark, located in Jersey and that he was well. He did express some remorse over his past behavior, and even that small regret was a great admission from our Jack. We heard from others that he had joined the newly formed New England Army. Jack never mentioned that in his letter. I found out that this was a voluntary militia army, formed by the Massachusetts Bay Colony, created shortly after the battle of Lexington. It was the first step in America's military action.

Word finally came from Congress on June 14, 1775 that the American Continental Army had been adopted.

In July of 1775, our first son was born. We christened him Cornelius Arent, but we call him Neil. He is a handsome, happy baby—auburn of hair as his mother and blessed with the blue green VanHameetman eyes. He was baptized by a traveling priest. What the future will hold for our new babe and us is undetermined.

Living on Long Beach Island, we are quite removed from the initial action. Ricardo and I have spoken about joining the local militia. We have not made a final decision, as to when.

Benjamin VanHameetman
His Journal

"I think things have come together just right for us," Ben told Sunny. "I know that I made the right decision to go into partnership with your brother. Ricardo is responsible and has great foresight. Father thinks we are biting off more than we can chew. We will see. Time will tell." Ben had made no mention to his father, that he and Ricardo had discussed joining the militia.

Andrew commented to Ben, "Mr. Cox is a very busy man. He has also expanded the Batsto furnaces and is manufacturing a variety of household and commercial articles. He foresees the necessities, not only for the soldiers' everyday needs, but munitions for the militia and the new Continental Army." Andrew handed him a copy of the advertisement that Cox had run.

Pennsylvania Gazette of June 7, 1775:
MANUFACTURED AT BATSTO FURNACE in West New Jersey, and to be sold either at the works or by the subscriber, in Philadelphia, a great variety of iron pots, kettles, Dutch ovens and oval fish kettles, either with or without covers, skillets of different sizes, being much lighter, neater and superior in quality to any imported from Great Britain; Potash, and other large kettles from 30 to 175 gallons, sugar mill gudgeons, neatly rounded, and polished at the ends; grating bars of different lengths, grist mill rounds; weights of all sizes, from 7 to 56 lb; Fullers plates; open and close stoves, of different sizes; rag wheel irons for saw mills; pestles and mortars, sash weights, and forge hammers of the best quality. Also Batsto Pig Iron as usual, the quality of which is too well known to need any recommendation.

The VanHameetman Lumber Company was already supplying the much in demand cedar to the local shipyards. Supplying the Batsto furnaces in West Jersey with various indigenous woods would be a separate undertaking, but still under the auspices of the family's lumber business. The furnaces heated the raw iron, making the iron malleable enough to shape into musket shot, swords, and other weapons. Huge amounts of wood would be needed to keep the furnace temperatures hot enough. Ricardo would manage the new business, supplying timber from the Pine Barrens near Batsto for the furnaces.

Ben would continue to supply cedar to the shipyards and builders up and down the coast of Jersey and to their small family shipyard in Tuckerton. Batsto was located approximately 12 miles from Tuckerton and about 25 miles from Manahawkin.

Ricardo held off signing the agreement with Mr. Cox, unable to decide how they could run everything and still join the militia. They could not unload their responsibilities on Andrew.

"By the way, father, what is going on with the navy?"

"They are dragging their feet, or should I say their anchor?" Ben laughed at his father's pun. "Seriously, though, I will get in touch with them. They have to discuss their needs with us."

"Supplying cedar to our shipyards and other yards and filling Mr. Cox's needs for the local lumber to keep those big furnaces running will be a lot of work." Andrew questioned Ben and Ricardo's proposed new commitment to Cox. Ben changed the subject. He really did not care to hear his father questioning him about what they could do and what they could not do. Ben was inclined to be a control master; however, rather than pass an uncalled for remark to his father, he kept his mouth shut.

"I can hire twenty additional men or more, just to fill Mr. Cox's orders. Ben will stay with the local cedar orders. I know that we can do the work." Ricardo was sure that he could manage his end at Batsto.

July 10, 1775

Rumor has it that France is very sympathetic to the Colonists' quest for independence. Word reached Philadelphia earlier this month that the Marquis de Lafayette, not yet twenty years old and wealthy in his own right, would soon join Washington. He will aid our General in the battle for independence. I surmise that the marquis will contribute to the cause monetarily, as was intimated. Rumor has it that General Washington is not happy with foreign countries or foreigners themselves, personally buying commissions.

Benjamin VanHameetman
His Journal

1775

The Continental Congress has elected Benjamin Franklin first Postmaster General of the United Colonies, and a mounted courier system has been established.

Ben could hardly wait to read more about the recent battle of Lexington and Concord. "Listen to this," he said, raising his voice to his father, who had moved into the parlor. He joined him to continue the discussion of the engagement at Lexington, then they moved on to discuss Ticonderoga.

"The militia has taken back Fort Ticonderoga in New York and the fortress at Crown Point from the British. Benedict Arnold and Ethan Allen led the battle. This is a great victory for us. They have captured cannons from the fort, which is more good news." Andrew continued to tell Ben the history of Fort Ticonderoga which had changed hands many times over the years.

"Your memory amazes me, father." How can you keep all of that information in your head?"

"It really interested me, and I have followed the battles closely over the years." Andrew changed the subject. "By the way, Ben, Mr. Cox seems to be doing an admirable job. I commend him, but it is dangerous work; I want you two boys to be very careful in your dealings with him. I know that you and Ricardo are angry with him, but I feel he was correct in his decision."

"Who told you about that?" Ben was annoyed. He and Ricardo were still harboring resentment toward Colonel Cox, who had recently secured the forced exemption of both Ricardo and Ben from military duty.

Captain Huro, superior officer of the local militia company, had spoken to Colonel Cox about Ben and Ricardo's thoughts of joining his company. It had come to Huro through others who had heard it. Huro knew that they were working with Cox and had approached him, regarding Ben and Ricardo's work at Batsto.

"How necessary are these two?" Huro had asked Cox.

Cox was irritated that the two had not spoken to him about their potential plans. The furnace outputs were urgently needed for their ore to supply the militia and the newly forming Continental Army with the necessary weapons and equipment. Ben and Ricardo could not walk off. Cox needed to confront the two, quickly.

Lieutenant Colonel Cox of the militia's Philadelphia Second Battalion was a formidable, no nonsense man. Physically, he was of a medium, well built stature, not a big man but he had a huge presence which made up for his average size. His muscular physique backed up his loud mouth and once he had you in his sights, there was no getting away. He was trustworthy, loyal, and extremely direct. He spoke the truth, which bothered more than a few. He was a good friend to have watching your back.

Ben and Ricardo complained loudly to Colonel Cox, who responded just as loudly. "The need to supply men with arms is more important than you two joining up and serving in the militia. The furnaces must be kept running at all costs, night and day. We have a contract and I am holding you to it!"

Ben wondered who had snitched on them and grumbled softly. Cox told them both, "Remember, the furnaces demand huge amounts of wood to keep the temperature up to melt the raw pig iron. We need to make the shot for the muskets. I need an output of two hundred tons of bar iron per annum. Who else can fill this demand for wood? You, Ricardo need to keep those furnaces running! Ben, you have commitments to me for overseeing the delivery of weapons to the military and tracking what and where they need the weapons. The navy will also need weapons and cedar for their new ships. I did what I thought was best. That is the end of it. It is too late to get anyone else to fill my contracts. You two have an obligation to me. I am holding you both to the agreements and your consciences," he stated. Then he stopped speaking.

Cox was also aware that Ben was supplying the cedar for the shipyards, which was part of his decision to ask for exemption for the both of them.

"Curses," Ricardo whispered to Ben. "We almost made it. If Huro had not spoken to Cox, we would have been signed up with the Jersey militia and long gone."

"Who would have supplied the lumber for the furnaces then? Who would supply the shipyards?" Ben mumbled. They both realized that Mr. Cox was right. Ben also realized even though he had figured it would not take more than one day a week traveling to Batsto to do his scheduling for the weapons, this was already escalating.

"I know, I know," Ricardo moaned. "But I do not have to like it!"

"I guess we will learn to live with it. Let us move ahead and put this to rest. I have to agree, Cox was right." Ben came to see the truth of the matter.

After further computations, Ricardo had to change his forecast. He would need at a minimum, fifteen more woodcutters, along with the teamsters and wagons to haul the lumber to Batsto, to supply wood to feed the hungry furnaces at their peak demand. "I hate to admit it, but we were wrong." They spoke of it no more.

Not only did Ben worry about his contracts, his family and the war—he felt slavery was an abomination. As far back as he could remember his father and grandfather, Kurt had hidden runaway slaves traveling north. The *Marta* would pick up the escapees from the seaport town of Lewes across the Delaware Bay. The slaves had run there from the southern colonies—usually Virginia and the Carolinas. The *Marta* would then sail them to Tuckerton.

They would then be routed to Manahawkin, only a few miles away. From Manahawkin, they would be handed off to a conductor, as the contact was called and the conductor would route them into the Pine Barrens, or further north, usually to Canada. The Barrens in Jersey reportedly held over one million acres of dense forest throughout southern Jersey and could be reached along old Indian trails. The Barrens offered the runaways the freedom to set up their own trade and housing, that is if they wanted to stay. There was no slavery as such in the Barrens, an available supply of lumber for houses and land to farm was theirs for the taking.

The small village was deep in the Barrens and few ever saw it. Many truly wondered if it were not all talk, but Ben knew better; he had been there. The Barrens also held escaped prisoners and deserters; but they did not bother the runaways. The British stayed on the peripheries, cautious to enter, not knowing what they would find or rather who or what would find them. Outsiders, particularly law officials, were extremely hesitant to venture into the heart of the Barrens. They were afraid that they would never be seen again. Jersey law was usually not inclined to help any of the coloreds. The Pine Barrens seemed to be off limits to Jersey law officials. They let the Barrens take care of the runaways.

Ben knew that the work of his father and grandfather before him was never discussed openly, nor written of in detail in the family journals. Some members of the family had no knowledge of the runnings, except for those conductors personally involved and it all was a well kept secret.

Congress had now fully established the Continental Army as well as a Continental currency. This army was not a volunteer army. The men would be issued uniforms and paid wages, so they were told. In July, the Second Continental Congress issued the *Declaration to Take Up Arms.*

"Why Congress cannot come forth with a strong declaration proclaiming independence is beyond my understanding," Ben remarked to his father. "At least they have appointed General Washington Commander-in-Chief. Best move in a long time. I heard that it was at John Adams' suggestion. Maybe now the southern colonies will come into the independence movement. They all respect Washington. Yes, it was a good move." Andrew agreed.

"Sorry to say that there is further bad news," Ricardo announced and told them of the terrible battle at Bunker Hill near Boston, on June 17, 1775—the first battle since Lexington.

The actual site of the fighting was Breed's Hill, and approximately a fifth of the men were African American. Instead of fighting as the British fought, in lines, the militia dug trenches and hid behind trees. They were mostly farmers and shot fierce and deadly volleys that shocked the British. However, The British managed to turn the tables and defeated the militia. When news reached England, surprisingly, sympathy was with the ordinary farmers.

Henry Knox had met and impressed Washington previously. He had been in the militia before; he supported the *Sons of Liberty* and had been at the Boston Massacre. Washington commissioned Knox to Colonel and appointed him to head the expedition to retrieve the captured cannons from Fort Ticonderoga. Henry Knox left for the Fort on December 1775 and returned in January 1776. The captured cannons were put on ox drawn sleds to be pulled along the west bank of the Hudson River from the Fort to Albany and then across the Hudson, through the Berkshires and then to Boston. It was a gigantic task that Knox had accomplished.

"And a huge thanks to Colonel Knox, who transported the cannons from the victory at Ticonderoga and then used them well in March of 1776 on Dorchester Heights, outside of Boston, finally helping to end the siege of Boston." Andrew commented after reading the news. He laughed at the irony of it—Fort Ticonderoga—that fort had been captured and recaptured so many times one could hardly keep track. "You should read the expedition facts. Knox certainly had a challenge ahead of him, bringing the cannons through those Berkshire Mountains on sleds was enough, but then crossing ice choked rivers, was another great challenge. He must have the constitution of an ox."

"I bet you all did not know that Colonel Knox owned a bookstore before he joined the militia," Sunny commented. "More of a scholarly man I would think—certainly not an outdoors man to be forging through mountains; he is a brave and competent man indeed."

On March 17, 1776 the British abandoned Boston; they advised that they would leave the city as it was found.

In June of 1776, Richard Henry Lee introduced a resolution:

Resolved: That these United Colonies are, and of right ought to be, free and independent States, that they are absolved from all allegiance to the British Crown, and that all political connection between them and the State of Great Britain is, and ought to be, totally dissolved.

On July 1, Congress reconvened.

On July 2, twelve of the thirteen colonies passed Lee's Resolution; New York did not vote. Congress began to consider a declaration regarding independence from Britain. Once Jefferson completed the draft, the committee of Jefferson, Franklin and Adams made their changes and submitted the document to Congress. Congress also made numerous alterations and deletions, but Jefferson's basic document stood. Congress worked on the document all day July 3, and into late afternoon of July 4. John Dunlap, who was the official printer to the Congress, printed the first copies of the Declaration of Independence from his shop. On the morning of July 5, copies were authorized and dispatched by members of Congress to various assemblies, conventions, and committees of safety as well as to the commanders of the Continental troops.

"I heard that the Bells did not ring on July 4. The Declaration is dated July 4, 1776." Andrew explained to his family, "But the Declaration was at the printers. Can you believe that?" He laughed. "The first time the Declaration of Independence was read to the public, on July 8, all of the bells throughout Philadelphia rang that day. I wonder how loud our Liberty Bell rang."

"Well, I heard too, that the bells of Philadelphia were rung on July 8 to summon the citizens of Philadelphia to the *first public reading* of the Declaration. However," and Sunny paused for emphasis; "remember when we discussed this? About the rotted wood on the rack where the bell is hung? More than one person thought that the steeple that houses the Liberty Bell is so rotted that they were afraid to ring the big bell for fear it would fall off its rack. People heard all the other bells ringing, and I bet they thought the Liberty Bell was among those. I would suppose that July 4, the date the Declaration was formally completed, will be the day we celebrate the Declaration of Independence. They really ought to fix that rack."

On July 9, 1776, the New York Convention officially approved the action of Congress. All thirteen colonies had now signified their approval. "*We are united at last*," Sunny commented loudly, but she knew that the war was far from over. "Congress has formally declared the independence of the Colonies from Britain. Now the declaration needs to be officially signed." Sunny shook her head. "God knows how long that will take." She was not alone in her frustration with the length of time it took Congress to accomplish anything.

Congress recessed for three weeks and gave the drafting job to the *Committee of Five*. On July 22, 1776, the Declaration of Independence itself was passed by twelve of the thirteen colonies, with New York abstaining. Congress made refinements and planned for the distribution of copies to citizens and to the soldiers in the field.

August of 1776 brought 30,000 British troops into New York. "Dark days are ahead for our militia and Washington's Continentals." Andrew was concerned and upset after hearing of the enormous number of new British troops that had arrived in New York.

The Americans were defeated in Long Island, Harlem Heights, Lake Champlain, White Plains, and Fort Washington, New York. They were also forced from Canada.

Marie opened the door to her son, Jack, who arrived home on a sunny, cold day in November of 1776. Andrew later remarked, "I am amazed and full of gratitude to see the changes in my son. He has lost his cockiness, and in its place has risen the character of a self assured young man, confident in himself and somewhat humbled."

Jack spoke of his travels, his comrades, and the battles he had fought. He seemed anxious to mend the rift between himself and his brother.

"Our Jack has lived through a terrible time." Marie reminded them. Her voice broke with emotion. "We will not linger on his previous departure and the discord surrounding it. We know that it was an immature boy who had left us and in his place a man has returned."

"Sunny and I are happy to see him. We have our brother back, and that is all that matters." Ben agreed.

Jack did not stay long. He was anxious to return to his unit and as quickly as he had arrived, he was gone—off to serve his country now, as an enlisted man in General Washington's Continental army.

"It will be interesting to see which captures my son, politics or the army life." Andrew wondered. "Time will tell where our Jack lands. Most times though, it is on his feet. God be with him."

Washington found himself commanding an estimated 4,000 discouraged, poorly equipped Continentals, some near starvation, some in tatters, and some with their feet wrapped in rags. The blood on the snow told their story. The British were on the Continentals' backs, following them much too closely. Washington started his march southward during November. He had left Newark in Jersey after five days and reached Brunswick, where he picked up a small group under Brigadier General Lord Stirling. Washington had been hoping for a much larger force, but all he found was a small unit of Jersey militia, who had volunteered to assist him. They pushed on to Princeton, arriving on December 2. From there, they quickly continued and posted in Trenton.

Cornwallis, hot on Washington's heels, arrived in Brunswick and asked General Howe's authorization to forge ahead and raid Washington before he could cross the Delaware River into Pennsylvania. Howe was undecided however, and this would cost the British dearly. It was thought that they probably could have ended the war at that time, if Howe had made an immediate decision.

Washington had ordered his men to search the Jersey shore side of the Delaware River for boats, especially for the Durham boats.

Robert Durham, an engineer at the Durham Iron Works in Reiglesville, Pennsylvania had built the Durham boat around 1757. The large open boats could haul enormous amounts of cargo, including ore, pig iron and produce from farms, output from upcountry mines, and timber from forests down the Delaware River to the Philadelphia port and market places. Philadelphia was second only to London in their imports and exports. The largest Durham boats (up to 65 feet long and 8 feet in the beam) could transport up to 20 tons of iron or 150 barrels of flour downstream. Smaller loads of manufactured goods such as sugar and molasses were carried in these boats upstream from Philadelphia.

The Durham boat moved swiftly downstream with the current, aided by a pair of 18 foot oars and a 25 to 30 foot long sweep to steer through the rapids. The boat could be fitted with a 30 foot mast and triangular sail, to travel swiftly and silently downstream. Traveling upstream against the current and through the treacherous rapids of the river above Trenton required a crew of six men and a captain. The crew captain at the stern wielded the long steering sweep, while two to four men pushed against the river bank or bottom with iron tipped setting poles (12 to 18 feet long), and the rest of the crew oared against the current. Along each side of the vessel was a narrow gangway, which provided footing for the crew as it poled the boat upstream. When weather did not encourage sleeping in the open, the crew slept in the forward cabin—which were on the larger Durhams. These boats were able to travel down the river through its many shallows because when fully loaded, they drew only about 24 inches of water. They were able to travel against the current and through the treacherous rapids up the Delaware River; because when partially loaded with a cargo of about two tons, they drew only about three inches of water.

The Durham boats filled the bill exactly for what General Washington needed to transport his men and supplies across the Delaware River. After scavenging the Jersey shore line for the boats, his men found what they needed and on December 7 and 8 Washington moved his men, guns and equipment to the Pennsylvania side of the river. He had accomplished his crossing just in time, as Cornwallis was already near Trenton. Cornwallis attempted a crossing on December 9, but to his surprise, the entire area was devoid of any kind of craft. The Americans had already confiscated all the boats, barges, rafts, or pontoons available in the area. The Durham boats and others had been ordered to be put under heavy guard on the Pennsylvania side of the river.

Cornwallis could do nothing but wait for the river to freeze so that he could cross his men and equipment. It was later found that there was material in Trenton for Cornwallis' men to build rafts, pontoons or boats. However, there was no effort made to do so.

Howe halted operations for the winter and Cornwallis formed several temporary encampments in the area around Elizabethtown, Brunswick, Princeton, Trenton and the 1,500 Hessian troops in Bordentown. Not a Brit realized that placing a Hessian troop encampment, unfamiliar with even the very language of the patriots was not a good idea. On December 11, Colonel Von Donop left Trenton and marched to Bordentown to take command.

In December of 1776, there were three, full, Hessian infantry regiments consisting of German auxiliary soldiers ensconced in Trenton. Included in that infantry regiment was a detachment of Artillery, fifty Hessian yagers and twenty light dragoons. These soldiers, numbering around 1,400, were under the command of Colonel Johann Gottlieb Rahl; the accompanying officers were Von Knyphausen and Von Lossberg. These German soldiers were part of the British purchase of 30,000 men from the Landgraff of Hesse Cassel, mercenaries who quickly became known as Hessians. Reportedly, the British had paid more than a half million pounds to the Landgraff princes of Hesse Cassel for these Hessian soldiers.

General Washington knew that the Colonists were depressed and losing faith, as was the Congress. Colonel Joseph Reed, Adjutant General of the Continental army urged a crossing of the Delaware and a march on Trenton. He felt that the action would uplift the American hope and trust in Washington, who had never lost his resolve to do something for the people. Washington was ready to move on the Trenton Barracks. It was finally agreed upon—to act.

At the final American Council of War on Christmas Eve, General George Washington, Major General Nathanael Greene, Generals Sullivan, Mercer, Major General Lord Stirling and Colonel Henry Knox were counted among the officers. They had planned a raid on the Barracks Christmas day when they would make a three offensive move on the Hessians. Washington would cross at McConkey's Ferry in Pennsylvania, to north of Trenton in Jersey with about 2,400 men and march upon the Hessians; Brigadier General James Ewing's division would cross the river at the Trenton Ferry, cutting off Rahl's retreat with a force of approximately 1,000 men and prevent Von Donop from dispatching reinforcements from his station at Bordentown. The 1,800 man force of Cadwalader would cross the Delaware further south and aim directly at Von Donop. Assuming Rahl and Von Donop were defeated, and that the Continentals were controlling Trenton as well as the British encampments in the area of Bordentown, they planned to advance the full Continental army on the British in Princeton and Brunswick.

Washington and his officers may have heard that the Hessians celebrated Christmas with heavy Yule drinking. On Christmas morning, despite terrible winter weather, General Washington issued orders for the march on Trenton. Washington ordered his officers to set their watches by his. Food rations were adequate for each man, along with forty rounds of ammunition. Their clothing and foot coverings were woefully inadequate. Lacking shoes or boots, they tied their feet in burlap and rags and marched through the snow. However, this was Washington's opportunity to launch a surprise raid on the Hessian Barracks in Trenton and his mind was set in accomplishing this mission. The password that night was *Victory or Death.*

General Washington had appointed Henry Knox to command the entire march of the troops directly under Washington's authority. Henry Knox was a well organized man and he had become Washington's personal friend. He was steadfast in completing a challenge and could be depended upon. In preparing for the attack, Washington had previously ordered the confiscation of as many Durham boats as possible, along with any adequate boats, rafts or barges that could be found. He knew that the Durham boats were the most adaptable to a river crossing and he would use barges and rafts for the horses and artillery. He had stored the seized boats under heavy guard, just below McConkey's Ferry in Pennsylvania.

John Glover's Marbleheaders, rough, rugged men of the 14th Continental Regiment from Marblehead, Massachusetts and all seafaring men, were chosen to man the boats against a river half frozen with chunks of ice and heavy snow. These seafarers would be depended upon to get the men across; their yeoman's knowledge, abilities and grit did just that, *without a single loss.*

Thanks to the Marbleheaders, Colonel Knox had brilliantly managed to get the raid force of men, officer's horses and artillery across the river on barges and Durhams, with no losses.

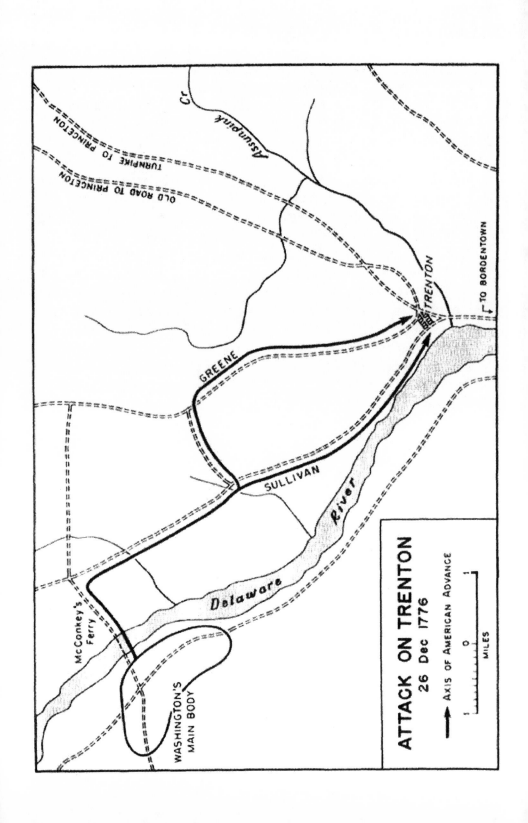

ATTACK ON TRENTON
26 Dec 1776

→ AXIS OF AMERICAN ADVANCE

TRENTON

TO BORDENTOWN

Assunpink Cr

TURNPIKE TO PRINCETON

OLD ROAD TO PRINCETON

GREENE

SULLIVAN

River

Delaware

McConkey's Ferry

WASHINGTON'S MAIN BODY

MILES
1   0   1

Washington had hoped to get his men across and landed around midnight, Christmas night. However, the horrendous weather would change history for the General, and upset his exact plans. It would actually be four o'clock in the morning, on a cold December 26, before they were across the river, organized and ready to march. Daylight would be upon them before they reached the Barracks.

In the meantime, General Ewing could not launch boats at the Trenton Ferry because of the ice, snow and howling winds; Colonel Cadwalader, landing some 600 men at Dunk's Ferry, just below Bristol, met icy walls and surrendered to the elements.

After crossing to the Jersey side, Washington's men marched down the Pennington Road pressed by violent winds with rain, sleet and snow rendering them nearly frozen. But marched they did, with a tremendous snowstorm engulfing them and winds pushing them the nine miles south, along the Bear Tavern and Pennington Roads. They reached the Hessian Barracks in Trenton about an hour after sunrise on the morning of December 26, and set up their artillery on two main streets in Trenton.

Washington was heard shouting, "*Stay with your officers, men!*" to his army of raggle taggle men—many barefoot, some without outer coats, most nearly frozen—as they commenced their attack. The Continentals announced their attack with the loud thundering of the cannons. Washington led his troops to the juncture of King and Queen Streets. Here Captain Forrest set six cannons to cover both thoroughfares, and the Prince Road was taken to prevent escapees. General Sullivan chased von Knyphausen and his men and captured the bridge on the Bordentown Road. The Hessians made ready two cannons, but they were deterred by Captain William Washington and Lieutenant James Monroe. Colonel Rahl came forth on his horse to gain control of his men, but was shot and fell. Countless Hessians were killed or wounded.

Previously at the Hessian Barracks, those not required to stand guard were drinking and singing, joined by

Colonel Rahl, their commanding officer, so it was reported. Rahl had been warned by his superior officers that an advance raid was likely to take place and to use extra caution; Von Donop at Bordentown was also advised to be on the alert against a raid on Trenton. A patrol had been sent to Trenton by General Leslie advising that Trenton or Princeton were at high risk of an attack.

The Hessian troops in Trenton all but laughed at this news, so confident were they of their own military strength. They continued to make merry, drinking until late into the night and partying with the locals.

On Christmas morning, Colonel Rahl had been sent a warning that Lord Stirling might raid the village during the day. Rahl ignored the warning and stopped at Stacy Potts house, where Rahl had his headquarters. They had started to play checkers when shots were heard. Rahl took a number of his men and went out to see where the firing was. He was told that the Americans had attacked a picket on the Pennington Road who had been run off and then could not be found. It was later discovered that the party that had attacked the Pennington guard was a small Continental detachment scouting through the county under General Stephen. Stephen was censured later by Washington for allowing one of his men to carry on independently as he did. He had come close to warning the Hessians of a major attack. However, Rahl again ignored the firing, thinking it to be an isolated incident, thus to Washington's favor.

Rahl did not return to Pott's house to resume his game of checkers. Instead he visited Abraham Hunt's home. Hunt was a rich merchant, always good for a bounteous meal and drink. Rahl was so drunk, it was reported, that he had no idea what was happening when Washington stormed into town on that freezing morning of December 26. Shortly before Washington had arrived, a Pennsylvania Tory had knocked on Mr. Hunt's door to advise Rahl of the Americans in the area. Mr. Hunt's servant refused to let the Tory in, but took a note from him and delivered it to Rahl, who promptly put it into his waistcoat pocket without opening it.

The assault was so unexpected that the Hessians were in disbelief that the raid was real. Commanding officer Rahl failed to respond quickly, probably feeling the effects of his Christmas celebrating, but the delay was long enough for Washington's men to fire three volleys, assuring a quick victory.

The raging weather continued, making Washington's intended strike next on Princeton, impossible. Washington ordered his men to return to Pennsylvania. Colonel Knox was again challenged to cross the river and a nine mile march back to McConkey's ferry. It would have been impossible to drag the Durhams, the barges and other conveyances through the icy river those nine miles to the nearby Paddy Colvine's ferry crossing from Trenton to Morrisville, Pennsylvania. This crossing was less than two miles from the Trenton Barracks. However, if they had used this ferry initially, certainly they would have been spotted quickly, by the Barracks, or other Loyalists or Hessians in Trenton. Colonel Knox accomplished the nearly inconceivable task of ferrying the same Continentals, along with hundreds of Hessian prisoners, captured supplies and boats, back across the river into Pennsylvania on the afternoon of December 26, via McConkey's ferry. Washington promoted Knox to brigadier general for his great achievement. One of Washington's officers wrote:

> *"It is a glorious victory. It will rejoice the hearts of our friends everywhere and give new life to our hitherto waning fortunes. Washington has baffled the enemy."*

Later, Andrew told them the news that he had heard of General Washington and his staff being headquartered in Newtown, Pennsylvania, just west of Yardley and the river. "The General is using the Widow Harris' home for his headquarters. I hear he returned to the Harris House right after the battle; he sent notice of his victory to the Congress from Newtown. The man certainly needs a decent place to stay after what he and his men have endured this past winter. Then that terrible march to Trenton in the ice and snow—remarkable, remarkable," Andrew commented softly.

"Newtown is quite lovely and not far from where General Washington crossed the river." Sunny knew the area in Bucks County.

"Newtown has been an important depot for supplies for the Continentals," Ben added. "The Half Moon Inn serves wonderful food if you are looking for a good place to eat."

"I hear that the frightened Hessian prisoners of war were paraded through Newtown right after their capture. The Hessian officers were housed at some of the inns and private homes in Newtown. The Bird in Hand house was used as an extra jail for the overflow of the captured Hessian officers. They took the soldiers in the ranks to the Presbyterian Church and the Session House. I guess we will hear something later in the newspaper. I know it is not right to feel this way, but I am rather sorry for those men—so far from home. I am sure that it was not pleasant to be paraded through town, as they were."

Sunny has it in her mind that the Hessians are poor misguided soldiers; Ben did not have the same thoughts. "I heard that General Washington's Staff and Hessian officers were hosted by Amos Strickland in his two story brick mansion." Ben was surprised. "I wonder what that was all about. I just do not understand the military."

A month after General Washington had defeated the Hessian troops, Ben read a few accounts of the battle and summarized his thoughts to his father and Sunny.

"There are many stories being put forth. I think a lot of those stories are hogwash. It was reported that John Honeyman, an American spy, working with General Washington and posing as a Loyalist, misled Colonel Rahl, the Commanding Officer himself."

Ben laid the newspaper down. "I had wondered where they crossed coming back into Pennsylvania. It was impossible for them to cross over to Morrisville, as some suggested, when all their conveyances were left at McConkey's ferry. I see where the February 5th Packet reports that 750 prisoners were crossed back over at McConkeys. What a

378 JEANETTE H. FUSCO

terrible march back to the ferry that must have been," Ben
was amazed at the final accomplishment.

"I have read some about Honeyman's background in
another report. Honeyman was born in Ireland and was
of Scottish descent. He was a farmer until he was 29
years old and then he joined the British Army during the
French and Indian War in 1758. Around that time he had
saved the life of a Colonel James Wolfe while on the frigate
Boyne. Honeyman had caught Colonel Wolfe, as the Colonel
tripped at the top of a stairway. Wolfe had firmly believed
that the young private had saved his life. Colonel Wolfe was
promoted to general shortly after that event. He sought out
the young private and made him his bodyguard. After the
war, Honeyman moved to Philadelphia. He had fought for the
British, but he was sympathetic to the Colonists' cause. He
had met George Washington during Washington's meetings
with the Continental Congress. There is much more to the
story, but that is the way that Honeyman met General
Washington. Honeyman posed as a Tory for Washington and
had previously told Colonel Rahl that the Continental Army
had such a low morale, that they would never raid Trenton.
Many people felt that Honeyman was a double agent."

Andrew stopped speaking, gathering his thoughts.
"According to one statement, Rahl was playing checkers
with Stacy Potts, the owner of the house being used for the
Hessian military headquarters. Rahl was handed a note
from a local Loyalist who warned Rahl of Washington's
troops gathering, but Colonel Rahl pocketed the note without
reading it. Why did Rahl not read the note? Was he that
confident that his barracks could not be invaded? Could this
have been Honeyman who handed him the note?"

"All of this is yet to be confirmed," Ben told them. "It
was also reported that Rahl did not return to Stacy Potts
house after investigating the firing incident of the picket,
but went to visit Abraham Hunt's house and this is where
Hunt's servant refused an informant entrance. The servant
did take the warning note from the informant and delivered
it to Colonel Rahl, who promptly put it into his pocket,
unread. *Who was this informant?* Again, was Rahl that

confident? And was Honeyman the informant? What does Hunt's servant have to say? I do not see any reporting of that. Were there really two informants? At Stacy Potts and or at Abraham Hunt's with notes, or just one informant?"

Sunny interrupted. "Notice that the editor says *not being able to confirm* this information. I would find it difficult to believe that a commanding officer would just ignore something like that! Has it been proven that there were two informants as it was reported? Although I wonder why that would be written in the newspaper, if it were unconfirmed."

"You are being naïve Sunny. I think a lot of the newspaper reportings are unconfirmed; probably to sell more issues, and the leanings of the editor are coming forth. I agree. I do not think that this should have been printed." Ben read on, where the newspaper gave a short biography on Rahl. "Colonel Johann Gottlieb Rahl, known as the *Lion*, was a formidable enemy and the son of Captain Joachim Rahl. Johann rose quickly through the ranks to his current status as Colonel."

"That is interesting," Andrew added. "Now I wonder about a career officer like Rahl not getting out of bed immediately, which is what I heard too. Moreover, one of the younger Lieutenants, Andreas von Wiederholdt, had ordered the last guard detail that was on duty that night to take safe haven from the weather in the copper shop. That would have been Christmas night."

Ben took up the story. "I read that the duty officer, Major Friedrich von Dechow had called off the next morning's pre dawn patrol because of the bad weather. That would have been in the very early morning of December 26. They certainly had no notion at all that Washington would be on the attack. While all this was going on, or rather not going on in the Hessian barracks, General Washington was probably in the midst of crossing the river."

Andrew was not sure what to believe of the plethora of information coming forth. Everyone was silent, trying to digest all the reports.

Ben shrugged, waited for a minute and then continued reading. "Shortly after sunrise, Lieutenant von Wiederholdt went outside, probably to check the weather, and saw multiple troops advancing toward him. The 24 Hessian guards exchanged fire with General Washington's oncoming troops, but of course they were hugely outnumbered. The sounds of the muskets and cannons from General Washington's men finally sent the garrison into action. All three Hessian regiments responded."

"Bloody hell!" Andrew was amazed at what he was hearing. "I read that Colonel Rahl had ridden out first to find Lieutenant von Wiederholdt for a report and was told that the enemy was not only above the town, but was also around it on both the left and the right. I am sure that those were not his exact words, but you get the gist of the conversation and the information given to Commander Rahl. The Lieutenant also told Rahl that four or five enemy battalions had been spotted."

"The editor of this paper," Ben pointed out another article, "said that the report from Lieutenant von Wiederholdt was not altogether true. I do not know where this editor got his information, but I would think that he would try to report the truth, or am I very innocent?" Ben was stymied. "The editor suggests that General Washington had not blocked the southern route out of Trenton. If Rahl had been privy to that information, he probably would have acted differently and could have saved much of his brigade. If this information was true, as reported to Rahl by Lieutenant von Wiederholdt, why did Rahl not guide his men out the open southern route?"

Ricardo walked in on the discussion and heard Ben's last comment. "I heard that civilians, camp followers and probably about 500 men did escape using the southern route. It seems that Washington did leave the southern route open; perhaps only allowing civilians to escape. Rahl however, upon hearing the half truth of the situation and in a true Hessian code of belief, set up a counterattack, which of course failed. It was then too late for escape. The 18 pieces of artillery that the Americans used had already decided the victory." Ricardo shook his head.

THE PENNSYLVANIA PACKET
JANUARY 4, 1777

PHILADELPHIA, JANUARY 4

It was determined some days ago, that our army should pass over to Jersey, in three different places, and attack the enemy. Accordingly about two thousand five hundred men and 20 brass pieces, with his Excellency Gen. Washington at their head, and Majors Gens. Sullivan and Green, in command of two divisions, passed over on the night of Christmas, and about three o'clock, A.M. were on their march, by two routs towards Trenton. The night was sleety, and the roads so slippery that it was daybreak when we were two miles from Trenton. But happily the enemy were not apprized of our design, and our advanced party were on their guards at half a mile from the town, when Gen. Sullivan and Gen. Green divisions came into the same road. Their guard gave our advanced party several smart fires, as we drove them; but we soon got two field pieces at play, and several others in a short time; and one of our Colonels pushing down on the right, while the other advanced on the left, into the town. The enemy, consisting of about fifteen hundred Hessians, under Col. Rohl, formed and made some smart fires from the musketry and six field pieces, but our people pressed from every quarter, and drove them from their cannon. They retreated towards a field behind a piece of wood up the creek, from Trenton, which I expected would have brought on a smart engagement from the troops, who had formed very near them but at that instant, I came in full view of them, from the back of the wood, with his Excellency Gen. Washington, an officer informed him that the party had grounded their arms, and surrendered prisoners.

I was immediately sent off with the prisoners to McConkey ferry, and have got about seven hundred and fifty safe in town and a few miles from here, on this side the ferry, viz. one Lieutenant Colonel, two Majors, four Captains, seven Lieutenants, and eight ensigns. We left Col. Rohl, the commandant, wounded, on his parole, and several other officers and wounded men at Trenton. We lost but two of our men that I can hear of, a few wounded, and one brave officer, Capt. Washington, who assisted in securing their artillery, shot in both hands. Indeed every officer and private behaved well, and it was a most fortunate day to our arms. Which I the more rejoice at, having an active part in it. The success of this day will greatly animate our friends, and add fresh courage to our new army, which, when formed will be sufficient to secure us from the depredations or insults of our enemy.

Colonel Rohl died at Trenton on Thursday the 26th of December, of the wounds he received in the engagement that morning.

The Pennsylvania Gazette, February 5, 1777

Philadelphia, February 5

RETURN of prisoners taken at Trenton, the 26th of December, 1776, by the army under the command of his Excellency General WASHINGTON.

Regiment of ROHL:

"On the second instant the enemy began to advance upon us at Trenton; and, after some skirmishing, the head of their column reached that place about 4 o'clock, whilst their rear was as far back as Maidenhead (Lawrenceville). They attempted to pass Sanpinck creek, which runs through Trenton at different places; but finding the fords guarded, they halted and kindled their fires. We were drawn up on the south side of the creek. In this situation we remained till dark, cannonading the enemy, and receiving the fire of their field pieces, which did but little damage.

At twelve o"clock, after renewing our fires, and leaving guards at the bridge in Trenton, and other passes, on the same stream above, we marched by a round about road to Princeton. We found Princeton about sunrise, with only three regiments, and three troops of lighthorse in it, two of which were on their march to Trenton. These three regiments, especially the two first, made a gallant resistance, and, in killed, wounded and prisoners, must have lost five hundred men. Upwards of one hundred of them were left dead on the field; and with those carried on by the army, and such as were taken in the pursuit, and carried across the Delaware, there are near three hundred prisoners, fourteen of whom are officers—all British.

From the best intelligence we have been able to get, the enemy were so much alarmed at the apprehension of losing their stores at Brunswick, that they marched immediately thither from Trenton without halting, and got there before day."

"You all know, of course that Colonel Rahl was mortally wounded during the battle. He was hit twice in his side by musket balls. They moved him to a church nearby and later brought him to Stacy Potts house. He died during that night.

Three Hessian Regiments surrendered. General George Washington and Major General Greene visited the dying Colonel Rahl before he passed over, or so it was reported. They provided Rahl a last military honor before he died."

"I wonder if we will ever know the exact truth of that night," Sunny questioned. "There is a discrepancy in where and who handed Colonel Rahl the note that he pocketed without reading. It was reported that he received it while playing checkers with Stacy Potts; it was also said that an informant came to the door while Rahl was at Abraham Hunt's and tried to deliver a note to Rahl himself, but Hunt's servant would not let the informant in. The note was delivered though, and Rahl also pocketed that missive. I guess that does not make a huge difference, how or where it was delivered, Rahl did not open it. Colonel Rahl, so it was reported, addressed his neglect about the note while he was dying and said about the note, *If I had read that at Mr. Hunt's, I would not be here.*" So I would say that Rahl was at Mr. Hunt's when the note came; it seems more credible, and there were witnesses, the doctor attending Rahl, and perhaps the servant. I wonder what those two have to say. Have we heard from them?"

"I have heard nothing," Ben told her. "General Washington evidently accepted Rahl's defeat as honorable, and provided him with military honors before he died. It would seem to me that Rahl was an irresponsible man who let drink come before duty. However, it came down individually to military man to military man, even though Washington was a stickler when it came to obeying army regulations. Obviously he was satisfied that Rahl was an honorable man. Not so of the Hessian Court, who wanted to try Rahl in abstentia."

"It is over now, however it happened. We can rejoice in General Washington's victory. We can hold up his brave young men who followed him into victory after that cold and miserable march." Andrew stated this with conviction.

"Circumstances sometimes dictate unexpected endings," Ben made the last comment.

General Washington's coup brought great excitement to the Colonists and a much needed boost to his men. The people read and reread the battle account in the newspapers and discussed it for weeks. Hope had been restored.

A few weeks later, Andrew told them, "I heard that Colonel Rahl was buried in the cemetery of the First Presbyterian Church on East State Street in Trenton. They inscribed on his grave, *Here lies Colonel Rahl, for him, all is over.*"

For the next six months, the talk was of Colonel Rahls' censure in absence. "For God's sake," Sunny exclaimed. "Let the poor man rest in peace."

"What are they demanding?" Andrew asked.

"He is being charged with Negligence by the Landgraff Princes; a listing of the negligence charges has been shown."

"Wonderful," Sunny said. "Those are the Princes who sold them to the British, right?" Ben shrugged his shoulders. "Do you think they care one fig? Those Princes of Hesse Cassel are just happy to have all that British money."

"Remember Sunny, it was also their decision to come over here to fight for the British."

"You do not know that for sure, Ben."

He did not answer her, hoping that would end that conversation.

Landgraff Friedrich II of Hesse Cassel had immediately ordered an investigation, questioning how it happened that Rahl's three regiments had been so quickly overwhelmed. A deposition was ordered from every survivor from privates to Lieutenant Colonels, asking them what they had seen and done that morning. If the soldier was illiterate, he was to dictate and make his mark when finished. Even the captured had to submit. It probably would be some time before the Landgraff would issue a very thorough critique of how the defense was handled. There were strong rumors that Rahl would not be court martialed. Some felt that the British wanted to find him innocent to cover themselves. They, of course had brought the Hessians to America.

Sometime later it was reported that there would be no court martial. Rahl's downfall had been his over confidence. His failure to take commonly applied precautions when garrisoning any place for more than a day or two, such as preparing earthworks and a strong point or redoubt. This would have allowed them to take refuge to buy time, should there be an enemy attack of superior numbers.

Andrew had a different take on the event. "Perhaps in the very end of this, Rahl was made a British scapegoat. After all, the Brits had brought those Hessians to America. One wonders."

In June of 1777, Cox showed Ben and Ricardo a notice he had just received from the General Assembly in Haddonfield, in Jersey, stating that his ironworkers had been given military exemption. Furthermore, the Assembly had authorized Cox to put together a company of fifty men and two lieutenants, with himself as captain. Their primary military duty, short of a military invasion, was to be armed to defend the Batsto works. "Consider yourselves in that company of fifty men. You are now in the militia."

In July of 1777, a military band of Hessian prisoners of war returned to Philadelphia and performed at the first Fourth of July celebration. "It must have been quite humiliating to those men," Sunny remarked.

"For god's sake Sunny." Ben was irritated. "You forget that many of those Hessian soldiers were responsible for the deaths of hundreds of our militia and Continentals. I get tired of you feeling sorry for the enemy!"

"I am sorry Ben. I guess I just look at them as poor, uneducated men, risking their lives and receiving such little monies from the British. Remember Ben, these men were not volunteers. They were conscripted. They had no choice."

"Maybe they were not humiliated at all. Perhaps they found it better to be here and have the opportunity that they did not have in their own homeland. I have heard talk that a great number of the Hessian soldiers have decided to stay here after the war is over. I doubt that they appreciated that the British had paid big monies to the Princes in Germany for their services. Certainly, the Hessians saw very little of that money, as they fought and died for the British."

"The talk is that some 13,000 of these Hessians had lost their lives and of course, many of them are still prisoners of war. Such a shame," Sunny remarked. "I still feel bad for them, but now I will take into account all of the history behind these men."

In July of 1777, the British took control of the Delaware River and won the important battle of Brandywine.

The important, decisive American victory at the Battle of Saratoga finally stopped the English in their advance down the Hudson River.

It did not take long for Colonel Cox, along with Richard Wescoat and Elijah Clark, to organize the running of the British blockade on the Delaware. "Cox is now Lieutenant Colonel of the Philadelphia Second Battalion. Did you know that?" Ben asked his father.

"Yes I did and he deserves it. Running the Batsto munitions plant is a huge and responsible job."

The British also had control of the Mullica River basin and Lieutenant Colonel Cox had resorted to running supplies overland to Valley Forge and other posts in that area very successfully. "Mr. Cox has done himself proud by loading wagons from Batsto in southern Jersey and maneuvering around the British blockades. I hear he crosses into Pennsylvania at different points." Ben was becoming worn out. They all knew that he was helping Cox with delivery of the Batsto munitions, but no one spoke of it.

The British blockade of the Delaware River continued to cause serious problems for the Colonists. It was necessary to salt food to preserve it; the troops had to eat. The Colonists were unable to import salt and as a result they were forced to erect several new salt works. This included a large works at Coates Point on the meadows at the north bank of Toms River, where it merged with Barnegat Bay, opposite Cranberry Inlet. "Someone asked me the other day, who is the Tom in Toms River? I do believe it is common knowledge, locally anyway, that the river was supposedly named after the farmer Tom Luker, who ran a ferry across Goose Creek." Ben told them.

"Sounds the same as I have heard." Andrew was always on top of things.

Water was always saltiest opposite an inlet and there, long, shallow ditches were dug into the meadows. A floodgate or sluice gate was erected at the bay end. At high tide, the ditches filled with water and the gate closed. The water was exposed to the sun and gradually evaporated and became brine. The brine was scooped into big iron kettles and boiled down to salt. Then the salt was packed in wicker baskets and any remaining brine could ooze, leaving edible salt. A windmill for pumping water from the bay into the ditches or vats on the meadows was erected. Movable covers were used to keep the rainwater out of the saltwater vats.

"Was this the way salt was extracted by my ancestors in Holland?" Ben had asked his father.

"Most of the men who built the salt works were Dutchmen, so I have heard. I would guess that the know how has been passed down and thank God for that."

In May of 1777, Sarah and Ricardo had their first son, a strapping dark haired baby that had been an easy birth for Sarah. They named him Andrew Emilio for the babe's two grandfathers.

Ben was aware that there was an Underground Railroad operating near Manahawkin, although he had never become involved with the Underground. On August 10, 1777, Ben was secretly contacted by an acquaintance, Eli Jones, a member of the group. Ricardo had delivered the message to Ben when he arrived back on the island from Batsto.

Eli had written to ask Ben to meet him at the Manahawkin Tavern about Underground business. Ben was surprised to hear the request from Eli telling him that he needed help in conducting six slaves fleeing from Virginia. They would route the fugitives as far as Manahawkin in Jersey. The slaves would remain hidden there until plans could be made to move them north. Ben wrote Eli that he could meet him in the early morn on August 11 at the Manahawken Tavern in Jersey.

"This run will be a new experience for me," Ben told Eli later at the tavern, "Still, I am acquainted with the immediate area, and I have more than a few contacts at my disposal which may be useful. Why did you ask me?"

"I see that I was right in contacting you," Eli responded, but did not answer his question. Ben knew that this was a necessary precaution, but he was curious.

Eli told him that he was not sure when the runaways would arrive in Manahawkin. "However," Eli continued, "I do have a local safe house at my disposal should it be needed." He felt that the runaways would arrive between August 18 and August 20.

Ben paused for a few minutes; he needed to mull over the route he would follow and calculate the time involved. "I will contact you as soon as I can, through Ricardo. I have some reckoning to do." Ben left the tavern to do a few errands in Manahawkin and thought, a*nd more than one reckoning to do.*

A few days prior to his meeting with Eli, Ben had received a note from Lieutenant Colonel Cox, again through Ricardo. Cox had asked for a meet in the Manahawkin Tavern, on August 11 around noon.

Cox had another meeting that morning at the tavern with Captain Reuben Randolph, Monmouth, New Jersey Militia's 5th Company, Second Regiment. Ben was relieved that the meeting with Eli had been scheduled early. He did not want to run into Cox or Captain Randolph. His relationship with Eli at this point needed to be protected and he did not want to make two trips to Manahawkin.

Ben could not imagine what Cox wanted of him. He usually saw the Colonel out in Batsto. *I am curious to see what he is up to now.*

Colonel Cox walked into the tavern around noon and spotted Ben at a table in the back. "Have you eaten yet?"

"Waiting for you, Sir." They ordered drinks and something to eat and moved to a more isolated corner table.

Cox got into it immediately. "I would like you, personally, to deliver an important document for me. It will be a dangerous mission, Ben, but I need someone reliable whom I can depend upon."

Good god almighty, Ben thought. He tilted his chair back, unconsciously putting more space between himself and Cox. Immediately, he assumed that this would be about Batsto. His plate, once more, would be too full. *Either feast or famine* came to his mind.

CHAPTER EIGHT

Mission Impossible

1777-1787

The cool water refreshed his body and quenched his thirst. He remembered the bible telling the holy attributes of water; he understood now what that truly meant.

B en was right in his assumption. Cox leaned forward. "I want you to find General Washington and deliver a list of munitions out of Batsto available immediately to the General. Washington's appeal is a little out of the ordinary. He has requested that this be a priority." Cox sat back in his chair, waiting for a reply.

Ben drew in a deep breath to collect his thoughts. He had not finished his strategy for his upcoming plans with Eli. However, he did not hesitate to answer Colonel Cox. "I know how important this is, but first tell me the dates you need me and exactly where I have to go." *He knew that priority meant right now, immediately.*

"This may be a little difficult." Cox appeared agitated. "The request has come up suddenly. The General is not sure what his next move will be. Information is forthcoming as to where the British General Howe is headed. On July 25, Washington was camped near Morristown, in Jersey. He was informed that the British fleet had left the New York harbor. On a hunch, Washington proceeded towards Philadelphia and marched to the Delaware River in Jersey. A courier arrived and reported that the British were seen off Delaware Bay."

Cox pushed back in his chair, collected his thoughts and continued. "The General then ferried his troops across the river into Pennsylvania and marched until that evening. He camped at the Cross Roads in Warwick Township and then continued marching toward Philadelphia and arrived near Germantown. The General inspected Philadelphia's defenses and conferred with Congress. He attended dinner that evening in his honor where he met the Marquis de Lafayette."

Ben took a long swallow from his tankard and waited for Cox to continue. "They broke camp shortly thereafter to return to Coryell's Ferry on the Delaware River. Washington felt that this area was close enough to defend Philadelphia. If General Howe was starting north, this would also give Washington and his men a head start north." Cox was silent for a moment and then continued.

"Washington is a stickler for keeping his troops on the straight and narrow," Cox told Ben. "He wanted them away from the city to avoid temptation and indulgences. They finally reached their encampment around dinner time and dug in."

Cox called to the barkeep for two more tankards.

"I will try to give you the lay of the land as best I can. The General was last camped at the Cross Roads, in Pennsylvania with 11,000 of his men. The Cross Roads is located in Warwick Township, where the York and Bristol roads intersect; York running north and south, Bristol running east and west. York Road is the main highway to Philadelphia. I will continue to use the Cross Roads intersection as my reference point. The men will be encamped in that area if the General is still there."

"I am familiar with the Cross Roads."

"The main bodies of men are camped on Carr's Hill, I was told. Carr's Hill is on York Road, where the Moland House stands. Washington is using the house as his Headquarters. The Hill runs from York Road along the northern shore of the Neshaminy Creek to the small Warwick Presbyterian Church which sits west of the Cross

Roads on Bristol Road. The Hill continues along the Bristol Road, and then ascends.

Lord Stirling's Division will probably be occupying the farm of Major George Jamison and the Ramsey farm on Bristol Road." Cox hesitated, trying to be even more specific. "I would say that Stirling's camps would be spread out, starting a mile or so east of the Cross Roads, up to the Cross Roads intersection. Conway's Brigade of Pennsylvania Troops will be encamped directly across from Stirling's men. You will be traveling west, out of Newtown and you will come upon the beginnings of Stirling's camps first, just off the Bristol Road. I am sure that you are familiar with Lord Stirling, who is considered a staunch patriot and a great asset by General Washington."

Ben nodded his head. "Any other camp locations I should know about?" He was trying to write down what Cox was telling him.

"There will probably be a few camps just west of the Cross Roads. It is difficult to say, where the camps will be exactly—they are probably all over that area. Just watch yourself as you come west, up to the Cross Roads. You do not want to get spotted until you are near the Moland House." Cox lit a cigar. "You do not have to write this all down, Ben. I have a map for you." He pushed a parchment across the table.

"The Widow Moland's house, on the east side of York Road is a stone's throw from the actual intersection. You need to cross over the Little Neshaminy Creek to get to the house. You will probably have passed Stirling's camps before you reach the intersection."

Ben interrupted. "That is if I make it to the Cross Roads! Bloody Hell! 11,000 men—camps scattered all over! And now I hear it may be up to13,000 men. 11,000 or 13,000 in the grand scheme of things, what does 2,000 more matter? It only takes one bullet!"

Cox did not answer. He shrugged his shoulders at Ben. "You should leave the Bristol Road slightly before the intersection and head on a northwest trek, making your way across the creek in the woods. Try to come up behind the house, which will be, needless to say, well guarded. I will leave the approach up to you." Cox pushed back in his chair, stretching his legs.

"That is the approximate layout of the land. You can play it anyway you want, as to how you approach the Moland House. You must be at the Cross Roads on August 21. I will set your meet with the General on that date." Cox fell silent, waiting for Ben's reply.

Ben's mind raced. He was stunned and thought both undertakings would be roughly in the same area. *Can I manage the two missions?*

He had tentative plans to be in Manahawkin on August 21 to meet the party of runaways. He had not told Eli that he would definitely help him, but now he knew that he would; that is, if he could coordinate the two missions.

It was approximately fifty miles from Manahawkin to Trenton for the meet with the conductor; then, north with the runaways, sending them on their way to Canada. *50 miles is too much traveling in one day with two women and a child,* he acknowledged. Eli had informed him that the runaways would be sent on the northern route through Pennsylvania to Ontario, Canada. Where in Ontario, Eli did not mention and Ben did not want to know.

Ben pondered over how he could coordinate Eli's request and the request from Cox. He had decided to follow a route from Manahawkin to Trenton in Jersey and cross the Delaware River into Pennsylvania at Trenton. If the Trenton crossing presented any problems, they would have to continue in Jersey a few more miles north, along the river and then cross over into Yardley, Pennsylvania.

This river crossing into Yardley would certainly be more beneficial for him. He could take the road directly from the ferry landing in Yardley, through to Newtown and then straight to the Bristol Road. He would continue on the Bristol Road all the way to the Cross Roads.

He calculated that he could make it to the Cross Roads from Yardley in one day *at the least,* but he would give himself that amount of time. He could even journey at night. However, if he did not have enough time to find General Washington, that is, if he was still there, then all would be for naught.

Ben could not and would not disclose to Cox his other mission regarding the runaways. He would have to leave on August 19. There was no other way. He decided to do it, and felt his heart skip a beat. *I cannot turn away from a challenge like this.*

He would have to camp the night of August 19 in the woods immediately before Trenton, he decided. Ben saw Cox in Batsto soon after and told him, "I can leave August 19. That will put me there in plenty of time. Just pray that I can find the General and his troops." Cox breathed a sigh of relief.

"You have the map with the layout of the land, which should give you a good route for avoiding the larger camps. *Good lord,* Ben thought, *I certainly cannot miss 11,000 men, but I could get killed in the looking.*

"Remember where I told you the majority of the camps should be located. I have marked them well on the map. I will have Ricardo bring you the documents," Cox continued. "I trust him to deliver the packet to you without questions?"

"Of course," Ben answered and they both left; Cox happy and Ben apprehensive, aware of the danger that he would be flirting with. He had new respect for Cox, who was taking on an important assignment for General Washington. He would certainly accord him, and address him, by his new rank, Lieutenant Colonel Cox; or as commonly expressed, Colonel. The Colonel had been right to chastise them both.

When Ricardo returned to Batsto, Ben would send his note to Eli with him. Right now he would prepare for his two fold trip to the Delaware River and then to the Cross Roads.

Ben had left some rough maps in the envelope with the letter for Eli to give to the conductor. There was always the safe house in Yardley, which Eli had mentioned, along with old friends at the Yardley Gristmill, should plans go awry. Ben had breathed more easily when he heard this.

Eli:

> *I have heard that there have been some problems at Paddy Colvin's Ferry crossing from Trenton to Morrisville, Pennsylvania. I will decide when we arrive if we can cross there or go further north, crossing over into the town of Yardley, Pennsylvania. I have asked Samuel, who is heavily involved in the cause to accompany me. He is well trusted. We will leave from the small shack, behind the Manahawkin Tavern on August 19 at sunrise. We can bring the group from there, via the old Shamong Indian trail, to Mount Holly, then to the Kings Highway. We will work our way to Trenton, just off the road, staying well hidden in the woods. We will meet at the small abandoned tavern as we previously discussed.*

> *Ben*

On August 19 at sunrise, Ben and his friend, Samuel collected the fugitives from Manahawkin, then started their long journey north on horseback. The group included two women, three men, and an eleven year old boy. Samuel noted that the group was all very brave, but extremely frightened. "The men ride well, as does one of the women. The boy and the other woman will be quite sore I am afraid, by the time we reach our destination."

Ben was still not sure which ferry crossing into Pennsylvania he would take. "The Redcoats have pulled back to Brunswick in Jersey, but I would like to add suspenders to my belt." He grinned at Samuel. He realized that he sounded like his father.

They camped that night a few miles south of Trenton and were up early the next morning of August 20. Ben and Samuel received the first bit of bad news when the group passed through the heavy woods outside of Trenton.

Ben was surprised when he saw Eli behind the deserted tavern. He had not told Ben that he would be their conductor. "Eli," Ben greeted him. "I did not expect to see you here."

"You have to understand that I must keep my part strictly secret until the meet is made, for fear of being followed. I received your note, and thanks for spelling out the route—I agree and would have chosen the same way. Word is out that some of the Trenton crossings are being closely watched. I heard that a Tory was killed, and a runaway was suspected. The British and the Loyalists are out in number. I do believe that they are looking south, though," Eli shared. They decided that Paddy Colvin's ferry crossing was out. The ferry crossing was too close to the city of Trenton.

Samuel overheard the conversation. "We have to be very careful. We should move further inland to escape detection, then head north to the ferry and cross over into Yardley."

It was less than a mile extra, but it was tiring to the already weary travelers. When they finally reached the ferry in the center of Yardley, they hunkered down in the grass and woodlands so Samuel and Eli could watch the crossing for a short time.

When they saw no one in the area except the ferryman, they moved out of hiding. Both Eli and Ben knew that this hired ferryman could be bought. Eli had been in accord with Ben when he had chosen this crossing because of the ferryman. The barge was large enough for two horses, and a few passengers. They would leave the other horses on the Jersey side and pay the ferryman to come back for them. The ferryman it seemed, owed no allegiance to either the British or the Colonists, and cared not about the escaped slaves. He was a mercenary and did not deny it. He would cross the river for anyone for a price; he could be trusted. If that trust were broken, that would end his lucrative business.

"There is an old shed, just down the road after we cross, where I will hide our party until the ferryman returns,"

Eli advised. "I do not want to stay there too long, but I have to wait for the other horses. Then we will head out for the barn, which is about a mile from there and quite deserted. Tonight we will start out again."

Ben's participation in the journey ended. He handed the six people over to Eli, wished them good luck and rode on from the ferry. Ben murmured, *"Thank you for riding with me,"* to Samuel. "Bless Eli for helping those poor souls. I will see you back on the island or in Manahawkin." Ben headed his horse to the west and Newtown.

He turned back to ask Samuel, "I nearly forgot. I have been requested to locate and look over a possible safe house. I was told that it was near the Thomas Craven farm, at the Four Corners in Johnsville on Street Road. Do you have knowledge of the Craven farm?"

Samuel looked at Ben, then asked him, "On Street Road, you say? Yes I know the place. Nice people, the Cravens. It is a good landmark for you. And yes, your directions are good."

Ben estimated that it would take him a few cautious hours to reach the Cross Roads if he did not encounter Tories. He wanted to give himself plenty of time. He would work his way over to the Bristol Road and ride just off the roadbed, where he could dash into the shelter of the woods. There was no place to hide the important papers he was carrying, if he was stopped and searched. Safety of the documents was paramount.

He had heard that most of the local inhabitants living near the Cross Roads were Scots Irish and patriotic Colonists. At least that particular area was not overrun with Tories. He did see a few people walking on the Bristol Road and one coach went by, but it was from a distance. He passed few houses. Cox had told him of a farmer, in the immediate area, where he could leave his horse; the farmer asked no questions. Ben did so and then continued on foot.

A short time later, traveling west, he suddenly heard muffled noises and the clink of cooking utensils in the distance; then distinctly human voices in the quietness of the countryside. The voices seemed to be coming from the right side of the road, or from a northwest direction.

He must be coming upon some campsites, he thought; they were deep in the woods but more important, that meant that General Washington was still in the area. He knew that he could not long avoid 11,000 men bivouacked over the area; he was on high alert. He prayed that he would not be shot, and felt his God was with him.

General Washington and his officers were reportedly occupying the Moland House as their headquarters. John Moland had been a prestigious and well known attorney in Philadelphia and Bucks County. His widow, Catherine ran the Moland house efficiently but at that time food was scarce and Washington certainly would have paid her for the use of her home and for food for himself and his staff.

The soldiers bivouacked in the area would be on their own, depending to an extent on the local farmers, who were usually quite generous to the troops.

Ben was greatly relieved that at least, if the men were there, so was the General. He had made it safely past the first encampments. He now stood near the Cross Roads intersection. He turned north on the York Road. There were brick buildings on the Cross Road corners, but he saw no activity.

Ben took to the shelter of the woods on the east side of the road, and just a spit down the York Road he saw the Little Neshaminy Creek. He was closer to the Moland House than he had anticipated. He quickly dropped down and retreated into heavier woods for cover. He realized immediately that he was in the thick of it. Keeping the creek in sight, but remaining well hidden, he followed the water into the woods. He hesitated, thinking he would like to jump in; the heat was so oppressive. However, he knew that the creek would be heavily used for water in this close area. He continued following the creek further into the woods and he smelled cooking and heard laughter. He gave that camp a wide berth and realized that evening was falling. He would wait for a few hours. He had not realized how tired and tense he was. He needed to rest and he lay down in the heavy underbrush, well hidden.

Darkness was gathering when Ben made camp a safe ways from the creek, in a densely wooded area. He looked up and saw that the moon was nearly full and he was able to see about him quite well as night fell. It was good for his maneuvering, but it was also good for the pickets. He had to be careful. He would cross the creek out in the woods near dawn and come up behind the house in the morning light. He wanted to be seen clearly as he got closer, rather than be shot, half seen in the bushes and high undergrowth. He did not make a fire, he ate what he carried. He would meet General Washington early, that is, if he could get close enough without being shot. He needed to think positive.

Ben was both anxious and excited thinking of meeting General Washington. He had some time now to ruminate as he rested. He knew a little of the General's background and felt that Washington was not as most people saw him. The General was born in Fredericksburg, Virginia, not into great wealth, but his family was comfortable. It could be considered second tier gentry. The General's father, Augustine, died on April 12th, 1743, when George was eleven years old. George was devastated. He, like his older brother had anticipated being educated in England, but with his father's death, there was no money to send George for further education. Always resourceful, he went to work as a surveyor, choosing a bold career path, which would enable him to be in contact with influential people. At the age of 21, Washington had joined the Virginia military. He was bold, clever and very ambitious, which carried him a long way in his promotions. He was shrewd in his military career and this shrewdness served him well. It was said that he had even tricked Cornwallis. During the Trenton/Princeton Campaign, where he was grossly outnumbered, he had his men light numerous campfires, making Cornwallis think that these were actual campsites of his Continentals. When Cornwallis hesitated, trying to verify the number of campsites and men, Washington's men slyly slipped through Cornwallis' lines. Cornwallis never forgot that Washington had made a fool of him—he would become his arch enemy. Washington was a master of duplicity, always alert and at the ready to take any advantage that came his way. He was a self made, gifted strategist—determined, courageous and his resourcefulness carried him forward—his common sense and dependability more than made up for what others thought he lacked in heritage and upper gentry. He was really a man of many faces; winning was foremost in his every effort. However, Ben believed that Washington had a kindness about him and truly cared for his troops.

The sun was just beginning to rise on that warm, sticky August day when Ben packed his gear and started out for his appointed meeting. He moved through the woods until he could make out the line of the Moland House roof, which was almost completely hidden in the dense surrounding foliage and trees. Now he could hear more sounds drifting toward him, becoming louder. It was still half light, as he crept cautiously onward.

He made his way further up the Neshaminy Creek and crossed at a narrowing, dunking himself quietly. He slid on his belly up the opposite bank and on to the dry wooded land. The cool water both refreshed his body and quenched his thirst. He remembered the bible telling the holy attributes of water; he understood now what that truly meant. He sprawled out for a few minutes to rest on the warm earth.

Ben knew that he could be wounded or killed on the spot; that of course, was his biggest fear. He hunkered down to acclimate himself to his surrounds and waited for full sunrise. He stayed quiet for a time until daylight spread over the area. He still did not move. He needed to get the lay of the land and make sure that he was not walking into an encampment. He still felt he had a better chance if he showed himself when he was near enough, rather than creeping up in the undergrowth.

He made his move and was immediately spotted. He assumed that this would happen and was why he had waited until daylight—so that they would know that he was alone.

Suddenly, armed soldiers appeared from all sides and circled him with bayonets at the ready.

"Give me a minute," Ben yelped. "Hold fire! I am not the enemy! I am only the messenger! Hold fire!" he pleaded with those who were now grabbing him roughly. "I have documents for General Washington, sent by Lieutenant Colonel Cox of the 2nd Philadelphia Battalion." *He thought he should mention Cox's full rank.*

"Search him, men," ordered a captain. "Search him thoroughly," he commanded. The soldiers took Ben's pistol, brusquely disarmed him of everything that he was carrying, and found the waterproof courier's pouch containing the documents. When they saw the official wax seal on the papers addressed to General Washington, they hastily shoved it back into the pouch and then into Ben's inner waistcoat.

Ben was quickly escorted up to the house by Captain Caleb Gibbs, Commander of George Washington's Guard, and the first officer who Ben had encountered. Captain Gibbs told him that the men on duty were from the Commander-in-Chief's Guards and had sounded the alarm. He was rushed through the entry way into the vestibule, where he was now inside the house, noting that there were two rooms. Ben was nudged forward into a sizable reception room and told to wait. A group of officers, seated at a large round table were in an intense and very loud discussion. Ben smelled coffee and his mouth watered. A young private, not much more than a boy, brought Ben a container full. Empty pewter mugs, along with open maps, were scattered about. Ben recognized General Washington immediately. He had not realized yet, that he had walked into a Council of War. It was August 21, 1777.

While he stood waiting, Ben thought about what Cox had told him. On Washington's eleventh day at the Cross Roads, the General had called a Council of War in the Moland House. Many of his major and brigadier generals would be present. This would be Lafayette's first inclusion into this decision making group. The group conclusion was that Howe probably was planning a strike on Charleston. Washington knew that there was no possibility of reaching Charleston soon enough. They would proceed to the Hudson River now, and make an effort on New York, or assault General Burgoyne. Colonel Alexander Hamilton would take a copy of the Council's discussions and conclusions and carry them back to the Congress. *Hamilton had been ordered to bring back the results of their opinions.*

Ben was escorted by Captain Caleb Gibbs, who then approached General Washington to advise him of a courier's early arrival from Lieutenant Colonel Cox, out of Batsto. Ben stood quietly and continued to peruse the room. He took notice of several Officers and wondered who they were. He had probably seen artists' drawings of some of the men, but to recognize faces from drawings was difficult.

General Washington rose from his chair, motioned Ben closer, and offered his hand. Ben was taken aback by his height—it was reported that he was six feet four inches tall at least; he was a big man and his feet were very large. He met Ben eye to eye and then some. Perhaps he was six foot plus; the former may have been exaggerated. He was a splendid specimen of a man, Ben observed, looking at Washington's long, well proportioned body. His strong face was serious, except for his bright blue eyes, in which Ben thought he detected a sense of humor. His rather large nose was well set above a firm, strong mouth and chin.

"Benjamin VanHameetman, General," Ben stated, collecting himself and nodding quickly in respect. He shook the General's offered hand and gave over the documents from Cox. General Washington nodded his head in return, took the papers, and walked over to a large table, where he spread out the documents.

He motioned Ben over and commented, "I hope your journey was a safe one? No enemy encounters?" He turned to the Batsto lists.

"No. Thank you Sir, for your concern. My trip here was uneventful. I was most cautious." *I am just happy to be alive,* he thought, but did not say it aloud. Suddenly he noticed that he was dripping water on the floor from his creek crossing. He dared not move; he waited for the General to dismiss him.

Washington continued to read the list of munitions that he could depend upon from Batsto. Ben scanned the room as he stood there, waiting to be released.

The General turned toward Ben. "This is excellent news, Sir," he stated, "My compliments to Lieutenant Colonel Cox. Please tell him, that I will be in touch with him soon."

Suddenly, Washington spotted the water on the floor. He looked intently at Ben, and said, "I hope that is just creek water, son," and he ordered a towel for Ben.

"Yes Sir, it is. Although, the thought of getting shot can do that Sir." The General smiled. "I will pass your compliments and message on to Lieutenant Colonel Cox, Sir," and he thanked the General for the towel. Washington turned back to the table and Ben knew that he was dismissed. Ben was right when he initially thought that the General had a sense of humor. He had heard that the General loved dogs and had quite a few: a pack really, of dogs with interesting, sometimes odd names, so his nephew had told him. His hounds were named Chloe, Captain, Forester, Lady Rover, Searcher, Taster, Tippler and Vulcan. In addition he had a Dalmatian named Madam Moose, and a Foxhound named Sweet lips.

As Ben stood there, waiting for the towel to arrive, his glance hovered over a nearby round table where several officers sat. His eyes rested on a dapper, young man, probably not yet past twenty years. Ben noted his smart, long, navy blue colored coat, faced in buff with gold epaulets on his shoulders. Ben was taken by his youth and demeanor as he sat at the table with the older officers.

The young man caught Ben's scrutiny. He stood up and approached Ben. "Bonjour, Monsieur VanHameetman." Ben quickly recognized him as the much talked about Marquis de Lafayette and nodded his head to Lafayette in respect, as he had done to General Washington. The Marquis held out his hand in greeting, and asked, "Parlez-vous français?" Ben shook his head no, to the question from the Marquis, asking him if he spoke French. He wished Sunny was with him. At this answer from Ben, the Marquis held up his hand for Ben to wait and he motioned to another young man.

"Lieutenant Colonel Alexander Hamilton at your service sir." Hamilton, a slightly built, fair haired young Continental officer and newly appointed Aide-de-Camp to General Washington, spoke French fluently. His mother, Rachel Fawcett Hamilton was the daughter of a Huguenot physician and French was spoken in the home. Hamilton introduced himself to Ben. "The Marquis sometimes needs some help to express his English correctly; although he is coming along nicely." Hamilton smiled, as the Marquis communicated something to him in French. "The Marquis told me that General Washington has been waiting for your news, Monsieur VanHameetman. We are thankful that you are here and did not encounter the British."

The Marquis said something else to Hamilton, who then told Ben, "They had managed to alert the pickets of your mission."

Ben was surprised that the Marquis knew his name, and that the troops had been alerted that he was in the area. "Thank you Sir, for warning the men of my arrival. It was somewhat dangerous trying to avoid 11,000 of them," and Hamilton started to interpret, but the Marquis laughed and held up his hand to stop him.

"I can do that. I think you did rather," pausing, he looked to Hamilton for the word he needed, "*superbly*, in avoiding the troops and sentries as long as you did."

Ben looked at Hamilton and asked him, "Should I address the Marquis as General?" He remembered reading that Lafayette had secured his commission from an American agent in Paris. He had joined the American ranks as a major general, but the gossip was that he would soon be one of Washington's full generals, despite his youth. *Oh lord,* Ben thought, as he remembered that there was some controversy surrounding the Marquis' desired appointment as general. *Washington initially was not in favor of awarding high ranks to foreigners. Evidently this situation is somewhat different,* Ben acknowledged. *I hope I have not overstepped myself here.*

The Marquis, after hearing what Ben had asked, picked up on his faux pas and discomfort. Lafayette smiled and said something in French to Hamilton, and then to Ben in English.

"News travels fast in your country, Monsieur. We are fortunate, indeed, to have brave men as you fighting for the cause." *But he chose not to answer Ben's question.*

"I do what I can," Ben replied, thanking God that the Marquis, too, had a sense of humor. "General Washington is the real hero," Ben stated, and Lafayette nodded his head in acknowledgment. "I am honored Sir, to have helped in some small way. I consider it a great privilege to have met you."

Lafayette smiled again and told Ben through Hamilton. "You may address me as Major General," and he bid Ben farewell. Ben turned to leave and one of the officers advised him that they were hopefully breaking camp soon. More information was forthcoming.

Captain Gibbs escorted him out. "I am your escort out of this area, Sir," he told Ben.

"Thank you," Ben replied. "I am happy to be alive." He grinned at Captain Gibbs.

"They passed the word through the camps that a courier would be riding in this morning to see General Washington. Glad you made it, Sir." The captain grinned back.

"Wish I had known that. Is there a chance that someone could retrieve my horse?" Ben told the captain where he had left him.

"Certainly Sir, I am familiar with the farm. I will send someone after him. Your name is Hameetman, Sir?" Ben nodded his head. He sat down on a bench and wiped his forehead in the heat. He had been at the Moland House longer than he had thought. He got up and sat down under a shade tree. The heat was stifling. He watched a private lead a large, dark brown gelding, recently saddled from the barn.

"A rider is leaving?" he asked the captain.

Ben turned and saw Lieutenant Colonel Alexander Hamilton. Again, Ben nodded in respect.

Hamilton acknowledged Ben. "A fine day for a ride, except for this blasted heat." Lieutenant Colonel Hamilton quickly mounted his horse and rode off. Ben was curious as to where Hamilton was going, but he dared not ask.

In short time his own horse was brought back and Ben was on his way. He had been requested to inspect a house that was under consideration to use as a safe house for the Underground Railroad. He passed the Craven Farm and in no time he came upon an empty house with a small barn behind it. Eli had told him that the house would look deserted, by design. The description fit, and after stopping and inspecting the house, he paused to jot down some notes and then started on the long return journey to his home on Long Beach Island. Days later, Ben heard from Colonel Cox just how eventful the day had been for the fledgling country.

On the afternoon of August 21, Colonel Hamilton had rushed into the Hall of Congress with Washington's informational conclusions. Congress read the report and adjourned for two hours. Only that morning word had been received in Philadelphia that upwards of one hundred sailing ships of the British fleet had been spotted the night of August 14 in the Chesapeake Bay. However, it was concluded that the courier had passed Hamilton en route.

No further news had been received and when Congress reassembled later that day, they had passed a resolution approving Washington's plan and gave him permission to act as *circumstances require.*

General Washington's departing date had been changed to August 23—their marching destination was Wilmington, Delaware, through Philadelphia.

Ben told Cox that he had seen Lieutenant Colonel Alexander Hamilton riding out in the early afternoon. "I heard reports that he carried the results of the Council meeting to the Continental Congress for their perusal and advice. Hamilton waited for a reply to carry back to Washington. Evidently the Congress told General Washington *to use his own discretion.*"

Cox smiled. "Lots going on that day."

Another important visitor had shown up at the Moland House headquarters. Count Kazimierz Pulaski had arrived with a letter from Benjamin Franklin, who introduced Pulaski as a gentleman of *character and military abilities.* Major General Lafayette welcomed Pulaski warmly. Pulaski had brought the Marquis news of the Marquis' wife and little daughter. His wife was expecting her second child and he was anxious to hear how she was faring.

"Methinks that Pulaski will be a general before long," Colonel Cox had told Ben. "The letter written by Benjamin Franklin had made quite an impression. I do believe that was the first meeting between Washington and Pulaski." That was all Cox knew. Count Pulaski had offered to fight and die for American freedom.

Too bad I missed him, Ben thought, but then I did meet General Washington and the Marquis and had a few words with Hamilton. I saw and met some very important men. Ben stopped in mid thought. If Pulaski had to wait for his letters of introduction, *perhaps he was there when I came into the room.* No one said anything, but of course, that was not my business and it was secret as well. He tried to remember who was in the room, but realized that he did not know the Count's appearance.

"Goodness, Ben," Sunny interrupted his ruminating. "I think you were most fortunate to meet General Washington and then the Marquis de Lafayette. That is quite a coup in itself!" She had no idea about Pulaski, or even Hamilton.

"I guess so," Ben replied. "Good god, woman. You have quizzed me about meeting these men until I can no longer breathe." In jest, he gasped for air. "Enough, madam, enough," he pleaded. He did not dare mention that Count Pulaski could have been there without his knowledge and that he had a few words with Lieutenant Colonel Hamilton. Sunny would never have stopped her interrogation. Cox told Ben, that General Washington had dispatched Pulaski soon after with an introductory letter to President Hancock and George Clymer.

Word had finally been received on August 23 in Philadelphia, that the British ships had again been sighted, this time in the northeast part of the Chesapeake. It was obvious that General Howe intended to land in Maryland, then march on the city. With this news, the men were aroused from their doldrums and became highly active.

Ben then heard from Cox that General Washington and the main body of the army began to move out of the Neshaminy encampment. It was said that the men were ragged looking and some were wearing British uniforms that had been taken from the dead. They slowly trekked down the York Road to Philadelphia, carrying the Stars and Stripes, which were said to have been unfurled at the Moland House for the first time. Congress had adopted the flag officially two months previously. Pulaski had been appointed First General of the cavalry forces.

September 1777

The war has moved closer to the Philadelphia area. Local citizens in that area were warned that the British would confiscate anything that they could use. The Colonists were advised to hide any items of worth—anything metal would be targeted. The iron bells could be melted and cast again into cannons. The Liberty or State House Bell was removed and hidden in the basement of the Zion Reformed Church in Allentown, Pennsylvania. Colonel Thomas Polk of North Carolina was in charge of the bell's journey to the church. The citizens of Philadelphia had moved the bell just in time, because the British under General Howe entered Philadelphia on September 26, 1777.

We pray that the bell will be returned one day to its rightful place in Philadelphia.

Benjamin VanHameetman
His journal

Ben remained faithful in updating his maps with the latest reports of local skirmishes and larger battles. By the end of August, the main British army had sailed into Chesapeake Bay to come ashore at Head of Elk, Maryland and was skirmishing toward Philadelphia. Washington had his 11,000 men to Howe's 15,000. Difficult times were ahead for the General. Sunny included the troops in her prayers at the dinner table that night; she also remembered them in her nightly prayers.

Washington did risk battle with Howe, and they met at Brandywine Creek, near Wilmington, Delaware, on October 11. Washington was outmaneuvered and defeated. However, the troops under Nathanael Greene and the militia held on tenaciously and Washington's men regrouped. "By god, that Nathanael Greene is some fighter," Ben remarked to Sunny and reiterated what he had just read.

"Yes, but how many men were lost?"

Ben did not answer her.

"It is a sad day indeed to hear that Philadelphia has been captured, and our Congress will have to flee again," Andrew lamented.

The British blockade of the Delaware River was still causing problems, cutting off most supplies going north.

Ben commented, "Now, more than ever, military capability is vital. Lieutenant Colonel Cox knows this and is spending most of his time in Batsto. I just learned that he has committed to contracts with the navy."

Sunny sat down and opened one of the many newspapers that she read. "I am amazed that I have been able to get my hands on those scarce copies of the *Pennsylvania Evening Post* and the *Pennsylvania Gazette*. The paper has managed to survive and get the news out under dire circumstances. I hear that a few of the papers have gone underground. Ben Franklin fled to Yorktown with his *Pennsylvania Gazette* some time ago. I assume he is still in Paris, France."

"I cannot blame them. Their presses have been vandalized, and their lives are under attack. I also heard that others have also gone underground." Andrew shook his head.

"Cox is holding multiple contracts with both the army and navy to furnish an increased quantity of cannon shot, musket shot, camp kettles, and other necessities," Ben announced. "Both the Continental army and navy had been rather loosely formed; both need to be beefed up, especially the navy. And rolling mill at Mount Holly could be a huge contract. I hope we can handle an agreement that large." He turned to see Ricardo walk through the door.

"I just overheard you and I agree." Ricardo sat down at the table and Sunny brought her brother coffee. "Our lumber contract would be greatly increased. I know that Cox will expect us to step it up. We have to do what we can do, and then one step further. I do know that we will have to start advertising for more wood cutters."

"You look tired Rico," Sunny told him, using her childhood name for her brother.

"Nothing that a week of sleep could not fix." He grinned at her.

Long Beach Island's nearest skirmishes with the British at that time, took place in Chestnut Neck and Tuckerton, which were still hotbeds of pirate activity. Both harbors sheltered the "bloody pirates," as both the British and Colonists called them.

The pirates burned and pillaged the smaller British ships and attacked any other ship sailing too close. They avoided any of the British Men-of-war and the larger sloops-of-war. They were mercenaries and taking the prize was their only goal.

The latest rumor was that the Continental Congress had encouraged smugglers to turn to privateering. "*Privateering,* mind you." Ben grinned. "Not pirating, which, in other words, makes privateers legalized pirates? We are no match by ourselves for the English navy, so this is a scheme to halt the British shipping and capture some much needed supplies. Not a bad idea, not bad at all." Andrew added that the privateers were being officially sanctioned to seize British cargo and ships and sell them at auction.

"Did you know that investors are backing these privateers? Mr. Ball, the furnace manager, so I have heard is an investor and guess who else? Benjamin Franklin, himself!" Ben had to laugh. "I guess there are no holds barred in war. Whatever it takes, we will do. Who can judge what is right or wrong?"

Friend Samuel advised Ben that there had been thirty five privateer captured ships berthed at the Tuckerton docks a few weeks ago. "Just think of that, Ben. Tuckerton is the largest port in the country. Did you know that the port harbors pirates, turned privateers, along with other captured ships that were built here in the shore area? I guess nothing is off limits to the privateers!" Ben was surprised to learn that Tuckerton was now a major harbor for captured British ships; they would have to enlarge their holding slips.

The war and the continuing slavery issues caused great consternation to many Colonists in the northern areas of population. Some even felt little hope for the future of the newly founded America. The Colonists in Virginia and parts south were not concerned about slavery, nor saw it as a detriment to America's success.

"I pray that a law be enacted to stop this horrendous treatment of human beings." Sunny was angry. "Did you know that the British offered freedom to all slaves and indentured servants if they joined their ranks?" She knew that this presented unsolvable problems to those who took the British offer. Those slaves who had bargained to fight alongside the British soon found that it was the same cause that enslaved them. In order to regain their freedom, they took risks. Few who bargained with the British upheld their agreement and the English had a difficult time trying to enforce the contracts.

"A number of slaves joined the British ranks and then ran directly off into the Pine Barrens in southern Jersey. The Barrens are increasingly more dangerous since the war, which is such a shame. They used to be a godsend for the runaways but since the war, that has all changed. The Barrens have become a haven for deserters, escaped prisoners and fugitives," Ben reminded them. "The runaways who live in the Barrens have banded together to protect themselves. I certainly hope that they are well armed and can stand against anyone who threatens them."

"You will never guess who recently escaped into the Barrens." Ben quizzed Sunny, who was busy with her cooking. "Captain John Bacon, our famous Loyalist, who is nothing but a brute and a robber, along with his gang of toughs. They have raided from Middletown to Long Beach Island. Now he is holed up in the Barrens. Bacon claims to be a Loyalist to cover his dirty deeds. Loyalist, my foot. Loyalist to whom? Certainly not to Great Britain as he proclaims. Loyalist to himself, that is what he really means. What kind of asylum can the Barrens offer the runaways with Bacon and others like him hiding there? He should be shot." He shook his head in disgust.

"He had better watch out," Sunny said. "Perhaps we will all be lucky and the Jersey Devil will get him!"

Ben laughed a long time. "You cannot be serious, Sunny. That is just an old wives' tale," and he laughed again.

"Well, I made you laugh," Sunny smiled, hoping that her remark would break up the seriousness of the conversation.

Andrew was in the parlor and heard them laughing, and he joined them. "I have read a bit about those tales—and of witches too. Imagine a devil like creature inhabiting the Pine Barrens. People keep talking about it. I heard where the tale originated, near Leeds Point. People swear that they have seen this devil that flies about," and he too, laughed.

"You two better not laugh," Sunny said, trying to hide a grin. "Be careful at night if you go into the Barrens, less the Jersey Devil gets you! I just hope it swoops down and grabs that awful Bacon person."

1777 brought numerous defeats to both the Continental Army and the militia. Ben expressed his concern to Sunny. "I wonder how our troops can keep fighting. They are willing to lay down their lives, not only for their own freedom, but also for the freedom of all of us. I wish I could do more. Everyone is working as fast as he is able at the munitions plant so that our soldiers can defend themselves." Sunny could certainly testify to that by the amount of time Ben was away.

On November 16, 1777, Sunny and Ben joyously announced the birth of their daughter, Hannah, a beautiful, healthy baby girl, who joined her older brother, Neil. They named her after a Dutch ancestor of Ben's who was among the early settlers in South Jersey. "Well I guess I really did have some time at home," Ben grinned at Sunny. "Where did she get those dark eyes?" Ben asked.

"Those are Spanish eyes from my side. She is such a beautiful baby," Sunny answered, smiling down at her daughter.

In December of 1777, General Washington chose Valley Forge, a windy, desolate plain as his winter encampment. "Heaven help Jack if he is with Washington at Valley Forge. From all reports, it is a terrible place. Pray for his survival," Marie asked.

They had not heard from Jack in some time and his mother constantly worried about him. Marie was not in good health; she seemed to be going downhill too quickly. The doctor suspected consumption.

The fighting continued throughout 1777; the Americans were defeated at Princeton in Jersey, but were victorious in Bennington, Vermont. Finally, Lafayette's French volunteers arrived in America, and Ben felt that now they had a fighting chance. "We intend to give our men all the munitions they need and then some." He was committed.

January 1778

We are consumed by the war. At times, we are unable to receive news for days. No riders come from Philadelphia, the mail is seized, and packages are confiscated. We are thankful that our Indian friends carry a newspaper to us whenever they can.

Ricardo was wounded badly and is recuperating. He and three friends encountered Loyalists, disguised as American militia, outside of the Batsto Munitions Building. He feels the intruders were spying on the works there with intentions of violence and that he and his friends surprised them. Before they had a chance to pull their weapons, they were all shot. Ricardo's friends were mortally wounded, and he played dead. Workers came running when they heard the shots and the intruders ran away.

Ricardo is very depressed and feels responsible for the deaths. They had taken all precautions, and marauders had not been reported in the area. Adding to that loss were the deaths of two of his cousins in the battle of Brandywine. Our friends and neighbors have suffered great losses. A cousin on my mother's side from the Tuckerton area was killed, and a second cousin was injured and will never walk again.

Sunny and the children remain on the island, where our Lenape friends watch over them. I have been in Batsto for the last month, afraid to leave for fear of the destruction of our buildings. Ten militiamen have been assigned to guard the works, night and day.

I fear that my journals are nothing but a timeline of the war. We pray for a swift victory. I have copied the following from one of the newspapers:

Americans are bold, unyielding, and fearless. They have an abundance of that something, which urges them on and cannot be stopped.

Major Baurmeister, a Hessian officer,
January 20, 1778.

Benjamin VanHameetman
His Journal

February also brought the signing of treaties with France and Holland. "The Dutchmen think Benjamin Franklin is a hero," Ben commented. "Perhaps we can be hopeful again. Maybe this will be our turning point. Mr. Franklin seems to be an excellent negotiator, although I guess some would disagree."

In February 1778, an outright skirmish ensued in Newtown, Bucks County, Pennsylvania.

Andrew asked Ben and Ricardo if they had heard what had happened in Newtown on February 18. They told him that they had heard talk about a Tory raid, but not the details. "One of my friends had the report from a Tory newspaper. A raiding party of forty Loyalists, consisting of British Light Dragoons and Bucks County volunteers left Philadelphia for Middletown, Bucks County to raid Jenk's Fulling Mill who were makers of cloth for uniforms. They captured a guard and stole 2,000 yards of material from the mill. They continued on to Newtown to the Bird in Hand house, led by Major Francis Murray where they overcame 16 Pennsylvania militiamen, took prisoners and killed five men. Besides the stolen 2,000 yards of material, they confiscated two wagons filled with timber and took 32 prisoners. In an aggressive move, they had marched 26 miles, stole goods and took from the poorly dressed soldiers of the 13th Pennsylvania Regiment, the cloth they so badly needed for uniforms. A Tory newspaper in Philadelphia referred to the raid as the "Newtown Skirmish," and called the attack the gallant action of the Loyalists, which was met with applause from the Tories. They feel that it showed commitment of Americans loyal to the Crown." Andrew shook his head in disgust.

"If these people feel this grand commitment to England, let them go back to England. They have no right to call themselves Americans." That was Ben's take.

In April of 1778, a meeting to exchange prisoners was held in Newtown. The ten day exchange talks were steered by an American, Elias Boudinot, Commissioner of Prisoners and Colonel Alexander Hamilton.

In May of 1778, Sarah, Ricardo's wife, came to Sunny and reported that they heard news from one of Ricardo's friends, who lived in Pennsylvania. "There was a terrible battle in Bucks County in Pennsylvania at the beginning of the month," Sarah reported. "It started near the Crooked Billet Tavern in the village of Hatborough."

Ben interjected, "I know that town. Friend Samuel spoke a great deal about it. At one time it was called the Crooked Billet. The village was discovered early, around 1715 by John Dawson. I remember asking about the history of the town when Samuel and I stopped at the Tavern. I do know that Dawson was a hat maker in England before he came here. They say that Dawson also made hats for the Continentals. I rode through there once or twice. Nice little village. Samuel told me that Washington and his officers stopped for supper at the Crooked Billet Tavern on their way to the Moland House last August. I heard that Washington used the gristmill in town for his troops. The Crooked Billet Tavern has been there a long time."

"That's where the battle started; right at the Tavern," Sarah reported. "Our militia, led by young General John Lacey, was in the area, trying to protect the local farmers from the marauding bands of General Howe's regulars and the local Loyalists. We have all heard about that before—General Howe's men foraging the countryside farms, confiscating foodstuff to supply his troops in Philadelphia." Sarah sipped some water and continued. "More than 900 British were in the vicinity and ambushed a contingent of 500 of our militia. The Redcoats shot and wounded or killed many of the militiamen and then chased the remaining men across the Craven farm in Warminster. Some of the wounded tried to hide under the buckwheat straw. The Brits bayoneted them and then set the stacks on fire, burning them alive. It was a terrible act of cruelty."

Sarah stopped for a moment not to forget anything. "The local people and of course neighbors, tried to help the wounded after the British left. They managed to get a few of the survivors into the Craven farmhouse. Such cruelty," she spoke softly as she shared the terrible news. "We have to thank God for the survivors. I pray that they will live. Some of the British soldiers have such black hearts. Bayoneting wounded men! Such evil. I, for one, will never forget this," she repeated and broke down and wept. "Those poor men."

"I passed the Craven farm last year on my way home from the Moland House," Ben said softly.

The Battle of Crooked Billet and the skirmish in Newtown were the only outright fighting fought on Bucks County soil during the war.

American militia tried to protect the farmers, even though there were some turncoats among the farmers, selling their foodstuffs to the British.

"I suppose the farmers have to live, too." Sunny commented about the traitorous farmers.

"It is wonderful to be so liberal minded, Sunny, but this is war. Would you like the food taken out of your children's mouths?"

Sunny pulled back at the harsh words from Ben. "I really did not mean it that way. I know they are traitors; but how were their children to be fed if the parents have no produce from their farms?"

"They could eat what their parents were selling to the British, while many of their neighbor's sons were out fighting for us." Ben was extremely annoyed by her attitude.

"I probably spoke too soon, not thinking about the entire picture. I am sorry." Ben calmed down, realizing that she had a soft heart.

"I would not know what to do if we could not feed our children. I would lie, steal, or do anything to keep their stomachs full." Now she was upset.

Ben agreed. "We will speak of it no more."

"And I will be more careful of speaking aloud without thinking!"

On June 18, 1778, the British evacuated Philadelphia. "There was really no reason for them to stay," Sunny stated. "I am so happy that my parents are out of the city and with us. I wonder if their house is still intact." Ben noticed a lone tear rolling down her face. "You know the old ancestral bell standing behind the house? My father had it put down in the basement, hidden behind one of the walls. Do you think that the British found it anyway?"

Sunny was beside herself. From the old journals, she knew what that bell had been through, coming over on Sergio's ship, then being buried in Manahawkin near Captain Weber's place. "Did you know when Sergio came back from Lisbon the second time, he had stopped on the island to see Captain Weber and he picked up the bell. He brought it to his early trading post near the Fort Nassau settlement, close to Philadelphia." She looked at Ben. "I do believe it was Sergio's son, Mario who brought the bell from there to Town Bank and then it was brought to our home in Philadelphia for safekeeping."

"The British would confiscate the bell for its metal—that is, if they can find it. Right now there is nothing we can do."

"I have asked Father if we could move the bell down to the island. I thought that appropriate. Our Captain Sergio washed up here, along with the bell. What do you think?" She waited for a moment. "The bell's story would come full circle then."

"I agree. That is a nice thought, about the bell coming full circle." *Good god almighty, will this war never end?* Ben thought, but said nothing. He wondered about the family held property near the city. Had the British destroyed it all? Why bother worrying; there was nothing they could do.

"Where did you read that the British had abandoned Philadelphia? With all the talk, I forgot to ask you."

"Here, right here." Sunny pointed to an item in the newspaper. "But who knows if it is true? You better inquire as soon as possible if you are thinking about going to the city to check the family's holdings."

They did confirm that the British had left Philadelphia. Ben waited a week and then traveled to check on their properties. He was pleased that everything was intact. There was minimal damage, probably because their properties were on the far outskirts of the city. He checked the Scarlatti's empty house and found the bell untouched, still hidden in the basement.

"You need to speak with your father," he told Sunny. "The bell should be moved before it is vandalized. Local scavengers may start roaming the city, searching empty houses."

Later, Ben brought home a copy of the May 16, *Pennsylvania Gazette*, which contained the military report of the *Battle of Crooked Billet*. "I see that Mr. Franklin is still getting his paper out. Good for him!" he commented, and handed the paper to Sunny. "Then look at the report from the Royal Pennsylvania Gazette, which of course is from the British. And I've clipped out the article about the British and Loyalist reports of atrocities. Some difference."

"You know Ben, that battle in Hatborough has never left my mind. I cannot understand how people can be so cruel; soldiers or not—those men have no consciences. Bayoneting and burning others who are unable to defend themselves is not human. They must be extraordinarily bent toward evil. I wonder whether people are born that way or they have been sorely mistreated by others to become so twisted."

"I do not know," Ben sighed. "I do agree, that evil itself exists."

PENNSYLVANIA GAZETTE

YORK TOWN, MAY 16 1778

(Published in York Town, Pennsylvania during the British occupation of Philadelphia.)

Extract of a letter from the Militia Camp near Neshaminey Bridge, York Road, dated May 4, 1778 (copied from the May 16, 1778 original in the Library of Congress)

"This camp, which lay near the Crooked Billet was surrounded on the morning of the first instant, by daylight, with a body of the enemy, who appeared on all quarters; the scouts had neglected the preceding night to patrole the roads as they were ordered, but lay in camp till near day, tho' their orders were to leave it by two in the morning; one of the parties, commanded by a Lieutenant, met the enemy near two miles from the camp, but never gave us the alarm. He makes his excuse, that he was so near before he espied them, that he thought himself in danger of being cut to pieces by their light horse should he fire, but sent off a man to give notice that the enemy were approaching, who did not come. On the disobedience and misconduct of this, and the other officers of the scouts, we have to lay our misfortunes.

The alarm was so sudden, we had scarcely time to mount our horses before the enemy was within musket shot of our quarters. We observed a party in our rear had got into houses and behind fences; their numbers appearing nearly equal to ours, we did not think it adviseable to attack them in that situation, especially as another body appeared in our front to the east of the Billet; and not knowing what numbers we had to contend with, we thought it best to open our way under cover of a wood to the left of our camp towards Colonel Hart, for which our little party moved in columns, the baggage following in the rear. We had not passed far, before our flanking parties began to change shot with the enemy, but kept moving on till we made the wood, when a party of both foot and horse came up the Biberry road, and attacked our right flank; the party from the Billet fell on our rear; the horse, from the rear of our camp came upon our left flank. A body of horse appearing in our front, we made a stand in this wood, and gave them some warm fires, which forced them to retire; their horse suffered considerably, as they charged us, and were severely repulsed; their strength gathering from all quarters, we thought it best to move on, which we did with the loss of the baggage, the horse giving way in the front as we advanced.

We continued skirmishing for upwards of two miles, when we made a turn to the left, which entirely extricated us from them. We came into the York road near the Cross roads, and moved slow down towards the Billet, in hopes to take some advantage of them on that quarter, where they must least expect us, but we found they retired towards the city. Our people behaved well; our loss is upwards of thirty killed and wounded; some were thrown into buckwheat straw, and the straw set on fire; the clothes were burnt on others, and scarcely one without a dozen of wounds with bayonets and cutlasses. Fifty-eight are missing. The enemy-loss is not known, but it is currently reported one field officer is among the slain; we took three of their horse, five were left dead on the field, the riders either killed or wounded. We learn, that of the enemy in this attack, were 400 horse, with each a footman (chiefly light infantry) behind them."

ROYAL PENNSYLVANIA GAZETTE, PHILADELPHIA, MAY 5, 1778

The clash occurred on May 1, during the British occupation of Philadelphia. The militia, commanded by Gen. John Lacey and assigned to cut off British supplies, was encamped here. Surprised by British troops, they were defeated and driven off with heavy losses. On Thursday night last, a small party of the British infantry, dragoons, and Queen's rangers, with a few of Capt. HOVEDEN's Pennsylvania, and Capt. JAMES's Chester dragoons, left the city about eleven o'clock, and proceeded up the Old York road.

About a mile beyond the Billet they fell in with Lacey's brigade of militia, consisting of about 500 men, and immediately attacked them: Lacey, at first, made some appearance of opposition, but, in a few seconds, was thrown into confusion, obliged to retreat with precipitation, and were pursued about 4 miles. They left between 80-100 dead on the field; and on Friday, between 50-60 prisoners, besides waggoners, with 10 of their waggons loaded with baggage, flour, salt, whiskey, &c. were brought in by the troops on their return: What number of rebels were wounded, we have not been able to learn. Besides the above waggons, 3 were burnt after taking out the horses; also all the huts and what baggage could not be brought off. The royal party did not lose a single man on this occasion, and have only 7 men wounded, and 2 horses killed.

British Loyalists/Tory Report

REPORTS OF ATROCITIES COMMITTED BY BRITISH AND LOYALIST FORCES

Almost immediately, reports surfaced that British and Loyalist troops had committed atrocities, including the murder of prisoners of war and setting fire to the American wounded. On May 7, Washington ordered Brigadier General William Maxwell to conduct an inquiry into these allegations so that a report could be made to British commander General William Howe. Andrew Long, a justice of the peace in Bucks County, took the depositions of Colonel Watts and four residents who witnessed the battle: Samuel Henry, William Stayner, Thomas Craven and Samuel Erwin. Watts reported *"we found the bodies of the dead usid [sic] in a most inhuman & barbarous manner"* and that *"the most cruel Barbarity that had ever been exercised by any civilised Nation; nay, Savage barbarity in its utmost exertion of cruelty could but equal it."*

Lacey's report to Major General John Armstrong further documented the atrocities: *"Some of the unfortunate, who fell into the merciless hands of the British, were more cruelly and inhumanely butchered. Some were set on fire with buckwheat straw, and others had their clothes burned on their backs. Some of the surviving sufferers say they saw the enemy set fire to wounded while yet alive, who struggled to put it out but were too weak and expired under the torture. I saw those lying in the buckwheat straw—they made a most melancholy appearance. Others I saw, who, after being wounded with a ball, had received near a dozen wounds with cutlasses and bayonets. I can find as many witnesses to the proof of the cruelties as there were people on the spot, and that was no small number who came as spectators."*

Then came some much needed good news. The British General Howe had resigned. Andrew read later that the British felt that Howe had not moved forward strongly enough and that he had been unable to weaken the Colonists' cause.

"I have just finished reading about General Howe. He has left the Country, probably in disgrace. Washington has outlasted two British commanders, first Gage, now Howe. What fortitude the General has. No wonder his troops admire him as they do." Ben recalled what a strong personality Washington projected and his genuine concern for his men. He understood why Washington's troops were so loyal.

In June of 1778, General Washington and his men left Valley Forge. They had survived more than six months, through a terrible winter, starving, and many barely living through the cold.

June 1778

The latest headline is wonderful news. *"Washington defeats the British at Monmouth, in Jersey."* This is one of the largest, if not *the* largest, battle of the war to date, from the point of the number of fighting troops. Washington is claiming victory, but the British did not actually surrender; they abandoned the battlefield and continued to travel up to New York. Our men needed this victory for their morale—abandoned battlefield or not."

Benjamin VanHameetman
His Journal

Ben reported that later, in October of 1778, the British had sent an army raiding party from New York to wipe out Chestnut Neck, at the entrance to Little Egg Harbor, the seat of the privateering. Too many British ships had been captured or destroyed and the British had had enough. They landed their troops at Chestnut

Neck and burned docks and shipping along with many of the privateers' ships. They had intended to wipe out the Batsto works, but that never happened. It could have been disastrous.

Colonel Procter's Pennsylvania Artillery regiment was sent to the area and General Pulaski was ordered to march to Chestnut Neck under the command of Major General Stirling. Pulaski was in good position, but that Judas, a Hessian Lieutenant by name of Juliat gave the British important strategic information, betraying Pulaski. Because of Juliat's deed, Pulaski's troops were massacred." Andrew put his paper down, unable to say another word.

"May Juliat burn in hell!" Ben was vehement in his outburst.

"The British are calling this *The Egg Harbor Expedition.* There was an exposé in one of the papers I read recently about Juliat, who has some interesting background. I will see if I can find it."

In 1778, the British turned their energies to the south and captured Savannah, Georgia.

1779 brought the Americans a victory at Vincennes in Illinois and the capture of Stony Point, New York.

August of 1779 brought happy news once more when Sunny and Ben's third child and second son, Matthew arrived—a thriving, husky baby, with a ravenous appetite and a loud, demanding cry.

The battle continued to rage over Savannah. October 9, 1779, Brig. General Kazimierz Pulaski, with the rebel cavalry, led an aggressive but foolish charge between the British redoubts. He led 200 horsemen and reached the abatis and was struck down by enemy cannons and was mortally wounded. His cavalry was confused by Pulaski's demise and scattered. The effort to capture Savannah had been thwarted.

"Oh my goodness," Sunny drew in her breath. "Did you see this Ben?" She asked, on one of the few days Ben was home. "Our troops have wiped out forty Indian villages because of uprisings. Why did they wait until now to report this in the newspaper?"

"Where did this happen?" Ben was surprised. "And whose command was responsible?"

"They are calling this the Sullivan Expedition, or the Sullivan Clinton Expedition. It is an American campaign led by Major General John Sullivan and Brigadier General James Clinton against Loyalists and the four nations of the Iroquois who had sided with the British. The first battle was in Western New York; about 1,000 Iroquois and Loyalists were defeated by an army of 3,200 Continentals. It is reported that Sullivan's army then carried out a systematic killing campaign and destroyed at least forty Iroquois villages throughout western New York to put an end to attacks against American settlements. Thousands of Iroquois refugees starved or froze to death that winter. Evidently this campaign was ordered and sanctioned by General Washington to stop the Indian killings of settlers and Continentals."

Sunny had heard stories of the Iroquois violence but felt the group she knew had broken away from the main Iroquois tribe years ago. No wonder they would never speak of their homelands. Sunny got up, visibly shaken. She handed Ben a screaming baby Matthew and left the room.

The southern campaign became active and was waged heavily in the southern Colonies. General Gates, who had recently led the Continental troops in the Camden, South Carolina battle, was defeated. Gates swore that many circumstances were against him. He reported many other instances of what he thought were infractions against him.

"I heard that he was recalled and Nathanael Greene is replacing him," Andrew reported. "Good luck to him. You know that it is funny that General Gates wound up in the Continental Army. He was born in England and was once in the British Army. I guess he decided that it was better to be over here, in our army. And what are they saving those French troops for? Samuel told me that they had arrived in Newport, Rhode Island."

"Really?" Ben was surprised. "I hope that they will utilize the French in the next big battle. I just wonder how long this damnable war will go on. 1781 will be upon us before we know it. It has been nearly six years since the war began."

The furnaces of the munitions plant in Batsto were running at full capacity. Colonel Cox had retired and Mr. Ball, the former manager, had bought the furnaces. The salt factory continued to turn out huge amounts of salt, sorely needed to preserve rations for the troops. Ben, Ricardo, and now even Andrew were away most of the day, carrying heavy loads out of Batsto for the Colonists' cause. Ricardo had appointed one of his cousins to supervise the tree cutting for the furnaces.

"I am so tired of it," Sunny told Ben when he was home for two days. "I am happy that the children are too young to be aware of your long absences."

Two weeks later, Sarah, Sunny, Ricardo and Ben were together. It was unusual for all of them to be home at the same time. Sarah and Ricardo were visiting at Ben's house. The talk turned to Benedict Arnold. "And now this traitorous fool, Benedict Arnold. And a Continental officer to boot! Can you imagine his concocted plot to surrender West Point to the British? This is far beyond what I could have imagined. It is just too awful. What would possess a man to plan such treachery?" Sunny could not believe the news about Arnold that she had read recently.

"You know the story behind this? I have read a bit about this so called hero, Benedict Arnold." Ben joined in. "Washington gave him the rank of colonel and then brigadier general. Now, I am sure General Washington rues the day he called Arnold *the bravest of the brave*. Ethan Allen and Benedict Arnold fought over who would have the honor of being the first to enter Fort Ticonderoga. Can you imagine that they finally agreed to march together, side by side, into the fort? Such childish behavior I cannot believe."

"Arnold has had a very shady record throughout his career. He just could not get himself on the right track. I read that he came from a very poor background and I think he craved wealth. He has put himself in hot water more than once and he has disappointed General Washington a number of times." Ricardo could not figure out Arnold.

Sarah joined in. "I know at one time, Arnold was under General Gates. He made a name for himself at the battle of Burgoyne and some feel as a direct result, France came into the war on the American side. Arnold had lost his seniority before, but it had been restored. He had been badly injured when his horse was shot and fell on him wounding him once more on the same leg that had previously been damaged. As a result, he was crippled for life."

"How could Benedict Arnold have turned?" Sunny wondered. "Washington honored him with the military command of Philadelphia, once we regained control. Good lord, he certainly had many chances to prove himself."

Sunny thought for a minute. "You know, he married that Peggy Shippen. It is said that she was a boisterous young woman and the youngest of three daughters. Her father, Edward Shippen was a Judge and spoiled her rotten. She and her family were prominent in Philadelphia and the family was loyal to the British Crown. Funny though, the Judge's cousin, William Shippen was Surgeon General to the Continental Army." She lifted her eyebrows. "I have seen more than a few times when the families have been split, taking sides."

Sarah jumped in. "You know Arnold bought Mount Pleasant House for Peggy as a wedding present. You wonder where he got the money. Perhaps borrowed from his father-in-law? Mount Pleasant is certainly one of the most elegant homes in Philadelphia. Captain John Macpherson, who built the house, was a privateer. According to Mister John Adams, the Scottish captain had *an arm twice shot off.* The captain certainly must have lived well. He had to have loads of money to build such a home. Captain Macpherson called the house *Clunie*, for his ancient forebears' original clan in Scotland. However," and she paused here, making sure all were listening, "Benedict and Peggy never lived there! Because of the treason charges, they eventually fled Philadelphia and went to England."

"I wonder whatever happened to Mount Pleasant," Sunny asked and no one responded, so she continued on with more information. "You know Major André once kept company with Peggy, but she must have been very young, really just a child, if she married Arnold when she was eighteen. André was Aide-de-camp then to the British General, Henry Clinton. I guess that Arnold just moved in."

"When she married Benedict, Peggy was only eighteen. He was thirty eight, and Peggy was his second wife. Peggy's father had misgivings about the marriage but gave in to her. Benedict had been married, first in 1767 and that marriage resulted in three sons. His wife died in 1775. People said that Benedict and Peggy lived above their means, probably supported by her family. She had social status, and I guess that was a big attraction to him," Sunny shared, pursing her lips. "And that she was only eighteen! He was more than twice her age, and maybe that was his attraction to her!"

Ben laughed. "You are bad Sunny."

"I only say what everyone else is thinking. Maybe Peggy was a spy in her own right." Sunny paused, collecting her thoughts of all she wanted to tell. "Benedict was the commander of Philadelphia when the British held it. I wonder how much Loyalist influence the family wielded over him. You remember we discussed his court martial for using his post to further his personal ambitions. They said he misused government wagons and issued an improper pass to a ship. He was cleared, but he must have been bitter. I have heard, too, that he is rather arrogant. Maybe that was what triggered his treason, or one wonders if his wife instigated the relationship between Benedict and John André to that end."

"Perhaps Arnold was bitter that he had lost the use of his leg to the cause. He was redeemed by General

Washington who appointed him to the Continental Congress and sent him to head the Canadian Invasion. Washington gave Benedict the rank of brigadier general during the Quebec battles." Ben expressed his take on the gossip.

"I do believe he lost the commission and then had it restored two years later. He must have been an angry man; he felt slighted by the army and evidently did not take responsibility for things that he had done. I think this may have been one of the reasons he defected to the British." Ricardo's statement was strong and he continued.

"During the time when Arnold was involved with John André and West Point, Arnold heard that André had been captured. Arnold had made his escape in the Vulture, the same ship that had left André high and dry." Sarah had been taken aback when she first heard of André's abandonment.

Andrew jumped in. "Benedict then defected to the British and received a large sum of money. They also gave him ongoing pay, land in Canada, pensions for himself, his wife and his five surviving children with Peggy, and three children from his first marriage. Plus—and I am not finished: a commission as a British Provincial brigadier general. Pretty grand what say you? However, the British never trusted him. He moved back and forth between Canada and London and failed miserably at everything he tried to accomplish. The last that was heard of Benedict was that he was living in London."

"I think Benedict Arnold's head became too big," Ben offered. "He wanted revenge." He looked at Sunny. "And where do you get all this information?"

"From the Philadelphia and local papers that you bring home. What an uproar this is causing in Philadelphia. The writers have really dug up a lot of background information about the entire affair," Sunny smiled. "Those newspapers are hard to come by. I have to pay a premium to get my copy." She was rather enjoying the attention this plethora of information was drawing to her. "And for Arnold to conspire with John André! Can you believe that? He really took a chance, and see what happened in the end? I am sure Benedict Arnold's wife, Peggy, had something to do with fostering their relationship."

"Why do you say that, Sunny?" Sarah wanted to know.

"Remember, John André was a major in the British Army and held a very prominent position with General Henry Clinton. John André was, for a time, a very important Brit, who distinguished himself at the battle of Bunker Hill. He was privy to all of Clinton's personal information. And they named him second in command to British General Howe and then promoted him to a lieutenant general. He was knighted after the battle of Long Island. What could John André have gained by going along with Benedict Arnold? How did this happen?" Sunny was appalled.

She got up from the table where they all were sitting and made sure everyone had full glasses. "John André's parents were Huguenots. His father was from Geneva, Switzerland, and his mother, from Paris, France. He was only twenty when he joined the British Army, hardly more than a boy, but evidently very worldly. His accomplishments as a painter are well known and he could cut beautiful silhouette pictures." Sunny looked around the table and saw that they were all hanging on her words. "And John André was a talented singer and a writer. You know, I think it takes an extraordinary memory to be a good liar. I do not think that John André possessed such a memory. I guess all of André's accomplishments did not contribute toward making him an honest man."

"You said one big mouthful, Sunny. But it still sounds like he was indeed a sensitive sort of a fellow," Sarah added.

Ben smiled and shook his head. "I am amazed at your knowledge of John André, Sunny. You could write his biography! How much are those newspaper premiums costing us?" They all laughed.

Ben had more to say. "André felt the sting of prison when he was captured at Saint Johns in Canada in 1775 and later held prisoner in Lancaster, Pennsylvania, for a year, before being exchanged," Ben continued. "I still cannot understand how those two communicated without getting caught." Ben shrugged his shoulders in disbelief that someone of Benedict Arnold's so called caliber could have behaved so foolishly. Perhaps Sunny was right; Peggy Shippen had arranged their meetings. Perhaps she wanted to draw Benedict over to the Loyalist side.

"Arnold probably communicated through his wife and then after plans were made, he arranged a meeting with John André," Sunny offered. "I am sure there was no problem doing this as those Shippen Loyalists probably had contacts in the right places."

"I did read where André was a favorite in society during that time," Sarah shared. "Another bizarre twist is that Peggy had kept company with John André, or had a previous affair, or whatever you want to call it, with André and then married Benedict Arnold—then John André and Benedict Arnold became fast friends. How bizarre is that?"

There was silence while everyone digested Sarah's statement. She was sure that they all thought the same thing, but she had said it aloud.

"Here's something I bet you ladies have not heard," Ben said and smiled at the women, feeling caught up in the gossip and rather liking it. "John André occupied Benjamin Franklin's house during his stay in Philadelphia. It is said that Benedict Arnold told André that he was ready to help defeat the Americans."

"That is so hard to accept as truth, Ben." Sunny found that hard to believe.

Ben rolled his eyes at her and said, "*I* have the full story, everyone. Benedict Arnold was passed over a number of times for promotion, and he was believed to be resentful, making matters worse. He just skirted his way around scandal and was a smooth talker. He somehow talked General Washington into making him Commandant of West Point back in August, as we all know. He probably had a strategy in mind then, because just seven weeks later he set up a secret meeting with John André on the banks of the Hudson River to conclude their plans."

Anticipatory faces watched Ben closely. "The night of the meeting, John André sailed up the Hudson on the British ship, the *Vulture*, under cover of darkness. The *Vulture* cast anchor to wait until André returned from his meet with Benedict Arnold in the woods just south of Stony Point, New York. They agreed that Arnold would give up the plans to West Point for 10,000 pounds sterling, although it was reported the sum was between 10,000 and 20,000 pounds sterling. But who really knows the truth of the amount?"

"It was speculated that this was a twofold move by Benedict Arnold," Andrew said. "If the British could take over West Point, it would allow them to cut off New England from the rest of the rebelling Colonies. Benedict Arnold would receive the monies to pay off, I presume, major personal debts that he had incurred. I wonder if we will ever know the truth of the matter."

"This talk has worn me out!" Ben said.

"Or the true story," Sunny interrupted, in response to Andrew. "And you know that you are enjoying the gossip as much as we are." She laughed at her husband.

Not to be outdone, Ben offered more information. "Here is the worst and most ridiculous of all André's moves. After the agreement was fulfilled, it was morning. They had talked all night, which was a bad mistake. It was extremely important that John André leave in the darkness of the night. What was he thinking to stay so long? Incredibly stupid," he stated and paused a moment.

"In the early morning light, the Americans started firing on the *Vulture*, and the ship left without Major André," Ben added. "I heard this part of the escapade from a friend who was up in that area when this was transpiring. Major John André had been left high and dry. Arnold had given him common clothes and a passport, with bogus papers made out to John Anderson—and six papers, written in Arnold's hand, of plans for taking West Point. And guess what? John André hid the plans in his stocking!" Ben slapped his forehead, mocking the stupidity of it.

"André traveled as far as Tarrytown, New York, and was stopped by three men with guns. André thought they were Tories and asked them if they belonged *to our party*. He was asked, *what party*? John André had replied, "The *lower party*," meaning the British. "*We do,*" was the answer, and André then told them he was a British officer. He certainly was easy to fool."

"And how smart was that?" Sarah interrupted this time.

Ben gave her a look of annoyance for interrupting. "To John André's surprise, they responded that they were American scouts and patriots and that he was their prisoner. Major André then tried to trick them and said he was an American officer. However, it was too late; their suspicions were aroused. They searched him and found Benedict Arnold's six pages of plans in his stocking. How dumb could he have been, carrying those plans on his person? André tried to bribe them with his horse and watch, but they would not listen; and this was very unusual. Bribes went on all the time. I guess that they realized that this was too big an involvement for them."

"This is so hard to believe," Sunny replied. "Arnold and André's behavior was almost childish.

"I heard that the scouts took him to the American army's headquarters in Tappan, New York. André was tried as a spy in October, found guilty of being behind American lines under a feigned name and in a disguised habit and was sentenced to be hanged," Ben replied and shook his head.

"Sir Henry Clinton, you remember him? André's superior? He had just moved his command to New York. He and other officers, it was said, did all they could for John André, but Clinton refused Washington's request to surrender Benedict Arnold to him in exchange for John André. André appealed to General Washington to be shot, rather than hanged, but that was refused because of the rules of war." Ben paused, still finding the entire event almost ludicrous. André was hanged last week in Tappan,

New York, on October 2, 1780. He was only 31 years old. Dear god, the consequences of war."

Sunny ended the conversation with her view from a woman's side. "It is said that John André endeared himself to all the American officers, with his charm and likableness. His hanging saddened the Americans, as well as the British. The day before André's death, it was reported, he drew a likeness of himself with pen and ink."

"That is indeed sad," Sarah said. "Even though he was our enemy, I feel that perhaps he was too much influenced by Benedict Arnold. Too bad that John André did not inform General Washington of Benedict Arnold's plan. Arnold used André."

"I think the whole thing is rather weird," Sunny commented, rolling her eyes. "And Peggy was not that pretty," she said, and they all laughed. "She must have had assets to offer that were well hidden." Sunny grinned.

"Sunny!" Sarah said. "Shame on you!" But she laughed too, and Ben laughed with them.

"Well," Ricardo got up from the table and announced, "I have to get back to Batsto. This has been quite a learning experience for me; although I do not know if the information holds any importance in the overall scheme of things." He laughed and he and Sarah left.

1781

I find it too depressing to report here all the deaths in our extended family. The early year brought a British defeat at Cowpens, North Carolina. The victory of General Daniel Morgan over the British many felt was the battle that turned the tide in the south.

In March, the Americans were defeated at Guilford Courthouse. Major General Nathanael Greene was in command of approximately 4,500 American militia and Continentals. However, he was tactically defeated by Lord Charles Cornwallis' smaller British army, numbering only about 1,900 veteran regulars and German allies.

After more than two hours of intense and brutal fighting, Cornwallis forced Greene to withdraw from the field. This, in the end, served Greene well, preserving his army from many fatalities. Cornwallis' victory had cost him more than 25 percent of his army. Weakened in his campaign against Greene, Cornwallis abandoned the Carolinas and hoped for success in Virginia. Here are two quotes I felt worthy to include in my journal.

Great generals are scarce—there are few Morgans around.

Nathanael Greene

I never saw such fighting since God made me. The Americans fought like demons.

Lt. General Charles Earl Cornwallis

Benjamin VanHameetman
His Journal

In the beginning of 1781, Sunny and Ben's third son was born. They named him Horatio. "This is definitely the last one," Sunny said. However, baby Horatio was welcomed warmly into the family.

Once Ben had time to analyze and digest the Guildford Courthouse, North Carolina battle, he decided that he was happy over this last Greene Cornwallis encounter because Nathanael Greene had managed to clear the interior of South Carolina and Georgia of Cornwallis' troops. Even though Cornwallis had technically won, he had abandoned the Carolinas for good, probably due to his terrible losses in that last meeting with Greene. Nathanael Green's clearing of these southern states, was a sure sign that the war was ending. The talk ran wild about Cornwallis leaving the Carolinas.

"Hold on to your breeches, Ben," Sunny told him. "The best is yet to be realized. I just know it. The war will soon be over." Ben prayed that she was right.

In October of 1781, General Washington knew that the British were digging in at Yorktown. He recognized his chance to finish them off and requested the aid of the French fleet from the French admiral. The admiral agreed, on his own, to come to Washington's aid; there was no specific authorization from the French government.

The French admiral had played a dual role: he prevented the British fleet from coming to the aid of the British troops at Yorktown, he helped in the battle that was waged there. The plan worked. The British found themselves defeated at Yorktown and surrendered. They evacuated Charleston and Savannah.

Washington finally had defeated his arch enemy, Cornwallis. Lord Cornwallis surrendered his seamen and soldiers on October 19, 1781 at Yorktown, Virginia to the combined American and French forces, commanded by General George Washington.

In 1782, the British still occupied New York; despite this, peace talks began. "The English are unable to conquer the north and are defeated in the south. Their home support has dried up, and they have had enough," Ben declared.

"Yes, indeed," Andrew gloated. "The Redcoats have had enough. I heard that they sent Thomas Grenville, the British politician, into negotiations in Paris with John Adams and Ben Franklin for the Americans. You know trouble is afoot between Adams and Franklin. They can barely tolerate one another. The two had better put aside their petty differences, settle down, and get on with the peace treaty."

"Nothing will happen overnight. The talks will halt the war and we have to be thankful for that," Ben offered.

In October of 1782, a terrible event took place on Long Beach Island. Sunny lowered her head. "I cannot believe that this has happened under our very noses—right up in Barnegat. For heaven's sake, the peace is being negotiated. I feel so sorry for Andrew Steelman's family and the rest of his slaughtered men. They all came through the war and then to end like that."

"What happened? I am afraid to ask." Andrew waited patiently.

Sunny could not speak for a moment. "Captain Andrew Steelman and his crew of twenty five men happened upon a cutter out of Ostend, Belgium that had run aground off the Barnegat shoals. You know how bad that northern inlet is. She was bound for St. Thomas in the Dutch West Indies and had come too close to the inlet. I heard the rumor that Captain Steelman has become a privateer on his boat, the *Alligator* out of Cape May. Steelman seized the Belgium cutter and discovered that it was carrying, among other cargo, a load of Hyson tea which would fetch a nice price. Any tea has been practically impossible to obtain because of the British still controlling the seas. It was a large cargo, and Steelman needed help to unload the booty. He sent some of his crew to canvas the local area of the island and the mainland, hoping to find volunteers to help them offload the cutter."

"I did not hear anything about anyone looking for volunteers from the island," Andrew offered. "They probably went off island to the mainland right away to see who they could collect to help them."

Ben had just walked in and heard Sunny telling his father the story. "I just heard about this. And of course, we have the notorious John Bacon, the proclaimed Loyalist involved. I heard that Steelman and his men, along with some volunteers they were able to solicit, unloaded the cargo up among the dunes near the inlet and guarded it through the night. Evidently, when the crew went to look for volunteers, it was reported that the miserable rat, William Wilson of Waretown left the crew and went to look for John Bacon, probably to make a deal to Wilson's advantage. I guess he found that robber and brute, Bacon. The same one who ran and hid in the Pine Barrens so the law could not get him? The self proclaimed Loyalist? Self proclaimed for his own damned convenience!" Ben asserted, anger cracking his voice. "Bacon, along with his gang of toughs, attacked Steelman, killing him as he slept—*yes, as he slept*—then those rotten cowards proceeded to murder most of Steelman's crew. Only five escaped. It was outright slaughter. Bacon announced, once again, the convenient cry that he was a Loyalist. Loyalist, my behind!"

"I am outraged," Andrew was fuming. "And so are the rest of us. We know that Bacon is hiding under a cloak of loyalty to the King. He is certainly not fooling anyone and thank God the Governor saw through his cry of *Loyalist* and put a reward on his head."

"How did Bacon get onto the island so quickly?" Sunny was surprised.

"I did hear that Bacon and his motley crew sailed on his ship, *Hero's Revenge*, and landed on the bay side. Can you believe the name of his ship?" Ben had to stop and laugh before he went on.

"They must have sneaked from the bay side across the beach to the ocean side under the cover of darkness, like the snakes that they are. The cowards! Surprising Steelman and his crew, along with the volunteers, who were helping. I would say that Steelman's men were tired after all that unloading and with a goodly ration of rum, they were caught sleeping in the dunes. Bacon probably slew anyone in his path, volunteers and crew alike." Ben lowered his voice to a whisper. "It is a massacre of horrific proportions."

Sunny stared at Ben in disbelief. "I pray that it will never be forgotten. And those Loyalists call themselves refugees! What nonsense. If they love England so much that they call themselves refugees here, let them go home."

"A few of Steelman's men survived. I did not hear just who, but I did confirm that Bacon himself, killed Steelman," Ben stated. The story was finished, but they all knew that it would never be forgotten.

The following January of 1783, Andrew received a letter from relatives who lived in Manahawkin, with a newspaper clipping from the *New Jersey Gazette*. He read the letter aloud and he could hardly believe what he was reading.

"What is going on?" Simon had entered the room with Ricardo.

Ben opened the *New Jersey Gazette* to show them an account of a battle in Manahawkin in Jersey. "Look—here is exactly what the Gazette reported from the American side."

One of the Lenape men told me about this only yesterday, Ricardo mentioned. "I have the Loyalist paper also, showing the British side."

"Notice that it was the Jersey Gazette that published the event according to the militia report." Sunny was holding the copy of the Gazette.

"This is difficult to believe." Ben sputtered angrily. "Another battle? By god, the treaty is about to be signed, ending this war, and yet, another fight has broken out. They are calling it the *Battle of Cedar Bridge*, in Manahawkin. The skirmish took place on Friday, right after Christmas.

"Guess who was involved? John Bacon, once again, the hero Loyalist. The people hereabouts are saying that Bacon is the person most hated by the Jersey militia. I am amazed that it has taken them so long to capture him. He seems to be involved in any fight or murder or theft going on in the area. I would guess that he has many spies on the lookout for him so that he can invite himself into any money scheme, even if it means murdering; then he runs. The man has no soul."

On Friday, the 27th of December, Capt. Richard Shreve and Capt. Edward Thomas, having received information that John Bacon with his banditti of robbers, was in the neighborhood of Cedar Creek . . . collected a party of men and went immediately in pursuit of them. They met them at the Cedar Creek Bridge. The Refugees [Loyalists] . . . had greatly the advantage of Capts. Shreve and Thomas' party . . . but it was nevertheless determined to charge them. The onset on the part of the militia was furious, and opposed by the Refugees . . . for a considerable time . . . on the point of giving way when the militia was unexpectedly fired upon by a party of the inhabitants, who had suddenly come to Bacon's assistance. This put the militia into some confusion and gave the Refugees time to get off . . .

(January 8, 1783, *New Jersey Gazette*)

"I heard that the refugees, as the Loyalists are now calling themselves, along with other town inhabitants jumped into the fray and backed Captain Bacon. I cannot believe these people," Ricardo said. "They know what this man has done; they still think he is one of them—a Loyalist! Are they stupid? He would cut anyone of them down if it suited him. I think this time these supporters of Bacon have gone too far when they attacked our militia."

The *New York Gazette and the American Weekly Mercury* reported that Colonel Shreve of the militia did not have much luck in routing out Bacon. The towns people had jumped into the fray and backed Bacon.

"They will pay for doing this." Andrew could hardly believe what these towns people had done. He hoped they would be punished.

"As usual our Captain Bacon celebrated his victory. One wonders what several trophies Bacon had that were mentioned in the newspaper. I hope he does not mean dead militia. Perhaps it would have been better if Shreve had a little more fear when he met Bacon on the Cedar Creek Bridge. Obviously, they knew of the reputation of this man and his murderous ways. A number of their militiamen were wounded." Ben was angry.

January 13, 1783
Loyalist Account of Cedar Bridge
"Last Battle of the American Revolution"

Captain BACON, of the Black Joke whale boat, with six men, who left this place about the 20th of November last, retook, in little Egg harbour Bay, the sloop—, then in the possession of Capt. Badcock, and one from Philadelphia said to have been bound for Halifax; but the ice stopping him in the mouth of the inlet from bringing her off, was obliged to abandon her (having lost his Boat) and taken to the shore.

Col. SHREVE being informed of this circumstance, dispatched a party of 20 men, seven on horses, and an officer, in quest of Captain BACON and his party, who were by that time reinforced by six of General BURGOYNE's soldiers, and being apprized of the enemy's design, did not much fear the number. On the 24th ult. both parties met at Cedar Creek Bridge; the enemy, in three different attempts to charge Captain Bacon's party, killed Mr. JOHNSON, (a refugee) wounded the Captain and two of the soldiers slightly.

The other eight, not expecting any great civilities from their enemies, were determined not to be taken prisoners, and instantly charged both horse and foot, who seeing them desperate and determined, retreated, but not without loss, three horsemen and their horses, and four footmen, killed; three horsemen and six footmen badly wounded. William Cook, who commanded the horse, was among the dead. Capt. Bacon's party arrived in this city on Saturday last, with several trophies of their victory.

Simon joined in and gave his opinion. "I am somewhat surprised that the British General Burgoyne lent his men to Bacon. Just because this murderer claimed to be a Loyalist? I truly wonder if General Burgoyne knew who this person really was and all of his black dealings. I am sure that you all have noticed that the account from *The

New York Gazette and the *American Weekly Mercury* does not mention any help from General Burgoyne. I wonder what that is all about."

"This account from the Loyalist's side must have been written by the British. It smells to high heaven. What a laugh," Andrew commented. "This man, Bacon was so hated by the New Jersey militia for all his murders that after he was killed recently, *resisting arrest*; the militia threw his corpse into a cart and dragged it over fifty miles of dusty roads, throughout the countryside. They let Bacon's murderous head hang out over the end of the wagon for all to see. His grieving widow was finally given his torn and mangled body to bury, and that is how the *Gazette* summed it up. Bacon and his band raided and terrorized families who did not remain loyal to the crown. Perhaps his ending was brutal, but fit."

1783

The force of the war is over; physical and emotional wounds may take a lifetime to heal—perhaps never. Life moves forward and the VanHameetman and Scarlatti families survive and continue to grow. Our future generations will have journals full of family and historical information to show that their ancestral kinsmen were industrious, brave people. Let us hope that this trait is inherited and carried into our future generations. Let us pray that Americans one day will have more together that unites them, than divides them.

Benjamin VanHameetman
His Journal

Humanity has won its battle. Liberty now has a country."

Marquis de Lafayette

January 1784

General George Washington resigned as Commander of the Continental army on December 23, 1783.

My brother, Jack VanHameetman decided on a lifetime career in the army. He has not married. My mother has never given up hope.

The United States Constitution was adopted on September 17, 1787.

The original thirteen States as
they entered into the Union

1. Delaware	December 7, 1787
2. Pennsylvania	December 12, 1787
3. New Jersey	December 18, 1787
4. Georgia	January 2, 1788
5. Connecticut	January 9, 1788
6. Massachusetts	February 6, 1788
7. Maryland	April 28, 1788
8. South Carolina	May 23, 1788
9. New Hampshire	June 21, 1788
10. Virginia	June 25, 1788
11. New York	July 26, 1788
12. North Carolina	November 21, 1789
13. Rhode Island	May 29, 1790

New Jersey became the third state to ratify the U.S. Constitution and the first state to sign the Bill of Rights.

CHAPTER NINE

Peter Cadiz Hamilton
the Young Man

1914-1942

"You two are Americans? And what are you doing in Paris?" she wanted to know. Peter suddenly noticed his uniform hanging on the door. *Rats! No lying,* he thought as he maneuvered into unknown territory.

Okay, guys," Peter announced with gusto. He propelled himself out of his chair, throwing himself into the middle of his classmates who were sitting on the floor of the dorm lounge. "It's time to make our mark. We're up against the wall! We need to put our heads together and do something unforgettable for the class of 1914!" He emphasized *unforgettable*, punching his right fist into his left hand. "C'mon, guys! Who has a suggestion? All ideas will be heard," he continued gleefully. "Remember though, nothing destructive. A caper which can be easily reversed, a senior act, outstandingly memorable!"

Peter Cadiz Hamilton was in his senior year of high school, attending Saint John's Military Academy in Western Pennsylvania. He would graduate this year. It was a late graduation—scheduled for the beginning of July because of the multiple snowstorms that Western Pennsylvania had suffered that winter. The dorms had to be shoveled out twice that year and the main furnace had broken down twice. Class time needed to be satisfied.

Academia came easily to Peter. He had breezed through his lower grades, as well as his four years at the academy. The school was a distance from his home in New Jersey, but he enjoyed being on his own and carrying on the family tradition.

He had loved growing up on Long Beach Island; although most thought the island was dreary and deserted during the winter, Peter disagreed. He looked forward to returning to Seagate for his holiday breaks. He had many friends on the island; he kept in touch with all of his buddies who had been former classmates in the lower grades. His father belonged to the *Island Gun Club;* later, the club would change its name to the *Island Yacht and Gun Club.* At that time, the Hamiltons still owned a shipyard near Philadelphia, founded originally by Peter's VanHameetman ancestors. The Hamilton boys were all seasoned seamen and enjoyed sailing their own boat year round. When the Gun Club and Yacht Club came together, they were delighted. Peter and his brothers, Ray, Jerry and Malcolm were active in the island sports; trap shooting was popular, as was hunting the wild game birds and both surf and deep water fishing. They enjoyed the camaraderie the club offered. Then there was ice boating on the frozen lower waters of the bay, and the lake in Manahawkin. The brothers worked part time in the family shipyard during the summer. However, they still found time to enjoy the island's offerings in the wonderful salt waters that surrounded Long Beach Island.

When his parents, Joseph and Madeline visited St. John's Academy, they had ridden the train through from Beach Haven on the island, to Whitings. Then they made their way to the ferry to Philadelphia where they caught the train to Columbia, Pennsylvania and Saint John's Military Academy.

This year however, the new causeway bridge opened on June 20, 1914 linking the island to the mainland. Peter's parents could now hire a driver to motor them across the new bridge and on into Philadelphia to the Pennsylvania Railroad station. Here they would catch the train to Columbia. They ceased using the Beach Haven train, which took much longer.

Joseph, Peter's father, a tall, slim man with dark hair, dark eyes and a kind smile remembered when he was young and attending the academy, how he had ridden the trains. There was no bridge to the island then; he would pick up the train in Beach Haven and ride to Whitings, New Jersey. Then it was a hassle getting into Philadelphia to catch the train to Columbia. He was happy that now he could take a car to the mainland and then into Philadelphia and the train station.

Peter's mother, Madeline, a petite woman, with dark auburn hair and bright blue eyes, enjoyed her visits and always opted to stay in one of the smaller hotels near the academy. "My mini vacation, Cherie," she would say to Joseph. She always expressed herself with great enthusiasm. Madeline was French born and still carried a slight accent.

Peter was outgoing and charismatic. He definitely had a mind of his own, which sometimes led him down the wrong path with his instructors. However, most of Peter's teachers enjoyed his bright, challenging mind and quickly became his mentors. Peter's thick, dark hair complimented his piercing brown eyes, which were always on the alert to his surroundings and to other people. He missed nothing. When he smiled or laughed, his slightly full lips presented straight white teeth. His modified Roman nose was perhaps a throwback to his Spanish heritage on his father's side. He displayed a strong physical presence at more than six feet tall with broad shoulders, probably from his love of athletics. His smile melted young women's hearts and he had the reputation of being quite the ladies' man. But he was kind and sensitive to others. This part of his personality moved him forward, whether he was aware of that or not. His mother knew that genuine kindness flowed through his entire personality. He was not motivated to use this asset as anything but what it appeared to be. He tried, on a daily basis to fulfill his motto of *Do unto others.* Peter's sense of humor drew others to him; his benign mischievousness was contagious and resulted in his popularity with fellow students.

As president of the Class of 1914, he felt that it was time to plan a caper that would be memorable. He wanted his class to be remembered in the chronicles of the academy and spoken of, for years to come.

His father, Joseph, and his Grandfather Theodore had graduated from the same prep school; Peter would be the third Hamilton to matriculate from Saint John's Military Academy. Joseph had gone on to a military college and then into the military. Theodore had graduated from the academy in 1863 and had joined the Union army to fight in the Civil War.

Peter was undecided about his future. His father had used his education to further his career in the military. After an early retirement, he continued to work part time as a consultant to the Government in foreign affairs—a large miscellaneous tag that covered much. Joseph tended to be closed mouth about his business affairs and his contacts. Peter had deduced that his father was involved in military weapons, or something similar. Joseph traveled frequently, not only in the states, but also to those foreign countries where the United States was ensconced.

Peter and his friends sat in the dorm lounge now, hunched around the radio, listening to the most recent news of the war in Europe. They had met to discuss their plans for the end of the year caper, but the news dominated. They listened awhile, then retreated to Peter and Hank's room.

"Today is Monday," Peter announced, looking at the calendar on the wall. "I can hardly believe that graduation is here. Our parents will be up this weekend. We have to have our plans in place before then, so let's get the ideas rolling. Remember, something benign. We don't want to destroy any property. Something that will make the Class of 1914 stand out above former capers!" He looked at his friends and smiled broadly.

"I have an idea," Hank, Peter's roommate stood up. "Let's put the school up for sale!" *Hear, hear* and applause came from the gang for that super proposal.

"Excellent," Peter saw that the group was enthusiastic about the suggestion. "Think about it guys. We'll meet after dinner, at the shack."

The group gathered later at the edge of the campus, in the old grounds keeper's hut. Hank offered his ideas first. "This will work out superbly if we use the front lawn of the main building to set up a huge sign, *School for Sale, Best Offer.*"

"Great thinking, Hank—colossal!" All agreed.

"What if we string a big banner between the main building lamppost and the post on the walkway? That would make it easier than us putting in posts," Feeney offered.

"Good thinking, my man Feeney," Peter agreed.

"Okay, there are six of us here. I think we would need about ten senior men to help us pull this off." Hank looked at the group.

"Do we need that many?" Feeney was skeptical.

"Let's make a list of what has to be done, then we can see for sure." Peter always wrote everything down and had his friends sign it. This held those involved responsible for their part of the bargain and no one could duck out.

"We should first decide on the banner's size, material and lettering." Sam was the pragmatist of the group. "We need to plan ahead, in detail."

"Canvas would probably be the best bet. It would be easy to paint and it's neutral in color." Peter said.

"What size are you guys thinking?" Hank was wondering where they could purchase such material.

"How about either a canvas six foot by nine foot, or a six foot by three foot?" Skeeter spoke up.

Feeney chimed in. "What color paint should we use?"

"Hold it, let's summarize. Someone will have to check out where we can buy a piece of canvas. I would try the local fabric store." Skeeter looked around. "Who has a sister or a girlfriend here? I want to use a woman to go into the material store. If they see the banner they'll remember anyone who came in to purchase a piece of canvas that large. If the store doesn't carry it, they could tell us where we can get it. Second, I think the six foot by nine foot would be too large to handle. I feel that we should stick with the six foot by three foot canvas and make up a bunch of smaller signs. We can do all of that right in one of our rooms. The smaller signs could say, books, pencils, desks, and on and on and stick them in the ground around the central banner." Skeeter paused.

"The paint should be red. Feeney, our artist can take care of the lettering. What say you all?" Peter asked for other ideas, but they all felt that this scheme was the best.

"You all know Marion, my girl friend. She has a close mouth. We can use her to visit the material store." Skeeter was sure about her; Peter wrote her name down on his list.

"I still think the less men involved the better. You can be sure a leak will happen if we have too many guys involved." Sam was being real.

"Do you think that six of us can do it?"

"Yeah, Pete, I do." Skeeter was sure.

Peter called for a vote for the go ahead and then the work was divided up. "Let me know in another day how you make out," he told Skeeter, who was to be responsible for the canvas. "After we clear that, we can go ahead with the paint and the plans for installation. I can front this and then when we get the total spent we can split it up. Any objections?" There were none; they broke up and returned to the dorm.

"Don't forget the police," Sam reminded them as they left. "We need two lookouts—one on Main Street, and one on Mercer Street where it meets Main. I will see if I can come up with their routes this week."

Peter walked into his room, and picked up a message from the office switchboard that his father had called and left a message when his family would arrive.

Peter's parents and Grandfather, Theodore, were making plans for the long trip from southern New Jersey. Grandfather Ted, a stocky man of medium height, with gray hair and clear hazel eyes was getting on in age, but still hearty and looking forward to his grandson's graduation.

Ted's Grandfather Neil had built Seagate House in the early 1800s and Seagate had been home to generations of VanHameetmans, before the name change to Hamilton. Peter and his three brothers along with his father, Joseph and Grandfather Ted, had been raised in Seagate House, where they all still resided. Peter often asked Grandfather Ted to tell him about the building of Seagate. "Do you remember Neil building it?" Peter would ask when he was a child. And when his Grandfather Ted started speaking of Neil, Peter would ask how he was related to Neil.

"Let me see now, Pete. Neil was my grandfather. Jon, his son and Cerise were my parents. They died very young, in a drowning. I was six years old and only have a few memories of them and the oil painting hanging in the library. Neil and Johanna, my grandparents raised me in Seagate House. They nearly lost their minds when my father and mother drowned in the ocean. It was so sad. My parents were in their small Chris Craft, about a mile out when a squall line came up suddenly. It quickly swamped their boat and it sank. My mother was an excellent swimmer, but they found out later that she had suffered a severe head injury, probably from the boat itself. They had no rubber raft with them and evidently their life jackets were no match for that stormy ocean. Knowing my father, it was said that he had probably tried to save her, but he was no match for that rough ocean and they both drowned. The medical examiner proclaimed drowning and after reading all the evidence, my grandfather told me that he believed that it was correct. They found both my parents a few days later, washed up on the beach, with their life jackets still on. I don't think my grandfather and grandmother ever recovered from the loss. Jon was their first and only child. I was their only grandchild.

I am your grandfather, so you would be the fifth
generation down from Neil; who was Sunny and Ben's
son. I wasn't even alive when Neil built Seagate house,
Pete. His given name was Cornelius, but they called him
Neil. He was an infant when the old war ended, around
1790. That's the Revolutionary War, son," he reminded
Peter. "Neil had siblings you know. Hannah, Matthew
and Horatio. I do know that Horatio was killed in a tree
cutting accident; perhaps one of the family can look up
the genealogy of Hannah and Matthew."

"Neil used the magnificent cedar from the island and
wonderful, indigenous woods from the Tuckerton area to
build the house. I just remember my grandfather being
almost militant in his upkeep of Seagate over the years.
The humidity was hard on the house, but the wonderful
cedar stood up to the brunt of the shore weather. It was
quite a feat in those years when Neil built Seagate house.
There were few homes, perhaps some out buildings and
fishing huts on the island and a few old whaling shacks
further north. Seagate House has held up well, for being
as old as she is." He paused to swat a fly that had been
bothering him and yelled to please keep the screen doors
closed.

"What was the island like, back when you were a boy
grandfather?"

"In the very early days, way before I was born, the
ocean was rife with pirates. Our ancestors' journals tell
of the pirate activities—more so from 1750 through the
Revolutionary War. Not that I was living then. The family
had the Lenape and Iroquois Indians as protectors or I
don't know how they would have survived. Evidently the
island had the reputation of the ferocious Iroquois Indians
being frequent visitors and the pirates rarely set foot upon
Long Beach. The better for our ancestors. But some pirates
were more bold. They even killed cattle here and there, to
feed their men. These were the cattle that mainlanders
swam over to the island and turned loose to graze in the
fresh water grasses of the Great Swamp. Our cattle also
grazed there. During that time there was so much piracy

and then privateering going on right off the coast that it made it all but impossible to sail the ocean waters. It was whispered that the coast off the Barnegat inlet should be avoided at all costs. There were reports of seeing pirates burying chests of booty in that area. Treasure hunters searched for years, but nothing was ever found. The rocky low bottoms were threatening enough, but it was said that the Devil held reign there. To destroy the ships sailing on the ocean route, the island squatters would tie a lantern around a mule and lead him in a circle around a haystack simulating a light house beam—when the mule walked past the stack, the light would disappear for a second. It was thought that this would be mistaken for a lighthouse and lead ships in further to the beach to wreck and then plunder. It also was said that the first settlement was made near the Great Swamp. The exact date of the first whalers on the island was unknown, but a patent was given to the family Soper in 1690." He paused for a minute. "I do believe the VanHameetmans were here earlier than that. Again, I would have to look at the journals. I wonder why the VanHameetmans never received word about a land patent. That probably was why there was no record of our family settling on the island earlier. I wonder who gave the Soper family their patent. That's something else I need to look into."

"Let's see now, Pete." His grandfather paused a moment to collect his memories. "I was schooled on the Island in a private home, as your father had been. One of our ancestor cousins was an early graduate of the College of New Jersey, chartered in 1746 and then moved to Princeton, New Jersey in 1756. This cousin established and ran one of the first schools on the island. The tradition of teaching continued for many years. That part of the VanHameetman line had the reputation of turning out excellent educators. The island was very fortunate to have them. The school rooms were in the community building in the family compound. It was only after I had graduated did I realize what an excellent education they had given me. Then I was sent to Saint John's Academy and graduated in 1863 in the midst of the Civil War." Ted stopped to gather his thoughts. "Where were we? Oh, yes, the Civil War years. In the 1860's the Civil War came. The War had been raging about two years after much of the South had seceded from the Union—after Lincoln was elected. Without advising my parents, I joined the Union army. When I look back now, I realize what a daring and pigheaded young man I was," Ted admitted to Peter. "And because I was a graduate of a military academy, the Union army took me as a second lieutenant."

Peter felt honored that his grandfather spoke to him of the war. He rarely spoke of it, usually only saying, "I hope that I will not live to see another war so bloody, where brother is pitted against brother and father against son."

Not only had the war taken so many lives, but the yellow fever epidemic hit parts of the South with such viciousness that entire towns were wiped out. "My first cousin was lost in that yellow fever epidemic in Wilmington, North Carolina, helping to care for the sick. It nearly killed his father and mother. He is buried in the National cemetery there."

Ted had suffered a severe leg wound from a musket shot and had been sent to a large hospital in the north to recuperate. More than once, he had said, "*The medicine of today would have been some impossible, futuristic dream back in the middle 1860s.*"

He could not wait to get back to Seagate House, to the peace and sanctuary near the water to distract himself from the terrible memories that he would always carry. His very soul had been wounded. Ted could never purge or escape the demons that continued to live deep within. His only recourse was to repress those horrors, but never could he wipe his memory clean, or soften them when they seeped through into his consciousness.

Ted's wife, Lucy, Peter's grandmother, had passed away at a young age from disease of the throat, probably diphtheria, leaving Ted with their only child, Joseph to raise. Ted always thanked God that Lucy's mother, Della, a strong, determined Scots woman and a widow, had come to live at Seagate. Yet, she was kind and caring and raised Joseph well. Ted had stayed at Seagate House to ease his grief and to help raise his son. *It is the most restful place in this world,* he would declare. He had his solitude when he desired; he also had family and friends near. He never remarried.

In 1914, just before Peter's graduation, the world heard of the assassination of Archduke Ferdinand and his family. The students and their history professor kept close tabs on the volatile events that the world experienced because of the attack. The students met in the assembly room and discussed the history leading up to the assassination.

The Archduke Franz Ferdinand had been heir to Austria Hungary's throne. The assassins, a group of seven young Serbian anarchists, did their dirty, cowardly work on June 28, 1914, in Sarajevo, in the Balkans.

The students had discussed the incident intently. Many felt the explosion of world tensions would cause a domino effect that could bring about total war. Certainly, this had put a dark cloud on their graduation; they felt that war would come to the states without a doubt.

Peter had commented, "Do you realize the number of countries involved? It certainly cannot be a straightforward matter. I have been trying to decide whether to enlist now, or wait until the United States becomes involved. Let's think about it." He looked around at his silent friends. They had recognized the validity of what he had said.

When Peter's parents, grandfather, and three younger brothers had arrived on Friday afternoon, they met for dinner in the small hotel near the Academy. After the greetings and small talk, the conversation turned to the international unrest, which many foresaw as a prelude to imminent war. Peter noticed that his grandfather was visibly upset. "But Pop Pop," Peter said falling back to the childhood name he had called his grandfather, "the war will be here and we will have to deal with it. It's not going to go away."

"I'm not that much out of touch," the old man had responded, somewhat miffed. "I lived though one nightmare of death and it is very difficult to hear talk of another war upon this country—my country! Enough is enough!"

Peter looked at his father and decided not to carry the conversation further. He had thought of mentioning the plans that he and his group had discussed, of joining up. His grandfather's face had deterred him from speaking further.

Madeline quickly jumped in and changed the subject. "Do you need any help with your packing up, son?" She did not want to discuss war. She had four sons—Peter was the elder—and any talk of war took her thoughts in an unbearable direction. "Would you like your brothers to stay after graduation and help you pack and ride home on the train with you? I think it would be wise to stay in Philadelphia overnight in the apartment. We can send someone for you the next morning." Joseph maintained a small apartment in the city. He was often in Philadelphia on business, and he found it more convenient to stay in his own place.

Peter responded with an enthusiastic nod of his head. "That's great, Mom. I would be glad to have them help me." He didn't enjoy the cleaning up and packing.

After dinner, Grandfather Ted excused himself early, saying he was tired and wanted to retire. "Good night to all," he said as he got up to leave. "I hope you have no thoughts Peter, of getting involved in this monstrosity, that will soon have a life of its own," he said, referring to the impending war. Peter did not respond, and his grandfather left them. Madeline dismissed his younger brothers and asked them to accompany their grandfather up the stairs to his room.

Joseph looked at his son and Peter saw concern on his face. "Are you thinking of joining, son? You are too young, Peter, and far too naïve in life to go into this war. There is a very good chance that you would not come back, or come back severely wounded. At least wait until your own country is drawn in. I'm asking you to think about that."

Madeline watched her son across the table and shook her head, knowing how strong willed he was. "I don't know what to say to you, Peter. This war is not ours yet. I don't think I could live if I lost you," her voice broke. "You know that your Aunt Gina and Uncle Claude still live outside of Paris. I hope my sister and her family leave there if the danger comes to her door. I have not heard from her recently. Please tell us that you're not thinking of voluntarily enlisting, my dear." Tears overcame her.

Peter sat quite still for a moment. "I won't lie to you. My friends and I have spoken about joining up when we turned eighteen. We'll all have that birthday by the fall; but Mom, nothing is written in stone. Let's not speak of it now. And I will think about what Father has asked me to do." He reached over and patted her hand.

Madeline kissed her son good night and stood up to leave, only to hesitate. Peter could see that she was upset. "I must write to Gina tomorrow or try to call her. I'm going to offer Seagate as a refuge. I think that they should leave Paris now, before events escalate."

Peter bade his parents good night and walked back to the dorm.

He did take his father's counseling under advisement and spoke with his friends that night. "You know, my parents are right. I guess we're all fired up and ready to go. But would we be fighting for America? I don't even know. My father wants me to wait until when and if our country becomes involved. Let's think about that." There were no rebuttals.

After midnight, Peter and his friends sneaked off and did their dirty deed. Feeney unrolled the piece of canvas which he had worked on in his dorm room. The group stood back to admire his handiwork, congratulating themselves on a job well done. They did not push their luck or the time however, and got right to it. They strung the large banner between the planned posts and stuck about fifteen little banners in front of it and then hot footed it back to the dorm. They were well pleased with their work.

At 2:00 a.m., police sirens screamed, and bedlam ensued in Peter and Hank's room. "Holy Moses!" Hank yelled. "The cops are here for us," he cried as he jumped out of bed. He was halfway to the window to look for the police car when he tripped over a chair and screamed in pain as he hit the floor, hard.

Peter was half asleep and wrapped in the sheets. He tried to get out of bed when he heard Hank scream. He struggled to free himself and rolled off the bed. "Damn it!" he yelled as he hit the floor. As the sirens continued, he was still in the grip of the sheets. Peter's blood ran cold. *Someone surely saw us hanging our work,* he thought. He sent a stream of obscenities flying through the air and stubbed his toe on the bedpost, trying to break free from the bed wrappings.

Hank was already at the window. "Damn, I can't get the blinds up." They were trying to peek through the slats. They stood there, out of breath, Hank from his tripping, and Peter from his fight with the sheets. Hank tried to pull up the wooden blinds too roughly and the entire works came completely off the track. "Look out!" he yelled, but it was too late. They were both hit in the head and face with the Venetian blinds. That was the final insult.

"What the hell is going on out there?" Peter asked.

"I don't see anything," Hank answered, peering right and left.

"There it is," Peter whispered. They saw the red flashing lights from the police car, now far off, racing down the road. They sat there looking at each other in the half lights of the outside shining through the window. "I thought they were coming for us!"

"Must have been an accident or someone sick," they decided.

"I guess they didn't even see the banner from that angle of the road; it's black as pitch out there." Hank offered.

"Maybe they did see it and left it alone. One of the cops is pretty neat. Maybe that's what happened," Peter speculated.

"Man that was a close one!" Hank caught his breath and they both collapsed, rolling on the floor, howling with laughter now. "How great was that? The law going by and not spotting our handiwork."

Hank came to breakfast the next morning with a black eye; Peter could hardly walk his toe hurt so badly. Both had abrasions on their heads and faces from the blinds.

As predicted, that Sunday morning drew crowds of locals, students and parents. They all stood laughing at a banner that could not be missed. Whispers and guesses flew around the dorm. Who could have done this? *Congrats to those men,* they applauded. Not even the seniors knew the answer, but many of them would have named Pete and his crew. It was one of the best senior capers that had ever been pulled off.

Feeney was with his parents at the Purple Rooster Restaurant near the dorm and came outside when he saw Peter and Hank. "What do the other guys look like?" Feeney inquired with a straight face.

"Don't even ask. You would never believe it anyway. Move on, man." Peter could not get his shoe on over his toe.

"We were busting, man." Hank told Feeney about the police. Feeny grinned, rehashing their mishap and then excited at the outcome of their work. "I'm sure the parents heard all about it. I bet the Purple Rooster Restaurant was crowing," Hank laughed.

"My folks are over at the Gateway Inn. I told them I would see them after the ceremony. They'll fill me in. I'm sure they must have seen the banner. I'll hear about it later. Right now, we have to get moving. Graduation first, lunch and then packing up this afternoon. I'll have to wear a slipper or cut out the top of a sneaker." Peter was still annoyed about his toe. The he recapped the previous night to Hank again and allowed himself a laugh. Then, they both became hysterical with laughter.

"I thought I'd wet myself," Hank confided, once he stopped laughing.

"I think I did," Peter could hardly get the words out, setting them off again.

"What a gas!" Hank commented after they had calmed down. "What a night to remember!"

At lunch in the main hall later, Madeline remarked to Peter that the graduation ceremony had been lovely. Joseph and Ted grunted their agreement as they stuffed themselves from a variety of food set out buffet style. "Hey Pete, did you hear anything about who put that big banner up?" Malcolm, his younger brother asked.

"What do you mean? I didn't hear anything," Peter tried to keep a straight face.

"We know that the seniors put that banner up. We just wonder who it was. We heard the people in the restaurant talking about it. We could see it from the Inn. Do you know who did it?"

Peter looked at his brothers. "How would I know?"

His father and grandfather looked at Peter and held their silence.

"What?" Peter asked, trying hard not to crack up.

"Nothing," Joseph answered. "Nothing at all." His father tried not to smile and continued eating. "We'll be leaving after we finish here. Pop is ready to go home. By the way Pete, what's that on your foot? A new style or do you need money to buy yourself a new pair of sneakers? I think that's what they call running shoes now."

"I'll be packed and out of here fast, with all the help." Peter ignored the comment his father had just made. "See you at home. Hank's driving us to the station this afternoon. We'll be on the 3:00 p.m. train. We can take a cab to the apartment."

"You have your key? And money for the train?" Peter nodded his head. He was anxious to get underway. "Here, take this," Joseph slipped him a twenty dollar bill. Peter accepted it when he remembered that he had four tickets to buy.

In August of that year, 1914, Austria Hungary declared war on Serbia; Russia entered the war, allying with the Serbs; France joined Russia. Germany, an ally of Austria Hungary, then tried to reclaim territory from France, lost in 1871 and invaded French Alsace Lorraine. England immediately joined with the French and the Russians. As the war took on momentum, it also took on a life of its own, as Grandfather Ted had predicted.

During that summer, Peter remarked to his father, "I think that we need a scorecard to remember who is whose enemy, and who is allied with whom." He and his father felt strongly that it would only be a matter of time until America would be targeted, or another incident would force President Woodrow Wilson to jump into the fray.

"I pray with all my heart that America stays out of it," Joseph said to his son. "Nevertheless, if American lives are at stake, I do realize that Wilson will be forced to act."

On May 7, 1915, German torpedoes sunk the British ship, *Lusitania*, killing more than one hundred Americans. Although there was no United States Declaration of War, four young men reported to the enlistment office that June.

"We have all honored our parents' request, and we have waited to enlist. You know what happened on May 7. Americans are dead," Peter declared to his parents. "We're going to the recruiting office together. I don't know if we will be able to stay together, but at least we can enlist together."

"What about university? You could be a sophomore this fall."

"We have one year under our belts, father. The rest of College will have to wait."

Not all who applied for military duty were accepted. Some were physically impaired; others were under age, or the only means of support for their family. Some were too old and some were mentally unfit. The four young men were assigned to Camp Greene, a new army camp in Charlotte, North Carolina which had been named after the Revolutionary War hero, Nathanael Greene. The area selected to build the base was once a cotton and vegetable growing area. Suddenly tents and wooden barracks, along with new roads, changed the entire face of that rural area. Camp Greene's location had been chosen specifically by the army for its available transportation system, its great source of water and the amount of open land. The camp had been built in less than ninety days and had soon become a city unto itself. Troop trains continued to pour in, carrying young men from all States, along with supplies.

Peter and his friends reached Camp Greene in the middle of the day, on a troop train out of Philadelphia. "Dear God," Peter remarked, wiping the sweat from his face. "This humidity and heat will kill us before we even see any action!" He thought of the cool environment of his academy in the Pennsylvania hills and of Seagate House with its ocean breezes flowing through the house all summer. It was June, 1915.

The first long weeks of training were rough on the body and mind, but eventually completed. Peter was assigned to communications; his buddies were assigned to several other areas. They grumbled at the separation, but they knew that this had been anticipated; soldiers were assigned to meet the army's needs, not the enlistees.

Peter's background was quite different from his friends, because of his mother's roots. French was the second language spoken in Seagate House. Peter was fluent in French, and after studying German at the academy for four years, he could converse in German as well. He was a self taught, proficient typist. He typed his school assignments on his small, portable Remington typewriter. He found it easier than writing long hand. The army would further train him in code, portable and mobile radio equipment, wireless telegraph communications, FM radio and advanced field telephones. Peter was not happy with his first assignment to Washington, D.C. Then his assignment had been extended six months. His friends had shipped out to France. His parents however, were delighted. Their son would be in D.C. for a time, within visiting distance.

During his next assignment Peter was trained expansively, including heavy indoctrination into all aspects of military code. His training touched the periphery of French and Belgian intelligence. The Army did not usually snag a bright, young man who spoke both French and German; they took advantage of his assets. After his last assignment in military code and considering his prior military academy background, his year of college and his language abilities, Peter was given a top secret clearance. He would be working in Army Intelligence, although he was only twenty years old. It was wartime—he was promoted to second lieutenant.

His father thought that advancements were coming too quickly for Peter. He communicated his concerns off handedly to one of Peter's superiors on a visit to D.C. The officer told Joseph clearly, that it was wartime and that Peter was well qualified and well trained. They needed men of his caliber. Qualifications, not age, dictated assignments and promotions. Madeline had been greatly annoyed and told Joseph in no uncertain terms, that it had been none of his business about Peter and that he had stepped over the line, questioning his son's superior. She asked him not to mention this to Peter.

When Peter had completed this training, it was late 1916. His entire background now would fit like a glove with his next assignment. He was approaching his twenty first birthday and he was promoted to First Lieutenant.

In the beginning of January 1917, the headquarters office of the United State's Intelligence operation was attached to Folkestone, Kent, in England, as an adjunct of the British intelligence effort. One of the American offices was located in a Paris suburb, under Captain Hon. G. J. G. Bruce. The British Captain Bruce's chief function was recruiting agents from among Belgian and French men and women. Peter was eventually assigned to Captain Bruce in another, smaller branch office and he left for France in January. Peter's office was cloaked as a local U.S. Government commodity store, in charge of foodstuff and other supplies. A mixed group worked in the office. They recruited and then worked with only French agents; although half of the group were French Americans—French, but not native born.

In February 1917, British Intelligence issued a high level report that a plot had been uncovered between Germany and Mexico to invade the United States across its southern borders. One month later, German submarines sank five American merchant vessels. The war was creeping closer.

"Listen up, guys!" Peter was openly agitated. "It's happening. The President has requested the United States Congress to declare war. I hope Congress approves the request quickly." His friends in the office cheered.

On April 6, 1917, Congress approved the request, and President Wilson declared war on Germany. "Good for Wilson. No one can just go about sinking our ships," Peter declared loudly. He sat at his desk and made a list of the Central Powers—America's enemies, which included Austria Hungary, Bulgaria, Germany, and Turkey. He wanted to understand who was involved.

"Let's make a list of our allies," a colleague suggested. By the time they were finished, their list of U.S. allies included Belgium, Brazil, China, Cuba, France, Great Britain, Greece, Italy, Japan, Liberia, Montenegro, Portugal, Romania, Russia, San Marino, Serbia, and Siam.

"Quite a list," Peter acknowledged. Then he threw out a question to his co-workers. "What's going to happen to those countries not on either list?" There was silence.

One of the senior officers walked in during the middle of the discussion. He spoke up. "Those countries not declaring themselves will probably be either affected due to their geographic locations, or will lose their diplomatic relations. This war, I'm afraid, will have even more far reaching effects than we first had thought."

Peter set up contacts and communication procedures for the newly recruited agents. Within a short time, he had established the agents' locations and their duties.

They would now be passed on for more intensive training.

The neighbors in the area of the small military offices where Peter worked had no idea what was truly transpiring in their neighborhood.

"I guess the ruse of the office being involved with foodstuff has worked," Peter declared. He worked with, and became friends with Robert, a young, second generation Belgian from the United States east coast. Robert spoke French, German, and Flemish fluently. He was near Peter's age—tall and slim with light brown, curly hair and gentle, blue eyes.

"Why don't you stop looking for an apartment?" Peter asked Robert. "We do okay together. My apartment has two bedrooms and it's close to the office. With the army's off base living allotment, we should do better than okay, sharing costs."

"Thanks, old man," Robert said, jumping at the offer. "This makes my life easier. We can split everything. Looking for an apartment is a pain. This will work out and I like company."

On a frosty morning that winter, Peter had decided to visit his Aunt Gina and Uncle Claude who lived in the outskirts of Paris. He called his aunt and she invited him to the house. He remembered her and his two cousins vividly from their visit to Seagate a number of years before. She gave him directions via public transportation and he quickly found the house. His aunt greeted him warmly in French. "Peter, my nephew, I would know you anywhere, even though you are now a grown man. Come in, come in," she said and took his arm to steer him into a large front room.

He handed her his coat, sat down and asked how she, Uncle Claude, and the boys had been over the years. "Your elder cousin, Jon, attends University in Basel, Switzerland. Your younger cousin, Yves, is here in the local school, in sixth grade. They are both doing fine. How they would love to see you." She offered him coffee and a plateful of small cakes and cookies from the buffet. "My, how handsome you are in your uniform, Peter. I see that you have already gained the first lieutenant's bars?"

"Yes. I am grateful that my mother insisted that we speak French at home. It's been a great asset. Poor Father had to learn French too," he said and laughed. "You speak so rapidly, Aunt Gina, but I can keep up!"

He took a minute to look at his aunt more closely. She was petite like his mother, with dark hair, dark eyes, and a full, red mouth; she was stylish in her red dress and tasteful in her jewelry. He noticed the good sized diamonds ornamenting her ears and the lovely, diamond necklace containing small, matching rubies.

She laughed and spoke English, "You know I do speak English, but then I am not around too many English speaking people now. But I will yield to English if you are more comfortable."

"It's all right, however you want."

Gina nodded to him and continued to speak rapidly in French, asking him, "How is my sister? And your father and grandfather? And how is the rest of the family? And your brothers? I think one of them was just a little ahead of Yves in age, no? And have you found a nice place to stay? Your mother wrote that you were not in the barracks, but in town? And you have a nice roommate? Too bad you are in the other side of Paris. I know it is a trip, but then, here you are. Please, please, Peter, tell me all." She drew in a deep breath and sat down.

Peter did respond to her rapid fire questions, and only then did he say to her, "Yes, I would like some coffee and something from that wonderful plate you offered me."

"I hope you like these raspberry tarts. They were freshly baked this morning. My younger son cannot get enough of them." She smiled at him.

As they sat and ate their sweets and drank their coffee on that cold morning, they were suddenly startled by explosions in the far distance, or what Peter thought were explosions. "Good lord, what was that?" he almost jumped out of his chair to get to the window. Then came another muffled noise and another, not as loud, but loud enough that Peter could identify that the sounds were definitely from big guns. He and Gina hurried out and in the distance they still heard the shelling.

An elderly neighbor suddenly appeared. Peter nodded to him. "What's going on? Do you know anything about the shelling, which is what I presume it is?"

"Yes, it is German artillery; I just heard from another neighbor that the Germans have broken further through the French line. They have their artillery aimed at the outskirts of Paris. Thank God, we are still out of their range." The old man stood there in the cold, wringing his hands.

Peter turned quickly to his Aunt. "You and your family can't stay here any longer. Just trust me when I say that. I have information that I cannot discuss with you—but you must leave now. You have no choice. If the Germans overrun Paris and occupy the city, you cannot stay. They are cruel and fanatical. I mean it Aunt Gina, you must leave. Go to Switzerland, where Jon is. I'm quite sure the rails to Basel are still open." His Aunt suddenly realized the danger that would be upon them.

"Call Uncle Claude, Aunt. Ask him to pick Yves up from school and come home. Get out while you still have the time. Too many people stay too long, not believing that the enemy will invade and then it's too late. They cannot leave."

"Merciful heavens, Peter. I do believe you; we will leave. I could never take the chance of staying too long." Her face was pale and she hung onto his arm.

"Come in the house now, Aunt. It's very cold out here," and he led her back inside.

She immediately telephoned Claude. They had a private telephone in the house because of Claude's business. Peter heard her say, "Yes. I can do that. I will see you in a few hours." She was silent for a moment, and then turned to Peter. "We are leaving for Basel this afternoon. Claude has already taken action. We will not risk our lives for material things. We are leaving; that is settled. If things work out, we will come back." She burst into tears. "I am to pack one suitcase for each of us," she sniffled. "I can take Flossie with me. Claude will pick up Yves from school; we will take a taxi to the train station. He will reserve the tickets over the telephone, and stop at the bank to close our accounts and transfer the monies to our account in Switzerland. We will carry some with us. Claude had opened that account in Basel some months ago. He wanted to be prepared for any outcome. Thank God he did, even though his friends laughed at his cautiousness. They told him Paris would never fall. I'm beginning to doubt that now."

"I am afraid that many people believe this. What kind of business is Uncle in?"

"Investments. There is nothing material there if they shut the doors."

"Who is Flossie?"

She smiled and went to open the bedroom door. "Flossie? Flossie, where are you, my dear one?" A little white dog ran out of a bedroom and into the living room. "I put her in the bedroom when you arrived. I didn't want her getting dog hair all over you. They do allow dogs on the train in carrying cases—I will have no trouble with her. I could never leave her behind."

The artillery booms had abruptly stopped. Peter assumed that the Germans had a contact in the immediate area to assess the damages. The German gunners would then adjust the guns' range. *God knows exactly how far reaching their guns will become*, Peter thought.

"Claude doesn't know it, but I decided weeks ago, to pack up a suitcase for each of us, just in case. He kept saying to me that we should have a plan in mind if we had to leave, but the discussion never went any further. So, a few weeks ago, on my last trip to Switzerland to see my son, I rented an apartment in Basel with a six month lease, just to be on the safe side. The manager agreed to accept incoming packages. Just recently, I shipped out what I considered important to us: picture albums, family heirlooms, and other miscellaneous items. We will have to buy some furniture. I had some doubts when I

JEANETTE H. FUSCO

did this, but now I am exceedingly glad." She tightened her lips. "I know that Claude will be relieved too."

Peter was surprised. "I know that most of the French people think a direct attack will never happen. I can tell you that I know to the contrary. You are truly remarkable, Aunt," he declared and hugged her. *She is so like my mother.* Always at the ready, always implementing plans on her own and surprisingly, her strategy turns out well. Gina had considered this an emergency and she had acted.

Within the hour, Claude and Yves burst through the door. "How are you, nephew?" Claude hugged Peter. "It certainly has been a long time; our meeting is not under the best of circumstances." Peter turned toward the young boy standing behind his father. "This is Yves." Claude nudged his son forward.

"You were just a little fellow when last I saw you." Yves grinned at Peter and offered his hand.

"Gina, are those suitcases packed?" Claude was becoming anxious.

"I've had them packed for over a month." She sent Yves to the closet to retrieve the cases.

"I can't believe that you packed these cases awhile ago, Mama," Yves struggled with the luggage. He was a tall boy, about twelve, with fair hair and light eyes and resembled his father.

Gina turned to her husband. "I have rented an apartment in Basel that should be ready for us. I have already shipped important items out. I am sorry that I did not tell you, but I just knew that I had to do it. Now I am more than glad that I went ahead with it."

"You are truly magnificent, my love, and very wise to have suggested the apartment. I am the one that is sorry that I did not follow through. Write down the address in Basel for Peter, please. We have to get going."

"I'll call mother later from work, Aunt Gina. You have enough to do," Peter offered. She thanked him and mentioned that his mother had offered them asylum at Seagate.

"All right, everyone," Claude said, "pick up your belongings and let's get going. I will leave the car in the garage. If the Germans want it, they can take it. I told the cab to wait downstairs, so let us leave."

"Going on a trip?" the cabdriver asked.

"Just going to see our son in school, and a little vacation," Claude answered, as he noticed the driver looking at the suitcases. *Who knew who the driver might be?*

The main station was a madhouse. Crowds of people were leaving. "Look at that line!" Gina commented, checking the long lines through the large glass windows of the station. "Good thing you booked over the telephone."

"And I charged the tickets to our company." Claude grinned.

Peter felt relieved that his uncle had chosen to leave immediately. Tomorrow and the next day would be even more chaotic, and the trains would be crammed.

Yves guarded their bags on the sidewalk. "Bring me that small blue bag, Yves. Yes son, the bag in your arms." Claude whispered, "Our money is in there. I will be responsible for that."

Claude remembered as a child, before his parents were lost in the atrocities of war, how they spoke of their beloved Serbia being overrun and the terrible killings and the fear. Claude and his brother had been sent ahead to Paris, to an aunt. Sadly, his parents had not gotten out in time. Now Claude berated himself again, that he had not moved more quickly this time to leave Paris. He was thankful that Gina had the courage and fortitude to take matters into her own hands.

"Goodbye, Peter," Gina said, embracing Peter tightly. Claude and Yves moved in to shake hands and hug him.

"There will be a time in the future when we will see you again. If you ever get to Basel, you have our address," Claude paused, looking at Peter. "But then, hopefully we will meet again at Seagate—such a lovely place."

Peter picked up their bags, put them in an empty pushcart and followed the little family into the station.

Peter said goodbye, wished them well, then left to find his train.

The following morning, Peter arrived late at his office and saw visitors there. "What's going on, Robert?" He watched the disruption caused by two men dressed as civilians and a third in military uniform. "What the hell's happening?"

"We may have to move if the office has been compromised," Robert told him. "That blatant attack yesterday has made the military a little jumpy about our security here. I don't know if we'll be staying at this location; although I think it would be a mistake if we moved."

"I agree," Peter nodded. "Anything that draws more attention to us is not good."

"They'll probably make a decision today," Robert offered. "I haven't heard any big guns this morning. Have you?"

"I heard the guns at my aunt's yesterday and that was enough. My aunt and her family have left Paris. I think the Germans are still too far for their artillery to reach us yet. I heard that the French ordered more troops to the front. The agents will be busy."

"As a matter of caution, I think I'll pack a rucksack tonight with the bare necessities in it. Maybe you should do the same." Robert was concerned.

Later in the day, the news came that the office would remain open, for the present anyway. They were on high alert that night, nervously puttering around the apartment, expecting to be called back to the office at any time, should some of the French agents be called into active duty.

Around 9:00 p.m., there was a knock on their door. The two moved quickly. Robert stood hidden behind the door to the kitchen, pistol at the ready. "Okay?" Peter mouthed as he walked slowly to the door, turning first to see that Robert was well placed. "I'm opening the door. You all set?" he whispered. After a nod from Robert, he opened the door.

"Sorry to bother you. My telephone is not working. It is a business phone. Do you have one? Is it working, yes?" Peter found himself staring at the pretty, green eyed blonde standing in his doorway, speaking rapidly in French.

"Who is it, Peter?" Robert called, interrupting his friend's staring at the lovely, young woman standing in the doorway.

"Sorry about that, old man," Peter responded, breaking his gape.

"Forgive me. Do come in." He held the door open and continued to smile at her.

Robert appeared, and tested the phone. "I overheard you. Yes, our phone is in order, so it's not the phone center. Perhaps the problem is right in your phone itself. This is such new technology, not everyone even has a telephone. Ours is a business phone too."

"Do you need to call someone? Do come in, please." Peter stepped aside to let her in. He noted that Robert had referred to their phone as a business phone, rather than one that the military had supplied. Good for Robert—always one step ahead.

"Perhaps I need a new one," she sighed, and came into the living room. "My mother lives south of Paris, in Belfort, and I just wanted to make sure she was all right. I heard at work that the Germans are shelling close to her village. There is nothing there that the Germans would want, but it is close to the front. I have to gather my mother and get her out of there." Her voice trembled with emotion. "My mother does not have a telephone. I would like to call the general store in Belfort. The owner lives over the store. That is the only way I can get through to Mother."

Peter handed her the telephone and stood aside to watch as she asked the operator to ring the number. She was quickly told that the lines into Belfort were down. "What do you think is really happening?" Her face had turned pale.

"Peter, get her a little sherry, would you?" Robert asked, watching her face as she heard the operator. "Or would you rather have a nice hot cup of tea?"

"Thank you. I don't want to bother you, but a cup of tea would be nice. I'll be all right. I will try to get through to Mother tomorrow from the office. If all else fails I will send a telegram to the store."

"By the way, I'm Robert Monet and this is Peter Hamilton. May I ask your name and which apartment is yours?"

"I'm Denise deBusse. I live in number four upstairs, probably directly above you. I work for the Paris Transport System."

The two men were silent. Peter stood and stared at her, again thinking that he had never seen anyone quite as beautiful; he just couldn't help himself. He thought her a real stunner—her body was slim, rounded in the right places and her long, naturally, blonde hair was swept back and up. Her big, green eyes, edged with heavy, dark lashes, looked directly into his. Her lovely features were combined beautifully in her oval shaped face, enhanced further by her flawless, ivory coloring. She suddenly smiled at Peter, showing her even white teeth. She continued to smile at him, aware of his scrutiny of her. Peter blushed, knowing that he had been caught.

"You two are Americans, no? And what are you doing in Paris?" Her color had returned.

They hesitated. Suddenly Peter noticed that his uniform was hanging on the door. *Rats! No lying,* he thought as he maneuvered into unknown territory. He caught Robert's eye and glanced toward the hanging uniform. "We're here with the American Government commodity store up the street, and we're enjoying Paris as a bonus," Peter answered. "And what's your story, Denise? I'm sure you have one." He turned the conversation back to her.

"I was raised in Belfort, which is a small suburb. I came into Paris to work, to be part of the city, and to meet new people. After graduating university, I attended a special training course that the city transportation runs. Now,

I work on designing and refurbishing train car interiors and I love it."

Peter could not carry on a trivial conversation with her. He remained silent; he was still too taken with Denise. Robert asked her if she had family nearby.

"I have one brother, Armand, in the French Army. I am so concerned about him. He is an infantryman and I am sure that they ship the infantry to the front, first. My poor mother worries about him constantly. I try to visit her every other weekend at least. What do you think will happen?" She shifted to the front of her chair, anxious, asking them both again.

Peter glanced at Robert. "I don't know what will happen. But I think that you should be cautious and perhaps have a plan made," Robert told her.

"Well, I have to go." She got up from the chair. "I'm really tired. Thank you, again."

"Whoa," Peter turned to Robert, once the door was closed. "What do you think?"

Robert smiled. "She certainly was taken with you. I saw those glances that she was sending you."

"What do you mean? She is quite sophisticated. What would she want with someone unworldly, hardly into manhood? But we do have an old saying in our family," Peter told him. "*There is a lid for every pot.*" They both laughed.

"She cannot be more than twenty two," Robert said. "You're almost there," he grinned.

Peter shook his head and thought he must watch himself. He really didn't know anything about the woman. His inner antenna was up and alert. He decided not to pursue her, for many reasons. He did not trust strangers. Job training had instilled that mode of thinking in him; perhaps one day it would save his life.

The announcement came that the Germans were near the front lines at Reims and Château Thierry. Peter looked at a map and found that this was near Belfort. He wondered how Denise's mother was doing. The answer came within the week. He heard a knock on the door—really more than a knock, a banging. When he opened the door, Denise burst through, highly agitated and in tears. "I have to get my mother out and somewhere safe. Belfort is too near the shelling. I am afraid those big guns will hit her house, by mistake or not. I need help!"

"Come in and sit down," Robert took her arm. "Tell me how you know this."

"I was able to get through by telephone to the general store in Belfort. Mr. Danner, the proprietor knows just about everyone in Belfort." She hesitated. "But I cannot ask him to get a message to my mother, until I figure out how I will get to her. One German shell already has landed in Switzerland, near the border, so Mr. Danner told me. Probably by mistake, because the Swiss are neutral. But mistake or not, when you are dead it doesn't make any difference!" she wailed. "What am I to do? My friends at work have checked all the trains, and most are still running into Basel, Switzerland. Belfort of course is on the French side and I would have to drive from Basel back to Belfort. The local train across the border has been stopped, because of the shelling on the French side; I was told by Mr. Danner. I remember it is about an hour or so drive from Basel back to Belfort. I don't have a car, and they cannot promise how long those trains near the border will continue to run if the Germans target that exact area. I just have to get her out," she persisted.

"Let me see what I can find out." Peter was still not sure if this was a ruse on Denise's part, but he needed time to check her story. "We might be able to get your mother out of Belfort into Basel. "If I can make arrangements, would you be able to move her quickly?"

"Oh, how good of you Peter." She got up from the chair and threw her arms around him. "I am having such an awful time, alone. Only my mother and brother are left. My father died two years ago," then she started to stutter. "I ca ca cannot get in touch with my brother either and I haven't heard from him in weeks."

"Come up and see me tomorrow night after I get in. Where will your mother go? Bringing her into Paris would not be too smart. You're liable to have to move her again. Are there relatives elsewhere?" Peter offered her something to drink.

She took tea, and thanked him profusely again. "My mother has two elderly cousins who live in a large house in Basel. I will call them tomorrow from work and see if they will take her. They have a telephone. I will not try to reach Mother until I speak with you."

After Denise left, Robert was sharp with Peter. "Are you crazy? She could be setting you up for disaster."

"I intend to check her out tomorrow. I would not be that foolish. I don't think that she's up to anything, but I intend to take a close look into her background. If she's clean, then I will go ahead and make arrangements to get to her mother."

"Be careful, Peter. You're treading on dangerous ground," Robert warned him.

The following day, Peter drew on his connections and thoroughly checked Denise's background. He requested a picture to confirm her identity. He secured other information, found her clean and by the end of the day he had all that he needed and left the office.

At 6:00 p.m. that night, Denise was at his door with news. "I called my cousins in Basel. They are more than willing to take mother into their home. I wanted to speak with you first, Peter. Then I can contact Mr. Danner at the store in Belfort. He can send someone to my mother's house with a message. What shall I do? What shall I tell Mother?"

"I've checked the trains," Peter shared. "The Paris-Basel train is running only once a day. It leaves Paris at noon and arrives in Basel at 3:30 p.m. I can arrange for a friend in Basel to leave a car for me." He told her no more of the car. An agent friend of Peter's in Basel would leave a benign looking car at the train station as a favor.

"We will stay overnight, Tuesday, in Basel. We have no other choice of trains. Then, early the next morning we will drive to Belfort, pick up your mother, drive back to Basel and drop her off. Then we can take the Basel-Paris return home. It leaves at 4:00 p.m. I would like you to go into work tomorrow, that's Tuesday and call the store. Ask Danner to send a message to your mother that we will be there on Wednesday. I cannot give your mother a definite time, but tell her to be ready from 8:00 a.m. on, Wednesday morning."

Denise was beside herself. "I cannot thank you enough, Peter. I could never do this by myself. I am indebted to you for life," she was overwhelmed and put her arms around him once more.

"You need to leave work on Tuesday early enough to catch the noon train," Peter told her. "Will that be a problem? And Wednesday too."

"No," she told him. "My superior knows what's going on, but of course not the details. He offered his help, so I know that I will be able to take the time off."

"I will see you at the Paris Nord station tomorrow morning by 11:30 a.m.," Peter said and she left.

"Be careful," Robert cautioned. "It's very close to the German line. Wouldn't it be safer driving into Belfort under cover of darkness?"

"I will have to take that chance. I am more concerned about getting lost in the dark or being on country roads with headlights on."

Denise was on the train platform on time Tuesday, as Peter had requested and they caught the noon train from Paris and arrived in Basel near 3:30 p.m. *All right,* Peter thought when he recognized the car that had been left for him by the license plate. It certainly was nondescript. They drove to the hotel to check in and have dinner. Denise told him that she wanted to rest for a while; she had slept badly the night before, and she went straight to her room. Before she left, Peter told her to call him when she got up, and they would go for dinner.

"Oh, Peter," Denise said later, after they sat down for dinner in the hotel dining room. "I'm just too anxious to eat much. I cannot wait until we fetch mother tomorrow and get her into Basel." She paused, looking at the menu. "I'll just order something light." Instead, she turned from him and began to cry.

Peter was not sure what to say or do because there was a real element of danger in what they were doing and he could not deny that. He reached across the table to take her hand. "Everything will go well tomorrow; we'll be back in Basel with your mother before you know it."

"I will stop being such a baby," she sniffled. "Thank you for caring."

"Let's have a nice bottle of wine and something light to eat." Denise nodded her head. "My birthday is coming up soon. We'll celebrate a little ahead of time. Okay?" *I've known this woman for only a short time. How did this come about anyway?* Suddenly it seemed surreal to him, sitting there, eating dinner in a beautiful Basel hotel and tomorrow, driving to Belfort along dangerous roads to pick up her mother. It certainly had a dreamlike quality about it—like an old movie. However, he recognized that he was smitten with her.

They finished dinner near 7:00 p.m. Peter took Denise's arm as they walked toward the elevator. She was flushed from the wine and a little unsteady. She leaned heavily against him and Peter felt the length of her body. His heart skipped, as he drew in a quick breath. He looked down at her. She met his eyes and he realized that she had leaned deliberately. She straightened herself up—Peter knew that she had not had that much wine. He was sure that she was aware that he was powerfully attracted to her—she had certainly sent out signals to him, or had he read her wrong? He had never stepped over the line with her. *What is she doing now?* He thought, trying to clear his head. *What is she thinking? What does she want from me? Does she want to move ahead with me?* He decided to take her lead. His mind grabbed hold of the possibilities and his excitement mounted. He held her as they stepped into the lift; she did not pull away. In the empty lift, he pulled her closer to him; once more, she did not resist. He buried his face in her lovely, long hair and smelled the faint sweet smell of flowers, and it was more than he could bear. He moved to her smooth, white neck and kissed her; then he found her soft lips and his passion escalated. The lift stopped and so did Peter. She opened the door to her room, and he swept her up into his arms, carrying her inside. She was receptive to him and he kissed her while she clung to him, trying to remove his jacket. He put her down and moved further into the bedroom as she held tightly to him. He thought his heart would burst with the heat of excitement as they merged into togetherness.

He woke up next morning and found her gone. "Denise," he called. "Where are you?" He thought suddenly, that she had left him. *Oh god, have I played the fool? Did she just feel indebted to me?*

"I'm here. In the bathroom," she called. "I didn't want to wake you up." She walked back into the bedroom and smiled down at him. He reached up for her, but she backed away. "We have to get going. We have a schedule to keep. It's 6:00 a.m. And thank you for a lovely night."

He thought it certainly was more than a lovely night, and if he died right then, he wouldn't have cared. He agreed to get up. "Okay. Let me at the shower. I'll be ready in fifteen minutes." His mind switched to high alert.

It was nearly 7:00 a.m. when they left the hotel. "You'll have to direct me when we get to Belfort. I've given us plenty of time, should we run into any problems," Peter was anxious.

"Oh lord, Peter. Do you expect problems?" She felt his anxiety.

"Not really," he said to comfort her, but thought to himself, *I always anticipate problems.* The artillery booming grew increasingly louder as they approached Belfort on a country road, nearly an hour later. "We have to make this quick. If there is another breakthrough, the first thing they'll do is block the roads."

Denise looked at him. "I am terrified. I feel I cannot breathe!"

They crossed over into Belfort. "It's not that far." Denise was clearly agitated. She directed him to the house and she hurried inside and came out with her mother in only minutes. Her mother carried one large suitcase; Denise hauled a carrier holding her mother's cat.

Peter got out of the car, now thankful the he could put his suspicions aside and Denise introduced him to her mother, Beatrice. "I couldn't leave Tippy," Beatrice cried. "I just don't understand all of this." Denise tried to calm her. "I know I'm never coming back here," she cried, and Peter felt sorry for her. She was probably right. Peter helped Beatrice with her suitcase and the cat carrier while a frightened Tippy meowed loudly.

"My neighbors have all left," Beatrice wailed. "Most of the village is deserted. All of my neighbors have left," she repeated.

"I think we're here just in time." Denise was watching in all directions as they drove out of Belfort. They reached Basel without incident at a small border crossing into Switzerland; only then did Peter breathe a sigh of relief.

"Mother, you know that I will be back to see you," Denise said before they dropped her off. Her cousins were happy to see Beatrice and they crowded around. "Mama, I can call you here and you have my telephone number. She kissed her mother goodbye and hugged her cousins. "I cannot thank you enough for taking Mama into your home. She has some money with her, and I will send her more. Thank you so much." She started to sob.

"You mustn't worry about me," her mother said softly.

"Come now, Denise," Peter put his arm around her. "Everything is going to be fine. She's safe now." He leaned down and kissed Beatrice on her forehead and they left.

It wasn't a week later when Denise was at Peter's door near 7:00 p.m. She was hysterical and told him, "My brother, Armand, has been killed. He has been shot, and *he is dead!* An army officer was just at my door. He'll be back later to let me know about the arrangements." She collapsed on the floor.

Peter and Robert quickly picked her up and laid her on the couch. Robert gave her a glass of sherry. When she was able to calm herself, they asked her where and how Armand had died. "Armand was right at the front," Denise moaned softly. "I knew it. I just knew it." The

Army officer had told her that he was only aware of what the report stated. Armand was driving one of the supply trucks when he was blown up. "What am I going to do? I will have to tell Mother. Oh, what shall I do, what shall I do?" she wept and fell back onto the couch.

Peter knew that nothing he could say would comfort her. It was a tragedy and it was wartime. Denise was devastated. Now all he could do was help her in the weeks ahead, through the burial and the loss itself. Suddenly, he thought about home and how beautiful and peaceful springtime was at Seagate.

He stayed close to Denise and tried to support her in any way that he could. She finally took a leave from work and went to Basel to stay with her mother while both were recovering from Armand's death. Peter visited her when he could, and when he could not visit, he wrote letters to her. Their relationship blossomed and given the on rushing inevitability of war, they were drawn closer.

Without notice, Peter and Robert were ordered back to the field barracks located in the far west of France; the bogus offices where they had worked, closed. They were needed in the communications division to intercept and decode German radio messages.

Before leaving, Peter gave Denise his home address in New Jersey, his aunt's address in Switzerland and Robert's contact information. He told her that he would return for her and that he wanted to marry her. "Please wait for me, my sweetheart," was the last thing he asked of her.

She put the contact information into her wallet for safekeeping. She had known this day would certainly come, but she had not realized until now that she truly loved him. "Oh, Peter," she cried, through tears. "Come back to me. I will wait forever." She kissed him goodbye; and when she did, an ominous feeling welled up inside of her; she felt she would never see him again.

"My Denise, my sweetheart; I cannot bear to leave you, but I have no choice. You can't write to me, because I don't know where I will be. I will try to get mail out to you somehow." He held her, and kissed her goodbye. "Just wait for me, Denise," he said, and after he had left her, the faint smell of flowers lingered with him.

He and Robert were on the next troop train heading west. Once at the field barracks, they fell into long nights and days, until time moved in one continuous blur.

On May 23, 1918, German shells landed directly on Paris.

On May 31, 1918, American forces at Château Thierry stopped the Germans on the banks of the Marne near Paris.

July was upon them before they knew it. "German troops are being shipped from the Eastern to the Western Front," Robert said. "The German soldiers are deserting in massive numbers from the troop trains."

Then terrible news reached them. On July 16, the Bolsheviks, who had taken over the Russian government, had murdered Tsar Nicholas II, his wife, his children and members of his entourage.

"Murdering innocent women and children," Robert felt great sadness. "What unholy people these executioners truly are."

Peter was severely wounded in the second battle of the Marne. Their barracks were bombed and a fragment of metal from an explosion lodged deeply in his leg when German shells hit the barracks; he nearly bled to death before the medics pried him loose from the rubble. Two of his buddies died instantly.

After surgery, Peter was heavily medicated and shipped out on a Red Cross troop ship to New York. His letters to Denise in Basel were returned months later, marked *unknown* at that address. The small store where Denise had made contact with her mother had been wiped out, as had most of the town of Belfort, by the nonexistent German shells? *Who would ever know the truth? The*

Germans would never have admitted shelling civilians while intending to reach their destination.

Peter had taken a trip to Basel after the war to visit the home where he had left Beatrice. The house was now occupied by another family. The realtors who had sold the house told Peter that they knew nothing of a Denise. They had heard though, that the two elderly cousins had passed away, and a year before that, an elderly Beatrice had died suddenly. That was all they could tell Peter. The post office in Basel had no information. He spoke to the Paris Transit System, and all they could only tell him that Denise had left their employ. They had no forwarding address.

He had lost touch with his friend Robert and later found out that Robert had been killed while operating an emergency field telephone near the front. His mother wrote that there had been a Memorial Service. Peter told her that he had been severely wounded but if he had known, he would have made his way there. He promised her that he would stop sometime to see her. It was a while before Peter could stop ruminating over the death of Robert. *Such a gentle soul; he had no business being in a war,* Peter thought.

The Armistice was signed, the war was over. His Aunt Gina and Uncle Claude had moved back to Paris. He did not know if he would ever see them again. Perhaps they would come to Seagate to visit.

After a long, exhaustive search for Denise, Peter had given up. He had tried every avenue he knew, networking with former buddies in his division and even hiring a detective in France. Death and cemetery records were in disarray from the war; he did not know the aunts' last names and there was no deBusse listed anywhere. Between losing his best friend Robert and his sweetheart Denise, Peter could not be consoled. It took him a long time before he started to come back into the world.

Two years later, Peter married Mae Mulholland, a close friend, who he had known since grade school. Loving her in a steadfast way, they looked forward to raising a family together. He would never be able to forget his Denise; he knew this with absoluteness. He tucked her away in a special place in his heart and in time, managed to move forward.

In 1941, more than twenty years later, during World War II, Ethan Hamilton, Peter and Mae's only offspring was with Special Operations in London at the beginning of World War II. General Charles DeGaulle, who was based in London, led the Free French, composed of approximately half of the country of France. Marshall Petain, considered a traitor by the French led Vichy France or Independent France, occupied by the Germans. Ethan had gained a reputation in the Special Operations group, specializing in ferreting out the missing or the dead, encamped, or murdered by the Nazis.

Towards the end of 1941, Martine LeClair was still searching for her husband, Oliver who had remained missing for over a year. She was one of the hundreds of French who had managed to get to London. Martine was more fortunate than most; she had worked with the French underground in Paris and she still had many connections. Her Government considered her at high risk of being either assassinated or kidnapped by the Nazis. They transferred her to London to work with the Free French.

Still, with all of her connections, she could not find any information about Oliver's disappearance. She had a few old photographs and other small items that Oliver had been given by his family, along with a slip of paper with a name and address on it. However, the name and address was from some twenty years prior. When she did check this out, she found that the person was deceased, so she placed the paper back in the box with the other items. She had run out of leads, places and names that had been given to her. Her supervisor, Melvyn Osterman stopped at Martine's desk one day and asked her how it was going.

"I am disappointed and discouraged to tell you that I have gotten nowhere." She proceeded to tell him of all her failed contacts.

"Here's a shot in the dark, but perhaps you should call this man, right here in London. He is with Special Ops and from what I hear, he has quite a reputation for ferreting out the missing. His name is Derek Blackstone." Melvyn paused. "Do you want his phone number?"

Martine hesitated, then shook her head, yes. *What the hell*, she thought, *I will exhaust all possibilities.*

Martine called the number the next day, but was told Mr. Blackstone had been transferred six months earlier. Martine asked the operator for anyone else in that office, or the person who had filled his position. She was told she was being transferred to a Mr. Ethan Hamilton.

Ethan was at his desk, still trying to catch up after Derek Blackstone had moved on. A call was transferred to him from a Martine LeClair. Ethan did not recognize the name, but he did recognize Melvyn Osterman's name, who had done the referring, so he took the call.

She had a French accent and she told Ethan that she was with the Free French in London and needed his help. She had been referred to a Derek Blackstone specifically, by her supervisor, Melvyn Osterman. Her husband had been missing for over a year in France and perhaps Mr. Blackstone could help her. "I am desperate, Mr. Hamilton," she whispered, after learning that Mr. Blackstone was no longer in that office. No surprise, she thought. Everything else has failed. *Why should this be any different,* yet she doggedly held on.

Ethan had hesitated. Her voice had something in it, something that he could not identify, but it moved him. "I will need some background information, Mrs. LeClair."

"I have been in London only a few months. When the Germans occupied France, my Communications Group closed. I was fortunate enough to be transferred to London," Martine told him. "It was a tough journey out of the country, but I managed with my Government's help. I have a son, and I am thankful to God that we are here in London." Ethan heard her breathe a sigh of relief. However, she failed to tell him that her office had feared for her life and had gotten her out of the country, secretly. She held too much classified information.

"My husband, Oliver LeClair has been missing since June of 1940. He was only twenty one years old when he disappeared. When I first met him, he told me that he worked for the French Government with a specialty in inner city structures. I had no reason not to believe him. We were two orphans facing the storm together. I am an only child; I had lost my parents in the 1920 worldwide flu epidemic and my grandmother took me to the country to live with her. When I met Oliver, I was happier than I had ever been. By then, I had lost my dear grandmother and I had no other relatives," she told him. "We were both very young when we married. Oliver and I had a wonderful, happy courtship for a year and then we were married. Relatives had raised Oliver; he did not know his parents and was told that they went missing during the war. Our son, Marcel Antoine was born a year later and of course, he is with me. Marcel will soon be two years."

"Tell me a little more of the circumstances of your husband's disappearance," Ethan prompted.

"In May of 1940, right after the German blitzkrieg broke through the French line and drove northward, I'm sure you remember the fall of France. The armistice was signed on June 15, between France and Germany, which by the way was a total farce. In July, my husband Oliver vanished from the face of the earth. He just didn't come home one night. After an extensive search by his office and the local police, we began to suspect something more sinister had happened to him. My personal communications network was unable to obtain any information, which was strange. I could not understand how Oliver could vanish so completely and with such finality. Then I had another thought. Suppose he, like me had not confessed that he was involved in some other type of work with the government. Had he lied the same as I had lied?" she paused.

Martine told him that she knew that the Free French offices in London still maintained a close liaison with the French resistance.

"I knew the Free French offices were based in London, and it was then that I asked for a transfer and my supervisor's help. My London offices, under General DeGaulle maintained a close liaison with the French Resistance. It took a lot of paperwork and my boss calling in favors to get me out of France, into London. But, viola, here I am." Once more Martine did not divulge that her life was at risk if she had stayed in France.

"I only hope you did not come here in vain. I will do my best for you, but to tell you the truth, I don't hold out much hope." Ethan wanted her to know the odds.

"I was told that your particular unit was well known for its experience in finding lost, captured, or murdered victims. And you also had connections—through payoffs—to the lists in the growing German concentration camps." Her voice wavered. *Perhaps it is destiny*, Martine thought. *Maybe this man, Hamilton, can help me find Oliver after all.*

Time was passing now, since Oliver had gone missing. She was losing hope. She had known in her heart that if Oliver had any way to contact her, he already would have done so. Rather than be caught in the horrors of a camp, Martine prayed that Oliver had been killed immediately after his capture, which she felt at this point had been a kidnapping.

"Let me get back to you, Ms. LeClair," Ethan told her and took her number. "There are a few things I want to check out. I will call you back as soon as I can."

Ethan discussed Martine's call with his supervisor. "I think that this is a lost cause, given the time that has passed. Her husband is either dead or lost in a German concentration camp. It will be nearly impossible to find him." Ethan shook his head. "She has told me that Oliver was connected to the French government. Perhaps there was more to that than he told her." He paused, thinking. "Or perhaps the Germans made a mistake and Oliver was truly an innocent? Although she seems pretty clear in assuming that it was a Nazi grab. I am beginning to agree with her."

Within a few days, Ethan called Martine. "I do have some news for you. Your husband *was* with the Resistance, and quite active I might add. I was able to trace his contact in Paris. We still have some of our people active there," and Ethan paused, waiting for Martine to catch her breath. "They knew that he has been missing for quite some time now. They feel it was a grab and that he probably had been shot, if he had refused to give the Germans information. Paris has been looking for him through other contacts, and has pretty much ruled out the camps, and exhausted several other avenues."

"I knew it. I just knew it," she sobbed quietly, then was silent for a time. "I am really not surprised Mr. Hamilton."

"Please, call me Ethan."

"What will you do next?" she asked.

"Why don't we meet and discuss further plans. There is other information that I would like to have you answer personally."

"That sounds fine. Where shall I meet you?" Martine asked.

"I think you should come to my office." Ethan gave her directions, and they set the first meeting. He had an old photo of her from the files; but he wondered what she looked like now. He soon found out that she was a very pretty woman of medium height, dark brown, curly hair and clear blue eyes.

Ethan did not realize that Martine too, had wondered about his physical appearance.

She watched as he leaned back in his chair to give his long legs some room. Martine noted how good looking he was with his dark hair and dark eyes, that missed nothing. His lips were full and he had a slight European look, probably Spanish or Italian heritage.

Frequent meetings followed during the next months. A personal relationship was forming for them that they had not anticipated. Ethan began to worry about her and the daily stress she was experiencing. He made no romantic move toward her. He respected her circumstances. He had no way of knowing that Martine had strong feelings for him. When he met her little son, Marcel, for the first time at her small apartment, he fell in love with the child. Marcel had Martine's bright blue eyes and curly brown hair. He had hugged Ethan when they met and asked Ethan, "Papa?'

Ethan again perused the lists of killed, captured, missing in action, along with other pertinent records. He hoped that he would see Oliver's name among them. He knew that Martine needed closure, and although he did not give up looking for Oliver, he was becoming more doubtful of finding an answer.

Finally, there was a break. Ethan came across an interesting list that had come in from one of the field units. A shallow grave had been discovered and among the skeletons of burned victims, were ID tags. Oliver LeClair's tags were in the bundle. He had been found at last. After delving deeply into the report, Ethan could only confirm that Oliver was connected with an active Resistance group, and that he had been murdered in a group assassination. Beyond that, Ethan did not probe. What would be the use? *Strange that the assassins had slipped up and left his tags.* The tags had probably been well hidden in a secret seam pocket. It was a lucky break. He gave Martine the information, while trying to keep his voice from wavering and told her that evidence showed that all of the victims had been shot, execution style, and then burned. "He died quickly," Ethan assured her, hoping that knowing this would help in some way. He knew that the body, or what was left of it, would come back in a body bag. He did not mention this to Martine, but he would tell her later that the bag would be sealed for burial.

"I am devastated over his death," Martine sobbed, "Even though I thought I would be prepared for this, I need a few days to myself and then I will arrange for a memorial service and a burial. I thank God that he was found. I needed to know what happened to him."

A few weeks after the services, Ethan told her, "I will be transferring back to Washington, D.C., soon. I'm not sure just when, but soon."

Martine was now well acquainted with the difficulty of being on her own with a child. She and Ethan had become close, after working together these past, long months. The thought of his leaving devastated her. She dreaded the day, but it eventually came.

"I just found out that I will be sent to the States within the next month, Martine," and he pulled her to him. "You have been through so much. I want to take care of you and baby Marcel," he whispered. "Marry me, Martine. I love you and want you and Marcel with me."

She had to decide quickly. Ethan was arranging transportation for three German engineers defecting to the States, and the reason Ethan was being transferred back to Washington, D.C. It had been a coup for the Americans, securing these brilliant men who were scientists working on new weaponry. He would be working with them, extracting their voluminous information, which was expected to be a long and tedious job. "I want you and Marcel to travel with them," he told her. She had experienced some guilt feelings, but those feelings were counteracted by her need for security for herself and her son. And she did love Ethan, which surprised her in its intensity. When she realized that he was leaving, those feelings had come forward. She had not thought that she could feel as strongly for anyone, again.

"I do love you, Ethan," she told him a week later. "I will marry you, dearest."

"I would like to adopt Marcel, before we leave London. It will make it much easier to enter the States. It's up to you, my sweet; you know I love him as if he were my own."

When Martine accepted his marriage proposal, Ethan included her and the baby in the travel plans. He had advised his superior that Martine would be a valuable asset to the United States Government. After checking her credentials, his superior agreed.

"It's all set," he told Martine. "You and Marcel will be traveling with the three men. I will meet you in the States. I don't want to tell you where. You will find out in time." He hesitated. "We did the right thing, Martine. Getting married and finishing the adoption here was the wise thing to do. It eliminated a great deal of red tape that we would encounter in the States."

Martine found herself extremely upset when Ethan left her, even though she knew that they would be together, soon. She couldn't understand why she felt this way because she did trust him with her life, and her child's life. She suddenly realized that unconsciously she feared losing him; and she finally realized that her fear was normal after the losses she had suffered. Still, she was anxious to start her journey to America and Ethan.

The trip was long, but fortunately Marcel traveled well. The three engineers kept him busy. She was grateful that she was with them. She was exhausted when they finally reached the States safely. They arrived at their destination somewhere on the east coast, not far from Washington, D.C. She realized how very weary and stressed she really was. Suddenly she saw Ethan hurrying towards them. She carried Marcel in her arms when she ran to meet him. "Ethan! Oh, Ethan—we are both fine, but it has been a very long journey. I am so glad to see you, Cherie."

"I had to meet you, my love," Ethan said as he hugged Martine and baby Marcel to him. He had told her before she left London that he did not know if he would be able to meet her when she arrived. Plans had been made to bring Martine and the baby to his apartment in Washington, D.C., and he would be there to meet them, that is if he could not meet her when she arrived.

"My plans have changed," he told her. "I have to stay overnight here to finish some business, but I will see you tomorrow. Come, I want you to meet Lieutenant Juniper with the FBI. He will take you to my place, and I will see you there. If you need to stop during the trip, just ask him." Ethan gestured to a large, black van that would carry them on the final leg of their journey. "Let's get you going. We have a time constraint. I am so sorry, but we have to keep moving. We'll have all the time tomorrow and then always." Martine kissed Ethan goodbye and placed Marcel on the middle seat of the van then climbed in beside him, breathing a sigh of relief. She had been given a bag with sandwiches, drinks and something for baby Marcel to eat along with the use of a bathroom. She was surprised how hungry and tired she was. She would try to get a little sleep. The three men settled themselves in the large back seat. She felt her body grow limp; finally, she was able to relax, dozing to the hypnotic drone of the van's engine. She knew that Ethan had taken care of everything and they would be together in just a matter of hours.

A jolt of the van woke her on the outskirts of Washington, D.C. "Where are we?" she asked the lieutenant.

"You are in the capital of the United States of America," he answered quietly.

"I cannot believe I am here." Martine looked at her still sleeping son and said aloud, "Thank you God, for watching over us."

She heard a soft *Amen* from the back seat.

CHAPTER TEN

Closing the Circle—the Reunion

October 1988

"It is very difficult dealing with family when you are involved in matters that you cannot discuss," Ethan admitted.

Ella and Gussie had been in the kitchen Friday evening with Kate, going over a simple lineage chart, that Ella had made for the reunion for those friends and family not often seen. "There are so many of us Mom, that I thought it would be helpful for our friends and relatives. Just the Hamilton Family—I'll leave a stack on the hall table and let our guests pick one up, if they like. I kept it small and not too involved."

They were suddenly startled by the thumping and bumping noises from the area of the stairs leading to the second and third floors.

"Good lord, what's that noise? Quick, Gus! Go out and see what's going on. If that's your uncle, I hope he hasn't fallen down the stairs!" Kate always worried about him.

Gussie rushed down the hall and spotted Uncle Peter struggling with what looked like a large frame covered with a canvas. He was having a hard time maneuvering the stairs, bumping the frame down, one step at a time. He saw her coming at him. "I did well, once I negotiated the attic steps. I'll be down these damned stairs in a minute. Not to worry."

"Uncle Peter, let me help you before you fall and break a leg," Gussie warned him.

"I'm okay. I'm all right," he puffed, out of breath, but then relented. "Here, take the other end and we'll carry it into the living room." Peter had managed to carry the large frame down two flights by himself, even though he was in his nineties.

"For heaven's sake Peter, why didn't you ask for help?" Mae was aggravated. "That's all you need to do, break a hip or your bad leg. What's so important that it couldn't have waited until somebody came to give you a hand? I swear, Peter, you will be the death of yourself and me!"

"You'll see. Just wait and see. I can handle it." Peter walked the frame over to the wall and pulled the canvas covering off.

"Great balls of fire!" Charles exclaimed. Hattie echoed his surprise. "I had forgotten about that painting. I haven't seen it in years."

"He looks just like Ethan; or Ethan looks just like him." Kate declared. "Have you ever seen such a likeness?" She stared at the portrait and turned to Peter. "Is that Ethan dressed up in a costume?"

Peter was enjoying himself immensely. He took in the gaping faces standing in a semicircle in front of the painting. This was the first time any of the family had seen it. He had shown the oil only to Charles, Hattie and Mae years ago.

"Amazing," Ella whispered. "It's Ethan's twin. What a likeness!" She stared at the beautiful young man dressed in his Spanish naval regalia.

Peter stared at the painting. "It's the Captain Scarlatti himself; full name Captain Sergio Cadiz Scarlatti, our ancient ancestor who started it all. He's back amongst us. I've brought him down to join the party before I put him back into safekeeping."

"Don't say such things, Uncle Peter," Gussie shook her head. "It's too creepy!"

"Ella remembers what I told her about Captain Sergio when she was little. Right, Ella?" Peter winked at her.

"Of course, I remember all that you told me, Uncle Peter. How could I forget? Especially *that* ancestor, because when I was just a kid, I thought his ghost was ringing the bell out on the beach that dark night." She turned from the portrait. "I just cannot believe Ethan's resemblance to the painting."

"How old is that portrait, Uncle?" Gussie asked.

"It's from the 1600s. It has come down through the generations. I retrieved it from storage to show everyone. I used to keep it here in the house years ago, wrapped tight, but I was worried that the damp sea air would seep in. When I took it to the storage place initially, I was offered a pretty penny for this one!" he bragged, "Just brought him home for the party."

"Shame on you—bumping a valuable 1600 painting down the stairs. You would never sell this priceless piece of family history, would you?" Mae was stunned.

"Oh, no, my dear," Peter told her, putting his arm around her waist. "I have the same blood running through my veins as Sergio. Without him, there would be no me, or really, no family. I could never part with the painting or the journals. I've picked out a few of those ledgers too, to read while we're all together. They're full of family history, you know."

"What a great idea." Gussie grinned with enthusiasm. "I can hardly wait. This is just like an old movie!"

"Why don't you hang the picture up, Uncle Peter? Just for the party. Put it right here in the living room where everyone can see it," Ella suggested. The group continued staring; no one could believe that this was not Ethan.

"My, what a handsome man our captain was," Ella remarked.

"And what colors in that canvas," Gussie observed. "I think it's in great shape, considering its age. I am so glad that you brought the portrait downstairs before all the guests arrived, Uncle Peter, so that we could all have a close look at it."

Peter was silent, admiring this grand work of art.

Ella and Kate went back into the kitchen. "I'm so pleased Mom, that your sisters will be here."

Kate sighed. Everyone knew how much she missed her siblings. "I've made motel reservations for them. They like their space."

"When you live in California and Oklahoma, it's hard to get together," Ella offered. "I am happy, though, that they're all going to be here."

"Peter?" Kate asked, as he came into the kitchen for something to drink. "How many guests did you invite on your own?"

"Not more than fifteen or twenty." He was casual about it.

"Excuse me?" Kate was shocked.

"What's the matter? What does a few more matter?"

Kate gave up. "I have things to do," he told her and left the room.

"Remember when we were all together and slept up in the dorm?" Gussie smiled, lost in memories. "What good times we used to have."

"I remember getting yelled at for all the noise we used to make! And yes, we certainly did have good times." Ella remembered the chaos that ensued when all the cousins were together. "I can never forget the lectures Hattie gave us for leaving wet suits and towels on the floor and chairs."

"Rightly so, Ella. It's a wonder you didn't leave marks all over the furniture from the wet stuff. But I forgive you." She gave her just a little smile.

"Thanks. I needed to hear that," Ella smiled back. "All right, gang. I think that's it." She turned to see Uncle Peter back again, closing the refrigerator. *I hope I am doing that well when I get to be his age, that is, if I do live that long."* She admired his energy. He was elderly, but still fit and completely cognizant. He saw them looking at him and he presented himself to the women with a sweeping bow.

"I see you're still the cavalier gentleman." Kate laughed.

"Always," he responded with a grin to his daughter-in-law. "How are the plans coming along, ladies? I think there'll be a big crowd and we love to interact," he said and then smiled, "and all good looking too."

"Where did that sage saying come from?" Gussie asked.

"I remember Aunt Mae used to say that, and more than once," Kate replied. "I do believe it's an old Irish saying. They do have a few good ones, you know!"

"But the Irish can be quite morbid; they seem to revel in their morbid," Kate added. "Just listen to *Danny Boy*, and keep from crying! You know my Irish background."

Ella changed the subject and looked at Uncle Peter. "How's Aunt Mae feeling?"

"She's all right. I have a few years on her, you know. The old gal just needs her snoozie time and I surely don't begrudge her that. Well, I'll leave you gals alone. I know you have lots of things to do." He turned to leave. "Today is still Friday? Right?"

"You are correct, Uncle. It's Friday. We have to hustle. Most of our guests will be here tomorrow." Ella stood up from her chair. "Uncle Peter, you're sure Ethan and Martine are coming? And how about Holly and Marcel?" Ella asked about Ethan's daughter and son, second cousins to her. "I am looking forward to seeing all of Ethan's family." Ella tried to hide her anxiousness.

"Well, of course, they're all coming, as far as I know," Peter responded. "I heard from Ethan last night, and I might add he asked if you'd be here."

"Really." Ella was going to say more, but then left it alone. She knew that her uncle remembered that long ago October night and he recognized that it had to be finally settled this weekend—with both of them.

"I haven't seen that grandson and granddaughter of mine in a while. I forget that Marcel is my step grandson; makes no difference to me. I just love him for himself." Peter paused, collecting his thoughts. "I don't think I've ever said that to him, but I should have. You know he's the apple of my eye, besides you, Ella. Guess I never thought about it. Did you know that Ethan had told me that they were not going to tell us that he had adopted

Marcel? He said they did the adoption in London to cut the States' red tape. *"Good lord, I am getting dotty, always reminiscing."*

For a moment, Peter had been off in another world, remembering the past. "And speaking of Marcel, I hear that he and Julia are expecting! Why, I'll be a great grandpa! And high time, too. Good lord, Marcel is getting on. I guess it takes some of us Hamiltons a little longer. Good thing Julia is younger," he reminded Ella.

Peter thought of his granddaughter, Holly, who was Marcel's sister. He remembered her as a child too, as bright as her brother Marcel. *Rather sophisticated though, even as a young girl,* he recalled. "Who knows what Holly is up to? Maybe we'll get a clue while she's here." As he exited the room, he remarked to no one in particular and to the space around him, "Well, I have things to do—I had better get on with them."

"I didn't know that Marcel and Julia were expecting," Kate remarked a little later to Ella. "I guess it's time that Ethan and Martine were grandparents. I wonder how far along she is."

"I hadn't heard that either." Ella sighed, and then thought to herself, *but then no one really hears that much from Ethan and Martine.* "I have to run some errands, so I'll see you later. I'll help you this afternoon, Gussie, if that's okay." Gussie nodded her head. "I'm taking Tucker with me," she told her sister. Her border collie was already at her heels.

Ella let herself out the back door and into the driveway. She stopped before she slid into her car and looked up at the sky, happy to see the sun shining. She opened her car window and smiled at the gentleness of the wind. She had the sudden urge to walk down to the beach and look out at the ocean to see *if it was still there,* which the family would say when they had been away from Seagate for a time.

Yes, she thought to herself, the grand old ocean. It was still there and will always be there, forever. She recognized how many different moods the sea offered. She had seen the earth's spinning spawn a hurricane within the ocean's midst, frightening in its hugeness, intensely blue, throwing its huge breakers onto the shore. At other times, it was warm and gentle, spilling ponds of water onto the beach for the children's tidal pools. *I will ask the heavens to give us wonderful weather this weekend.* Finally, she took off to complete her errands.

The Boulevard was practically empty. It made driving a snap. Negotiating the Boulevard which ran the length of the eighteen miles of island was becoming nearly impossible in high summer. The island was overwhelmed with cars. Starting in September after Labor Day, it was a pleasure to be able to go out and drive without the masses. She rode off island to the big department stores to purchase her few items, enjoying the ride. She glanced at the huge shopping centers and remembered when that entire land was empty, except for the wild landscape.

She then switched her thoughts to Matt. She knew in her heart that she truly loved him, but she was afraid to take the leap and tell him so. Where would that lead? *Marriage?* Good lord, she thought. She stopped herself. *You haven't even been asked yet, my girl.* What makes you think he will ever ask you? *Even if he did ask, would I accept?* She quizzed herself.

The thought of marriage made her anxious. Even though she loved Matt, being tied to him, left a knot in her stomach. *Move on, my girl,* she told herself aloud. *Good lord, enough is enough.* Yet Ella knew now, that she could never give him up. She would not let old memories rule. Matt was a wonderfully, kind, caring, gentle man and she was not the same Ella now. She was mistress of her own ship—she could take care of herself.

Undecided if she should risk it all and ask Matt to drive down tomorrow, was her choice. Matt could certainly hold his own with this raucous group of Hamiltons. Suddenly, she wanted him to meet them. *He should be back from Spain by now,* she thought. She hoped that he had not physically joined the crazy bull running. She just could not understand. Just like his trip to Mount Kilimanjaro the year before. *I wonder what he will think to do next year and if I will go with him, that is, if we are still together.* She took a deep breath. She wondered exactly how much they really had in common. I will call him when I get back to the house.

She pulled into a slot in front of the store. "Now you watch the car," she told Tucker and assured him that she would be back soon. She knew that he would never leave the car. Tucker owned everything and was responsible for everything or so he thought, *like his mistress* she acknowledged and laughed inwardly. She called him her director of everything. *It keeps him busy,* she thought. She noticed a payphone in front of the store and abruptly decided *I will call Matt right now on that phone, before I chicken out.* She headed to the booth and left him a message.

Her mind switched back to the day ahead. Today I will put an end to another one of my demons. I will confront Ethan—it has gone on long enough. It will feel good to clean my house.

Not far away, in Washington, D.C., Ethan and Martine were getting ready for the trip to the reunion at Seagate House. "I don't know if I'm going to enjoy this reunion or not. It's been such a long time." He was somewhat uncomfortable. Ethan was fortunate that his wonderful good looks had followed him through his aging years. The fact that he took care of himself physically, further enhanced his presence. His hair was salt and pepper now, thick and abundant; his dark eyes were always at the ready. He certainly did not look his age, nor did he feel it. He found it hard to believe that so many years had passed.

"We'll have a great time," Martine declared confidently. She had also aged gracefully and was still a pretty woman. Her dark brown hair was streaked with an attractive gray at her temples, her blue eyes were clear and direct, and her body slim and she still had the remnants of a French accent. "And why wouldn't we?" She reassured herself and went on. "I'm just sorry that we haven't seen more of your family. You are very fortunate that you have them. You know I lost everyone close to me during the war." She was silent for a moment, thinking. "Why haven't we seen your family more often? Your father is getting on. Good lord, he's still going strong. And your mother, too, although she's younger," Martine paused. "Well, I'm happy Mae saw us whenever she could. Now, it's too hard for her to travel alone on the train." She paused looking for the right words. "I feel badly that your father hasn't taken the opportunity to see his grandchildren more often. He truly loves Marcel and Holly. Well, at least, they speak on the phone quite often." She turned away and started to pack her suitcase.

"I know." Ethan confessed. "He does treat Marcel well. He's never asked questions about the boy's father; I appreciate that. Not that we could have told him anything more than you knew. I've always been glad that I did tell him about the adoption," he paused, thinking about the long gone years. "My father and I never did see eye to eye. It's just been hard," Ethan admitted. "He was inclined to try to run my life, and I guess I wasn't having any of it. Perhaps we should have spent more time with my family, but it's very difficult dealing with family when you're involved in situations that you cannot discuss. My father knew that, but he kept pushing on and on, telling me that I ought not to be involved so deeply in the Government; even though he had done the same thing. That's why we had heated arguments all the time. He knew I couldn't speak of my business; but that never stopped him from trying to extort information from me. He knew in general what I was doing, but I think he would have been surprised how deeply I was involved; but that was years ago."

"He's your father, and he loves you and only wants the best for you." She was determined to let him know how she felt.

"I know. I know," Ethan relented.

"And you have been a true father to your son. Marcel loves you so, as does Holly. You've done a splendid job with both of them," she smiled. "And speaking of Marcel, my dear, I think it will be good for him to be a father." She acknowledged Julia's pregnancy. "I guess Julia didn't want to wait until she was past her childbearing years. You know Marcel has some years on Julia. Maybe this will prompt a proposal from him. He's no kid for heaven's sake. He's been with Julia quite some time. Perhaps the baby *will* bring on a wedding."

"Have you discussed this with Marcel? Who's the holdout?" Ethan was rather annoyed. He snapped his suitcase shut. "By god, the younger generation certainly does its own thing today. Can you imagine if it were in our time? There would have been no question about having a choice whether to marry or not."

"I don't know. Personally, I think it's Marcel." Martine shrugged. "I don't understand why he can't make a commitment. He's fortunate that Julia stayed around, waiting for him to make up his mind. I just don't understand," she repeated. "Maybe Julia gave him an ultimatum? Maybe he feels life is too dangerous and unpredictable out there. Why risk it?"

"Perhaps he should have made a trip to the drugstore, if that's the way he felt about having a child," Ethan said, shaking his head.

Martine frowned at him, but didn't address his statement. "I was talking to Julia last night. She wasn't feeling well. I hope she's okay for the car ride. Maryland is a good ways from the Jersey shore. If she isn't feeling well, she may not come." Martine was concerned.

"I hope they work things out." Ethan wanted to sound positive.

"She has a while before she shows; I know that she would like to work a bit longer. It's a different world—you're right," Martine conceded. "I know I'm still old fashioned."

"Well anyway, Holly is moving along nicely. The Master's in Biology will get her on track for that university research job, if she wants it. There's still time." She was quiet, looking at a picture of Holly on her dresser. "Such a pretty girl with that gorgeous dark red hair—takes after your cousin, Ella, in looks, except that Ella's hair is dark. Speaking of Ella, you need to have a long sit down with her. You know what I am speaking about."

"I know. I know. I'm aware of that. I know that I have a lot of explaining to do to my little cousin. I'll get her alone," he promised. "I had no choice that night. Nevertheless, that event needs to be cleared."

"My goodness, Ethan. How many things did you have going on? You need to get a broom into that dark closet of yours and sweep it out. So much happened so long ago. I would sieve through it all and take care of the things that really matter."

"You're right. I know. Well, I have to admit," Ethan revealed, "that I am looking forward to seeing everyone, especially my mother." He paused. "I guess even the old man." They both laughed. "Now let's get finished in here, and I'll bring the suitcases to the car. We'll get an early start in the morning."

Back on Long Beach Island, Ella went into the kitchen. "How's everything coming along?" She glanced around the large room. Piles of serving dishes and paraphernalia for the party were everywhere. "I'm anxious to see Luke and Hope and their kids," she told Gussie. "We haven't seen them since last Christmas," Ella reminded Gussie about their first cousins. "We really ought to have a reunion every year." She remembered how close they had been as children.

""I don't think I could survive that." Kate rolled her eyes at her daughters, after overhearing Ella.

"I'm off to bed," Kate announced. "Need my sleep for the big day."

The rest of the gang would arrive tomorrow, Saturday. The food was ordered, the house was ready; preparations were complete. Ella's sons had told her that they would arrive early in the morning, but one never knew for sure what time. They would show up eventually. Time held no significance for them.

The moon was riding high when Ella and the last of the stragglers turned in. She needed her sleep, and drifted off quickly, although she awakened twice during the night.

The alarm clock went off from somewhere far away. Ella's dreams had been discombobulated and colorful, but made no sense, so she thought. She regained her wits and reached over to turn the damned thing off. She lay there, unable to move again, thinking of Matt. With great effort, she finally rolled out of bed and made her way to the shower. *Just one more hour*, she thought. How she would have liked to have slept, just one more hour. She appeared in the kitchen twenty minutes later, energetic, after her shower and ready to face the day. It was 9:00 a.m.

The back kitchen door suddenly burst open with a bang, and a cool wind blew in, along with Polo and Adam, Ella's two sons. Their physical energy immediately filled the room. "Hi, Mom." Polo grabbed Ella, swinging her off the floor. "Here we are, bright and bushy tailed!"

"Apparently!" She laughed and hugged him, surprised to see them this early, then turned to Adam to do the same.

"How was the drive down? Where's Michele?" she asked Polo.

"The drive was fine. No traffic—it's October, Mom. No one comes down this early on a Saturday morning in October. Michele will be down later. She wanted her own car because she's going to work on Monday from here," he mumbled as half of the fresh blueberry scone he was stuffing into his mouth fell onto his shirt.

"Blueberries stain, Polo," his mother reminded.

"Where are Sonya and the kids?" Adam asked, referring to his sister. "Is Tim coming?"

"She should be along any time now, and I don't know about Tim," Ella confessed. "You know what's going on," speaking of her son-in-law, Tim. *Things are not that happy in paradise*, Ella knew. *I hope that they can work it out.* "Your sister had planned to drive down with Grandma Kate yesterday morning, but she had too much to do with the children's schedules and all. Sonya should be here soon."

"And where is Hattie?" Polo demanded. "Ooops, there she is!" He spotted her and gave her a big hug too, lifting her off the floor. "Hattie, don't ever leave us. I could not get along without your scones." He swallowed the sweet, mopped himself up, and turned to look for Tucker. "Where's my guy?" he boomed, looking for the dog. Tucker had heard them come in and scampered down the hall, wiggling his behind and wagging his tail with great excitement. He jumped up into Polo's arms, as Polo encouraged him to do. "Here he is! The best dog ever!" He laughed and hugged Tucker.

"Polo, I have asked you repeatedly not to have Tucker jump up on you. He will do that to the little ones and my friends. I've been working with him to stop his jumping."

"Yeah, Polo," Adam butted in. "Are you stupid or something?"

"Ooops. Okay, Tucker. You have to get down."

"Where are we bunking?" Adam asked.

"Where are *you* bunking, you mean?" Polo answered. "Michele and I decided to stay at a motel or a bed and breakfast. Any reservations made for us?"

"Ask Charles. He was checking into that." Hattie heard him ask.

"My goodness," Kate complained, entering the kitchen. "What's all the noise about?"

"Guess who's arrived?" Ella asked, pulling back from the door to avoid getting hit, as her sons hauled in various items.

"My boisterous grandsons, of course. I should have known. Coffee ready yet? And where are Sonya and my two great granddaughters?"

"I'm sure they're on their way."

"Nana, banana," Polo smiled, pushing in through the door again with more bags. "How are you and what's cooking?" He gave Kate a great bear hug.

"I am just fine. What's going on with you and your brother? Are you behaving yourself? How does Michele put up with you?"

"Because she loves me, Nana! I'm a great guy! She's getting the best of me and she knows it!" and Kate laughed because she loved him and his brother with all of her heart.

"Come give me a kiss, then see what your mom needs you to do."

"The day progressed, bringing joy, noise, laughter, and hugging. Peter's younger brothers arrived together, Jerry, from California, and Ramon, both widowers. They were hale, hearty and happy in their old age. Ella's cousins, Luke and Hope, along with their spouses and teenagers, came through the door, excited to see Ella and Gussie. Kate's sisters and offspring arrived, and there was more hugging. The adult children mingled noisily, catching up on childhood memories.

Marcel and Julia pulled in, parked along the street, and Marcel started to unpack the car. Ella spotted them and hurried out to help. Tucker followed her to check out all the commotion. "Hi, you two. How are you?" Ella greeted them. "Are congrats in order?" she asked when she hugged Julia.

"I'm happy with it." Julia smiled as Marcel started for the house. She lowered her voice and confided to Ella, "I've been asked and have accepted. Do not say a word, Ella. I think Marcel wants to make the announcement to everyone today."

"When did I see you last, Marcel?" Ella asked when he returned to the car to carry in another suitcase. "Last year I think. We really ought to get together more often. I've seen Julia here and there a few times. And I'm looking forward to seeing your father and Martine."

"They should be here pretty soon," Marcel answered as he headed up the driveway, hauling in the last of the suitcases.

"Mum's the word, Julia," Ella whispered. "Hey, everyone! Look who I've found." Ella raised her voice, opening the door and alerting everyone to Marcel and Julia's arrival.

"My goodness, Julia, you look fit and happy! How are you feeling?" Kate hugged her and the women crowded around her. They needed to get all the pregnancy details.

Peter arrived on the scene and boomed, "Where is that handsome grandson of mine?" Marcel had just entered the door with arms full. "Ho there, Marcel," Peter greeted him. "And where is my soon to be legitimate granddaughter-in-law, Julia?" He pulled no punches and always hit the mark.

"Hi, Grandpa," Marcel greeted Peter with a big hug. "How have you been?"

"I'm fine now, seeing you two. When are you going to make an honest woman of Julia?"

"You'll have to forgive your grandfather, Marcel. You know he thinks that getting old gives you leave to say whatever you want." Aunt Mae rolled her eyes at her husband and gave Marcel a hug, and then kissed Julia.

"That's okay. I know you're all talking about us. Oh, what the hell! I've asked Julia to marry me. Let her tell you though. No more now. That's the deal. I'll announce it later and then answer all the questions."

"Thank God! My lips are sealed. Where's your father? When did he leave?" Peter was insistent, referring to Ethan.

"He should be here soon. He was leaving around the same time we did, or so they said, but D.C. is a little further than Maryland," Marcel reminded him.

Ella heard Marcel's answer, and she felt her heart beat a little faster. She had to keep herself together and get Ethan alone, or confront him with Uncle Peter in the room. She hadn't decided just yet how she would do this. It seemed incredible that she had not seen Ethan for so many years. After all, they were first cousins, even though there was a large gap in their ages. Ella recalled Uncle Peter mentioning that Ethan and Martine had visited Seagate a few times over the past years. She concluded that the visits were few and far between.

Holly, Ethan and Martine's daughter arrived. After all the hugging and greetings were finished, she made for the beach where the teenagers and young adults were playing touch football. Ella heard the noise from the beach and yelled down to her sons, "Remember, you're playing with the girls. No rough stuff, guys!" Gussie's two teenage daughters had also arrived and were with them; Ella didn't want anyone getting hurt. She knew how enthusiastic the young men became when running the beach.

It wasn't more than a half hour later when Ethan and Martine arrived. Ella's stomach turned over; she took a deep breath and headed for the front door. The two were just exiting a dark green Jaguar. She saw Ethan first. *Oh well* she thought, *better have at it*. Ella could not believe how little age had taken its toll on him—his hair was streaked with gray, but still quite dark; he had carried over his tan from the summer and he had kept his lean, wiry build. Ella was sure that he still worked out.

"Ella!" he greeted her with a big smile, flashing his pearly whites. *Still as handsome and roguish as ever,* she thought.

She moved into his arms, and he hugged her tightly. She leaned back to look up into his dark eyes, which had once been so mesmerizing. *My goodness*, she thought, *he's only a man!* Of course, Ella was now a mature woman. All of her black memories of the event had been built upon the perspective of a nine year old. She could see now how powerful he had looked to her then, in his boldly charismatic manner.

"Let me look at you, Ella," he held her back from him while he gave her the once over. "You certainly look well," he complimented her. "Beautiful as ever. I hear you have three children? I am looking forward to meeting them." He turned to Martine and asked Ella if she remembered his wife.

"Of course I do, although it has been a long time." Ella turned to hug Martine. "You are as pretty as I remember." Ella smiled. "Come in. Come in. May I help you carry anything? By the way, this is Tucker. He loves people and is our official greeter!"

"Hi there, Tuckerie boy." Ethan reached to pet him and with his head still down, he asked her, "Do you remember my father's three Scotties?"

"You mean Winkin, Blinkin, and Nod? I certainly do. How I loved those dear, little dogs," Ella recalled, and was silent for a moment. Tears clouded her eyes, remembering her beloved little friends.

"They were wonderful little dogs and great company for my father and mother. Martine and I had two Scotties years ago. We loved them dearly and thought of them as members of the family." Ethan's expression was sad as he turned his face away, emotionally moved by the memories. Ella was surprised that he was so affected.

"Come in, come in." Kate held the door open. She was pleased to see them. "How are you two? It's been a long time."

"We're doing fine, Kate," Ethan responded, and Martine stepped ahead.

"How are you, Aunt Kate?" My goodness, you haven't changed a bit." Martine smiled and hugged her.

"I'll get one of the boys to help you upstairs," Ella excused herself. "I need to see Gussie about something. I will see you after a bit. I'll tell your mother Ethan, that you've arrived."

The door banged open again and Sonya pushed through, holding the door for her two little daughters. "C'mon, girls. Keep moving."

Sonya was attractive, like her mother, and married to Tim, a successful attorney. Sonya did a great deal of volunteering and was in local politics. She had her degree in Education, and was working on her Masters. Right now, trouble was brewing in her marriage.

"Where's Nana," the little ones kept asking. "Where is she?"

"Try the kitchen, girls. Nana's usually in there," Sonya said, referring to Kate. "Oh Oh . . . Here he comes. Here he is," Sonya said to the girls. "Tucker's been waiting for you." They screamed and were all over the dog.

Kate heard them from the kitchen and came to greet them. "Here they are! My good girls," and she hugged and kissed them both.

"Look, Nana. "Look what I made for you in school," the little one said and shoved a drawing, now rather tattered from her holding it in the car.

"Did you make that in Kindergarten, for me, my sweetness?" Kate asked, and her little great granddaughter was all smiles.

"She carried it all the way," the elder great granddaughter confirmed.

"Ooops. There's the doorbell. Let me go answer it and when I come back we'll hang up your picture," and the little one smiled broadly.

"I'll see you later, Sonya," Kate said to her granddaughter, as she headed for the door. "Your brothers are here and your mother is floating around somewhere. How are things?"

"Tim is with us," she smiled, and Kate thought, *thanks be*. Perhaps things will mend themselves. She hated to see Sonya and Tim part.

Minutes later, Kate called Peter to the front door. As he approached, Kate was welcoming yet another group, one that Peter did not recognize.

"Yes, my dear," Peter said to her. "Here I am. And who do we have here?"

"These are relatives of yours, Peter. Ella did well, tracking down your cousins that you probably haven't seen in years."

Peter searched the two men's faces and suddenly he knew. "I don't believe my eyes! It's Yves! The French have arrived! Yes, of course, my first cousins. Am I correct? I think I have about ten years on you, right?" Peter thought silently of his mother, Madeline now long gone, and of Aunt Gina, her sister and Claude, Gina's husband. How they would have loved to have been part of this grand reunion. *I have lived a long time* Peter acknowledged. He was thankful that he was still here to enjoy his wonderful large family.

"Hello Peter," Yves hugged him. "And this is my brother, Jon, whom you've never met, but he was spoken of that day when my parents and I left Paris."

"Of course, of course. You left for Basel. Jon was already in school there; you left because of the bombing. I did see your parents once more, years ago, but not you, Yves. And this *is* my first meeting with Jon." Peter remembered all of it.

"Right," Yves agreed. "My one son lives in California now. I visit him part of the year and then travel back to Paris, where my extended family lives. Jon has a place in Basel with his family. Your niece, Ella, tracked us down and we decided to come to the family reunion. How my mother and father would have loved to have been here."

"This is just too grand," Peter replied, and Kate saw tears gathering. "Come in and get acquainted with everyone. We'll get together later so I can hear all about your families." Peter showed them into the large parlor, and turned to Ella.

"My dear, how did you find them? I am amazed."

"I knew that you had lost track of them. I found them in the Paris phone book. It wasn't too difficult, Uncle. I dropped Yves a note. His elder son received the note and called him in California where Jon and Yves were both visiting, and then, viola, they showed up!" She laughed at her uncle's astonished face. "Well, actually, it wasn't quite that simple. They did call me. Arrangements were made; they flew in to Philadelphia and took a limo here. I knew you would enjoy seeing them."

"How can I thank you, Ella?"

"No need. We are family, and I knew you'd be surprised. Did you see Ethan and Martine? I think they're in the living room."

Peter hugged Ella and headed for the other room to see his son and daughter-in-law. He found them in the enclosed front porch, watching the young people on the beach. "Ethan, son," he greeted him. "And Martine—how are you, my dear?"

"We're good, Dad," Ethan hugged him. "It's always good to be here at Seagate. Brings up great memories of my growing up years." Ethan was staring out the window, watching the touch football game going on.

Martine stood with her arm around her father-in-law. "It's good to see you, Dad. I am sorry that we don't come to visit more often. And you know you're always welcome at our home." Peter saw her look over at Ethan.

"Sure, Pop. We're both getting on in age, although you're doing okay. Hope I've inherited your genes. I promise that we will get together more often."

Peter's face lit up. "I would like that, son. Before we get lost in the crowd here, we need to set a time for a meeting with Ella. I don't have to tell you why. It's been a long time that she's held her anger over that childhood incident, and you know she needs closure. She has been unable to do that. I would like some closure too. I would think that restraints would have been lifted on any information that had to do with that incident. Am I correct?"

Ella had been circulating and spotted an old friend. "Good lord, Rita, is that you? You look tremendous!"

"I saw the blip in the classified about your reunion. I live in Toms River now and I just couldn't resist coming."

They chatted for awhile and Ella retreated into the past recalling memories of summers at Seagate. "Remember we used to call ourselves the grand foursome. Weren't we something else? Or at least we thought we were. And the old two piece bathing suits, and riding the waves in. They call that body surfing now. Weren't those the days?"

"I wonder about the rest of the foursome," Rita was lost in thought.

"I keep up with Lee and June," Ella offered. "Lee is in Florida and June is in California. Too far to come, but I correspond with both of them on holidays, and I have been able to see Lee a few times a year, which is a treat. You know Megan passed away a few years ago. I think there are some pictures of all of us in the den. Let's go and look and have ourselves a good laugh," and they headed off. "Don't forget to give me their addresses," Rita reminded Ella.

Ella left Rita in the den to mingle with the other guests; she greeted her mother's family in from Oklahoma, and spotted another friend of hers that she had not seen in awhile.

"How have you been, Pat?" And she and Pat had a wonderful trip down memory lane. "Remember the ice cream dipper was square at Millside Farms near Loveladies? Or was that Harvey Cedars? I remember that you had just gotten your driver's license and a new tan convertible. You were just sixteen. Didn't we think we were something," and they both laughed.

"And the Drive in Theatre over in Manahawkin, and the stock car races. What fun times we had those summers," Pat smiled, remembering.

Ethan had given a lot of thought to how he would approach Ella. "Dad, I would like to have a private meeting with Ella and her family, Gussie, Kate, Marcel, Holly and you. The information we need to discuss can be given out later to others, as Ella sees fit. Gussie was no more than a baby at that time, but I want to include her because she has grown up with Ella, knowing Ella's perspective. The same reason applies to her daughter and sons, who have been around Ella their entire lives. I don't know if you want Mom to join us."

"I don't think that's necessary. She would get a little confused." Peter paused, thinking of Mae. "Let me ask Hattie if that small office on the second floor is being used. We can meet there right after lunch if you like. I think it will do nicely."

Peter cleared the use of the room with Hattie. She had promised to bring coffee to them. He told Ella there would be a 2:00 p.m. meeting. He advised Ella who he thought should be there and asked her if there was anyone else that she wanted to include. Ella passed the time on to her mother, Gussie, Sonya and her two sons. She hoped that she wouldn't get sick or die of anxiety. However, she knew *nothing could stop her from being in that room at 2:00 p.m.*

The house was still full of people, but by 2:00 p.m., Ella, Gussie and Kate had greeted everyone. They asked Hattie and a friend of Kate's, who knew most of the guests, to take over.

The group filed into the small, upstairs office and took seats. Ethan sat behind the large desk; Peter was with Martine, Marcel and Holly; Ella, Gussie, Sonya with her brothers and Kate grouped toward the side. The room was quiet until Hattie knocked on the door with the coffee. She set water, the coffee pot and cups on the table and asked them to help themselves and she left. Silence kept watch for a few minutes while they all prepared their coffee.

Ethan jumped in. "Well, it's been a long, long time since that incident in October of 1941 happened here at Seagate. It's strange how each person perceived the event. I want you all to know what actually did happen that night on the beach and why I could not discuss the incident with any of you. I do apologize sincerely to those most affected." He looked first at Ella and then at his father.

"I hid the truth from Ella and my father; for that, I am sorry. I knew the ramifications of that lie, but I had no choice." Ethan looked at Ella and again over at Peter. "My father, as you know, was in the army in World War I, through the second battle of the Marne where he was severely wounded and sent home. After he had healed, he worked for the Government. He knew all about secrets. He also knew that years had to elapse before the covert dealings that demanded high security could be discussed. My father never spoke about that side of his life. When I was young, he was gone a lot. However, I knew that he was heavily involved with our Government. I also knew that he could never reveal exactly what he did. I accepted that, as my mother did." His voice had risen.

Ethan took a swallow of water, trying to calm his emotions. He knew that he was treading on dangerous ground with his father, and really did not want to hurt him. "Therefore, I still to this day, cannot understand why my father held the attitude he had about my affairs." Ethan heard his voice escalating; he stopped to check himself. "I could never disclose what happened that night to anyone, except to those directly involved, or to those who held some sort of security clearance. I was dealing with defectors, for god's sake," Ethan said, glancing at his father.

Ella drew a quick breath in, catching the slight sharpness in his voice.

Ethan poured coffee and continued. "After I joined the army at the beginning of the war and went through extensive training, I carried a high level security clearance. I eventually reported to London and was assigned to a Government operation for a time, involving American and French underground agents. I was finally assigned back to Washington, D.C. This you all know," he looked around at each of them.

Polo and Adam sat in silence, fascinated at the conversation that was unfolding.

"I was still in London during the bombing. The Government had given me the responsibility of transporting three very important, defecting, German engineers to the United States. They had made it out of Germany and we had to get them to D.C. These engineers had expert knowledge of advanced weaponry which they had been working on in Germany. I was asked to oversee their travel to the States." Ethan continued. "Mind you, they were extremely important defectors who had promised to give valuable research information to our Government, who in turn, promised them asylum in the States."

"Question please, Dad," Marcel interrupted. "Was this the FBI, CIA, or what?"

"Like that, Marcel. I really don't want to pinpoint. Let us just say it involved covert Allied operations. I had other considerations at that time. I had met your mother," he said, looking at Martine. "When Paris was overrun by the

Germans, the free French Government where she had worked got her out of Paris and into London. Because of her work, they felt her life was at risk. She called my office shortly after she had arrived in London, but did not get to me directly. She had been referred to another person whom I had just replaced. I was then in the business of finding lost agents, among other things, and my department had been very successful." He took another sip of coffee.

"Martine had been assigned to DeGaulle's department in London after she had transferred out of Paris. She had heard of my department through her friends at work and thought, that perhaps we could help her. She had lost her husband Oliver, your biological father, Marcel, shortly after you were born," he looked at Marcel. "Your father Oliver, had vanished one day and had never been found. He had worked in a different area of the French Government than your mother. Time had passed and because he was not found, your mother suspected that he had some ties to the Resistance, that he had not disclosed to her, although she could not prove it. After more than a year, we had nothing," he paused and looked at Martine. "Agents finally found his I.D. tags in a shallow, mass grave, filled with many bodies. They had all been shot in a mass execution." Again, Ethan paused. "Are you all right?" he asked Martine.

"I'm okay. Go on. Truly, I'm all right."

He looked toward Marcel. "When your father was finally declared dead by the French government, your mother knew it to be true. She also found out then, that your father had been involved in the Resistance and had not told her. This confirmed our suspicions that the Nazis had grabbed him."

Ethan paused. "During that time, I was setting up transport for the three German engineers to the States, and I wanted to get Martine and you, Marcel, with them. I knew that I would be transferred back to D.C., to carry on with the interrogation of these men. There was so much information that they were willing to dump, that I knew it would take at least six months or more to confirm and work with the information forthcoming. Martine was alone, really an orphan, without any relatives or family to help raise her child. We had known each other for over a year and had become close. Martine and I discovered that we loved each other, and I asked her to marry me. Oliver had been gone a long time and finally, his death had been confirmed." *Silence reigned.*

Adam leaned toward Polo to whisper, "I feel as though I am in a novel. Can you believe all of this? Mom never told us anything other than that night at Seagate."

Ethan continued his story. "Martine had a solid background with the French government. I managed to get her into our offices in D.C., and they were happy to have her. We were married in London before we left and I signed adoption papers for you, Marcel. These procedures do not happen now as easily as they did for us. It was wartime, and the red tape had to be cut." He paused, reflecting on dangerous past times.

"You're getting dry. Would you like more coffee?" Kate asked Ethan at his pause. He accepted the coffee and was silent for a few minutes trying to recapture every detail. Ella could not believe what she was hearing. The transport of the defectors and Martine and Marcel was so simple an explanation. Of course, it had to be kept quiet.

Ethan observed Ella watching him. Her face mirrored her surprise. "I know that it sounds simple, Ella, but there was a great deal at stake. The defection could have been compromised, if I had told my father about the engineers. My father, quite possibly could have known them through his former government dealings. This operation was top secret."

Peter was taken aback and sat silent, finally realizing the ramifications of that night.

"I left London to meet the group here, on the East Coast. But now I can tell you Ella, what happened on that October night when you were at Seagate." Ethan shifted in his chair. "As a barrier island, Long Beach Island fit the bill nicely as a landing place. Not only that, I was familiar with the island, and I had contacts here. We had originally planned to hit the island more north, in a deserted part of Barnegat. I had called my father previously to let him know that I was in the area just to make sure nothing was going on at Seagate. However, that was before I knew that Malcolm was sick. If I had known that, we would have kept to our plans to come ashore at Barnegat. However, when I learned that Uncle Malcolm was in the hospital, and that my father and mother would be out of the house overnight, I moved quickly. I had no idea that you and Gussie would be there."

Ella listened intently and leaned forward in her chair, not to miss a word.

"The engineers, Martine and baby Marcel had already started their journey on a merchant marine ship out of London. They were to meet a submarine at a designated location in the Atlantic Ocean, about two miles from the New Jersey coast. When I learned that Seagate would be deserted, except for Hattie and Charles, I spoke to my contact in the navy, who accessed the ship and spoke to the agent who was escorting the group. We were able to change the submarine's specific surfacing location. It did not make too much of an interruption in their plans; they adjusted the course of the sub slightly so it would be a straight in shot to the center of the island."

Ethan got up and moved about. "Charles had some time in the army years ago, and I trusted him to help us." He paused and looked at his wife. "Martine can tell you better about the journey." He turned toward his wife and sat down next to her.

"Goodness, Ethan, it was so long ago." she said. "I know that it's important to you Ella, so I will try to remember all of the details. When I learned that I would be traveling with the three defecting Germans on a merchant marine ship and then a submarine to a relatively remote area off the eastern coast of the States, I was quite anxious," she admitted. "And I was only told the night before I left. I said to Ethan that I didn't mind sailing on the large merchant ship, but I was concerned about traveling with Marcel in the submarine."

She reached for her coffee. "He told me not to worry, that all would go well. I was in safe hands. We would transfer to the submarine somewhere in the Atlantic Ocean. From there, we would head for a barrier island off the New Jersey coast. That's all I was told of the secret destination. A large, rubber raft with an outboard motor would be launched from the sub to take us into shore. I remember praying that the waters would be calm. It frightened me to think about being out on that huge ocean in a rubber raft, steered only by a small motor—maybe in unexpected rough waters and with a young child!"

"Good Lord, Martine, you were certainly brave to do this," Ella interrupted.

Martine smiled at her. "It was past midnight when the sub surfaced. They inflated the raft, we all got in and the first mate launched it," Martine recalled. "He started the motor and steered by a compass for awhile, because the fog was pretty bad—I don't know how long he had to steer like that. I would guess that we were about a mile or so from the coast when I realized that no light would be allowed from the shore. I had forgotten about the blackout conditions. Ethan told me later that they were hoping for a full moon that night. There was nothing that they could do about that. The compass would have to do until we were in closer and could hopefully see the beach. To make matters worse, there was a half moon, so light was not optimal. The fog and mist grew heavier as we approached the shoreline. I recall that we couldn't see anything. Certainly a compass could not be that accurate in pinpointing our exact landing spot."

She hesitated, shivering; trying to remember the exact course of events. "At first, I thought I was hearing things and asked what it was. I knew I heard a bell ringing in the distance and noticed the first mate adjusting our course to the sound. I realized that someone was ringing a bell to guide us in."

"I felt relieved that we had some guidance now and that the water was relatively calm. Of course, there were swells out there, but not large. I could not even think about what could have happened to us if that ocean had been rough that night," she shuddered now, remembering the darkness. "The moon moved in and out of the clouds and it was so black, we could not see the shoreline, because of the blackout. So you could not imagine how comforting the sound of that bell was. After a time, we glided in swiftly and the water was gentle. The soft waves breaking onto the beach were more like hills of water. Then the raft caught the water's pull toward the beach and the mate cut the engine. I remember the raft ran over the gentle breakers before coming to a hard stop, half in the water and half in the soft, wet sand."

She recalled more. "The men got out of the raft quickly and pulled it into the low, sandy waters. I handed Marcel to the first mate. Marcel had been asleep and he woke up when we moved him. He didn't know where he was. He was just about two years old and very bright. When he didn't recognize his surroundings, he started to scream. I tried to hurry getting out of the raft and told him that Mommy was coming. I reached out to take him from the first mate and lost my footing in the watery sand. Marcel slipped some in the transfer, and when his little feet hit the cold water, he screamed loudly again. I tried to comfort him and whispered to him that he was all right. He stopped crying and looked around. By that time the fog had lifted and there was a moon, not much, but it reflected off the white sands and we could see—not sharply, but I could see outlines and close ups fully."

She leaned back, overcome by the memories flooding her mind. "Suddenly I saw someone running toward us on the beach and I recognized Ethan. I hurried to him and he hugged us both. I don't remember what we said, but I do recall that we were so happy and relieved to see each other." She paused to catch her breath.

Ella looked over at Ethan and was surprised to see tears in his eyes. "Are you okay?" she asked him, suddenly realizing how emotionally affected he was by Martine's story.

"I'm all right. I never permitted myself to feel things back then. If you did, you could not do whatever you had to do. I realize now what a traumatic event this must have been for Martine. Having the baby with her made it doubly difficult."

"I knew everything was fine when Marcel recognized you and laughed. I remember now, you taking us all into the big house, where we found towels and a change of clothes. I remember this was the first time I had seen Seagate and from what I could see, I thought how truly lovely the house was," Martine smiled. "You know Ethan, you spoke of the house many times, and your description was grand, but it didn't do justice to the house. I thought that I had never seen such a lovely home. I think I forgot that part of the story."

"It has always been a safe haven for the family and you must have felt that when you came through," Peter offered.

Hattie interrupted and knocked on the door. She asked if they needed anything.

"Come in Hattie," Ethan stood up. "Hattie was helpful throughout that night. We had to tell her what was going on. We had no choice, but I knew she could be trusted. There was just no other way." Hattie nodded her head. "We also had to notify the Coast Guard and the local police."

"It was truly a very difficult time for me," Hattie said. "But I had to be quiet about it," and she looked at Ella's astonished face.

"I don't know what to say to you Hattie, except now I understand what you had to do."

"It bothered me greatly, especially lying to you, Ella. Now you know why I had to do it. I felt it was a matter of life or death." Hattie felt relieved to unburden herself after these many years.

There was silence, as they all turned to Martine to hear the rest of her story. Martine looked at Ethan. "Before we left the house, you said to me that we were on a tight schedule and needed to hurry. Then Marcel started to cry. Just whimpering, not all out crying."

"You gave him a cookie, remember?" Ethan reminded her.

"I do, now," Martine said, and went on to finish her story. "There was a large, black van and it had colors and a paint brush on the side. It was by the house, waiting for us. You know something?" She had a puzzled look on her face, and glanced over at Ethan. "I thought *what was a van, advertising painting, doing there?* I finally realized that the van was disguised. The vehicle would take us to Washington, D.C. and you introduced me to the driver, a Lieutenant Juniper of the FBI, if I remember correctly. You told me that he would take care of us and that you had to stay at Seagate for the night. You said you would see me the next day, and you kissed me goodbye. And that's all I can remember."

"You had taken something for a headache, if my memory serves me correctly. I recall now that Juniper told me later, that you had slept almost all the way to Washington. It's a wonder you didn't have a nervous breakdown, but you handled the situation exceedingly well." Ethan reached over and took her hand.

Marcel stared at his mother. "*Judas Priest* mother, you are one brave lady. What a fabulous memory you have."

"You were only a baby, Marcel," she smiled at him.

"Who rang the bell?" Ella wanted to know.

"That was Charles," Ethan answered. "I came up from Washington to meet the group at Seagate. The sub would contact the Coast Guard by radiophone when the raft was launched so that they would be aware of any local activity in those waters. The Coast Guard had to let the local police in on the event, should anyone report anything suspicious. It was a dark night with pockets of heavy fog, so we decided to use the bell to guide them in. We could not use any kind of signaling light. This is what Ella heard: *Sergio's bell, ringing out once more to guide a craft safely in.*"

Ethan was silent. "I don't think that you know this Ella, but beings we're disclosing all, I will tell you. Charles took the dogs in their crates to a kennel in Manahawkin and came back to ring the bell if he thought it necessary. He went back for the dogs early next morning.

"So I did figure that right," Ella confirmed, "about other people being involved. Then I heard a baby crying and thought you were involved in a kidnapping. That had to be Marcel crying. Right?"

"Yes, you're right," Martine said. "I tried to hurry out of the house when he started crying again."

"Can you imagine?" Ethan looked at Marcel and laughed. "Coming all the way across the ocean and then afraid of a little water!"

"How embarrassing." Marcel joined in the light banter. "Of course, I don't remember any of this. I was just a toddler."

"And I heard voices drifting up the stairs," Ella remembered.

"Right again," Ethan confirmed. "We came into the house to use the telephone. It was late, and no one was awake to interfere. One of the Germans slipped in the seaweed and wads of it stuck to his shoes. That's what you saw high up by the garage, Ella. He was complaining about his wet feet as we walked from the beach into the house. Soon after the group left for D.C., I stayed overnight to handle any problems that might have come up and I buried the rubber raft. And later Ella, you told my father what you thought had gone on."

"It all seems so simple now," Ella acknowledged. "But you have to remember, that I was only nine at the time. When I didn't have the facts to interface with what I had heard, my mind tried to interpret. Now I understand why you could not speak of this sooner. I was in the wrong place at the wrong time."

"Good explanation, Ella," Ethan agreed. "And I am so sorry."

Ella looked him in the eye. "I would like to know, why you didn't contact me sooner. I can't believe that you were held to secrecy all these years."

"Pretty close, Ella," Uncle Peter jumped in. "When you're dealing with events like this, especially defections, it takes a long time before the veil is lifted. Governments and even supporters of fallen governments, have long memories. And then, there was the witness protection program for the defectors to deal with."

"Thank you, Father," Ethan said. "What did you think I was involved in? You knew that it was something that I could not discuss. Landing here was the best possible solution. When your brother, Malcolm was away at the hospital, and you and Mom and Aunt Kate went to visit, that left Charles and Hattie in the house. I had no way of knowing that Gussie and Ella had been dropped off that night. The group had already started their journey, and we had to go through with it."

"I had no way of knowing the importance of the event. I should have trusted you, son. I am sorry that I didn't realize or give you credit that what you were doing was extremely important." Peter leaned over and put his arm around Ethan's shoulder. "I know that this has caused a rift between us for years and I should have stepped forward sooner."

Ethan met his father's eyes. "It wasn't only your fault. It seemed to be an impossible situation, and then when the time came when I could come to you, I couldn't bring myself to do it."

"You have my gratitude for finally clearing the air," Peter told his son and turned to Ella. "Have you any questions? God knows that it has been hard on you for so many years. In your mind, your fear and your anger were legitimate. You had a right to be frightened by what you heard and saw. Do you think you can move forward now that you know what really happened?"

Ella could only shake her head in disbelief. Nothing could have prepared her for this explanation. "I must go forward. I've been stuck for so long, in so many things; it's good to bring this piece of my life to a resolution."

Kate spoke up. "My goodness, Ella, I knew that you had been scared nearly witless; but I didn't know what to do about it because no one knew what went on that night, except Hattie and Charles. They couldn't speak of anything then. I don't know what I thought. I was always sorry that I could not help you."

"Glory be Ella," Gussie said. "It's finally solved. I don't mean to be flip about this. It has gone on far too long. I know that the event came up for you much too often. I am really glad it's finished!"

Sonya turned to her mother. "I am relieved too. Finally a valid explanation for you."

"You're relieved?" Ella said. "I am elated that there is an explanation for that night. At times, I thought it was all a hallucination!" and she turned to Hattie. "What's the matter Hattie? You seem perplexed."

Hattie frowned. "Ethan just said that Charles rang the bell. He didn't ring the big bell. He left for Manahawkin that night about 7:00 p.m. with the dogs. He didn't get back until early morning—about 3:00 a.m. Winkin got lose over there and they had to hunt for him. Charles figured the landing would be over and done with by 3:00 a.m., so he brought them back home then. He never went back the next morning."

"Who else was here?" Ethan asked, quite surprised.

"No one," Hattie said, "except the girls and me. And I stayed in the room with Gussie and Ella did not get out of her bed."

Ethan was startled. "I have no idea who could have been ringing the bell. Only the two of us knew—Charles and myself. We had planned to ring the bell if the fog rolled in. Perhaps Charles called someone else to do this when he knew that he could have been stuck in Manahawkin. I will ask him."

The quiet continued for a moment or two. Each was engrossed and trying to digest the large amount of information that had just been revealed to them.

Kate finally broke the silence. "What time is it? We need to get back to the others."

Marcel pulled his watch from his pocket. "It's 3:15," he announced and clicked shut the cover of his watch.

Peter was watching Marcel. "My, that is a handsome old watch. May I look at it?" Marcel handed him the watch and its chain.

Peter turned the watch over to examine it. "Looks like there are initials on it," he said, and then he suddenly turned pale. He looked at Marcel. "Where did you get this watch?"

"Why do you ask? Are you all right?"

Peter lost his breath. "Just tell me where you got it, Marcel."

"My father, Oliver, left it to me. My mother kept it until I was old enough to appreciate it. She gave it to me a few years ago. Why do you ask?"

Peter appeared unable to breathe, move or speak. Ethan got up from his chair. He thought his father was having a stroke or a heart attack. "Here, take some water, Dad. What's the matter? Are you feeling sick?" Ethan leaned over to loosen his tie.

Peter waved him away. "Just give me a minute."

Now Kate and Ella got up and stood by Peter. "Shall we call a doctor? Uncle! Uncle!" Ella put her arm around him. "What is the matter? Tell us."

"That's my watch!" Peter gasped.

Martine was stunned. "*What?* What are you saying Dad?"

"*That's my watch!* Those are my initials there," he showed Martine the back of the watch. "My father gave me this watch when I was eighteen. It was a graduation present. There is no doubt in my mind that it's my watch!" His fingers repeatedly traced the scrolled initials cut into the back of the watch, like a blind person reading Braille. His face was the color of chalk and he couldn't take a deep breath. "Those are my father's initials," he paused to trace once more and confirm his discovery. "And there was a tiny chip out of the braid around the face. I dropped the watch by accident on a marble floor." He looked and felt for the chip. "By god, here it is. *This is mine without question!*"

Ethan could not understand. He knew that Martine had kept mementos for Marcel from his father, Oliver, but he had not seen any.

Martine spoke up. "When I married Oliver, he told me that his elderly cousins, who raised him, had *saved a watch and two photographs* in a little chest. This was all that Oliver's father had left him." She paused, trying to remember what Oliver had told her. "His father, who was an American soldier, gave his mother this watch. At the time, he had nothing else to give her. He told her he would return for her, but he never did.

Martine took a deep breath. "Shortly after Oliver was born, his mother was killed on a train, bombed by the Germans—it was a mistaken bombing, they had claimed. That's all that they could tell him. I kept the watch and the photos in our bank box, so they would not be lost and I gave them to Marcel when he was twenty one. Oliver had asked me to do this if for some reason, he was not around. Perhaps he had a premonition of his early death," Martine offered.

Ella whispered, "And Marcel has had the watch and the photos all these years?"

"Exactly," Martine replied, shaking her head. "Marcel never used the watch when he was young because it was rather large for a young man and it had to be repaired. He decided to put it back into the bank box and have it fixed later. Later became nearly twenty years. He wore it occasionally after it was repaired."

"*Where are the photographs*?" Peter asked, barely able to speak. He lay back in his chair, spent, his voice a whisper. "Do you know Oliver's mother's name, Martine? Did Oliver ever tell you?"

"Why, yes, and I have told Marcel. Her name was Denise deBusse."

Peter collapsed and they had to hold him in his chair. "Sweet God and all the saints in heaven! What has happened?" He could barely get the words out. Ethan bent over his father and asked if he wanted a little brandy. Peter nodded, pointing toward a cabinet.

Adam and Polo got up to help their great uncle. "*Judas Priest*, what is going on? I cannot believe what I'm hearing here," Polo said.

Peter sipped the brandy for a minute and some of the color came back into his face. His mind raced; he knew that he had given this same watch to Denise so many years ago. He had told her that he had nothing else to give her. He had told her he would come back for her. He had told her to consider the watch an engagement memento. "Dear God," he sobbed her name, "Denise, Denise, I didn't know," and he was lost in his sorrow. "How has this come about after all these years?" he asked; he could not understand what had happened.

Ethan asked Marcel, "Do you still have those pictures?"

"As a matter of fact, I carry them with me," Marcel reached for his wallet.

The group was shocked into silence—listening, hanging on to every word, as the unbelievable story unfolded. "Here, Grandpa," Marcel said and handed the pictures over to Peter. "They're rather worn, but I think you can still see the people."

"Oh, Lord, *it's Denise and me.* It was the only picture we had taken together." Swift, discombobulated thoughts ran through Peter's head. *She wanted to keep it,* he remembered. He scrutinized the other picture feeling it looked like Oliver as a baby with Denise. "What does this mean? *I never knew she was pregnant!*" Peter was traumatized at the turn of events. "I am speechless and confused. How could this have happened?"

"I don't quite understand what's going on," Ethan was also confused. "What's the date on that picture with the baby?"

Peter held silent, trying to unravel the course of events, but it was coming too fast for him to make any sense of it. He turned the picture over to Ethan. March 1919, Ethan read and turned to Martine. When was Oliver's birthday? Do you remember?"

"Of course," Martine turned white. It was January 10th, 1919.

"*Oliver was my son*! He must have been three months old in that picture. I never knew Denise was pregnant! How can this be? I left her in late May of 1918." *And then the memory of that night in Basel flooded his mind.*

"What is it Uncle Peter? What is it?" Ella was upset for him.

"I am recalling more. Those dates are correct. I was wounded and shipped out sometime that early summer of 1918—I think. Just give me a minute."

Marcel spoke up. "I am remembering more now too," he said to his mother, Martine. "What you told me as a child about my father. It's been so long, and I never spoke of it to anyone. I know that my biological father, Oliver vanished during the war. His father was an American soldier. When he never came back, the family thought he was probably lost in the war. Oliver's mother, Denise, who would be my grandmother, was killed in the bombing of a train near the Swiss French border. Evidently the watch and photos were not with her when the train was bombed."

"I can't believe that I am remembering all of this," Marcel said, shaking his head. "Any contact information about the American soldier disappeared then, in the train wreck and none of Denise's family could remember the American's last name. The watch and the two photos were all that had been left of the American, along with a contact name of Robert Monet and his address in Connecticut."

"That was my friend Robert," Peter interrupted. He was terribly wounded by a grenade around the same time that I was injured. I am sorry to say that Robert never made it. He was a wonderful friend," and Peter was silent, remembering past times. "I recall speaking to his mother many years ago. He was from a very small family. It was a tragedy."

Martine piped in. "Marcel had told me that he tried to contact Mr. Monet, but he found that he had been a war casualty. Mr. Monet's mother was somewhat out of it after Robert died; she was not really cognizant of her surroundings and didn't know anything. She was his only family left."

"My mother, Martine and father, Oliver, were both working in the French Government; that's where they met. I remember my mother telling me that my father vanished one rainy, cold night. She concluded that the Nazis had killed him." Marcel continued.

"Oliver's elderly cousins had told him Denise's story when he was very young. All identification had burned with her in the train accident, except an I.D. bracelet she always wore. When her mother, Beatrice heard the news, she knew that Denise was on that train, returning home, and she went into shock. My father Oliver, an infant at that time, was at home when Denise was killed. The elderly cousins sold their house and along with Denise's mother, Beatrice moved into something more accommodating to a child. However, Beatrice's memory had been affected by the shock of her daughter's death. She was never the same after Denise was killed, and she died a year or two later. She never did regain much of her memory. That's all Oliver knew. When he was twelve, he was sent to boarding school by his elderly cousins and then university."

Marcel sat in silence. "Where did that all come from? It had to be deep down in my memory. My father, Oliver, took the name, LeClair, from one of his elderly cousins who had raised him."

"That was what I told Marcel about his father. And all that his father, Oliver had told me of his parents, the American soldier and Denise deBusse." Martine said. "I never hooked it up; because Oliver's last name was LeClair.

"*Oliver was my son!*" Peter cried, again. "And I knew nothing of him, and I missed his entire life." Peter was overwhelmed. Tears poured down his face, grieving not only for the lost son that he had never known, but also for the woman *he had loved and lost* in the war. Of course, he now wondered how his life would have been if he had married his first love, Denise.

Ethan commented softly, "All the time I was looking for Oliver, *I didn't know, that he was my brother.*" He too, was in shock, realizing that both he and Oliver were Peter's sons.

"And that makes Marcel your biological grandson, Peter," Kate declared.

"That's the one thing that isn't shocking," Peter revealed. "There was something there, a connection, if you will. Probably I'm crazy, but I felt an unexplainable tie with him from the beginning."

"I would guess the reason for that would be that the child carried some family trait that reminded you, unconsciously, of a relative or family member." Kate told him. "Usually there is a time of bonding, bringing the love for the adopted child, but there may be something to what you say. Once you bond with a child, however, most times it doesn't make any difference about the biological connection or not." Kate spoke from her background in psychology and what she had seen.

Peter sat and stared at the photograph of Denise and him. How beautiful she was. Then he stared for a long time at the second photo, of Oliver as an infant with Denise.

Finally, he handed the pictures to Ella, who drew in a deep breath as she scrutinized the black and white photos. "What a beautiful woman she was, Uncle Peter. Looks like she had light blonde hair. Oliver looks like he had lighter hair; almost a pale brown. Now you know where Marcel got his light brown hair." She handed the photos back to him.

"What of Mae, Uncle Peter?" Ella wanted to know. "Does she know about Denise?"

"Denise was in another lifetime. It was a matter of timing. Evidently, I was not meant to be with Denise. Perhaps I will meet her in another time or place. I'm thinking all different things, Ella. I just thank God that I found out about this before I left the earth. I had known Mae since childhood, but I didn't get serious with her until I had reached a dead end in my search for Denise. I even took a trip back to Paris and Basel, but I could not find anyone. I did not know that the one cousin's name was LeClair. Death certificates were lost—I would think until this day. Many, many French were killed, and many didn't have death certificates."

The others sat silent, trying to figure out what had just happened. Now Holly spoke. "Good lord, everyone. Can you believe things like this can happen? It's as though the events took on a life of their own. Only in story books or perhaps in our family?" She turned to her brother, Marcel, "What in the world would our relationship be, Marcel? I think I will keep you as a brother and just forget about trying to figure that out. But then, we are truly half brother and sister. We both had the *same mother*. Does this make us cousins, too?"

"Write a book one day Holly, and ask your readers to figure out these relationships!" Marcel shook his head in awe at Holly and her thought processes.

"Maybe I will do just that," Holly said. "How about since my biological father is also Oliver's half brother, and my mother was married to my step uncle, what am I to you?" She had stumped Marcel.

"Just as long as there's no incest here, we're all right," Holly added.

"For heaven's sake, Holly. Was that necessary?" Kate shook her head.

"Well, I knew everyone was thinking that, but afraid to ask."

"Do you want to tell the rest of the family about this?" Ella asked her uncle.

"I'm not sure. I have to think about it. Let me speak to Mae first, so that she doesn't get this shock in a crowd." Peter still seemed confused.

"That's strictly up to you, Uncle Peter," Ella said. "If you want to tell everyone this unbelievable story, which has flabbergasted me; you should do it. We're all family, although somewhat intertwined—I am still stunned," she repeated. "Last word though, it is up to you—only you. However, beings you asked me, I would say that it is not for everyone assembled here at the reunion. The immediate family, yes. For all to know? I would say, no."

Before they left the room, Holly, who sometimes had a weird sense of humor, but always seemed to hit the mark, said to her Grandmother Kate, "Aren't you sorry you asked what time it was?"

Kate didn't answer, but she had to hold back a smile.

A short time later, Peter came downstairs, his arm around Mae, who looked red eyed, but smiling nevertheless.

He asked Hattie to have the rest of his friends and family come into the library. He had changed his mind and felt that he wanted his close friends, along with his family to hear his story. Ella felt that this turn of events should be only for family; however, it was her Uncle's call.

"The more I think about this revelation and look at the photos, the more I find it amazing and synchronistic," Peter said when he had finished. "Things fell together almost as though they had been predestined by the universe for me to understand." The group was speechless, and then they all started talking at once. One by one, they came over to Peter and thanked him for sharing such a personal journey. They wished him well.

"Ethan," Ella said. "Wait a minute. What happened back then was no one's fault; it was circumstances that neither of us caused purposefully. I don't really think that anyone else was involved or even had any inkling of that night. I am satisfied with what you told me; I can put it to rest now that I know the truth. I wish you would too," she said, looking at Ethan to see what response that would bring.

"That's the way you want it?" he asked. "Then it's okay with me. We will put the entire episode to rest, deal?" He smiled at her. "I agree. As long as those involved know, that satisfies me."

"You know something, my cousin? You really aren't that scary, from where I'm standing now," Ella told him and they both laughed.

Ella felt that Ethan had cleared his dark shadows of hurt with his father and had finally reached a resolution with her. He had let light into his closed circle of mistrust and anger with his father and had dissolved her long standing fear that had arisen from that dark night on the beach.

Ella looked across the room and noticed that, even as others spoke to him, Uncle Peter was in his own world. She felt that his psyche had been shocked to its very depths. She tried to imagine how she would feel. It was hard to believe that a chapter of his life, that had never resolved itself, was now shown in a way that was so stunning and unimaginable. She wondered if it were beneficial to her uncle to relive all this sadness that had happened so long ago and share it so openly. As the startling past was brought into the light, it had touched his family deeply. Ella felt that at least the revelations brought forth today had united Uncle Peter and Ethan, and she and Ethan. She knew that she would never be close to her cousin, but now she could understand him. Her memory demons would finally be put to rest. It would take her some time, but she felt lighter. Her childhood anger, which she had held so long, would defuse in time. Perhaps the universe had played some pretty mean tricks on everyone involved, Ella thought—but then, it also had brought more than one person including herself, into the light of understanding. *I will have to let it go at that, and remember that everything is as it should be.*

As everyone calmed down, Marcel stood up and declared that he had an announcement. "Julia and I will be married quietly next month. After the baby is born, we will celebrate both the marriage and the arrival of our child. We hope that everyone will share in our celebration."

Ella lifted her eyes upward, and thought *some wonderful happy news.*

Hattie passed around glasses for the toast.

"I'm committed," Marcel said and raised his glass. "I love Julia very much. I hope she can put up with me!" Everyone clapped and hooted.

"What took you so long, son?" Ethan asked to more laughter, as the family toasted Julia and Marcel.

"Thank you, Marcel, and thank you, God," Martine said as an added toast, to still more laughter.

Later, needing a breath of air, Ella sat on the patio, looking out at the ocean. Peter came out to join her. "I am stunned over this turn of events," he declared. "I have no doubt, that this was meant to be revealed to me before

I died." His mind wandered a bit as he tried to focus on how to express himself. "When I spoke with Mae, she was astonished. I had never told her about Denise, only that I was looking for someone that I met during the war. But Mae is very perceptive. I'm sure she knew there was more to it than I had divulged."

"Telling her must have been a difficult thing to do, Uncle Peter. Although, I must say, Mae seems to be handling it well."

"I had to let the past go after I married Mae. At least, I thought I had. I love her, and she has been a good wife and an excellent mother all these years."

"How could you forget something so dramatically memorable as your relationship with Denise? It's a part of your life, a part that never was resolved. I think you handled it beautifully."

"Come with me, Sweet Pea," he addressed her with his childhood name for her.

"What?" she asked, as he took her hand.

"Come, I want to show you something."

"I don't think I can take anything else in. I am so overwhelmed with information that my brain is on overload."

He led her into the back storage room, which held some boxes. "Just open one."

"What is this?"

"Here, just open it." He pushed a carton toward her and watched her lift the top off the box.

"Oh, Uncle Peter," she whispered. "This is phenomenal! All the family journals. Did you get them out of storage for the reunion?"

"Yes, for that and for another reason."

She looked at him.

"I want you to carry on the family journals. You'll be at Seagate another few days. Get into these journals. Look and see what priceless family information is stored under their covers. And then I'll have them copied and bound for you and put the originals back into storage." He smiled at her.

Ella was stunned. She remembered what she had asked him when she was a child: Who will be asked to carry on the family history and lineage? And now she knew. She was extremely pleased.

"I would be honored to keep the history," she turned to hug him.

"There. Another chapter in my life coming full circle. Thank you, my dear niece. I know you'll respect and keep the history going."

"I have a question, Uncle." Ella turned serious and lowered her voice. "Have you wondered who rang the bell on that night? Ethan said he would find out, but I don't think he will get an answer. I asked Charles just now and he told me exactly what Hattie said. He didn't get back until after 3:00 a.m."

"At least not an earthly one," he winked at Ella.

"Are you thinking the same thing I am? I could never reveal my thoughts to anyone except you, about who rang the bell."

Peter looked at Ella with his *gotcha smile*. "You know Ella, Baby Marcel was on that raft. The baby carries the ancient Spanish bloodline—disaster could have happened out on the ocean. You decide who came to the rescue, and who rang the bell. That's all I'm going to say." He paused remembering something else. "We are in 1988. It is exactly 400 years that Sergio and the Spanish Armada started out. You know that we are connected to that and the bell through Sergio." Ella stared at her uncle. He had verbalized thoughts that had run through her head and although she wanted to dismiss them, she could not.

"Just turn around, Ella and see who's looking at you."

"This is too, too creepy."

"I brought the painting out to the garage to put into the car. I intend to put him back into safe keeping tomorrow, after I have shown it to all my friends." The door to the garage was open and the portrait was leaning against the car. Peter exposed the portrait again, and turned the canvas towards Ella.

She studied Sergio's face once more and turned to her uncle. "I need to clear my head," Ella told him. "I'm going to take a walk on the beach with Tucker. I am exhausted with all that has happened, and I need some sea air."

She turned to leave and saw Aunt Mae at the door.

"I know. I know what that old bugger is up to. He's always wanted you to have those journals. He hasn't decided who will inherit the painting, but I suspect it will be Ethan—and rightly so."

"If I don't get out of here right now, I will cry," Ella said and left for the beach. Twilight was descending and she wanted to walk and breathe in the wonderful smell of the ocean and look up at her beloved Seagate from the beach. What tales that big ocean could tell of the wonderful things it had seen, marking those memories on a segment of time. But right now, she wanted to walk in her ancestors' footprints—perhaps they were there—just below her feet, hundreds of years old, under new layers of sand. The tiny grains covered the old prints but didn't hide their memories, which were told so well in the family journals. Perhaps Willem and Maggie had trod here too; maybe Sergio and Captain Weber and old Davey had laid down their tracks. How she would have loved to have met Sunny and her beloved Ben. She felt a kinship with all of them, especially Willem and Maggie who started it all on the island. Ella carried the family DNA and she felt she had known them in her ancient memories. Perhaps she *had* met them in another time.

Tucker ran wild, picking up sticks here and there, turning his face into the soft wind, sniffing the briny smell. He loved the beach and the surf and now he ran helter skelter though the still warm October water.

"If only you could speak, my boy," Ella looked at the dog and she swore he smiled at her.

"Let's go back, Tuck." She laughed and spun herself around a few times. They headed toward Seagate to join her family. She saw someone in the distance approaching. She couldn't make out who it was until he came closer, and her heart leaped into her throat.

"Matt," she said aloud, first softly. "Matt, Matt!" she shouted, hardly believing her eyes. It was really him! All of the surprising events of the day had driven him right out of her mind, but now she realized, that he had received the telephone message that she had left for him. She was overwhelmed with joy.

Matt saw her and started running to meet her.

"Come on, Tuck. Look who's here!" she yelled. "Go get him, boy!"

Tucker ran like the wind to Matt and jumped high on the run into his arms. She heard Matt laugh as he hugged the wriggling dog to him.

"Ella!" he shouted. "Here I am!" He put Tucker down, grabbed her, and held her tight. "Ella, my love," he whispered. She was beset and without words. "I should have spoken sooner. I don't want to lose you." He smiled down at her. "I have great faith in us. Do you want to be with me for the rest of our lives?"

She couldn't speak. This was so unexpected. Now she knew that this was something she had truly longed. She thought she would drop right there on the sand. It was almost heaven.

"I will tell you that I don't believe in long engagements," he whispered. "Let's share thoughts of marriage—on Pikes Peak in Colorado?"

Oh well, at least it was in the States. Suddenly, she laughed because she was truly pleased. She laughed until her stomach hurt.

"What? What?" he asked, laughing with her.

Leave it to Matt. But then, life with him would not be for the fainthearted. "I love you," she whispered. "Come back to the house and meet my family, if you dare." She smiled up at him, realizing that she too, had come full circle.

FURTHER READING

Andrist, Ralph K. (Edited by) *George Washington, A Biography in His own Words.* New York, NY: Newsweek 1972.

Bailey, John Lloyd, *Eighteen Miles of History on Long Beach Island.* Harvey Cedars, NJ:Down the Shore Publishing. 1994.

Beck, Henry Charlton. *More Forgotten Towns of Southern New Jersey.* New Brunswick, NJ: Rutgers University Press. 1963

Blockson, Charles L. *The Underground Railroad in Pennsylvania.* Jacksonville, NC: Flame International, Inc. 1981

Cunliffe, Marcus. *George Washington, and the Making of a Nation,* American Heritage Publishing Co, Inc. New York, NY: Harper and Row. 1966

Davis, W. W. H., A.M., 1876 and 1905 editions. *The History of Bucks County, Pennsylvania, Chapter XL, Bucks County in the Revolution, 1774 to 1783. from the discovery of the Delaware to the present time.*
Contributed for use in the USGENWeb Archives by Donna Bluemink.
dbluemink@cox.net

Encyclopedia Britannica: *Spanish rulers, Spanish Armada Cadiz, Spain*

Fisher, Sydney George. *The Making of Pennsylvania*. Port Washington, L.I., N.Y.: Ira J. Friedman, Inc. Reissued 1969.

Ferris, Frederick L. *The Two Battles of Trenton*
The Trenton Historical Society
http://trentonhistory.org/His/battles.htm

Haley, K.H.D. *The Dutch in the Seventeenth Century*. London: Thames and Hudson Ltd, 1972. Harcourt Brace Javanovich, Inc. (on first page after title) First American edition 1972, Printed and bound in Great Britain by Jarrold and Sons Ltd, Norwich

Hawke, David Freeman. *Everyday Life in Early America*. New York, NY:Harper and Row. 1988

Howarth, David. *The Voyage of the Armada*, The Viking Press, New York, NY: 1981

Johnson, Donald S. *Charting the Sea of Darkness*. Camden, Maine: International Marine/McGraw-Hill Book, 1993

Kross, Peter. *New Jersey History*. Wilmington, DE: A Middle Atlantic Press Book 1987

McCormick, Richard P. *New Jersey from Colony to State. 1609-1789*. New Brunswick, NJ:Rutgers University Press. 1964

McMahon, William. *South Jersey Towns, History and Legend*. New Brunswick, NJ:Rutgers University Press. 1973

Nash, Charles Edgar. *The Lure of Long Beach, By* the Long Beach Board of Trade

Newton, Gerald, *The Netherlands: An Historical and Cultural Survey 1795-1977.* London: Ernest Benn Limited, 25 New Street Square, Fleet Street, London EC4A 3JA 1978, and Sovereign Way, Tonbridge, Kent TN9 1RW and West view Press, 5500 Central Avenue, Boulder, CO.

Ocean County Principals' Council, *Tides of Time.* Toms River, NJ:Ocean County Principals' Council. 1940

Olsen, Victoria. *The Dutch Americans; The Peoples of North America.* New York, Philadelphia: Chelsea House Publishers, a division of Main Line Book Co. 1989

Oxenford, David D. *The People of Ocean County.* Brick, NJ: George Valente. 1992

Pierce, Arthur D. *Iron in the Pines.* New Brunswick, NJ:Rutgers University Press. 1957

Pomfret, John E. *Colonial New Jersey, A History.* New York:Charles Scribner's Sons. 1973.

Times Books:*Spanish Armada*

Weigley, Russell F. et, al, *Philadelphia, A 300 Year History.* New York, London:W.W. Norton and Company. 1982

Wilson, Charles. *The Dutch Republic and the Civilisation of the Seventeenth Century.* New York, Toronto:McGraw-Hill Book Company, World University Library. 1968.1

Wold, Edwin II, *Philadelphia, Portrait of an American City.* Philadelphia, PA:Camino Books. 1990

WEBSITES OF INTEREST

(To access site, place cursor on website name, control, click.)

13 Days of August, by Helen Gemmill
http://www.earlyamerica.com/review/winter96/august.html

15th and 16th Century Discoveries in the New World
http://www.xtinahs.org/generalhistory/Scharf4.html

Arnold, Benedict
http://www.ushistory.org/valleyforge/served/arnold.html

Barnegat Lighthouse
Barnegat Light Historical Society Museum and Edith Duff
Gwinn Gardens
http://www.nealcomm.com/nonprof/blhist.htm

Batsto Village
Wharton State forest
Washington Township Historic information
http://www.co.burlington.nj.us/info/history/township/
washingtontownship.htm

Battle of Crooked Billet
http://www.myrevolutionarywar.com/battle/780501

Black History in Canada
http://www.osblackhistory.com/history.php

Boston Tea Party
http://www.boston-tea-party.org/

Camden, New Jersey
http://www.ci.camden.nj.us/history/earlysettlement.html

Carrack, The mid 15th Century
http://www.greatgridlock.net/sqrigg/carrack.html

Cornwallis surrenders at Yorktown
http://www.eyewitnessstohistory.com/yorktown.htm

Cox, Daniel reference Appendix II full text
Tatham, John, New Jersey's Missing Governor
http://www.westjerseyhistory.org/books/smith/
smithappendix2.htm

Craven Hall Historical Society, Inc
Craven-Hall.org

Crooked Billet, the Battle of
http://www.myrevolutionrywar.com/battles/780501.htm
http://www.battleofcrookedbillet.com/premiere.htm

David Library of the American revolution
http://www.dlar.org/

Delaware Bay History
http://www.tydb.org/a_history.php
Ferries, Ancient in Philadelhia
http://www.phillyh2o.org/backpages/Ledger_ferries_1882.htm

Durham Boats
http://www.ushistory.org/washingtoncrossing.
asp?d=history&f=crossing.htm

Flanders, History of
http://www.theotherside.co.uk/tm-*heritage/background/*
flanders.htm

General History
http://www.xtinahs.org/GENERALHISTORY/Scharf4.html

Gloucester County, NJ History and Genealogy
*http://www.nj.searchroots.com/Gloucesterco/*fortnassau.

Half Moon Press and Henry Hudson
http://www.hudsonriver.com/halfmoonpress/stories/
hudson.htm
Full text of Robert Juet's Journal (Henry Hudson's Navigator)
From the collections of the New York Historical Society,
Second Series, 1841 Full Text of Robert Juet's Journal and
Newsday.com

Hessian Information: Johannes Schwalm Historical Assn. Inc.
http://jsha.org/
Also see Captain Johann von Ewald Diaries
http://library.bloomu.edu/Archives/Maps/mapindex.htm
Also see:
http://www.revolutionarywararchives.org/Rahl.html
Also see:
History of Bucks County, Pennsylvania
W.W.H. Davis, A.M., 1876 and 1905 editions
(USGENWEBNOTICE) see under further reading: Davis

Holland or the Netherlands
http://www.archimon.nl/general/holland.html

Jersey Cape, History of
http://members.tripod.com/scott_mcgonigle/history.htm

Long Beach Island History and Timeline
http://www.nealcomm.com/lbihistory/timeline.asp

Marquis de Lafayette
http://www.marquisdelafayette.net/

Mey, Cornelius Jacobsen
http://en.wikipedia.org/wiki/Cornelius_Jacobsen_Mey

Moland House, Warwick Township, PA
http://www.poles.org/Moland.html

Native American Names
http://www.snowowol.com/swolfNamesandmeanings.html

Navigation, finding latitude, noonday sun, longitude
http://www.phy6.org/stargaze/Snavigat.htm

Newtown, Bucks County, PA Battle of
http://www.newtownhistoric.org/birdinhandraid.html

New Jersey Pinelands
http://www.usgennet.org/usa/nj/county/atlantic/
Pinelands/ChestnutNeck.htm

Newtown, PA, Historic Association
http://www.newtownhistoric.org/historicalnotes.html

Paris Falls to the Germans
http://century.guardian.co.uk/1940-1949/
Story/0,6051,128218,00.html

Patriot Pirates
http://www.patriotpirates.com/events/id4.htm

Pirate's Cove, Rob Ossian
ThePirateKing.com

Privateering during the American Revolution
http://www.shsu.edu/~his_ncp/Privat.html

Rahl, Johann Gottlieb, Commandant Hessian Barracks,
Trenton, NJ
http://www.revolutionarywararchives.org/Rahl.html

Revere, Paul, and his famous ride:Map of Paul Revere's Ride
http://www.theamericanrevolution.org/ipeople/prevere/
mid_ride.asp

Revere's (Paul) Account of his own Ride
http://www.laughtergenealogy.com/bin/histprof/misc/revere.html

Revere's (Paul) Ride, the Poem by Henry Wadsworth Longfellow
http://poetry.eserver.org/paul-revere.html

Revolutionary War Information
www.AmericanRevolution.org

SailingAhead.com
A list of sailing terms
http://www.sailingahead.com/information/glossary.htm

Sailing Vessels; Complete list of Rob Ossian's Pirate's Cove
http://www.thepirateking.com/ships/ship_types.htm

Scenic Byways in New Jersey, State of New Jersey,
Department of Transportation
http://www.state.nj.us/transportation/community/scenic/pinelands.shtm

Society of Colonial Wars in the State of Connecticut
http://www.colonialwarsct.org/1614.htm

Sons of Liberty
http://www.revolutionarywararchives.org/Rahl.html

Ship's Bells (Watch Schedules)
http://www.boatsafe.com/nauticalknowhow/shipbee.htm

Signaling at Sea
Http//mysite.verizon.net/vzeohzt4

Spanish Armada and Philip II of Spain and Elizabeth
http://www.spartacus.schoolnet.co.uk/TUDarmada.htm

Spanish Ships, their Parts, Wrecks and Treasures
http://all-kids.us/ship-parts-page.html

Statehood entry listings:
http://.50states.com/statehood1.htm

The Two Battles of Trenton
Frederick L. Ferris
The Trenton Historical Society
http://trentonhistory.org/His/battles.htm

Trenton, Battle of
http://www.doublegv.com/ggv/battles/Trenton.html
http://www.theamericanrevolution.org/battles/bat_tren.asp

Trenton Historical Society
http://trentonhistory.org/
Tuckerton, New Jersey
http://www.tuckerton.com/tuckerton-history.htm

Tuckerton Railroad
http://en.wikipedia.org/wiki/Tuckerton_Railroad

Washington Crossing State Park
http://www.fieldtrip.com/nj/97370623.htm
Washington's "Not-So-Wooden" Teeth,
http://www.goodteeth.com/gwteeth.htm

West, Thomas
http://www.answers.com/topic/earl-de-la-war

Edwards Brothers Malloy
Thorofare, NJ USA
April 9, 2012